Theatre in Europe: a documentary history

This is the third volume to be published in the series Theatre in Europe: a documentary history. This book makes available for the first time an overview of a significant segment of European theatre history and, with few exceptions, none of the documents presented has been published in English before. Gathered from a rich variety of sources, including imperial and municipal edicts, contracts, regulations, architectural descriptions, playbills, stage directions, actors' memoirs, among others, the book sheds light on one of the most fascinating areas of cultural life in the German- and Dutch-speaking countries. Explanatory passages put these documents into their historical context, and numerous illustrations bring the material even more vividly to life.

Through the presentation of key documents, Brandt and Hogendoorn trace the relatively early rise of Dutch theatre during Holland's Golden Age and the later development of German-language theatre, the theoretical battles for the definition of a national style of drama, and the practical problems – meeting the taste of various audiences, coping with architectural, administrative and financial matters – which had to be solved. The volume also reveals how the cross-currents of European theatre – English, French, Italian and Spanish – met in this area.

The book contains numerous illustrations, the source location for each document and a substantial bibliography. It will be of interest to scholars and students of theatre history, German and Dutch history, language and culture, art history and sociology.

Theatre in Europe: a documentary history

General editors:

Glynne Wickham
John Northam
John Gould
W.D. Howarth

This series will present a comprehensive collection of primary source materials for teachers and students and will serve as a major reference work for studies in theatrical and dramatic literature. The volumes will focus individually on specific periods and geographical areas, encompassing English and European theatrical history. Each volume will present primary source documents in English, or in English translation, relating to actors and acting, dramatic theory and criticism, theatre architecture, stage censorship, settings, costumes, and audiences. These sources include such documents as statutes, proclamations, inscriptions, contracts and playbills. Additional documentation from contemporary sources is provided through correspondence, reports, and eyewitness accounts. The volumes will also provide not only the exact source and location of the original documents, but also complementary lists of similar documents. Each volume contains an Introduction, narrative linking passages, notes on the documents, a substantial bibliography and an index offering detailed access to the primary material.

Published

Restoration and Georgian England, 1660–1788, compiled & introduced by David Thomas and Arnold Hare, edited by David Thomas

National Theatre in Northern and Eastern Europe, 1746–1900, edited by Laurence Senelick

Theatre in Europe: a documentary history

German and Dutch theatre, 1600–1848

Compiled by

GEORGE W. BRANDT
Professor Emeritus
Drama Department
University of Bristol

and

WIEBE HOGENDOORN
Professor Emeritus
Instituut voor Theaterwetenschap
Universiteit van Amsterdam

Edited by

GEORGE W. BRANDT

CAMBRIDGE
UNIVERSITY PRESS

Published by the Press Syndicate of the University of Cambridge
The Pitt Building, Trumpington Street, Cambridge CB2 1RP
40 West 20th Street, New York, NY 10011–4211, USA
10 Stamford Road, Oakleigh, Melbourne 3166, Australia

First published 1993

Printed in Great Britain at the University Press, Cambridge

A catalogue record for this book is available from the British Library.

Library of Congress cataloguing in publication data

German and Dutch theatre, 1600–1848 / compiled by George W. Brandt and
Wiebe Hogendoorn; edited by George W. Brandt.
    p.   cm. – (Theatre in Europe)
    Includes bibliographical references and index.
    ISBN 0 521 23383 6 (hardback)
    1. Theater – Germany – History – Sources. 2. Theater –
Netherlands – History – Sources. I. Brandt, George W. II. Hogendoorn, Wiebe.
III. Series.
PN2641.G47   1992
792'.0943 – dc20   92-4417   CIP

ISBN 0521 23383 6 hardback

SE

Contents

List of documents

Asterisks before titles indicate illustrated documents

General editors' preface

In appointing appropriately qualified editors for all the volumes in this documentary history it has been our aim to provide a comprehensive collection of primary
source materials for teachers and students on which their own critical appraisal of
theatrical history and dramatic literature may safely be grounded.

Each volume presents primary source documents in English, or in English
translation, relating to actors and acting, dramatic theory and criticism, theatre
architecture, stage censorship, settings, costumes and audiences. Editors have, in
general, confined their selection to documentary material in the strict sense
(statutes, proclamations, inscriptions, contracts, working-drawings, playbills,
prints, account books, etc.), but exceptions have been made in instances where
prologues, epilogues, excerpts from play texts and private correspondence provide
additional contemporary documentation based on author's authority or that of
eyewitnesses to particular performances and significant theatrical events.

Unfamiliar documents have been preferred to familiar ones, short ones to long
ones; and among long ones recourse has been taken to excerpting for inclusion all
passages which either oblige quotation by right of their own intrinsic importance
or lead directly to a clearer understanding of other documents. In every instance,
however, we have aimed to provide readers not only with the exact source and
location of the original document, but with complementary lists of similar
documents and of secondary sources offering previously printed transcripts.

Each volume is equipped with an introductory essay, and in some cases
introductory sections to each chapter, designed to provide readers with the
appropriate social background – religious, political, economic and aesthetic – as
context for the documents selected; it also contains briefer linking commentaries
on particular groups of documents and concludes with an extensive bibliography.

Within this general presentational framework, individual volumes will vary
considerably in their format – greater emphasis having to be placed, for example,
on documents of control in one volume than in another, or with dramatic theory
and criticism figuring less prominently in some volumes than in others – if each
volume is to be an accurate reflection of the widely divergent interests and
concerns of different European countries at different stages of their historical

development, and the equally sharp differences in the nature and quality of the surviving documents volume by volume.

The editors would like to thank Sarah Stanton and those members of Cambridge University Press whose unwavering interest, encouragement and practical support has brought this enterprise forward from first thoughts to publication of this third volume in the series.

Glynne Wickham (Chairman)
Bristol University, 1992

Editor's preface

The authors of this volume have divided their joint task along straightforward geographical lines. George Brandt collected and edited the material covering the German-language theatre for the period 1600–1848, Wiebe Hogendoorn that covering the theatre of the Low Countries over the same period. George Brandt has been responsible for the overall shape of the volume.

As the overall editor I wish to express my deep indebtedness to two institutions whose financial assistance was crucially important in enabling me to extend the scope of my research. Indeed but for their generous help, work on this volume could not have been undertaken, or at any rate carried to a (one hopes, successful) conclusion. The first of these institutions is The British Academy, the second The Leverhulme Trust. I should particularly like to thank Miss Jane Woods of the former and Miss J.E. Bennett of the latter for their immensely helpful interest in this exploration of aspects of European theatre history which had not hitherto been fully documented in English.

Both authors would like to express their gratitude for all the advice received and the long-suffering patience shown by the general editors of the series, *Theatre in Europe*, especially Professors Glynne Wickham and Bill Howarth, during the period of preparing this volume. The overall guidance we were given during its gestation by Sarah Stanton of Cambridge University Press has also been greatly appreciated. I wish to thank Professor Hans Reiss and Miss Janet Arnold for their willingness to supply some recondite information, and Miss Alison Booth for translating a difficult passage from the Italian (27). I am glad to acknowledge all the help I was given in my work by the University Library, Bristol, and the University of Bristol Theatre Collection, especially its Curator Mr Christopher Robinson; the Arts Faculty Photographic Unit of the University of Bristol, especially Mr Martin Williams; as well as the staff of the British Library, including its Photographic Service. The Library of the Institute of Germanic Studies proved to be an invaluable source for my research, and I should like to thank Dr John Flood, the Deputy Director, Miss Jane Lewin, the Secretarial Assistant, and Mr William Abbey, the Librarian, for all their help; the generous bibliographical advice of the latter, in particular, saved me a great deal of time on several occasions by pointing me in the right direction in the early phases of my research. I also owe a great debt of gratitude to Frau Fryda, Herr Kohlmannsperger and Frau Dr Balk of the Deutsches Theatermuseum (Munich); Herr Dr Junginger of the Bayerische Staatsbibliothek (Munich); Herr Dr Hans Haase, Herr Professor Dr Paul Raabe and Herr Christian Hogrefe of the Herzog-August-Bibliothek (Wolfen-büttel); and Herr Dr Matthes of the Niedersächsisches Staatsarchiv (Wolfenbüttel) for their scholarly advice and expert guidance around the relevant sections of their respective collections. Finally, I should like to thank Harald and Andrea Clemen for all the help extended to me during my stay in Munich.

ACKNOWLEDGEMENTS

The authors wish to express their appreciation of the kindness of the following institutions in giving permission to reproduce material, which is separately acknowleged for each item.

Germany

The British Library; the Deutsches Theatermuseum (Munich); the Gesellschaft für Theatergeschichte e.V. (Berlin); the Herzog-August-Bibliothek (Wolfenbüttel); the Museum für Geschichte der Stadt Leipzig; the Nationale Forschungs- und Gedenkstätten der klassischen deutschen Literatur in Weimar; the Niedersächsisches Staatsarchiv; the University of Bristol Theatre Collection; the Württembergische Landesbibliothek (Stuttgart); the Max Niemeyer Verlag (Tübingen), and Verlag Georg D.W. Callwey (Munich).

The Netherlands

Archives Générales du Royaume, Bruxelles; Chatsworth House Trust Ltd, Baslow; Gemeente-archief Amsterdam; Gemeente-archief 's-Gravenhage; Gemeente-archief Leiden; Hamburger Staatsarchiv; Nederlands Theater Instituut, Amsterdam; Prentenkabinet Universiteit, Leiden; Rijksarchief, Utrecht; Stedelijk Museum 'De Lakenhal', Leiden; Stichting Atlas Van Stolk, Rotterdam; Universiteitsbibliotheek Amsterdam.

The following publishers have kindly allowed some passages of translations from German into English to be used: Penguin Books Ltd; the University of Miami Press; and Cornell University Press.

Abbreviations

ADT	*Annalen des Theaters* (Berlin)
BL	British Library
CUP	Cambridge University Press
DLD	*Deutsche Literaturdenkmale des 18. und 19. Jahrhunderts*, ed. Seuffert/Sauer (Heilbronn/Stuttgart/Berlin)
DNL	*Deutsche National-Literatur*, ed. Kürschner and others (Stuttgart: W. Speemann)
DSB	*Die Schaubühne* (Emsdetten)
DTM	Deutsches Theatermuseum (München)
ELT	*Ephemeriden der Litteratur und des Theaters* (Berlin)
LTZ	*Litteratur- und Theater-Zeitung* (Berlin)
KSGTG	*Kleine Schriften der Gesellschaft für Theatergeschichte* (Berlin)
M&K	*Maske und Kothurn* (Vienna, later Graz & Cologne)
MBGDKL	*Monatliche Beiträge zur Geschichte dramatischer Kunst und Literatur* (Berlin)
NA	*Schillers Werke/National-Ausgabe* (Weimar: Hermann Böhlaus Nachfolger)
SGTG	*Schriften der Gesellschaft für Theatergeschichte* (Berlin)
SJB	*Shakespeare-Jahrbuch* (Weimar)
TIE	*Theatre in Europe* (Cambridge University Press)
TJD	*Theater-Journal für Deutschland* (Gotha)
TGF	*Theatergeschichtliche Forschungen* (Hamburg/Leipzig)
WA	*Goethes Werke/Weimarer Ausgabe* (Weimar: Hermann Böhlau)

German theatre, 1600–1848

EDITED BY GEORGE W. BRANDT

Introduction

This volume in the series, *Theatre in Europe*, covers the period 1600 to 1848; it is divided into two parts, the first dealing with German and the second with Dutch theatre. Obviously one cannot hope to give more than an overall picture of a complex development over so long a time-span. In the case of German theatre history, the impossibility of quoting every relevant document is due not only to the great social and political changes Germany underwent in the course of two and a half centuries – something that could equally well be said of other countries – but more particularly to some specific characteristics of German society which were reflected in the development of its theatre. Inevitably the documentation presented here is selective with no claim to exhaustiveness.

The history of German theatre is, of course, interconnected with that of many other European countries. *Vis-à-vis* the West (England, France, the Netherlands, Italy) Germany received more than it gave, at least in the formative period of its theatre; *vis-à-vis* the East it was to play a more seminal and giving role. Yet for all its links with neighbouring countries, there are significant differences which distinguish it from the pattern of theatre elsewhere, particularly in England and France.

While it is not the case that *all* of English theatre was entirely confined to London nor *all* of French theatre to Paris during this period, the crucial events as regards playwriting and stage performance certainly did take place in those two metropolises. After the demise of locally based religious mediaeval drama, provincial English and French theatre had to look to the centre for inspiration: success was gauged by the extent to which playwrights, managers, actors and other theatre workers made their mark in the capital where the political, social and cultural energies of their respective nations were concentrated.

This was by no means the situation in Germany. There was then no single theatrical or indeed cultural centre for German-speaking countries – and this is to a considerable extent still true today. So as we follow the evolution of the German theatre, we see the focus of our interest shift repeatedly. Certain major centres do indeed stand out over long periods of time – notably the deeply Protestant, flourishing commercial city of Hamburg at one end of the territory and the devoutly Catholic Imperial city of Vienna at the other. But though these and other cities such as Leipzig, Berlin, Brunswick, Munich also have their key roles to play at various times, no single place can be said to encapsulate the story of German theatre as a whole. The theatrical significance even of these major cities fluctuates according to the whims of rulers, the varying degree of enlightenment of their citizens, the fortunes of war and trade, and other fortuitous factors. In this checkered history relatively minor centres of population such as Ulm, Schwerin, Gotha or Weissenfels come to the fore momentarily. Indeed there are times of greater or lesser duration when the most remarkable theatrical developments are due to the enterprise and initiative of certain individuals of exceptional administrative or creative gifts – such as Baron v. Dalberg in Mannheim, Goethe in Weimar or Immermann in Düsseldorf. The result of this lack of any one single gathering-point for the cultural, or more specifically the theatrical, energies of the German-speaking world is that no presentation of documents can cover absolutely every aspect of what is a local and regional as much as it is a national phenomenon: what we are dealing with is a mosaic rather than a single, well-composed picture.

The principle of selection of documents here is the tracing of a slow ascent, which lagged well behind that of neighbouring countries, of a specifically German theatre with its own style and organisation and, above all, its own repertoire. Admittedly there is some bias in this presentation in favour of the process by which a national corpus of drama came to be forged. It would have been possible to organise the wealth of available material according to different principles. The editor would, however, like to think that facets of the story not wholly subservient to the main thrust of the book have not been neglected.

The decentralised nature of German culture is rooted in history. The Holy Roman Empire ('neither Holy nor Roman nor an Empire', according to a well-known witticism), a loose confederation of states with no clear-cut natural frontiers, from which some Swiss cantons had begun to break away as early as at the end of the thirteenth century and the beginning of the fourteenth; torn asunder in the sixteenth century by the Reformation and then, as a result of that religious schism, devastated in the following century by the Thirty Years' War, a catastrophe with disastrous long-term physical and cultural consequences – this political structure had in fact always lacked internal cohesion. In his *De statu imperii germanici* (1667), the jurist Samuel Pufendorf described its constitution as irregular, indeed as resembling a monster. We recall the tipsy students in Auerbach's cellar, in Goethe's *Faust*, mocking the Holy Roman Empire. The Empire's centrifugal nature did not allow any one court (not even that of the Emperor) nor any one administrative, ecclesiastical or commercial centre unquestionably to represent all the cultural energies of such an extensive territory in the heart of the Continent. The spread of absolutism in the seventeenth and eighteenth centuries strengthened the power of electors and princelings; it only further debilitated that of the Emperor. By the eighteenth century, the Empire was little more than a legal fiction; it consisted of some 300 states with a greater or lesser degree of virtual independence; if the territories of local magnates were to be included in this list, this number would come to well over 2,000 states and ministates. We find Germany divided by borders, customs regulations, laws, religion, dialect and lifestyle. Weights and measures differed from territory to territory. The profusion of different currencies (*Gulden, Taler, Schilling, Kreuzer, Batzen, Ablus, Stüber, Groschen, Pfennig, Mark, Heller*) indicated the depth of *Kleinstaaterei* (little-statism) throughout the Empire. (This monetary chaos among the German states also complicates theatre history in that it makes it harder exactly to assess the precise meaning of sums of money involved in contracts, ticket prices, travel costs etc.)

The particularism which forms such a striking contrast to the more centralised administrations of Britain and France was a political fact that for a long time inhibited the development in Germany of a *professional* theatre, the very art form which depends more than any other on basically urban, intellectually curious mass audiences sharing broad cultural values.

The stress here is advisedly on the word 'professional'. Non-professional types of performance public or private abound from the beginning of our period. There were courtly and aristocratic types of celebratory, largely emblematic, theatre couched in an essentially international idiom, very similar to those flourishing at the courts of Italy, France, England and Spain; these continued to exist in some form or other up to the latter part of the eighteenth century. People at the other end of the social spectrum were also entertained by nonprofessional theatre. The *meistersinger* drama of an earlier period had not disappeared; although this type of guild drama was already in its decline by the beginning of our period, the meistersingers of Augsburg built a theatre of their own as late as 1665 and in some towns continued their existence until the eighteenth century. A more important aspect of nonprofessional theatre were the school performances which played such a conspicuous role in seventeenth- (and even eighteenth-) century education.

But the plays of Protestant schools and those staged, often with considerable scenic sophistication and enormous casts, at Jesuit colleges (the latter sharing a playmaking style and ethos with similar institutions in other Catholic countries) had primarily didactic rather than purely aesthetic aims. The main point of the exercise – apart from advertising the merits of the school – was to teach the pupils eloquence and decent deportment by making them perform in specially written plays that would convey sound lessons of conduct and doctrine to actors and spectators alike. (To be sure, apologists for the professional theatre would stress until the latter part of the eighteenth century that it, too, was 'useful' in that it exalted virtue and either ridiculed or castigated vice.) Now, all this was a far cry from the ideal of a professional class of actors performing in fixed venues who would provide the nation, or at any rate the educated section of it, with vivid images of life as nourishment for its imagination.

It was in this sense of theatre as a vital cultural institution that Germany, because of its social structure, made its entrance upon the scene markedly later than its Western neighbours. The German bourgeoisie, politically weak compared to that of France, let alone that of England, was unable to assert itself confidently against the cultural dominance of the ruling classes and did not manage until the last quarter of the eighteenth century to find its own voice, at any rate in the theatre. To say this is not, of course, to decry middle-class German cultural development as such. It is a striking fact that German music, with its deep folk roots and inspired by religion, flourished greatly at a time when drama was still quite underdeveloped. The patricians of Hamburg supported German opera in a specially built opera-house from 1678 to 1738. German opera even enjoyed the patronage of *minor* courts though the greater ones tended to favour the more expensive and prestigious Italian variety. One simple comparison will make clear the relative states of musical and theatrical culture. The city of Leipzig witnessed the first performance of Bach's *St Matthew Passion*, that profoundly dramatic oratorio which is one of the crowning glories of European music, in 1727; the première in the same city in 1731 of the first German 'regular' play, the local university professor Gottsched's *Der sterbende Cato*, which after its performance by the Neuber company was hailed as a milestone in German drama, ranks as a cultural feat on an incomparably lower level, of minor significance in the wider European context.

It is not surprising in view of the lack of a single cultural centre that German professional theatre over long stretches of its history was open to foreign influence. The first fully professional actors seen in German-speaking lands on a relatively massive scale were the Englishmen who toured many parts of Northern and Central Europe from the 1580s onwards. The keen competition among companies in an England bursting with dramatic vitality made theatrical virgin territories abroad seem a tempting business prospect. These players, often referred to in Germany as 'English Comedians', would sometimes be employed by a court; at other times they would play for the general public in whatever performance spaces they could secure. Bringing with them an exciting repertoire of new plays, these visitors were to confront their barely professional German confreres with much higher standards of skill, even though their offerings were probably greatly inferior to what English audiences would have seen in the playhouses of London.

A performance in an *ad hoc* venue to spectators unable to grasp the literary subtleties of the dialogue, which therefore had to be coarsened in order to be visually readable, was bound to be a more rough-and-ready entertainment than one offered of an afternoon at the Globe.

English influence was in the ascendant in the first half of the seventeenth century (the companies continuing to bear the English label in the latter part of the century were essentially German). In the second half of that as well as the following century French and Italian players were the dominant influence, at least as far as courtly audiences were concerned. After the Thirty Years' War, German courts prided themselves on being able to maintain a company of French actors: Hanover and Celle shared the services of such a company as early as 1668; and this aristocratic fashion of aping the court of Versailles continued well into the latter part of the eighteenth century. The Italian presence came on the one hand in the shape of *commedia dell'arte* troupes who had first made their appearance in the sixteenth century. (The stock figures of the Italian comedy and their *lazzi* were taken up by German actors; as in the case of the English Comedians, many of the best-known later commedia players were in fact German, e.g. the Harlequin J.F. Müller and the Pantaloon J.P. Hilverding in the eighteenth century.) On the other hand – and this was a more profound and long-lasting influence – there were the imported singers, composers and librettists who had made Italian opera the principal court entertainment, ever since the performances in 1618 of this new kind of spectacle in the Prince-Archbishop's 'rock theatre' of Hellbrunn in Salzburg. Opera, on which princes would squander vast sums of money, by far outshone the spoken drama at court. (But intimately linked as the operatic and the dramatic stage are in German theatre history in terms of theatrical architecture, repertoire-planning and the skills expected from actors as well as singers, this book, not being concerned with it as such, will only refer to opera incidentally.) In the related field of ballet, professional dancers also tended in the main to be either French or Italian.

The Italians led the way in other respects too, in Germany as elsewhere: theatrical architecture followed the guidelines laid down by the Italian scenic stage, in the first instance applying them on a large scale more to opera-houses than to playhouses. Italian architects and designers were active in the German lyric and dramatic theatre for a very long time: the Burnacini – father and son – in the seventeenth, Giuseppe Galli-Bibiena in the eighteenth and the Quaglio family up to the latter part of the nineteenth century are merely representative examples of this crucial cultural exchange. We even find Italians such as Nicolini or Bellomo as managers of German companies until well into the eighteenth century.

Stimulating as these external influences may have been, they did nothing to advance the prestige of the indigenous player. The origins of German professional acting are wrapped in obscurity; such companies as existed before the Thirty Years' War remain faceless and are traceable in the main only through their applications to the authorities for permission to perform. It is not until the second half of the seventeenth century that certain *Prinzipale* or actor-managers – for example, Treu, Paulsen and Velten – begin to emerge somewhat more clearly.

These men ran companies which gained a wide reputation not only at courts but also among the theatrically inclined public at large, the latter of course only amounting to a small proportion of the still predominantly rural German people. The fact that some actors had been to university suggests a certain increase in the prestige of the profession. In the early part of the century, German companies seem to have been composed entirely of men, as had also been the case in England (though not in the Latin countries). But now women were at last beginning to be accepted on stage; indeed towards the end of the century there were women in charge of some companies. In the following century, Frau Neuber, the actress who did much to raise the standing of what was still a marginalised profession, not only ran a company jointly with her husband but actually enjoyed a greater reputation and authority than he did.

The main respect in which German actors differed for a long time from their English and French confreres was the peripatetic nature of their calling. Strolling players were a not insignificant part of the profession elsewhere; but in Germany even the leading actors were condemned exclusively to a touring mode of existence until the middle of the eighteenth century. Even after (usually brief) experiments of working as resident companies such as Schönemann's company being established as court actors by the Duke of Mecklenburg at his Schloss in Schwerin in 1750 or the actor-manager K. A. Ackermann building the first ever privately managed theatre in Königsberg in 1755, the life of German actors continued by and large to be one of constant travelling. This meant that companies, generally consisting of some sixteen or seventeen actors working under the direction of a *Prinzipal*, had to spend a great part of their lives on the road, carrying with them their necessarily rudimentary scenery and home-made costumes as well as their families, and perform either in existing venues only roughly adapted to theatrical purposes or else in temporary wooden booths specially erected at their own expense. Since audiences were small in any but the largest cities, players had to be ready to offer a wide and varied repertoire. Theatrical discipline tended to be poor, rehearsals few and little more than walk-throughs; the company's own jealously guarded stock of texts would be all too often supplemented by more or less skilled improvisation. This was obviously not the way to achieve the highest standards of performance, nor was it an encouragement to German men of letters to write for the stage. The repertoire was extremely heterogeneous and of generally inferior literary quality. Instead of being original German creations, most plays would be directly or indirectly derived from English, French, Dutch, Italian or Spanish sources; frequently they were adaptations from opera libretti. It is this state of affairs that made Luigi (Louis) Riccoboni assign a distinctly modest place to the German theatre of his day and age when comparing the theatres of Italy, Spain, France, England, the Low Countries and Germany in his *Réflexions historiques et critiques sur les différens Théâtres de l'Europe* (Paris: Guerin, 1738).

The distances covered by these touring companies were often considerable. It must be remembered that up to our century, German speakers – either as the majority population or as an influential minority – were more widely dispersed throughout Europe than they are today. Theatrical performances in German might be given in places as far apart as Strasbourg and Hermannstadt (in Transylvania), in Agram (Zagreb), Prague or Pressburg (Bratislava), in Buda, Riga, Reval (Tallinn) or Warsaw, as well as in the German heartland. At various times there were German companies playing in the Netherlands, in Scandinavia and in Russia where they might find themselves in competition with or serving as a stimulus to actors performing in the national language.[1]

But this wide dispersal should not suggest unconnected work by isolated individuals or groups. In fact, companies were constantly breaking up and reforming, with some members leaving and others joining; experiences were exchanged, traditions established. This frequent turnover of personnel made for a good deal of continuity of approach throughout the profession.[2] To take the example of the Neubers: after beginning their career with the Spiegelberg troupe, they worked with the company of Sophie Elenson-Haack which then became the Elenson-Haack-Hoffmann company; when the latter was disbanded in 1726 the Neubers founded their own company, taking on some of their former colleagues. This company was in turn to produce a number of other leading actor-managers – Schönemann, G.H. Koch, Döbbelin – and, in spite of rivalries between the parent company and these breakaway upstarts, to influence acting styles for some time even after 1750 when the Neubers finally went out of management. Such interchanges, often cemented by marriage, created a network of style and tradition among strolling players, extending over large areas of the German-speaking world. It is thus possible to trace fairly direct lines of descent by which an acting tradition, albeit in a constant state of flux and evolution, was passed on from generation to generation in the eighteenth century. Konrad Ekhof, the

---

[1] For the impact of German companies on Bohemia, Hungary and Rumania at a rather later date, see Laurence Senelick (ed.), *TIE: National Theatre in Northern and Eastern Europe, 1746–1900* (Cambridge: Cambridge University Press, 1990), pp. 231–2 & 240–1, 278–80 and 301–2 respectively.

[2] For further details on the composition of companies of strolling players, see Eike Pies, *Prinzipale* (Ratingen-Kastellaun-Düsseldorf: Henn, 1973), and W. H. Bruford, *Theatre, Drama and Audiences in Goethe's Germany* (Cambridge University Press, 1950), esp. pp. 30–8.

outstanding actor of the middle years of the eighteenth century, worked with the Neuber pupil Schönemann. Both Iffland and Schröder, the premier actors of the following generation, had in their turn worked with Ekhof in the early stages of their brilliant careers. Gradually something like a German style of acting began to crystallise, although German actors clearly did share many of their stage conventions with those of colleagues in other countries.[3]

Since there were, and indeed still are today though perhaps to a somewhat lesser extent, many variations of pronunciation and speech rhythms throughout German-speaking territories, there was a real incentive for actors to cultivate a standard diction: this was 'bühnendeutsch', a stage German equally intelligible and acceptable anywhere. Though frequent criticisms make it clear that even by the end of the eighteenth century provincialisms had by no means been expunged from stage speech, such standardisation as was achieved represented a bond between the different parts of a culturally diverse area. Indeed, with the progress of drama around the middle of the eighteenth century, theatre was increasingly felt to be more than just a polite entertainment in which Germans wished to emulate their, in this respect, more advanced French and English neighbours; it was seen as an assertion by the nation of its own cultural distinctiveness. Hence the number of National Theatres that sprang up in the second half of the century as the result both of private and government initiative. Initially this ambition to create a German theatre before the nation had found its own appropriate political and cultural form seemed to be putting the cart before the horse. The collapse in 1769 of the first of these ventures, the short-lived Hamburg Enterprise, after less than two difficult years of existence, caused Lessing, its resident playwright, to comment with bitter irony, in the final instalment of his theatrical bulletin, the *Hamburgische Dramaturgie*:

> Alas for the naive idea of creating a National Theatre for the Germans when we Germans are not yet a nation! I do not speak of our political constitution but only of our moral character. One might almost say that this is not to have any. We are still the sworn imitators of everything foreign, in particular the humble admirers of the never sufficiently admired French ... (19 April 1768)

But emancipation from overwhelming external influence was at hand: the 1770s saw a qualitative change in the German theatre. As the young Goethe entered upon the playwriting scene together with the other exciting new dramatists of the *Sturm und Drang* generation, not to mention numerous other playwrights all but forgotten now but popular at the time, the public became

---

[3] See Dene Barnett, *The Art of Gesture: The Practice and Principles of 18th-Century Acting* (Heidelberg; Carl Winter Universitätsverlag, 1987).

aware that the German theatre was no longer merely a pale imitation of foreign models.

From this decade onwards, German theatre was to find its feet quickly; theatrical organisation improved, more and more playhouses were built by private and official enterprise, the Vienna Burgtheater was raised to the status of a National Theatre by Imperial edict in 1776, acting standards everywhere came to be subjected to more informed criticism and, a particularly important point this, a native body of drama of real stature sprang up. The première in 1782 of *Die Räuber* signalled the appearance of Schiller as a playwright of the first magnitude whose further development was to place German drama on a European level of achievement. Goethe's role in this development was crucial, not only as a dominant figure on the literary and intellectual scene but also in a practical capacity as the director of the Weimar court theatre from 1791 to 1817. There he set the example of a director in the modern sense, a man of the theatre not himself a performer but the co-ordinator of all the elements of production. With quite limited means at his disposal he managed to establish new standards of repertory planning; he systematically educated the taste of his audience and – perhaps his principal contribution – he supported Schiller in the creation of a series of dramas which were to become the bedrock of a national repertoire. The patriotic upsurge of the Napoleonic Wars, especially the War of Liberation of 1813–14, set the seal on German theatre as an expression of national culture indispensable not only to the middle class but acceptable even to the hitherto French-inclined upper classes.

One effect of the increasing hold of theatre upon the public's imagination was the growth in the 1770s of a theatrical press. The Gotha court librarian H.A.O. Reichard, who served as administrative director of the Gotha court theatre between 1775 and 1778, published the annual *Theater-Kalender* from 1775 until 1800 (with the exception of the year 1795), as well as the *Theater-Journal für Deutschland* which, planned as a monthly, appeared irregularly from 1777 to 1784. In Berlin C.A.v.Bertram brought out a number of publications – the weeklies *Litteratur- und Theater-Zeitung* (1778–84) and *Ephemeriden der Litteratur und des Theaters* (1785–7) as well as the half-yearly *Annalen des Theaters* (1788–97) – which like his friend Reichard's journals aimed at a nationwide readership. Although these papers devoted a good deal of space to apologetics for the theatre as an institution and to simply chronicling performances or listing the composition of companies rather than providing theatrical reviews in the modern sense, they constitute, together with the numerous other local or regional theatrical journals of the time,[4] an invaluable primary source of information. Vienna, which

---

[4] For a selective though by no means exhaustive listing of German theatrical magazines and journals, see part 4 (periodicals) of the German bibliography, pp. 519–23.

had long been well served by a number of ephemeral theatre journals, was at a somewhat later date to establish a record for continuous stage documentation with the *Wiener Theaterzeitung*, founded by A. Bäuerle in 1806: this journal was published until 1859 although it repeatedly changed its name.[5]

If we were to summarise the evolution of German acting during the period covered by this book, we might, in a highly simplified and schematic way, describe it somewhat along the lines adopted by Eduard Devrient in his canonical survey of German acting, *Geschichte der deutschen Schauspielkunst* (1848–74) – while bearing in mind the regional variations and the overlaps of the old and the new that blur such an over-neat pattern, as well as the difficulty of deducing the living reality of theatrical performance from its perhaps never wholly reliable verbal and pictorial documentation.

During the seventeenth and the early years of the eighteenth century, professional acting appears to have been a fairly unsophisticated affair, tending towards slapstick in comedy and bombast in tragedy, with scant respect for playtexts which were frequently interlarded with improvisation. At this stage of development, the acting of aristocratic amateurs or well-trained pupils of the Jesuits may indeed have rivalled professionals in histrionic skills. The improvements introduced by the Neubers in the 1730s and 1740s were academically inspired and largely modelled on French example: this meant an essentially declamatory style which in the long run did not suit the taste of German audiences. In the second half of the eighteenth century a style of modified realism was achieved, largely on the basis of prose drama, with Ekhof as its greatest exponent. This style, committed to a highly expressive language of gesture, was however still far from latter-day naturalism. In the 1770s, a more emotional type of acting evolved to accommodate the *Sturm und Drang* dramas of the younger playwrights as well as the growing vogue for Shakespeare. The *Ritterstücke* (plays of chivalry) popular in the latter decades of the century in the wake of Goethe's *Götz von Berlichingen* were often blamed for a renewed coarsening of acting. It is also the case that Goethe's attempts in Weimar to create a high theatrical style, an outstanding feature of which would be the noble delivery of verse, were widely noted; but these had only a limited influence upon other theatres not under his jurisdiction. In a parallel though somewhat later development, the Vienna Burgtheater was to develop a high style of its own, one marked by refinement and an easy conversational tone. In the early years of the nineteenth century, the highly emotional performances of romantic star actors caught the public's imagination, much as they did in other countries; later in the century this was to yield to a more sober style. After Goethe and Schiller had passed from the scene it

---

[5] See pp. 521–2.

became a commonplace of criticism to deplore the decline of the German theatre. (It should be remembered though that the work of Georg Büchner, now regarded as one of the high points of German playwriting, was unknown at the time of his death in 1837 and did not reach the professional stage until the twentieth century.) But if the complaints were largely true as far as new dramatic output was concerned, there was actually a wealth of talented actors in this epigonal period. Nevertheless stages of greatly increased size, more and more given to spectacle and sensationalism, were not calculated to favour the subtler portrayals of character. This loss of intimacy can of course be paralleled in theatres other than those of Germany during the nineteenth century.

Summarised like this, it is obvious that the German theatre, particularly in the later phases of this history, had much in common with that of other countries. A great difference remains however between its development and that of the theatre in England, France and Spain – and that is the fact that for well over a century, it was not shaped in the first place by the demands of staging homegrown texts of high quality: the theatre preceded the drama, literature was a relatively late arrival on the scene. Only with the marriage of stage and literature did the German theatre truly emerge as a vital cultural, indeed national, institution. The documents presented in the first part of this volume are intended, above all, to illustrate this development.

The periodisation of the German part of the book calls for a word of explanation. Although it covers the longest era, Period I – 1600–1726 – has the briefest story to tell: it is an account of the infancy of German theatre. The year 1600 is an arbitrary date; the year 1726 saw the Neubers beginning to form their own company. The latter event, although not appreciated as a watershed at the time, can in retrospect be regarded as the end of one age of theatre and the start of another.

Period II – 1727–1814 – takes us from the year in which the Neubers were given official recognition with the grant of the patent as Royal Polish and Electoral Saxon Court Actors to the end of a major historical era with the defeat of Napoleon. This period, during which a classical German literature, including an important body of drama, was forged, gives us the longest section, and it is in the nature of things that chapter 14 (repertoire, dramatic theory and criticism) turns out to be by far the fullest chapter of any.

Period III covers the post-Napoleonic era, from 1815, the year of the Emperor's final overthrow at Waterloo – and, more immediately relevant to theatre history, the year of the appointment of Schreyvogel as theatre secretary to the Burgtheater which inaugurated the latter's great age – up to the revolutionary year 1848. This section can be regarded as the post-Weimar period (although Goethe was not actually dismissed from his post as director of the grand-ducal theatre until 1817); it is dealt with relatively briefly here.

The spelling of English quotations has been modernised. The translation of all quotations is by the editor unless otherwise indicated. There is some inconsistency in the spelling of German names beginning with C (e.g. Conrad, Carl) which were changed to K in the nineteenth century: whilst the modern spelling has been adopted in direct quotations, the older spelling had to be retained in the titles of books. Another inconsistency needs to be pointed out. The names of rulers have been given either in their Anglicised form (e.g. the Elector John Sigismund, King Frederick of Prussia) or in their German form (e.g. Duke Karl August) following the somewhat erratic normal English usage.

One final point. *Taler* or *thaler (from Joachimstaler)* has been consistently translated as *dollar*, the name of the latter having, after all, been originally derived from the former.

Period I: 1600–1726

I   Contractual and organisational documents

A. RELATIONS WITH COURTS & OTHER AUTHORITIES

As companies of strolling players travelled from place to place within the Holy Roman Empire, they depended on the gracious permission of local authorities before they were able to perform anywhere, usually in venues in the gift of these authorities. Permission if granted at all was often grudging, valid only for a limited period of time and hedged in with provisos as well as demands for monetary contributions. An example of the numerous applications still preserved in various municipal archives is the following one addressed by the managers of a German company to the City Council of Danzig (now Gdansk).

I   A German company pleads for permission to play, 1615

From the Danzig city archives. Reproduced in Johannes Bolte, *Das Danziger Theater im 16. und 17. Jahrhundert* (The Danzig Theatre in the 16th and 17th Centuries) (Hamburg/ Leipzig: TGF 12, 1895), pp. 42–3

Worthy, right honourable, estimable, most sagacious, gracious Gentlemen, Worshipful Mayor and Councillors. [...]

Having been graciously permitted by our Elector and master, His Grace the Elector of Brandenburg,[1] whom during the winter just past we most obediently served with our performances of plays [...], to travel abroad to other places during the current summer season and perform our plays, we thereupon resolved to come to this royal seaport whose fame flourishes everywhere [...]. Now having safely arrived here with our company three days ago, we address our humble plea to Your Gracious Worships to be so generous as to deign to permit us to perform fourteen plays here [...]. Since there is no place suitable for our performances to be found here other than Your Worships' premises where fencing lessons are given we beseech Your Worships most humbly to do us the great favour of suggesting to the widow who is now in possession of this house to let us have it [...] for a fair and reasonable fee. [...][2]

Humbly commending ourselves to Your Gracious Worships in the hope of a favourable reply, Your obedient servants

Johannes Fridericus Virnius, poeta Caesarius[3]

Bartholomeus Freyerbott

Read 20 July 1615. And the honourable Council agreed to [allow] seven plays and that they may not take more than two groschen per person.

---

[1] The Elector in question was John Sigismund of Brandenburg (reigned 1608–19).
[2] Fencing-schools were frequently used for theatrical performances by strolling players.
[3] The post of *poeta Caesareus* (not Caesarius) was that of a poet laureate and carried considerable prestige.

When the English actor-managers John Green and Robert Reynolds applied to the City Fathers of Danzig for permission to perform plays there some fifteen years later, they had to use a similarly persuasive style in order to obtain a licence. (See also 2, 5–7, 28–31 and 287–9 for other documents relating to English Comedians.)

2   An English company pleads for permission to play, 1616

Danzig city archives. Reproduced in Johannes Bolte (1895), pp. 48, 49.

Worthy, gracious, honourable and most sagacious Gentlemen,

Your Worships' high reputation draws many foreign nationals hither and tempts those that have acquired some arts to let them be seen and heard in this goodly city. Now it is certain that the ways of the world cannot be pictured with greater art than by way of comedies and tragedies which represent and picture all men's lives and their very being, good and evil, as it were in a mirror so that everyone may see and recognise himself [. . .] Since our bent and inclination has led us to perfect ourselves in this art and to endeavour to the best of our ability to exhibit the same in all manner of countries and cities, we have at this moment arrived hither from the goodly Kingdom of Denmark in the knowledge that excellent gentlemen are in authority [here] who have visited, seen and had experience of the world, thereby earning much praise and reputation abroad. Hence we do not doubt that Your Worships will not take exception to our offering and presenting our art and services, beseeching Your Worships most urgently that Your Worships may grant us their special favour and permit us to act and present our useful and pleasing comedies and tragedies to this famous city and its honourable citizens [. . .]. We beg most humbly as we have stated before that Your Worships will not allow us to have undertaken this journey with its high expenses in vain but instead will favour our art and kindly allow us to exercise it, to your greater glory and praise amongst all potentates and countries that we shall visit. We shall not make the least unreasonable demands on anybody but shall be satisfied with whatever Your Worships may regard as equitable, wishing that God's Eternal Majesty may grant Your Worships long and healthy lives, successful governance and ever flourishing trade and commerce. Dated 28 July 1616. [. . .]

Your humble servants,
Johan Green
Robert Reinald
and the whole company
of English Comedians

Read in Council on 29 July 1616 and resolved to grant their request for the space of one week on condition that they take not more than three groschen per person, that they do not perform anything indecent and do not continue when the week has expired, either here or outside the city, but cease and discontinue playing.

More than half a century later, the position of strolling players was still so insecure that they had to submit humble petitions to municipal and other authorities to be allowed to stage their plays in a given place. Indeed, the need for such petitions, generally formulated in terms of cringing servility, continued far into the following century. Frequently these petitions were reinforced with economic arguments, as in the case of this petition by the well known actor-manager Andreas Elenson who addressed this petition to the Salzburg Council in September 1675. (See **35**.)

3   Andreas Elenson pleads for permission to play, 1675

Salzburg *Hofratsprotokoll* (Council minutes) of 23 September 1675, f.237. Reproduced in Friedrich Johann Fischer, 'Wandertruppen des 17. Jahrhunderts in Salzburg' (Seventeenth-Century Strolling Players in Salzburg), in the Festschrift *100 Jahre Gesellschaft für Salzburger Landeskunde 1860–1960* (Centenary of the Salzburg Local History Society) (Salzburg, 1960), p. 459

Andreas Elenson, actor, humbly petitions to be [...] permitted like last year to erect a booth not far from the tennis-court and then to give public performances together with a company to be gathered; thus enabling him to escape from his debts.

This petition was granted on 14 October 1675.

Once a Council's favour had been won it was the usual practice for a company to give a free performance for the councillors and their families, the so-called '*Ratskomödie*'. One of the purposes of this was a plea to be relieved of local taxes. The custom persisted into the following century, a clear indication of the strolling players' insecurity in German-speaking countries. The example quoted below is the dedication to the Councillors of Nuremberg on the title page of a printed play text offered by the actor-manager Benecke several days before the actual performance.

4   Announcement of a 'council performance', 1709

Municipal Library, Nuremberg, nor. 4475. Reproduced in Bärbel Rudin, 'Der Prinzipal Heinrich Wilhelm Benecke und seine "Wienerische" und "Hochfürstlich Bayreuthische" Schauspielergesellschaft' [The Actor-Manager H.W.B. and his Viennese and Electoral Bayreuth Company of Players], in *Mitteilungen des Vereins für Geschichte der Stadt Nürnberg* (Bulletin of the Historical Society of the City of Nuremberg), vol. 62 (Nuremberg, 1975), p. 185

For your most gracious pleasure/
And in due and humble gratitude for/
The high honour received/
There/
Will be performed in all humility/
In the ordinary playhouse/
For the Most Noble and Sagacious Council/
Of the World-Famous Imperial Free City of Nuremberg/
Our gracious all-commanding MASTERS/
An entirely new play
Entitled:
The Theatre of the Fortunes/
Of the Emperor Otto the first of that name/
A Tale of War, Love and Valour/
With the unconquerable Adelaide:
By the High German Players
Currently in residence here.
Monday 23 September 1709.

For strolling players letters of recommendation from highly placed persons, such as the princes whom they had served, were invaluable either in obtaining service with another prince or in overcoming local obstacles and opposition to their being allowed to perform in public. The following example shows the protection given by John Sigismund, Elector of Brandenburg, to the company of English Comedians led by John Spencer (whom he had dismissed), in a letter addressed to John George I, Elector of Saxony and dated 16 April 1613.

5   A letter of recommendation for English Comedians, 1613

Dresden Archives. Reproduced in M. Fürstenau, *Zur Geschichte der Musik und des Theaters am Hofe der Kurfürsten von Sachsen* (Contributions to the History of Music and Theatre at the Court of the Electors of Saxony) (Dresden: Rudolf Kunze 1861–2), and Albert Cohn, *Shakespeare in Germany in the Sixteenth and Seventeenth Centuries* (Oxford, 1865, reprinted Wiesbaden: Dr Martin Sandig, 1967), p. lxxxvii (translation taken from Cohn)

Bearer of these, the English comedian Johann Spenzer [John Spencer], has been a considerable time in our service, and in his humble waiting on us has so borne himself that we have derived a gracious pleasure therefrom. But when he purposed to visit other places, and among the rest also to exhibit his art and his comedies in Dresden, we have wished to give him this our recommendation. We request Your Highness will be pleased not only to give him permission to do so for four weeks or more, but also to show him all favour in other respects.

Testimonials and letters of safe conduct continued to be highly desirable when the activities of strolling players, including English actors, resumed after the Thirty Years' War. The following letter of safe conduct was issued by the Emperor Ferdinand III (reigned 1637–57) on 10 November 1650 for a company of English Comedians who had performed at court that year. (Compare the letter of safe conduct issued in Holland in 1618 to a French company – 290.)

6   An Imperial letter of safe conduct for English Comedians, 1650

Julius Max Schottky, *Unterhaltungen für das Theater-Publikum* (Entertainments for the Theatre-Going Public) ed. August Lewald (Munich, 1833), p. 135. Reproduced in Cohn (1865), pp. ci–cii

We Ferdinand the Third, by the Grace of God etc. publicly declare and make known to all men by these presents: After the bearers of these, Wilhelmb [William] Roe, Johann [John] Waide, Gedeon Gellius [Gideon Giles?], Robert Casse and their companions, being English Comedians, had most humbly given Us to understand how that they for a considerable time past had publicly exhibited and acted all sorts of amusing plays [...] at the courts of various high potentates, as also at other places, humbly beseeching that We would likewise grant them Our gracious permission publicly to act such things for a certain time in Our Imperial residence, and We graciously granted them the said permission [...], whereas they now further humbly announced to us that they were desirous of leaving this place and of practicing and exercising their said profession in various other places, as well in the Holy Roman Empire as in our hereditary Kingdoms, Principalities, and countries, and to this behoof [...] have humbly begged our aid, permission and protection.

Graciously regarding this their humble and respectful petition, but more especially taking into consideration that all the time in which We have graciously permitted them to act their plays here in Our city of Vienna, and yet more, in Our Imperial Court itself, they have comported themselves in such a manner that no complaints have been made against them; We [...] have shown them this

Imperial grace and given them licence that they may without hindrance publicly exercise, carry on, and use this their intended profession in all places [...] and that they suffer no damage intended or otherwise or impediment; provided however that they conduct themselves quite honourably in so doing, and are sure to abstain from all unseemly speeches and actions.

Hereupon We order each and everyone, Electors, Princes spiritual and secular, Prelates, Counts, Barons, Lords, Knights, Squires, Landmarshals, Captains General, Viceregents, Burgraves, Prefects, Wardens, Administrators, Stewards, Bailiffs, Burgomasters, Counsellors, Citizens, Commonalties, and all other lieges and subjects of Ourselves and of the Empire, as also Our hereditary Kingdoms, Principalities and lands [...] seriously and solemnly by this letter, and decree that they not only allow the aforementioned company of English Comedians, together with their people, horses and effects to pass and pass again at all places, by water and by land, freely, safely and without hindrance, and [...] afford them all convenient aid, and render them all assistance and good will, but also allow them quietly to enjoy this grace, freedom and permission granted to them and to use the same at all places freely and without hindrance nor complain against the same, nor allow others to do so in any manner or wise: this is Our serious intent.

In witness of this letter, sealed with our seal attached thereunto, given in Our city of Vienna the tenth day of the month of November in the sixteen hundred and fiftieth year after the birth of Christ, in the year of our sovereignty, the fourteenth of the Roman Empire, the twenty-fifth of the Kingdom of Hungary, and the twenty-third of the Kingdom of Bohemia.

(signed) Ferdinand

B. OFFICIAL PAYMENTS

Acting companies attached to German courts would receive gratuities for their performances at their master's pleasure, either for particular performances or for service over a period of time. The following payments were made to the company of John Spencer who was known as Hans von Stockfisch – evidently a clown role – and who worked for a while for the Elector of Brandenburg (see 5).

In 1618 this company accompanied the Elector on a journey from Berlin to East Prussia and played at Elbing, Balge and Königsberg. The following accounts were connected with this tour.

7   Payments by the Brandenburg Court for English Comedians, 1618

Accounts of the Electoral Court. Reproduced in Cohn (1865), p. xciii. (Translation taken from Cohn.)

19 marks, at the gracious command of His Electoral Grace, being 50 dollars and 36 groschen, to a certain Stockfisch, whom His Electoral Grace sent to Elbing to bring from thence the English Comedians, paid March 17.

112 marks 30 sh. which His Electoral Grace has graciously ordered to be given to the English Comedians as a second gratuity, in addition to the 50 rix-dollars which they have previously received. Paid November 8.

To the High Counsellors of the Duchy of Prussia. We, John Sigismund, by the Grace of God, etc., have granted, once for all, two hundred Polish florins to the actors for their trouble, who, as is well known to you, have at different times at Our gracious command, acted in Our apartments at Königsberg and Balge, and hereby graciously order you to pay them the said 200 florins out of Our treasury. Dated Elbing, June 20 1619.

150 marks to 18 English Comedians who acted several comedies before His Electoral Grace, paid June 22 1619.

C. CONTRACTS WITH FOREIGN GOVERNMENTS

In the eighteenth century, German companies performed not only in the German heartland but also in predominantly non-German-speaking countries – even at times at foreign courts. Russia which was beginning to turn to the West for cultural guidance under Czar Peter I ('the Great') was a case in point. Peter wished to lay the foundations of a professional and secular theatre in his country. In 1701 his emissary Jan Splavsky engaged the actor-manager Johann Christian Kunst in Danzig to go to Moscow with his wife Anna and eight actors, in order to become the director of the Czar's court theatre at a salary of 5,000 dollars in cash. The negotiations for this enterprise were far from smooth.

8   Kunst negotiates with a Russian envoy, 1701

Danzig archives. Reproduced in Bolte (1895), pp. 153–4

The Honourable *Joannes Slawski* [sic], with a lieutenant's commission from His Majesty the Czar in Muscovy etc. etc. etc., has personally appeared at the Mayor's office to complain that Johan Christian Kunst, an actor, who was also present, had promised him in good faith to travel with him to Moscow together with his companions in order there to serve His Majesty the Czar with all manner of plays, having already received and taken from him 30 rix-dollars cash in hand and at the same time having promised him and his company free travel and living costs until arrival at the destination [...], however, now that the date of departure had come and all was arranged, the aforementioned actor had gone back on his promise and did not want to travel with him; he therefore desired the latter to make a categorical statement concerning this matter at the office.

Whereupon said Johan Christian Kunst [...], after a serious admonition to bethink himself well what he had done so far and was still bound to do, stated publicly that because of his wife and his little children he could not travel and was therefore prepared to return the 30 rix-dollars cash. But if in future sufficient security was put up for him here in Danzig so that he together with his company could travel back at any time freely, safely and without hindrance, he would then decide without any further ado to travel to attend [upon the Czar] as expected but with his accommodation costs en route paid for. [...]

The presiding Mayor agreed, following the pleas by the aforementioned lieutenant, to note this down for Your Noble and Gracious Highness and, so that it may be delivered under the seal of the City, to show it to Your Most Noble Excellency's Council.

Done on 4 October 1701. [...]

Delivered on 6 October 1701.

In fact, Kunst did go to Moscow in 1702 where his company at first performed in an existing playhouse inside the Kremlin. Then Peter had a theatre erected specially for him in Red Square. However, Kunst died shortly after, in 1703, and another German – the goldsmith Otto Fürst, who was a Moscow resident – became the head of the company. Performing in Russian as well as in German, Fürst introduced items from the German repertoire (Lohenstein, Gryphius) as well as Italian and French plays (including several by Molière), which had been translated into Russian not from the original texts but from the German versions.

II Playhouses and performance venues

The illusionistic staging methods developed in Italy during the sixteenth and early seventeenth centuries were taken up in Germany from the beginning of the period under review. While playing spaces tended to be adaptations of existing venues – tennis courts, riding-houses, fencing-rooms, guildhalls – there were also some purpose-built theatres. The first of these was the 'Ottonium' erected in Kassel between 1603 and 1606 by Landgrave Maurice of Hesse (1572–1632), himself a composer, playwright, patron of the arts and employer of Robert Browne's company of English Comedians. This building continued to be in theatrical use until 1696.

But not all theatrical venues were indoor stages: there was a lively interest in outdoor performances as well which was to continue into the next century. The first example of a specially designed open-air venue was the 'rock theatre' built in 1616 in the park of Schloss Hellbrunn by Marcus Sitticus von Hohenems, Prince-Bishop of Salzburg. Seating hundreds of spectators, the theatre, which exists to this day, was used both for sacred dramas and for operas. It was described in the following terms by the chronicler Johann Stainhauser in his life of the Prince-Bishop.

9   An open-air theatre described

MS in the Studienbibliothek Salzburg. Reproduced in Artur Kutscher, *Vom Salzburger Barocktheater zu den Salzburger Festspielen* (From the Salzburg baroque theatre to the Salzburg Festival) (Düsseldorf: Pflugschar-Verlag Klein Vater & Sohn, 1939), p. 35, and in Heinz Kindermann, *Theatergeschichte Europas* (Theatre History of Europe) vol. 3 (Salzburg: Otto Müller Verlag, 1959), p. 484

A sight well worth seeing on the aforementioned hill in the park is the beautiful large theatre hewn out of the rocks and handsomely equipped, which has been pierced and fitted for the acting of pastorals with such skill and art that persons can enter prettily anywhere out of the rocks whereat spectators are not a little amazed [...]

10   Rock theatre in the park of Schloss Hellbrunn, Salzburg

Margarete Baur-Heinhold, *Theater des Barock* (Baroque Theatre) (Munich: Georg D.W. Callwey 1966), p. 153. Photograph by Helga Schmidt-Glassner

When the idea of illusionistic perspective staging as practised particularly in Florence became known in Germany, it was felt to be a most exciting innovation. Joseph Furttenbach the Elder from Leutkirch (1591–1667) spent ten years in Italy – in Milan, Rome, Genoa and Florence – on an extended study tour; when he was appointed to the post of municipal architect in Ulm on his return to Germany, he applied the new architectural and scenic techniques to building a theatre in the orphanage in 1641 and to staging school dramas there. The ideas deriving from his stay abroad he committed to paper in *Architectura civilis (Civil Architecture)* (Ulm: Jonas Saur, 1628), *Architectura recreationis* (Recreational Architecture) (Augsburg, 1640) and *Mannhafter Kunst-Spiegel* (The Noble Mirror of Art) (Augsburg: Johann Schultes, 1663). These works, which cover a very much wider field of architecture and mechanics than merely that of theatre, do not simply reflect what he had learnt from Parigi and other masters of the scenic art: they are the works of a practitioner who did his best to put these innovations into practice himself, though of necessity on a scale far more modest than that possible at a court in Renaissance Italy. Most of his ideas are directly traceable to Italian example, but some of his solutions to architectural problems encountered at home are not without interest in their own right. The following two extracts from his last book deal not so much with problems of staging as with problems of lighting, ventilation and seating.

II   Ensuring proper ventilation in a theatre, 1663

Furttenbach, *Mannhafter Kunst-Spiegel* (1663), pp. 113–14. Reproduced in somewhat modernised translation by George R. Kernodle in Barnard Hewitt (ed.), *The Renaissance Stage* (University of Miami Press, 1958), p. 206

[…] it is a matter of the highest importance that the windows in the entire building be placed in such a manner that when large numbers of people are assembled there, sitting very close to one another, they may not perish, collapse or faint with so much breath, vapour, and heat (as I know from my own experience, hence my point is to be taken seriously and heeded), nor should windows, out of sheer carelessness, be cut away only after the building has been completed, or the upper stage be mutilated and spoilt with air vents in order to get rid of vapours; an event which would be a disgrace to the architect and the mark of a botched job. So it will be no bad idea to have small air vents at various places in the ceiling which could be closed with shutters, so that when the weather is hot they may be opened, and the vapours and the heat let out […], whereby both the spectators and equally the actors may enjoy good clean air.

Therefore, after much thought and deep consideration […] a couple of windows facing east […], another couple facing south […], and a third couple facing north were installed, which not only light the dressing room but at the same time bring good fresh air to the actors concealed there,[1] but since the rear pit[2] needs daylight if one wishes to play without any oil lamps during the daytime, two pairs of windows must be installed […] on either side, corresponding to each other. These will suitably let in the light from south to north and thus provide enough light for the rear pit.

But no windows are to be placed on either side of the front pit[3] where the walls should remain entirely unbroken so that the spectators are not blinded but, left in darkness, they may enjoy as a peculiar delight to the eyes and with great amazement the daylight entering the stage along the streets,[4] shining like the dawn through the clouds, as well as alongside the house fronts painted upon the *telari*,[5] and they are bound to be astounded at these ingenious arrangements.

Although it would actually be best not to have any windows by the seats or benches on which the spectators are sitting […] so that the audience sitting in darkness will turn their faces towards the stage whereby the daylight on the stage will appear all the more charming to them, it may nevertheless do no harm to have by the side of the said seats, i.e. along the aforementioned side walls, a couple of windows at every tenth bench, so that when a large crowd, especially in summertime, is seated together there before the start of the performance, it may nonetheless enjoy some fresh air […]; but as soon as the trumpets and drums are sounded, but before the curtain is dropped,[6] all the [...] windows opened next to the spectators' benches must have their shutters closed so that everything is made dark again, or alternatively the window openings may be densely covered with green foliage which will darken the place somewhat and yet allow the air to pass through.

[1] The dressing room in Furttenbach's scheme was immediately behind the stage.
[2] The rear pit was a pit at the back of the stage, designed to accommodate such effects as passing ships.
[3] The front pit was immediately behind the parapet which formed the front of the stage facing the auditorium.
[4] 'Streets' or 'lanes' in Furttenbach's terminology were the spaces between the wings, or rather the *telari*, which were used for entrances. For the use of daylight illumination in seventeenth-century theatres, see also 272.
[5] *Telari* – three-sided prisms used for scene changes, in supposed imitation of the *periaktoi* of antiquity – were a borrowing from the Italian scenic theatre.
[6] Drums and trumpets were a conventional way of announcing the start of the performance. Note that in Furttenbach's plan, the front curtain instead of being raised was to be dropped into the front pit.

12   Seating arrangements in a theatre, 1663

Furttenbach (1663), p. 114. Reproduced in Hewitt (1958), p. 216. (Translation taken from Hewitt.)

The seats for the spectators must be planted with care. A floor is erected on strong pillars, and over this a sloping floor. The seats of the benches are $1\frac{2}{3}$ feet from the sloping floor and $1\frac{1}{4}$ feet wide, with backs $1\frac{1}{3}$ feet high. A space $1\frac{1}{4}$ feet is left between the benches for entering and for comfort when sitting. The fact that the benches are set on a sloping floor enables all the spectators to see the stage clearly [...].

In the space between the first benches and the front pit are placed sixteen well-appointed chairs for the most distinguished spectators with their wives, and for their youths.

This space is separated from the front pit by a parapet $2\frac{1}{4}$ feet high.

In the second half of the seventeenth century a large number of opera-houses were built in major centres of the German-speaking world – in Dresden (1664–67), Vienna (1666–8), Munich (from 1651), Hanover (1687–9), and Wolfenbüttel (1688). The high cost of erecting and running such a building normally made it an affair of the court of Emperor, Elector or Prince; and the interior unambiguously reflected the social hierarchy in its structure. The best sightlines were reserved for the Prince, either seated in the front row immediately facing the stage or in a centrally placed box at the back of the house. (See 71.)

13   Interior of the Munich Oper am Salvatorplatz, 1686

Graphische Abteilung, Deutsches Theatermuseum, Munich

In this opera-house the Elector's box was at the back of the house, which afforded the noble spectators a clear and undistorted view of the perspectively designed scenery. The stage of this large theatre, the first free-standing opera-house in Germany, the building of which began in 1651, had up to eight pairs of wings by 1654; from 1657 onwards, these could be moved on wagons below the stage. The auditorium was rebuilt in 1685 in the form shown.

III   *Stage presentation*

A. STAGING METHODS

Like the courts of other European countries, the aristocracy of German-speaking countries organised court festivals of an essentially theatrical type in the seventeenth century, which were comparable to the Italian *trionfi*: see Michael Anderson, *TIE: Italy, 1476–1789* (CUP, forthcoming); the French *ballets-mascarades*: see W.H. Howarth, *TIE: France, 1550–1789* (CUP, forthcoming); or the English masque: see Glynne Wickham, *TIE: England, 1530–1642* (CUP, forthcoming) – self-celebrations in which the participants and performers were in the main the courtiers themselves.

Essentially allegorical, these festival plays were based on patterns initiated in Italy in the late fifteenth century and then developed there as well as in France throughout the following century. The festivities from 10 to 17 March 1616 at the court of Württemberg in Stuttgart in celebration of the baptism of Frederick, son of Duke John Frederick, which consisted of processions, ballets, songs, tournaments etc. were the last major event of this kind before the Thirty Years' War (1618–1648) for quite some time put a stop to a tradition which in a variety of forms was to survive well into the eighteenth century.

Most of the songs and poems which formed part of the spectacle were contributed by the Württemberg court poet Georg Rodolf Weckherlin (1584–1653) who was also the author of the book subsequently published in Stuttgart to describe the proceedings. (The practice of embodying such an event in printed form was resumed when such festivities were taken up again after the long interruption of the war. Note that such official descriptions may give an idealised version of the proceedings and therefore have to be taken with a pinch of salt.) Weckherlin, who was to settle in England in 1626 and serve as Latin secretary under the Commonwealth, wrote the description both in German and in (slightly faulty) English – the latter version as a tribute to Elizabeth, the daughter of King James I of England, who was the wife of the Prince Palatine Frederick.

14   The Stuttgart masque described, 1616

G. Rodolphe Weckherlin, *TRIUMPHALL SHEWS* Set forth lately at Stutgart. *WRITTEN* First in German, and now in English (Stuttgart: printed by John-Wyrich Resslin [Johan-Weyrich Rösslin] 1616), ch. 3, pp. 8–12. Reproduced in Ludwig Krapf and Christian Wagenknecht (eds.), *Stuttgarter Hoffeste/Texte und Materialien zur höfischen Repräsentation im frühen 17. Jahrhundert* (Stuttgart Court Festivals: Texts & Materials on Courtly Spectacles in the Early

17th Century), Neudrucke deutscher Literaturwerke, Neue Folge 26 (Tübingen: Max Niemeyer 1979). (The spelling and some of the punctuation have been modernised.)

Of the mask.[1]

The supper being done, all Princes, Princesses, and the gentry went from the castle into the palace in the garden, where a great room is in, that for beauty's and largeness' sake scarce can be compared. As soon as they were entered, a music of many instruments entertained the time till everyone was placed, and then four trumpeters did appear in the shape of ancient Romans very bravely apparelled all in white satin, covered with gold and silver, their helmets garnished with great bunches of red, yellow, blue and white feathers. Another like dressed Roman followed who did proclaim the ordinance that (after the custom of German chivalry) should next day be kept at the running to the ring, and publish a challenge of King Priamus, that did defy all other knights and would be defendant against all adventurers.

This being denounced, and everyone falling again to feed his eyes of that he did like best, the ears were presently filled with as pleasant [and] as strange a sound of music, where all eyes were again withdrawn by to the place that resounded of. There they saw come in four huge great but also well-formed heads, going the one after the other, and was each of them so big that six men could be therein at their ease and walk withal.

The first head was (as it were) a lodging of three Western nations: the second of three Northerly: the third of three Easterly: and the last (and it was a blackamoor) of three Southerly nations. Those four heads after they had done three turns about, stayed themselves right over against the Princes, and there having made a low curtsey (inclining their monstrous noses to the ground) their consort of music that was within ceased: and there came out of the first head but one player on the lute alone, in a red suit, almost like an English shipman. To the sound of his lute came forth after him a gentleman that did represent the English nation. His hat was white embroidered with silver, with a white feather, being the fashion of his habit that was of white silver cloth, as English Lords were wonted to use some twenty years ago. He danced a galliard after the English manner: and as soon as he was near the Princes, a wild Scottishman danced out from that same head at the sound of a drum another Scottishman played on. Now the Englishman seeing him come against him, began to dance likewise after his fashion, and was the one on this, and the other on that side, when they did see come out of that same head an Irish harper, to whose play followed another Irishman that by his dancing caused the first two to imitate his sport too.

The second head (a dwelling place of three Northerly nations) gave issue to a Frenchman, apparelled in carnation satin, and dancing a coranto that another

French fiddler, coming out with him, did play. After him hopping forth a High-Dutchman in a red Dutch garment with puffs, his player was a fluter in like an apparel. The third that came forth of the second head was a Lapponian, covered with the skin of a bear, and trampling about at the sound such another fellow of Lapland did tune with a sackbut.

The third head was big of a Spaniard, who came forth strutting and roaming most bravely, attired in a habit of purple laid with gold laces: his head and hands were richly set in great ruffs. Another Spaniolized fellow played his measures on a bandora.[2] The Italian did follow, with his gown, even as a signor Pantalone is commonly to be seen at Venice: and another played him with a cithern[3] a dance, he did perform with pretty tricks, when out of that same head appeared a Polonian in a garment of blue satin, of his country shape, with his bag-piper, and caused all the foresaid nations to imitate his kind of dancing.

A blackamoor came out of the fourth head, richly adorned with jewels about his arms, and another one of that country played on a little tabor full of bells a measure after their custom. Then followed a Turkish piper, and another Turk jumping to his play brabbled with his unsheathed scimitar. Lastly came forth an Indian or American all bare and painted over his body, having only a fair cloak of coloured feathers, and upon his head likewise a hat made of feathers. Another American made him move to a strange noise he made with a very big horn.

The eleven nations that were come in before him did presently counterfeit his demeanours and countenances [...]: and then the whole consort of their twelve musicians with their several nature of instruments began to play a new dance, which was lively and strangely performed by the maskers. And there shall be known that still one nation did imitate the other, so that he that was the Englishman, being the first, did countefeit the eleven nations that came after him: he that played the Scottishman, ten: the Irishman nine: the Frenchman eight, and so forth. [...]

---

[1] Note that the word 'balleth' in the German version of the text is rendered as 'maske' in the English, which suggests that the various national forms of court spectacle (combining text, spectacle, music and dance) were seen as being essentially mere variants of the same thing.

[2] The bandore is a guitar- or lute-like instrument.

[3] The cithern is a kind of guitar played with a plectrum.

15   Illustration of the Stuttgart masque, 1616

Esaias van Hulsen and Matthäus Merian, in *Repraesentatio der Fvrstlichen Avfzvg vnd Ritterspil* (Depiction of the Princely Progress and Chivalrous Games) (Stuttgart: Johan-Weyrich Rösslin, 1616). Reproduced in Krapf & Wagenknecht (1979), Neue Folge 27, p. 7

Like other aspects of theatre technology, stage lighting in indoor theatres in seventeenth-century Germany was inspired by Italian example. Furttenbach has left detailed descriptions of several lighting methods in *Mannhafter Kunst-Spiegel* (see 11 & 12), following the guidelines laid down by Buontalenti, Sabbattini, and other Italian innovators – see Anderson, *TIE: Italy* (CUP, forthcoming).

16   Methods of stage lighting, 1663

Furttenbach (1663), pp. 123–3. Reproduced in a somewhat modernised translation in Hewitt (1958), pp. 234–6. (Translation taken from Hewitt.)

For lighting the stage a glass oil lamp of medium size is used, 5 inches high and 4 inches wide above at the mouth, but tapering to 1 inch at the bottom – just the sort that is ordinarily used in church. This lamp is filled with fresh spring water up to the widest neck, leaving 1½ inches at the top of the container for oil. A quarter of a pound of heavy olive oil will float on the water and fill the vessel almost to the top. A floating wick is prepared as follows. For a base a brass wire ring is made 2½ inches across; to this ring are fastened, at equal distances, six little cork blocks about the size of a small hazelnut. A little ring or collar, the size of a feather quill, which will hold the wick rather loosely, is fastened above the brass ring by twisted wires. A cotton wick, about 3 inches long and no thicker than a little quill, is inserted. When the entire float is set down in the lamp on the olive oil, the top of the wick will stand ⅓ inch above the little ring for burning and the rest will remain below to draw up the oil by the heat. Then the lamp is ready to light. [...]

The whole lamp is placed in a wrought iron ring with a 4-inch screw to fasten it where it is needed. There should be a number of these rings ready for the lamps at the back of the parapet,[1] back of the side walls of the proscenium, between the sections of the heavens,[2] at the rear pit,[3] and at other places. [...]

For greater effect and safety, we use behind each lamp a piece of gold tinsel 5 by 8 inches marked out in lozenge shapes with cross lines. Or better, behind each lamp a flat thin piece of mica [...] is set up or fastened on so that it throws out a glowing reflection of the lamp. [...]

In practice such an oil lamp has often given a good light as long as twelve hours with ¼ pound of olive oil, for water is continually poured in to raise the oil and the floating wick until the last drop of oil is burned and only water is left. [...] As many as 50 lamps can well be distributed around the stage and up in the heavens to light a scene. [...]

---

[1] The parapet divided the stage from the auditorium. (See 11, note 3.) The lights placed behind it were, in fact, footlights.
[2] The sections of the heavens are the borders and cloud machines.
[3] See 11, note 2.

There is some evidence that in addition to, or perhaps in the absence of, a front curtain, a traverse curtain dividing the stage into two halves – downstage and upstage – was a frequent piece of stage equipment during the seventeenth century and again later, in the latter part of the eighteenth century. This usage, which made possible both swift scene changes and discoveries on the inner stage, is conjectured by some to derive from the practice of English companies touring in Germany. See W. Flemming (ed.), *Das Schauspiel der Wanderbühne* [The Theatre of the Strolling Players], Leipzig: Philipp Reclam 1931), pp. 34–49. The following stage directions are one example out of many indicating the use of such a traverse.

17   The use of the traverse curtain

Johann Georg Schoch, *Comoedia Vom Studenten Leben* (The Comedy of Student Life) (Leipzig: Johann Wittigauer, 1658). Reproduced in Robert Eduard Prutz, *Vorlesungen über die Geschichte des deutschen Theaters* (Lectures on the History of the German Theatre) (Berlin: Duncker & Humblot, 1847), p. 139; also in editions of the play by W. Fabricius (Auswahl litterarischer Denkmäler des deutschen Studententums, Munich: Seitz & Schauer, 1892), p. 5

Exit Mercury quickly at this point and the curtains are lowered.[1] Instrumental music is played. Thereafter the curtains both on the stage and the inner stage are raised, and the first 4 scenes of Act One are shown in postures and *tableaux vivants*, except for Pickleherring who is not present.

Here there may be a brief pause until another signal for action is given with drums and trumpets.[2]

[1] The literal word for curtains is, significantly, 'Teppichte' (carpets).
[2] Compare 11, note 6.

18   Unattributed mid-seventeenth-century German stage.

Frontispiece of Isaac Clauss's *Teütsche Schawbühne* (German Theatre) (Strasbourg, 1655)

The engraving shows a perspectively designed *scène à l'italienne* such as might have been used by the more successful sort of strolling players: there are two chandeliers, four sets of wings and four borders. Note the traverse curtain which is clearly visible in front of the backcloth.

Court performances – opera, ballet, or whatever – continued throughout the seventeenth and indeed much of the eighteenth century to be on a scale of sumptuous spectacle that strolling players could not hope to match out of their meagre resources. Special performances celebrating particular dynastic or political occasions were mounted lavishly by courtiers, sometimes supported by professionals; all the resources of the scenic theatre were employed. The example quoted below was part of the birthday celebrations in July 1687 of Frederick, Duke of Saxe-Gotha, at the Friedenstein theatre.

19   Scene changes in a court spectacle, 1687

Scenario of *Ballet von dem beglückten Rauten-Krantz* (Ballet of the Fortunate Wreath of Rue) (Gotha: Christoph Reyher, 1687). Herzog-August-Bibliothek, Wolfenbüttel, Textb.4°6

The Scene changes are:
1. The heavens with clouds.
2. A landscape at the back of which the earth is pictured upon a hill.
3. A pleasant garden.
4. A landscape and a field of grain.
5. A forest.
6. A ravine.
7. A different sort of landscape at the back of which there is the sea and in the middle of which [there is] a rock whereupon lies an image of water.
8. A large chamber.
9. Another more magnificent chamber or gallery, with equestrian statues on both sides.

The Machines or Spectacles are:
1. A gloomy cloud filling the entire stage.
2. The chariot of Phoebus drawn by two horses.
3. Mercury's flight from the clouds.
4. Flora's chariot hung with wreaths and flowers.
5. Ceres' chariot.
6. Diana's chariot drawn by two stags.
7. The ascent of the 7 planets from underneath the earth.
8. The miners' [or mountaineers'?] journey.
9. The sea and rocks with living water dropping into the sea.
10. The crossing [of the sea] by the Water Goddess and two Naiads upon sea-shells.
11. The throne, out of one of whose steps another seat is produced by a pulley, sitting upon which 4 citizens and artisans appear and rise.
12. The live horse on which a knight presents himself in full armour.

Princely family occasions which took on a public character would make use of theatrical (as well as other) entertainments. An outstanding event of this nature was the gathering in Dresden during the whole month of February 1678 of various branches of the ruling house of Saxony at the invitation of the Elector John George II. The entertainments offered included processions, hunts, chivalrous exercises, fireworks as well as operas, plays and ballets. The plays were performed by the company of Johannes Velten (1640–1692/3?), the most distinguished actor-manager of German-speaking countries of the period. The *Ballet of the Reunion and Effect of the Seven Planets*, performed on 3 February 1678, i.e. only a few days after the arrival of the guests on 31 January, was designed by Johann Oswald Harms (1643–1708), the greatest of seventeenth-century German set designers for opera and ballet who had been employed as court painter in Dresden since 1675. See Horst Richter, *Johann Oswald Harms/Ein deutscher Theaterdekorateur des Barock* (J.O.H./A German Stage Designer of the Baroque Period) (Emsdetten: Verlag Lechte, 1963, *DSB* 58), esp. pp. 28–41. For an account of the entire festivity, see Gabriel Tszchimmer, *Die Durchlauchtigste Zusammenkunft etc.* (The Princely Gathering etc.) (Nuremberg: Hoffmann, 1680).

20   Scene of Bacchus, Ceres and other figures

Ballet von Zusammenkunft und Wirckung derer VII. Planeten (Dresden: Melchior Bergens, 1678). Herzog-August-Bibliothek, Wolfenbüttel, Textb. 4°22

Such mythological/allegorical spectacles under court auspices continued well into the following century. A notable example was *Angelica Vincitrice di Alcina* (Angelica's Victory over Alcina), an outdoor show staged at the command of Emperor Charles VI at the Favorita palace (now the Theresianum) in Vienna on 14 and 20 September 1716 in celebration of the birth of his son Leopold. The Italian libretto of this opera was by Pietro Pariati (many texts of performances at the Imperial court in the seventeenth and eighteenth centuries were in Italian); the music was composed by Johann Josef Fux; and the elaborate staging of the performance was the work of Ferdinando Galli-Bibiena (1657–1743) and his son Giuseppe (1696–1757), members of the famous Italian family of scenic designers, stage technicians and architects active in Italy, Spain and the Holy Roman Empire throughout the century. (Details of the production are to be found in *Hofzeremonial-protokoll, 1716*, ff. 210, 214–15, Haus-, Hof- und Staatsarchiv, the Imperial Archives, Vienna.) *Angelica Vincitrice di Alcina* was witnessed by the English traveller Lady Mary Wortley Montagu, who reported her impressions in a letter from Vienna dated 14 September 1716 to her then friend Alexander Pope.

21   Lady Mary Wortley Montagu describes the production of 'Angelica Vincitrice di Alcina', 1716

Robert Halsband (ed.), *The Complete Letters of Lady Mary Wortley Montagu* (Oxford: Clarendon Press, 1965), pp. 262–3. (The spelling has been modernised here.)

[...] Don't fancy [...] that I am infected by the air of these popish countries, though I have so far wandered from the discipline of the Church of England to have been last Sunday at the opera, which was performed in the garden of the Favorita, and I was so much pleased with it, I have not yet repented my seeing it. Nothing of that kind was ever more magnificent, and I can easily believe what I am told, that the decorations and habits cost the Emperor £30,000 sterling. The stage was built over a very large canal, and at the beginning of the 2nd act divided into 2 parts, discovering the water, on which there immediatedly came from different parts 2 fleets of little gilded vessels that gave the representation of a naval fight.

It is not easy to imagine the beauty of this scene [...]. The story of the opera is the Enchantments of Alcina, which gives opportunity for a great variety of machines and changes of the scenes, which are performed with a surprising swiftness.[1] The theatre is so large that 'tis hard to carry the eye to the end of it, and the habits in the utmost magnificence to the number of 108. No house could hold such large decorations, but the ladies all sitting in the open air exposes them to great inconveniences, for there is but one canopy for the Imperial family, and the first night it was represented, a shower of rain happening, the opera was broke off and the company crowded away in such confusion, I was almost squeezed to death.

[1]   The story of Angelica, daughter of Galafron, King of Cathay, and the witch Alcina was taken from Ariosto's *Orlando Furioso*.

22   Various monsters occupy some lonely islands by the enchantment of Alcina, 1716

Angelica Vincitrice di Alcina (Vienna: Van Ghelen, 1716, with five engravings by Franz Ambros Dietel, Galli-Bibiena, Elias Schaffhauser & Johann Ulrich Biberger). Herzog-August-Bibliothek, Wolfenbüttel, Textb.230

23   Figures in a procession: Antiopa Giustificata. This court spectacle celebrated the birth of a son, Maximilian Emmanuel, to the Elector Ferdinand Maria of Bavaria and his wife Henrietta Maria Adelaide, 1662

Dragons ridden by trumpeters. (Munich: Gioann Iekelino 1662). Herzog-August-Bibliothek, Wolfenbüttel, 18.12 Eth.(2)

Spectacular ballets, particularly but by no means exclusively as part of an opera performance, were an important feature of the German theatre in this period and well into the latter half of the eighteenth century. The new opera house erected in Brunswick by the great patron of the arts, Duke Anthony Ulric, was opened on 4 February 1690 with *Cleopatra* (libretto by Friedrich Christian Bressand, music by Johann Sigismund Kusser and sets by Johann Oswald Harms who had been working for the Wolfenbüttel-Brunswick court since 1686). This lavish production to which ordinary spectators were admitted for an entrance fee (something by no means to be taken for granted at such a princely entertainment), boasted a number of ballets, as listed in the published libretto.

24   Figures in an operatic ballet, Brunswick, 1690

Friederich Christian Bressand, *Cleopatra, Sing = Spiel/Auf dem grossen Braunschweigischen Schauplatze vorzustellen/ im Jahr 1691* (Cleopatra, Opera presented in the great Brunswick Theatre in 1691) (Wolfenbüttel: Caspar Johann Bissmarck, 1691). Herzog-August-Bibliothek, Wolfenbüttel, Textb.397.

Dances.

At the end of every scene change there will be one dance; as follows.

Three Tutelary Goddesses (*Divae geniales*) of the three Serene Princely Houses of Brunswick-Lüneburg.

2 *Harlequins*, 2 *Scaramouches* and two *Polichinelles*.[1]

6 Boatmen, with oars.

6 Ladies-in-Waiting of the Queen, followed by

3 Pages.

6 Women Gardeners.

2 Old Men, 2 Old Women and 2 little Children.

6 Ghosts.

2 Flag-Wavers, with flags.

8 *Combatants*, or fighting Soldiers.

[1] Note that these figures were of Italian origin, either taken directly from the *Commedia dell'arte* or indirectly via the *Comédie italienne*. Polichinelle, for instance, is the French descendant of the Neapolitan Pulcinella (who was also the ancestor of the English Mr Punch). The Italian improvisational comedy with its masks had been known in German-speaking countries since the middle of the sixteenth century from the visits of Italian companies: note the Pantaloon figure in the Stuttgart masque of 1616 (see 14). The influence of the *Commedia dell'arte* was to be a factor in German theatrical development until well into the eighteenth century (see 94, 161, 162). For the dramatic, rather than strictly theatrical, significance of Italian comedic models, see Walter Hinck, *Das deutsche Lustspiel des 17. und 18. Jahrhunderts und die italienische Komödie* (German Comedy in the 17th and 18th Centuries and the Italian Commedia) (Stuttgart: J.B. Metzlersche Verlagsbuchhandlung, 1965).

B. COSTUMES

As might be expected, stage costumes in seventeenth-century German theatre differed on the one hand according to the nature of the theatrical occasion (popular farce, Protestant or Catholic school drama, court festival, high tragedy) and on the other hand according to the resources available to the performers (strolling players, well endowed colleges or princely courts). The costume conventions were not dissimilar to those obtaining in other European countries with an established theatrical tradition, allowing for differences in national dress styles.

Emblematic conventions deriving from Renaissance practice continued as an important influence throughout this and the next century. The following examples are taken from the political allegory, *Das Friedewünschende Deutschland* (Germany Longing for Peace) written in 1647 at the special request of the actor-manager Andreas Gärtner by Johann Rist (1607–1667), Lutheran pastor, poet and founder of the literary society, the Elbschwanorden (Order of the Swans of the Elbe).

25(i) Costumes, 1647: archaeological

Johann Rist, *Das Friedewünschende Deutschland* (Hamburg: Heinrich Warner's widow, 1649; Cologne, Andrea Bingh, 1649). Reproduced in Rist, *Sämtliche Werke*, ed. Eberhard Mannack, vol. 2 (Berlin/New York: Walter de Gruyter, 1974), p. 48. (Pagination taken from the Mannack edition.)

(The four heroes are dressed in an antiquated manner, with long hair gathered up, holding large maces in their hands, girded with broadswords [all of] which can be found in the illustrations of the learned Father Klueverius' Ancient Germany, a very useful work for this purpose.) – Act 1, Sc. 2.[1]

[1] Note the attempt at some kind of archaeological documentation for the costume of the ancient German heroes of the play.

Germany's fall from prosperity to wretchedness as a result of the war was suggested by means of costumes.

25(ii) Costumes, 1647: symbolical (a)

Rist (1649), p. 56

(Enter Germany, preceded by Peace in a snow-white gown, a golden wreath on her head, a green laurel branch in her hand and carrying a cornucopia under her arm. Germany is dressed in the most splendid modern fashion, holds a beautiful sceptre in her hand, wears a magnificent crown on her head [...], has many male and female servants, being followed especially by Lust who is dressed most wantonly in all manner of colours but who walks about all but half naked.) – Act 1, Sc. 3.

25(iii) Costumes, 1647: symbolical (b)

> Rist (1649), p. 156

(Enter GERMANY in the figure of a poor wretched beggarwoman dressed in torn old rags; she is leaning on a staff and carries a beggar's wallet around her neck.) – Act 3, Sc. 1.

The foreign nationalities devastating Germany were represented emblematically by one single figure with a composite dress.

25(iv) Costumes, 1647: national

> Rist (1649), pp. 104–5

As soon as the Gentlemen have left there must enter a person wearing rather a ridiculous outfit, such as a Spanish doublet, French hose, a Polish or Croatian cap and similar foreign clothes (...) – Act 2, Sc. 3.

The following quotation from the German version of *Hamlet* used by strolling players – *Der bestrafte Brudermord* (Fratricide Punished) – makes it clear that in the seventeenth century these professional companies often carried very incomplete wardrobes, a state of affairs which continued well into the latter part of the following century. Although the first publication (as late as 1781) of the complete text of *Der bestrafte Brudermord* was based on a manuscript dated 27 October 1710, it is certain that this represented a much older version of the play as performed by German actors in the previous century. The appearance in Act 2, Sc. 7 of a head of a company of players by the name of Carl (Charles) suggests that the text may well have been used by the 'Carlische hochteutsche Comödianten-Compagnie' (Charles's High German Company of Players) of Karl Andreas Paulsen (*c.* 1620–?). This doyen of German actor-managers toured tirelessly throughout German-speaking countries and even further afield between 1650 and the end of the 1670s (see **58**).

26   The inadequate wardrobes of strolling players

> *Der bestrafte Brudermord*, in *Olla Potrida*, (ed. by Reichard, 1781), Pt. II. Reproduced in A. Cohn (1865), and in W. Creizenach, *Die Schauspiele der Englischen Komödianten* (The Plays of the English Comedians), *DNL* 23 (Berlin & Stuttgart: W. Spemann, 1888); repr. Darmstadt: Wissenschaftliche Buchgesellschaft, 1967), p. 163

HAMLET When you were in Wittenberg you used to put on good plays. However, you had some fellows in your company who wore good clothes but black shirts, others who had boots but no spurs.

CHARLES Your Highness, you often cannot have all you want, perhaps they thought they were not to do any riding.

HAMLET Still it is better to have everything correct; [...] there were also some who wore silk stockings and white shoes but had on their heads black hats which were full of feathers, a plumage almost as full below as on top, I think they must have worn them in bed instead of nightcaps; now that won't do and is easily mended.

The costumes used in court spectacles were of an altogether more lavish variety. At the Emperor's court in Vienna, with resources beyond the reach of lesser mortals, Italian designers, notably Lodovico Burnacini (1636–1707), created not only dazzling stage sets but also extravagant and fantasticated costumes. A particularly splendid occasion from the costume point of view was the 'horse ballet', the *Contest of Air and Water*, held on 24 January 1667 in the inner courtyard of the Hofburg, the imperial residence in Vienna, to celebrate the marriage of Emperor Leopold I with the daughter of Philip IV of Spain. Both the scenario of the event and its published description were written by the Jesuit Francesco Sbarra; Alessandro Carducci was brought in from Florence and Carlo Pasetto from Ferrara to help organise the festivities. The splendour of the emblematic costumes used on that occasion can be gauged from the following description of the dress of Duke Charles of Lorraine, the Emperor's brother-in-law, who played the role of the leader of the dawn-coloured forces of the Air.

27   A costume for a horse ballet, Vienna, 1667

Francesco Sbarra, *La contesa dell'aria e dell'acqua. Festa a cavallo rappresentata nell'Augustissime Nozze delle Sacre Cesaree, Reali M.M. dell'Imperatore Leopoldo e dell'Infanta Margherita delle Spagne* (Vienna: Matteo Cosmerovio, 1667). Reproduced in Hilde Haider-Pregler, 'Das Rossballet im Inneren Burghof zu Wien' (The Horse Ballet in the Inner Courtyard of the Palace in Vienna), *M&K*, 15 (1969), p. 303

His Highness bestrode a noble grey steed whose dappled coat enhanced his beauty, on a silver-plated saddle embellished with gold and pearls, with matching headpiece and reins, stirrups and a gold bit [. . .]. His Highness wore a shining breastplate embroidered with gold, pearls and other precious stones which depicted in finely drawn designs and in many colours the beauty of the Breezes and a variety of birds [. . .]. Emerging from a belt of small but lovely plumes of many colours, his outer dress was marked out with the various faces of the Winds embroidered in relief which blew out breaths of silver and gold, and it cascaded all over the caparison which, embroidered with clouds with precious lace all around, was made entirely of silver cloth in hues of Dawn, strewn with stars [. . .]. Of the same quality was the mantle edged with lace of the finest gold and of the greatest width to be found, which cascaded down from his back and was encircled with rich jewels and English braid, gathering round his sides, then lying in spreading graceful flounces and held up by the Breezes, dwellers of the Air, who paid this reverent homage to her noble champion. To the whole hose in harmony with [the rest of] the apparel was joined the stocking in hues of Dawn covered to halfway up the leg with a silvery buskin in the manner of the ancient Romans, all spread with gold and gems; and above the helmet which rivalled the shining shield from which hung a sumptuous silk pennant shot with gold and edged with the richest lace, there rose in creamy plumes the ensigns of daybreak and in snow-white gauze the hues of Dawn [...].

IV Actors and acting

Known as 'English Comedians', the English companies touring on the Continent from the 1580s onwards played in German-speaking countries under the most diverse conditions – often but by no means exclusively as entertainers in the service of a prince. At such a court they might be working in a setting worthy of their novel and exciting talents. But they also performed for the public at large, in all kinds of venues which might be only roughly adapted for theatrical use. (For further information on English touring companies in this period, see 287–9, as well as Glynne Wickham (ed.), *TIE: England, 1530–1660* (CUP, forthcoming.) Working in a language not understood by most of their spectators, they soon learnt to acquire at any rate some German or to take on board a few German actors. But what made them so attractive to all strata of German society was the fact that they were all-round entertainers – clowns, musicians and dancers as well as 'mere' actors. If the company described below, which also visited Amsterdam and Cologne on the same journey that took it to Münster, was that of William Kemp (as has been conjectured), this visit would have come shortly after Kemp's leaving the Lord Chamberlain's Men in 1599.

28 The composition of an English company of strolling players, 1599

Joh. Janssen (ed.), *Chronik der Stadt Münster* (Chronicle of the City of Münster) (Münster, 1852). Reproduced in A. Cohn (1865), pp. cxxxiv–cxxv, and in H. Kindermann, *Theatergeschichte Europas*, vol. 3, (1959), p. 354

On 26 November (1599) eleven Englishmen arrived here, all of them young and lively fellows except for one rather elderly fellow who was in charge of everything. They performed five different plays in their English language in the council-house for five days in succession. They had with them many different instruments such as lutes, citherns, viols, fifes and the like; they danced many new and strange dances (not common hereabouts) at the beginning and the end of their plays. They had a clown with them who fooled around and jested in the German language during the performance, when they were about to start a new act and had to change their costume, so that he would make people laugh.

The impact of these experienced foreign actors on aristocratic audiences can be gauged from the following letter written in Graz in February 1608 by the eighteen-year-old Archduchess Maria Magdalena, whose betrothal to Cosimo, son of Grand Duke Ferdinando de' Medici of Tuscany, had just been announced. In this letter addressed to her elder brother, the Archduke Ferdinand (the later Emperor Ferdinand II), who was in Ratisbon at the time, she describes theatrical performances she had witnessed of English Comedians under the leadership of John Green who played at the court in Graz from 6 to 20 February.

29   Green's company in Graz, 1608

K.K. Staatsarchiv, Vienna. Reproduced in Joh. Meissner, 'Die Englischen Comoedianten zur Zeit Shakespeares in Österreich' (English Comedians of Shakespeare's Time in Austria), in *Beiträge zur Geschichte der deutschen Literatur und des geistigen Lebens in Österreich*, no. 4 (Vienna: Konegen, 1884), pp. 76–80, and in Willi Flemming (ed.), *Das Schauspiel der Wanderbühne* (The Drama of Strolling Players) (Leipzig: Philipp Reclam, 1931), pp. 71–2. (The translation cannot do full justice to the naivety and the wilful spelling of the original.)

Your Highness, loving and dearly beloved brother. I could not do other than drop Your Grace a line, and at the same time beseech you to forgive me for not having replied to Your Grace's letter any sooner [...].

[...] Now I must report to you what sort of plays the Englishmen have performed. First of all they came here on Wednesday after Candlemas, they rested on Thursday, on the following Friday they performed the *Play of the Prodigal Son*,[1] as they did at Passau, and on Saturday the one about *A Pious Woman of Antorf*[2] which was very nice and decent. On Sunday they played *Doctor Faustus*,[3] on Monday the one about a Duke of Florence *who has fallen in love with a nobleman's daughter*;[4] on Tuesday they played *Nobody and Somebody*[5] which was terribly amusing; on Wednesday they played the one about *Fortunatus' bag and magic hat*;[6] on Thursday they played the one about the *Jew*[7] which they had played in Passau; on Friday both they and we took a rest [...]. At five o'clock we then had dinner again[8] and the Englishmen again performed a play about *Dives and Lazarus*;[9] I cannot tell Your Grace how lovely it was, there was not the slightest bit of obscenity in it, it was very moving because they acted so well; they must surely be regarded as good actors [...]

---

[1] This may have been based on the anonymous *Pater, Filius et Uxor; or The Prodigal Son*, written some time between 1530 and 1534.

[2] This may conceivably stand for *Friar Rush and the Proud Woman of Antwerp* by John Day and William Haughton (1601) or the revised version of this by Henry Chettle (1602). The text of both plays has been lost.

[3] Clearly this is Christopher Marlowe's *Doctor Faustus* (see also **58**).

[4] This may be John Day's *The Italian Tragedy of . . .* (name lost; 1600), the text of which has been lost.

[5] This could have been any one of the three versions of this play, the dates of which are 1592, 1602 and 1606 respectively; the author of the original play is unknown.

[6] This is Thomas Dekker's *Old Fortunatus* (1599) or just possibly the earlier two-part play on the same theme, probably written by Robert Greene.
[7] This is more likely to be Marlowe's *The Jew of Malta* (*c.* 1589) than Shakespeare's *The Merchant of Venice* (*c.* 1596), though the latter remains a possibility as does Dekker's *The Jew of Venice*.
[8] This performance took place several days later than the previous ones.
[9] It is not clear which dramatisation of this theme, the earliest known English version of which dates from *c.* 1570, is being referred to here.
(The information for the above notes was kindly supplied by Professor Glynne Wickham.)

As a result of the War engulfing wider and wider areas of German-speaking countries, the visits of English Comedians to the Continent became increasingly rare.

30   Decay of theatre during the Thirty Years' War

Illuminirter Reichs vnd Welt-Spiegel (Illuminated Mirror of the Empire and the World) (1631). Reproduced in Cohn (1865), p. xcviii

This Monsieur Pickelherring was first introduced into Germany by the English while it was still in a state of prosperity, and everybody liked to amuse himself with comedies and other representations, which is now no longer the case.

In the second half of the seventeenth century more and more members of companies nominally termed English for prestige purposes were in fact German. One of the last mentions of English Comedians was as late as 1697.

31   The last of the English Comedians, 1697

Jakob Daniel Ernst, *Ausserlesene Gemüths-Ergötzlichkeiten; das ist, Funffzig sonderbare Lust- und Lehr-Gespräche* (Extraordinary Mental Diversions, That is, Fifty Curious Pleasant and Instructive Conversations) (Magdeburg: Lüderwald, 1697), p. 93. Reproduced in Reinhold Köhler, *Shakespeare-Jahrbuch (Shakespeare Yearbook)*, I, pp. 416–17, and in Creizenach (1888), p. 13

What about it, gentlemen, would you like to go to the playhouse this afternoon and see what good things the actors recently arrived here from England have to offer? I hear they are going to present their former King Charles Stuart's war with his subjects and his subsequent execution, which will be an interesting spectacle, especially because of the rockets and blank pistol shots they will fire off.[1]

[1] It is hard to know exactly what play this might refer to; if it was Gryphius' *Carolus Stuardus*, it would have been a German play dealing with an English political subject rather than a play of English origin.

B. DUTCH COMPANIES

In the second half of the seventeenth century some Dutch companies, notably that of Jan Baptist(a) van Fornenbergh (1624–1696), included Northern Germany in their foreign tours and met with a good reception there. (For further information on Fornenbergh's touring, see 293 and 333.) A particular characteristic of Dutch theatre which impressed German audiences were the *vertoningen* (i.e. *tableaux vivants*): these occurred at key points in the dramatic presentation when the actors formed themselves into a picturesque grouping and held it for a while, as it were constituting a painterly composition (see 277 and 278). This device was imitated by some German playwrights and performers (see 17 and 57).

32   Fornenbergh's company visits Altona, 1665

Johann Rist, *Die AllerEdelste Belustigung Kunst- und Tugendliebender Gemüther* (The Most Noble Entertainment of Lovers of Art and Virtue) (Hamburg: Johann Naumann, 1666), pp. 75–6. Reproduced in Rist, *Sämtliche Werke*, ed. Eberhard Mannack, vol. 5 (1974), pp. 275–6

[...] when we arrived in the famous city of Hamburg about a fortnight ago, we were told that a number of Dutch actors had arrived in the nearby royal city of Altona whose head or leader was named Jan Baptist, and that this company performed their comedies and tragedies so well that all experts praised them highly for it. We went out there together in order to discover the truth of the matter, and we found that the high reputation accorded this company by persons of high as well as low rank was no fable but corresponded to the facts; we therefore watched these excellent actors more than once.

C. FRENCH COMPANIES

If opera was regarded as a specifically Italian skill, it was the French who were considered the great exponents of dance. German princes in the second half of the seventeenth century often made a point of employing French dancing-masters and choreographers. More significantly, the French spoken drama of the Grand Siècle came to enjoy high prestige in upper-class circles. Not only did French plays, translated or adapted, form a large part of the German repertoire – it actually became the fashion at the greater courts, in the latter part of the seventeenth and throughout most of the eighteenth century, to keep under contract a full acting company imported from France. The assumption that the aristocracy would have fluent French was taken for granted. Thus, Frederick I, the first King of Prussia (1657–1713), who maintained a splendid court with French as its language, commissioned one George Du Rocher, a *directeur de spectacles*, to engage a French company to come and take up residence in Berlin (where they were to stay from 1706 until 1711). The terms of service offered can be taken as not untypical of the working conditions of such companies.

33   A French company's conditions of service in Prussia, November 1706

Kgl.Geheim.Staats-Archiv. Dramatisches Rep.9.L.L.7.C. (in 1902). Reproduced in Jean-Jacques Olivier, *Les Comédiens français dans les cours d'Allemagne au XVIIIe siècle* (The French Actors at German Courts in the Eighteenth Century) (Paris: Société d'imprimerie et de librairie, 1902), 2nd series, pp. 8–10

[...]

His Majesty the King of Prussia having resolved to establish in his city of residence a company of French actors whom Sieur du Rocher offers to bring here and to have in readiness to play on the first day of next month, has seen fit to grant them the following conditions. [...]

II.

Orders have been given to pay the said Du Rocher two thousand dollars to reimburse him for his expenses in bringing the company to this city.

III.

His Majesty will grant a stipend of six thousand dollars a year starting on 1 December of this year, and of this sum fifteen hundred dollars will be paid in advance for the first quarter as soon as the company arrive here, and the rest in three-monthly instalments.

IV.

The company will be obliged to perform at court twice a week, either in His Majesty's residence or in His country seats. The rest of the time they can perform in town, although not on any day whatever but only on prescribed days.

V.

When the company play at court they will be assigned a suitable place. The required candles will be supplied. But then the company will be in no position to ask for anything whatever to do with the play itself.

VI.

And when they follow the court into the country they will be transported, lodged and fed.

VII.

When they play in town, the King, the Princes and Princesses of the royal house and the persons named by the King will be able to enter free of charge. But all other persons of whatever quality who wish to go to the play will have to pay, as follows: for the first balcony one dollar per seat, for the second a florin, and for the third half a dollar, and for everybody in the pit 8 groschen. [...]

IX.

The company will be provided with a guard of soldiers free of charge to prevent any disorders in whatever place a play is performed. [...]

X.

Before the company gets ready to perform any play, the court will be presented with a list of all plays intended for public performance in order to know which ones will be permitted. [...]

XII.

Out of the above-mentioned sum of six thousand dollars a year which the King has promised the company, one hundred dollars will be kept back every quarter for distribution to the poor by order of His Majesty.[1]

XIII.

And in addition the company will pay the Excise one dollar every time they play in town, in consideration of which no other sort of actors will be allowed to play here. [...]

Given at Cologne-on-the-Spree, 2 Nov. 1706.

Frederick.

[1] It had been standard practice throughout the seventeenth century for actors to be taxed for permission to perform, generally in order to make a contribution to charity, a custom which continued well into the next century.

D. GERMAN COMPANIES

While German actors were frequently regarded as social outcasts, a condition which was to continue for a very long time (see 36, 37, 96, 97, 147), some among them – particularly in the second half of the seventeenth century – had actually enjoyed a good education. University students often took to the adventurous life of the road as strolling players. It was during this gradual rise to a somewhat more respectable status that women were allowed to appear on the professional stage.

34   Students become actors

Der bestrafte Brudermord (see 26), Act 2, Sc. 7, in Cohn (1865), pp. 264–6 (Translation taken from Cohn.)

HAMLET Were you not some years ago at the University of Wittenberg? It seems to me I have seen you act there.

CHARLES Yes, Your Highness, we are the self same company.

HAMLET Have you the whole of the same company still?

CHARLES We are not quite so numerous because some students took engagements in Hamburg. [...]
HAMLET Have you still got the three actresses with you? They used to play well.
CHARLES No, only two, the one stayed behind with her husband at the court of Saxony.

Some companies secured not only the protection of various courts but also achieved a degree of social recognition – e.g. the troupes of Johannes Velten (see **20**) and of Andreas Elenson (d. some time after 1706 – see **3**). Elenson founded a theatrical dynasty which ran through three generations, from the 1670s to the 1780s. His son Julius Franz who briefly took over his father's company after the latter's death and was famous in the role of Pantaloon, received the signal honour of having a black marble tombstone erected in his honour by the Elector of Cologne after his early death, with a Latin inscription.

35   An actor's epitaph, 1708

Reproduced in Philipp Eduard Devrient, *Geschichte der deutschen Schauspielkunst* (History of German Acting), vol. 1 (Leipzig: J.J. Weber, 1848), pp. 319–20, new edition by Rolf Kabel and Christoph Trilse (Munich/Vienna: Langen Müller, 1967), vol. 1, p. 199; also Eike Pies, *Prinzipale* (Actor-Managers) (Ratingen/Kastellaun/Düsseldorf: Aloys Henn Verlag, 1973), p. 121

> Hic jacet, et tacet
> qui stabat, et clamabat
> Ludens Comoediam
> Finit Tragoediam
> Viator, hic ora
> atque labora
> Ut ultima hora
> sit tibi Aurora [...]
> Obiit 1708. 7. Julii
> Julius Franciscus Elenson
> Comoediant annorum XXVIII

(Here lieth and is silent he who used to stand and declaim, playing comedy at first but tragedy in the end. Traveller, pray here and labour in such wise that your final hour may be a new dawn unto you. [...] Julius Franz Elenson, actor aged 28, died on 7 July 1708.)

But by and large German actors throughout the seventeenth century and well into the eighteenth century were regarded as rogues and vagabonds. Protestant clergymen, both Lutheran and Calvinist, often railed against them on moral grounds: series of pamphlets appeared from time to time denouncing the profession. Velten was denied holy communion in Hamburg in 1692, shortly before his death, and his widow, having taken over the management of the company, was attacked by the Rev. Johann Joseph Winckler who in 1701 published an anti-theatrical pamphlet in Magdeburg based on the writings St John Chrysostom. She replied the same year in a pamphlet entitled, *Zeugnis der Warheit Vor Die Schau-Spiele oder Comödien/ Wider Hn.Joh. Joseph Wincklers [...] Herausgegebenen Schrift/ Worinnen er Dieselbe heftig angegriffen/ um verhasst zu machen sich vergeblich bemühet [...]* (Witness of Truth in Favour of Plays/ Against the Pamphlet Published by the Rev. J.J. Winckler, in which he attacked them violently/ endeavouring in vain to make them hated [...]). The pamphlet quoted from below, by Precentor Martin Heinrich Fuhrmann of Berlin, was part of this long-running controversy.

36   A clergyman's attack on Frau Velten

M.H. Fuhrmann, *Die an der Kirchen Gottes gebauete Satans-Capelle* (Satan's Chapel Built Next Door to the Church of God) (Berlin, 1729). Text quoted in Carl Niessen (ed.), *Frau Magister Velten verteidigt die Schaubühne* (Emsdetten: H. & J. Lechte, 1940), epilogue, p. 6

Most commendable, too, was the zeal shown by Your Right Reverend's ministers in Magdeburg against the licentiousness of the actors at that time [...].[1] Because when the Velten company ([...] consisting entirely of people who had been to university) staged the most offensive farces and foolish obscenities, these priests raised the trumpet of their voices in the pulpits against the theatrical walls of this comedic Jericho so long and so loudly that the same were finally bound to collapse and perish. Now it so happened that when the widow Velten fell into a violent fever and, pricked by her guilty conscience and fearful of death hovering before her very eyes, wished to be reconciled with God on account of her sinful profession and asked for holy communion, no priest was prepared to give this blessed object to the bitch and cast the noble pearl before this swine, before and until she had promised on oath in future wholly to abandon her unhallowed way of life [...]. Which did indeed take place, but she kept her promise ill and devoured her vomit with the dogs.

[1] A reference to Winckler's campaign against Frau Velten.

Not only were actors reproached with following an immoral profession; their close affinity to other types of showmen – mountebanks, acrobats, animal tamers, puppeteers and the like – militated against their being accepted by respectable German society. Thus, Frau Velten was 'reduced' to staging marionettes instead of live actors at the end of her career, around 1711/12. The Augsburg preacher and deacon Ruprecht pointed out the 'base' aspects of showmanship in a pamphlet published as late as 1724; while ostensibly attacking only low-grade actors, he in fact echoed prejudices which had been current for a long time against any form of theatre.

37   Second-rate actors denounced, 1724

Georg Ruprecht, *Zeugnis der Wahrheit/Gegen der sogenannten/Curieusen und wohl-erörterten/ Frage: /Ob Comödien unter denen Christen geduldet (...) werden können?* (...) (Witness of Truth/Concerning the So-Called/Curious and Much Discussed/ Question/ Whether Comedies may be tolerated among Christians (...) (Augsburg: Paul Kühtzen's widow, 1724), pp. 50–1. Reproduced in Niessen (1940), from the Niessen Collection, Theatermuseum Cologne

But the reason why comedians are hated so much nowadays is that every puppeteer and juggler (nay, even people who exhibit for money unreasoning beasts such as baboons, dogs and horses etc.) will arrogate to themselves the appellation of actor. You see daily examples of puppeteers (who have no idea what a play, much less a player, might be), having earned a pittance with their wooden actors for whom they provide neither subsistence nor a wage, taking on, in despite of honest actors, a handful of vagabonds who have never seen a stage in their lives, let alone acted on one, and besides by their ill conduct and disgraceful behaviour render the name of actor so contemptible and hateful in a town that it is sometimes hard for an honest company to obtain another licence [to play].

E. NONPROFESSIONAL PERFORMANCES

The rise during the seventeenth century of professional acting, both native and foreign, in German-speaking countries did not mean the total disappearance of earlier, particularly religious, forms of amateur theatre. These evolved with changes of taste, religious orientation and theatrical technology but allowed their earlier origins in mediaeval scriptural drama to shine through, albeit at several removes.

School drama was a feature of both Protestant and Catholic education. In Catholic boys' schools, various teaching orders – Jesuits in particular, but Benedictines and Piarists as well – made theatre an important element of their teaching. Jesuit performances in the Catholic parts of the German-speaking world, in places like Vienna, Munich, Ingolstadt, Lucerne or Cologne, attained high forms of theatricality.

The link with mediaeval drama is apparent in the following extract from the *Perioche* (programme with plot summary) of *Vonn dem Todt oder Todtentanz* (The Play of Death, or The Dance of Death), performed in the great hall of the Jesuit *Gymnasium* of Ingolstadt on 6 February 1606. It is only fair to point out that if this text based on the image of the *danse macabre* seems backward-looking, not to say naive, the themes of later Jesuit plays covered a wide range of topics of contemporary interest, such as anti-Protestant polemics, the Turkish menace, problems of personal conduct as well as statesmanship inspired by Christian principles: see Elida Maria Szarota, *Geschichte, Politik und Gesellschaft im Drama des 17. Jahrhunderts* (History, Politics and Society in C17th-Century Drama) (Berne & Munich: Francke Verlag, 1976), esp. p. 11. Later, the sophisticated technical developments of baroque theatre and opera were fully incorporated into Jesuit school performances in this and the following century, until the suppression of the Society in 1773. For the acting methods of Jesuit theatre, at any rate in the latter part of the seventeenth century, see **41–7**.

38   Synopsis of a Jesuit play, 1606

Perioche (programme) of the above (Ingolstadt: Andreas Angermeyer, 1606), p. 2. Reproduced in Ruth Eder, *Theaterzettel* (Dortmund: Harenberg Kommunikation, 1980), p. 19

PROLOGUE

The prophet Isaiah considers the condition of mankind. He hears a voice summoning him to prophesy. He asks what he is to prophesy and hears this saying: All flesh is as grass, and all its glory is as a flower of the field which withereth and falleth away. This saying causes him to say more about the brief duration of life, and he is astonished that any man may walk in pride seeing he is at no moment safe from death by means of which he will be made level with the most contemptible of men. In confirmation of this he finds a skull which answers him, saying: Everyone great or small, rich or poor, noble or common, must die, and nothing is more commendable than the frequent thought: Consider how thou shalt die. Death appears and says, This sermon might displease some of the spectators, he would take on this office himself.

Some of the educational benefits to be derived from these school performances were mentioned by the architect and designer Furttenbach (see **11, 12, 16**.)

39   The educational benefits of school drama, 1663

Furttenbach, *Mannhafter Kunstspiegel*, pp. 111–12. Reproduced in a somewhat modernised translation in Hewitt (1958), pp. 203–4

[…] Hence this exercise is extremely useful, nay delightful for the younger generation and growing youth when it is used above all for the exaltation, praise and honour of God as well as [for the inculcation of] good conduct among respectable people. Acting on a well equipped stage, the young lads will acquire a good appearance and firm presence, which will greatly encourage in them brave, confident speech, and give them a bold and heroic spirit so that later on they will be able to hold forth all the more vigorously and forthrightly on religious as well as secular matters. Therefore it is exceedingly necessary as well as highly desirable even for persons of inferior rank […] to build such playhouses for the sake of the younger generation, so that our dear growing youth may be kept from sin, disgrace and vice, but may be brought up to decent conduct as well as useful virtues by such praiseworthy exercises.

Now it is not the case that one has [. . .] to build very large structures and plunge into immense expenditure on every occasion, but it is possible to do these things just as well at a low and reasonable cost. [. . .]

Since one cannot write (nor indeed speak) about anything better or more usefully than that which one has successfully carried out in practice before, so on this occasion I have seen no way around describing in some detail [. . .] the very stage or theatre which, with God's good help, I have had built and erected twice [. . .]. On the first occasion the noble and most learned Herr *Joan.Chunradus Merchius. Rector, Hist.Biblothec. & Direct.Mus.* with his students presented the very pleasing and memorable *tragi-comedy* of the life and history of Moses, especially his leading the people of Israel out of bondage in Egypt etc., with a cast of 120, a duration of six hours, and with three main scene changes. On the second occasion, in the year 1650, in celebration of the peace, there was acted and performed on the famous stage, with 5 scene changes, [a play] about the condition and nature of the ancient Christian Church during the rule of the Roman Emperors *Caius, Diocletian, Galerian, Constantine, Maxentius* and *Constantine the Great,* so charmingly and delightfully that the whole community has been talking about it ever since.

Since the purpose of school performances was largely didactic, the guiding principles of playwriting and casting were naturally entirely different from those governing the professional theatre. Christian Weise (1642–1708), headmaster in Weissenfels and Zittau in Saxony, who wrote and directed more than thirty school plays, explained his guidelines in the preface to *Lust und Nutz der Spielenden Jugend.*

40   The writing and casting of school plays, 1690

Weise, *Lust und Nutz der Spielenden Jugend* (Delight and Utility of the Acting of Young People) (Dresden & Leipzig: 1690). Reproduced in Robert Eduard Prutz (1847), p. 247

In these plays I had to accommodate far too many people who for the most part wanted a good role. And if one were to consider the purpose of the whole exercise, any one of the youths ought to be in it as well as the next. Indeed little boys should be suitably mixed in as well so that they might learn to acquire some social self-confidence at an early age. So it was not my fault if the plotting was somewhat forced. That is to say, persons who according to history should have been in one place had to stay away so as to give the others a chance to speak. And as a result many plots, many emotions and much comic business were introduced which would otherwise have been omitted, if it had been possible to arrange the characters according to the play and not the play according to the characters. Hence my greatest skill lay in hiding my art and as it were raising the whole edifice in an irregular place.

Furthermore I was well aware that plays calling for nearly one hundred persons could not easily be placed elsewhere. [...] in most matters I looked at the temperament of people to suit their [stage] character. Whether they were lively or lethargic, brash or timid, merry or melancholy, I accommodated the dialogue to their expression and their diction in such a way that they could not fail to act well.

Probably the first acting manual published in Germany – but written in Latin – was the *Treatise on Stage Action* by the Jesuit Father Franciscus Lang (1654–1725). This post-humously published illustrated book, the summary of a lifetime's experience in directing Jesuit plays, principally at the Jesuit school in Munich, represented an essentially backward-looking approach to acting by the time it was published. The drilling of boys of varied talents had entailed a somewhat mechanical approach designed to create pleasing stage pictures rather than plumbing any psychological depths. Though very different in intention, Father Lang's guidelines for actors were not unrelated to professional stage practice of the late seventeenth and the early eighteenth century.

41   How to stand and walk

Franciscus Lang, *Dissertatio de actione scenica, cum figuris eandem explicantibus, et observatio-nibus quibusdam de arte comica* (Treatise on Stage Action with Figures Explaining the Same and Some Observations on the Art of Acting) (Munich: Maria Magdalena Riedlin, 1727), pp. 21–2. Translated into German and reproduced by Alexander Rudin, *Abhandlung über die Schauspielkunst* (Berne/Munich: Francke Verlag, 1975), pp. 170–3

So the first thing to note in putting down the soles of one's feet is that they should never be set down on the boards in the same direction but always quite a bit turned away from one another, in such a way that while the toes of one foot point in one direction, the second foot should point in the other. Let me be permitted henceforth to call this manner of standing and walking the stage cross [...].

As regards standing, it is above all necessary to ensure that both feet never stand on the boards in a straight, uniform and parallel position; but let one foot always be at an angle to the other so that in standing [...] one sole is turned to the right and the other to the left; let one foot be advanced slightly, the other drawn back. That will happen if one's body is never kept in a straight and flat but always in a more or less oblique posture towards the spectators. [...]

So in walking and in moving the feet I demand a particular stage walk [...]. This stage walk is carried out with three or four steps in which the actor must proceed in such a manner that the stage cross [...] is observed meticulously. [...] If the actor wishes to move from one place to another on the stage, he will not be walking properly unless he first draws back a little the foot which was in advance of the other from the position in which he is standing. So let the foot which was in front be retracted and moved forwards again but further than where it had stood before. Let the second foot follow and be placed in front of the first: but let the first, lest it remain behind, again move in front of the second. But in this movement one should always remember to put down the feet at an angle. [. . .]

Some may say that this is a queer and artificial way of walking. [. . .] However, I maintain [. . .] that this stage walk is one of the great charms of the art of acting if the opinion of connoisseurs, my own experience and insight as well as the truth of the matter do not deceive me.

42   The proper management of arms, elbows and hands
Lang (1727), pp. 28–32; Rudin (1975), pp. 178–84

I move on to the discussion of arms, elbows and hands. Here the rule applies that in acting the arms are usually kept away from the trunk and moved freely without clinging to the hips or flanks [. . .]. Figure II illustrates the art in that he extends his right arm freely while he keeps his elbow away from his trunk while his left hand is propped up on his hip. Something similar can be seen in Figure III in which it is also to be noted that both arms should not be moved with the same extension and in the same manner, but let one be higher, the other lower, one more extended and straight, the other more bent even when it is raised [. . .]. It is essential that this be done, and experienced painters and sculptors observe this well in their works.

[. . .] the arms should neither hang down untidily nor be flung upwards like missiles; it is permissible to extend the right arm forwards freely from time to time but not to its full length unless one is pointing at a particular thing; the left arm though is mostly to be held in such a way that it is applied to the side in as it were the form of a handle, unless it is to accompany the movement of the right arm once in a while. Neither arm should be raised above the shoulders or the eyes (except during the strongest emotions).

It is first of all to be noted about the hands in particular, the mightiest tool of the art of acting, that they should be flexible and free at the wrist where they are connected to the arm. Furthermore, the fingers should be arranged in such a way that the index finger is mostly extended straight while the rest gradually begin to turn inwards and contract more and more towards the palm. See Illustration III. [. . .]

While discussing these matters let me briefly digress to the question of whether gloves should or could be worn by actors on stage. This new custom has begun to be introduced into theatres [. . .]. Having spent more than fifty years in the theatre either as a spectator or as a producer, I can testify to the fact that I have not once seen any person on stage covering his hands with gloves. Therefore let no innovator blame me if I fight against the introduction of this novelty with the authority of the ancients [. . .].

Nor does the argumentation of some who say this is the custom of court theatres, where all persons on stage have to appear wearing gloves, apply to our theatre. Indeed as long as directors at court look above all more to ostentation and outer show in their performances than to the true characteristics of the art of acting, they must not and cannot be an example to us.

43–44 The actor's use of his hands and arms

Lang (1727), pls. II, III, pp. 27, 29

Fig. III

Fig. II

45 How to express emotion on stage

Lang (1727), pp. 42–51; Rudin (1975), pp. 191–9

[...] But I say concerning this matter that it can be very useful for someone [...] frequently and diligently to study the paintings of experienced painters or the sculptures of artists so that by contemplating them he may train his own imagination and endeavour to imitate by living representation the images impressed on his mind.

[...] The skilful actor should always be attentive so that one may deduce from his expression and gesture what is going on in his mind, occupied as it is with the subject of the dialogue; without that the performance is useless.

Moreover, let the face and the chest be constantly turned towards the spectators, for since the whole performance takes place for the sake of the spectators, respect for the latter demands that the actor face them completely. This is all the more necessary whenever an emotion bursts out more violently which is to be shown to, and impressed upon, the spectators [...].

In speaking [...] it is necessary to take care the speaker's mouth be turned towards the spectators and not towards the partner he is addressing. [...]

[...] There is another point to be made about the emotion of grief. Often the hands are folded with fingers interlinked and they are usually raised aloft or dropped below the hips. In either case it is necessary to take care that the folded hands be held on one side or the other, to the right or the left as one pleases, but not in the middle of the body. For if this happens his face will be covered as long as the speaker holds his hands high, which is wrong

[...] Decency, however, does not permit the hands to be lowered straight down the front. [...]

[...] if somebody ponders a matter, which occurs in almost every play, care must be taken to illustrate the meaning of the business through all the actor's gestures, as far as possible, with the greatest liveliness. To attain this it helps not a little if posture, walks and gestures be frequently changed and well chosen. Now the actor may lean against the wings while reflecting quietly what to say, what resolution to adopt or what measures to take: now he may stand erect, one hand propped on a table while he uses the other to act with, thereby indicating the uncertainty of his mind [...].

In violent pain or in grieving it is not improper, nay it merits praise and arouses delight, if occasionally one completely covers one's face for a while, either with both hands held up against it or with the head concealed in the arms, and one leans against a wing the while [...]. It is however advisable to keep this sort of stage business brief so that the audience may not grow tired of it.

46   Positioning in dialogue scenes

Lang (1727), pp. 55–6; Rudin (1975), pp. 203–4

You might well ask how actors are supposed to stand in order as it were to talk to one another if, as has been demanded above, they have to turn their faces wholly towards the spectators, which is all the more difficult when there are several standing on stage. There are two answers to this question. Above all the action of the hands and some motions of the body should definitely be directed at the interlocutor, but the voice and the face, at least while speaking, towards the spectator. However, before beginning to speak, and equally after finishing a speech, you may look at the interlocutor for a while [...]. This way the listener can understand at whom the words and their significance are directed without ever losing the actor's looks and words. [...]

Another procedure is for the speaker to take up a position behind his partner and so to face the spectator's glances frontally with his full face and body [...]. Meanwhile the other person who is listening to the speaker can repeatedly look over his shoulder at him briefly and express a feeling appropriate to the conversation until it is up to him to reply. Then let them exchange their positions in such a way that he who previously was the listener and stood in front now becomes the speaker and steps behind the other one.

47   Positioning in dialogue scenes

Lang (1727), pl. VIII, p. 55

We may safely assume that some religious plays presented by amateurs outside a school context were fairly crude affairs, although the following description of a guild performance is clearly intended to be satirical rather than a sober factual report.

48   A guild performance of the play of Judith

Johann Rist, *Die AllerEdelste Belustigung Kunst- und Tugendliebender Gemüther*, pp. 90–7. Reproduced in *Sämtliche Werke*, ed. Eberhard Mannack, vol. 5 (1974), pp. 283–6

[...] but I think what was even funnier was the grand play of Judith and Holofernes as represented by some journeymen linen-weavers in a nice little town in the following manner. First there was to be seen the city of Bethulia which was a large painted poster depicting the city of Lübeck, very artistically done too [...], prettily bedaubed with thick colours. From behind this city at its highest point there peeped out a fellow with a small ruff [...] like the ones usually worn by old vergers, and he was meant to be Prince Ozias. Judith entered in the person of a rough, fat, thickset peasant lass who carried in her hand a wreath of oak leaves and a large basket full of eggs which she was going to present to Holofernes. She was followed by her maidservant, a short, swarthy, repulsive creature with a big hump on her back. She carried a bucket in her hand containing a large hunk of green cheese, rye bread and a wooden butter dish; in her other hand she held a dirty wooden beer jug, and around her neck she carried a barnyard rooster with his feet tied up together, because they intended to invite Holofernes to supper [...]. Fair Judith, having saluted the spectators, bidden them good evening and made a deep bow to them, as did her hunchbacked maid who copied whatever her mistress did, informed the audience what she was planning to do, viz., how she was going to knock off the villainous head of that filthy Holofernes, as sure as her name was Judith [...]. They had dressed Holofernes in a pair of soiled old leather breeches as well as large peasant boots. They had also put a breastplate on him which was so miserably rusty that you couldn't see what it was made of; it had been used as a trough for piglets for many a year. On his head he wore a casque in which hens had been laying their eggs for more than twenty years [...]; by his side he wore an old knife which, however, had only half a scabbard [...]. I only want to tell how the slaughter of Holofernes was contrived. [...] these enlightened and ingenious players had put into Holofernes's bed in his place a live calf with its four feet tied together. Now when Judith was about to perform her heroic deed she drew the bed curtains, threw off the blanket, and with a dagger hung up near the bed she thrust the poor innocent calf in the throat so that it began to bleat piteously [...] until at last she had chopped off his head altogether which she raised aloft, exclaiming in a loud voice, 'Look here, gentlemen and friends, this is the villainous head of the tyrant Holofernes;' and when the spectators burst out laughing immoderately at this and some shouted, 'Yes, a calf's head!', fair Judith began to reprove them with the following words, 'How can you fools stand there and laugh? Can't you imagine that this calf is Holofernes?' [...] which profound interjection only increased the laughter until at last, losing patience, she threw the calf's head into a basket and ran with it towards Bethulia as if she had lost her wits. Now when the grooms tried to wake up their [lord] Holofernes but the poor calf would not stir, they approached more closely and, seeing the dead calf's body to be headless, [...] they were in such a panic that they ran around the stage like madmen. But the citizens of Bethulia who had displayed the calf's head above the painted city [...] came rushing forth most boisterously, with that big peasant lass Judith in the lead. She was followed by Ozias with his verger's collar [...]; he had a rusty spear for pig-sticking with which he meant to finish off the Holofernian boors; the rest were all apprentice weavers both of the female and the male sex [...] with their tools and implements [...] and there began a vigorous skirmish. The poor Holofernian village louts wrenched the weapons out of the linen-weavers' hands, seized hold of their heads and they gave each other such a thorough drubbing that they bled out of their noses and their mouths. With that the siege was raised and the beautiful tragi-comedy [...] concluded.

Nevertheless nonprofessional performances, particularly of religious plays, were profoundly serious matters. The outstanding example which has survived to this day is, of course, the Oberammergau Passion Play. Not actually a mediaeval survival, this play was from its beginnings organised by an entire village community rather than by a trade guild. By 1770 at the latest it had achieved a more than local reputation and had even taken on something of a commercial character; the text underwent repeated revisions; and the staging was indebted more to Jesuit methods of open-air theatre than to more ancient forms. But though not a direct example of mediaeval drama, this passion play nevertheless represents a link with it in that its original text was based on two earlier sources from Augsburg: a *meistersinger* text of 1566 and a fifteenth-century play from the monastery of St Ulric and Afra. See Willi Flemming, 'Das Oberammergauer Festspiel als theatergeschichtliche Quelle' (The Oberammergau Festival Play as a Source for Theatre History), in *M&K*, 6 (1960), pp. 147–58.

49   The origins of the Oberammergau Passion Play, 1633

Preface of Anon., *Das Grosse Versöhnungsopfer auf Golgotha oder die Leidens- und Todes-Geschichte Jesu [...] aufgeführt zu Oberammergau*, (The Great Redemptive Sacrifice at Golgotha, or The Story of the Passion and Death of Jesus [...] performed at Oberammergau), published in connection with the 1830 performance (Munich: Mich. Lindauer, 1830). Reproduced in Otto Weddigen, *Geschichte der Theater Deutschlands in hundert Abhandlungen dargestellt* (History of the Theatres of Germany presented in a Hundred Essays) (Berlin: Ernst Frensdorff, n.d.), p. 941

In the year 1633 there raged in the neighbouring districts [...] such an infectious disease that only a few people remained alive. Although the Ammer Valley is separated from those districts by mountains and all precautionary measures and steps were taken to protect people from this terrible scourge, it yet arrived here unexpectedly when a local labourer [...] crept into his house having crossed the mountain by secret paths from Eschenlohe where he had been working in the fields during the summer, and brought the plague with him.[1] Only two days later he had died, and within three weeks 84 people with him. In this universal distress the local community sought help from the Almighty – with a solemn vow publicly to present the story of the passion of Jesus, the world's Saviour, for grateful adoration and edifying contemplation. The power of faith won out – not another person died of the plague although many had been struck down by the infection. In the following year, 1634, the story of Jesus' passion was performed for the first time in fulfilment of the vow. [...]

Faithful to their forefathers' vow, the community has not allowed any obstacles or difficulties to prevent this public performance once every ten years [...]

[1] Eschenlohe was one of the infected villages.

F. ACTING TECHNIQUE

It is not easy exactly to reconstruct the acting style used by strolling players in the seventeenth century; but the indications are that both in tragedy and in comedy it was lacking in subtlety, at least as far as the great majority was concerned. The following excerpts from German playtexts, based directly or indirectly on Shakespeare, suggest that these adaptations aimed at drastic and highly readable effects, tending towards sensationalism in tragedy and broad farce in comedy.

Three passages from the *Hamlet* adaptation, *Der bestrafte Brudermord*, demonstrate a considerable coarsening of the play in performance.

50   The German Hamlet: stage business

(i) Cohn (1865), p. 248. The following stage direction occurs in Act 1, Sc. 2

(GHOST gives the Sentinel a box on the ear from behind, and makes him drop his musket. Exit.)

(ii) Cohn, p. 288; Act 4, Sc. 1, a scene added to the original plotline in which the ruffians, i.e. the king's servants, offer to take Hamlet's life.

HAMLET   One word more: – as the meanest criminal is not refused his last request
     for time to repent him of his sins, I, an innocent prince, do beseech you to

grant me time to address a prayer to my Creator, which done I will willingly die. I will give you the sign: I will raise my hands to heaven, and fire the moment I spread out my arms. Level both pistols at my sides, and when I call, fire, give me as much as I require, and be sure and hit me that I may not suffer long.

RUFFIAN 2 Well, we may do that much to please him; therefore let us proceed.

HAMLET (*Spreads out his arms.*) Fire! (*Meanwhile he falls forward between the two servants, who consequently shoot each other.*) [. . .] Ha! the dogs, they move still. They have butchered each other, but to satisfy my revenge let them take the coup de grâce from my hand, else one of the rogues might escape. (*He stabs them with their own sword.*)

(iii) Cohn, p. 297; Act 5, Sc. 3, Hamlet in conversation with Horatio just before his duel with Leonhardus (Laertes)

HAMLET Come, Horatio, I go this very minute, and present myself to the King. Ha! What does this bode? See, these drops of blood which fall from my nose. I tremble from head to foot. Alas! alas! how is it with me? (*Faints.*)

HORAT Most noble Prince! O Heavens! what does this import? Come to your senses, my lord! My noble Prince, what is the matter with you?

HAMLET I do not know, Horatio. When I thought of going to court, a sudden swoon came over me. The gods alone know what it signifies.

HORAT Heaven grant this be no evil omen!

In comedy the same process of coarsening compared to the original text can be traced, as is apparent from some of the stage directions in Gryphius' *Herr Peter Squentz* (Mr Peter Quince), a farcical comedy based, albeit almost certainly at several removes, on the mechanicals' scene in *A Midsummer Night's Dream*. Gryphius' satire is aimed at literary and performance conditions in Germany during the Thirty Years' War, particularly such survivals from earlier non-professional forms of theatre as *meistersinger* plays. Although much of seventeenth-century German literary drama remained firmly in the closet, this particular piece, probably written between 1647 and 1649, enjoyed considerable popularity until well into the eighteenth century. It figured in the Velten company's repertoire; it was performed at Heidelberg Castle in 1730; it served as an afterpiece for Ackermann's company in Mainz as late as 1759. The stage business, however satirically sharpened, can be regarded as in some sense indicative of actual practice, at least at the time of composition. It must at any rate have reflected the audiences' sense of humour. The excerpts below are all taken from the third act, the play-within-the-play of *Piramus and Thisbe*. (For an illustration of a Dutch performance of the play, see 315.)

51   The 'Midsummer Night's Dream' mechanicals: farcical business

Andreas Gryphius, *Andreae Gryphii Freuden und Trauer-Spiele auch Oden und Sonette sampt Herr Peter Squentz Schimpff-Spiel* (Andreas Gryphius's Comedies and Tragedies as well as Sonnets and Odes, with Mr Peter Quince, a Farce) (Breslau: Johann Lischke & Jacob Trescher, 1658), pp. 20, 23, 31, 32–3, 38. The play has been reprinted many times, including in editions by Wilhelm Braune (Neudrucke deutscher Literaturwerke des XVI. und XVII. Jahrhunderts, No. 6), and Hugh Powell (ed.) (Leicester University Press, second edn 1969)

(i) Peter Quince sits down on a stool, takes his spectacles and puts them on his nose, but as he is about to look at his script a court lackey knocks the stool so that Peter Quince tumbles over [. . .].

(ii) Pickleherring punches Bully Bottom in the neck, then Bully Bottom knocks him over the head with the wall; they get hold of each other by the hair and pull each other about on stage, so that the wall comes to pieces entirely. Peter Quince tries to separate them.

(iii) She [i.e. Thisbe] wishes to throw away her cloak but she cannot because it is tied on too tight; when she has torn the strings at last, she beats the lion about the head and runs off screaming.

(iv) The Moon beats the Lion about the head with his lantern; the Lion catches the Moon by the hair; in this set-to they knock over the Well and break his pitcher; the Well knocks both of them about the ears with the pieces; P.Q. seeks to pacify them but is knocked down by all three of them and gets his share of blows.

(v) She [Thisbe] stabs herself under her skirt with the sword, then throws the sword away and falls onto Piramus [. . .]

Improvisation loomed large not merely in straight farces but also in the political melodramas known as *Haupt- und Staatsaktionen*, which did indeed often combine farcical interludes with scenes of high seriousness. A number of texts of these immensely popular plays have survived. One of these, *Karl der Zwölfte vor Friedrichshall* (Charles XII at the Gates of Fredriksten), is supposed to have been written between 1720 and 1730, i.e. not long after the Swedish king's death in 1718, by one Ludovici, a university man acting and writing for Johann Gottlieb Förster's company. The manuscript was rediscovered in Zerbst (Saxony/Anhalt), more than a century after its composition, by Heinrich Lindner who edited and published it. This play shows clearly how improvised scenes were intercalated into a written text. Note that the Harlequin scenes are cheek by jowl with the historical chronicle, and that action scenes of a serious character no less than farcical passages are left to improvisation.

52   Improvisation farcical and serious, c. 1720–30

H.L. Lindner (ed.), *Karl der Zwölfte vor Friedrichshall. Eine Haupt- und Staatsaction in vier*

Actus, nebst einem Epilogus (Charles XII at the Gates of Frederiksksten. A Political Melodrama in Four Acts and an Epilogue) (Dessau: Karl Aue, 1845), pp. 94, 104, 116, 131, 132

(i) Act I, Sc. 4

Improvised scene about getting married, Harlequin wants to go for a soldier, Plapperliese [Chatterbox Lizzie] wants to go to war as a sutler, they both agree, exit Plapperliese.

(ii) Act I, Sc. 5

The Lieutenant comes to an agreement with Harlequin because he likes him, promises that he shall want for neither meat nor drink, teaches him how to drill and after some lazzi takes him off to the recruiting station.

(iii) Act II. Sc. 4

Harlequin wants to marry Plapperliese. The Lieutenant disagrees. [...] they both pull him about; at last the Lieutenant orders them to be ready to march. Exeunt omnes.

(iv) Act III, Sc. 4

The middle curtain opens, soldiers eating and drinking.[1]

(v) Act III, Sc. 5

Harlequin dressed as a dragoon, feasts, refuses to pay, claiming it was in his terms of enlistment, the sutler insists on getting paid and boxes his ears. Harlequin draws his sword, the sutler screams. Harlequin takes fright and drops it, she takes up the sword and is about to stab Harlequin, he screams, she takes fright and drops the sword in turn; finally Harlequin smashes up her pots and everything. Exit.

(vi) Act IV, Sc. 6

Harlequin dressed as a woman with Plapperlieschen, is going to desert, goes through the drill with Plapperliese because they want to run off together, he tries to disguise his voice as a woman's in case anybody should recognise him.

(vii) Act IV, Sc. 10

Meanwhile there is heavy [artillery] fire. [King] Charles orders everything to be got ready for the bombardment, encourages his men to attack, is at last hit by shot and falls. [...] His body is removed, the Swedes gradually disperse.

---

[1] Note the use of a traverse curtain (see 17–18).

V Audiences

The repertoire of strolling players who travelled the length and breadth of the German-speaking world (and indeed further afield) may to some extent have transcended regional differences of taste, but there certainly were considerable variations in the theatrical preferences of the different social strata. Literary dramas requiring a public ready to catch classical allusions and to decipher complex allegories, or spectacular and musical entertainments calling for financial resources well beyond the reach of mere itinerant players were clearly the prerogative of the learned or of the aristocracy: hence school or court performances satisfying these needs were frequently (though by no means invariably) based on a repertoire quite distinct from that of public performances offered to ordinary folk in booth, guildhall or tennis-court.

This difference is clearly stated in volume 6 of *Frauenzimmer Gesprächspiele*, Georg Philip Harsdörfer's 8-volume guide to the social graces (publ. 1641–9). Harsdörfer, pastoral poet of Nuremberg and literary spokesman for the South German middle class of the Free Cities (he was one of the founders of the literary society, the Pegnitz Order), here employs the characters of Degenwert (D.), a scholar and a soldier, Cassandra (C.), a young aristocratic lady, and Vespasian (V.), an experienced elderly courtier, to state his views on audiences for different sorts of theatrical performances, including opera.

53 Theatrical preferences of different classes in the 1640s

G.P. Harsdörfer, *Frauenzimmer Gesprächspiele* (Ladies' Conversational Games), vol. 6 (Nuremberg: Wolfgang Endkern, 1646; repr. Tübingen: Max Niemeyer Verlag, 1969) pp. 42–4

D You can see from this that there is a good deal to poetry, which requires not merely the art of metrically combining words [. . .] but the knowledge of many, indeed of all other, sciences. Hence it follows that poetry is not the common man's meat, since it greatly exceeds his understanding and he judges it as the blind man does colour. He can appreciate and listen with pleasure to a tooth-drawer, a conjurer, a juggler, a comic master of ceremonies or a rhyming improviser, but a proper poem is not meant for the vulgar herd but is for scholars and other educated folk.[1]

68

c But tragedies and comedies are performed for the entertainment of the common man.

v You must make a distinction between the comedies performed for the sake of gain by actors trained to this work from their youth onwards, and the comedies, performed by gentlemen on special occasions in the Italian manner by means of song. In the former case, you can please the populace with farces, but in the latter of which we are speaking, it is essential to attend to the highest art of performance, and certainly things have now risen to such a height that it is hard to imagine how they could be raised any higher.

---

[1] These paratheatrical occupations were thought to be closely allied to the acting profession. See 37.

Seventeenth-century German audiences, in contrast to the audiences of other Western countries where theatre was flourishing at the time, did not regard verse as the indispensable hallmark of high drama, either comic or tragic. Later, in the eighteenth century, the relative lack of a verse-speaking tradition was to prove a technical problem when new literary trends increasingly made this skill a necessary accomplishment for the actor. (See 135, esp. paras. 3–33.)

The following dialogue, in which Johann Rist puts his point of view, clearly expresses a predilection for prose on the part of many German authors as well as spectators. (Compare 136.)

54   The advantages of prose dialogue, 1666

J. Rist, *Die AllerEdelste Belustigung* (1666), pp. 127–31. Reproduced in Willi Flemming, *Das Schauspiel der Wanderbühne* (1931), pp. 132–4, and Rist, *Sämtliche Werke*, ed. Mannack, vol. 5 (1974), pp. 310–13

It is no accident, said INGENIANDER,[1] that we are discussing at some length my most noble entertainment of art lovers, i.e. the performance of plays, comedies and tragedies [...] but I trust my honourable companions will forgive me for posing this question: is it better to present tragedies and comedies in verse or in prose?

This question is rather hard to answer, said The Hardy One,[2] all the more so in that those who express their inward thoughts in metre will maintain their preference as well and as vigorously as those who only speak freely and in prose, although in my humble opinion, the latter is rather to be preferred to the former, especially when using our German mother tongue. Now it is a well known fact that the ancients, Greeks as well as Latins, wrote their tragedies and comedies in metre or verse and no doubt recited them to the people in this manner on stage, wherein they have been followed by the Italians, the French, the Netherlanders and perhaps other nations as well [. . .]. Now I will let each man make out his own case, but if for my own person I were to give my views concerning this fair art and truly speak on behalf of the actor, I should never perform any tragedy or comedy in verse in our German language; for there is no question at all as to what an advantage freedom of speaking is for anyone who has actually to tie himself down to something so definite as verse or rhyme. Whoever speaks freely does not mind if at times he makes a mistake or gets stuck; he will soon recover himself and find such words as will convey the meaning of the play clearly enough, which cannot be done in verse plays. [. . .] Let us Germans therefore in all fairness stay with free prose dialogue which enables one to use much freer gestures too, since one often has to twitch when speaking in verse. But occasionally to mix in sweet and charming songs [. . .] with the prose dialogue is not unacceptable but is apt to add a sweet delight and grace to tragedies as well as to comedies.

[1] 'Ingeniander' – the name accorded to one Herr Neuberger by the Order of the Elbe Swans – was one of the four participants in this colloquy.

[2] 'The Hardy One' was Rist's own literary name; the view put forward can therefore be taken as his own.

VI Repertoire

Like their successful competitors the English Comedians, German companies of strolling players would offer a broad repertoire of entertainments. A typical early example is the following one taken from the Danzig (Gdansk) archives, an application from the otherwise unknown heads of a company, Paul Schulz, Michel Frantzoss and Johan Tiess, to the Mayor for permission to play during St Dominic's Fair in 1623.

55 Wide range of plays offered by strolling players, 1623
Bolte (1895), p. 58

Your Worship etc.,
We petitioners and actors having come here to this goodly city for St Dominic's and for the especial honour of the honourable [and] sagacious Council, with the intention and aim of exhibiting not only beautiful religious but secular comedies and tragedies as well, during all of which beautiful and pleasant music will be heard and performed, just as during said comedies and tragedies excellently beautiful ballets, disguisings and English dances will be seen, performed and exhibited. [...]

Some forty years later, the academically trained entrepreneurs Johann Casper Kempfer, Adam Koch and Wilhelm Haberman approached the Mayor of Danzig with the following offer of a comprehensive repertoire.

56 Large number of plays on offer, 1662
Bolte (1895), p. 94

[...] We therefore offer to perform such useful, edifying and instructive plays of which we have 90 and more with us and so to embellish them with our own music that no one might be annoyed or offended but rather everyone should be edified and the beloved citizenry strengthened in unity, obedience and valour.

Disappointingly enough, the offer proved resistible as the following note indicates.

Read in Council on 11 August 1662. The Honourable Council for good reasons does not see how the petitioners' request could be granted.

Not only was there little specialisation among strolling players in terms of comedy, tragedy, ballet, or musical drama – an evening's programme would contain generically different items; indeed the genres might be promiscuously thrown together within one and the same play. An example of this common practice is the playbill dated 6 January 1671 for a performance at Rothenburg-on-the-Tauber of a saint's play based on Dekker and Massinger's *The Virgin Martyr*, (1620), introduced into Germany by Robert Reynolds shortly after its English première.

57   Mixture of genres in strolling players' repertoire, 1671

Bärbel Rudin, 'Fräulein Dorothea und der blaue Montag/Die Diokletianische Christenverfolgung in zwei Repertoirestücken der deutschen Wanderbühne' (Miss Dorothea and the Jolly Spree/ Diocletian's Persecution of Christians in Two Repertoire Plays of German Strolling Players), in *Elemente der Literatur* (Elements of Literature) (Stuttgart: Alfred Krämer, 1980), vol. 1, p. 102

The High German Company of Players
With their entertaining
Pickleherring
Will be presenting and exhibiting
by Permission of the High Authorities
Of the Imperial City of Rothenburg-on-the-Tauber
all manner of New and Well Constructed Comedies, Tragedies, Pastorals, Ballets, [and] Dances on a Handsome Stage Lit by Candlelight, Pleasant Music, Beautiful Tableaux with Popular Entertainments: And today, Friday 6 January, we shall be presenting to our Well Disposed Spectators an Exceedingly Delightful Play entitled:
The Holy Martyr Dorothea,
How the same is beheaded in public and the Grand Chancellor Theophilus is torn apart with red-hot tongs, enlivened by
Pickleherring's Jests.
The Play will be followed by a Ballet by Six Persons.
The Performance will be in the Dancing-House immediately after Vespers.

Of all the plays taken over from the English repertoire, the one which was destined to play the longest role in the history of the German theatre was Marlowe's *Doctor Faustus*, itself derived from a sixteenth-century German chapbook and embodying a popular legend that has never ceased to have a wide appeal in the German-speaking world. (See **29** for the first recorded performance of Marlowe's play there.) This inexhaustible theme has continued to inspire both the puppet theatre and the living stage in widely different versions. In addition to Goethe's magisterial rehandling of the story there were to be further dramatisations by such nineteenth-century playwrights as Klingemann and Grabbe; and Faust has been haunting twentieth-century authors as well, not all of them German nor indeed all of them playwrights. For further information, consult Eliza Marian Butler, *The Fortunes of Faust* (CUP, 1952).

When the actor-manager Karl Andreas Paulsen (see **26**) visited Danzig from August to December 1669 and staged his version of the play there, an account of the performance was noted down in his diary by the well educated and widely travelled Danzig Councillor Georg Schröder (1635–1703). But before this, the first detailed description of a German *Faust* play, earlier performances are known to have taken place in Dresden (1626), Prague (1651), Hanover (1661) and Lüneburg (1666).

58   An early German play on the Faust theme, 1669

Georg Schröder's 'Quodlibet oder Tagebuch' (Miscellany or Journal), Danzig Municipal Library III A fol. 36, pp. 114b and 115a. Reproduced in Bolte (1895), pp. 108–9, in Flemming, *Das Schauspiel der Wanderbühne*, p. 202, and in Kindermann, *Theatergeschichte Europas*, vol. 3, pp. 396–7

First Pluto comes forth out of hell and calls one devil after another: the Devil of Tobacco, the Devil of Whoring, among others the Devil of Cunning, and gives them the order that they should deceive people as much as possible. Thereupon it comes to pass that Dr Faustus, not satisfied with ordinary scholarship, searches out books of magic and conjures the devils to do him service, testing their swiftness so as to choose the speediest. It is not enough for him that they should be as swift as deer, as clouds, as the wind, but he wants one that is as swift as man's thought, and the cunning devil having pronounced himself such a one, he desires him to serve him for 24 years and he would yield himself up to him, which the cunning devil will not do for dear life, taking the matter up to Pluto; with the latter's agreement, the cunning devil makes a pact with Dr Faustus who signs himself over in blood. Hereupon a hermit wishes to warn Faustus but to no avail. Faustus succeeds in all his conjurations; he has shown to him Charlemagne, (and) fair Helen with whom he takes his pleasure. At last his conscience awakes and he counts all the hours until the stroke of twelve, then he speaks to his servant and counsels him against magic. Soon Pluto arrives and sends his devils to fetch Dr Faust which indeed happens and they cast him into hell and tear him to pieces. It is also shown how he is tortured in hell being pulled up and down, and these words are seen in fireworks: *Accusatus est, judicatus est, condemnatus est.*

Period II: 1727–1814

VII   *Contractual and organisational documents*

In the first half of the eighteenth century, with more than a century of professionalism behind them, actors in German-speaking countries were still artists on the margin of society who sorely needed the protection of one or more of the numerous courts scattered throughout the Holy Roman Empire. While a patent (*Privileg*) from a prince neither gave a company of strolling players any automatic salary nor any assured rights to play within his territories, the status it brought was invaluable in that it carried a great deal of weight with lesser authorities; it might therefore be a condition of survival in the profession. Some companies managed to obtain more than one patent at a time: the title was not exclusive.

A typical such patent, both in form and content, was the one granted by Frederick Augustus I ('the Strong'), Elector of Saxony (1670–1733) – who was also King of Poland under the title of Augustus II – to Friederike Caroline Neuber (1697–1760), the leading German actress of her time. Together with her husband Johann (1697–1756), Frau Neuber ('die Neuberin') was the manager of what was going to become the most prestigious company of strolling players in German-speaking countries.

59   Award of a Saxon patent to the Neuber Company, 8 August 1727

(Former) Königl. Hauptstaatsarchiv, Dresden. Reproduced in Friedrich Joh.v. Reden-Esbeck, *Caroline Neuber und ihre Zeitgenossen/Ein Beitrag zur deutschen Kultur- und Theatergeschichte* (Caroline Neuber and her Contemporaries/A Contribution to German Cultural and Theatrical History) (Leipzig: Johann Ambrosius Barth, 1881), p. 56, and Sybille Maurer-Schmoock, *Deutsches Theater im 18. Jahrhundert* (German Theatre in the 18th Century) (Tübingen: Max Niemeyer, 1982), p. 208

We, Frederick Augustus by the grace of God King of Poland, Grand Duke of Lithuania, [...] Duke of Saxony, Jülich, Cleve, Berg, Engern and Westphalia, Grand Marshal and Elector of the Holy Roman Empire, Landgrave of Thuringia, Margrave of Meissen as well as Upper and Lower Lusatia, [...] etc. hereby certify that, the so-called Haack Troupe[1] of our former court actors having disbanded, We accept and adopt *Johann Neuber* and his wife Friederike Caroline as Our court actors and hereby and by virtue of this open letter publish this fact in such a manner that the same as well as their troupe shall be regarded and respected as Our court actors by one and all and they shall be entitled to act and perform at unprohibited times[2] anywhere in Our electoral and hereditary lands as well as at the Leipzig fairs and a week before and a week after the fairs. They will, however, have to discharge and pay the usual taxes but without being burdened unduly.[3] We therefore command the authorities in all places, in particular city councils, strictly to conduct themselves accordingly and to protect the said Neuber and his wife as well as their troupe as ordered. [...] Issued and decreed in Dresden on 8 August 1727.

[1] Johann Kaspar Haack (d. 1722), Harlequin in Andreas Elenson's company (see 3), who had stayed on under his successor Julius Franz Elenson (see 35) and by marrying the latter's widow Sophie Julie had himself become co-director of the company. Johann and Karoline Neuber worked for the Elenson-Haack company before founding their own company in 1726. Note that the patent uses the somewhat deprecatory term 'Bande' (troupe) which in later eighteenth-century usage was replaced by the word 'Gesellschaft' (company).
[2] Performances were not permitted on holy days.
[3] Compare 33, section xii.

The actors' continuing dependence on the favour of the great in this period emerges clearly from the following letter, written from Hamburg by the Neubers to Charles I, Duke of Brunswick (reigned 1735–80), shortly after his accession.

60   The Neubers seek to obtain a Brunswick patent, 22 June 1735

Niedersächsisches Staatsarchiv, Wolfenbüttel, 2 Alt 12313

[...] Your Princely Highness will graciously recollect that you accorded your most gracious permission for us once again most humbly to call upon you after the conclusion of the period of court mourning. In acknowledging this high princely favour with the most submissive thanks and obedience and greatly rejoicing in it, we also, in the most submissive confidence, take our refuge in your Princely Highness as our particularly gracious duke and lord and request that Your Princely Highness will be so gracious as to accept and adopt our company as your court actors, [...] and allow everybody to regard us as such and favour us with the gift of a specially drawn-up patent signed by Your Princely Highness. Such high princely grace will be acknowledged by us for the rest of our lives with the most devoted loyalty and obedience [...]

> Your Humble Servants
> Johann Neuber
> Friederica Carolina Neuber

Towards the middle of the century it became increasingly clear that if German-language theatre was to be improved, strolling players would sooner or later have to give way to resident companies working not in *ad hoc* accommodation but in specially built public playhouses (see 101). For this to happen, the authorities' permission was still essential, even if the money for the erection of such playhouses were to come from private sources. The actor-manager Johann Friedrich Schönemann (1704–1782), first an actor with the Neubers and from 1739 onwards the head of his own company, wished to establish a permanent theatre in Berlin in 1742. King Frederick II of Prussia ('the Great') much preferred French to German literature and theatre (see 203); but being opposed to the 'Strong Man' Johann Karl von Eckenberg and his Pantalone player Johann Peter Hilverding, who dominated the Berlin theatre at the time with crude theatrical fare, he was favourably disposed to this venture, as the following letter by Schönemann indicates. In the event, Schönemann's initiative, at that time a pioneering attempt at any rate in Northern Germany, did not come to anything.

61   Schönemann wishes to build a playhouse in Berlin, 22 November 1742

Original lost. Copy in the Geh.Staats-Archiv, Berlin, Manuskript König 295, Sheet 149. Reproduced in Hans Devrient, *J.F. Schönemann* (Hamburg/Leipzig: TGF 11, 1895), p. 72

Your Most Serene etc. Royal Majesty has most graciously ordered me through your Colonel Count von Hacke to build a large German playhouse by the so-called Kavalier-Brücke [Noblemen's Bridge]. I therefore beseech Your Majesty most humbly to have the goodness to cause someone to indicate to me the dimensions of the space so that I can draw up my ground plan accordingly; for the gracious supply of the timber I thank Your Majesty in deepest humility and beg to remain Your most submissive servant and

subject Johann Friedrich Schönemann.

Berlin, 22 November 1742.

The taxes imposed on actor-managers for permission to play were a constant problem for them (see 33, section XIII, and 59); not surprisingly, a recurrent theme of their letters to the authorities was a request to lighten this burden. A case in point is the following letter by Schönemann to King Frederick II from Breslau (Wroclaw), where he was working after the collapse of his hopes of permanently establishing himself in Berlin.

62   Schönemann appeals to Frederick II for partial remission of tax, 20 March 1748

Former Staatsarchiv Breslau P.A. IX, 75c vol. II, p. 1 *et seq.* Reproduced in Hans Devrient (1895), pp. 324–5

Having recently arrived again with my company in Your Royal Majesty's capital city and residence of Breslau in order to entertain the public with regular dramas arranged according to reason and morality following Your Royal command, I most humbly take the liberty of declaring that I have had great expenses not only because of the considerable costs of undertaking the long journey hither but also because of the costumes and other matters required for said plays, as a result of which money has become a scarce commodity for me. Also I have found on arrival so much to mend and improve at the local theatre [. . .], the maintenance of which according to the article in my patent is my responsibility, that I do not know where to find the money, since some evenings I do not take more than 8 or 10 rix-dollars but have to pay 11 and more rix-dollars every time for musicians, candles, playbills, tax, workmen and so forth, without reckoning what I need for myself and my company. [. . .] I address my most submissive request to Your Majesty that You might deign in Your benevolence to set a certain limit to my tax liability and fix it at, say, 10 rix-dollars a month, since owing to the aforementioned circumstances there are days when because of poor takings I lose 2 to 3 rix-dollars a day by way of expenses [. . .]. Living in hope of a most gracious concession I shall always strive most obediently together with my company to make ourselves worthy of such sovereign grace by our good conduct. But I in particular prostrate myself with the most submissive veneration etc. etc.

Breslau, 20 March 1748.

VIII Playhouses and performance venues

A. BOOTH THEATRES

Strolling players in the seventeenth and eighteenth centuries would normally perform in existing premises dedicated to quite different purposes, in venues which inevitably had built-in limitations for anything scenically elaborate – unless they happened to be fortunate enough to be summoned to play in a prince's private theatre. In the eighteenth century some companies chose to erect their own playing booths or huts – given municipal permission to do so as they often were in places like Frankfurt-on-Main, Berlin, Hamburg and Leipzig. These temporary structures which were at least custom-built had to be dismantled again when the permitted playing time had run out. The contrast between these huts on the one hand, and the lavish facilities on the other hand of palace theatres, not to mention the magnificence of princely or municipal opera houses, vividly illustrates the low esteem in which German drama was held up to the middle of the eighteenth century.

The following document gives some insight into the matter-of-fact attitude of municipal authorities towards visiting artists' requirements, even if they were people of the relative prestige of the Neubers, in a place like Leipzig which was conspicuously theatre-minded. In actual fact, three years earlier the Neubers had been outmanoeuvred here by their archrival, the Harlequin actor Joseph Ferdinand Müller (d. 1755), who had managed to wrest out of their control the municipally owned Shambles ('Fleischhaus'), a building which served as a dance and fencing hall outside the theatre season and which had been the Neubers' regular acting venue (see 113). Now, for their return to Leipzig, they were forced to erect their own temporary premises.

63 Site inspection for a booth for the Neuber Company, Leipzig, 4 September 1737

Leipzig Archives. Reproduced in Reden-Esbeck (1881), p. 209 and in Heinz Kindermann, *Theatergeschichte der Goethezeit* (Theatre History of the Age of Goethe) (Vienna: H. Bauer, 1948), p. 520

Report.

We have pleasure in informing the architects currently in charge that as ordered by them we have inspected the place where the Neuber troupe of actors intends to erect a playing booth and have established how the booth, which is planned to be

60 ells in length and 30 ells[1] in width, is supposed to be taken to the spot outside the Grimma Gate[2] where there are situated Bosse's Gardens as well as, at the moment, some dunghills carted out of town. The booth would thus be entirely free-standing so that it would block neither the thoroughfare nor the entrance to Bosse's Garden nor the stables, which we beg to report herewith. [...]

Johann Michael SenkEisen,
Chief Supervisor
Mathäus Küntzel
Chief Market
Supervisor

[1] Approx. 40m by 20m. (There were more than 100 variations in the length of the ell in different parts of Germany.)
[2] A noted Leipzig landmark at the time.

These conditions – flimsily built temporary theatres with wretched technical facilities – persisted even into the second half of the eighteenth century, although gradually more and more permanent theatres for the public at large were being built. Karoline Schulze-Kummerfeld (1745–1815) has described, in the memoirs written in her latter years but unpublished during her lifetime, the sort of temporary structures which strolling players still had to perform in while she was a young actress, i.e. in the period up to 1768.

64   Primitive performance conditions in fit-up theatres, middle of the eighteenth century

Karoline Schulze-Kummerfeld, 'Biographisches', in *Monatliche Beiträge zur Geschichte dramatischer Kunst und Literatur* (Monthly Contributions to the History of Dramatic Art and Literature) ed. Karl von Holtei (Berlin: Haude- und Spenersche Buchhandlung), vol. 3, no. 3 (June 1828), pp. 188–9. Herzog-August-Bibliothek, Wolfenbüttel, Sign. Wd 567i.

For a fuller version of these memoirs, see *Lebenserinnerungen der Karoline Schulze-Kummerfeld* (Memoirs of K.S.-K.), ed. Emil Benezé (Berlin: *SGTG* 23, 1915), and *Ein fahrendes Frauenzimmer/Die Lebenserinnerungen der Komödiantin Karoline Schulze-Kummerfeld 1745–1815* (A Travelling Woman/The Memoirs of the Actress, K.S.-K.), ed. Inge Buck (Berlin: Orlanda-Frauenverlag, 1988).

Almost as rare as permanent companies of actors were proper theatre buildings. When a director had received a patent or permission [to play], he would erect a light scaffolding in some great hall or a large empty room in which there were only two points to consider, the stage and the auditorium, and at most as an extra a meeting-room for the actors. Dressing-rooms as such were unknown, the corridors behind the scenes were used for that purpose, one side for the gentlemen, the other for the ladies. At best the people getting dressed were protected by screens against peeping Toms but not against the inclement weather; only too often, rain and snow which had found their way through walls and roof had to be shaken off one's clothes.

B. PLAYHOUSES

Public playhouses not under court direction and run along commercial lines began to make their appearance in the second half of the eighteenth century. In 1765, the actor-manager Ackermann built a theatre in Hamburg (the Theater am Gänsemarkt), inaugurated on 31 July; this was to play an important role in German theatre history as the home of the short-lived Hamburg National Theatre, 1767–9 (see 170). In 1766, Koch opened the Theater auf der Ranstädter Bastei in Leipzig. An anonymous author compared these two theatres designed to cater for bourgeois, not courtly, audiences.

65   The theatres in Hamburg and Leipzig compared, 1769

Anon., *Vergleichungen der Ackermann- und Kochischen Schauspielergesellschaften*[1] (Ackermann' and Koch's Companies of Actors Compared) (Hamburg/Leipzig, 1769), pp. 18–9. DTM, R 158

The Hamburg playhouse is attractive and well built but it is situated in a courtyard reached by two lanes which are so narrow that a coach has only just enough room to get through, and this exposes pedestrians to a good deal of inconvenience and not infrequently some danger. The Leipzig playhouse, however, which is as attractive, as good and perhaps even more beautiful than, though not as large as, the Hamburg one, is uncluttered and has quite a large courtyard which lessens the nuisance commonly caused by coaches to pedestrians. The interior arrangements of the two playhouses under consideration are much the same, so much so that I would not know which one to prefer to the other.

The boxes are laid out in a similar manner; the pits are similar but for the fact that in the Hamburg one which, in my view, is larger than the one in Leipzig, you can sit at your ease, a comfort which is very agreeable for elderly, weak and fat people [...]. Which of the theatres should I prefer as regards scenery? The Hamburg playhouse at any rate cannot boast anything made by the busy and skilful hand of that subtle artist Oeser.[2] The rest of the scenery both in respect of variety and beauty is much of a muchness. [...]

---

[1] Konrad Ernst Ackermann (1712–71), one of the German theatre's leading actors, an educated man whose style was more realistic than that of the more formal Neuber school and who played lovers, tragedy kings and comic character parts. He worked in Russia for several years. Although for much of his life he followed an itinerant career with his company, he was responsible for the building of a theatre not only in Hamburg but also in Königsberg (in 1755). For Ackermann's career, see Herbert Eichhorn, *Konrad Ernst Ackermann/Ein deutscher Theaterprinzipal* (K.E.A./A German Actor-Manager)

(Emsdetten: Verlag Lechte, *DSB* 64, 1965). Heinrich Gottfried Koch (1703–75) started his acting career with the Neuber company where he also worked as scene painter, adaptor of improvised comedies and translator. He always retained something of the Neuber style. He ran his own companies in Leipzig, Lübeck, Hamburg and Berlin.

2 Adam Friedrich Oeser (1717–99), who had studied painting in Vienna and settled in Leipzig in 1759, was appointed the director of the newly founded academy of art there in 1764. He taught art to the young Goethe during the latter's student days in Leipzig. One of Oeser's earliest tasks in his new post was that of painting the curtain and ceiling of the Leipzig theatre which opened in 1766. Whilst the ceiling decorations were destroyed some three decades later and the curtain described below was replaced at the beginning of the nineteenth century by a new one designed by Veit Hans Schnorr v. Carolsfeld, a picture of the latter by a student of Oeser's survives.

This type of allegorical curtain was not uncommon in the latter part of the eighteenth century: similar ones were to be seen in Hamburg, in Ulm, at the Burgtheater as well as the Kärntnertortheater in Vienna, and elsewhere. What is worth noting here is that in this allegorical depiction of the history of drama, French authors are *not* given pride of place and that Shakespeare is ranked among the world's great playwrights, although at that time he had not yet been fully adopted into the German repertoire.

66   Description of the allegorical curtain at the Leipzig theatre, 1766

Franz Wilhelm Kreuchauf, Festival brochure for the opening of the theatre, 1766, Museum für Geschichte der Stadt Leipzig, Sign. N 102 a. Reproduced in G. Wustmann (ed.), *Leipziger Neudrucke* (Leipzig, 1899), vol. 2, pp. 32–6, and in Gertrud Rudloff-Hille, 'Das Leipziger Theater von 1766', *M&K*, 14 (1968), pp. 224–5

Two colonnades of the Doric order surround the circular forecourt of the Temple of Truth which is seen far away in the middle. It is open on all sides and reveals the delightful goddess, bare of all drapery, showing her open arms to all comers. At the entrance to the forecourt, in the middle of the picture, stand the statues of Sophocles and Aristophanes, the greatest dramatic authors, cast in bronze. The tragic muse dedicates to the former, who stands to the left of her, a laurel wreath which she deposits on the pedestal at his feet. Behind her stands Socrates, accompanied by his friend Euripides whose plays he preferred to all others [...]. Among the Greek poets near whom [...] one also sees some of their leading German and French followers, History is seated with an opened book. Aeschylus bends down towards her [and] shows her the mask and the buskin which he intends to lend to her truths. [...]

A flat is propped up next to him which a boy is painting [...]. On the other side you see the Comic Muse wreathing the statue of Aristophanes with garlands; [...] Plautus leans on his staff and looks attentively at the scattered writings of his predecessors. Tender Terence stands next to him, bringing with him Cupid whose torch he gently wrests out of his hand. In front of them sits Menander by the statue of Aristophanes [...].

In the forecourt you see inimitable Shakespeare who has passed by the old exemplars, hastening straight towards the Temple of Truth. Aristophanes' gesture indicates that he is mocking the tragic poets. Sophocles seems to be answering him by pointing with one hand at Truth and with the other at the Graces who with linked arms are hovering above the Temple in the clouds from which are swooping a host of genii bringing laurel wreaths for latter-day poets wherewith the ancients have already been adorned.

67   Oeser's curtain for the Leipzig theatre, 1766

As copied by Christian Friedrich Weigand. Museum für Geschichte der Stadt Leipzig

Theatres in Vienna

Of all cities in the German-speaking world, Vienna in the eighteenth century was the place most devoted to theatre in all its shapes and forms. The Theater nächst dem Kärntnertor (Theatre Next to the Carinthian Gate), built as early as 1708–9, was to provide a venue for the entertainment of the ordinary Viennese citizen throughout the century for German (as against foreign-language) theatre, including improvised drama until this was banned in 1770.

The Theater nächst der Hofburg (Theatre Next to the Imperial Palace), known as the

Burgtheater, was created in 1741 by the conversion of a tennis-court; under the impresario Joseph Karl Selliers, it served to entertain the court: and that meant Italian opera and French drama as well as German, but certainly not popular, theatre.

The Kärntnertortheater burnt down on 3 November 1761 after the performance of Gluck's ballet-pantomime, *Le Festin de Pierre* (based on the Don Juan story). The restored building was described as follows by J.H.F. Müller, one of the actors there who was subsequently to play a leading role in the company of the Burgtheater when it was raised to the status of a National Theatre. (For Müller, see 104.)

68   The Kärntnertortheater in Vienna described, 1772

Johann Heinrich Friedrich Müller, *Genaue Nachrichten von beyden Kaiserlich-Königlichen Schaubühnen und anderen Ergötzlichkeiten in Wien* (Precise Information Concerning both Imperial and Royal Theatres and other Entertainments in Vienna) (Bratislava/Frankfurt/ Leipzig: Anton Löwen, 1772), pp. 1–6. BL 11795 b. 22

(Note that the measurements in German feet (Schuh) and inches (Zoll) only approximately correspond to imperial measures.)

After the old municipal theatre had burnt down the present new playhouse was rebuilt from the ground up at Her Majesty's orders, under the direction of His Excellency Count von Durazzo,[1] Acting Privy Counsellor of Her Imperial and Royal Apostolic Majesty and the then Director General of Spectacles, according to the ground plan by Nicolaus Baron von Pacassi,[2] Imperial and Royal Architect-in-Chief, and opened for the first time on 9 July 1763. [...]

It is situated at the end of town next to the Kärntnertor [the Carinthian Gate].

Above the main entrance there is an imperial eagle carved out of stone. A statue of Apollo as well as a genius playing a wind instrument adorn the portal. To the right of them there is a genius with a dagger representing tragedy, to the left of them a genius with a mask representing comedy.

In addition to the main entrance there are another eighteen side entrances, fifteen of them practicable, so as to save the spectators from any danger in case of accidents.

From the wall of the Carinthian Gate to the theatre an archway has been erected across the street as an entrance for the Imperial Court.

An alteration to the main entrance was undertaken in 1766. For the convenience of household servants who had previously congregated by the box office towards the end of the show, not infrequently causing a commotion by their coming and going, a spacious vestibule, 12ft wide and 34ft long, was built where they can now wait for their masters without becoming a nuisance to the spectators. The head porter's apartment is behind this vestibule.

As regards the interior dimensions, both the space for the spectators and that for the stage are fairly ample. Apart from two spacious pits, which taken together are 46ft 3in long, and the orchestra which is 7ft wide and 44ft long, it contains five tiers. In the first there are eighteen, in the second twenty-four boxes. The third tier has on one side eleven boxes as well, but the other side is a gallery as are the fourth and fifth floors. But in the latter there are 10 boxes for the dancers.

The stage itself is 44½ft deep, 62ft wide and 42½ft high.

Messrs Quaglio[3] and Riccini were responsible for the installations in the flies. Here there are three floors 9½ft apart from one another for hanging the curtains and backdrops and for working the flying machines. In order to have sufficient water needed in case of fire, there are four large copper pans on these floors, each of which holds 56 [...] buckets in which rainwater is collected by means of a gutter, the surplus draining off through hosepipes. There is a well on the stage itself.

The curtains and backdrops are 37ft high and 34ft wide. The wings are 27ft high, and four are 4½ft wide.

The stage floor can be opened in thirteen different places for the production of machines and for traps.

The installations below the stage are by the French engineer M. Duclos. Here there are three compartments, too, which are 9ft away from each other, from where the machinery in the cellar and the wings are operated. There are two large copper water vats here as well.

On the first floor of the house adjacent to the theatre [...] which the management has rented and opened up to the theatre, there are five spacious rooms where the actors meet and get dressed, and a room where a part of the wardrobe and other theatrical properties are kept.

The dancers have seven dressing rooms in the theatre. [...]

The box-keeper and a wardrobe assistant have their apartments in the theatre.

---

[1] Jacob, Count von Durazzo, formerly the Genoese Ambassador; an expert in French and Italian literature; in charge of theatres in Vienna from 1754.

[2] Nikolaus (Niccolò) Franz Leonhard Baron von Pacassi (1716–90) also built the Schlosstheater at Schönbrunn, in 1747 (see 70).

[3] Johann (Giovanni) Maria von Quaglio (1700–65), a member of the distinguished Italian family of painters and set designers who were active in Italy and in German-speaking countries from the early seventeenth to the late nineteenth century.

69 An English visitor's impression of the Kärntnertortheater, 1 September 1772

Charles Burney, *The Present State of Music in Germany, the Netherlands and United Provinces*, 2 vols. (London: Becket, Robson & Robinson, 1773), vol. 2, pp. 241, 243–4. Reproduced in Percy A. Scholes (ed.), *Dr. Burney's Musical Tours in Europe*, 2 vols. (Oxford University Press, 1959), vol. 2, p. 85

[. . .] those [theatres] of Florence and Milan, are, at least, twice as big as this at Vienna, which is about the size of our great opera-house, in the Hay-market. [. . .]

The admission into this theatre is at a very easy rate; twenty-four creutzers only are paid for going into the pit; in which, however, there are seats with backs to them. A creutzer here, is hardly equal to an English halfpenny; indeed, part of the front of the pit is railed off, and is called the amphitheatre; for places there, the price is doubled, none are to be had for money, except in the pit and the slips, which run all along the top of the house, and in which only sixteen creutzers are paid. The boxes are all let by the season to the principal families, as is the custom in Italy.

The size of the theatre may be nearly imagined, by comparing with any one of our own, the number of boxes and seats in each. There are in this five ranks of boxes, twenty-four in each; in the pit there are twenty-seven rows of seats, which severally contain twenty-four persons.

70   Interior of the Schlosstheater at Schönbrunn

Baur-Heinhold (1967), p. 203. Photograph by Helga Schmidt-Glassner

This handsome court theatre – one of several built for the entertainment of the Imperial family – exists to this day (see **68**, note 2).

71　Dr Burney at the Burgtheater, 31 August 1772

Scholes (1959), p. 77

The second evening after my arrival, I went to the French theatre, where I saw a German comedy [...]. This theatre is not so high as that at which I had been the night before,[1] but it is still better fitted up; here the best places seem to be in the pit, which is divided in two parts, and all the seats are stuffed, and covered with red baize [...]

　Three large boxes are taken out of the front of the first row, for the Imperial family, which goes frequently to this theatre; it was built by Charles the sixth.

[1] Dr Burney had visited the Kärntnertortheater on 30 August.

C. THEATRE FIRES

Theatres during this period were largely or wholly wooden structures: what with the use of large numbers of open candles for illumination, it is not surprising that a good many of them went up in flames. This of course was not peculiar to German theatres. The following passage from the best known and fullest German theatrical autobiography of the eighteenth century, that of the actor-playwright Brandes, shows that a fire – in this case one affecting more than merely a theatre – was not always due to the careless handling of lights; and that the destruction of a playhouse could have a disastrous effect on the fortunes of a company of players.

72　The burning down of the Weimar Schlosstheater, 6 May 1774

Johann Christian Brandes, *Meine Lebensgeschichte* (The Story of My Life) (Berlin: Friedrich Maurer, 1800), vol. 2, pt. 2, pp. 165–9

On the 6th of May, in the year one thousand seven hundred and seventy-four, a fire broke out in the castle at half past two in the afternoon, presumably ignited by a flash of lightning during a heavy thunderstorm which had been hanging over the town during the previous night. In a matter of a few minutes the entire roof of the castle was alight. The fire lasted for several days, and since here, too, the fire-fighting arrangements were far from good, the entire magnificent building – but for the archive and the tower – was reduced to ashes. [...] Whoever was not engaged in putting out the fire came hurrying along in order to snatch from the raging flames the cashboxes, the silver plates and whatever else of value came to hand. [...]

　The Duchess showed a good deal of equanimity and no less charity during these mishaps.[1] Disregarding the irreplaceable losses she had suffered herself she distributed generous rewards to all those who had shown themselves particularly active in trying to help during the fire and gave charitable gifts to the unfortunates who had lost their belongings as a result of it. Seyler, too, who had lost a considerable amount of his theatrical wardrobe stored in the castle was amply recompensed.[2] It is true that the actors now had to be dismissed since there was no theatre left; but the benevolent princess arranged at the same time for their employment elsewhere and recommended them to the Duke of Gotha who in fact took on the company very readily on rather favourable terms.

[1] The Duchess Anna Amalia of Saxe-Weimar (1739–1807), daughter of Duke Charles I of Brunswick (see **60**) and niece of Frederick the Great, was a keen patron of the arts, including the art of the theatre: it was she who had invited the Seyler Company to Weimar in the first place. Regent of her small principality at the time of the fire, she handed over the government to her son Duke Karl August in the following year; one of his first acts was to invite Goethe to take up residence in Weimar.

[2] Abel Seyler (1730–1800), Swiss-born businessman from Hamburg who invested and lost his money in the unsuccessful Hamburg National Theatre venture (see **170**) and then became the director of his own company. He managed to lure some of the best actors away from Ackermann's company, including the great Ekhof (see **108, 113, 115–17, 189 & 194**) and Mme Hensel (see **118–19, 188, 189**) whom he was to marry after divorcing his wife. The company stayed in Weimar to perform at the Schlosstheater for nearly three years until the fire at the Schloss forced them to resume a peripatetic existence.

Fire precautions came to be taken more seriously over the years (see **68**), but major conflagrations still occurred in the following century (see **235**). When Friedrich Ludwig Schröder took over the direction of the Hamburg theatre for the third time in 1811, the following fire precautions were laid down and publicised. (For Schröder as a director, see **90**.)

Well intentioned as they clearly were, they would not perhaps inspire a contemporary theatre-goer with unqualified confidence.

73   Fire precautions at the German Theatre, Hamburg, Easter 1811

Friedrich Ludwig Wilhelm Meyer, *Friedrich Ludwig Schröder. Beitrag zur Kunde des Menschen und des Künstlers* (F.L.S. A Contribution to Knowledge of the Man and the Artist) (Hamburg: Hoffmann & Campe, 1819), vol. 2, pt. 2, pp. 258–60

Uninformed persons have claimed all too often that there was no chance of escaping from the Hamburg German Theatre during a fire, but actually there are seven exits just for the audience. Three would be enough to prevent anybody coming to any harm, *provided he does not try to leave the theatre any faster than he would normally do*. If he were to go even more slowly there would be even less cause for worry.

The *dress circle* has two special exits [...]; but the one to be chosen is that on the right hand side since on the opposite side [...] one would get mixed up with the spectators from the gallery. Next to each emergency exit there hangs a key on an iron chain. The spectator closest by can open these doors himself and bring himself, as well as the rest of the spectators, to safety. [...]

The *pit* has an exit to the right of the orchestra which leads out into the courtyard; another one on the opposite side [...], the end of which is however joined with the gallery one. Next to these emergency exits there are also keys hanging on iron chains [...]; another one next to the second door through the bar; another one on the path of the usual entrance, through the door next to the second cashier's office.

The *gallery* has its special exit. Although not more than three hundred persons are admitted to it, slowness is to be particularly recommended here in that somebody might have an accident through merely stumbling when people are *pushing* each other downstairs. Therefore let no woman presume to hasten away first, but let her calmly give way to the men. It would be a highly meritorious act if in such a case some *strong* men took up positions by the stairs to prevent their fellow citizens pushing. [...] All doors quite properly open outwards and will not resist a man's pushing against them.

It may not be unhelpful to publish some of the measures taken by the management for the safety of the audience.

(1) There is a daily check to see whether the keys which are supposed to hang by the emergency exits are in place, the locks have been oiled, the doors do not jam and can easily be opened.

(2) In case of a fire alarm the gallery exit [...] will be opened at once and the inner door through which one goes up to the gallery will be locked [...]

(3) The street exit through which the spectators in the pit leave at the end of every performance will be opened at once in the above-mentioned case, and the inner door through which they enter will be locked. The closing of the inner door is highly necessary because otherwise everybody would be pushing towards the main door and blocking the exit. [...]

(5) If a fire breaks out with the curtain open, not only the front curtain but the next few curtains will be lowered as well; so that a) there will be no draught caused by open doors and fire-fighting will be facilitated; b) the audience will not be panicked by smoke. [...]

(7) There is a daily check to see whether fire-hoses and water tanks are in good order.

IX Stage presentation

A. STAGING METHODS AND SCENERY

The distinction between aristocratic theatre – extravagant in manner and self-glorifying in intention – on the one hand and a commercial theatre – either raucously popular or middle-class and refined – on the other, continued well into the eighteenth century. While the composer Karl Ditters (1739–99) (later knighted and called von Dittersdorf) was employed by the Imperial Field Marshal Josef Maria Friedrich Wilhelm von Hildburghausen (1702–87) as a violinist in the latter's private orchestra at his seat Schlosshof from 1751 to 1761, he witnessed the following lavish entertainment devised on the occasion of a visit by Emperor Francis I with a large retinue. The water festival as described by Ditters many years after the event was the sort of baroque entertainment that might well have taken place a century or more earlier. (Compare 14, 19–24 & 27.)

74 An Imperial entertainment at Schlosshof in the 1750s

Carl Ditters von Dittersdorf, *Lebensbeschreibung, seinem Sohne in die Feder diktiert* (Leipzig: Breitkopf & Härtel, 1801), pp. 65–70. English version: *The Autobiography of Karl v. Dittersdorf, Dictated to his Son*, tr. A.D. Coleridge (London: Richard Bentley & Son, 1896), pp. 64–70. (Translation taken from Coleridge.)

[…] I mean to tell you all about a water-fete, given on an artificial lake at Kroissenbrunn, which had been planned by Prince Eugene, and walled round with large blocks of freestone, by his orders.[1]

It was eighty feet broad and a hundred long. From bank to bank, in the centre of the lake, two galleries were thrown across; on each of these were seated a number of trumpeters and drummers, with other players on wind instruments; they were heard playing alternate strains.

In the lake itself, at a little distance from the shore, there stood, at regular intervals on each side, eight pedestals, painted so as to look like stone, and adorned with bronzed grotesques. On the first two pedestals, two live bears stood opposite each other, dressed as clowns; on the second two, two wild-boars, dressed as columbines; on the third, two big goats, dressed as harlequins; and on the fourth were two huge bulldogs. […]

The picturesque hills, on both sides of the lake, were thronged with some thousands of spectators. Opposite the fishing cottage stood a gallery, resting on pillars, with railings through which you could look. It was a wooden construction, but Quaglio, the famous stage architect, [. . .] had so disguised it with a coat of paint, that anyone, looking at it from a distance, would have taken it for stonework.[2]

After allowing his guests an interval in which to enjoy the scene, the Prince waved his handkerchief as a signal, and the show began.

Two gondolas emerged at either end of the gallery, and made towards the cottage; each was manned by four gondoliers, dressed in Venetian fashion. One of them sat on the beak of the vessel, with a bundle of spears, lances, and similar weapons, laid crosswise before him; two others rowed, and the steerer, turning the gondola wherever he chose, sat behind them. These two gondolas advanced, circling in different ways round the pedestals; they were afterwards joined by two others, then by two more, and then the last two. The eight went through their manoeuvres with such accuracy, that no ballet-master, marshalling his *danseuses*, could have improved upon them. When they had gone their rounds, they were ranged face to face, and a tournament began, in which each water-knight, seated on the beak, broke from four to five lances; then they went once more round the pedestals on which the comic actors stood. At one and the same moment, each knight, armed with a staff, struck at one of the grotesque masks, a spring gave way under the blow, and a trap-door fell. Numbers of white ducks and geese, and one swan as well, were concealed in each of the hollow pedestals, and you may fancy the alacrity with which these winged creatures took to their native element, though a marionette rode upon each of them. These marionettes were various figures, proportioned to the size of the birds which they bestrode – clowns, harlequins, Anselmos, Doctors, Leanders, Pasquins, Scaramouches, and other Carnival mummers.[3]

A fray ensued, and the knights seized their clubs and threatened one another. The gondolas darted about in studied disorder. When one collided with another, the knights dipped their clubs, which were hand-syringes, into the lake, and squirted their enemies. Whenever they neared a pedestal, the creature on it got the whole benefit of a shower-bath, and the animals loudly resented the rudeness of the whole proceedings. The effect on the audience may be imagined, for orders had been given to the musicians on either bank to blow in any key they chose. [. . .] Some of the drummers had tuned up, others had tuned down; oboists, clarinettists, bassoon-players, followed suit. What an infernal discord it was! The beasts growled, the ducks and geese quacked and spluttered, coming into collision with the moving gondolas every moment, and the three thousand spectators roared with laughter. [. . .]

When the scene had lasted long enough, the gondolas withdrew, and to the astonishment of all the spectators, the gallery was metamorphosed into a willow grove. Laughter died away on their lips. [...]

From the centre of the grove there slowly rose a pretty little garden, which looked like a floating island; it went on moving, as though of itself, for about a quarter of an hour, towards the fishing-house. It was fenced all round with palisades, painted white and green, half the height of a man. The garden was planted with regular borders of box, within which flourished all sorts of most lovely flowers that happened to be in bloom just then. Between the borders were vases, painted white and green, containing twelve pomegranate and orange trees, laden with ripe fruit. In the middle of the garden was a round basin, filled with shoals of little bleak. A small dolphin, too, was seen disporting himself, and throwing up a jet of water. [...] At the end of the garden was Parnassus, with the winged Pegasus. At the blow of his hoof, two streams bubbled out to the right and left of the rocks, and fell into the basin by means of a little canal.

Baron Beust, dressed as a gardener, and Mademoiselle Heinisch, as a gardener's wife, stood at the entrance.[4] The lady wore a white and green satin dress, covered with real flowers. The gardener had a gilded rake, and the lady a gilded watering-pot.

Two fishermen and fisherwomen, dressed in white and sky-blue satin, stood near the basin. [...] Each [...] had a small draw-net, with a handle of black fretted wood, the nets being composed of thin silver lace.

When the garden had reached them, the royal guests were invited by the gardener to enter and pick the flowers. They gathered several nosegays, and the Archdukes and Archduchesses [...] drew fish out of the basin, and threw them into the lake.[5] At last they sat down on the benches provided for them, along the palisade. The gardener and his wife retreated to Parnassus, where there were plenty of ices, which they handed round in the most dainty glasses.

[1] Francis Eugene, Prince of Savoy (1663–1736), had built Schlosshof.
[2] See **68**, note 3.
[3] See **24**, note 1.
[4] Baron Beust was the Prince of Hildburghausen's Equerry and Master of the Horse, Mlle Heinisch a famous soprano from Vienna.
[5] The Archdukes Joseph (subsequently the Emperor Joseph II) and Charles, the Archduchesses Mariane and Christine.

Compared with such munificently mounted outdoor spectacles, the commercial theatre catering to the bourgeoisie was a very much more modest affair. Inadequacies of stage design and technique were everyday experiences even well into the second half of the eighteenth century, which did not escape the notice of alert observers.

75   Anachronism in stage design

Brandes (1800), vol. 2, pt. 1, p. 52

In mentioning that tragedy, I must criticise one conspicuous error.[1] The ship on which Regulus arrived was built neither in the Roman nor the Carthaginian manner but was a fairly modern English frigate; nor had the insightful artist failed to provide on the visible side a dozen loopholes with as many cannon protruding.

[1] The play in question was *Regulus*, adapted from the Italian by Prince Frederick of Brunswick.

76   Inappropriate stage design, Stuttgart 1794

'Stuttgarter Theater, Kritik über "Die Jäger" ', *Rheinische Musen*, 1, 1, p. 132. Reproduced in Kurt Sommerfield, *Die Bühneneinrichtungen des Mannheimer Nationaltheaters unter Dalbergs Leitung (1778–1803)* (The Staging Conditions of the Mannheim National Theatre under Dalberg's Direction) (Berlin: SGTG 36, 1927), p. 2

The choice of decor was not appropriate for the play [Iffland's 'The Foresters'], the first room was far too magnificent for the ordinary living-room of a chief forester, the pier-glasses, the china service made rather an odd contrast with the oil lamp gracing the table and the huntsmen parading in nightcaps [. . .]. The hall in which meals were taken was such as not many counts of the Holy Roman Empire would dine in.

77   Faulty stage technique, Stuttgart 1794

'Stuttgarter Theater. Kritik der Oper "Caliroe" ', *Rheinische Musen*, 1, 1, p. 122. Reproduced in Sommerfield (1927), p. 2

But the effect of the best scene changes was marred by the sloppiness with which they were carried out. [. . .] Curtains got stuck, the wrong ones were used instead of the intended ones, a tomb appeared instead of a prison; and the borders were a veritable collection of samples of previously used hangings, entire pieces of the temple of Isis hung in the Turkish chamber [. . .]

In the German theatre as elsewhere in Europe, the lighting source both in the auditorium and on the stage were wax or tallow candles; auditorium lights were, of course, not extinguished during the performance. The disadvantages of this lighting system were not only the dripping of the candles and the sooty smoke they produced but, in many cases, the sheer inadequacy of the light output. True, princely theatres, operas in particular, could afford a very considerable outlay in order to overcome this problem. Not so the middle-class theatre, even in the permanent playhouses which were becoming increasingly common in the second half of the eighteenth century. Both auditoria and stages were often underlit, as the following extract from a theatre journal describing conditions in Leipzig indicates.

78   Inadequate house lighting in the Leipzig theatre, 1783

Raisonnierendes Theaterjurnal [sic] von der Leipziger Michaelmesse 1783 (Leipzig: Jacobäer, 1784). Reproduced in Gertrud Rudloff-Hille, *Das Theater auf der Ranstädter Bastei, Leipzig 1766. Geschichte des ersten Leipziger Theaterhauses* (History of the first Leipzig Theatre) (Leipzig: Museum für Geschichte der Stadt Leipzig, 1969), p. 38, and in Maurer-Schmoock (1982), pp. 68–9

I entered the pit, some five minutes short of a quarter to six, and nearly fell down the last few steps at the entrance because of the darkness, although both chandeliers had already been illuminated. – In one of them there were eight candles lit, in the other one only seven. How can such slight illumination do its proper job in the space of the amphitheatre here?[1] [. . .] It would be better to open the doors later when all the lights were fully lit, including the ones in front of and in the orchestra.

[1] The amphitheatre was the more desirable front part of the pit (see **69**).

In the last few decades of the eighteenth century, German audiences like those of other countries increasingly demanded some degree of realism, consistency and historical accuracy in theatrical presentation. The première of Goethe's drama of chivalry, *Götz von Berlichingen mit der eisernen Hand* (Götz von Berlichingen with the Iron Hand), which took place in Berlin, set a new standard in terms of what was taken at the time to be authenticity of design. The announcement in a leading Berlin newspaper of a play important both as a piece of dramatic literature and as a milestone in theatre history is quoted here in full. Note that the commissioning of sets and costumes – the latter by the artist J.W. Meil, an expert in costume history – for a particular production, rather than just taking these out of stock, was deemed sufficiently unusual to be worthy of particular notice. (For comments on various productions of *Götz*, see **197–9, 203**.)

79   Announcement of first production of 'Götz von Berlichingen', Berlin, 14 April 1774

Berlinische privilegirte Zeitung (also known as the *Vossische Zeitung*), Berlin, 14 April 1774. Reproduced in Julius W. Braun, *Goethe im Urtheile seiner Zeitgenossen* (Goethe in the Judgement of His Contemporaries), 3 vols. (Berlin: Friedrich Luckhardt 1883–5; reprinted Hildesheim: George Olms Verlagsbuchhandlung 1969), vol. i, p. 31

Tonight Koch's Company of German Players, graciously patented by His Majesty the King of Prussia,[1] will present:

Götz von Berlichingen with the Iron Hand

An entirely new play in five acts which has been penned by a learned and ingenious author according to a very special and hitherto unaccustomed plan. It is said to be written in the Shakespearean manner. There might have been some reluctance to stage such a play but the requests of many friends have carried the day and such efforts as time and place permit have been made to perform it.[2] In order to oblige the esteemed public no necessary expense has been spared for the needed decorations and new costumes of the kind customary in those days. There will also be a ballet of gypsies in this play. The programme of this play is obtainable at the entrance for one groschen.

[1] Koch (see **65**, note 1) had been established in Berlin since 1771. He died in 1775, i.e. the year after the production of *Götz*.
[2] Berlin had previously been a citadel of French taste in the theatre, and staging so irregular a play as *Götz* was clearly felt to be a daring venture.

By the end of the eighteenth century, the traditional indoor set was felt by some critics to be no longer adequate for creating a theatrical 'illusion'. Although the box set only came gradually to be accepted in the first few decades of the nineteenth century, the idea of using angled walls rather than successive sets of wings was in the air much earlier, as the following excerpt from a series of magazine articles shows. For Schröder's use of a box set in Hamburg as early as 1790, see Maurer-Schmoock (1982), p. 50. For Goethe's objections to that kind of scenic realism, see Alois Maria Nagler, *Sources of Theatrical History* (New York: Theatre Annual Inc. 1952), p. 435.

80   Use of box sets suggested, 1785

A. Baron v.K. (von Knigge), 'Über die deutsche Schaubühne' (Concerning German Theatre) in *Ephemeriden der Litteratur und des Theaters* (Ephemerides of Literature and the Theatre), ed. Christian August v. Bertram (Berlin), vol. 2, no. 29 (16 June 1785), p. 40. DTM, Per 81 (1.2)

I consider it a prejudice to think that single standing wings are more advantageous for [creating] perspective and representing a greater distance. A skilful painter will know how to paint entire side walls just as perspectively. [...] Furthermore, even in the best built theatre it is unavoidable that [spectators in] some side boxes at any rate can see through the downstage wings and there become aware of candles, candle-snuffers, the other actors and actresses together with their friends, maids, hairdressers etc., which spoils the illusion. I would therefore like to suggest experimenting with two complete side walls. Scene changes would undoubtedly be effected more swiftly, for the whole thing could be dropped in all at once like a curtain; though there might be some lighting problems. But even these could be remedied, especially when the scene represents a room. Perhaps daylight might be imitated better, false shadows avoided and indeed some savings made, with real windows through which the light fell artificially amplified by mirrors. I seem to have heard that there is such a theatre in Italy.

By the end of the century, the leading theatres – in Mannheim, Berlin, Weimar, Hamburg and elsewhere – saw to it that playtext, costumes and setting were fully integrated so as to create a unified aesthetic impression. Exemplary work along these lines was carried out at the Weimar theatre, despite the small duchy's limited financial resources, during the directorship from 1791 to 1817 of Johann Wolfgang von Goethe who worked in close collaboration for part of this period with his friend and fellow playwright Friedrich Schiller. Both men firmly believed in creating a stage picture which should be both picturesque and at the same time appropriate to the action of the play – but without 'declining' into naturalism. The detailed care that went into the planning of the décor of their own productions, or productions of their plays mounted elsewhere, is apparent in the following practical notes in a letter by Schiller. He was writing from Weimar to the actor-manager Iffland, at the time the director of the Royal National Theatre in Berlin, detailing his ideas for the proposed production in Berlin of *Wilhelm Tell* (William Tell), which as yet only existed in draft form and which was to be Schiller's last completed play. These elaborate scenic suggestions (note for instance the request for sophisticated atmospheric lighting effects) were made in view of the resources of the Berlin theatre which were considerably greater than those available in Weimar. They do not in fact exactly correspond to the scenic indications of the final text.

81   Schiller's scenic suggestions for *Wilhelm Tell*, 5 December 1803

Schillers Briefe (Schiller's Letters), ed. Fritz Jonas (Stuttgart/Leipzig/Berlin/Vienna: Deutsche Verlags-Anstalt 1892), 7 vols. vol. 7, pp. 99–101, letter 1,921. Reproduced in English translation in Marvin Carlson, *Goethe and the Weimar Theatre* (Cornell: Cornell University Press, 1978), pp. 214–17

[...] I enclose a list of the scene changes needed for Tell, but one or the other might be added which I cannot as yet determine precisely.

Act I. 1. High bluff above the Lake of Lucerne, the lake forming an inlet, across the lake you clearly see the green meadows, the villages and farms of Schwyz lying in the sunshine. Beyond (to the left of the spectators) the Haken with its two cloud-capped peaks. Still farther off and to the right (of the spectators) shimmer, blue-green, the Glarus mountain glaciers. On the rocks, represented by the wings, are steep paths with railings and ladders on which huntsmen and shepherds are seen climbing down in the course of the action. So the painter must represent the boldness, grandeur and danger of the Swiss mountains. A part of the lake must be movable, because it is shown during a storm.

2. Stauffacher's newly built house (the exterior), painted with many windows, heraldic figures and mottos. It is at Steinen, next to the highway and the bridge. It may be painted entirely on the backdrop.

3. A Gothic hall in a nobleman's seat decorated with escutcheons and helmets. This is the residence of Baron von Attinghausen.

4. A public square in Altdorf. In the distant background you see the new fortress of Zwing-Uri being built, already so near completion that the overall shape is apparent. The rear towers and curtains[1] are completely finished; only on the nearer side work is still in progress. The wooden scaffolding is still up on which workmen are climbing up and down. The whole rear scene is a lively representation of a great building project with all its equipment.[2] The workers on the scaffold must be represented by children, for reasons of perspective. N.B. This scene is significant because this very Bastille being built here will be razed in the fifth act.

5. Walter Fürst's dwelling represents a room in a well-to-do Swiss house.

Act II. 1. A public square at Altdorf, at the discretion of the painter.

2. A room.

3. The Rütli, a meadow surrounded by high cliffs and forests (the wings can be the same as those for the first scene of Act I). In the background is the lake, with a *lunar rainbow* above it, high mountains close the backdrop, with even greater glaciers beyond. It is completely dark, only the lake and the white snow-capped mountains shine in the moonlight. N.B. This scene, which represents a moonlit landscape, closes with the spectacle of the rising sun; the highest peaks must therefore be transparent so that at first they may appear white when lit from the front, and later, when the morning sun appears, be lit red from behind. Since the red morning sky in Switzerland really is a magnificent spectacle, the inventiveness and art of the designer can be manifested here in the most pleasing manner.

Act III. 1. The vestibule in Tell's house, with costumes of the period.

2. A square at Altdorf planted with trees. In the background the hamlet, in front of it the hat on a pole. The space must be very large, since it is here that Tell shoots the apple.

Act IV. 1. The Gothic hall of knights.

2. Lakeshore, cliffs and forest, the lake in a storm.

3. Wild mountains. Ice fields, glaciers, and glacial currents, all the fearfulness of a desolate winter region.

4. The gorge near Küssnacht. The path winds between rocks from background to foreground so that persons travelling on it can be seen up above from afar, disappearing again and then reappearing. In one of the downstage wings there is a bush high up and a *projecting point* from which Tell shoots.

5. The Rossberg fortress at night with a rope ladder for scaling.

Act V. 1. The setting of Act I, 4. The scaffolding is being pulled down, the populace is at work destroying Zwing-Uri, beams and stones are heard crashing down. The fortress could also be set afire – signal fires on eight to ten mountains.

2. Tell's entrance hall. Hearth with fire in it.

3. As yet uncertain.

[1] That is, walls connecting bastions or towers.
[2] Note that the division of the stage into the downstage and upstage (rear) parts mentioned earlier (see 17) still persisted up to this period.

Goethe, who had a lifelong interest in the visual arts, had spent much of his time during his extended stay in Italy from 1786 to 1788 in associating with painters, studying, sketching, and collecting. It was natural then for him as director of the Weimar theatre to be very much concerned with the appearance of productions. His interest in design and scene painting was very practical and well informed.

In the latter years of his life, long after he had severed his connection with the stage, Goethe touched from time to time on matters theatrical in his wide-ranging talks with his friend and biographer Johann Peter Eckermann (1792–1854). In the following conversation recorded as having taken place on 17 February 1830, he was referring to experiences some fifteen years or so earlier.

82   Goethe on colour contrast in scenic and costume design

Johann Peter Eckermann. *Gespräche mit Goethe in den letzten Jahren seines Lebens. 1823–1832.* vols. 1 & 2 (Conversations with Goethe in the last Years of his Life) (Leipzig: Brockhaus, 1836), vol. 3 (Magdeburg: Heinrichshofen, 1848). English translation by John Oxenford, *Conversations of Goethe with Eckermann and Soret*, 2 vols. (London: Smith, Elder & Co., 1850), reprinted Everyman's Library no. 851 (London/Toronto: Dent, 1930), p. 350. (Translation taken from Oxenford.) Reproduced in Nagler (1952), p. 442

We talked of the theatre – of the colour of the scenes and costumes. The result was as follows:

Generally, the scenes should have a tone favourable to every colour of the dresses; like Beuther's scenery, which has more or less of a brownish tinge, and brings out the colour of the dresses with perfect freshness.[1] But if the scene-painter is obliged to depart from so favourable an undecided tone, [. . .] the actors should be clever enough to avoid similar colours in their dresses. If an actor in a red uniform and green breeches enters a red room, the upper part of his body vanishes, and only his legs are seen; if, with the same dress, he enters a green garden, his legs vanish, and the upper part of his body is conspicuous. [. . .]

'Even when the scene-painter is obliged to have a red or yellow chamber', said Goethe, 'or a green garden or wood, these colours should be somewhat faint and hazy, that every dress in the foreground may be relieved and produce the proper effect.'

¹ Friedrich Beuther (1776–1856), a scene painter Goethe had engaged for Weimar in 1815, who in his first year produced no fewer than thirty-nine new settings. See Carlson (1978) pp. 275–6.

B. COSTUMES

As in other theatres in Europe, costume conventions in German theatre for the greater part of the eighteenth century were full of anachronisms. While this did not seem to trouble most spectators, Johann Christoph Gottsched (1700–66), Professor of Poetry at the University of Leipzig and during the 1730s the virtual dictator of literary taste, demanded reform in this, as in so many other areas, of theatre. His guiding principle was that of 'reason', interpreted in a narrowly literal way. His dogmatic neo-classicism was attacked by the Swiss critics Bodmer and Breitinger and later ridiculed for all time by Lessing; nevertheless, his call for costume authenticity in fact anticipated those developments in the latter part of the eighteenth century which were to become the dominant costume doctrine in the following century.

83   An early call for authentic stage costumes, 1742

Johann Christoph Gottsched, *Versuch einer Critischen Dichtkunst* (Essay on the Criticism of Poetry) (Leipzig: Bernhard Christoph Breitkopf, 1729, 1737, 1742 & 1751). The following quotation is from the third (1742) edition, pp. 725–6. Reproduced in Joachim Birke and Brigitte Birke (eds.), *Johann Christoph Gottscheds ausgewählte Werke* (Berlin/New York: Walter de Gruyter, 1973), vol. 6, pt. 2, pp. 332–3

[...] characters should properly appear on stage according to the nature of the plays, now in Roman, now in Greek, now in Persian, now in Spanish, now in Old German dress; and this should be imitated as naturally as possible. The more nearly perfection is attained in this the greater will be the verisimilitude, and the more the spectator's eye will be delighted. Hence it is absurd when simple-minded actors represent Roman citizens wearing a rapier at their side; seeing they wore long and ample white clothes. It is even odder when one goes so far as to put full-bottomed wigs and tricorns with plumes on ancient Greek or Roman heroes in camp and deck them out with gloves; to represent an American princess in a whalebone corset and a fleeing Zaïre in the Orient with a three-ell-long train;¹ nay, even the ancient Germans Arminius, Segestes and others dressed like their mortal enemies the Romans, that is to say with wigs, white gloves, dress-sword etc.² Here a sensible stage manager must look to antiquity and study pictures of the costumes of all the nations he intends to put upon the stage.

¹ These are clearly references to Voltaire's plays *Alzire* and *Zaïre* respectively.
² Arminius (Hermann) and Segestes were princes of the Germanic tribe of the Cherusci. The exploits of the former had just been celebrated in Johann Elias Schlegel's play, *Hermann* (1741).

Gottsched's demand for archaeological exactitude in dress was premature: the taste for conventionalised stage costume along French lines was still too strong. This underlay the incident on the Leipzig stage on 12 June 1741, described some time after the event in the following letter, dated 17 February 1744, from Johann Peter Uz (1720–96) to his fellow Anacreontic poet Johann Wilhelm Ludwig Gleim (1719–1803), in terms suggesting some sympathy with Gottsched. The background to this particular theatrical polemic was the fact that Frau Neuber, who had been closely allied with Gottsched and had championed his dramaturgic principles, had fallen out with him by 1741, when the influential academic had come to favour Schönemann's company instead.

84   An attack on the idea of authentic stage costumes, Leipzig, 12 June 1741

Richard Daunicht, *Die Neuberin. Materialien zur Theatergeschichte des 18. Jahrhunderts* (Frau Neuber. Materials towards Eighteenth-Century Theatre History) (issued by the Ministry of Culture, GDR, 1956), p. 87. Reproduced in Maurer-Schmoock (1982), p. 58

Mme Neuber [. . .] was criticised in the issue of the *Beiträge*[1] that came out during the previous Easter Fair, in particular her and her company's frequently offending against verisimilitude on stage, especially with her Paris fashions, white gloves, full-bottomed wigs, plumes etc. About a fortnight later when the principal play was finished,[2] an actor appeared on stage in the usual way in order to announce the play to be performed the following day; which he did in this manner: tomorrow, he said, they would perform a play arranged according to the strictest rules of verisimilitude such as had been established by the greatest critics of our times, which would be taken from Cato.[3] The tremendous burst of laughter which arose from all sides prevented his saying any more.

The following day the auditorium was packed out; and first the curtain raiser was performed [. . .]. Thereupon the third act of Cato was presented: all the characters wore the costumes of their country; Roman men and women appeared in bare feet: which was not ridiculous or only seemed so because one was not used to it.

---

[1] The magazine, *Critische Beyträge* (Contributions to Criticism), was published by Gottsched from 1731 to 1744.
[2] A normal evening's programme consisted of a curtain raiser, then a main play followed by an afterpiece, which would frequently be a ballet.
[3] Gottsched's tragedy, *Der sterbende Cato* (The Death of Cato), largely based on Addison's *Cato*, had been premièred by the Neuber company in 1731 and was a regular item in its repertoire until the outbreak of this controversy.

In contrast to the rich and varied costumes employed in court entertainments and operas, the wardrobes carried by companies of strolling players were modest. (Their hard-to-transport stocks of scenery were of course even more limited.) Until the middle of the eighteenth century costumes were stereotyped according to character; they followed French fashions in contemporary as well as in classical and exotic roles. In some companies, actors were largely responsible not only for keeping their own dresses in good order but for providing them in the first instance, except for particularly elaborate or costly ones. A vivid picture of these conditions is conveyed by Karoline Schulze-Kummerfeld who joined Ackermann's company in 1758 and stayed on until 1766. The leadership of the company was at times in the hands of Ackermann's wife, Sophie Charlotte Schröder, herself an actress of distinction and the mother by her first marriage of Friedrich Ludwig Schröder – the man who was to be the leading actor and director of the German-language theatre in the last quarter of the eighteenth century.

85   The wardrobe of a company of strolling players in the 1760s

Karoline Schulze-Kummerfeld, 'Biographisches', in *MBGDKL*, vol. 3, no. 3 (June 1828), pp. 196–7. Herzog-August-Bibliothek, Wolfenbüttel, Sign. Wd 567 i

Skilful and extremely hardworking as she [i.e. Mme Ackermann-Schröder] was, she raised the splendour of the wardrobe by her embroideries. At that time there were still various dresses in the theatre entirely made by her, which from the stage looked like rich elegant materials, in great flowery patterns made up of many small pieces of silk and gold fabric sewn together. Audiences were not used to a wide range of costumes. Managements only provided court dresses and exotic costumes, and as is well known these included very few other than, perhaps, countryfolk, shepherds, Chinese, or Turks. Clytemnestra and an ancient Danish princess were not very different in their outfits, wearing hoopskirts and lace cuffs as much, and according to the same pattern, as any fashionable lady at the court of Louis XV. (Cf. 286.) In the Ackermann wardrobe there were for the use of younger actresses, apart from rich gowns and black dresses, one made of rose-coloured silk, [and] one in multi-coloured silk for light-hearted lovers, [as well as] a mauve and an all-white one for sentimental ones. If the new wearers did not quite fill them out as the former ones had done, they were sewn and patched into them.

Where actors had to supply at any rate part of their own wardrobe, some theatres offered a cash allowance enabling them to make their own purchases. This was the case at the Weimar theatre under Goethe's direction.

86   Actors' costume allowance in Weimar under Goethe's management

Eduard Genast, *Aus dem Tagebuch eines alten Schauspielers* (From an old Actor's Diary), 4 vols. (Leipzig: Voigt & Günther 1862–6). Also Robert Kohlrausch (ed.), *Aus Weimars*

klassischer und nachklassischer Zeit. Erinnerungen eines alten Schauspielers von Eduard Genast
(Weimar's Classical and Postclassical Period. Recollections of an old Actor by Eduard
Genast) (Stuttgart: Robert Lutz, 1904), p. 88. Reproduced in Maurer-Schmoock (1982),
p. 62

In order to circumvent the constant though not unjustified demands of the actors
concerning costumes, the regulation had been passed that each one playing a
leading role would be given an annual wardrobe allowance of 500 dollars, for
which he would have to purchase not only his everyday dress but also his knightly
accoutrements together with all properties: sword, boots, spurs, gloves, headgear
and the requisite adornments.[1]

[1] The need for the latter was the result of the rash of plays of chivalry that flooded the German stage in
the wake of *Götz von Berlichingen*.

In parallel with set design at the turn of the eighteenth century, costume design was
becoming more and more 'realistic' and atmospheric – in others words: romantic. A very
similar development can of course be traced in the theatre of other European countries of
the period. These illustrations of leading characters in plays by Schiller as performed on the
well-endowed Berlin stage show this trend at its most lavish.

87   Early nineteenth-century costumes

*Kostüme auf dem Königl. National-Theater in Berlin. Unter der Direction des Herrn Aug.Wilh.
Iffland* (Costumes at the Royal National Theatre in Berlin. Under the management of Herr
A.W.I.) (Berlin: L.W. Wittich, 1812), pls. 5 & 72. BL 11795 g. 12

(i) Joan of Arc (*Die Jungfrau von Orleans*)   (ii) Wallenstein (Iffland in the title role)

X   *Technical jobs and theatre regulations*

In the latter part of the eighteenth century repeated attempts were made to formalise the responsibilities of the technical staff in theatres, largely because companies were beginning to achieve a greater degree of permanence, staying in one place at a time for longer periods. When Schönemann's company was given a home at Schwerin and Rostock from 1750 to 1756 by Duke Christian Louis II of Mecklenburg-Schwerin – a hitherto unprecedented appointment of *German* players as court actors – the leading man in the company, Konrad Ekhof (1720–78), founded an 'academy' in an attempt to raise the company's artistic standards in the teeth of much indifference on the part of his fellow actors. While this academy mainly concerned itself with repertoire planning and acting technique during its brief life (1753–4), it did not altogether neglect technical tasks, as we can see from the minutes it kept. The amendments of 9 February 1754 to the academy's constitution defined some of these tasks in the light of then current practice.

88   The duties of the stage manager and the wardrobe staff, 1754

The original minutes, kept in the Herzoglich Gothaische Bibliothek, were lost during World War Two, but had been previously photocopied by Professor Kindermann. Reproduced in Heinz Kindermann, *Conrad Ekhofs Schauspieler-Akademie* (Konrad Ekhof's Acting Academy) (Vienna: Rudolf M. Rohrer, 1956), p. 35

[...] 4. It will be the stage manager's task to see to it that wings, backdrops and borders as well as all machinery required for illumination are in good order at all times, to mend them constantly or, if they are damaged, to report this to the director immediately on penalty of being liable for the damage. [...]

5. The supervisors of the wardrobe and everything connected therewith shall be responsible for constantly brushing clothes, hats, etc. [...], for checking them carefully and for making good any damage, and for providing the actor or actress at all times with a complete and undamaged costume, on penalty of a fine of 4 dollars. On the other hand, the actor or actress shall be required, if he or she has an accident with a costume or tears it, to report this to the supervisor, on penalty of a 4 shilling fine. The supervisors are to report this at once to the director so that he

can examine the damage or the causes thereof and have it mended again. Similarly, all required objects or properties needed for each play and itemised at rehearsal, must without any excuse be laid out in readiness for each actor or actress at the dressing place or put inside the costume, on penalty of a 2 dollar fine, and actors and actresses who last used them shall be required either to return them to the supervisor themselves or to leave them in their place with their costumes, on penalty of a 2 dollar fine.

The prompter was an important member of the technical staff in eighteenth-century German theatre, with a rather wider range of functions than those of today. He would pen all the letters used in a play and indeed whatever had to be read out aloud in the course of the action; he would give the signal for scene changes; and he would keep a record of all the plays performed and of their technical requirements – tasks now carried out by stage management. The Mannheim theatre, opened in 1779 under the title of 'National Theatre' which it retains to this day, was led in its early stages by Wolfgang Heribert Baron v. Dalberg (1750–1806) who laid down precise regulations for the conduct of the staff. Here are some of the prompter's important responsibilities (apart from the basic duty of prompting) as laid down in Article XVI, par. 3 of the revised regulations under the Dalberg regime. Compare the even more detailed enumeration of responsibilities of the prompter at the Hamburg theatre (90).

89   The prompter as record keeper, Mannheim, 27 March 1797

Mannheimer Nationaltheater, Akten, Litr.G.III, Fasz.1. Reproduced in Sommerfeld (1927), p. 33

Apart from other clerical duties in connection with the theatre, he [i.e. the prompter] also has to keep the record [*Hauptbuch*] of the plays performed on the stage here. In this he must note down with all needful clarity [...]: (1) the day of performance, (2) the play's running time, (3) the casting and any alterations, (4) the number of costumes, (5) the number of walk-ons and supers according to their casting and their costumes, (6) the scenery, and (7) finally the props.

Friedrich Ludwig Schröder (1744–1816), dancer and improviser in his early years, then a star actor of immense versatility, author and adaptor of plays (particularly from the English) as well as the leading German champion of Shakespeare on the stage (see 102, 120–1, 124, 134, 193, 199–200 & 204 for different aspects of his work), was also – as a complete man of the theatre – a distinguished director. Being Ackermann's stepson, he took over the latter's Hamburg company in 1771 and served as its director until 1780. He then left to go on extensive tours and to play at the newly founded National Theatre in

Vienna, but he returned to Hamburg and resumed running the playhouse from 1786 to 1798. His last period as its director (1811–1812) was a brief coda following his retirement from the stage in 1798.

The detailed regulations he laid down for the Hamburg theatre during his second period of office are quoted at length below. Of course, other theatres – not only in Germany but elsewhere – also had such official codes of conduct. Compare for instance the regulations which governed the conduct of actors at the Amsterdam Schouwburg (307, 361). See also David Thomas (ed.), *TIE: Restoration and Georgian England, 1660–1788* (CUP, 1989), pp. 240–5 for analogous rules in England and Scotland, and Laurence Senelick (ed.), *TIE: National Theatre in Northern and Eastern Europe, 1746–1900* (CUP, 1991), pp. 192–3, for Lipski's rules for Polish actors (1766). But the Hamburg regulations, covering technical functions as well as the conduct of actors, afford a particularly good insight into the day-to-day running of what in its day was regarded as an exemplary German theatre. If a listing of the transgressions of which theatre personnel were then routinely expected to be guilty and against which it was thought necessary to offer deterrents seems to cast a poor light on the profession, it is as well to remember that conditions were much the same in other countries. Perhaps more worthy of note are such democratic safeguards against the abuse of directorial authority as Schröder saw fit to build into his statutes. (Note by the way that it was still common at the time for a theatre to combine the spoken drama with opera and ballet in its repertoire.)

90   Hamburg theatre regulations under Schröder, 1792

Annalen des Theaters (Annals of the Theatre), ed. Christian August v. Bertram (Berlin: Friedrich Maurer), no. 9 (1792), pp. 4–22.[1]

1. Everybody is obliged to acknowledge these regulations by his signature on being engaged [...].

2. No beginner is to be accepted as a member of this company whose previous life is not known and whose parents or his next of kin are not agreeable [to his joining the theatre].

3. Each member will receive a printed copy of these regulations in order to be guided by them.

4. No new regulation shall be valid unless approved by two-thirds of the company.

5. No one shall be allowed to reject a role nor to object to any of his fellow actors. If he has any reasons for such a refusal, let him write to, or have a cool discussion with, the director who will never refuse either to give in to substantial arguments he had overlooked or to persuade him by a majority vote of the senior company members. Thus all causes for grumbling about this matter will cease; anyone persisting nevertheless will be lacking in respect and will pay two shillings out of every dollar of his monthly salary. [...]

7. Nobody should take offence if the director switches roles or assigns a role played before by one actor to another: because it is possible to be excellent in one business and very mediocre in another. Any actor rendered aware either by his own feelings or the coldness of the public that he is not in the right place and voluntarily offers to resign will merit the director's gratitude in that he will spare him an embarrassment.

8. The spreading of excessively favourable rumours concerning plays, the publication of the casting and other matters that are none of the public's business will if proven be punished by [a fine of] two shillings in the dollar out of the monthly salary.

9. The spreading of unfavourable rumours of plays, operas and their casting [...] can be damaging to [the company's] peace and effectiveness and will if proven be punished by the loss of a quarter of the monthly salary.

10. Anyone who notes anything that might promote the general welfare, either through his own or other people's observations – no matter whether this concerns the director, the actors, the wardrobe supervisor or the scene painter – and fails to divulge it, gives evidence of indifference towards the group, that is to say an inclination to quit the theatre, and entitles the director to consider finding a substitute for him. [...]

11. Nobody involved in a play or in an opera is allowed to mingle with the audience either in the first nor the last acts when free. If he does so he will pay two shillings out of every dollar of his monthly salary. [...]

13. No servants are permitted to stand around the stage; they must either stay in the dressing-room (if their master is changing) or go home and return only at the end of the performance in order to fetch his things.

14. Nobody is allowed to miss a read-through without a substantial reason, no matter how small the role. If he does so he will pay one shilling out of every dollar of his month's salary. [...]

15. Since mental effort cannot be enforced no specific time is laid down for learning a new part. But if anyone, having signed the casting circular, delays the performance of a play through negligence, he will pay one-twelfth of his monthly salary.

16. Every one is obliged to dress in conformity with his character and following the director's instructions. A dress once chosen and registered must not be changed without authorisation. [...]

17. Rehearsals will be announced at least two days in advance by means of a circular which everybody will have to sign; [...] In order to save the call-boy [*Probenansager*: literally, 'rehearsal announcer'] any needless journeys, the actor will instruct somebody in his apartment to sign in his absence.

18. Anyone arriving late for the first rehearsal of a play, thereby delaying the

start, or missing a scene will pay half a shilling out of every dollar of his monthly salary. Anyone missing a rehearsal altogether will pay two shillings [...].

19. At the last rehearsal but one (if it is held the day before the opening) everyone must rehearse without a script and clearly delineate the character to be played.

20. Silence and good order must be observed at all rehearsals; especially the dress rehearsal must be held with all the precision of a real performance, and nobody other than the players are to be allowed on stage. [...]

22. Anyone who does not know his lines at the dress rehearsal, i.e. who cannot continue the lines started by the prompter without another prompt, will pay two shillings out of every dollar of his monthly salary.

23. Anyone who does not know his part during performance; enters late or too soon; enters from or exits on the wrong side – will pay one-twelfth of his monthly salary.

24. Nobody is allowed to make any alterations in his part to the disadvantage of the play – to introduce any immoral business or gags – to laugh or do anything that spoils the illusion. Other points under this paragraph are:

(a) Unless called for by the author there must not be any kissing.

(b) No woman must on any account be lifted up and kissed.

(c) Under no circumstances is a man permitted to kiss a woman on her mouth. If the author has introduced a kiss into the action, the kiss is to be on the cheek or the forehead.

(d) A kiss between men as a form of greeting in a comedy is unseemly and must be avoided; it is to be tolerated only for serious emotions.

(e) Also there are particular contacts that must be avoided by all means; e.g. when a man on clasping a woman gets too close to her bosom. –

Anyone contravening one of these regulations will pay two shillings out of every dollar of his monthly salary.

25. Anyone who misses an entire scene during an actual performance or who is responsible for a play not starting at the right time will pay one quarter of his monthly salary.

26. Anyone who misses a performance altogether in which he plays a part which cannot be cast differently at all, or only to the great disadvantage of the play, will forfeit one month's salary.

27. If anyone deliberately, out of ill humour, neglects a role, especially one played previously, to such an extent that the audience notices and becomes indignant, and such an event cannot be excused on grounds of illness, he will forfeit one month's salary. [...]

28. Anyone talking, laughing or singing so loudly in the wings during the performance of a play or an opera, or behind the front curtain between the acts,

that the audience or the actor on stage can hear it, pays two shillings out of every dollar of his monthly salary.

29. Anyone who has to change during an act is obliged to remind the director of this; if he fails to do so, thereby causing confusion, the actor will pay two shillings out of every dollar of his monthly salary; but the director will pay ten dollars, whether or not he has been so reminded.

30. [...] anyone provoking a quarrel during a rehearsal or a performance, in the dressing-rooms or on stage, will pay two shillings out of every dollar of his monthly salary.

31. It is sometimes highly necessary to cast actors in mute roles. Nobody is allowed to refuse such a role for it cannot demean anybody. [...] Anyone in such a role who arrives late, misses some scenes or stays away altogether during rehearsals or performances, pays a fourth part of the fines to which the actor is subject in speaking parts.

32. Anyone who heedlessly or even deliberately damages a costume or a piece of scenery will pay for the damage; this, however, is to be decided not by the director but by a majority of the older actors.

33. Although the wardrobe supervisor and the designer [*Decorateur*] are instructed to hand each actor the right props, it is nevertheless necessary for the actor to check his props before the beginning of the play. If there is anything missing during performance [...] he will pay one-twelfth of his monthly salary.

34. Nobody may leave town for twenty-four hours without warning, on penalty of one-twelfth of his monthly salary. [...]

35. Any proven immoral conduct entails the loss of a month's salary; or in extreme cases, cancellation of the contract. However, this is to be decided by a majority vote of the whole company.

36. If there is no written contract, either party has four months' notice. No one can leave or be dismissed any sooner.

37. An actor is entitled to disobey the regulations and to regard his engagement as cancelled if he does not duly receive his salary on the first day of every month. [...]

41. The director may not cancel or mitigate any penalty without consulting the five oldest actors. Also, if the director infringes the regulations he will pay double the fine.

42. Every member with a salary of three hundred dollars or more will pay half a shilling out of every dollar monthly into the poor-box which is combined with the penalty box. Anyone paying nothing into the poor-box has no vote at general meetings; however, those with smaller salaries are free to contribute.

43. The fines and charity fund are deducted every month by the cashier and remain in the director's hands [...]. Two of the oldest actors keep the book, and at

the end of each theatrical season an account will be rendered to the entire company.

44. It is up to the company to decide the future use of the fines and charity fund on a majority vote.

45. No one can receive a pension from this fund who has not served the theatre with distinction for several years. [...]

Regulation concerning opera in particular

1. Everyone is obliged to appear at the rehearsal time set by the music director. Anyone arriving more than fifteen minutes late will pay a fine of one mark; anyone failing to turn up altogether, three marks. The music director will pay a double fine. [...]

5. Nobody is entitled to omit or change an aria, or to replace it by another, without the director's authorisation. [...].

6. The music director, or whoever is entrusted with a score, may not pass it on, have it copied, or make any individual items public without authorisation.

Concerning the prompter

1. Seeing he is at the same time the librarian, he has to keep the texts in good order and must not give away any scripts without authorisation at the risk of forfeiting his honour, and he must try to prevent any theft so that neither the author nor the director suffers any damage.

2. He shall therefore have the scripts copied out by two or more persons.

3. He keeps the following books in good order:
   1) The casting record, in which will also be entered the sets and props, the running time and each performance of every play.
   2) The wardrobe record.
   3) The little prop book.
   4) The little scenery book.
These books will be brought up to date as soon as possible after the first performance.

4. He receives all circulars from the director which he passes on either himself or through the call-boy. If an actor is absent and has not signed he pays the latter's fine. [...]

5. He writes a list for the scene painter in which the scene changes following the last speech are clearly marked, which is completed by the director before the first rehearsal.

6. He sketches out the wardrobe schedule which is also completed by the director and which the wardrobe supervisor hands to the cast at the last rehearsal but one.

7. He hands a prop list to the scene painter as well as the wardrobe supervisor. For each prop forgotten by him (if the fault shows up in performance) he will pay two marks.

8. He writes the letters which are part of his props as are all writings and books on stage. [...]

10. If he has the time and inclination to write out parts himself he will receive [extra] payment for this.

Concerning the wardrobe supervisor

1. He is obliged to ask the director for the small objects and props needed [...] before every dress rehearsal and to return them after the performance to the rehearsal room. If he forgets a prop for which he is responsible and the fault shows up in performance, he will pay two marks.

2. He is to lay out the costumes well cleaned and undamaged in everybody's place and to insist politely that they be not thrown down soiled and higgledy-piggledy when they are taken off. [...]

5. If anybody damages or soils a costume he is to report this at once; failing which he is to be responsible for replacing it. [...]

8. Under no pretext is he to send anybody's trousers or any other items of clothing to put on at home, without the director's permission, nor to allow anybody to go home with any items of clothing, on penalty of two marks. [...]

11. The day after the performance he is to enter the costume list in his record, likewise every new costume.

Concerning the stage manager

1. As soon as the music begins at 6 o'clock without any previous signal, he is to send a message to that effect to the dressing rooms.

2. He is to make sure that he receives his promptbook in good time and that the last speeches after which he has to do the scene changes are not too short [...]. For each scene change which is either too late or too early he will pay a fine of three marks.

3. It is his duty every afternoon to examine the curtains and wings required for that evening [to see] whether they are in good condition. If a curtain gets stuck he will pay three marks. If during a scene change a wing gets stuck, the stage hand on whose side this takes place will pay two marks. [...]

7. He is to make sure that no stranger, regardless of person, loiters on the stage and he is to allow no actors' servants to be in the wings, on penalty of two marks.

8. The day after the performance he is to enter the stage directions into the appropriate book. [...]

12. No lamp may be put out until the house has been cleared of spectators.

Concerning the hairdresser

1. He is to be on stage at half past five at the latest [...].

2. He is to keep a register of the numbered wigs and write down which ones are used for each play and by whom.

3. He is to ensure that the powdering gowns he is to be supplied with are always clean, and not to powder anybody (other than in very quick changes) in the dressing room but in his [own] room.

4. He is to arrange the supers' hair according to the costume allocated.

Any infraction of any of these points will entail a fine of one mark.

---

[1] Compare Schröder's rather briefer regulations of Easter 1781, published in *Litteratur- und Theater-Zeitung*, 24 February 1781, pp. 116–18.

XI Actors and acting

A. FRENCH COMPANIES

Like his grandfather before him (see **33**), King Frederick II of Prussia loved French culture, including French theatre. In 1742 he imported a French company of actors as well as a ballet company. The actors, who performed regularly in the royal palaces in Berlin, Charlottenburg and Potsdam, were an important cultural influence in the Prussian capital and formed a major obstacle to German companies trying to establish themselves there (see **61**). These government-supported and highly prestigious actors were described individually and somewhat irreverently by the young Gotthold Ephraim Lessing (1729–81), later to become the father of German criticism, and his cousin Christlob Mylius (1722–54) in the quarterly theatrical magazine, the first of its kind in the German language, which they had the enterprise to publish while still in their early twenties.

91 The French actors in Berlin, 1750

Lessing & Mylius, *Beyträge zur Historie und Aufnahme des Theaters* (Essays on the History and Improvement of the Theatre) (Stuttgart: Johann Benedict Metzler), pt. 1 (1750), pp. 126–31; reprinted Leipzig: Zentralantiquariat der Deutschen Demokratischen Republik, 1976

Some of them [i.e. the French actors] are incorrigible; but some could be much better. In fact they exert themselves very little when the court is not present; and then they bellow out everything so hastily that a regular five-act comedy including music barely runs for an hour and a quarter. The actors are the following.

Mons. Rosambert. He is rather tall and well built, about 30 years old. He specialises in the role of the lover which he does rather well. But one wishes he would eliminate from his gestures a frequent sideways flinging out of his arm followed by a semicircular movement of it. [...]

Mons. Rousselois, a rather stout forty-year-old fellow of medium height and a sober expression. We do not hesitate to name him the best actor on that stage. His versatility is almost boundless: [...] One of his outstanding good qualities is his loud and clear diction which causes him to be understood even when he is talking rather quickly and when there is a good deal of byplay among the spectators. [...]

Mons. Favier [. . .] is the same age as the aforementioned, of medium height, not too fat and not too lean, and has a round face from which shines out the jolly and merry character which he generally has to adopt in comedies. [. . .]

Mons. Duportail is not the worst [actor], but less good than the three preceding ones. [. . .] His diction, though at times quite audible, is rather disagreeable. He is suited neither for very merry nor for very sad characters: but he acts the inbetween ones tolerably well. [. . .]

Mons. Marville, a fifty-year-old living skeleton, is stiff, indolent and wooden, with poor and totally incomprehensible diction. [. . .] In short, Mons. Marville was not meant for the stage.

Mons. Thomasin is [. . .] the comic person. Experts in these matters say that he does his business quite well [. . .]

Mad. Rousselois, the wife of the above-mentioned Mons. Rousselois. She shares the characteristic with most stage queens of looking handsome at a distance but not so good at close quarters: [. . .] She is of medium height and seems to be closer to thirty than twenty. [. . .] One would appreciate her skills twice as much if she did not endeavour to express some emotions, e.g. sadness, tenderness and rage by means of a most repulsive howling noise [. . .]

Mad. Marville. She is far better than her above-mentioned husband. She is tall, well built, with a generally impressive figure and face, and she must be the wrong side of thirty. She best expresses her talent in the character of serious matrons.

Mlle. la Motte excels all other Berlin actresses. [. . .] She is a good height and somewhat thin but not skeleton-like. She is exceptionally vivacious and portrays the merriest of persons, other than servants, outstandingly well. All her expressions are eloquent, there is no facial trait, no movement of her body that does not express something specific. [. . .]

Mad. Giraud is actually a dancer, and one of the best: but she also treads the boards occasionally as an actress. But it is just as well for her to be given the minor roles which in fact she performs as badly as could be. [. . .] As soon as she has delivered her lines she will look at the people standing in the wings and burst out laughing; indeed she is often overcome by laughter in the middle of a speech. She only rarely moves her hands and her head, and she does so in an absolutely puppetlike manner. It is amazing how a reasonably talented dancer turns into a statue the moment she is supposed to act. [. . .]

B. GERMAN COMPANIES

(i) Strolling players

The way of life of German actors in the eighteenth century had much in common with that of other peripatetic professions, both nontheatrical ones like quack surgeons, dentists and oculists, and theatrical ones like shadow puppeteers or marionette players. As had been the case in the previous century, the borderlines between these different kinds of travellers were fluid: actors had to be versatile to survive. A typical example of this ambiguous status was the actor-manager Johann Ferdinand Beck (d. after 1745). Although decried by many for his sensational *Haupt- und Staatsaktionen* ('principal plays' dealing with political events), Beck at times enjoyed great popularity in the character of the Salzburg clown, Hanswurst (Jack Sausage); but he also went in for puppeteering and such other sidelines as the occasion demanded. And yet in 1731 he claimed his company enjoyed the honourable title of being Saxon, Polish and Waldeck court actors.

92   Actors as puppeteers: Johann Ferdinand Beck, 1743–4

'Geschichte der Maynzer Bühne' (History of the Mainz Theatre), in *Theater-Journal für Deutschland* (Theatre Journal for Germany), ed. Heinrich Ottokar Reichard (Gotha: Carl Wilhelm Ettinger), no. 1 (January 1777), pp. 63–4; reprinted Munich: Kraus Reprint, 1981

Beck appeared in the years 1743 and 1744. He had put together a company which had already gone bankrupt as the result of various mishaps in the Netherlands. When he came to Mainz he played for a while with large puppets and was enabled by large audiences and a few charitable people to play again with living persons. He built a spacious booth in which he presented all sorts of Hanswurst plays with reasonable success for a while. He and his daughter won the spectators' complete approval. But as people grew tired of him in the course of time and he was dogged by further misfortunes, he was forced to leave Mainz and his company failed a second time.

93   Beck as Hanswurst, engraving by C.F. Fritzsch (*c*. 1730)

Katalog (Armamentarium), Herzog-August-Bibliothek, Wolfenbüttel, Portr.ii/293

Beck's costume in this illustration is based on that worn by Josef Anton Stranitzky (1676–1726), who first created the character of Hanswurst, a comic pig-gelder from Salzburg, at his regular venue, the Kärntnertortheater in Vienna (see **68**). Typical features of this Austrian clown figure were the pointed green hat, the pleated collar, the open red jacket, the large initials 'H.W.' on his chest, the yellow trousers braided along the side and the tough leather shoes.

The caption at the bottom of the picture reads:

> [. . .] I am an artist, whoever does not believe me,
> Let him sit in a chair and keep still,
> I shall delicately and swiftly take out his teeth,
> Then his aches and pains will be finished all at once.
> [. . .]

93

94

94   Josef Ferdinand Müller as Harlequin, engraving by Bäck

Katalog (Armamentarium), Herzog-August-Bibliothek, Wolfenbüttel, Portr.II/3562

This illustration shows that, side by side with the native Hanswurst figure, the Italian Harlequin flourished in Germany – impersonated not only by the numerous *commedia dell'arte* players coming up from Italy but also by German actors. Both the costume and the posture in this print are entirely in the commedia tradition. J.F. Müller (d. 1755), an improviser notorious for the coarseness of his material, was the bitter rival of Frau Neuber in the 1730s (see **113**). His wife was the daughter of the Pantaloon player Julius Franz Elenson (see **35**).

The caption in macaronic German reads:

> This sprightly attitude can cheer up melancholy people,
> My ever waggish spirit puts everyone in a good humour.
> Even Heraclitus cannot but laugh at my simplicity
> When I play Harlequin in his mask.

Strolling players might spend as much of their time travelling, often in tiring, disagreeable or even dangerous circumstances, as acting. Quite apart from the hazards of coming close to scenes of military conflict, as during the Seven Years' War, there were many tense and perilous moments on the road, especially when companies went on their not infrequent tours abroad – to Scandinavia, the Baltic countries, Poland or even as far afield as Russia (see **8**). The actor-playwright J.C. Brandes reports a potentially disastrous encounter while travelling through Poland en route to Breslau as a member of Schuch's company, some time in the early 1760s.

95   The hazards of touring, early 1760s

Brandes (1800), pp. 284–5

On our journeys, which we often made with hauliers, I was always in the habit during fine weather of walking part of the way by the side of the coach or even ahead of it. So one morning as usual I went ahead of the coach just as it was setting out and finally lost sight of it in a forest. The road was passable, and I could not go astray on the highway; so I followed it without any worry in the hope of soon reaching a village where I should be awaiting my travelling companions at breakfast; however, my serenity was soon shattered when, after a while, I caught sight through a glade of a considerable pack of wolves which came closer and closer, cut off my path some fifty paces ahead and trotted past without noticing me. Very fortunately for me the wind was blowing in quite the opposite direction so that these terrible beasts of prey could not catch my scent; and I squeezed behind a tree in good time to be out of their field of vision. As soon as they were sufficiently far into the forest I flew, shaken and terrified, in the direction of the coach I had left behind, and indeed I did manage to reach it after about half an hour. In fact the danger had been even greater than I had thought; for in the next village where I told my story, some people had already gone missing, having ventured into the woods unaccompanied and without taking any precautions.

Until the end of the eighteenth century strolling players, especially those with small artistic pretensions, enjoyed very little social esteem (See 36 & 37). This is clearly apparent in an order issued by the Duke of Brunswick to Philipp Nicolini, a ballet-master, mime artist and actor-manager, probably of Italian origin, who was famous for his children's ballets and who was the ducal 'directeur des spectacles' in Brunswick from 1752–63.

96   Strolling players equated with puppeteers and acrobats, Brunswick, 13 August 1762

Niedersächsisches Staatsarchiv, Wolfenbüttel, 2 Alt 12499

Seeing that all those people who have exhibited their persons or their skills in public for money at the local fairs have hitherto reported to the *directeur des spectacles* Nicolini, and the City Council has not been informed as to how many and what people of this sort are staying in the city,

The *directeur des spectacles* is to consider whether it would not be better to lay down the following regulation –

1) that no actor, marionette-player and puppeteer, equilibrist and rope-dancer, nor anyone exhibiting strange animals and human beings of extraordinary shape [. . .] shall be permitted to put on a show at times when plays are being performed in the princely theatres –

2) that all actors, marionette-players and puppeteers, as well as equilibrists and rope-dancers must have a certificate from the *directeur des spectacles* Nicolini, whereas

3) all those who put on display strange animals or human beings of extra-ordinary shape, likewise jugglers, conjurers, and raree-showmen are to be left entirely to supervision by the City Council.

The contempt in which official bodies held strolling players even at the end of the century, i.e. at a time when resident companies had already won a considerable measure of respectability, was expressed with brutal frankness in this submission made by City Syndic Ben. von Loess to the Council of the Prince-Archbishop of Salzburg on 1 June 1796.

97   Strolling players decried as rogues and vagabonds, 1796

Salzburg Government archives, University of Salzburg. Partially reproduced in Rudolf v. Freisauff, *Zur hundertjährigen Jubelfeier des k.k. Theaters zu Salzburg* (The One Hundredth Anniversary of the Imperial and Royal Theatre at Salzburg) (Salzburg: publ. by the author, 1875), p. 48 and following pp., and in F.H. Wagner, *Das Volksschauspiel in Salzburg* (Popular Theatre in Salzburg) (Salzburg, 1882), pp. 27–32, and completely reproduced in Richard Maria Werner, 'Das Theater der Laufner Schiffleute' (The Plays of the Laufen Sailors), *TGF* 3 (1891), pp. 8–10

Duty compels me to draw the authorities' attention to a class of people who not only endanger public safety but also deeply undermine morality, particularly among the common people; – and these are the [...] companies of German actors, as they call themselves, or rather – troupes of comedians as the populace tend to label them rather more fittingly.[1]

[...] They consist largely of bone-idle dissipated young people of either sex and of elderly good-for-nothings – of people either entirely without any education, or who if they were fortunate enough to have had a decent education, had run away from their parental home as adventurers; of seducers or the seduced; – of people who do not understand their own mother tongue but who nonetheless all look down on the ordinary hardworking citizen with the most ridiculous pride. [...] With all this, the squalor they live in is indescribable. The common man, who quite reasonably prefers real food and drink to such intellectual fare, only visits their theatre if he can do this with the least sacrifice possible [...], and not infrequently an evening's total takings will come to 3–6, or at most 10–12 florins. This is not enough for a company of 10–12 members, not to mention children and servants, to live on without worrying where the next meal is coming from. They are forced to importune the public with impudent begging, and it makes a truly lamentable contrast when the dictator, who with proud mien controls the lives of thousands in the theatre – when the millionaire who wastes fortunes on the stage

– after the end of the show begs for a piece of bread and a bowl of soup at the inn in order to stave off hunger for himself and his family. It is a very rare exception to the rule when a company departs without [leaving behind some] debts [. . .]. The supplementary source of income of the female sex can easily be guessed at. What fills their cup of misery to overflowing is the fact that most of them, once committed to this way of life, dazzled by its seeming freedom and lack of constraint, never or only with extreme difficulty find their way out of it. [. . .] Their end may be deemed fortunate if they are allowed to die in some hospital, the victims of extreme deprivation or a dissolute way of life – but their common lot is to die despairing and unlamented in some village inn or maybe wandering the open fields.

[1] The word 'comedians' (*Komödianten*), which had been the common term for actors in the seventeenth and early eighteenth centuries, had by now taken on a derogatory flavour.

Despised by their more solid fellow citizens they might be – but strolling players had their own usages, their own way of life: a very strong hierarchical tradition linked to an actor's 'line of business' (*Rollenfach*). Many years after these customs had passed away, August Wilhelm Iffland (1759–1814), the leading actor, director and playwright of the end of the eighteenth and the beginning of the nineteenth century, described them, clearly with some ironical condescension, as they had been in the days of his youth.

98   Customs and usages among strolling players

Iffland, *Almanach für Theater und Theaterfreunde auf das Jahr 1807* (Almanac for the Theatre and Friends of the Theatre for the Year 1807) (Berlin: Wilhelm Oehmigke, 1807), pp. 141–7. Reproduced in Eduard Devrient, *Geschichte der deutschen Schauspielkunst*, ed. Kabel & Trilse (1967), vol. 1, pp. 219–21

The second hero had to greet the leading tragic hero first whereas the latter only returned the greeting. Those who played the confidant took their hats off the moment the first hero or the one who played the tyrant turned up. In public places the leading actors kept to themselves, the others withdrew of their own accord and were only allowed to approach when condescendingly invited to do so. [. . .] Only after years of service could a novice win the right to appear covered in the presence of senior members. Any comment on the acting of senior members was regarded as a sign of madness. Criticism of a play that was about to be or that had been performed was a crime resulting in isolation or expulsion. The admission of a new member into the actors' guild took place with a great deal of fuss and bother. The first question put to the newcomer was, 'Can you do the sceptre business, sir?' Hereupon he would be handed a marshal's baton which he had to try either resting solemnly on his hip or pointing imperiously into the far distance with. If he showed any hint of talent in this he would be asked to rant out a thunderous speech. If this could win a nod of approval from the old fellows, the manager would step forth, approach the novice and speak the following words, 'Do you, sir, possess a pair of black velvet breeches?' If this question could be answered in the affirmative, that at least opened up a chance of being accepted. This only followed after an admonition to, and a promise of, *obedience, hard work* and *humility*. [...] But rarely did the leading tragedy heroes appear in ordinary life without a sword, and the managers might allow all manner of coloured stones to show on the sword-belt protruding flashily from their coat-tail. Only the leader would wear a gold-embroidered scarlet waistcoat, also known as a 'patent waistcoat' [*Permissionsweste*] because it identified the owner of the patents. [...] These men had no laws among themselves but traditional usages and customs to which they clung rigidly. [...] But even though their acting remained basically stiff or lifeless, indeed vastly exaggerated at times, the externals were brought into harmony by firmly laid-down rules. The way they entered or stood together, whereby no character was allowed rudely to encroach on the space of the others, the outward salutations by means of which they knew how to make careful distinctions of rank, the manner in which they let new arrivals join in the semicircle,[1] the manner in which those not allowed to enter the circle were nevertheless kept in the spectator's eye, how characters left the circle and how they exited from the stage – the precision with which they practised *coups de théâtre* to the point of making them foolproof – all these things had definite forms and rules which gave smoothness to everything.

[1] Placing the main actors in a semicircle facing downstage in key scenes was a standard stage grouping, which ensured equal visibility for all and kept them in contact with the audience (see 142).

On arriving at a new place, a company of strolling players would advertise their, possibly very brief, presence by means of a parade which would be as noisy as possible, though not all municipal authorities would permit this. Such a parade was described by Goethe in Book 2, chapter 4 of his novel, *Wilhelm Meisters Lehrjahre* (Wilhelm Meister's Apprenticeship). Though a work of the fiction rather than a piece of reportage, this novel – a drastically revised version of his earlier draft, *Wilhelm Meisters theatralische Sendung* (Wilhelm Meister's Theatrical Mission; published posthumously as late as 1911) – gives a vivid impression of theatrical conditions in the 1770s.

99   A company of actors advertise their arrival in town

J.W.v. Goethe, *Wilhelm Meisters Lehrjahre*, vols. 1–4 (Berlin: Johann Friedrich Unger, 1795–6). Reproduced in *Goethes Werke*, WA (Weimar: Hermann Böhlaus Nachfolger, 1898), section 1, vol. 21, pp. 143–4

Their conversation[1] was interrupted by the clatter with which the motley crew set out from the inn in order to announce their play to the town and make it eager to behold their arts. A drummer was followed by the director on horseback, behind him a female dancer on a similar worn-out nag who held out a child well adorned with ribbons and tinsel. Then came the rest of the troupe on foot, some of them lightly and easily carrying children on their shoulders in extraordinary postures [...].

The clown ran up and down among the crowd pressing in on him and handed out his playbills with very obvious japes, now kissing a girl, now cudgelling a boy, and aroused among the people an invincible desire to get to know him better.

In the printed advertisements the various accomplishments of the company, especially those of a Monsieur Narcisse and of Demoiselle Landrinette, were extolled, both of whom as principal personages had been canny enough to absent themselves from the procession in order to give themselves a nobler air and to arouse greater curiosity.

---

[1] That is, the conversation of the hero, Wilhelm Meister, with a stranger he had just encountered at a country inn.

The inadequacy of German theatre and drama up to the middle of the eighteenth century (the two were obviously interconnected) was not remedied by the efforts of Professor Gottsched and his wife and co-worker Luise Adelgunde Viktoria, his 'able friend'. He propagated theoretical ideas for reforming the stage, not very original ones to be sure; their joint aim was to advance good taste by holding up the French stage as the great model to be followed and by providing a repertoire of plays translated from other languages, principally from the French. But though these translations and some timid efforts at writing original 'regular' dramas in German by the Gottscheds and their acolytes made the stage somewhat more acceptable to the educated middle class, the German theatre still seemed to rest on flimsy foundations around the middle of the century. Lessing put this view with characteristic bluntness in his famous 81st Letter of the weekly *Briefe, die neueste Litteratur betreffend* (Letters Concerning the Most Recent Literature), a series which he published, together with the philosopher Moses Mendelssohn and the bookseller Friedrich Nicolai, from 4 January 1759 to 4 July 1765.

100   German and French theatre compared, 7 February 1760

Lessing, *Briefe, die neueste Litteratur betreffend* (Berlin: Friedrich Nicolai, 1760). Reproduced in Lessing, *Werke*, 25 vols., ed. Julius Petersen & Waldemar v. Olshausen (Berlin/Leipzig/ Vienna/Stuttgart: Deutsches Verlagshaus Bong & Co., 1925), vol. 4, pp. 213–15; reprinted Hildesheim/New York: Georg Olms Verlag, 1970

We have no theatre. We have no actors. We have no audiences. [...] At any rate the Frenchman has a theatre; whereas the German barely has booths. The

Frenchman's theatre at any rate is the entertainment of a very large capital city; whereas in the German's main cities the booth is the mockery of the populace. The Frenchman at any rate can boast that he diverts his monarch, an entire splendid court, the greatest and worthiest men in the realm, the highest society; whereas the German has to be satisfied if a few dozen honest private citizens, who have timidly sneaked up to his booth, are prepared to listen.

But let us be quite honest. The fact that German drama is still in such a wretched state is not perhaps solely and exclusively the fault of princes failing to give it their protection, their support. Princes do not care to concern themselves with matters for which they anticipate hardly any, or no, successful outcome. And when they look at our actors, what can the latter offer them? People without any education, without any breeding, without any talents; a master tailor, a creature that was a washerwoman but a few months ago, etc. What can princes see in such people that is in any way like themselves and that might encourage them to raise these stage representatives of themselves to a better and more highly respected status?

In the final decades of the eighteenth century, the cry for permanent as against peripatetic companies was heard again and again. Not that permanent theatres had invariably been successful. But it was clear that true long-term progress could only be made on the basis of playhouses with resident companies, as the following article in a theatre magazine argued.

101   A call for permanent companies in fixed venues, 1790

'Fragmente über stehende Bühnen und die Vortheile die sie stiften' (Reflections on Permanent Theatres and the Benefits they Bring), in *ADT*, 6 (1790), pp. 36–42

Let companies of strolling players be never so well constituted, let them include the greatest artists in their ranks, the benefit to be expected of them is very limited, indeed a travelling company's very existence often inhibits the good a resident company might do. [...]

Only rarely does a touring company come to a larger town without being obliged to pay back debts already contracted elsewhere on the expectation of rich pickings here; this money leaves the town, and nobody has a pennyworth of benefit from it; but supposing the daily income does not equal the costs which as a rule are considerable, then the companies will depart burdened again with new debts, and experience tends to show that creditors will not usually get any of their money back.

The strolling player has infinitely greater expenses than the resident actor. The local citizen who goes to the trouble of letting his room to strangers for the sake of profit, naturally demands more from the stranger than he would from a local citizen; this cuts into the actor's income so much that he is often obliged to incur debts whether he would or no.

You will rarely find any moral standards in the theatre among strollers, and the authorities should not be indifferent to the fact that, members of travelling companies for the most part being persons who have found their last refuge in the theatre so as to escape destitution or for fear of a musket,[1] intercourse with them has the most harmful influence on the morals of local people. [...]

You may call it a miracle but it is well nigh incredible that resident theatres have sprung up in so many major German cities all of a sudden before anyone had dreamt of such a possibility. – One might in all justice have written: *Festina lente*[2] high up on these playhouses, for the all too swift demise of these theatres clearly shows that neither reflection nor care had gone into ensuring their survival. Often the direction would fall into the hands of men who were either too greedy and in an effort to make big profits lost everything, or [...] the managers were not knowledgeable enough and therefore allowed things just to drift along [...].

Truly, strolling players are as harmful for the commonwealth as were the Jesuits in their day. Let the princes of Germany agree that each one tolerate but one theatre in his principality and favour this with such privileges as will secure it against failure: soon the most beneficent blessings would flow hence over the entire country.

[1] I.e. men trying to escape conscription.
[2] Latin: Make haste slowly.

(ii) Resident companies

The formation of resident companies in the second half of the eighteenth century brought with it not only an improvement in ensemble playing – it also meant rising prestige for a profession that had been very low in public esteem from its very beginnings in the early seventeenth century. To become socially acceptable was no easy matter; and thoughtful directors like Schröder invested much effort in raising the moral and cultural tone among their actors in order to open hitherto closed doors for them. (Note the emphasis on decent conduct in his regulations for actors, as in 90, paras 2, 24 and 35.)

102   Schröder's beneficent influence on his company

'Fragmente über stehende Bühnen und die Vortheile die sie stiften', *ADT* 6 (1790), p. 39

Hamburg never forgot the gratitude that has always been the lot of deserving artists there. Members of the theatre company were never denied access to the best society because there were never any such complaints about their conduct as were heard elsewhere [...]. People encouraged them with presents, and they in turn vied to show themselves grateful to their benefactors by tireless diligence. At every performance one could say here with Iffland, 'Audience and actors together constitute a society.'

No sooner had Schröder's spirit taken leave [from the company] than it began to vacillate; the spirit of anarchy threatened to descend until Schröder returned and with renewed zeal caused it to be what it is now: a temple of art and a school of good conduct.

It was in Vienna more than anywhere else in German-speaking countries that actors – at any rate some of the stars of the Burgtheater – achieved a socially prominent position. The distinguished actor Johann Franz Hieronymus Brockmann (1745–1812), director of the Burgtheater from 1789 onwards, insisted on the social dimension of actor training, in a manuscript not published until 1955. (For Brockmann, see **199–202, 204, 220.**)

103   The importance of actors moving in good society

Brockmann, *Briefe zur Bildung eines angehenden Schauspielers* (Letters on the Training of a Novice Actor) (n.d., MS in the Österreichische Nationalbibliothek); published for the first time in *M&K* I (1955), pp. 56–7

Unforced good manners, the easy forms of polite society are also a significant part of the qualities demanded of an actor. But these can never be learnt by study, only by social intercourse. [...] But where, you may ask, are these unforced good manners, these easy forms of polite society to be learnt, while the actor is regarded not as an artist but as a hired clown who for his weekly wages is obliged to amaze the spectators' eyes six times a week [...]? Here is the answer to your question. Honesty, purity of morals, and a noble pride springing from the consciousness of these virtues will smooth his path through the antechambers into the closets of the great. People will value not only your talents in the theatre but your company outside it as well, you will be allowed to participate in the more elegant entertainments of society. Here it will be an easy matter to model yourself on these examples. [...] You will not be embarrassed in the role of a prince [...]. You will appear in such parts, and people will think they see not a comedian pretending to be a prince but the very prince in person.

[...] I repeat, it is only the noble pride arising out of the consciousness of one's virtue that makes one charming. This pride [...] will never permit him to choose any company that would disgrace him, will spur them [*sic*] always to seek to associate with people superior to themselves. This pride will save them from base servility and precisely for that reason gain them general respect.

The actor Johann Heinrich Friedrich Müller (1738–1815), a founding member of the National Theatre ensemble at the Burgtheater, strikingly embodied the new social esteem which some actors at any rate were achieving in the last two decades of the eighteenth century. His glittering lifestyle was described in the following terms, not altogether uncritically, by Johann Caspar Riesbeck (1754–86), whose *Letters of a Travelling Frenchman about Germany to his Brother in Paris* maintained the fiction of a foreign observer's account of German life.

104   A star actor's life in Vienna in the 1780s

J.C. Riesbeck, *Briefe eines Reisenden Franzosen über Deutschland*, 2 vols. (Zürich: Gessner, 1783), vol. 1, pp. 263–4. Reproduced in Kindermann, *Theatergeschichte der Goethezeit* (Vienna: H. Bauer Verlag, 1948), p. 537. English translation by the Rev. Maty, *Travels through Germany; in a series of letters*, 3 vols. (London: T. Cadell, 1787), vol. 1, pp. 297–8

Among all the actors, none has so many well-wishers and friends among the principal people at court as Herr Müller. He is an immensely versatile man. He has set up lotteries for the balls in which even the Empress is interested,[1] keeps a fancy-goods stall, has a charming wife and a beautiful daughter who often plays the piano at great people's houses, and he knows how to profit from anything. He is alleged to have so much credit that some 50,000 florins of other people's money are circulating in his business dealings, though I think this sum is somewhat exaggerated. [...] His apartment is in the best and most expensive square in town and consists of a suite of rooms which have costly wallpaper in excellent taste. He has rented a pretty suburban garden where in summer he keeps open table for all the world. [...] All men of intellect throughout Germany are in touch with him, and he takes them all into his apartment. The acquaintances he has made here among the aristocracy and men of erudition repay this hospitality [...].

[1] The Empress Maria Theresa (1717–80).

(iii) Welfare: payments and health

For the greater part of the eighteenth century most German actors remained at the bottom of the financial ladder. Courts preferred to lavish vast sums on Italian opera and only somewhat less on French companies. The establishment of permanent public theatres meant some improvement; but in contrast to the distinctly happier situation at the government-supported National Theatre in Vienna, private enterprises working without any state subsidies continued to be beset with great difficulties. The speedy failure of the Hamburg Theatre is a case in point.[1]

In addition to benefit performances (an equally common practice in French, English and the early American theatre), there was a way for German actors to supplement their

meagre wages: by 'acting fees' (*Spielhonorare*). These were paid over and above the basic
wage for such special services as singing, acrobatics or slapstick.

[1] See Maurer-Schmoock (1982), pp. 112–18.

105   Special fees for singing, 1750s

Schulze-Kummerfeld, 'Biographisches', in *MBGDKL*, vol. 3, no. 2 (June 1828), p. 188.
Herzog-August-Bibliothek, Wolfenbüttel, Sign.Wd 567 i

There was an extra payment for every song in comedies [...], as well as for every
change of costume in the pantomimes [*Zauberstücke*] and machine plays popular
at the time which for the most part were improvised, and in one of which [...] my
mother had to change some 30 times. In Vienna they paid one florin for an aria
and 30 crowns for a song (both sung without any accompaniment), 20 to 30
crowns for a costume change; in minor theatres they paid less although the work
was very much harder there.

106   Special fees for slapstick, up to the 1760s

Burney (1773), vol. 2, pp. 218–9, and Scholes, *Dr Burney's Musical Tours in Europe* (1959),
vol. 2, p. 77

Premiums are now no longer given, as heretofore, in this theatre,[1] to actors who
voluntarily submit to be kicked and cuffed, for the diversion of the spectators.
However, it is but a few years since bills were regularly brought in to the managers
at the end of each week, in which the comic actors used to charge: 'So much for a
slap on the face;' 'So much for a broken head; and so much for a kick on the
breech, &c.' But, in process of time, the effect of these wearing out, it became
necessary to augment their number, and force, in order to render the pleasure of
the spectators more exquisite; till the managers, unable any longer to support so
intolerable an expense, totally abolished the rewards for these heroic sufferings.

[1] At the Hofburg-Theater which Dr Burney visited on 31 August 1772 (see 71).

Salaries varied considerably, of course – the hierarchy of the different lines of business being
expressed in terms of differential remuneration. This can be clearly seen in the budget of the
Mannheim National Theatre, a leading company, for the year 1779, among whom we note
the Brandes family, Mme Seyler (Hensel), Mme (Schulze-)Kummerfeld, Boeck and young
Iffland.

107   Actors' wages in a leading resident company, 1779

Theaterakten, Mannheimer städtisches Archiv, A 12, No. 77. Reproduced in Bernhard Diebold, *Das Rollenfach im deutschen Theaterbetrieb des 18. Jahrhunderts* (Lines of Business in German Theatre in the Eighteenth Century) (Hamburg/Leipzig: TGF 25, 1913), p. 61, and in Maurer-Schmoock (1982), p. 160

1. Queens and Tragic Leads	Mme Seyler	1000fl.
2. Female Juvenile Leads in comedies and tragedies, also Sprightly Characters	" Brandes	1200fl.
3. Tender Characters and Second Female Juvenile Leads	" Toscani	1200fl.
4. Soubrettes and Comic Characters	" Kummerfeld	600fl.
5. Grotesques and Naive Characters	" Wallenstein	500fl.
6. First Singer in operettas, also minor beginners' roles in comedy	Mlle Brandes	300fl.
7. Second Singer in operettas, also minor Utility roles in comedy	Mme Baëchel	400fl.
8. Heroes and Male Juvenile Leads in tragedies and comedies	Herr Boeck	1400fl.
9. Second Juvenile Lead and Lively Characters	" Opitz	800fl.
10. Sprightly Juveniles	" Beck	500fl.
11. Comic Old Men and Grotesques, also Jews	" Iffland	700fl.
12. Comic Servants, Peasants and Sprightly Characters	" Beil	600fl.
13. *Raisonneurs* and Even-Tempered Characters	" Meyer	800fl.
14. Low Comedians	" Backhaus	500fl.
15. Officers and Even-Tempered Characters	" Zuccarini	600fl.
16. Bad-Tempered Characters	" Brandes	900fl.
17. Old Officers and Second *Raisonneurs*	" Herter	300fl.
18. General Utility roles, really stop-gaps	" Haferung	
	" Trinkle	together
	" Toscani	1206fl.

The low wages of actors made retirement when they might find themselves penniless, a daunting prospect; after the breadwinner's death, widows and children would often be left in dire straits. But pension funds were unknown until the latter part of the century; the first to draw an old age pension was the actor Heydrich in Vienna in 1777: see Maurer-Schmoock (1982), p. 117. One man particularly concerned to remedy this profoundly unsatisfactory state of affairs was Konrad Ekhof, ever anxious not only to raise the artistic standards but also to improve the welfare and status of his fellow actors. One of his last actions before his death in 1778 was to write to the director Schröder in Hamburg with the following suggestion.

108   An actors' pension scheme suggested by Ekhof, 1778

F.L.W. Meyer, *Friedrich Ludwig Schröder* (1819), vol. 2, pt. 2, pp. 23–5

I shall submit my plan to you, and the circular to all companies known to me about a general pension and burial fund for all German actors will be drafted accordingly. [...] You shall be my aide-de-camp in this [...] so that, if death should overtake me in executing it you will be able to complete what I cannot.[1] I shall arrange the contribution to this pension and widows' fund not, as has happened hitherto, according to the wages [earned] but straightforwardly according to the number of years served. E.g. each one pays one pfennig for every year he has been on the stage; that is, one pfennig the first year, two pfennigs the second year and so on as the years mount up. For this the widow he leaves behind will enjoy, or conversely the husband, a pension for life proportionate to his contributions which will be paid quarterly in advance: at any rate to pay for the funeral expenses if necessary. [...] If an actor dies single and there are no children left, his eldest brother or sister or next of kin will enjoy the pension, for life if they have reached the age of forty, for ten or twenty years if they are younger, in proportion to their age [...]. As for children, if they are minors the eldest will benefit until he comes of age [...]. What a joy for me to think on my death-bed: Thank God! No longer will want insinuate itself between any German actor and his grave! The prospect of an assured income even after his death will give him credit and sustenance, and he will no longer be forced to go begging, or go herding the farmers' geese, as alas! [...] I found out after his death was the case with my late brother-in-law [...].

[1] Ekhof died before his plan could be realised; but Schröder did in fact set up a pension scheme at the Hamburg theatre (see **90**, paras. **42–5**).

The gradual rise to respectability of the acting profession, together with the increasingly emotional acting style of the *Sturm und Drang* period, made the question of the health of actors a matter of serious medical concern. Professor Franz M. May (1742–1808), court physician to the Elector Palatine and Ordinary Professor of Medicine at Heidelberg University, was so impressed by a performance of Schiller's *Die Räuber* (The Robbers) he had witnessed at the Mannheim National Theatre (see **207**) that he wrote a widely noted essay on actors' illnesses and how to cure them. Quite a few of Professor May's health hints still make reasonably good sense today. His comments on stage make-up point to the dangers of the methods then in use.

109   A health regime for actors, 1783

'Über die Heilart der Schauspielerkrankheiten vom Hofrath Mai in Manheim' [sic] (The Therapy of Actors' Illnesses, by Councillor May in Mannheim), in *Litteratur- und Theater-Zeitung*, ed. by Christian August v. Bertram (Berlin: Arnold Wever), 1 February 1783, pp. 67–76, & 8 February 1783, pp. 81–90. The *Litteratur- und Theater-Zeitung* has been reprinted in the series: *Das deutsche Theatre des 18. Jahrhunderts* (Munich: Kraus Reprint 1981). The essay itself was incorporated in *Vermischte Schriften von Franz May* (Franz May's Miscellaneous Writings) (Mannheim, 1786) and partially reproduced in *M&K*, 6 (1960), pp. 289–93

[...] I have repeatedly noticed as regards the illnesses of emotional actors that their nerves are more sensitive than those of the most delicate female. [...] But it is precisely this quite extraordinary nervous sensibility peculiar to good actors which is the mighty adversary against which the physician has to fight when they are ill. [...] Necessary as nervous sensibility is for their profession, to overtax it is damaging and results in convulsive contractions and hence the inhibition of salutary evacuations. It is this unhappy sensibility of the eccentric nervous system of actors that has forced me at times to combine strong doses of poppy juice (*opium*) with the rest of the evacuants when I wanted to bring about therapeutic evacuations by means of sweat or urine, bowel movements or vomiting. [...] This same excessive nervous sensibility is also the reason why most actors are melancholiacs. [...] Count Karl and Franz Moor in The Robbers spend their nervous juices for at least a week and weaken body and soul. Is it surprising then that after such violent roles there follow relapses into feverishness and debility? Is it surprising that the day after such taxing emotional labours they float around pale as ghosts, since this enfeeblement of the spirit is followed by restless sleep haunted by dreams. This is the reason why good actors so often suffer from indigestion [...].

If the actor's performance is to convince, his imagination must banish all calmness, all indifference from his inner being, he must turn into a waking dreamer, think and transport himself into a totally different situation. This condition is immensely debilitating for the nerves since it does violence to them.

The sole difference between true and pretended passion is the fact that the agitation of the blood and the nervous shocks last longer in the former than in the latter [...].

In addition to the passion he must act out, the unexceptionable desire for glory gnaws away at the sensibility of the star actor. [...]

From these sources [...] it will now be an easy matter to determine the way of life and the diet a good actor has to follow if he is concerned to keep his good health, so necessary for living on one's emotions, in his demanding profession. The actor must therefore

(1) Avoid any kind of excess.

(2) After a violent part he must not put too much trust in his feeling of exhaustion and his need to recruit his strength, otherwise he will overburden his stomach and disturb his sleep which is the best strengthener for his depleted physical and emotional resources. Let his supper consist merely of a good meat soup with toasted white bread and the yolks of a few fresh eggs, a piece of tender roasted meat, a good glass of wine with well baked white bread. Stewed fruit is seldom advisable since it acidifies the stomach. Any kind of salad is unhealthy for weak stomachs, but fruit in season may be taken in moderation.

(3) The best breakfast for actors in winter is a good soup consisting of beef-tea and rusks; a cup of chocolate without any seasoning. In summer, Schwalbach or Pyrmont water[1] with fresh unboiled cow's milk, and some grated lemon sugar. [...]

(4) Lunch may consist of a good meat-soup with rice, sago grains, pearl barley, oatmeal and rusks; of a light wine soup; of vegetables which are neither too rich nor too highly seasoned. Highly flatulent vegetables [...] are harmful for melancholics. I would rather permit good potatoes taken in moderation than any so-called invalid food and steamed apples. Asparagus is particularly detrimental for sensitive nerves. The whole family of sausages, with all other titbits of pork [...] are to be banished from the actor's table. [...] Most sweets for dessert are dangerous. There should be no more than three healthy dishes on the actor's table, the rest is excessive, damaging both to his stomach and his purse. Milk puddings with no butter added, e.g. rice pudding, pap with a little cinnamon and sugar are permitted dishes, however, after milk puddings no wine other than sweet is to be drunk. All pastry and doughy things, e.g. pies and tarts, are indigestible. [...]

(5) Hot drinks are generally damaging for the stomach. Pure well water is to be served at table, with or without wine. [...] If one experiences any heartburn or acid flatulence, bad temper, irritability and quarrelsomeness after drinking wine, it is to be avoided altogether. In these cases, Schwalbach water is the best thing to drink. In the summer the actor ought to put his beverage in ice water. [...]

(6) Untroubled sleep is balm for the nerves of the martyrs of the stage. Cold bedrooms are more salutary than heated ones. Staying awake at night is extremely damaging. The actor should never sleep lying on his back [...].

(7) Riding or coach travel in the open air filled with the exhalations of fields in bloom [...] is the very balm of life for actors. [...]

(8) It is dangerous to burden the memory on a full stomach.

(9) A cold beverage taken after a violent performance, in which the soul has been raging and the body sweating, is harmful [...].

(10) Washing all over in cold water in summer [...] strengthens the nerves immeasurably. Cold foot-baths after a strong mental effort are very salutary [...].

If his hair will stand it, the actor should get used to washing his head in cold water several times a day.

(11) Marriages without the priest's blessing and all the other follies of voluptuaries are an insidious poison for actors. Let no one mock this statement: it is the pure irrefutable truth. A good dose of religion and a healthy philosophy should [...] be the two bosom friends and companions of all bachelors. The commandments of the Christian religion are venerable, if for nothing else, in that they are the most excellent rules for healthy living.

(12) Let the actor use his leisure hours far from all debauchery, reading such books as cheer his heart without troubling his head. [...]

To prevent actors' illnesses even better, the following measures are to be taken:

(1) The theatre should be closed at least twice a year for some three or four weeks. Spring and autumn should be chosen for this.

(2) The actor should employ these weeks of rest not for debaucheries but for recruiting his spent vital powers [...].

(3) Preventive blood-letting and laxatives are to be avoided by actors; they weaken the nerves and should be applied only in extreme emergencies.

(4) These above-mentioned weeks of rest should be employed with riding, coach travel and other honourable diversions. Through these prophylactics the stage would be supplied with blooming lovers and enchanting daughters of the muses, with vigorous heroes and manly fathers, in fact with healthy actors and actresses.

It is not merely the actor's fate to have his health undermined and weakened by acting; often they [sic] are also exposed to the danger of contracting diseases through noxious make-up and paints. [...]

All kinds of white make-up prepared with mercury and lead are a danger to health.

However, the finest Venetian white lead, filtered repeatedly, is less noxious if previously the skin has been covered with an ointment made up of an ounce of virgin wax, an equal quantity of rose pomatum and a quarter of an ounce of spermaceti.

Powder of bismuth (*magisterium marcasitae*), that of oyster-shells, ground chalk filtered several times, starch, and a fine white bolus are harmless.

For red make-up the so-called make-up pads [*Schminkläppchen*], vermilion, dried dyer's red, bugloss root, juice of pigeon-berries, besides [...] cochineal, can be used safely; minium with which Roman victors smeared their faces is unsafe. In any case it is advisable to anoint the skin with the above-mentioned ointment before applying any make-up.

Yellow colours can be obtained from curcuma, liquorice and saffron juice.

[...] the burnt shells of apricot stones, mixed with powdered chalk, make a safe grey colour.

Brown colours are best made with [...] rust.

For a blue colour indigo and Prussian blue are to be used.

Finally, a black colour can usefully and safely be made with burnt cork or with the shells of apricot stones.

[1] Two kinds of effervescent natural spring water.

(iv) Nonprofessional performances

Side by side with the growth of professional theatre, based increasingly in the last quarter of the century on resident companies, nonprofessional drama continued to play its part. Whereas in the Northern, Protestant part of the German-speaking world, middle- and upper-class amateurs pursued essentially social and aesthetic aims with their theatricals, the Catholic South still performed religious folk dramas, though these might have altered considerably since their mediaeval origins. (See **39, 49**.)

A traveller's account, in a popular encyclopaedia, of such a folk play performed in Austria in the last decade of the eighteenth century suggests that there was considerable continuity in this tradition, however debased it had become.

110   A religious folk play, 1790

Anon., *Dr. Johann Georg Krünitz's Ökonomisch-technologische Encyklopädie* (Dr J.G.K.'s, Economic-Technological Encyclopaedia) 141, ed. J.W.D. Korth (Berlin: Paulische Buchhandlung, 1825), pp. 114–19, under: 'Schauspiel' (Theatre'). Reproduced in Heinrich Lindner, preface to *Karl der Zwölfte vor Friedrichshall* (1845), pp. 65–67. Partly reproduced in Philipp Eduard Devrient, *Geschichte der deutschen Schauspielkunst*, vol. 1 (Leipzig: Weber, 1848), pp. 400–1

Before my departure from Innsbruck a theatrical performance was given in a nearby village such as you would not find in Northern Germany. A printed folio sheet announced this for 25 July 1790 on the part of an honourable commune at Ambras. It was a grand tragedy entitled, The young hero and martyr St *Pancras*, which was to begin at half past one in the afternoon and finish at 6 o'clock. In spite of its being the tenth performance, a good many citizens of Innsbruck started the pilgrimage to Ambras at 1 o'clock on this sultry summer's day. The amphitheatre was a lawn by the inn [...]. Sitting in the shade cost six kreutzers. The three entrances were guarded by peasants with halberds. The theatre was a fairly permanent wooden construction, very tall and long; furthermore, two side curtains, which were alternatively opened besides the pretty main curtain, gave the stage manager some scope. Above these there issued from the sacred mouth of a wooden angel the life and death of the blessed Pancras in a golden smoke. The dissonant duo of two violins, a French horn and a cello induced pious feelings in the audience [...]. A prologue was delivered with songs in the Greek manner, in which the good shepherd, continually waving about his shepherd's crook, described the godlessness of our times in doggerel verse. The play itself opened with Gustav, a Phrygian nobleman, lying in state, and with the mourning of his fifteen-year-old son Pancras [...]; the costume of Pancras resembled that of a household hussar [...]. I was interested in browsing through the manuscript of the tragedy before it went back to the mayor's archive. It seemed to date from the last century and was written fairly legibly. [...] Everybody assured me with the honesty and candour typical of the Tyrolese that they had not had quite the opportunity of showing off their talent as would be the case next Sunday for which a secular low comedy [...] was being announced. Among religious plays they particularly praised *St Magdalen* and *St Sebastian* which were in the repertoire of the neighbouring village.

Very different from such village presentations of religious themes were the amateur theatricals in court and upper bourgeois circles. The repertoire of the latter might well overlap with that of the commercial theatre, but attempts were also made to supply original material. The outstanding example of an author of the highest distinction participating in such entertainments was that of Goethe who was to take an active part in court theatricals shortly after his arrival in Weimar on 7 November 1775; these in fact were the only form of theatre then available there in the absence of a professional company (see **72**). From the start, they gained a reputation far beyond the confines of the little duchy. For a detailed description of the Weimar amateur theatricals, see Carlson (1978), pp. 13–50.

111   Amateur performances at Weimar, 1776

Berlinisches Litterarisches Wochenblatt (Berlin Literary Weekly) (Berlin/Leipzig), 3 August 1776. Reproduced in Julius W. Braun, *Goethe im Urtheile seiner Zeitgenossen* (Goethe in the Assessment of his Contemporaries), 3 vols. (1883–5), vol. 1, pp. 289–90

(News) concerning private theatricals in Weimar

There are a great many performances here. I shall report as much to you as I have been able to gather during my stay which was rather brief. – The aristocracy put on French plays. Count von *Putbus* wins general applause in elderly roles both in plays and operettas [...].[1] The bourgeois private theatre, on which Herr Kraus, a member of the same, in his drawings of *Das Milchmädchen* and *Der Postzug*, bestowed the un-German name of *amateur theatre*, similarly plays in both dramatic genres but does so in German.[2] I have seen *Erwin und Elmire* done with *Goethe*'s additions and the beautiful music by the dowager duchess, and I must commend the performance.[3] [...] – Apart from that the society has played *Minna von Barnhelm, Das Milchmädchen* [The Milkmaid], *Der Postzug* [The Set of Horses], and *Der Fassbinder* [The Cooper].[4] Now they are rehearsing *Die heimliche Heyrath* [The Clandestine Marriage].[5]

   Der Westindier [The West Indian] has been performed by the court, and *His Highness the reigning Duke* himself played the role of the Major, and *His Highness*

Prince Konstantin the role of Earl Dudley. Herr Goethe was the West Indian.[6] [...]
The performance went uncommonly well, as many friends had told me previously
before I heard it confirmed in Weimar.

(Extract from a letter. Weimar, 15 July.)

[1] The Lord Chamberlain Count Moritz Ulrich von Putbus had led the private court theatricals before
  Goethe's arrival.
[2] The bourgeois amateur society was headed by the translator, editor and publisher Friedrich Justin
  Bertuch (1747–1822). *The Milkmaid* was a German version of Louis Anseaume's operetta, *Les Deux
  Chasseurs et la laitière*, and *Der Postzug*, a comedy by the Viennese playwright Cornelius Hermann
  von Ayrenhoff (1733–1819), which was translated into English in 1792 under the title, *The Set of
  Horses*. The artist Georg Melchior Kraus (1737–1806), director of the ducal school of drawing in
  Weimar and a friend of Goethe's who collaborated with him on a number of productions, illustrated
  several plays of the Weimar theatre both amateur and professional over a number of years. The
  writer of the article clearly objected to the use of the neologism, 'Liebhaber-Theater' (amateur
  theatre), as against the established word, 'Gesellschaftstheater' (society theatre).
[3] A new score for Goethe's operetta *Erwin und Elmire* had been composed by Duchess Anna Amalia
  (see 72, note 1).
[4] Lessing's *Minna von Barnhelm*, still a fairly recent repertoire item, had become an instant classic (see
  189–91). *The Cooper* was a German version of Nicolas Audinot's *Le Tonnelier*.
[5] A translation from the English of *The Clandestine Marriage* (1766) by George Colman and David
  Garrick.
[6] Richard Cumberland's *The West Indian* (1771), another translation from the English, which enjoyed
  considerable success on the German stage. The reigning duke was Goethe's lifelong friend Karl
  August (1757–1828), the Prince Konstantin his younger brother.

Middle and upper-class amateur theatricals continued to be of some importance in
Germany from the time of the Weimar amateurs to about 1830, as German literary and
indeed national self-awareness developed. Although the movement went through a
recession as a result of the Napoleonic Wars, it was stimulated again in the early years of
the nineteenth century when the immensely successful Weimar-born playwright August
von Kotzebue (1761–1819) (see **212**) issued a number of theatrical almanacs for
amateurs. The influence of the amateur movement was at first held to be benign, even by
professionals, in that the social elite set an example of sophisticated manners on stage to
actors from humbler backgrounds. The small town of Weissenfels in Saxony-Anhalt was
an outstanding example of amateur activity in the early nineteenth century, with three
drama groups in a total population of around 5,000. One of these, an upper-class group of
nineteen men and twenty women, was run from 1810–19 by the playwright Gottfried
Adolph Müllner (1774–1829), who was to become famous particularly for his 'fate
tragedy' *Die Schuld* (Guilt) (1815 – see **246**). The regulations he issued for the guidance of
this amateur company early on in his regime suggest problems of discipline not uncommon
in amateur work.

112   Regulations of an amateur company, 16 November 1811

Herzogliche Bibliothek Gotha, Adolph Müllner papers, vol. 19. Reproduced in Walter
Ullmann, *Adolph Müllner und das Weissenfelser Liebhabertheater/Die Inszenierung* (A.M. and
the Amateur Theatre at Weissenfels/Mise-en-scène) (Berlin: SGTG 46, 1934), pp. 152–6.

1. Art and pleasure only flourish in the realm of freedom. There is therefore no *legal obligation* to permit the exercise of dramatic art on the local amateur stage nor any *legal claim* to the enjoyment of this pleasure.

2. It is all the more necessary to observe the *social* obligations owed to one's fellow members according to the rules of decorum, politeness, discretion and courtesy, a breach of which is usually castigated by public opinion with the reproach of *rudeness*.

3. Members will be good enough to declare by signing these regulations to what extent they are prepared to accept parts for this winter so that the director will be in a position to know whom he can bear in mind in the choice and casting of plays. [...]

4. The choice of plays, casting of parts and *distribution* of plays (i.e. the determination of the time and order of their performance) although *suggested* by the director, will be decided by all the members [...]. The wishes of those who are keen to *rock* with laughter in the theatre can only be taken into consideration to the extent that members of the society are inclined to demean themselves as clowns.

5. The director has the prerogative of inviting the dramatic personnel to come and listen to a reading of the play. Those members whom he is hoping to cast in various parts and whom he has therefore invited by name to listen to the reading, will be good enough to attend regularly as should be the case with rehearsals.

6. After the reading members will be good enough to come to an agreement among themselves and with the director concerning the casting of the play [...], and to state their wishes and decisions without any reservations, while the director must strive to cast all parts if possible to every player's satisfaction. [...] This meeting will also be a suitable occasion for discussing the matter of wardrobe expenditure, which must always be arranged in such a manner that the players, in following their inclination, will both be as economical as possible and will enrich the wardrobe with usable items.

7. Whatever has been decided as regards casting and distribution is one of those social duties mentioned in par. 2, which no one will be guilty of neglecting by *wilfully* going back on his word, thereby impeding the execution of the plan. Anyone doing this commits a *discourtesy* and cannot complain if the company is made aware of it. [...]

9. If the performance can be saved by casting a role differently, anyone unable to play it will *himself* be good enough to request whichever person in the director's view would be able to play his role to take it over.

10. If the distribution of the plays must be altered because of him it will be up to him to request the parties concerned to accept this alteration.

11. If neither is feasible the performance will be cancelled and the cause of this

cancellation will be made known to the entire society by a public notice or a circular. [...]

17. Ladies are entitled not to be treated too rigorously with regard to these duties. All the aforementioned points are therefore primarily addressed to the *gentlemen*, and it is only for the latter that a *written* version [of the regulations] has been necessary, since ladies as a rule manage these things well with their naturally more delicate *feeling for propriety and decorum*. It is taken for granted that lady members of the dramatic society are not required to *go and see* the director if a need for discussion were to arise according to the above regulations. He will take great pleasure in calling on *them* at their request in order to hear their commands. [...]

(v) Some individual actors

Friederike Caroline Neuber (Die Neuberin)

Caroline Neuber played an important role in the history of German theatre in the first half of the eighteenth century. (See **59, 60, 63, 161, 163–5**.) At a time when strolling players were living a precarious life of financial insecurity and social disesteem, she attempted, together with her husband and fellow director Johann Neuber (1697–1759), to build up a repertoire of high literary quality. She was associated in this endeavour for a time with Professor Gottsched and modelled her acting on what she conceived to be a classical French style. Although she enjoyed great prestige in the 1730s, her career was in the end a frustrated and unhappy one. Against that it must be remembered that such leading actor-managers of the following generation as G.H. Koch, C.Th. Döbbelin and J.F. Schönemann came out of the Neuber company.

The great Konrad Ekhof supplied the following, not uncritical, brief biography of Frau Neuber, in a letter dated 7 March 1766, to Johann Friedrich Löwen who at the time was gathering material for the first history of the German theatre (see **161, 165, 170**).

113   Ekhof's view of Frau Neuber's career in the theatre

'Noch etwas aus Eckhofs Brieftasche' (Yet Another Item from Ekhof's wallet) in *TJD*, no. 17 (1781), pp. 88–90

[...] After Frau Neuber had set up the company in her husband's name and presumably at first played in a booth, she tried to settle in Leipzig, made an agreement with the Council and built a stage at the Shambles [Fleischhaus].[1] The King of Poland etc. died in 1735 and the Neuber Company had to leave during the period of mourning.[2] She went to Hamburg and finally to Brunswick [...]. The Duke protected her and gave her a patent.[3] Hoffmann had meanwhile disbanded his company and Müller had set up a new one.[4] The latter kept a close eye on the new government, asked for and got the patent his father-in-law had held and at the same time an order to play at the Shambles. The Council petitioned against this; Frau Neuber arrived with her company and found her theatre usurped, or at any rate shut. Here she composed several petitions in verse to the Queen and Count Brühl and subsequently to the Duchess of Brunswick as well, some of which I possess.[5] [. . .]

The law suit against Müller continued meanwhile and the upshot of it was [. . .] that both retained the patent, Müller kept the Shambles and got permission to play in Dresden as well, Frau Neuber on the other hand was allowed to play in Leipzig outside the [time of the] Fairs as well but she had to look for another place, and so built the little theatre in Nikolai Street [. . .].[6] On 20 February 1737 she was granted the title of the Schleswig-Holstein Company by Duke Charles Frederick in Kiel.[7] [. . .] In 1737 she went to Strasbourg,[8] at the end of June to Hamburg, and then again to Leipzig at the end of that year, and to Kiel up to Lent 1738, and to Hamburg before and after Michaelmas 1739. Here she received the invitation to Russia. Criticisms, the building in Leipzig, and despair had made her irritable, poor, and lazy and morally lax. Now pride was added and laid the foundation for her renewed failure. [. . .] She went to St Petersburg at the beginning of 1740 and returned to Leipzig in 1741 for the Easter Fair; from this time onward her reputation declined as did her fortunes. A debauched way of life, the fairly normal consequences of pride and poverty, finished off her management and her reputation. For about 10 years her reputation was in the ascendant, for 10 years it was in decline, and the last 10 years she spent in misery. She complained about injustice and abused her enemies without finding any pity. [. . .]

[1] The Leipzig Shambles were a much sought-after venue for theatrical performances.
[2] The Elector Frederick Augustus I was also King Augustus II of Poland from 1697–1733. See **59**.
[3] See **60**.
[4] Karl Ludwig Hoffmann, Sophie Julie Elenson-Haack's third husband (see **59**, note 1), became the director of her company after her death in 1725. In 1726 he disbanded it and went to Russia, returning in 1728 to found a new company. After his death in 1732 this was taken over by the Harlequin player Joseph Ferdinand Müller (see **94**; not to be confused with the actor J.H.F. Müller – see **104**). Müller, who had married Susanne Katharine Elenson, Sophie Julie's daughter by her first marriage, was Frau Neuber's principal rival in Leipzig.
[5] Heinrich Count von Brühl (1700–63) was the chief architect of Saxon state policy under the Elector Frederick August II. Ekhof, a keen collector of early documents of German theatre history, had also preserved a text of the strolling players' version of *Hamlet – Der bestrafte Brudermord* (see **26**, **34** & **50**).
[6] See **63**.
[7] Actually, the patent was issued on 28 February 1736. For the wording of the decree, see Wolfgang von Gersdorff, *Geschichte des Theaters in Kiel unter den Herzogen zu Holstein-Gottorp* (History of the Theatre in Kiel under the Dukes of Holstein-Gottorp) (Kiel: Mitteilungen der Gesellschaft für Kieler Stadtgeschichte 27/28, 1912), p. 213. Reproduced in Maurer Schmoock (1982), p. 209.
[8] See **153**.

The Neubers disbanded their company in 1743, started yet another one in the following year – but this in turn was disbanded in 1750. A final attempt at running a small company in 1755–6 ended in failure and total impoverishment of the couple. Frau Neuber's attempts in the 1750s to regain her former reputation by touring as an actress rather than as a company manager showed that her style was out of date. A letter from Vienna, dated 27 June 1753, by one Herr von Scheyd to Frau Neuber's former protector and present enemy Gottsched indicates as much.

114   The decline of Frau Neuber's acting, 1753

Reden-Esbeck (1881), p. 338. Reproduced in Kindermann, *Theatergeschichte Europas*, vol. 4 (1961), pp. 499–500

Frau Neuber has been summoned from Frankfurt and when she came on stage one did indeed perceive her to be a reasonable actress, but her voice was so weak that she could barely be understood. Then again she screamed and bellowed so excessively that her voice broke. Also she will not conform in her dress with Viennese taste. She appeared as a queen *nescio qualis*[1] like a dolled-up Neapolitan princess. Her head resembled the mane of a sledge horse.

[1]   Latin: I know not what sort.

Konrad Ekhof

The actor-playwright Johann Christian Brandes (1735–99) knew Konrad Ekhof (1720–78), the 'father of German acting', personally: he worked together with him in the companies of Schönemann, Ackermann and Seyler. His tribute – which matches the assessments of other observers – therefore carries a good deal of weight. (See also 189 & 194 for roles played by Ekhof.)

115   Konrad Ekhof characterised

Brandes, *Meine Lebensgeschichte* (1800), vol. 2, pp. 269–72

As early as 1757 when I dedicated myself to the theatre with Schönemann, Ekhof was the distinguished actor who could rightfully be called unique in Germany and who also enjoyed the rare honour of being seriously put on the same level as their Garricks and Lekains by several Englishmen and Frenchmen, who are so proud of their artists. His figure was but small and unimpressive, and his stage appearance by no means predisposed in his favour those who did not yet know him as an artist; but it took only a few moments for him to win over decisively even the most unfeeling of spectators; you forgot what his body was short of by way of symmetry and shapeliness, you only listened to him speaking, saw in him not the actor but the very person he embodied in such masterful fashion; and whenever he appeared he aroused at will any feeling whatsoever in anyone. Only in a few quite indifferent scenes did you have time to stand back and notice now and again some lack of polish, especially if he had to play a person of quality. His memory was admirable! A part running to four or five sheets he would learn by heart in almost as many hours before acting it. His theoretical study of the art was limited since he could devote but little time to consistent study of the subject on account of his ceaseless activity on the stage; in a sense, too, it was just as well that he never chose any models to copy; otherwise we should not have got to know him as such an admirable, original and practical artist who created everything only from nature and from himself. Though he made every character he had to represent completely his own, he only rarely gave himself up entirely to the emotion called for by the action. In tragic parts he appeared to be feeling far more than anyone's actual natural sufferings; even when in particularly moving situations a some-what stronger feeling sprang up within him at times, he nevertheless always remained self-aware and in control of his performance. But even without any empathy he knew how to move people's hearts. In the play, *Der Zweikampf* [The Duel], by the Reverend Schlosser, he had taken the father's role.[1] On one occasion his otherwise excellent memory failed him over the last few words in a dialogue with his daughter which he was about to finish, in which he suggests to her a husband worthy of her. Not being an experienced improviser he dried and sharply expressed his displeasure with the prompter who had not spoken loudly enough; at last the latter guided him back into the text, and having repeated his proposal in a slightly altered form, he ended his speech more or less with the following words: 'My daughter has always been obedient, now she is aware of my views and wishes, so this time she will not depart from her usually most affectionate conduct either and deprive her old father of the joy of seeing himself live again in his grandchildren.' The spectators were still disturbed by his lapse of memory, and the illusion had been wholly disrupted by this incident; even his fellow players were thrown off their stride; Ekhof at this moment was certainly not speaking from his heart; but his moving tone of voice, his eloquent eye and expressive face won back everyone's sympathy so quickly and overwhelmingly that his words caused everybody to burst out sobbing, and even his fellow players, deeply moved at this, had to regain their composure in order to carry on with the performance.

Ekhof played almost all types of roles; not, it is true, always with the same degree of success, but even those parts not wholly suited to his character gained far more in his performance than at the hands of any of his fellow actors: because he infused them with a life which the others, for all their efforts, were unable to give them. [...]

His loss has been irreparable! But how fortunate for the German theatre that at any rate some pupils worthy of his instruction have become masters of his art, outstanding among whom are the actors Iffland, Borchers and Meyer.[2]

[1] Schlosser's play, written while he was a student of theology at Jena in 1758 but not premièred until 1766, triggered off a famous controversy when the Rev. Goeze attacked it. (See 147.)

[2] August Wilhelm Iffland, one of the leading German actors after Ekhof's death, was noted for his powers of self-transformation. He was also an outstanding director and a highly popular playwright. (See 76, 87, 122–4, 208, 211–13 & 223). David Isaac Borchers (1744–96) triumphed over defective diction and poor memorising by sheer force of personality – a star actor with a notoriously wild lifestyle. Christian Dietrich Meyer (1749–83) was, like Iffland, a member of the company of the Mannheim National Theatre; but his inclusion in this list of distinguished followers of Ekhof is somewhat surprising.

116   Ekhof's voice

Pius Alexander Wolff, 'Bemerkungen über die Stimme und ihre Ausbildung zum Vortrag auf der Bühne' (Notes about Voice and its Training for Stage Declamation) in *MBGDKL*, vol. I, no. 1 (October 1827), p. 10. Herzog-August-Bibliothek, Wolfenbüttel, Sign. Wd 567a

Ekhof who, as is well known, lacked all physical beauty, triumphed through the mellifluousness of his voice over all his rivals whom nature had endowed with the fairest gifts of figure and face; his vocal magic swept the circle of his listeners off their feet and caused everything around him to be forgotten and to vanish.

As the dramaturg of the Hamburg National Theatre, Lessing was in intimate contact with Ekhof who was a leading member of the company. Ekhof played the role of Evander in *Olint und Sophronia* (Olindo and Sophronia) by Johann Friedrich von Cronegk (1731–58), which opened the National Theatre on 22 April 1767. Lessing paid him the following tribute in the *Hamburgische Dramaturgie* (Hamburg Dramaturgy), the news-sheet in which he discussed and analysed the company's productions from 1 May 1767 to 19 April 1768.

117   Lessing on Ekhof

Gotthold Ephraim Lessing, *Hamburgische Dramaturgie*, 5 May 1767. Reproduced in *Lessings Werke*, ed. Julius Petersen (Berlin/Leipzig/Vienna/Stuttgart: Deutsches Verlagshaus Bong & Co., 1925), vol. 5, p. 33

Herr Ekhof was Evander; Evander may be Olindo's father but at bottom he is not really much more than a confidant. However, let this man play whatever role he will; you still recognise him in the most minor one as the leading actor and regret not being able to see him in all the other roles at the same time. A talent altogether peculiar to him is that of being able to speak maxims and general reflections, those tedious digressions of an author at the end of his tether, with a decorum, a sincerity so that the most trivial things of this kind receive in his mouth some novelty and dignity, the most frigid some fire and life.

Sophie Friederike Hensel

An actress of impressive stature, with a universally acknowledged stage presence, Mme Hensel (1738–89) was a formidable character who tended to create dissension in the companies in which she worked. Her jealousy of other actors, and especially actresses, were a well known characteristic. Her second marriage was to the director Abel Seyler (see 72, note 1). See also 188–9 for some roles played by Mme Hensel.

118   Mme Hensel characterised, 1766

Johann Friedrich Löwen, *Auszug aus einem Briefe eines Freundes* (Excerpt from a Friend's Letter) (1766), in *J.F.L.s Schriften*, vol. 4 (Hamburg: Michael Christian Bock, 1766), pp. 75–6. Reproduced in Heinrich Stümcke (ed.), *Johann Friedrich Löwens Geschichte des deutschen Theaters/Flugschriften über das Hamburger Nationaltheater* (J.F.L.'s History of the German Theatre / Pamphlets about the Hamburg National Theatre) (Berlin: Ernst Frensdorff, 1905), p. 81

[. . .] You also asked for some news of Madame Hensel. Here is a brief description of her. She has the most pleasing, the noblest shape; her expression is lofty whenever she chooses: she has one of those Roman noses we so much like to see on our theatrical heroines and the King of Prussia's guardsmen. Her diction has not been spoilt by the Viennese dialect; she speaks beautifully, distinctly, she declaims in a most accomplished manner; rhyme becomes prose in her way of speaking.[1] She understands the full meaning of a part; she thinks it is necessary to know the contents of the entire play and not [merely] a single passage. Her deportment is beautiful, her manners grand and assured. She is almost stronger in the so-called *rôles de force*[2] in tragedy than in high comedy, although she always plays excellently. But this incomparable actress often does not know her lines; and being somewhat phlegmatic by nature, she is often deficient in fire in some of the great scenes which alone decide the merit of an author and an actress, e.g. [. . .] in Phaedra's remorse which is the soul of the action.[3] She sees Minos in hell with the dreadful urn which decides the fate of men; and she is amiable and charming when she should be terrible. In the meantime she is soliciting her friends' criticisms and she is improving. [. . .] In short, I am certain that Mme Hensel is currently one of the best German actresses.

[1] For the frequently stated German antipathy to verse drama, see 54 & 136.
[2] I.e., star roles calling for skill and energy.
[3] In Racine's *Phèdre*. The scene referred to is in Act 4, Scene 6.

A remarkable tribute was paid to Mme Hensel's declamatory powers by Lessing who personally had no reason to flatter her. It was she who, after the 25th instalment of the

Hamburgische Dramaturgie, insisted that Lessing drop all further comments in his bulletin on the acting of the company of the National Theatre. We can take it that this candid critic's laudatory comments were motivated not by any desire to conciliate a *monstre sacré* but to give credit where credit was due.

119   Lessing on Mme Hensel, 12 May 1767

Lessing, *Hamburgische Dramaturgie*, 12 May 1767. Reproduced in *Lessings Werke* (1925), vol. 5, pp. 41–2

Her principal asset is her very correct diction; hardly one false accent will pass her lips; she knows how to speak the most tangled, knotty, obscure verse with such ease, such precision that it receives through her voice the clearest elucidation, the most complete commentary. She not infrequently combines with this a refinement which bears witness either to a very felicitous sentiment or to very correct judgement.

Friedrich Ludwig Schröder

This outstanding man of the theatre (see **73, 90, 124, 134, 142, 157, 193, 199–200**), who was associated for the greater part of his career with the city of Hamburg, made a deep impression on his contemporaries. He inspired the character of the actor-manager Serlo in Goethe's novel, *Wilhelm Meister's Apprenticeship*. The following thumbnail sketch of Schröder is taken from one of the important sources of information about eighteenth-century German actors, *Gallerie von Teutschen Schauspielern und Schauspielerinnen der ältern und neuern Zeit* (Gallery of German Actors and Actresses of Former and Recent Times), allegedly composed by the (probably fictitious) Portuguese Jew Abraham Peiba.

120   Friedrich Schröder characterised

Gallerie von Teutschen Schauspielern etc. (Vienna: Ignatius Nepomuk Edler von Epheu, 1783). Reproduced in edition by Richard Maria Werner (Berlin: SGTG 13, 1910), pp. 131–3

He is an actor who feels and thinks. His soul is always active and his glance full of spirit. His carriage, his expressions, his gestures show breeding. Even in the most violent torrent of passions he observes a temperance whereby these acquire something attractive. He always speaks naturally, his words are suited to his actions, and the actions to his words. He does not overdo his comic roles in order to make the vulgar laugh [. . .]. He does not distort his face in order to express pain; he does not stand around insignificantly when he has nothing to say. He never lapses out of his role [. . .]. He has an intellectual physiognomy, is tall, slim and well built, dresses elegantly for each role and has easy manners. [. . .] Everything comes easily to him as if given by nature; he makes everything his own, even that which he has received from art, the author's very thoughts and words. His voice is not particularly pleasant, he lacks vocal melody and range, but he manages to hide these defects well; his pronunciation is correct and intelligible. He feels every situation and has the art of communicating his feelings, for he has deeply pondered every word he speaks as well as his part and the entire play [...]. His spirit is equal to any role, but those of high tragedy have a greater claim to his figure and education.

The following listing by F.L. Meyer, Schröder's friend and biographer, of parts played by him throughout his stage career gives an idea of the man's range.

121   Schröder's roles from 1748 to 1795

Meyer (1819), pt. 2, section 2, pp. 139, 159

In 1748 he spoke his first words on stage as a three-year-old child, in the character of Innocence at St Petersburg, in a prologue [...]. In the next few years he appeared frequently in children's, including some girls', roles, in tragedies, comedies, *Haupt- und Staatsaktionen* [political melodramas], and prologues [...].

Some six hundred parts [played by him in his stage career] could be traced. It is therefore certainly no error to assume that, in view of the many parts not listed and those relearnt because they were newly adapted or translated, the actual number of parts played by Schröder would run to more than seven hundred.

August Wilhelm Iffland

Together with Schröder, Iffland was seen by many of his contemporaries as *the* outstanding German actor of his age – a self-transformer with meticulous attention to detail of character creation (see 207). One of his admirers was Goethe who invited him four times – in 1796, 1798, 1810 and 1812 – to come to Weimar as a guest artist to give as it were exemplary performances. (See 208 & 211–3.)

122   (a) Goethe on Iffland, 18 April 1796

Goethes Werke, WA, ser. IV (letters), vol. 11, pp. 53–4, letter to J.H. Meyer of 18 April 1796 (3296). Reproduced in part in Carlson (1978), p. 90

Iffland has been playing here for three weeks now, and through him the all but lost idea of dramatic art has been revived; what is praiseworthy about him is that which indicates the true artist: he *separates* his roles from one another in such a way that in each successive one there appears not a trace of what went before.

This separation is the foundation of everything else; each person receives his character by virtue of this sharp outline, and just as the actor thereby manages to make his audience forget the one role while playing the other, he manages to separate himself from his own individuality whenever he chooses, allowing it to emerge only when imitation fails him, in jovial, affectionate and dignified passages. [...] He has great physical suppleness and is master of all his organs, the defects of which he knows how to conceal, nay even to make use of.

The great capacity of his intellect for noting the peculiarities of people and to reproduce them in their characteristic features causes amazement, as does the breadth of his imagination and the speed of his representational talent.

122   (b) Goethe on Iffland, 2 May 1798

Goethes Werke, WA (Weimar: Hermann Böhlau), ser. IV (letters), vol. 13 (1893), p. 130. Letter of 2 May 1798 to Schiller (3786)

Iffland continues to do his business extremely well and distinguishes himself as a true artist. Laudable features are his vivid imagination, by means of which he knows how to discover whatever his part calls for, then his talent for imitation by means of which he knows how to represent what he has found and as it were created, and finally the humour with which he carries out the whole thing in a lively manner from beginning to end. The distinguishing of the roles from each other by means of costume, gesture, language, the separation of the situations and the breaking down of these into clearly felt smaller parts is excellent. [...]

For me it was very important to observe that he has the most pure and appropriate mood perfectly at his command, which indeed is possible only as the result of the conjunction of genius, art and craftsmanship.

123   Iffland in the part of Harpagon in Molière's *L'Avare*

Pencil drawings by the Henschel brothers. Reproduced in H. Haerle, *Ifflands Schauspiel-kunst. Ein Rekonstruktionsversuch auf Grund der etwa 500 Zeichnungen und Kupferstiche W. Henschels und seiner Brüder* (I.'s Acting. An attempted reconstruction based on the approx. 500 drawings & etchings by W.H. and his brother) (Berlin: *SGTG*, vol. 34, 1925)

It was tempting for contemporaries to compare the relative talents of Schröder and Iffland, the two leading actors of the latter part of the eighteenth century. From the perspective of an insightful critic – the romantic author Ludwig Tieck (1773–1853) – writing after both actors had died, the advantage clearly lay with Schröder.

124   Schröder and Iffland compared

Ludwig Tieck, *Die geschichtliche Entwickelung der neueren Bühne und Friedrich Ludwig Schröder* (The Historical Development of the Latter-Day Stage and F.L.S.), Introduction to *F.L. Schröder's dramatische Werke* (F.L.S. Dramatic Works), ed. Eduard v. Bülow (Berlin: Reimer, 1831). Reproduced in Ludwig Tieck, *Kritische Schriften* (Critical Writings), 4 vols. (Leipzig: F.A. Brockhaus), vol. 2 (1848), pp. 344–6, 374

[...] And it is this strong, noble nature, this simplicity and truthfulness that characterised Schröder so that he adopted no seductive mannerisms, never needlessly raised and lowered his pitch in declamation, never pursued effects merely for the sake of excitement, never sang out any lamentations in [moments of] pain or emotion but always led natural speech through correct shades of meaning from which he never departed. [...]

In his youth Iffland was excellent in gay and exaggerated comic roles, later his talent developed for the subtly comic as well as for high comedy. In many of these parts he was certainly unsurpassed [...]. Everything he presented was drawn from observation, and whatever his humour and his imagination could do to weld these details into a whole showed him to be a master. But his imagination was not creative, his humour was not poetic. His acting was genteel and intelligible and commended itself to those well-meaning people who like to grasp and explain everything rationally, because he could fully account for every gesture, every transition [...]. Now when Iffland with his genuine but limited talent tackled great subjects and tragedy, these semi-philosophers admired him here as well. [...].

Schröder was not only superior to Iffland but [...] often diametrically opposed to him. And so the old school founded by him and Ackermann [...] stands in the sharpest contrast to the newer sophistical one called into being by Iffland.

(vi) Acting technique

Lines of business

The members of German theatre companies, itinerant or resident, had their specific lines of business, a custom which they shared with their Italian, French and English confreres. The composition of the company of the Mannheim National Theatre gives a good idea of the range of actors needed to constitute a well balanced company able to cope with the repertoire needs of the time (see 107). A degree of stereotyping – lovers, pedants, villains, comic servants, parents comic or dignified etc. – was inherent in the material that was staged. As characterisation became more complex with the development of dramatic writing in the latter part of the eighteenth century and the beginning of the nineteenth, these traditional role demarcations were felt to be losing their *raison d'être*.

The passing of the traditional idea of the villain as seen on the eighteenth-century stage was welcomed by the authors of an encyclopaedia of the theatre which admittedly was published later than in the period here under review: but the description of the earlier state of affairs is illuminating.

125   The stage villain

Robert Blum, Karl Herloszsohn & Hermann Marggraff, *Allgemeines Theater-Lexikon oder Encyklopädie alles Wissenswerthen für Bühnenkünstler, Dilettanten und Theaterfreunde*

(General Dictionary of the Theatre, or Encyclopaedia of Everything Worth Knowing for Stage Practitioners, Amateurs and Friends of the Theatre), 7 vols. (Altenburg/Leipzig: H.A. Pierer, C. Heymann, 1839–46), vol. 4 (1841), p. 295

Gone are the days when, as he first entered, a black and red bunch of plumes signalled to the audience, 'Look, here comes the malefactor!', gone the days when the villain shouted even louder than the first lead and put soap in his mouth in order to have foam on his lips when he was finally defeated, or had heavy carriage chains wrapped around his body so that he might be dragged off to punishment rattling to maximum effect. On the contrary, the villain is now generally the calmest, most calculating, most thoughtful figure, who speaks quietly and emphatically, does not dress conspicuously, operates slowly by means of intellectual superiority and uses this against all other characters.

A particular line of business represented perhaps more fully on the German stage than on that of some other countries was that of Jewish roles. Iffland was considered something of an expert in this field although obviously that was a very subsidiary element in his broad spectrum of parts (see 107). According to the nineteenth-century theatrical encyclopaedia quoted below, these portrayals often had an element of broad caricature; the fact that this article had a brief Judaeo-German bibliography appended to it for the guidance actors of such roles (which is not included here) suggests some desire for greater authenticity.

126   Jewish roles

Ph.J. Düringer & H. Bartels, *Theater-Lexikon. Theoretisch-praktisches Handbuch für Vorstände, Mitglieder und Freunde des deutschen Theaters* (Theatrical Encyclopaedia. Theoretical and practical handbook for committees of management, members and friends of German theatre) (Leipzig: Otto Wigand, 1841), p. 608

Jews only belong to a particular class of dramatic characters inasmuch as in representing them it is intended to demonstrate the peculiar characteristics of their nation in terms of speech and gesture; for the rest their treatment depends on the characters of the roles themselves. [...]

The imitation of Jews, normally of the lower-class ones [...] is often abused and exaggerated in our farces and comedies. The inflection is something of a sing-song; the manner in which so-called Judaeo-German is spoken must be copied from nature, i.e. learnt from Jews, and this is not very difficult since it is very noticeable. The language itself [...] offers rather greater difficulties.

Even before the turn of the century there were calls for the loosening of role demarcations, in line with changing practice. The example below culled from a leading theatre magazine is indicative of this progressive trend.

127   A call for the abolition of lines of business, 1790

Christian August von Bertram, editor's footnote to J.F.H. Brockmann's article, 'Rechen-
schaft dem Wiener Publikum abgelegt über die Direktion des Kais. Königl. National=
Theaters im verflossenen Theaterjahre 1789' (Account rendered to the Viennese Public
concerning the Direction of the Imperial and Royal National Court Theatre of the Past
Season of 1789), in *ADT*, 6 (1790), pp. 25–6. Reprinted Kraus Reprint (Munich, 1981)

According to the present constitution of our theatre it is not possible to lay down
any lines of business, and the theatre in which every actor has his particular line
will certainly always be worse off than another in which the actor has to take
whatever role he is best suited for. – Leading actors in the above sense should not
exist at all, for wherever what really matters is better casting [. . .], in short the
general good which will never flourish among a group of leading actors only, no
distinction should be made between first and last actors. In my view he who best
carries out his duty is the first actor.

Improvisation

Throughout the seventeenth century and for a great part of the eighteenth, German actors
and audiences often preferred the joys and hazards of improvisational acting to the
recitation of a precisely memorised text. But with more and more German playtexts of high
quality – original or in translation – becoming available, this subordination of literature to
theatrical effectiveness came increasingly to be frowned on, and it passed out of fashion in
the latter decades of the eighteenth century. But what was a clear gain in textual terms was
in many ways a loss from the acting point of view. This regret was articulated by many
observers, including Goethe (in Book 3, Chapter 2 of *Wilhelm Meister's Theatrical Mission*
and, in somewhat different terms, in Book 2, Chapter 9 of *Wilhelm Meister's Apprenticeship*).
The following extract from Brandes' autobiography, in which the actor-author looks back
over his theatrical experiences some three or four decades prior to the time of writing, is a
defence of an all but vanished histrionic skill.

128   The usefulness of improvisation

J.C. Brandes (1800), vol. 2, pt. 1, pp. 49–51

I am bound at this point to add a comment about improvised acting. It is true that
in those days quite a bit of nonsense, quite a bit of immoral trash in the guise of a
play was offered, and perhaps still is being offered here and there, by many a
company of strollers; but that was extremely rarely the case on Schuch's stage
[. . .].[1]

Admittedly even the best farces acted by good actors did not contain much that
was instructive; but nonetheless they afforded a pleasant entertainment,
especially at the time when the elder Schuch was still playing the role of

Hanswurst, because his wit was always quick, sharp and incisive. Since he always knew how to place his lazzi in just those situations where they were bound to arouse loud laughter; and since moreover, as a man of naturally delicate feelings, he never indulged in smut, the end of this kind of play: decent entertainment – only very rarely failed to be achieved [...].

In fact, improvisation in those days served as a very useful preparation for young novice actors. Being as it were left to their own devices on stage they quickly gained confidence; they acquired good diction, their bodies improved in ease and deportment since they were also mostly employed in ballets, and in regular dramas, if they dried, they could immediately help themselves out by a few improvised words appropriate to the actual text [...].

Some people may frown on my taste; but in all honesty [...] I must admit that very often – since genuine comedy has almost entirely been replaced by domestic dramas and historical plays – I long to have those improvised performances back again [...]. I think I need be all the less ashamed of this wish in that Lessing remarked more than once that he would much rather see a sane lively farce than a lame or sickly comedy or tragedy.

¹ Viennese-born Franz Schuch the Elder (1716–64) was a strolling actor-manager who, playing principally in Northern Germany, combined a repertoire of regular plays (Racine, Molière, Voltaire, Holberg, Gottsched) with improvised farces; he was considered the 'last German Harlequin'. The dynasty of actors he founded was active for the rest of the century. Brandes had worked for Schuch early in his career, from 1760 to 1764.

Acting theory and actor training

With the rise of original playwriting in German and the considerable improvement in the level of acting in the second half of the eighteenth century, interest in the theory of acting increased. But for a long time ideas emanating from France led the debate. Lessing frequently referred to acting problems but never wrote the complete essay on the subject he had intended to. However, when Antoine-François-Valentin Riccoboni's *L'Art du théâtre* appeared in 1750, Lessing and Mylius's theatrical magazine, *Beyträge zur Historie und Aufnahme des Theaters* (see **91**) published a translation in the same year. This essay by a member of a family of distinguished Italian theatre practitioners, which argued the case for conscious theatrical craftsmanship, aroused a good deal of interest in Germany: thus, it was used as a standard text for study and discussion by Ekhof's theatrical academy (see **88** & **129**), and as late as 1810 it formed the basis of a lecture by Schröder in Hamburg on the art of acting (see **134**, **142**). Lessing also translated Pierre Rémond de Sainte-Albine's *Le Comédien* (1747), which in contrast to Riccoboni's book took a more internal approach to the actor's art, and he published an excerpt in vol. 1 of his *Theatralische Bibliothek* (Theatrical Library) (Berlin, 1754, pp. 209–66). Perhaps as a counter-balance, he published a translation of Riccoboni's *Histoire du Théâtre Italien* in vol. 2 of the *Theatralische Bibliothek* (Berlin, 1755, pp. 135–214). Another influence on Lessing were Diderot's theoretical writings (excluding his *Paradoxe sur le comédien*, now considered a key text of acting theory but not published until 1830).

Complaints about the non-existence of a theatre school and suggestions for how to found and run one were recurrent debating points in the latter part of the eighteenth century and the first half of the nineteenth, but all actual attempts in this direction, invariably linked with existing companies, proved to be short-lived. Ekhof's 'academy' actually only consisted of some (not all) members of Schönemann's company to which he belonged at the time. He intended to fill the gap in the education of these working actors who had had no systematic craft training, and thus to raise the artistic standards of the company. The purpose of theorising about the art of acting was basically practical rather than philosophical.

The following paper was read by Ekhof to members of the academy while they were in session in Hamburg (not in Schwerin, their then headquarters), and it summed up the transactions of the institution to date. If Ekhof's guidelines to the art of acting strike us as simplistic today, it is only fair to suppose that basic principles may well have needed stating in the circumstances of the time.

129   Ekhof on basic principles of acting, 15 June 1754

Kindermann, *Conrad Ekhofs Schauspieler-Akademie* (1956), pp. 39–40

Gentlemen and Ladies!

So, at the end of our year's sessions, we have concluded the fourth part of our deliberations as well. We have examined in them the art of representation and all that forms part of it, or the actor's duties on the stage. We have from the very start considered the aptitudes and faculties they [*sic*] need if they are to be of any use to the theatre, such as reading and writing, a good memory, eagerness to learn, an inexhaustible urge to constant self-improvement and the strength to be intimidated neither by flattering eulogies, pride, nor by unreasonable disparagement. Furthermore, we have indicated the sciences they must needs seek to acquire, and then noted the arts and devices, meaning [those] whereby some mechanical actions may be carried out decorously, such as walking, standing, kneeling, laughing, interrupting someone else's speech etc. Then we penetrated into the inner nature of the art of representation and we have perceived that the latter in fact consists of this: *the imitation of nature*, but were persuaded at the same time that the theory of this has not been learnt until one *can make one's imaginary or pretended soul state credible as real, by dint of skilful movement and disposition of one's body* and that it was possible in the exercise of this to go so far as to *appear in this assumed state to exceed by art the powers of the human soul*. In this we have taken as our basic text the Art of Acting by Riccoboni the Younger [...]. We have given the French full credit for having been our predecessors in this difficult art, for having reached a fair degree of perfection as a result of time, effort and practice, and therefore we who are late-comers have not been at all ashamed to regard them as our instructors and to follow in their footsteps. In doing this, however, we have diligently striven to separate their errors from their good points and firmly resolved neither to hang onto nor to accept anything from them in this art that is not in accord with nature and has been approved by the touchstone of verisimilitude.

Nearly half a century later the situation had not changed in that German actors were still trained 'on the job' rather than by any formal instruction.

130   Call for an acting school, 1795

Anon., 'Briefe über die Hamburgischen Bühnen. Geschrieben in den Sommermonaten des Jahres 1795. Eilfter Brief' (Letters about the Theatres in Hamburg. Written in the summer months of 1795. Letter the Eleventh), in *ADT*, 17 (1796), p. 37

Believe me, dear friend, a chief reason why our German actors are still so backward both in their education and in the esteem of the public is this: nowhere in Germany are there any acting schools. After all, we have academies for draughtsmen and painters, why not one for the art of acting as well? As long as there is no such thing, it will unhappily remain something halfway between an art and a craft – lean or rich remuneration, hissing or applause, the hum of disapproval or noisy cheers will continue to be all that the actor in general has to fear or to hope for.

An early German contribution to the theory of acting, *Kurzgefasste Grundsätze von der Beredsamkeit des Leibes* (Concise Principles of Bodily Expression) (Hamburg, 1755) by Johann Friedrich Löwen, the author now best remembered for his unfortunate attempt to run the Hamburg National Theatre, made little impact and was dismissed as worthless by the first important German theorist of acting, Johann Jakob Engel (1741–1802). The latter, an academic and playwright who served, none too successfully, as director of the Berlin Royal National Theatre, from 1788 to 1794, attempted in his treatise, *Ideen zu einer Mimik* (Ideas on Mimesis), to establish an exact equivalence between inner (emotional) states and their external (physical) expression by a detailed examination of the manifestation of key emotions.

131   Engel on the congruence of feeling and expression on stage, 1785–6

Johann Jakob Engel, *Ideen zu einer Mimik* (Ideas on Mimesis), 2 vols. (Berlin: August Mylius, 1785–6). Reproduced in *J.J. Engels Schriften*, 12 vols. (Berlin: Myliussche Buchhandlung, 1804), vol. 8, pp. 4–5. Note also the book by Henry Siddons, Sarah Siddons' son, *Practical Illustrations of Rhetorical Gesture and Action, adapted to the English drama. From a work on the same subject by M. Engel* (London: Richard Phillips, 1807)

If the task were to be the following: to combine the expression of two conflicting passions contending within a man's soul; then, I maintain, you need only know the two desires and the expression which is appropriate to each one of them taken singly, need only know whether they keep each other in balance or whether one of them, and which one, predominates [...] and it will be no trouble at all to discover the true, fitting expression portraying the entire sentiment of the soul.

132   Hamlet's gesture in his soliloquy in Act 3, Sc. 2: 'Ay, there's the rub'

Engraving by Johann Wilhelm Meil. In Engel, *Schriften*, vol. 7 (1804), fig. 12, p. 150. Note that Hamlet's costume is that worn by Brockmann in the role. (See 201. For Meil, see p. 237.)

Towards the end of the century, the historical and ethnographic authenticity which Gottsched had demanded earlier but in vain (see 83–4), now seemed a desirable goal for actors to pursue. (Compare 379.)

133   The actor's need for historical and ethnographic knowledge, 1785–6

Engel (1804), vol. 7, pp. 47–8

It would be a blessing for the actor which as yet he lacks if somebody were to put down for him some notes about the customs and manners of different periods and nationalities. The more fully reasoned this were to be; the more deeply it were to lead him into the general spirit of those times and nations: the more easily and completely his imagination would be able to picture things; the more fittingly he could portray them in his performance.

While Schröder was not a theorist of acting as such, his vast practical experience entitled him to have his views listened to with respect. In his lecture of 17 November 1810 in Hamburg he noted disapprovingly that the fourth-wall convention of acting, which had been advocated by Diderot (and with which we are still familiar today), was being contravened in the early years of the nineteenth century.

134   Schröder on the actor–audience relationship, 17 November 1810

F.L.W. Meyer (1819), vol. 2, pt. 2, pp. 207–8

Since my departure from the theatre[1] a habit has grown up which destroys not only all ensemble playing but all verisimilitude [. . .], of which neither I, the oldest German actor, nor any predecessors I am aware of had any knowledge. It is this: directing one's speech at the pit, to talk with and even to make eyes at the pit. [. . .] The multitude will get used to anything, even to poor functioning of the machinery: but let no one think that the educated part [of the audience], who would prefer to forget that they are standing in front of a stage, will take any pleasure in this intimacy with the pit. When I framed the laws of the local theatre, it was quite free from this abominable abuse, this gross interference with the illusion: otherwise I should certainly have commented on it.[2]

[1] Schröder had retired from the stage in 1798, i.e. twelve years before giving this lecture.
[2] For his theatre regulations, see 90.

The views of Goethe on the art of acting are of exceptional importance: as a playwright-director he was in a position to try to mould the Weimar company to fit in with his and

Schiller's idealistic concept of theatre. The famous 'Rules for Actors' arose out of his regular teaching of twelve young actors, starting with Karl Grüner and Pius Alexander Wolff, from 1803 onwards; he handed over the papers codifying these rules to Eckermann on 2 May 1824. In them Goethe formulated explicitly what formerly he had only done intuitively as a director. His idealistic bias clearly inclined him towards a more classical, almost French, concept of acting. He laid particular emphasis on diction, including the much neglected art of verse-speaking, and made a clear distinction between recitation (beautiful diction *without* characterisation) and declamation (diction *with* characterisation). In reading these rules it is important to remember that they were a grammar of acting for the use of a private theatre school: hence their didactic tone. Some of them, especially pars. 82–91, also throw a light on Goethe's ideas on direction. Wolff's own notes on Goethe's instruction were only found after the Second World War.

135   Goethe's rules for actors, 1803

Reproduced in Hans Böhme, 'Die Weilburger Goethe-Funde: Blätter aus dem Nachlasse Pius Alexander Wolffs' (The Weilburg Goethe discoveries: pages from the papers left by Pius Alexander Wolff), in *DSB*, 36 (Emsdetten, 1950), pp. 45–63. A less complete version can be found in *Goethes Werke*, WA, section 1, vol. 40, pp. 140–68, with notes on the MSS on pp. 420–9. Reproduced in English translation in Carlson (1978), pp. 309–18, and in a shortened version in Nagler (1952), pp. 428–33.

Dialect

1. When a provincialism is heard in the middle of a tragic speech, it makes the most beautiful poetry ugly and offends the spectator's ear. Therefore the first and most essential task for the actor entering into training is to free himself from all faults of dialect and to seek to attain a completely pure speech. [...][1]

2. He who is accustomed to struggling with dialect holds closely to the general rules of German speech and attempts to enunciate new acquisitions very clearly, indeed more clearly than is really required. Even excesses are advisable in this case, without danger of any setback; for it is human nature to turn back readily to old habits and the excess will balance out automatically.

Enunciation

3. Just as in music the pure, true, and exact striking of every individual tone is the basis for all further artistic development, so also in acting the pure and complete enunciation of every individual word is the basis of all further recitation and declamation.
[...][2]

10. When a consonant is followed by another similar in sound, as when one word ends with the same letter that begins the next, there must be a break that clearly separates the two. [...]
[...]

12. Particular care should [...] be given to the enunciation of key words, proper names and conjunctions.

13. A stronger emphasis in expression than is customary should be laid upon proper names [...]. It is very often the case that a person is spoken of in the first act who first appears in the third or often even later. The public should have been prepared to take notice of him [...].

14. In order to develop expression to its fullest, the beginner should speak everything very slowly, the syllables, and especially the final syllables, clearly and strongly, so that the syllables that must be spoken softly remain understandable.

15. Also, in the beginning, it is advisable to speak in as deep a tone as one can manage and then intermittently to go higher, as this gives the voice a great range and develops the various modulations that are needed in declamation.

16. It is also very good if in the beginning one speaks all syllables, whether they are long or short, for as long and in as deep a tone as the voice permits, because otherwise in rapid speech one tends to lay emphasis only on the verbs.

[...]

Recitation and Declamation

18. By recitation is meant a delivery that lies halfway between the coldly restful and the highly elevated, without a tragic elevation of tone and yet not entirely without tonal modulation. [...]

19. It is [...] necessary that in passages calling for recitation one rely on a measured expression and deliver them with the sensitivity and emotion that the poem inspires in the reader by its content; yet this should be done with moderation and without that passionate self-expression which is called for in declamation. The actor doing recitation follows with his voice the ideas of the poet and the impression made on him by gentle or horrible, pleasant or unpleasant subjects [...]. He alters nothing of his individual character thereby; he betrays nothing of the nature of his individuality [...].

20. Declamation, or heightened recitation, is quite another matter. Here I must lay aside my innate character, disavow my nature, and place myself entirely in the circumstances and disposition of that role I am declaiming. The words I speak must be delivered with energy and the most lively expression so that every passionate impulse appears to arise authentically just as it is experienced. [...]

21. It is possible to use a prosaic tone in declamation, which truly has many analogues with music. But one must make the distinction that music [...] can develop more freely, while the art of declamation is from the outset much more limited in tone and subject to an external aim. The actor declaiming must always keep this axiom firmly in mind. For if he develops his tone too rapidly, speaks either too low or too high or with too many halftones, he begins to sing; on the

other hand, he may fall into a monotone, which is incorrect even in simple recitation – two reefs, each as dangerous as the other, between which yet a third lies concealed, namely a preaching tone. In watching out for one or the other of the former dangers, it is easy to fall into the latter.

22. In order to achieve a proper declamation, one should observe the following rules:

When I first completely understand the sense of a word and inwardly feel it completely, then I must seek to fit it with a suitable vocal tone and deliver it strongly or weakly, quickly or slowly, as the sense of each sentence requires. For example:

'The crowd murmured' must be spoken half loud, murmuring.

'The names rang out' must be spoken clearly, ringingly.

'Dark forgetfulness,' [...] must be spoken in deep, hollow, fearful tones.

[...]

25. When a word appears which because of its meaning requires a heightened expression [...], it is well to bear in mind that one does not tear it out of an otherwise relaxed speech as if it were a thing apart and put all the stress on the significant word, then fall back again into a relaxed tone. Rather one prepares the hearer by a careful distribution of the heightened expression, by placing a more articulated delivery on the preceding words and thus building to the key word so that it is delivered in full and rounded relation to the rest. [...]

26. When the expression *O!* is followed by other words, a pause is necessary so that the *O!* is a cry by itself. For example: 'O! – my mother! O! – my son!' Not 'O my mother! O my son!'

[...]

28. The person declaiming has the freedom to select his own places for dividing the phrases with pauses and so on, but he must not depart from the correct meaning in doing so; for it can be as easily destroyed here as with an omitted or poorly enunciated word.

[...]

Rhythmic Delivery

31. All the rules and observations made concerning declamation are also fundamental here. The particular character of rhythmic delivery, however, ensures that the subject will be declaimed with an even more elevated and emotional expression. Indeed, a certain weight will now be given to the expression of every word.

32. The arrangement of syllables, however, and the rhymed end syllable must not be too conspicuously indicated; coherence must be observed just as in prose.

33. If iambics are to be declaimed, care should be taken that the beginning of

each line is marked by a small, scarcely noticeable pause, though it must not disturb the flow of the declamation.

Placement and Movement of the Body on Stage

34. A few general rules can be given concerning this part of the art of acting, too, and although there is of course an infinite number of exceptions, all come back finally to the basic rules. These one should try to incorporate into oneself so completely that they become second nature.

35. First the actor must consider that he should not only imitate nature but present it in an idealised form, and thus unite the true with the beautiful in his presentation.

36. Therefore every part of his body should be completely under his control [...].

37. The body should be held thus: the chest up, the upper half of the arms to the elbows somewhat close to the torso, the head turned somewhat toward the person with whom one is speaking – only a bit, however, so that three-quarters of the face is always turned towards the spectators.

38. For the actor must always remember that he is there for the sake of the public.

39. For the same reason, actors should also avoid playing to one another, out of a sense of misunderstood naturalness, as if no third person were present; they should never act in profile nor turn their backs to the audience. If this is done for the sake of characterisation or out of necessity, then let it be done with care and grace.

40. One should also be careful never to speak upstage in the theatre but always toward the audience. For the actor must always divide his attention between two objects: the person to whom he is speaking and the spectators. Instead of turning the head entirely, make greater use of the eyes.

41. It is very important, however, that when two are acting together, the one speaking should always move upstage and the one who has ceased speaking should move a bit downstage. If the actors skilfully use this advantage and learn through practice to do it with ease, then their declamation will have its best effect for both the ear and the eye. [...][3]

42. When two persons are speaking together, the one on the left should be careful not to approach too closely to the one on the right. The more honoured person should always stand on the right – women, elders, nobility. Even in everyday life one keeps a certain distance from those one respects; contrary practice suggests a lack of breeding. The actor should show himself well bred and therefore adhere strictly to this rule. Whoever stands on the right should insist upon his privilege and not allow himself to be pressed towards the wings, but

should stand fast and with his left hand give a sign to the person pressing him to move back.

43. A beautiful contemplative pose (for a young man, for example) is this: the chest and entire body held erect, standing in the fourth dance position, the head turned somewhat to the side, the eyes fixed on the ground, and both arms hanging loosely.

Positions and Movements of the Hands and Arms

44. In order to ensure the free movement of hands and arms, the actor should never carry a cane.

45. When a long coat is worn, the modern fashion of placing one hand under the lapel should be avoided entirely.

46. It is most improper to place one hand on top of the other, or to rest them both on the stomach, or to stick one or even both in the vest.

47. The hand itself must never form a fist, or be placed flat against the thigh, as soldiers do; rather some of the fingers must be half bent, others straight, but never held entirely stiff.

48. The two middle fingers should always remain together, the thumb, index finger, and little finger remain somewhat bent. In this way the hand is in its proper position and ready to execute any movement correctly.

49. The upper half of the arm should remain rather close to the torso and should move much less freely than the lower half, which should have the greatest flexibility. [...]

50. Nor should the hands ever retire from action to their position of rest until the speech is concluded, and then only gradually, as the speech draws to a close.

51. The movement of the arms should always proceed in order. First the hand moves or rises, then the elbow, then the entire arm. Never should it be lifted all at once without this sequence, because such a movement would appear ugly and stiff.

52. It is a great advantage for the beginner to keep his elbows as close as possible to his torso. [...] He should practise this posture in daily life and always hold his arms back [...]. When walking or in moments of leisure he should allow his arms to hang freely, never press the hands together, but keep the fingers always in motion.

53. Descriptive gestures with the hands should be made sparingly, though they cannot be dispensed with entirely.

54. When referring to a part of the body, one should beware of indicating with the hand that part of the body [...].

55. Descriptive gestures must be made, but they should be made as if they were

spontaneous. There are certain exceptions to this rule [...], but in general it can and should be followed.

[...]

57. When gesturing, one should avoid as much as possible bringing the hand in front of the face or covering the body.

58. If I must extend a hand and the right is not expressly called for, I can extend the left just as well, for there is no right or left on the stage. One's only concern should be not to destroy the pictorial composition by any awkward position. If I am forced to extend the right hand, however, and am in such a position that I must pass the hand across my body, it would be preferable for me to step back a little and extend it so that I am facing the audience.

[...]

60. Whoever stands on the right side should act with the left arm, and contrariwise, whoever stands on the left side should act with the right, so that the chest is covered by the arm as little as possible.

[...]

62. For this very reason and so that the chest will be turned toward the spectator, it is advisable for the actor who stands on the right side to place his left foot forward, and the actor on the left his right one.

Gesticulation

63. [...] One should stand before a mirror and speak what one is to declaim softly or preferably not at all, but only think the words. In this way one will not be distracted by the declamation but rather easily observe every false movement that does not express one's thought or softly spoken words. Thus one can select the most beautiful and most suitable gestures and can express through the entire pantomime a movement analogous with the sense of the words [...].

64. At the same time it must be assumed that the actor has previously made completely his own the character and the entire circumstances of what is to be presented and that his imagination has correctly worked through this material; for without this preparation he will be correct neither in declamation nor in gesture[4] [...]

Observations for Rehearsals

66. In order to acquire an easier and more appropriate movement of the feet, one should never rehearse in boots.

67. The actor, especially one who plays young men, lovers, and other light roles, should keep a pair of slippers in the theatre for rehearsals, and he will very soon observe good results.

68. Nothing should be allowed during rehearsals which could not also occur during performance.

69. Actresses should lay aside their small purses.

70. No actor should rehearse in his topcoat but should have his arms and hands free, as he will in the play. For the coat not only prevents him from making the appropriate gestures but compels him to assume incorrect ones that he will unwittingly repeat in performance. [. . .].

71. The actor should make no movement in rehearsal which is not appropriate to his role.

72. He who sticks his hand in his bosom during the rehearsal of a tragic role is in danger of seeking an opening in his armour during performance.

Avoiding Bad Habits

73. A very serious error to be avoided: when a seated actor, wishing to advance his chair somewhat, reaches through between his open thighs to seize the chair, then raises himself slightly and pulls it forward. This is an offense not only against beauty but still more against propriety.

74. The actor should never allow his handkerchief to be seen on the stage, still less should he blow his nose, still less spit. It is terrible to be reminded of these physical necessities within a work of art. One can carry a small handkerchief, which is in fashion now anyway, to use in case of need.

Conduct of the Actor in Private Life

[. . .]

76. He should be careful of his normal gestures, postures, placement of the arms and body, for if his attention during the performance has to be directed toward avoiding his customary gestures, he will naturally not be able to give his full attention to the principal matter in hand.

77. It is thus absolutely necessary that an actor free himself from all habits so that he can concentrate totally on his role during performance and occupy himself only with those concerns related to the part.

78. On the other hand, it is an important actor's rule to strive to adjust his body, his behaviour, indeed his whole external appearance in everyday life just as if he were involved in a continuous exercise. [. . .]

79. The actor who has chosen to play emotional roles will improve himself greatly if whenever he speaks he attempts to produce an expression that is both accurate and discreet in tone and which is accompanied by a certain heightening of all his gestures. This of course must not be overdone, because it will then cause laughter in those with whom one is speaking. The artist who is developing himself can nevertheless be recognised in other ways. This will by no means bring him into

disrepute, indeed the idiosyncrasy of his behaviour will be readily tolerated if by this means it comes about that on the stage itself he is able to impress others as a great actor.

80. For on the stage one wishes everything to be presented not only with truth but with beauty, for the viewer's eye desires to be charmed by attractive grouping and poses. Thus the actor should also strive to maintain those attitudes offstage; he should always consider himself as being before spectators.

81. When he has committed a role to memory, he should continue to perform it before imaginary spectators; indeed, even when he is sitting alone or joining his fellows at the table to eat he should seek always to create a picture, to pick up and set down everything with a certain grace, and so on, as if he were on stage, and thus he will appear always artistic.

Grouping and Positions Onstage

82. The stage and the auditorium, the actor and the spectator form a whole.

83. The stage should be considered as a figureless tableau for which the actors supply the figures.

84. Therefore one should never perform too close to the wings.

85. Nor should one step under the proscenium arch. This is the greatest error, for the figure thereby leaves the space in which it makes a whole with the painted scenery and the other actors.[5]

[...]

87. As the augurs with their staffs divided the heavens into various areas, the actor can divide the stage into various spaces in his thoughts, which for experimentation can be represented on paper by areas in rhomboid shape. The stage floor thus becomes a sort of chessboard. Then the actor can determine into which squares he will enter, can note this pattern on paper, and can then be sure that in emotional passages he will not rush here and there inartistically but will join the beautiful with the significant.

88. Anyone who enters for a monologue from the upstage wings does well to move diagonally down to the proscenium on the opposite side, since in general diagonal movements are very pleasing.

89. Anyone who enters from an upstage wing to join somebody already on stage should not come downstage parallel with the wings, but should move slightly towards the prompter.

90. One should always determine all these technical-grammatical rules according to one's own understanding and practice them until they become habitual. All stiffness must disappear and the rule become merely the basis of living action.

91. [...] these rules should be particularly observed when one is portraying

noble, dignified characters. On the other hand, there are characters for whom this dignity is totally unsuitable, for example, peasants, boors, and so on. Yet one will portray these characters much better if one carries out with artistry and calculation the reverse of what decorum suggests, while always remembering that this should be an imitative appearance and not dull reality.

[1] The question of correct German stage diction is one that was frequently discussed in the latter part of the eighteenth century: not unnaturally in a country where provincialisms coloured – and continue to colour to this day – the speech not only of the man in the street but also of the educated classes.

[2] Paras. 4–9 have been omitted because they deal with diction problems peculiar to the German language.

[3] Compare Father Lang's directions on how to conduct duologues (46–7).

[4] Note that the aesthetic formalism on which Goethe insisted by no means excluded individual characterisation or delving into the psychology of the role.

[5] Note the total commitment here to a picture-frame concept of staging – compare Schröder's similar views (134).

In contrast to the sustained efforts Goethe and Schiller made in Weimar to create a high tradition of well spoken and flexible verse drama, the old antipathy to verse on the part of German actors and audiences alike had by no means disappeared (see 54). Engel as a theorist of acting had little time for verse-speaking.

136   Engel on verse drama, 1785–6

Engel (1804), vol. 8, pp. 231–2

The soul's sentiments, as they spring up, change and vanish in the midst of a tangled action, are only approximations; if the [speech] rhythm is to be brought into harmony with these sentiments as unquestionably it ought to be, it must likewise consist only of approximations: these approximations cannot be expressed otherwise than by a free, diverse mixture of feet and rhythms; however, such a free, diverse mixture is prose: and so [...] prose is embedded in the very idea of drama.

XII   Direction

Towards the end of the eighteenth century the need for a co-ordinator of the stage action, in other words a director, came to be felt increasingly. But directors – as against actor-managers wishing to give a high profile to their own roles – were still few and far between, as Engel pointed out in his *Ideen zur Mimik*.

137   Engel's call for the director to be the key person in the theatre, 1785–6

Engel (1804), vol. 8, pp. 268–9

I fully realise that this entering into the spirit of one's role in concert with the others, this feeling for the highest effectiveness of the whole [. . .], this explanation of each separate character from the context of everybody [else] calls for a certain penetrating deeper insight which nature has not granted to every artist, however talented in other respects [. . .]. But precisely this should, in my opinion, be the principal business of every head of a theatre so that he might guide the less insightful actor, instruct him in the idea of the whole, assign to him his true place in every group, keep him within bounds where he might go astray. – But of course, these are mere dreams as long as most of our theatres are governed either by complete anarchy or by an ignorant dictator.

Although Goethe lacked a background of hard professional experience before taking over the direction of the Weimar theatre, his charismatic person made him a key figure in German theatre history. He set the example to nineteenth- and indeed twentieth-century theatre practitioners of a director, not himself an actor but a man with broad artistic perspectives, able to shape a company and build up a repertoire for the long-term aesthetic education of the audience.

We have already noted some of Goethe's directorial principles – for instance the composition of a picture within the proscenium frame (see 135, pars. 82–7). He also had firm views concerning the selection, handling and training of actors. In the following conversation with Eckermann on Thursday, 14 April 1825, years after he had left the theatre, he looked back on his directorial practice. (For other ideas on auditioning and training, see 170, 251 and 252.)

138   Goethe on auditioning and actor training, 14 April 1825

Eckermann (1930), pp. 100–1. (Translation taken from Oxenford.) Reproduced in Nagler (1952), pp. 427–8

Since conversation upon the theatre and theatrical management was now the order of the day, I asked him upon what maxims he proceeded in the choice of a new member of the company.

'I can scarcely say,' returned Goethe; 'I had various modes of proceeding. If a striking reputation preceded the new actor, I let him act, and saw how he suited the others; whether his style disturbed our *ensemble*, or whether he would supply a deficiency. If, however, he was a young man who had never trodden the stage before, I first considered his personal qualities; whether he had about him anything attractive, and, above all things, whether he had control over himself. [...]

If his appearance and his deportment pleased me, I made him read, and in order to test the power and extent of his organ, as well as the capabilities of his mind, I gave him some sublime passage from a great poet, to see whether he was capable of feeling and expressing what was really great; then something passionate and wild, to prove his power. I then went to something marked by sense and smartness, something ironical and witty; to see how he treated such things, and whether he had sufficient freedom. Then I gave him something representing the pain of a wounded heart, the suffering of a great soul; that I might learn whether he could express pathos.

If he satisfied me in all these, I had a hope of making him an important actor. If he appeared more capable in some particulars than in others, I remarked the line to which he was adapted. I also now knew his weak points, and, above all, endeavoured to work upon him so that he might strengthen and cultivate himself here. If I remarked faults of dialect, provincialisms, I urged him to lay them aside, and recommended to him social intercourse and friendly practice with some member of the stage who was entirely free from them. I then asked him whether he could dance and fence; and if this were not so, I would hand him over for some time to the dancing and fencing masters.

If he were now sufficiently advanced to make his appearance, I gave him at first such parts as suited his individuality, and desired nothing but that he should represent himself. If he now appeared to me of too fiery a nature, I gave him phlegmatic characters; if too calm and tedious, I gave him fiery and hasty characters, that he might thus learn to lay aside himself, and assume foreign individuality.

A principle to which Goethe attached great importance was that of the cast having a read-through as the first stage in rehearsals – a practice that was by no means universally accepted at the time. The hero of his novel, *Wilhelm Meister's Apprenticeship*, echoes his own views in this respect.

139   Goethe on the importance of read-throughs

Goethe, *Wilhelm Meisters Lehrjahre*, vol. 3 (Berlin: Johann Friedrich Unger, 1795), bk 5, ch. 7, pp. 77–8. Reproduced in *Goethes Werke*, WA, section 1, vol. 22, pp. 179–80

Now a read-through was to be held, which Wilhelm looked forward to with keen pleasure. [. . .] All the actors were acquainted with the play, and he only tried, before they began, to convince them of the importance of a read-through. Just as one required of any musician that he should be able to play to some extent sight unseen, so should any actor, indeed any educated man, train himself to read sight unseen, to catch at once the character of any drama, any poem, any narrative, and to recite them skilfully. Learning by heart was no use unless the actor had first entered into the spirit and meaning of the good author; the letter could avail nothing.

Goethe, seconded by Schiller, saw the director's function not merely as that of putting on excellent performances but also as that of creating an exemplary repertoire, thereby raising the cultural importance of the theatre.

140   Goethe's approach to direction, 22 March 1825

Eckermann (1850, 1930), pp. 93–4, 22 March 1825. (Translation taken from Oxenford) Reproduced in Nagler (1952), pp. 426–7

The main point [. . .] was this, that the Grand Duke left my hands quite free; I could do just as I liked. I did not look to magnificent scenery and a brilliant wardrobe; I looked to good pieces. From tragedy to farce, every species was welcome; but a piece was obliged to have something in it to find favour. It had to be great and clever, cheerful and graceful, and at all events healthy and containing some pith. All that was morbid, weak, lachrymose and sentimental, as well as all that was frightful, horrible, and offensive to decorum, was excluded; I should have feared, by such expedients, to spoil both actors and audience.[1]

By means of good pieces, I raised the actors; for the study of excellence, and the perpetual practice of excellence, must necessarily make something of a man whom nature has not left ungifted. I was also constantly in contact with the actors. I supervised the read-throughs and explained to everyone his part; I was present at the chief rehearsals, and talked with the actors as to any improvements that might be made; I was never absent from a performance, and I pointed out the next day anything that seemed wrong. By these means I advanced them in their art.

But I also sought to raise the whole class in the esteem of society, by introducing the best and most promising into my own circle, and thus showing that I considered them worthy of social intercourse with myself. The result was, that the rest of the higher society in Weimar did not remain behind me, and that actors and actresses gained admission into the best circles. [...]

Schiller proceeded in the same spirit [...]. Like me, he was present at every rehearsal; and after every successful performance of one of his pieces, it was his custom to invite the actors, and to spend a merry day with them. All rejoiced together at whatever had succeeded, and discussed how anything might be done better next time.

[1] For details of Goethe's repertoire planning, see **179**.

While Goethe's direction of the Weimar theatre had a wide influence – out of proportion to the limited means at his disposal – he was not without his critics. One of the most incisive was Karoline Jagemann (1774–1848), an actress and opera singer of outstanding talent in the Weimar company, which she joined in 1797 after having played with much success at the Mannheim National Theatre for five years. Her opposition to Goethe proved to be only too effective: as the mistress of Duke Karl August she was largely instrumental in bringing about his dismissal from his post as director in 1817 (see also **217, 221 & 228**).

141   A negative assessment of Goethe as a director

Eduard v. Bamberg (ed.), *Die Erinnerungen der Karoline Jagemann* (The Memoirs of K.J.) (Dresden: Sibyllen-Verlag, 1926), pp. 98–101. Reproduced in Kindermann, *Theatergeschichte der Goethezeit* (1948), pp. 690–1

I came from a theatre which was governed by regulations and which was also exemplary in that the tone obtaining among the artists was decent and refined, whereas here arbitrariness and despotism prevailed. The personnel with few exceptions were unbelievably crude, the general tone not very different from that of an itinerant company. [...] it was one of the Court Councillor's [i.e. Goethe's] principles to tie up actors by means of advance payments; the deductions put them in the most wretched situation, and so I had to carry out my tasks with poor dissatisfied people and insignificant talents – I am not speaking only of opera – with the result that I took no pleasure in new roles. I ascribed these defects to the head of the theatre and was angry that he allowed things to happen which could easily have been mended, and that he was not interested in minor matters which are nevertheless important for the actor [...]. If for instance there had been prescribed for a play a grotto which would be adorned with wreaths, an arbour in which one was to eavesdrop, a waterfall by the margin of which one was to fall asleep, none of these props would be provided or even just indicated during rehearsals, on the contrary, Goethe would call from the stalls where, occasionally but not often, he used to attend rehearsals, 'Just suppose it to be so!' [...] These details of Goethe's personality and theatre practice will account for my [...] having been more repelled than attracted by him at the time.

The pictorialism favoured by Goethe tied in with a good deal of conventional stage practice, such as that explained here by F.L. Schröder.

142   Conventional composition of a stage group

Meyer (1819), vol. 2, pt. 2, p. 209

If there are several persons on stage, they must stand in a semicircle, which can very easily be formed by the one standing in the middle *only just* seeing everybody and *only just* being seen by everybody. One actor can make speech and action infinitely easier for another if the listener moves downstage a little.

143   **Painting by Friedrich Matthaei of Schiller's** *Die Braut von Messina*, **Act V (Weimar production of 1808–9).**
Nationale Forschungs- und Gedenkstätten der klassischen deutschen Literatur in Weimar, Fotothek

Note the typical Goethean tableau – a balanced composition with the main actors downstage centre and the two choruses forming a semicircle around them. (See also **225**.)

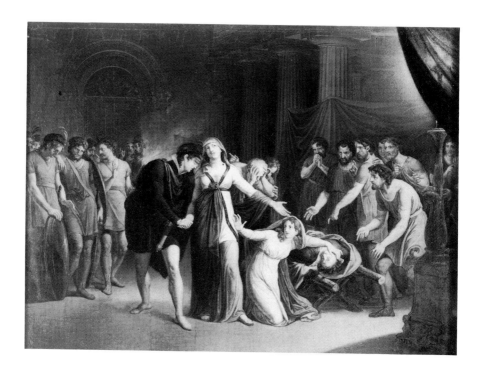

XIII   Audiences

A. OPPOSITION TO THE THEATRE

Up to the middle of the eighteenth century, German theatre companies – dependent on the favour of princes and the tolerance of municipal authorities, without fixed venues and often barely able to make ends meet – did not enjoy the esteem of the educated classes. The efforts of the Neuber company to attract audiences to a more literary repertoire had not by themselves had any long-lasting effect on taste; nor were the experiences of J.F. Schöne-mann, who after acting with the Neubers for ten years had become their bitter rival on founding his own company in 1739 with similar high-flown ambitions, very happy ones either. In the prefaces to four out of the five volumes of the *Schönemannische Schaubühne* (Schönemann's Theatre, 1748–51), collections of plays in his company's repertoire, he attacked both the tastes and the conduct of the audiences of his day and age. The preface to vol. II itemises some of the main difficulties that German actors had to contend with; it has been suggested that Ekhof, the outstanding member of the company, had a hand in writing this.

144   Unfriendly or ignorant audiences, 1748

Johann Friedrich Schönemann, *Schönemannische Schaubühne*, vol. 2 (Brunswick & Leipzig, 1748). Reproduced in Hans Devrient, *Johann Friedrich Schönemann und seine Schauspielerge-sellschaft* (J.L.S. and his Company of Actors) (Hamburg/Leipzig: TGF 11, 1895), pp. 147–9.

My preface shall contain nothing beyond a few justified reproaches and complaints about the mighty obstacles by which the German theatre is still oppressed. My own experiences in the nine years in which I have endeavoured to the very best of my ability, as the manager of a company of actors, to lead my fellow countrymen towards a purified taste in plays, being the most excellent, agreeable and useful products of wit, have given me the right, as the sole outcome of all my efforts, to grumble about my native land. [...]

Schönemann lists three 'prejudices which seem as it were to have conspired against the improvement of German theatre':

[…] the commonest of these is: whatever I do not understand is no good. So-called polite society is so strange and ignorant in what should actually constitute its politeness and forms the culture of our neighbours, viz. poetry, eloquence and drama, that it cannot understand how it is possible to take any delight in such matters. […] People of that sort laugh when they see their neighbour weeping at Zaïre.[1] […] In short, they conclude: I feel nothing in the playhouse, I take no pleasure in it. Hence the playhouse must be a thing of no worth. […]

The French theatre has acquired so many advantages over ours by virtue of time, practice, good fortune, nature and [the favour of] monarchs that we shall never be so impudent as to put ourselves on the same level with it. Those true teachers of wit and good taste who have visited it in their travels have had the goodness to instruct us by reporting the perfections of the theatre of Paris to us. They improve us. […] While we can never sufficiently exalt and venerate such well-wishers, we are bound to complain about those Frenchified Germans whose good fortune of having been to France is a veritable misfortune for the German stage. They have been to see plays in Paris because there you are not considered well bred unless you go to the theatre. […] They return home. They no longer feel any external pressure to go to the theatre. It is not the general fashion [here]: and if one does go, one does not pay such unwavering attention […] as would inspire the actor […] and force the least sensitive of spectators to applaud. Consequently they come out as cold as when they went in. So in order to demonstrate the experience they have supposedly brought back from Paris, they will pronounce: The German theatre is not worth anything, never will be worth anything and is incapable of being worth anything. It is not French. Since people are in awe of anybody who has been abroad, these oppressors of the German stage are accounted so many oracles. […]

Even more damaging for us is the prejudice which some moralists are labouring hard to instil in their listeners. – There are still some respected theologians who declare plays to be sinful and who thereby hold back the coming of dawn in the arts. […] It is due to their merciless condemnations that clever young people who devote themselves to the theatre are from time to time most cruelly persecuted and contemned for this by their parents, their relatives and other stubborn and ignorant people. But how many clever people are not thus kept from the stage! How are they not suppressed, and how much are not the pleasure and honour of our nation suppressed at the same time!

[1] Tragedy by Voltaire (1732).

In his comedy, *Die Komödianten in Quirlequitsch* (The Actors in Quirlequitsch), premièred in 1785 but written in the early 1770s, Brandes ridiculed (among other things) the blindly pro-French bias of the German aristocracy in matters of taste. The author admitted in his preface that by the time the play was published, his satirical shafts were somewhat wide of the mark. – In this scene, a backwoods aristocrat is discussing with his wife and daughter the arrival of a troupe of German strolling players.

145   Aristocratic contempt for German theatre, 1770s

Johann Christian Brandes, *Die Komödianten in Quirlequitsch* in *Sämtliche dramatische Schriften* (Complete Dramatic Works), vol. 8 (Hamburg: Dycksche Buchhandlung, 1791), pp. 24–6

ADELGUNDE I hear, dear Papa, that the players who have arrived here will be putting on a perfectly splendid play today.

[...]

BARONESS [...] I have heard of those people but I don't know very much about them. Are they French or Italian?

ADELGUNDE They are Germans, dear Mama.

BARONESS (ASTONISHED) Germans?

[...]

BARON German actors?

ADELGUNDE Yes, dear Papa!

BARON Whoever gave those fellows permission to come here to Quirlequitsch?

ADELGUNDE Unless I mistake, dear Papa, it was you granted them permission via the justice.

BARON So I did – but those were puppeteers, not actors.

ADELGUNDE They are the same people. Sometimes they perform plays with live human beings.[1]

BARON German actors! I just will not have any such riffraff sneaking in here! Anyone with the least courtly pretensions in Germany keeps, if not an opera, at any rate a French company!

ADELGUNDE A few years ago that was indeed the fashion, dear Papa; but nowadays ...

BARON (IGNORING HER) It would give the ancient house of Quirlequitsch a fine reputation if we were said to have such low taste as to keep a German company! Everybody would think we couldn't afford any foreigners.

[1] Compare 37 and 92.

It is only fair to point out that in the last quarter of the eighteenth century there was a growing body of opinion demanding – partly for reasons of financial policy, partly on national grounds – that the German theatre should feature German plays and employ

German actors. The following article in a theatrical magazine is typical of the arguments being put forward with greater and greater urgency at the time. (See also **167**, **170**, **174**, **197**, **199**.)

146   An argument in favour of German theatre, 1777

G. (G.W.F. Grossmann?), 'National = Theater, einmal ökonomisch betrachtet', (National Theatre, just seen from an economic point of view), in *TJD*, 3 (1777), pp. 59–60

The Minister of Finance says: that country is rich which hangs on to its money, or at most imports as many foreign products as it exports of its domestic products; that country is richer which exports more of its domestic than it consumes foreign products. The Finance Minister need not be a Colbert[1] to see that; [...] and yet many a country consumes more by way of foreign [...] actors and opera singers than it exports of its own products. There are, thank heaven, not too many instances of a grand opera and a corps de ballet ruining a principality, but they do occur. However, the instances are common enough of forty, fifty thousand and more dollars being spent on a foreign company of actors, the bulk of which leaves the country, because the Italian *en mangeant ses maccaroni* and the Frenchman, *en mangeant son morceau de bouilli*, assuredly do not consume in Germany a third of the pensions granted them so generously in preference to German talent [...]. The proof of this is obvious; where has an Italian, a Frenchman settled down after having filled his gut with German beef and German wine and collected German money, where? He goes back to his own country and takes German money with him. [...] So how many German dollars must be leaving Germany, in view of the masses of foreign actors in Germany, for which we receive no compensation. Ah yes, says the financier, where there are grand spectacles, foreigners are attracted who consume their money here; let me concede this although I have but rarely seen any lords, marchesi and comtes at our carnivals; but why on earth should not these grand spectacles be German or these foreigners not be attracted by German drama? Mannheim proves that we can have great German opera, great German ballets danced by Germans; a great many good German companies prove that we can have good German plays.[2] In truth there is no lack of German brains, of German talent! But most of our nobility think about drama as our ladies think about fashion.

---

[1] Jean Baptiste Colbert (1619–83) reformed French government finance as controller-general under Louis XIV.

[2] The Elector Palatine and Elector of Bavaria Charles Theodore (1724–99) was a great patron of all the theatrical arts in Mannheim; he founded the Mannheim National Theatre in the year this article was published.

The theological attacks on the theatre mentioned by Schönemann (see **144**) were nothing new: compare the polemics against the widow Velten by the clergymen Fuhrmann (1729 – see **36**) and Johann Joseph Winckler (1701 – see Niessen, 1940). Such attacks were expressions of a deep and recurrent Protestant distrust of play-acting as morally reprehensible, indeed the work of the Devil. (For similar sentiments in the Netherlands, see **303**.) In 1681, a vigorous polemic had been launched in Hamburg against all theatrical spectacles including opera by the Rev. Anton Reiser's *Theatromania*. Note that in the following decade there was a similar puritanical attack on theatre in England during the Jeremy Collier controversy which began in 1698 – see David Thomas (ed.), *TIE: Restoration and Georgian England, 1660–1788* (CUP, 1989), pp. 189–92. Nearly a century later, there was to be a repeat performance of anti-theatrical pamphleteering in Hamburg, initiated this time by the Rev. J. Melchior Goeze, better known to literary history for his theological disputations with Lessing in the late 1770s. When the play, *Der Zweikampf* (The Duel) by Schlosser, a probationer for the ministry, was performed, Goeze attacked him as well as the theatre in general in a pamphlet, the long-winded title of which encapsulated his argument: *Theologische Untersuchung der Sittlichkeit der heutigen deutschen Schaubühne, überhaupt: wie auch der Fragen: Ob ein Geistlicher, insonderheit ein wirklich im Prediger-Amte stehender Mann, ohne ein schweres Aergernis zu geben, die Schaubühne besuchen, selbst Comödien schreiben, aufführen und drucken lassen, und die Schaubühne, so wie sie itzo ist, vertheidigen, und als einen Tempel der Tugend, als eine Schule der edlen Empfindungen, und der guten Sitten, anpreisen könne?* (Theological Investigation of the Morality of the Contemporary German Stage in general, as well as of the Questions whether a Minister, especially an Ordained Preacher, may without causing grave Offence visit the Theatre, write Plays and have them performed and printed, and defend the Stage as it is now constituted and praise it as a Temple of Virtue, as a School of Noble Sentiments and Sound Morals) (Hamburg: J. Christian Brandt, 1770). While the second part of this pamphlet was directed specifically at Schlosser, the first denounced what Goeze considered a corrupting repertoire – and this at a time when German authors were already producing original plays of real merit; indeed shortly after the (admittedly ignominious) end of the ambitious local attempt to found the first National Theatre, with Lessing as its dramaturg (see **170**).

147   Theological opposition to playgoing: Goeze, 1769–70

Goeze (1770), pp. 22–4. BL 11794 d. 17

If we ask for proof of this innocence, purity and great usefulness ascribed to today's theatre, we are referred to the plays of a Schlegel, Gellert, Lessing, Cronegk and Weisse.[1] [...]

Finding myself among the opponents, I must candidly confess that I object to this proof so strongly that I dismiss it as altogether invalid. I propose at a later stage to investigate more closely one play or another by these famous authors. However, let me concede for the moment that these may, broadly considered, be acceptable and useful. But can any sure conclusion be drawn from these as to the overall character and constitution of today's theatre? Is it solely, is it primarily these plays that are staged? Is there not reason to fear that the *comic afterpieces*, that the *mimes* which invariably conclude the show will altogether wipe out of the spectators' minds the few feeble impressions made by the exhibition of a play which complacent criticism may deem morally beneficial? Only today I looked in passing at a posted-up playbill; it first announced the principal play to be performed which was called *Das Caffeehaus* [The Coffeeshop], followed by a mime: *Doctor Faust* [Doctor Faustus].[2] Yesterday they showed Herr von Cronegk's *Codrus*, and the mime was *Der Triumph des Harlekins* [The Triumph of Harlequin].[3] The first play, *Das Caffeehaus*, I know nothing about, and I do not begrudge *Codrus* the praise bestowed on it by experts; but I fail to see what the two *mimes* are supposed to contribute to elevating the minds of citizens, to broadening their sympathies, to improving their morals. I have never actually seen things of that sort but I cannot imagine them to be anything other than a kind of wanton feast for the eyes, the very title justifying such a supposition. Whether or not they strike a good many offensive postures in these displays, whether or not they might by some positions and postures cause the spectators to entertain such notions as cannot be put into words without extreme immodesty, I must leave to the judgement of those who have witnessed these things with their own eyes. [...] My conscience, my office and my character do not permit me to be a spectator at these affairs myself, and I have other business on my hands than trying to collect playbills [...]. But I believe I have sufficient grounds for maintaining that the number of plays which should be condemned on the basis of merely rational, not to mention Christian, morality but which are nevertheless performed constantly with the highest applause, far exceeds the few good ones, and that all *mimes*, *comic afterpieces* and *dances* are calculated to leave none but harmful impressions in the minds of spectators.

---

[1] Johann Elias Schlegel (1719–49), uncle of the more famous authors, August Wilhelm and Friedrich Schlegel, wrote historical tragedies (*Hermann, Canut*), comedies and critical essays. Christian Fürchtegott Gellert (1715–69) was the author of fables, moral treatises and hymns as well as some comedies and a treatise in defence of sentimental comedy, *De comoedia commovente*. Gotthold Ephraim Lessing (1729–81) had already written *Miss Sara Sampson* (1755) and *Minna von Barnhelm* (1767) by the time of Goeze's pamphlet. Johann Friedrich von Cronegk (1731–58) was the author of *Codrus* and the unfinished *Olint und Sophronia*, both of which figured in the repertoire of the Hamburg National Theatre. Christian Felix Weisse (1726–1804) wrote versions of *Richard III* and *Romeo and Juliet*, as well as some very successful operettas.
[2] *Das Caffeehaus, oder die Schottländerin* (The Coffeeshop, or The Scotswoman): J.J. Bode's translation of Voltaire's *L'Écossaise* (1760). For the persistence of the Faust theme in the German repertoire, compare **29, 58**, p. 288.
[3] See note 1 for *Codrus*.

Goeze's immoderate attack on the theatre, though no doubt echoing the views of many religious zealots and perhaps successful in keeping some people away from the theatre, did not fail to draw speedy replies. The ensuing polemical exchanges, to which the Hamburg Council finally put a stop by taking Schlosser's part, have been listed in Christian Heinrich Schmid, *Chronologie des deutschen Theaters* (Chronology of the German Theatre) (Leipzig: Dyck, 1775), pp. 293–294; reproduced in a new edition by Paul Legband (Berlin: SGTG 1, 1902), pp. 185–6. See also Heinrich Alt, *Theater und Kirche in ihrem gegenseitigen Verhältniss historisch dargestellt* (Theatre and Church shown historically in their mutual relationship) (Berlin, Verlag der Plahnschen Buchhandlung, 1846), pp. 638–44.

A Hamburg professor of rhetoric, Johann Hinrich Vincent Nölting, a vigorous defender of Schlosser and the theatre in general, wrote as many as three anti-Goeze pamphlets.

148   Reply to Goeze: playgoing is morally acceptable, 1769

J.H.V. Nölting, *Vertheidigung des Hrn.Past.Schlossers wider einen Angriff, etc.* (Defence of the Rev. Schlosser against an Attack etc.) (second augmented ed., Hamburg: Dieterich Anton Harmsen, 1769), p. 16. DTM 4278

[. . .] So to visit the playhouse and to visit it often is no disgrace for anybody [. . .]. For here in Hamburg all sensible people, and in fact the majority of those who pass judgment on probationers, at least know our plays from [so favourable] an aspect that they cannot find anything improper in a probationer going to see them.

Although Gottsched had had some influence on opinion as an advocate of a respectable German theatre, the German academic establishment continued to frown on the performance of plays as being at best a waste of time. The enthusiasm of Christian Heinrich Schmid (1746–1800), Professor of Rhetoric and Poetry at the University of Giessen, for all things theatrical (he wrote *Chronologie des deutschen Theaters*, the second history of the German theatre after Löwen's) involved him in a good many difficulties with the academic authorities. The following excerpt from Brandes' autobiography illustrates anti-theatrical prejudices among academics even at a time when German theatre was coming to be more widely recognised as a culturally valuable institution. The actors referred to were Abel Seyler's company (see **72**, note 2) who were visiting the town of Wetzlar (Hessen) in the summer of 1771. Though Schmid won this particular battle with the university authorities he found himself in hot water again in 1778 when he promoted student drama in a special university theatre: this activity was banned after the fourth performance.

149   Academic hostility to actors, 1771

Brandes, *Meine Lebensgeschichte*, vol. 2 (1800), p. 134

A short time after our arrival at Wetzlar my friend Schmidt [*sic*] wrote a very flattering poem in praise of the outstanding members of the company, entitled:

The Appearance. The Rector of the University of Giessen took it very much amiss that a lecturer at this institution had so much desecrated his pen as to eulogise a troupe of actors passing through, and he started legal proceedings against the author of the poem in Darmstadt; the latter, however, paid no attention to the proceedings but, whenever his duties permitted, made brief excursions over to Wetzlar in order to have the pleasure of getting to know even better one of the best companies of actors in Germany.

After some time, as expected, the rector's case was dismissed by order of the Landgrave of Hesse-Darmstadt, and Schmidt [sic] could now write whatever he pleased about the theatre.

B. AUDIENCE ATTITUDES AND BEHAVIOUR; AUDIENCE
REGULATIONS

The commercial theatre naturally depended on the whims of the paying audience; not so the court theatre where, at any rate up to the middle of the century, admission was often free for invited guests of the sovereign. These would be drawn either from court circles or from a somewhat larger but still select section of the public. The following example from the diary of a highly placed official at the Imperial Court in Vienna illustrates the link between the life of the court and stage entertainments.

150   Free admission to Court opera in Vienna, 12 May 1743

Rudolf Graf Khevenhüller-Metsch & Dr. Hanns Schlitter, *Aus der Zeit Maria Theresias. Tagebuch des Fürsten Johann Josef Khevenhüller-Metsch, Kaiserlichen Oberhofmeisters 1742– 1776. vol. 1: 1742–1744* (In the Days of Maria Theresa. Diary of Prince J.J. Khevenhüller-Metsch, Controller-in-Chief of the Imperial Household 1742–1776) (Vienna: Adolf Holzhausen, 1907), p. 146

After dinner Her Majesty withdrew to her drawingroom in the same order as before and wearing the crown, and in the evening towards 6 o'clock, an entirely new opera was performed in the theatre erected by the Viennese impresario Selliers[1] in the royal tennis-court by the palace garden, where his company performs both operas and plays every week, and everybody was admitted free of charge at the expense of the Court.

[1] The entrepreneur Joseph Karl Selliers, together with Francesco Borosini, held a twenty-year monopoly on play performances in Vienna from 1728 onwards. He combined supervision of the Kärntnertortheater (see 68) on a purely commercial basis with the installation, in 1741, as well as the running of what was later to become the Burgtheater (see 71). There he had to provide a daily programme of plays and operas for the Court, but he obtained the right to charge admission prices for public performances in the same venue when it was not used by the Court.

Unlike the invited guests at court performances, paying audiences in the commercial theatre were unconstrained by any considerations of decorum. While university authorities often took a censorious line to theatre as such, the attitude of students was often objectionable in a different way. Their presence there was not an unmixed blessing, as Schönemann reported in the preface to volume III of the *Schönemannische Schaubühne*: both their boorish conduct and their intellectual inadequacy are described as appalling.

151   The boorishness of student audiences, 1749

Schönemannische Schaubühne, vol. 3 (1749). Reproduced in H. Devrient (1895), pp. 158–9

Among all the spectators who have honoured me by attending my plays I have seen none more ill-mannered than those at the universities where I have put up my stage, only Leipzig which is distinguished for its polished manners making an exception. [. . .] Without having seen it himself, who can imagine people in Germany so far forgetting all respect for themselves, for a large gathering, for the womenfolk present and for the best products of wit, as most impudently to pour out tobacco smoke all over the playhouse, to drive whole clouds of it onto the stage and to envelop the performers in it? [. . .] Their other manners can be deduced clearly enough from this behaviour. [. . .]

The following examples will give further powerful proof of their ignorance concerning things of the mind. The performance of Corneille's *Cinna* at some universities has caused many pittites to speculate whether *Cinna* should be called a tragedy or a comedy; the performance of *The Miser* why Harpagon, being represented with a small beard, should be a Jew and not a Christian. You might have spent a few years at university and still wonder after a performance of M. Voltaire's *Mahomet* whether this was the story as it really happened among the Romans.[1]

Absurd as these anecdotes are, they are true and at the same time terrible for someone who would like to be proud of his country, even in matters of taste. But Germany will not change its neighbours' notion that nature has deprived her children of wit until all her pedants begin to set aside their philological probings and their rote learning in favour of the nobler, more fruitful and intellectual sciences.

---

[1] Note the prevalence of translations from the French in the Schönemann repertoire, as in that of other companies with some literary pretensions.

Often enough the attitude of students to actors and particularly actresses was objectionable in a different way – overly familiar rather than hostile, as Brandes relates in describing the same theatrical tour as above (**149**).

152   Obnoxious student attitudes towards actors and actresses, 1771

Brandes (1800), pp. 132–3

On this occasion I took no small pleasure [. . .] in seeing Göttingen too; however, immediately on entering it, my joy and the high expectation I had cherished of the place and its academic denizens was taken down several notches; for we had barely reached the gate when several students, probably just emerging from a lecture, came hurrying alongside the carriage with their lorgnettes to inspect us. 'Quite a pretty phiz!' cried one. Quick as lightning a couple of these madcaps jumped onto the steps of the coach in order to view my female companions at close quarters; others pulled them away in order to satisfy their curiosity in turn, and so we arrived at last at an inn. I ordered a meal for my family since it was lunch-time, and asked the landlord for a private room where we could lunch undisturbed, and indeed we were at once shown into one; but we kept open table just the same, because at every moment somebody would open the door of the room, peek in and after a few words of apology about mistaking the room, slam it shut again. Some of the most forward of these young people pushed their rudeness even further, coming in with their tobacco pipes and with their hats on, walking up and down a few times as if looking for somebody, eyeing us in turn, whispering their comments in one another's ears and then decamping to make way for others. I was thoroughly glad when the post-horses came at last and I readily abandoned my intention of calling on some professors for whom I had letters of introduction, only to make my escape with my family.

Strasbourg, which was then part of France as it is again today, was considered hospitable to German actors, at any rate in the first half of the eighteenth century. The fact that the coexistence of French and German companies favoured rather than harmed the latter at the time is made clear in a letter written by Johann Neuber from Strasbourg to his mentor Professor Gottsched in Leipzig. (This state of affairs does not seem to have obtained later in the century when no permanent German company was allowed there: see *Theater-Journal für Deutschland*, 5 (1778), pp. 92–3.)

153   Favourable performance conditions in Strasbourg, 1736

Reden-Esbeck (1881), pp. 200–1

Most Noble, Most Learned,
Most Reverend Sir and Patron,

[. . .] We are now living under the protection of the King of France who has been so gracious as to allow us to perform in this city. We are doing well, thanks be to God, and all we lack is a good supply of tragedies.[1] We have had a good reception for four weeks, performing every day although it was Advent. The French players perform here three times a week, but we play every day. [. . .] The leading citizens often come to see us, glad that the Germans, too, are following their nation in this respect. [. . .] Strasbourg has two playhouses, we play in the one, the French in the other one in the Horse Fair: both can be heated in the current winter weather. [. . .] Many Frenchmen who do not understand a word of German came and watched very attentively. The officers of the hussars as well as other officers are more polite than I can say, quite unlike our German officers. The *Lieutenant du Roy M. Trelans* has given us a guard of four men with the exceedingly strict command to keep a close eye on any drunks or servants or anyone else who is about to make a noise and to remove them from the playhouse forthwith. Also, no person whatsoever is permitted to cause an uproar or the slightest disorder at the entrance, either on account of the price of admission or the seats, and anyone resisting a soldier runs the risk of being shot down on the spot or at any rate of being arrested. It is a different state of affairs here from that in our country, and in view of such good arrangements it is no wonder that the French players are doing so well. [. . .]

I am My Most Noble and Highly Revered Master's

and Patron's

Obedient and Grateful Servant,

Johann Neuber.

Strasbourg, 24th December 1736.

---

[1] For a part of their theatrical career the Neubers looked to Gottsched for the supply of 'regular' drama (in the main translations from the French) – from their first arrival in Leipzig in 1727, throughout their travels to various parts of Germany, France and Russia, until the final breach in 1741 between them and their patron.

Nearly fifteen years later, when the Ackermann troupe visited Strasbourg, Karoline Schulze-Kummerfeld, a member of the company, reported that audiences there were still as perceptive and as keen on theatre, both in French and in German.

154   The exemplary nature of Strasbourg audiences, 1759–60

Karoline Schulze-Kummerfeld, in *MBGDKL*, vol. 3, no. 3 (June 1828), pp. 202–3. Herzog-August-Bibliothek, Wolfenbüttel, Sign.Wd 567 i

Strasbourg was an excellent place in those days for the formation of actors. There was no audience as discriminating as that of Strasbourg, regardless of whether its applause or disapproval was targeted at the author, the director or the actor. It was not customary at the time to have the actors named on the playbill. Now if a play familiar to the public was presented, the public would cast it in their own minds. If this turned out as expected, the actor on entering would be welcomed with applause, if the opposite was true they did not take it out on the actor since he had to play the role he was given, but they made the director aware of their feelings. If the director or a member of his family had an unsuitable role, no matter how hard they tried they would not be rewarded with the slightest sign of approbation, which they might obtain that very evening if they appeared in an afterpiece or the principal play, and spectators wanted them to understand, here you are in your right place. Young budding talents were encouraged but not spoilt, and they were clapped only when they deserved it; nay, the most minor role was rewarded by applause if it was played properly. Even the public's favourite was not excused poor memorising or any sloppiness in dress, manner and deportment; in short, it was an audience as it ought to be. At the same time there was an opportunity of seeing the French company who were excellent in the spoken drama [. . .]

155   Audience behaviour in different cities compared, 1779

'Sincerus' (pseudonym), 'Fragment aus dem Tagebuch eines Reisenden' (Pages from a Traveller's Diary), in *LTZ*, no. 17 (20 November 1779), pp. 739–40

Since I happen to be talking about audiences, I must confess that those of Hamburg, Gotha, Berlin and Dresden are in respect of taste as well as silence and attention the best among those I have seen. In Leipzig they allow themselves to be guided by intrigue. People knock,[1] people clap, people may whistle at times, all according to how many supporters are sitting in the stalls, often perhaps even egged on by very famous actors. The best members are so disgusted that they are forced either to choose another theatre or live in constant irritation. [. . .] I would earnestly advise the Frankfurt audience to be more calm and quiet. There is no end of noise, whispering and chattering. In the first play I saw I did not catch twenty words of the first act. Here a lady was fanning herself with an almighty fan, there a few others were chattering about some pretty watch-charms they had bought at the Fair. Now a scented young gentleman comes along to unburden himself of his news, then others pound [the floor] with their canes for silence. 'But for heaven's sake,' my neighbour said to me, 'why do people go to the theatre, if all they want to do is chat?' I ground my teeth and said nothing.

[1] A traditional sign of audience disapproval.

The habit of spectators having access to the stage was an unfortunate fact of theatrical life in eighteenth-century Germany as it was in England and France. (See David Thomas, *TIE: Restoration and Georgian England* (CUP, 1989), p. 268, for Garrick's banning spectators from the Drury Lane stage in 1762.) When Koch opened the Leipzig Theater auf der

Ranstädter Bastei (see **65**) with a performance of J.E. Schlegel's *Hermann*, the playbill contained the following request to put a stop to this deplorable custom.

156   Spectators banished from the Leipzig stage, 10 October 1766

Playbill for J.E. Schlegel's *Hermann*, performed by the Electoral Saxon Court Actors. Reproduced in *M & K*, 14 (1968), p. 230

I am obliged to beseech you to be so good as to put up in future with not being allowed access to the stage while a performance is in progress, since the cramped space as well as the machinery will not permit this, there being several scene changes which might be hindered or cause some damage; and since furthermore the narrow space must for the time being be used as a dressing-room.

10 October 1766   Heinrich Gottfried Koch

In the latter years of the eighteenth century, conditions inside the permanent theatres became more orderly and disciplined. F.L. Schröder was as exemplary in front-of-house management as he was in backstage arrangements (see **73 & 90**). In 1786, when he took over the Hamburg theatre for the second time, he published an announcement in which, among other things, he spelt out his view of the proper role of the audience.

157   Schröder's audience regulations in Hamburg, April 1786

Anon., 'Aus Hamburg vom 16.April 1786' (News from Hamburg of 16 April 1786), in *ELT*, vol. 3, no. 17 (29 April 1786), pp. 270–1. DTM Per 81 (3,4)

[...] It will now depend on your support and your approbation, patrons, friends and fellow citizens, whether I shall devote my endeavours to you for all time or leave it to someone else to provide this sort of entertainment for you. I promise you good order, the strictest morality and as much costly display as the number of theatre patrons permits. You will never be put under contribution by any sort of begging. Neither your approbation nor your money will be wheedled out of you by means of large posters or prologues of any kind [...]. – Help me bear the costs by your frequent attendance; encourage the actors by your indulgence and appro-bation; help to establish the necessary good order and morality by yourselves suppressing the old habit (banished from every good theatre in Europe) of being more often behind the scenes and in the dressing-rooms than in the stalls. [...] – I most urgently request all patrons to order their servants to observe orderly conduct in the playhouse. Spectators in the gallery have been upset by them repeatedly. Such behaviour might oblige me to cancel all free admission for servants. – Half-price admissions for children were introduced a few years ago – I can agree to this only if the tickets are collected from my home. At the box-office only the standard price will be paid so as to protect me from fraud. – In order to spare anyone the embarrassment of being turned away I hereby announce that all previous free admissions have been cancelled and that nobody will be allowed in without a ticket.

During Goethe's direction of the Weimar theatre, his personal prestige ensured that the audience was extraordinarily well behaved. Spectators did of course appreciate the remarkable cultural efforts he was making on their behalf; but undoubtedly his sheer presence could exert an intimidating influence on the house, as the following incident, reported by several witnesses, illustrates. The occasion was the performance on 29 May 1802 of the verse tragedy *Alarkos* by Friedrich von Schlegel, a play which vanished without a trace after its unhappy Weimar première.

158   Goethe attempts to manipulate the Weimar audience, 29 May 1802

Q. (Martyni-Laguna), review of *Alarkos* in *Neue allgemeine Deutsche Bibliothek* (New General Germany Library) (Berlin & Stettin, 1802), vol. 74, no. 2, pp. 356-62. Reproduced in Julius W. Braun, *Goethe im Urtheile seiner Zeitgenossen*, vol. 3: 1802–1812 (1885), pp. 9–10

A highly trustworthy letter from Weimar reports the following concerning the performance of this play:

Herr v. Goethe [. . .] is alleged to have seated himself in his special armchair in the front stalls, as he has tended to do on other occasions, and now and then to have given the signal for applause by raising his hand, but the applause somehow never quite materialised. However, respect for *Jupiter tonans*[1] had [. . .] at least kept mouths from opening for laughter. But when Ricardo uttered the words:

For fear of dying he did die indeed!

there was a loud burst of laughter throughout the house. My correspondent asserts that at this moment Goethe furiously leapt up from his armchair and, turning towards the assembly with arms outstretched, exclaimed, 'Hush! hush! let nobody laugh!', whereupon the laughter did not indeed cease altogether but at any rate died down a little. We hope for the sake of a very famous poet that at least the latter part of the anecdote did not happen just like that.[2] [. . .] In any case rumour has it [. . .] that the *Journal des Luxus und der Moden* was about to publish a very mild criticism of the tragedy *Ion* by Herr A.W. Schlegel which was performed in Weimar, penned furthermore by a man who cannot be denied the ability and the competence to pronounce judgement on a tragedy which is clearly an imitation of a Greek play.[3] This criticism, it is alleged, was taken away from the printer's on Herr von Goethe's order and in its place a *favourable review* of Ion written by Herr von Goethe was inserted, it being announced at the same time that news of the Weimar theatre in the *Journal des Luxus und der Moden* would henceforth be supplied by the *management*, i.e. by Herr von Goethe. We again trust for Herr von Goethe's sake that it is not the case that he has pushed vanity and partisanship to the point of forbidding the Weimar stalls to laugh at a patent absurdity and to forbid a writer to judge a play performed in Weimar in the pages of the *Journal des Luxus und der Moden* according to his conviction.

[1] Latin: Thundering Jove.
[2] Unfortunately there is corroborative evidence that the event did take place as described, e.g. in Henriette von Egloffstein's *Erinnerungen* (Memoirs) – see Carlson (1978), pp. 176–8.
[3] The brothers August Wilhelm and Friedrich Schlegel (1767–1845 and 1772–1829 respectively), the leading spokesmen of the romantic movement, are remembered more as literary theorists and as Orientalists than as creative dramatists; August Wilhelm's greatest contribution to the German theatre was his translation of Shakespeare. The performance at Goethe's insistence of *Ion* on 2 January 1802 was no more successful than the somewhat later performance of *Alarcos*. On the former occasion, too, Goethe used his authority to silence unseemly laughter among the spectators. It is also a fact that Goethe did exert direct influence on the *Journal des Luxus und der Moden* (Journal of Luxury and Fashion), a magazine published in Weimar by Friedrich Justin Bertuch; the suppressed review in question was by Karl August Böttiger, a perceptive though argumentative critic (see 208, 211–13). For Goethe's interventions, see Carlson (1978), pp. 165–8.

XIV Repertoire, National Theatres, dramatic theory and criticism

A. REPERTOIRE

In contrast to the theatres of England, France and Spain, early eighteenth-century German theatre did not have a national body of drama to serve as the bedrock of a classical repertoire. The literary drama of the previous century – such as the plays by the Silesian School of Gryphius, Lohenstein and Hallmann – did not feature prominently in the performances of strolling players. There was no German equivalent to the writings of Shakespeare, Jonson or Fletcher, of Corneille, Racine or Molière, of Lope de Vega or Calderón, which continued to form a substantial part of the later repertoire in their respective countries and to serve as a touchstone for new productions. German courts were on the whole satisfied with foreign offerings, whether presented by foreign or native actors. The German popular repertoire was a heterogeneous mixture of borrowings or adaptations from France, England, Holland, Italy and Spain on the one hand or of native offerings of slight literary merit, often sensational or broadly farcical in character, on the other. So the theatre was caught in a vicious circle: there was hardly any indigenous drama which combined high literary quality with popular appeal, and this lack held back the development of the actors; conversely the generally low status and inadequate craftsmanship of the actors made writing plays for professional production an unattractive proposition for potential dramatic authors. It was in this context that Professor Gottsched of Leipzig decided, from the security of a highly respected academic position, to bring the German theatre up to the level of other Western nations by providing it with a rational and morally elevated drama.

159 The inadequacy of the German repertoire, 1724

Gottsched, Preface to *Der sterbende Cato* (The Death of Cato) (Leipzig: Teubners Buchladen, 1732), pp. 3–4. Reproduced in *DNL*, 42, Johannes Crüger (ed.), *Joh. Christoph Gottsched und die Schweizer J.J. Bodmer und J.J. Breitinger* (Berlin & Stuttgart: W. Speemann, 1882), pp. 43–4, and *J.C.G., Ausgewählte Werke* (J.C.G., Selected Works), ed. Joachim Birke (Berlin: Walter de Gruyter and Co., 1970), vol. 2, pp. 5–6

Although I had ready enough access to reading Molière, I nevertheless had no opportunity at home of seeing a tragedy or a comedy performed which my reading had made me exceedingly eager to do.[1] So I had to forgo this pleasure until I came to Leipzig in 1724 and had an opportunity there of seeing the licensed Dresden

court players perform.[2] Since the latter only visited here during the time of the Fair
I hardly missed [seeing] a single play that was new to me. Although I thus satisfied
my longing at first, I soon came to realise the great confusion in which this theatre
was entangled. Nothing was to be seen there but fustian political melodramas
mixed up with Harlequin entertainments, unnatural romances and love intrigues, vulgar farces and obscenities. The only good play performed was The
Quarrel between Honour and Love, or Rodrigue and Chimène, though merely
translated into prose.[3] Now this pleased me, as may easily be imagined, better
than any of the rest and showed me in the most striking manner the great
difference between a proper drama and an irregular play of the most curious
complications.

Now here I seized the occasion to strike up an acquaintance with the then
manager of the company and to talk to him occasionally about how better to
organise his theatre. I asked him in particular why Andreas Gryphius' tragedies,
as well as his Horribilicribrifax etc. were not performed.[4] The answer was that he
had indeed staged the former in the past; but now that was no longer feasible. No
one would want to see such verse dramas any longer, especially as they were too
solemn and did not feature any jester.[5] I therefore advised him to attempt another
verse play and promised to make an attempt myself.

[1] Gottsched was a native of Königsberg (now Kaliningrad) in East Prussia, from which he had to flee to
Leipzig in order to escape the attentions of Prussian recruiters.
[2] I.e. the company of Karl Ludwig Hoffmann (see 113, note 4).
[3] This refers to Pierre Corneille's Le Cid (1637), a popular play on the German stage ever since it had
been translated in 1650 by Johann Georg Greflinger (c. 1600–77) – the first German translation of
any French tragedy. This version in alexandrines must have been spoken as prose by Hoffmann's
troupe.
[4] The plays of the leading playwright of the Silesian School, Andreas Gryphius (1616–1664) – his real
name of Greif was Latinised into this form – had been intended for performance by Protestant schools
rather than professional, i.e. strolling, players. Nevertheless, his tragedies did feature in professional
repertoires from time to time: for instance Papinian, a tragedy of state, was performed by Treu's
company at Schleissheim (Bavaria) in 1685 and by Velten's company in Torgau (Saxony) in 1690.
But by the second decade of the eighteenth century popular taste had turned against such baroque
tragedies. Gryphius' Horribilicribrifax, a miles gloriosus type of comedy, did not achieve the long-
lasting success of his farce, Herr Peter Squentz (see 51).
[5] For the insertion of clown (i.e. Harlequin or Hanswurst) scenes into 'serious' drama, see 52 & 57).

The claim that the older German plays were no longer theatrically viable was confirmed in
a letter written to Gottsched by a correspondent of his in Silesia, precisely the part of the
country where much of this literary drama had originated.

160   Gryphius no longer in the theatrical repertoire, 1733

Letter by Abraham Gottlob Rosenberg from Herrendorf to Gottsched, 17 April 1733.
Reproduced in Reden-Esbeck (1881), p. 250

I cannot give you any particular news concerning the theatre in Breslau since I live at some distance away from it. But that much I can say that, since they have been performing operas there for a number of years, this perverted taste has been highly prevalent among the nobility … […] The tragedies of Gryphius have become altogether unknown and, as far as I can establish, have not been performed publicly for a long time except in several schools.

The chosen instrument for Gottsched's reform plans in the first instance was the company run by Johann and Karoline Neuber (see **59–60, 63, 113–14, 163–5**).

161   Frau Neuber banishes Harlequin from the stage, Leipzig, 1737

Johann Friedrich Löwen, *Geschichte des deutschen Theaters* in *J.F.L.'s Schriften*, vol. 4 (Hamburg: Michael Christian Bock, 1766), pp. 28–9. Reproduced in Stümcke (1905), pp. 30–1

[…] Gottsched was mightily prejudiced against this innocent creature;[1] and he showed *Frau Neuber* that the rules of good taste would not tolerate Harlequin on any well ordered and properly conducted stage. So he counselled her solemnly to banish this malefactor from the theatre. *Frau Neuber* yielded and promised *Herr Gottsched* not only to banish Harlequin but to bury him as well. What a joy for good taste and for *Herr Gottsched*! The day of execution was settled: the dreadful year was 1737, and a booth near Bose's garden in Leipzig was the scaffold on which *Gottsched's* strict sentence on the accused Harlequin was to be carried out.[2] *Mme Neuber* herself arranged the auto-da-fé in a curtain raiser, from which perhaps no one except *Gottsched* anticipated the happiest consequences.[3] However, *Frau Neuber* performed an even greater miracle. She went to Kiel shortly afterwards; there she resurrected the murdered Harlequin in person; for she played the part herself.[4]

---

[1] I.e. Harlequin.

[2] For the location of Frau Neuber's booth, see **63**.

[3] The suggestion of an auto-da-fé is not to be taken too literally. The frequently repeated story of the 'burning' of Harlequin on stage is probably based on a confusion between the words 'verbannt' (banished) and 'verbrannt' (burnt). For a discussion of this, see Kathe Reinholz, *Eduard Devrients 'Geschichte der deutschen Schauspielkunst'* (Berlin: Colloquium Verlag, 1967), pp. 51–2.

[4] After her break with Gottsched, Frau Neuber took great pleasure in flouting his principles in public (see **84, 163–4**).

For all of Professor Gottsched's thunderbolts, Harlequin refused to disappear from the stage. It was not only Frau Neuber who kept him alive: in one guise or another (as Hanswurst, Bernardon or Kasperl) he survived vigorously, particularly in Vienna where the improvisational tradition continued to flourish until its official abolition in 1770. But even in Leipzig, nearly half a century after his formal expulsion from the stage, Harlequin was still haunting the theatre (if not exactly flourishing), as we learn from the following report in a literary/theatrical magazine.

162   Harlequin lives on in Leipzig, 1785

Anon., 'Briefauszüge' (Excerpts from Letters), dated Leipzig, 12 November 1785, in *ELT*, vol. 2, no. 50 (10 December 1785), p. 378. DTM Per 81 (1,2)

[. . .] Now we have Italian comedy here in the taste of the fairground stages of Venice: Harlequin as an aerial spirit, as Skanderbeg, as a tailor's apprentice, as you may see for your further delectation from the enclosed playbills.[1] What do you say to that? Is it not a disgrace that a place like Leipzig has to make do in winter with such a miserable farce? But do not think that this is the taste of the citizens of Leipzig. The theatre is often empty, the maximum takings are 60 to 70 dollars, and only rarely does the manager get, say, 120 or 150 dollars. But occasionally people go there out of pity, since the company are in the greatest misery.

---

[1] In the eighteenth century Harlequin, particularly in the tradition established by the Théâtre Italien in Paris, characteristically went in for numerous disguises. See Allardyce Nicoll, *The World of Harlequin* (CUP, 1963), pp. 175–202. Skanderbeg (1403–68) was the national hero of the Albanians in their fight against Turkish domination.

The Gottsched-Neuber Quarrel

The alliance formed, for the improvement of the German repertoire, between the academic reformer and a company of working actors who had to earn their living by pleasing the public was bound to be unstable. The break came when Gottsched transferred his favour from the Neubers to the newly founded Schönemann company and denigrated his former protégés, whereupon Frau Neuber's previous servility towards the eminent professor turned to gall.

163   Frau Neuber attacks Gottsched from the stage, Leipzig, 18 September 1741

Christian Heinrich Schmid, *Chronologie des deutschen Theaters* (Leipzig: Dyck, 1775), pp. 95–6. Reproduced in *Chronologie des deutschen Theaters*, ed. Paul Legband (Berlin: SGTG 1, 1902), pp. 61–2

Gottsched's vanity was touched to the quick and his hatred now rose to the point of vindictiveness.[1] He was determined henceforth to damage Frau Neuber professionally, and to that end disparaged her in his critical publications as much as he had praised her before, and transferred to other companies the favour he had withdrawn from her. The wrath of the actor is as much to be feared as the wrath of the painter. For the vengeance of either strikes home all the more the wider his influence is. Frau Neuber, seeing that her daily bread was at stake, used the weapons at her command against Gottsched. She, who had written so many curtain-raisers, now penned an allegorical satire entitled: *Der allerkostbarste Schatz* (The Most Precious of All Treasures), and on 18 September of that year she put Gottsched on the stage in the character of The Fault-Finder. The Fault-Finder's very costume was meant to arouse laughter; he was dressed in a starry gown like Night, with bat's wings, he carried a dark-lantern in his hand and wore a sun of gold tinsel on his head. Gottsched had early warning of her intention and managed to have the performance of the curtain-raiser banned by the council. But Frau Neuber was not to be intimidated and applied to Count Brühl who happened to be present at the time.[2] Not only did the performance take place, but it was repeated on 4 October by special permission of the authorities.

[1] Gottsched had felt insulted by Frau Neuber's holding up to ridicule his ideas on costume authenticity. See **84**.

[2] For Count Brühl, see **113**, note 5. The court at Dresden supported opera whereas the spoken drama was favoured by the academic Establishment in Leipzig – a clear conflict of aristocratic versus bourgeois theatrical tastes.

This skit on the literary dictator caused a sensation. In the following year the satirical and pastoral poet Johann Christoph Rost (1717–65), a former protégé of Gottsched's who had turned against his mentor, anonymously wrote a mock epic poem in five cantos, *Das Vorspiel* (The Curtain-Raiser). This lampoon in which he gave a comic description of the famous incident, was first distributed in manuscript, then published in 1742: allegedly as many as 2,000 copies were sold on the first day. When Gottsched had the books confiscated, his enemies in Switzerland published it there in 1743, well out of his reach.

The poem in alexandrines, modelled to some extent on Boileau's *Le lutrin*, was an instant success. It must not, however, be taken as a literal eye-witness account since Rost was in Berlin, not in Leipzig, at the time of the notorious performance. The following lines (670–766) are taken from the Fourth Canto.

164   Frau Neuber's attack on Gottsched celebrated, 1742

Johann Christoph Rost, *Das Vorspiel. Ein Episches Gedicht* (1742; no place of publication or publisher given). Reproduced in *DLD* 142, ed. F. Ulbrich (Berlin, 1910), 3rd series, no. 22, pp. 34–7. Reprinted by Klaus Reprint, Nendeln, Liechtenstein, 1968

The auditorium was crowded, the boxes were full
And only one remained empty – the one kept for Gottsched.

In this respect, too, Frau Neuber merited praise
Because she had reserved the best seat for the author.
She was informed at once of his arrival,
And everything was made ready to begin the show.
The curtain went up, the play commenced.
O Gottsched, would thou hadst not come this time!
The moment Frau Neuber made her entrance as The Art of Acting,
She raised her eye proudly and triumphantly,
As if trying at once to advise her foe
That he should seek safety in speedy flight.
But fate would not allow the professor to escape,
Vanity, Viktoria and Schwabe restrained him.[1]
He thought his prestige would hold them in check,
If not, Corvin's plot would have to take effect.[2]
Alas, the plot was foiled. The Fault-Finder appeared
And Gottsched had to acknowledge to himself: that is I. [...]
Their greatest shock only came at the end of the curtain-raiser:[3]
Everybody applauded by clapping their hands.
What was Gottsched to do? Go home in a rage?
Not if he understood the worldly wisdom which he taught.[4]
He forced himself to watch the curtain-raiser with a straight face,
Otherwise his reputation would have been blighted.
But thunder often follows lightning.
At the end Frau Neuber appeared and said
That every time she was going to perform Cato in future[5]
The performance would start with this curtain raiser.

[1] Gottsched's wife Luise Adelgunde Viktoria, a playwright and translator in her own right, abetted his efforts at reforming the theatre. Schwabe, the editor of *Belustigungen des Verstandes und des Witzes* (Diversions of Reason and Wit), was a favourite disciple.
[2] According to Rost, the lawyer Corvinus, a friend of Gottsched's, was planning to start a riot in the theatre as a diversionary manoeuvre. A few lines later in the poem he actually does so, but the trouble-makers backing Gottsched are soon defeated by students of the opposite party.
[3] This final defeat of the Gottsched cabal takes place after the quelling of the riot mentioned in note 2.
[4] One of the subjects the polymath Gottsched professed – he had written *Erste Gründe der gesammten Weltweisheit* (First Foundations of Philosophy in its Entirety, 1733–4).
[5] See **84**, note 3.

One of the factors inhibiting the creation of a generally accessible repertoire of original German plays was the reluctance of actor-managers to have their scripts made available to rival companies. (Compare **90**, 'Concerning the prompter', par. 1.) In this respect Frau

Neuber, for all her ambitions to raise the literary standard of her company's repertoire, was no better than her competitors, as Löwen explained in his History of the German Theatre.

165   Frau Neuber opposed to the printing of playtexts

Löwen (1766), p. 29. Reproduced in Stümcke (1905), p. 31

The curtain-raiser I have just mentioned [i.e. *Der allerkostbarste Schatz*] has never been printed. She [Frau Neuber] was altogether against the printing of plays. This reluctance was at bottom nothing other than a mean desire not to have her plays known by any other companies. She had inherited this meanness from her predecessors; and it is still found among a good many managers.

Gottsched based his ideas for reforming the German stage entirely on the principles, and largely on the repertoire, of French neo-classical drama. In this imitation of the French theatre, German literary drama inevitably came off second-best, as Lessing suggested in a review. (Compare 100.)

166   The status of German tragedy assessed by Lessing, 23 August 1755

G.E. Lessing, review of Z.S. Patzke's tragedy, 'Virginia', in *Berlinische privilegirte Zeitung*, no. 101 (23 August 1755). Reproduced in *Werke*, ed. Fritz Budde, pt. 9. (Berlin/Leipzig/ Vienna/Stuttgart: Deutsches Verlagshaus Bong, 1925), p. 423. Reprinted by Georg Olms Verlag (Hildesheim/New York, 1970)

You can look at any German tragedy from two points of view: as a tragedy and as a German tragedy. It is one thing to be superior to Gottsched, Schönaich, Grimm, Krieger, Quistorp and Pietschel,[1] and quite another thing to earn a place side by side with Corneille. But between these two extreme limits there are still vacant places that a bright spirit might fill honourably. It would be unfair to deny Herr Patzke such a place. It is his first dramatic piece.

---

[1] These were authors who had, at one time or other, been in Gottsched's camp. Christoph Otto v. Schönaich (1725–1807), primarily a writer of epics, had been 'crowned' a poet by Gottsched in 1755. The dramatisation of Heinrich v. Zigler und Kliphausen's seventeenth-century novel, *Die asiatische Banise* (Asian Banise) by Friedrich Melchior v. Grimm (1723–1804) was published by Gottsched in Volume 4 of his collection, *Die Deutsche Schaubühne* (The German Theatre); actually, Grimm's real claim to fame were the letters he was to write in French jointly with Diderot from Paris, between 1753 and 1792. Krieger presumably stands for Johann Christian Krüger (1722–50), the author of numerous comedies and translator of Marivaux for the Schönemann company. Theodor Johann Quistorp (1722–76) worked in various dramatic genres; several of his plays were published in *Die Deutsche Schaubühne*.

The comic repertoire of the German theatre had long been dominated by Molière and other French authors – a circumstance if anything reinforced by Gottsched.

167   The predominance of French comedy deplored by J.E. Schlegel, 1747

J.E. Schlegel, *Gedanken zur Aufnahme des dänischen Theaters*, (Ideas for the Improvement of the Danish Theatre, 1747), in *Joh. Elias Schlegels Werke*, vol. 3 (J.E.S.'s Works), ed. by Johann Heinrich Schlegel (Copenhagen and Leipzig: Mummische Buchhandlung, 1764), pp. 296–7. Reprinted by Athenäum, Frankfurt-on-Main, 1971

The Germans have made the mistake of indiscriminately translating all manner of comedies from the French, without stopping to consider whether their characters applied to their own manners. So they have turned their theatre into nothing other than a French theatre in the German language. True, this theatre for all that is not altogether unattractive. For there is something in [human] follies that is general, in which all nations resemble each other, and the representation of which is therefore bound to please everybody. But a theatre which only pleases in a general way is not as attractive as it might be; and this in my view is the cause of the coldness with which comedies are received in Germany. They would be very much more popular if on the one hand the nation could ascribe to its own wit the beauties it notes in the plays performed; and if on the other hand everyone recognised in the manners depicted the manners of his own country with which he is familiar, and was amused every time he found something he could relate to someone among his acquaintances. [. . .] German actors have been the chief losers in this matter. For even though at first they would not have had such perfect plays as they could have from French translations, yet plays showing at any rate some spirit and gaiety would, for all their defects, have attracted far greater attention and brought in more money.

Around the middle of the eighteenth century more and more voices were heard calling for German theatre to follow the lead of English rather than French playwrights – at least as an interim measure before German playwrights had created a national drama of their own. Lessing's polemic against Gottsched, in his 17th 'Letter Concerning the Most Recent Literature', argued against the professor's pro-French bias and in favour of using English drama, particularly Shakespeare, as an inspiration.

168   Lessing recommends Shakespeare as a model for German drama, 16 February 1759

G.E. Lessing, *Briefe, die neueste Litteratur betreffend* (Letters Concerning the Most Recent Literature) (Berlin: Friedrich Nicolai, 16 February 1759). Reproduced in *Werke*, ed. Peterson (1925), vol. 4, p. 57

'Nobody,' say the authors of the Bibliothek,[1] 'will deny that the German stage owes a great part of its first improvement to Professor Gottsched.'

I am that nobody: I deny it outright. It would have been a good thing if Herr Gottsched had never meddled with the theatre. His supposed improvements either consist of unnecessary trivia or actually make matters worse.

When Frau Neuber was flourishing and a good many persons felt called upon to render both her and the stage a service, things did indeed look pretty wretched with our dramatic poesy. No one knew of any rules; no one cared for any models. Our *Staats- und Helden-Aktionen*[2] were full of nonsense, fustian, filth and vulgar humour. Our comedies consisted of disguisings and tricks of magic; and their wittiest invention was a beating. It did not exactly take the subtlest and greatest intellect to recognise this corrupt state of affairs. Nor was Herr Gottsched the first one to recognise it; he was only the first one with enough faith in his own powers to remedy it. And how did he go about it? He knew a little French and began to translate; he encouraged anybody who could rhyme and understand *Oui Monsieur* to translate as well; [...] he laid his ban on improvisation; he had Harlequin solemnly driven from the stage, which was in itself the greatest harlequinade ever performed; in short, he wanted not so much to improve our old drama as to become the creator of an entirely new one. And what kind of a new one? A Frenchified one; without investigating whether this Frenchified drama was or was not suited to the German way of thinking.

He should have realised sufficiently from our old dramatic pieces which he banished that we incline more to the taste of the English than of the French; that we want to see and think about more in our tragedies than the timid French tragedy gives us to see and think about; that the great, the terrible, the melancholy has a better effect on us than the polite, the tender, the amorous; that excessive simplicity fatigues us more than excessive complication etc. So he should have remained on that track, and it would have taken him straight to the English theatre. [...]

If the masterpieces of Shakespeare had been translated with some minor changes for our Germans, I know for a certainty it would have had better consequences than having acquainted them with Corneille and Racine.

---

[1] *Bibliothek der schönen Wissenschaften und der freien Künste* (Library of Polite Learning and the Liberal Arts) (Leipzig: Dyck, 1758), vol. 3, ch. 1, p. 85 – in a review of Gottsched's *Nöthiger Vorrath zur Geschichte der deutschen dramatischen Dichtkunst* (Necessary Material for a History of German Dramatic Poesy).

[2] I.e. plots of state and heroics, another name for *Haupt- und Staatsaktionen*.

In the second half of the century, a great many English plays – both contemporary and classical – were translated and staged in Germany. C.H. Schmid (see **149, 163**) published a volume of translations, in the preface to which he made a programmatic statement favouring English theatrical fare.

169   English drama closer to German taste than French drama, 1769

C.H. Schmid, Preface to *Das Englische Theater* (The English Theatre) (Leipzig, 1769). Reproduced in the Introduction by P. Legband to Schmid, *Chronologie des deutschen Theaters* (1902), pp. xvi–xvii

Instead of so many shallow French comedies, to which our actors take refuge for lack of good original plays, I have often wished to see English plays on our stages, and the acclaim received in Leipzig by Colemann's [sic] *The Jealous Wife*[1] strengthened my hope that the Germans would find more nourishment for their spirit in them than in the bulk of other weeping comedies. The final aim of *performance* has always seemed to me to be the chief purpose [of plays], and if it is useful to spread the dramatic taste of the English among us, it cannot be spread better than by the performance of English plays.

[1] George Colman the Elder's *The Jealous Wife* (1761), which was based on Fielding's *Tom Jones*.

National theatres

A recurrent theme of would-be reformers of the German theatre was the call for a National Theatre. This was clearly inspired by the example of the Comédie-Française; but that venerable French institution which had been set up by royal decree in 1680 did not really provide a pattern which could readily be imitated in German-speaking countries. There was neither the centralised state, as there had been in the France of Louis XIV, capable of raising a cultural institution to exemplary status by an exercise of political will; nor was there, as in the case of Paris *vis-à-vis* the rest of France, a metropolitan culture in any one German city that would be broadly acceptable as a pattern to be followed by all parts of a highly diverse Empire, divided by religion, dialect, dynastic interests and life style. The idea of a National Theatre contained a number of often not very clearly defined aspirations. It certainly meant a permanently domiciled company in place of strolling players and therefore higher artistic standards; a theatre, perhaps, with a regular programme of actor training and a pension scheme; which, though it might be supported by a court, would be open to and devoted to the entertainment of the public at large and not merely of an aristocratic coterie – open in other words to a middle-class audience; but above all, a theatre which would promote a predominantly (there was no chance that it would be an exclusively) German repertoire: a theatre, then, which would encourage native playwrights and begin to build up a national body of drama.

The first attempt at creating such a National Theatre took place in Hamburg. This venture arose directly out of the existing company of the actor-manager Konrad Ackermann who had built his own playhouse there in 1765 (see **65**). The critic and poet Johann Friedrich Löwen (1727–71), somewhat tenuously linked to theatre in that he was married to Schönemann's daughter, had conducted a polemic against the principle of companies being run by actor-managers rather than by directors not themselves engaged in acting. In 1766 he persuaded a group of twelve Hamburg businessmen, among them the later director Abel Seyler (see 72, note 2), to form a consortium for taking over financial responsibility for the theatre, with himself as its director. In fact, the somewhat grandiloquently named Hamburg National Theatre had a stormy career, from its opening on 22 April 1767 to its early demise on 3 March 1769; its principal claim to fame in theatre history is Lessing's having joined the staff as dramaturg, which led to his writing the *Hamburgische Dramaturgie*. Löwen's manifesto which he published in October 1766 outlined his ideas for this National Theatre; unfortunately he proved not to be a person capable of realising them in practice. For a full history in English of the Hamburg National Theatre, see J.G. Robertson, *Lessing's Dramatic Theory* (CUP, 1939).

170   A manifesto for the Hamburg National Theatre, 1766

J.F. Löwen, *Vorläufige Nachricht von der auf Ostern 1767 vorzunehmenden Veränderung des Hamburgischen Theaters* (Provisional Notice of the Changes Planned for the Hamburg Theatre for Easter 1767, Hamburg: Michael Christian Bock, 1766). Reproduced in J.F.L., *Geschichte des deutschen Theaters* etc., ed. Stümcke (1905), pp. 83–90 and Robertson (1939), (in German) pp. 20–23

We announce to the public the perhaps unexpected hope of raising the German drama in Hamburg to a dignity which it will never attain under any other circumstances. As long as this excellent, agreeable and instructive branch of the arts remains in the hands of such men, be they the most honest of men, who are forced to make of their art merely a bread-and-butter craft; as long as encouragement and the noble pride of imitation is missing among actors themselves; as long as people are not accustomed to inspire the nation's authors to [the writing of] national dramas; and above all as long as a theatrical policy, both as regards the choice of plays in the theatre and as regards the morals of actors themselves, remains totally unknown; so long any expectations of the German drama progressing beyond its infancy will be in vain.

We take for granted the great advantages that a national theatre can provide for the entire nation; nor do we need to prove them nowadays to anyone other than those stubborn enough not to wish it proved. If meanwhile it be true, what has long since been established, that, apart from the theatre affording a noble diversion, morality too is rendered the most signal service by it; it is certainly worth while to consider the true improvement of the stage with something other than that lethargy with which its inner perfection has been worked for hitherto. And it is precisely for this important reason [...] that we are pleased to have the means in our hands to offer our fellow citizens, apart from the most noble delight of which human reason is capable, the richest treasures of purified morality as well.

Let us enlarge on the possibility and certainty of this intention.

A small group of well-intentioned local citizens has been pondering the execution of this plan for several years; and since they are currently working towards maintaining a sufficient number of respectable people who are at the same time the most excellent and best of German actors, they are prepared, at a time to be announced in the public newssheets, to open the German theatre with all the perfection rightly demanded of a well run and instructive stage. To that end the direction of the same has been entrusted to the hands of a man whose blameless conduct and whose knowledgeable insights into the mysteries of this art are necessary for the improvement of the theatre.[1] Since this man will not be concerned with the actual work as an actor but has exclusively taken upon himself, in addition to the well known duties incumbent upon any director, the further highly necessary obligation of making himself responsible for training the heart, morals and art of young student actors, one can readily assume that the public will certainly not be disappointed in the expectations cherished of him. The intention is to procure for this company of respectable and intelligent people all the advantages to be had in a theatrical academy. To that end the director will be giving regular lectures [...] on the *principles* of physical expression, shortly to be published by him.[2] [...]

Since efforts will be made to give such excellent training to the actor; and since the latter is sure to be an honour to the German stage if this instruction be seconded by talent; we are also concerned to ensure that his material circumstances will be entirely comfortable. Thus we aim to make the status of these people as honoured as the art to which they have devoted themselves merits. They will be offered an annual salary proportionate to their talents, special consideration going to making decent lifelong provision for those actors no longer able to serve the theatre by reason of old age.[3] [...]

Finally, since according to a statement by Diderot,[4] [...] the utility of the theatre for a whole nation can only grow considerable when it has its own stage, our attention will be directed above all to making the German theatre in the course of time as national as all other nations have cause to boast regarding theirs. Everybody is aware that this must be the first business of our dramatic authors: but everybody is also aware of the causes which in part have obstructed this work up to the present time; and it is hoped to attain this end by encouragement and the offer of prizes.

True, no actual geniuses can be created for the theatre by rewards; but it has long since been of the most splendid use among all nations, beginning with the Greeks and Romans, to inspire the talents of those who already have genius by the active and generous applause of the nation. A prize of fifty ducats will therefore be offered annually for the best tragedy, be it heroic or bourgeois; fifty ducats for the best comedy; and to observe the same rules concerning submission with sealed names and mottos as are customary [. . .] among all learned societies. The decision which of the plays submitted deserves the prize will be made according to the opinion of people of known talent.[5] [. . .]

[1] Here Löwen was speaking about himself, with perhaps a little less than becoming modesty.
[2] In fact, Löwen had to stop his lectures after the first class because of the opposition of the actors. He had published a book entitled: *Grundsätze der körperlichen Beredsamkeit* (Principles of Bodily Eloquence) in 1755, a new edition of which he was proposing to bring out. 'Bodily eloquence', a matter of great interest to eighteenth-century theorists of acting, was the art of gesture rather than what nowadays would be called 'movement'. For other suggestions concerning actor training, see 138, 251, 252.
[3] Compare the pension scheme put forward over a decade later by Ekhof, who was the leading member of the Hamburg National Theatre (see 108).
[4] Denis Diderot (1713–84) had a strong influence on German theatre, both with his theoretical writings and his plays. His *Le Père de famille* (1758), in Lessing's translation (1760), was one of the Hamburg National Theatre's favourite repertoire items with twelve performances. See J.G. Robertson (1939), pp. 232–5.
[5] The proposed playwriting competition never took place. For other playwriting competitions, see 176–7.

The idea of the two theatres of the Imperial City of Vienna constituting a National Theatre in the sense of being exemplary and entitled to speak for the entire nation was not easily accepted elsewhere. In the year 1772 the young Goethe, together with G. Schlosser, J.G. Herder, and J.H. Merck, was working on the staff of the *Frankfurter gelehrte Anzeigen*, a journal of book reviews: it was probably Goethe himself who wrote the review, from which the following excerpt is taken, of Müller's recent book on the two theatres of Vienna (see 68) in which he had advanced such 'national' claims for them.

171   The claims of Vienna's having a National Theatre challenged, 1772

Review of J.H.F. Müller's 'Genaue Nachrichten von beyden K.K. Schaubühnen in Wien', in *Frankfurter gelehrte Anzeigen* (Frankfurt Learned Notes) (Frankfurt-on-Main: Eichenbergische Erben, 1772), 24 April 1772, pp. 263–4. Reproduced in *DLD*, 7 (1882), pp. 218–19, and in *Goethes Werke*, WA, vol. 37 (1897), pp. 344–5

[. . .] We are of course glad that at last they have banned extemporising and Hanswurst in Vienna; but to make the Viennese theatre into a National Theatre just for that is an insult to the entire nation. [. . .] for all the nice things Herr Müller is telling us, not excluding the busts of the actors and actresses which he has had engraved, we would ask him in the name of the nation not to bestow the title of a national company on the Viennese company of actors until further notice but rather to wait until we are a nation, until Vienna has become its representative, and until the company there has taken on the character of the same.

Nevertheless, the foundation in 1776 of an official National Theatre at the Burgtheater in Vienna was to have long-term consequences for the theatre not only of Austria but of

German-speaking countries generally. The fundamental difference between this venture and the hapless Hamburg Enterprise lay in the fact that this National Theatre was not the result of a private enterprise but of an Imperial edict. Franz Hadamowsky has shown – in 'Die Schauspielfreiheit, die "Erhebung des Burgtheaters zum Hoftheater" und seine "Begründung als Nationaltheater" im Jahr 1776' (The Freedom of the Theatre, the 'Raising of the Burgtheater to the Status of a Court Theatre' and its 'Foundation as a National Theatre' in 1766), in *M & K*, 22 (1976), pp. 5–19 – that this raising of an existing theatre to the status of a National Theatre was not seen at the time as having the significance that later generations have attributed to it. Indeed, its early history – government by committee – ran far from smoothly. But with the appointment of the star actor J.F.H. Brockmann (see 103, 199–202, 204, 220) as director in 1789, its rise to a position of importance in German-language theatre was assured, and a Burgtheater style of deportment and diction began to be developed. In the nineteenth century the Burgtheater was to become one of the leading theatres of Europe though not immune to criticism (see 256 & 264). While it may have lost some of its eminence in the rich variety of German-language theatres in the twentieth century, it is still a theatre with a distinctive profile.

172   The founding of the National Theatre at the Burgtheater, Vienna, 1776

'Fortsetzung des Fragments der Geschichte der Wiener Schaubühne, im Theater-Kalender von 1776' (Continuation of The Brief History of the Viennese Theatre, in The Theatre Calendar for 1776'), in *TJD*, 2 (1777) pp. 108–10

In spite of all the lamentable precedents set by theatre lessees hitherto, various schemes for new leases were nevertheless submitted to the Court.[1] Promises were given to continue maintaining foreign companies (at the expense of the German theatre). But Joseph II, that praiseworthy German Emperor, exclusively supported the German theatre against the expectation and to the surprise of all its German adversaries. His first intention was to hand over the German theatre to the administration of the company at its own risk and profit. To that end Stephanie the Younger drew up a scheme signed by all members, except the minor ones.[2] He submitted this [...] to the Emperor, requesting the severance of ballet from German drama.[3] They argued the disadvantage that ballets brought to drama so persuasively that the Emperor granted this petition. But they thereby antagonised all ballet-lovers (the majority of the public). [...] But the Emperor had resolved to lay a sure foundation for the future of the German theatre; he therefore offered them his most active help. The actors, it was said, cannot possibly govern themselves, the greatest disorders are bound to arise without a director in charge. – Furthermore it was said that without ballets, drama is too boring and nobody will go and see it. He gave the following commands in order to have both objections to his plan either decisively overruled or confirmed, without putting the actors at risk and seeing his own work undone at the outset. He took the

German company into his service, put it under the office of the Controller-in-Chief of the Imperial Household, set aside the Burgtheater for their performances which he commanded would henceforth be called the National Theatre; granted the company the permission to govern themselves according to the scheme submitted and hence to elect a *régisseur* from amongst their own ranks, the choice by lot falling on Stephanie the Elder.[4] The Kärntnertortheater was set aside for foreign performances in all languages and genres.[5] [...] The enemies of German drama to their annoyance now saw it under the Emperor's protection; it was out of the reach of their attacks, and a haughty turning up of their noses was the only way by which they were allowed to vent their bile with regard to this significant metamorphosis. This they did not fail to exhibit.

Enough – the Germans now have a National Theatre, and their Emperor has founded it. What a ravishing, splendid thought for anyone capable of feeling that he is a German! Full of deep reverence everyone will thank him for the great example he has set the German princes.

[1] The Italian entrepreneur Giuseppe d'Afflisio had run the theatres of Vienna from 1767–70 with a preference for spectacle and little sympathy for German drama; the Hungarian Count Kohary who succeeded him favoured 'regular' drama but failed to attract the public. What was lacking under the system of leasing out the theatres of Vienna was a long-term policy for German drama.

[2] Gottlieb Stephanie ('the Younger' – 1741–1800), actor-dramatist of Silesian origin, wrote or adapted a large number of plays, including *Die Werber* (*The Recruiters*, 1769) based on George Farquhar's *Recruiting Officer*, and a version of *Macbeth*; a member of the National Theatre from the start. His libretto for Mozart's *Die Entführung aus dem Serail* (see note 3) was an enduring contribution to German opera.

[3] The combination of drama and ballet had been a standard combination in the theatre up to that point. Ballets formed an important part of the repertoire of the Hamburg National Theatre. The Viennese public had become more ballet-minded than ever as a result of the seven-year activity in Vienna (1767–74) of the great French choreographer Jean Georges Noverre (1727–1810). Note however that the Emperor wished the Burgtheater to foster opera, and one of the National Theatre's early glories were the first performances of several Mozart operas: *Die Entführung aus dem Serail* (16 July 1782), *Le nozze di Figaro* (1 May 1786) and *Così fan tutte* (26 January 1790).

[4] Stephan Christian Gottlob Stephanie ('the Elder' – 1733/1734?–98): like his brother (see note 2), a translator and adaptor of plays and a member of the original Burgtheater ensemble. Neither Stephanie was a first-rate actor.

[5] See 68. When operas were removed from the repertoire of the Burgtheater in 1810, the Kärntnertortheater was made the Court Opera.

There was something none too clearly defined about the very term, 'National Theatre'. Was it a theatre given over to a predominantly German repertoire? Was it a theatre serving the needs of the public at large? Was it in some sense intended to be exemplary? The very notion kept being challenged time and again.

173   The term 'National Theatre' questioned, 1779

'Sincerus', 'Fragment aus dem Tagebuch eines Reisenden' (Pages from a Traveller's Diary), in *LTZ*, 20 November 1779, p. 738

A man who thoroughly knows his business was summoned to a place in order to establish a National Theatre; his portrait was to be displayed on the curtain; so why didn't the project come off? They say he did not have a free hand, and knowing quite well that too many cooks generally do not improve the dishes, he thanked them for the honour and put down his ladle. And what on earth do you mean by your 'National Theatre' anyway? If it is as much as to say, 'The German theatre in this town', I shall accept that, but it is one of those big words which makes one person think of one thing, another of something else and a third of nothing at all, and so we had better use ordinary language.

The founding of the Royal National Theatre in Berlin was the direct result of the death (on 17 August 1786) of the Francophile Prussian King Frederick II; his successor Frederick William II, who preferred German theatre to French, soon turned the Theater am Gendarmenmarkt, formerly occupied by a resident French company, into the 'Königliches Nationaltheater' (Royal National Theatre), to be run by the local actor-manager Karl Theophil Döbbelin. Ten years after the establishement of the Burgtheater as a National Theatre, Berlin had followed the lead given by Vienna. The opening spectacle described below indicates clearly enough the programme of this new Prussian theatre – the fostering of German drama. (For the literary-allegorical imagery typical of the period, compare 66 & 180.)

174   Allegorical ballet at the Royal National Theatre, Berlin, 5 December 1786

'Vom hiesigen Theater' (Local Theatre News), in ELT, vol. 4, no. 50 (16 December 1786), pp. 382–4. DTM Per 81 (3,4)

Performances at the Royal National Theatre then commenced on 5 December. On that day Herr Döbbelin[1] opened the theatre with a speech of his own composition which was followed by an allegorical ballet in two acts: The Celebration of the Art of Acting. [...] The contents in brief was as follows: 'Artists and dancers are busy completing a triumphal arch behind which looms up the Temple of the Art of Acting. The latter entertain themselves with merry dances and then finish decorating the triumphal arch which features the words: Hail to the German Art of Acting! The arrival of the Art of Acting is heard, and all rush to meet her. She appears in a triumphal chariot with a flowered canopy borne by dancers, the chariot being drawn by them and the artists. In her suite there appear various characters from German spoken and musical drama, such as Götz von Berlichingen and Elisabeth,[2] Paul Werner and Franziska,[3] Adelheid von Veltheim and Karl von Bingen.[4] They all move through the triumphal arch into the Temple. – The High Priest is awaiting the Art of Acting. She approaches with her retinue.

[. . .] The High Priest hands the chalice to the Art of Acting; she pours it out on the altar which is surrounded by busts of *Euripides, Sophocles, Plautus, Terence, Shakespeare* and *Lessing*.[5] At a signal given by the High Priest a curtain rises in front of which stands the altar, and now you see the most magnificent part of the Temple, in a sun above the altar the King's signature,[6] and above the sun a winding scroll which bears the inscription: *His heart is German, His desire is His people's happiness.* The High Priest then shows the Art of Acting under whose protection she now finds herself. After this most inspiring spectacle, the Art of Acting commands a sculptor to carve into the altar, for a perpetual memorial, the law to be followed by her retinue, *viz.: Follow Nature, and let your art ennoble it,* which being completed this merry festival is concluded with general dancing.'

[1] Karl Theophil Döbbelin (1727–93) who had begun his acting career with the Neubers, founded his own company on Gottsched's advice in 1756. He established himself in Berlin in 1767; in 1775 he took over Koch's company after the latter's death and obtained the Prussian patent. He owned two theatres in Berlin; in 1786, when the Royal National Theatre was founded, his company consisted of 49 members. But his regime there was unsuccessful and of short duration; in 1789 he retired from the stage altogether. See also **192, 196, 201 & 205.**
[2] The hero of Goethe's play, *Götz von Berlichingen*, and his wife.
[3] The former sergeant-major, now the orderly, of Major von Tellheim, in Lessing's *Minna von Barnhelm*, and the maid of the eponymous heroine.
[4] Characters in the operetta *Adelheid von Veltheim (1786)* by the actor-playwright-director Gustav Friedrich Wilhelm Grossmann (1743–96), with music by Neefe. A trained lawyer, Grossmann only went on the stage at the age of thirty and worked for the Seyler company before running his own companies in Bonn, Kassel, Hanover, Brunswick and Bremen. On friendly terms with Lessing and Schiller, he was a strong advocate of more indigenous German theatre and a champion of Shakespeare on the German stage.
[5] Note the absence, at any rate in this description, of any French playwrights.
[6] I.e., Frederick William II.

But there were considerable constraints on the repertoire of German-language theatres, including the so-called National Theatres – even at a time when German literature overall was gaining in self-confidence, authority and popularity. The limits as to what could or could not be shown on the stage differed widely from state to state, although anything deemed subversive would tend to be suppressed anywhere. The Burgtheater, while benefiting immensely from the Emperor's support, was at the same time especially exposed to censorship pressures. From 1778, this National Theatre annually published a selection of plays which had appeared in its repertoire. The preface to the first of these anthologies quoted below clearly spelt out the limits in matters of religion, politics and taste beyond which it was not permissible to go. It was owing to guidelines such as these that such plays as Goethe's *Götz von Berlichingen, Egmont* and *Stella* and Schiller's *Wilhelm Tell* did not figure in the repertoire of the Burgtheater in the first few decades of its existence.

175 Constraints on the Burgtheater's repertoire, 1778

Preface to *Kaiserl.-königl.Nationaltheater* (Imperial and Royal National Theatre), vol. 1 (Vienna, 1778). Reproduced in Heinze Kindermann, *Theatergeschichte Europas*, vol. 5 (1962), p. 97

1. Where the bulk of the audience is of the Catholic faith, certain plays acceptable to Protestant towns cannot be performed on the stage.

2. In the residential city of the first German court, the domicile of the highest nobility, plays are called for which have to be more than [mere] entertainment for universities and commercial cities.

3. At the present time, an enlightened public demands plays more perfect than those performed with acclaim some twenty or thirty years ago.

4. Experience has taught us to point out something else as well. It is improper to seek to spread certain libertarian sentiments in monarchical states. No less reprehensible are [the following]: any strange choice of subject; any style and characters of an exaggerated or eccentric kind; or whatever offends morality on the stage. To fly quite beyond nature, to depict only melancholy and choleric individuals; to enforce disgust and repugnant feelings instead of arousing fear and pity is, alas, a fashionable error these days to which even authors of genius are prone at times.

A major problem confronting any of these new-minted National Theatres – others were founded in Mannheim (1777), Munich (1778), Nuremberg (1789), Frankfurt (1792), Altona (1796), Breslau (1797) – was the lack of an adequate original German repertoire. Time and again efforts were made to remedy this shortcoming by means of playwriting competitions – e.g. at the Burgtheater in Vienna or in Munich (the latter under the auspices of a literary journal) – but these only yielded meagre results. Goethe in Weimar was no more successful with a prize offered in 1802 for a 'play of intrigue'. The Mannheim National Theatre, under the direction of the highly cultured Wolfgang Heribert Baron von Dalberg (1750–1806), ran a playwriting competition in 1784: Iffland, a leading member of the company, made a disenchanted reference to this in his autobiography.

176 The Mannheim playwriting competition, 1784

A.W. Iffland, *Über meine theatralische Laufbahn* (My Theatrical Career), in vol. 1 of *Dramatische Werke* (Leipzig: Georg Joachim Göschen, 1798), pp. 159–60. Reproduced in DLD 24, ed. H. Holstein (1886), p. 70

The German Learned Society in Mannheim had offered a sizable reward for the best comedy to be submitted to it.

That was a very good and laudable idea. However, it was rash and naïve on the part of the theatre to undertake to perform all plays submitted. Not much good material was sent in, and [our] time, our memory, all the public's and the actors' good humour were put at risk and sacrificed throughout the summer. As a result we almost came to loathe the theatre from Easter to Michaelmas.

The competition proved a total failure. Another effort was made the following year; this, too, was to prove unproductive. The would-be playwrights' task was defined in the following terms which clearly indicate the lack of an indigenous comic tradition.

177   The second Mannheim playwriting competition, 1785

'Zweite dramatische Preisaufgabe der Churfürstlich Deutschen Gesellschaft zu Mannheim' (Second Playwriting Competition of the Electoral German Society at Mannheim), in *ELT*, vol. 1, no. 52 (24 December 1785), pp. 413–15. DTM Per 81 (1,2)

Last year the Electoral German Society in Mannheim offered a prize of 50 ducats for the best comedy. [...]

None of these plays was deemed worthy of the prize. What was missing in them almost entirely was novelty of characters and situations, correctness, beauty and subtlety of expression, irresistible movement towards the climax and, furthermore, that which the Society had chiefly aimed at in setting the competition, a plot designed to involve the spectator.

[...]

The Society again offers a prize, augmented to 75 ducats, for a comedy for the year 1786. In addition, the management of the theatre offers the winner the receipts of the second performance of the play.

The public are reminded that comedy is to be understood in the proper sense of the term, and that the Society is interested neither in serious, sentimental comedy verging on sadness nor in farce.

The German Society neither rejects sentimental comedy nor any genre of stage plays. However, it is not minded to promote the taste for that genre by offering a prize.

It directs its attention principally to that which concerns our theatres most. The elaboration of comic characters, the invention of new and apt situations, philosophy in the guise of a jest, dialogue full of charm and salt, the varied design of one or several characters to create one prevailing mood, apt portraiture calculated to incite the fool to laugh at himself and to entertain the sage: in a word, comedy – is indeed a very difficult business: but victory in this matter is a great and glorious victory. The prize is immortality.

The most excellent of the plays submitted will be performed at the Electoral National Theatre, and the assessment and the award of the prize will only take place after their performance.

The name of the winner will then be publicly announced and celebrated at the following performance of the play at the theatre here.

Dalberg wished to foster not only the talents of new playwrights but also those of his actors, who were encouraged – within certain limits and not without some pedantry – to *think* about their profession, its demands and its implications.

178   Dalberg's educational efforts, Mannheim, 1784–6

i) 'Dramaturgische Preisfragen' (Dramaturgic Prize Questions), in *ELT*, vol. 1, no. 18 (30 April 1785), pp. 285–6. DTM Per 81 (1,2)

Baron von Dalberg in Mannheim having, as the public will long have been aware, through consistent enthusiasm for dramatic art and profound knowledge of the theatre, given the confused chaos of his German theatre the attractive form of an academic institution and made a thinker of the mechanical artist, he fell upon the excellent idea a few years ago of keeping the best heads of the Mannheim National Theatre busy by setting prize questions concerning the philosophy of their art and in this way to challenge them to give an account of their studies and their acting. Seven such questions have already been answered in the year 1784 [...], and the prize was decided in favour of Herr Beck[1] by Baron von Dalberg, several distinguished foreign dramatic authors and the Palatine German Society having been consulted. It consisted of a golden commemorative coin of twelve ducats.

The questions were the following:

What is nature, and how wide are its boundaries upon the stage?

What is the difference between art and temperament?

What is true decorum upon the stage, and by what means can the actor acquire it?

Can French tragedies please upon the German stage? And how must they be performed if they are to obtain general acclaim?

Are there any definite general rules according to which the actor can manage his pauses?

What is a National Theatre in the truest sense? How can a theatre become a National Theatre? And is there really any German theatre which deserves to be called a National Theatre?

[1] Heinrich Beck (1760–1803), a leading member of the Mannheim company. See Hans Knudsen, *Heinrich Beck* (Leipzig/Hamburg: *TGF* 24, 1912)

The success of this competition, in Dalberg's view, was such that he repeated the experiment in 1785, setting the following questions to be answered by Easter 1786.

ii) *ELT*, vol. 1, no. 18 (30 April 1785), pp. 287–8. DTM Per 81 (1,2)

First Question

In what way does a German public deserve to be called the best public in general, and with respect to the actors in particular?

Second Question

Can the actor as well as the management of a theatre give a true direction to a public's false taste, and by what class of plays is good taste best improved?

Third Question

Does the good actor, whom one is used to seeing acclaimed in tragic and in character parts, gain or lose by often alternatively appearing in comic roles?

Fourth Question

In what way does true comic acting differ from caricature? And what must the actor do so as never to go too far in the comic line of business? [. . .]

Sixth Question

Can a general fixed code of law be drawn up for all German theatres; how could it be instituted, and what are the means to give it force and weight?

In Weimar Goethe set himself the task of planning the repertoire in such a way as to educate the public's taste over time and thus give this theatre the exemplary force of a true National Theatre. He explained his principles in an article in a local publication.

179   Goethe on repertoire planning, 15 February 1802

'Weimarisches Hoftheater' (The Weimar Court Theatre), in *Journal des Luxus und der Moden* (Journal of Luxury and Fashion), ed. Bertuch and Kraus (Weimar: Verlag des Industrie = Comptoirs), 3 March 1802. Reproduced in *Goethes Werke*, WA, ser. 1, vol. 40 (1901), pp. 72–85, and partly reproduced in English translation in Carlson (1978), p. 169

If the versatility of the actor is desirable, the versatility of the audience is even more so. The theatre, like the rest of the world, is plagued by prevailing fashions which flood it from time to time and then leave it high and dry. Fashion brings about a momentary habituation to some manner which we follow enthusiastically, only to banish it presently for ever. The German theatre more than any other is susceptible to this misfortune, presumably because we have so far striven and attempted more than we have achieved and accomplished. Our literature, thank heaven, has not yet had a Golden Age, and like everything else our theatre is still in the process of becoming. Let any management check over its repertoire and see how few plays out of the great number performed in the last twenty years have remained stageable until now. Anyone planning gradually to regulate this disorder, to establish a certain number of existing plays on the stage and thereby at last to put together a repertoire which can be passed on to posterity, must above all things begin to educate the audience he has before him in versatility in its way of thinking. This consists chiefly of the spectator learning to understand that every play is not to be regarded like a coat that must snugly fit the spectator's body entirely according to his present needs. He must not always just seek to satisfy himself and the most immediate needs of his intellect, heart and senses on the stage; he should instead at times regard himself as a traveller who, in unfamiliar places and regions which he is visiting for his instruction and entertainment, does not find all the comforts he is accustomed to expect for his individual needs back home. [...]

In fact, the German is a serious character, and this seriousness manifests itself particularly when playfulness is on the agenda, notably so in the theatre. Here he demands plays which exert a certain simple power over him, which either move him to hearty laughter or to deeply felt emotion. True, a certain mixed kind of drama has accustomed him to see gaiety cheek by jowl with sadness; however, neither is then taken to its highest expression but shows itself more as a kind of amalgam.[1] Besides, the spectator is always annoyed when merry and sad things follow each other without any intermediate links.

As far as we are concerned, we do indeed wish in time to receive more plays of the clearly separate genres, since only in this way can true art be advanced; however, we also consider highly necessary such plays as remind the spectator that all theatre is only play above which he must rise without enjoying it any the less, if he is to profit by it aesthetically, nay morally.

---

[1] I.e., sentimental comedy.

B. DRAMATIC THEORY

The poet and literary theorist Martin Opitz (1597–1639), in his brief excursion into dramatic theory in chapter 5 of his *Buch von der deutschen Poeterey* (Book of German Poesy) (1624), had been guided by non-German example: he explicitly mentioned Aristotle and Daniel Heinsius. More than a century later, Professor Gottsched was still indebted to foreign theory. In seeking to purify the highly irregular German drama and make it suitable for the rising educated middle class, he borrowed most of his ideas not only from Aristotle and Horace but also from (principally French) neo-classical writers whose principles there is no need to restate here. But in addition to drama along strictly classical lines Gottsched did allow a form which was distinctly baroque in character: allegorical/mythological plays. These were still frequent in the Holy Roman Empire, with its multitude of courts as well as municipal, academic and other authorities demanding symbolical self-representation and self-glorification (see **174**). The passage quoted below is taken from the chapter on pastorals, curtain-raisers and afterpieces in Gottsched's major critical opus.

180   Gottsched on allegorical drama

Johann Christoph Gottsched, *Versuch einer critischen Dichtkunst durchgehends mit den Exempeln unserer besten Dichter erläutert* (Essay on the Criticism of Poetry illustrated throughout with the Examples of our Best Poets), 4th edn (Leipzig: Bernhard Christoph Breitkopf, 1751), pt. 2, ch. 6, pp. 780–1. Reprinted Darmstadt: Wissenschaftliche Buchgesellschaft, 1962. Reproduced in *J.C.G., Ausgewählte Werke* (J.C.G., Selected works), ed. Joachim Birke & Brigitte Birke (Berlin/New York: Walter de Gruyter, 1973), pp. 581–2

[. . .] these [curtain-raisers] tend to be performed on certain festive occasions, such as the birthdays or name-days of great lords, at the weddings or the birth of noble princes, at anniversaries of academies and schools etc. They are thus intended to manifest the general joy of the country, of the towns, of certain societies and classes and perhaps express [their] good wishes too. Hence one must resort to allegorical or mythological figures who would have no proper place in any other plays. You have the whole country, such as Germany, Saxony, Lusatia etc. appear as a female with an embattled crown; you bring on Cities, Religion, the Sciences, the Liberal Arts, Commerce etc. For the latter Apollo, Minerva, the Muses, Mercury etc. are usually employed. Sometimes Venus, Cupid, the Graces, Diana, Vertumnus, Flora, Pomona etc. may be used in order to represent Beauty, Love, Grace, the Chase, Spring, Autumn etc. All such persons must be furnished with the proper costumes and attributes according to mythology: and great care must be taken that no real or historical figures be mixed up with such allegorical or mythological ones.

Gottsched whose rationalism was offended by the absurdities of opera, frequently polemised against it. Johann Georg Sulzer (1720–79), a Swiss-born member of the Royal Academy of Science in Berlin, also criticised opera as it then was in his widely noted dictionary of aesthetics. But in this comprehensive survey of all the arts, a compendious reference book which nevertheless was dismissed by the young Goethe and his circle as old-fashioned, Sulzer argued for a new national form of opera which in some respects anticipated Wagner by nearly a century.

181   Suggestions for the improvement of opera, 1774

Johann Georg Sulzer, *Allgemeine Theorie der Schönen Künste* (General Theory of the Fine Arts), (Leipzig: M.G. Weidmanns Erben, 1771–4), vol. 2, pp. 842–51

[. . .] In the best operas one sees and hears things which are so silly and absurd that one might think they only existed in order to astonish children and or the infantile minds of the mob; and in the midst of this quite miserable stuff which offends good taste in every respect there occur things which enter deeply into one's heart, which fill one's mind in a most charming manner with sweet delight, with the most tender pity, or with fear and horror. [. . .] Opera can be the greatest and most important of all dramatic spectacles because all the arts combine their forces in it: but it is precisely this spectacle which shows up the frivolity of the moderns who have equally debased and rendered contemptible all the arts in it.

We may [. . .] take it that the author of tragedies and the author of operas draw on the same material. Both present us with a great action interesting by reason of the various passions in conflict with one another, which is of short duration and which ends in an interesting dénouement. But in dealing with this matter, the opera librettist seems to have made it his aim to leave the path of nature altogether. His maxim is that everything should be treated in such a way that the eye is amazed by frequent changes of scene, by magnificent processions and by a multitude of powerful visual effects, let these be as unnatural as you please as long as the spectator's eye is constantly moved by new and ceaselessly dazzling objects. Battles, triumphs, shipwrecks, tempests, spectres, wild beasts and the like must be presented to the spectator's eyes whenever possible. [. . .] This is the first absurdity which fashion forces upon even the best of poets. Would it were the only one!

But now come the singers' demands. In every opera the best singers are to sing most often, but even all the mediocre ones, nay the very worst, having been hired and paid for performing, must be heard once or several times in great arias; the two best singers, i.e. the male and female leads, needs must sing together one or more times; so the poet must provide duets for the opera; often trios, quartets etc. as well. Nay more: the leading singers can generally display their complete art only in one sort of character; one in a tender adagio, another one in a fiery allegro etc. Hence the librettist must arrange his arias so that each one can shine in his own manner.

The multitude of absurdities resulting from this is legion. One or two female singers must necessarily play the leading roles, no matter whether or not the nature of the action admits of this. If the poet cannot find any other solution, he involves them in amorous intrigues, however contrary to the plotline this may be. [. . .]

Finally, one has to spend most of the time in a good many operas listening to very boring songs wholly devoid of any trace of feeling, with trivial texts, for every scene is expected to have an aria. But since the drama does not consist entirely of expressions of feeling, the poet must also express commands, announcements, comments or objections in a lyrical tone, and the composer inevitably has to turn them into arias which are an intolerable bore for the listener.

Added to this is the indecorum of the external arrangements, turning many an opera into a vulgar spectacle. Equally great nonsense is produced either by opulence or by meanness. In every opera it is desired to have at least some scenes that arrest the spectator's eye, whether or not the nature of the action permits this. Kings often enter the audience chamber with their entire bodyguard. That unnatural retinue takes up its position for a moment; but as the conversation is supposed to be secret, it leaves again forthwith; and not infrequently the secret conversation, not one word of which the listener can hear distinctly, commences during the exit which is often accompanied by a great clatter. At other times a scene becomes ridiculous by reason of poor presentation. Attempts are made to present an entire army or even a battle, and this spectacle which is meant to amaze the spectator is effected by a few dozen soldiers, who, in order to make their defile really impressive, are made singly to march around in a circle three or four times so that nobody will notice how few of them there are: and the fearful battle, backed by violins, is produced by the warriors beating upon the enemies' cardboard shields with their wooden swords, making a dull noise. [...]

And yet, for all these absurdities, this spectacle has often delighted me in individual scenes: more than once I have forgotten that I was watching an artificial spectacle, unnatural in so many of its parts [...]. After such entrancing scenes you understand what a magnificent spectacle, far exceeding all others, opera could be. You are sorry that such deeply moving things occur in the midst of so many absurdities, and you cannot help pondering schemes whereby this spectacle might be cleansed of the ordure of childish matters which occur in it, and [...] how it could be employed for a nobler and greater purpose than being a mere pastime. [...]

Opera's firmest foundation, upon which to erect a splendid and glorious edifice, would be its intimate connection with the national interest of an entire people. But that is out of the question in our day and age. For the state has never been further removed than at present from the spirit formerly reigning in Athens and Rome. [...] Without soaring into boundless regions of sweet fancy, we shall only speak of the improvements which could be made to opera given the present condition of the arts and of the political order. For this it would [...] be necessary for a great prince beloved of the Muses to hand over all the arrangements connected with this spectacle to a man who, with good will and good taste, had sufficient prestige to direct according to his pleasure the librettist, the composer and all the virtuosi necessary for opera.

The main responsibility would now rest with the librettist. Paying no attention to the singers and the above-mentioned factors which at present tempt him into so many absurdities, he should take it as his principle 'to compose a tragedy the contents and conduct of which were suited to the nobility, or at any rate the sentiment, of the lyrical tone.' In truth any tragic subject is suitable, the only condition being that the plot is not fast-moving and has no great complications. The action cannot be fast-moving because that runs counter to the nature of song which presupposes a dwelling on sentiments which give rise to the singing mood. Great complications run counter to it even more because they engage reason more than feeling. When plots are hatched, plans concerted, and consultations held, one is as far removed from singing as could be.

Hence the librettist would differ from the writer of tragedies in that he would not, unlike the latter, present an action from start to finish with all its complications, plots, negotiations and intrigues and incidents but merely the feelings they arouse and whatever is spoken or done under the influence of those feelings.

In addition to these dramaturgic points, Sulzer also made some general suggestions for the improvement of opera in presentational terms.

A landscape or a prospect can make us happy, merry, tender, sad, melancholy or fearful; and the same thing can be effected by a building or by the interior furnishing of a room. So the designer can anticipate the poet at every point in order to give him easier access to the spectators' hearts. But he must not stray one whit from the path followed by the poet: [there must be] nothing insignificant, for the mere delectation of the eye; far less anything surprising that contradicts the prevailing tone of feeling.

The costumes of the characters contribute greatly to the [overall] impression; and it is nonsense merely to aim at foolishly dazzling the eye. [...]

We prefer not to speak at all of ballets which would more fittingly be omitted from opera altogether rather than have them, as is now the case, interrupt the action and wipe out the impressions it has produced ... [...]

Contemptible as opera is in its usual disfigurement, and little as it merits the great expenditure it involves, it could be significant and venerable if it were led towards the principal aim of all the fine arts and handled by genuine virtuosi.

In the same dictionary of aesthetics, Sulzer also had something to say about the relatively new form of operetta, sometimes called *Singspiel* in German. Operetta was clearly still in need of a certain degree of critical justification.

182   The uses of operetta, 1774

Johann Georg Sulzer (1774), vol. 2, pp. 851–2

Just as opera in the strict sense [...] has arisen from the union of tragedy with music, music united with comedy has produced the operetta, which has only arisen in the last forty or fifty years but which has recently taken over the German stage to the extent of threatening to displace real comedy from it. At first it was a mere ridiculous farce, the idea of which the Germans borrowed from the Italian *intermezzo* and *opera buffa*. In this, author and composer only sought to be as funny as possible. [...]

Recently attempts have been made to elevate operetta, which initially was merely comical, to somewhat greater dignity, and this has resulted in an altogether new musical drama which may be of real value once it has achieved its perfect form at the hands of skilful poets and composers. [...]

Just as grand opera deals with important and highly serious subjects, whereby strong passions are brought into play, music, which can take on any tone with equal ease, can also serve to depict gentle feelings, merriment and mere delight. In order to combine this with a suitable action, let a subject be chosen, as in comedy, from the pleasant or delightful incidents of common life. [...] We already have some examples of French and German operetta pitched somewhere in the middle which as it were stand midway between high tragic opera and the low intermezzo and which make us hopeful that this genre might gradually be developed further and finally reach its perfection. [...] The dialogue of the action would be in prose, hence without any music, as has already become established; and at suitable points the poet would introduce songs of all sorts, including the occasional aria. The songs would partly be taken from the story, and would partly come in as episodic songs. [...]

In this way there would arise a new very pleasant kind of drama, dealing more with manners than with passions, in which music and poetry would be combined. Apart from the immediate utility which it would share with other dramatic spectacles it would have this particular utility that quantities of good songs of poetic and musical value and pleasant little arias, which one can easily sing without exactly being a virtuoso by profession, would thereby be diffused from the stage into society and into lonely closets.

Johann Jakob Engel, playwright as well as a theorist of acting (see 131, 133, 136, 137), wrote the libretto of one comic opera, or operetta: *Die Apotheke*. Although he did not think sufficiently highly of this text to include it in his collected works, in his preface he tried to justify farce on theoretical (and curiously sociological) grounds. Farce, while being a regular ingredient of the German repertoire, had not recently enjoyed any critical esteem: it had been anathema to Gottsched.

183   The uses of farce, 1772

J.J. Engel, *Die Apotheke, eine komische Oper in zwei Aufzügen* (The Chemist's Shop, a Comic Opera in Two Acts) (Leipzig: Dyck, 1772), preface pp. vii–xv. Herzog-August-Bibliothek, Wolfenbüttel, Lo 1267 (1)

I think [. . .] it would be a good thing if all farces were turned into operettas. Our public likes to see these farces and yet would like to appear to despise them. [. . .] Perhaps it would be as well to respect this petty modesty and to allow the public the pretext of only going to see the farce for the music. Besides you can kill two birds with one stone this way. You make people laugh and you develop their taste for music. [. . .]

Quite apart from this, I believe that even farce can have a higher aim than I have been able to aim at in mine. – For what is the difference between farce and the other genres? Is it a description of the follies and the vices of the lower classes? Well then, it is a picture of one part of human life; and anything relating to that can be rendered significant. But it has to be a true and exact picture. It would be a very good thing for the higher classes if the lower orders were not so entirely unknown to them. It would be useful for the well-mannered and well-bred citizen if he were to learn that common sense, wit, every talent, every perfection can co-exist with rough manners and the lack of outer polish; it would be a good thing if he had occasion to observe the way of thinking, the language, the inwardness of ordinary folk at close quarters.

A particular advantage of these depictions might be the fact that the judgements passed about the rich and the great at the meetings of artisans and peasants, judgements which are as a rule very severe and often justified, were to become known to the former. [. . .]

Yet another advantage of farce resides in the rank of the person performing it. Good manners and decorum always consist of a kind of reserve which somehow retrenches every truth, gives a false addition to any opinion which might offend, and often passes in silence over the most forceful and useful aspects of the matter. The simple-minded or gauche person appearing in farce says all he thinks straight out, and he says it as he thinks. Though remaining very much a fool or very much a child, he might yet utter a good many useful truths.

If there was a dearth of high comedy in the German repertoire, there was an even greater absence of high tragedy. Lessing attempted to direct the attention of both the public and playwrights back to the fountainhead of the European theory of tragedy: Aristotle – but an Aristotle not mediated by (chiefly French) neo-classical theory. He used the performance at the Hamburg National Theatre on 22 July 1767 of *Richard III*, an original play not directly indebted to Shakespeare but written in 1759 by the popular playwright Christian Felix Weisse (1726–1804 – see **148**, note 1), as a spur or pretext for enlarging on his ideas on this subject. He devoted eleven issues of the *Hamburgische Dramaturgie* (12 January– 16 February 1768) to the interpretation of Aristotle. In an extended polemic against Corneille's tragic theory, Lessing insisted on a return to the Aristotelian categories of a catharsis brought about by 'pity and fear', a concept he claimed had been undermined by French precept and example.

184   Lessing's call for true tragedy, 1768

Lessing, *Hamburgische Dramaturgie*, 5 February 1768. Reproduced Petersen (ed.) (1925), pp. 332–3

What is the weary labour of the dramatic form for? Why build a theatre, dress up men and women, torture one's memory, invite the whole town to one place, if I do not intend to produce with my work and with its representation anything other than some of the emotions which a good story that people read in their nook at home would more or less produce as well?

The dramatic form is the only one in which pity and fear can be excited; at any rate, in no other form can these passions be excited to so high a degree: and yet people prefer to use it for anything other than that for which it is so eminently well designed.

The public puts up with that. – That is a good thing, and yet it is not a good thing. For one does not much long for the dishes which are always on offer.

Everybody knows how keen the Greek and the Roman nations were on their dramas; especially the former, on their tragedies. By contrast, how indifferent, how cold is our nation as regards the theatre! Whence this difference if it does not derive from the fact that the Greeks felt inspired with such strong, such extraordinary emotions *vis-à-vis* their stage that they could not wait for the moment to have them again and again: whereas we are conscious of such feeble impressions *vis-à-vis* our stage that we rarely consider it worth the time and the money to have them? We go to the theatre, nearly all of us, nearly always, out of curiosity, out of boredom, out of a desire to gape and to be gaped at: and only some few for any other reason, and those few but sparingly.

I say, our nation, our stage: but I do not only mean us Germans. We Germans confess candidly enough that we do not as yet have a theatre. I really cannot tell what many of the critics have in mind who, agreeing with this confession, are great admirers of the French theatre. But I know well enough what I have in mind. What I have in mind is this: that not only we Germans but also they who glory in having had a theatre for a hundred years, nay who boast of having the best theatre in Europe – that the French do not yet have a theatre either.

Certainly not a tragic theatre! For the impressions made by French tragedy are so flat, so cold!

Like Lessing, Johann Christoph Friedrich Schiller (1759–1805) was both a playwright and a theorist who investigated not merely drama but a wide range of aesthetic problems. His ideas evolved considerably over the years: the essay quoted below expresses views at variance with his more mature beliefs in that it stresses, more than later essays do, the direct *moral* function of the theatre. The essay was a somewhat amended version of a lecture entitled, 'Was kann eine gute stehende Schaubühne eigentlich wirken?' (What

Effect can a Good Permanent Theatre really have?') which he had read at a meeting of the Electoral German Society in Mannheim on 26 June 1784, i.e. during his residence in that city, from July 1783 till April 1785, most of that time as resident playwright at the National Theatre (see 176–8, 206–7, 209–10). Many of the ideas Schiller put forward derive not only from Lessing but are commonplaces of eighteenth-century thought, including ideas drawn from Louis-Sébastien Mercier's *Du Théâtre ou nouvel essai sur l'art dramatique* (Concerning Theatre, or New Essay about the Art of Drama) (Amsterdam, 1773). But he insisted more than earlier theorists had done on the *political* function of the theatre: he claimed that it had a nation-building task, that it showed the ruling classes what the lower orders were thinking (compare 183) and – perhaps the most striking idea – that it enabled rulers to influence their subjects by what we should now regard as subliminal propaganda.

185   Schiller's justification of the stage in moral and political terms, 1784

Friedrich Schiller, 'Was kann eine gute stehende Schaubühne eigentlich wirken?', in *Rheinische Thalia*, ed. Schiller (Mannheim: Schwan, 1785), no. 1, pp. 1–27. Reproduced under the title, which has since become standard, of 'Die Schaubühne als eine moralische Anstalt betrachtet' (The Stage Considered as a Moral Institution), in *Kleinere prosaische Schriften von Schiller*, (Schiller's Shorter Prose Writings) (Leipzig: Siegfried Lebrecht Crusius, 1802), pt. 4, pp. 3–27; and in *Schillers Werke/NA*) (Works of Schiller/National Edition) vol. 20, ed. Benno v. Wiese (Weimar: Hermann Böhlaus Nachfolger, 1963), pp. 87–100

[. . .] He who first made the remark that *religion* is the firmest pillar of a state, that without it the very laws lose their force, has perhaps, without intending or knowing it, defended the stage in its noblest aspect. Precisely this insufficiency, this vacillating quality of political laws which makes religion indispensable to the state, also defines the moral influence of the stage. Laws, he meant to say, only revolve around negative duties – religion extends its demands to positive acts. [. . .] But if we were now to suppose, which is by no means the case – if we were to grant religion this great power over every human heart, will it or can it achieve its entire cultivation? – Religion (whose political aspects I here separate from the divine) generally acts more upon the senses of the people – perhaps it is so unfailingly effective only through the senses. Its power is gone once we take that away from it – [. . .]. Religion ceases to mean anything to most men, once we demolish its images, its problems – once we destroy its depictions of heaven and hell . . . [. . .] What a reinforcement for religion and law when they ally themselves with the stage, where everything is vision and living presence, where vice and virtue, happiness and misery, folly and wisdom palpably and truthfully parade past the spectator in a thousand pictures [. . .].

The jurisdiction of the stage begins where the tribunal of secular law ends. If justice is blinded by gold and revels in the pay of vice, if the crimes of the mighty mock its impotence and human fear binds the arm of authority, the stage assumes the sword and the scales and drags vice before a terrible tribunal. [...] As surely as a visible representation has a more powerful effect than the dead letter and a cold narration, the stage as surely acts more profoundly and more lastingly than morality and the law.

Here, however, it only *assists* temporal justice – it has a much wider field open to it. It punishes a thousand vices which are tolerated by the latter; it recommends a thousand virtues which the latter ignores. Here it serves as a companion to wisdom and religion. From this pure source it draws its teachings and examples, and clothes strict duty in a charming, attractive garb. [...]

But the influence of the stage extends yet further. Even where religion and laws deem it beneath their dignity to accompany human sensations, *it* continues to work for our cultivation. The happiness of society is troubled by folly as much as by crimes and vices. [...] My list of criminals grows shorter with every day of my life and my register of fools more complete and longer. [...] I know of but *one* secret to guard man against depravity: and that is – to guard his heart against weaknesses.

We may expect a great part of this effect from the stage. It is the thing that holds up a mirror to the great class of fools and mortifies them in their thousandfold varieties with wholesome mockery. What it effected above by emotion and terror, it effects here (more speedily perhaps and more infallibly) by means of jest and satire. If we were to undertake to assess comedy and tragedy in terms of the effect achieved, experience might well decide in favour of the former. Derision and contempt will wound a man's pride more keenly than destestation will torture his conscience. [...]

But its wide-ranging effectiveness is far from exhausted. The stage more than any other public institution of the state is a school of practical wisdom, a signpost through civic life, an infallible key to the most secret approaches to the human soul. I admit that self-love and a hardened conscience not infrequently undo its best effects, that a thousand vices brave its mirror with a brazen front; that a thousand fine sentiments rebound unprofitably from the cold heart of the spectator – [...] but even if we put a limit on this great effectiveness of the stage, even if we should be so unjust as to deny it altogether – what an infinite part of its influence will it not retain? Supposing it neither does away with nor diminishes the sum total of vices, has it not acquainted us with them? – With these vicious, these foolish people we have to live. We have to avoid or to encounter them; we have to undo them or succumb to them. But now they no longer surprise us. We are ready for their plots. The stage has revealed to us the secret of finding them out and rendering them harmless. [...]

The stage directs our attention not only to men and human characters but also to the vicissitudes of fate, and it teaches us the great art of how to bear them. In the web of our life, *chance* and *design* play an equally great part; the latter *we* conduct, to the former we have to submit blindly. It is much to our benefit if inevitable calamities do not find us entirely dismayed, if our courage, our prudence had already been exercised by similar ones and our heart had been steeled for the blow. [...]

But not only does the stage familiarise us with the fates of humankind, it also teaches us to be more just toward the unfortunate man and to judge him more leniently. It is only when we have fathomed the whole depth of his tribulations that we may pronounce judgement on him. [...] Humanity and tolerance are beginning to become the ruling spirit of our age: their rays have penetrated into the courts of justice, and further yet – into the hearts of our princes. How great a share in this divine work is due to our theatres? Is it not *they* that have acquainted man with man and disclosed the secret mechanism which moved him to act?

One class of men in particular has good cause to be more grateful to the stage than all the rest. It is only here that the great ones of this world hear what they scarcely ever hear anywhere else – the truth; what they never or seldom see, they see here – man.

So great and varied is the merit of the better sort of stage with regard to moral improvement; it is no less deserving with regard to the entire enlightenment of the intellect. It is precisely in this higher sphere that the superior mind, the fiery patriot knows how to use it fully.

He casts a glance over the generations of men, compares nations with nations, centuries with centuries and sees how slavishly the great mass of the people lie fettered by chains of prejudice and opinion, which forever run counter to their own happiness – that the purer rays of truth illumine only some few *individual* minds that may have purchased the trifling gain with the expenditure of a whole lifetime. How can the wise legislator give the nation a share in them?

The stage is the common channel through which the light of wisdom pours down from the thoughtful better section of the people and from thence is diffused in milder rays throughout the entire state. More correct notions, improved principles and purer sentiments flow hence through all the arteries of the nation; the mist of barbarism, of gloomy superstition disappears, night yields to triumphant light. Among so many splendid fruits of the better sort of stage let me point out only two. How universal has the toleration of religions and sects not become in but the last few years! – Ere yet Nathan the Wise and Saladin the Saracen[1] put us to shame and preached to us the divine doctrine that resignation in God's will did not at all depend on our fancied beliefs concerning God [...], the stage implanted humanity and gentleness in our hearts, the horrid portraits of the fury of heathen priests taught us to avoid religious hatred – in this frightful mirror Christianity washed off its stains. With the same success we might combat upon the stage errors of education; we have as yet to hope for a play in which this remarkable subject will be treated.[2] [. . .]

No less could the opinions of the nation concerning government and governors – if only the rulers and guardians of the state understood this – be corrected from the stage. Here the legislative power might speak to the subject through strange symbols, might justify itself against his complaints before they were ever uttered, and suborn his doubts without appearing to do so. Even industry and inventive genius could and would be fired by the theatre, if poets deemed it worth their while to be patriots, and if princes condescended to listen to them.

I cannot possibly overlook the great influence which a good permanent theatre would exercise upon the spirit of the nation. A people's national spirit is what I term the similarity and agreement of its opinions and inclinations in matters concerning which another nation thinks and feels differently. Only the stage is able to bring about this agreement in a high degree, because it roams through the whole domain of human knowledge, exhausts all the situations of life and sheds its light down into all the crannies of the human heart; because it unites all ranks and classes within itself and has the most direct access to heart and mind. If *one* principal point were featured in all our dramas, if our authors would agree amongst themselves and form a firm alliance for the accomplishment of this end – if a strict selection should guide their works and their brush were devoted to national subjects only – in a word, if we should live to have a national theatre in our midst, we should indeed become a nation.[3] [. . .]

Human nature cannot bear to be uninterruptedly and unceasingly stretched on the rack of business; sensual excitement dies with its own gratification. Man, surfeited with animal enjoyment, weary of protracted exertion, tormented by the ceaseless craving for activity, thirsts for better and choicer diversions, or else he plunges without restraint into wild revelry which will speed up his ruin and destroy the peace of society. [. . .] The businessman is in danger of paying with the wretched spleen for a life so generously sacrificed for the state – the scholar of declining into a dull pedant – the mob of turning brutish. The stage is the institution where pleasure unites with instruction, rest with exertion, amusement with education; where not one power of the soul is strained at the expense of another, where no pleasure is enjoyed at the expense of the whole. [. . .]

---

[1] In Lessing's *Nathan der Weise* (Nathan the Wise, publ. 1779, premièred 1783 – see **196**).
[2] Curiously enough, this does not take into account J.M.R. Lenz's play, *Der Hofmeister* (The Tutor, 1774), which had dealt with the problems of a private education.
[3] This point amplifies the then current arguments in favour of a National Theatre and gives the term a clearly cultural-political dimension. Schiller's hopes for the unifying national impact of theatre contrast sharply with Lessing's disenchanted dismissal of such a notion in the final instalment of the *Hamburgische Dramaturgie* (see p. 10).

Just as Schiller departed radically in his later work from the socially critical manner of his early prose tragedies, so he also modified his theoretical notions in parallel with, and indeed in preparation for and in support of, this change in the style of his plays. During the ten-year intermission in his playwriting (1789–99) when, as a professor at the University of Jena, he devoted himself to the study of history and of aesthetics, he fell deeply under the influence of Immanuel Kant. The theoretical works on aesthetics which he wrote in the 1790s and the early years of the nineteenth century (including those dealing specifically with the theory of tragedy) clearly reflect his idealist orientation. According to these newly developed views, it was the function of tragedy to assert human freedom on an ideal plane in the dichotomy between the realms of freedom and necessity: tragedy therefore had to belong to an aesthetic, rather than a moral, category since the latter was still in the realm of necessity. Hence even villains, as long as they exhibited freedom, might be tragic heroes; but in Schiller's (implicitly aristocratic) scale of human capabilities, not all spectators would be capable of attaining the heights of a tragic response to such human borderline situations. His insistence on free will being put to the most rigorous test in the course of the tragic action, as the basis of tragedy, was a vital contribution to modern tragic theory.

186   Schiller on the nature of tragedy, 1792

Johann Friedrich Schiller, *Ueber den Grund des Vergnügens an tragischen Gegenständen* (On the Causes of Delight in Tragic Subjects) (1792) (Leipzig: Siegfried Lebrecht Crusius, 1802) pp. 75–109. Reproduced in *Schillers Werke/NA*, vol. 10, ed. Siegfried Seidel (1980), pp. 7–15

[. . .] The well-meaning intention of pursuing moral goodness everywhere as the highest purpose, which has led to and protected so many mediocre productions in the arts, has done a similar damage to the theory of art as well. In order to assign a very high rank to the arts, in order to gain them the favour of the government and the veneration of all men, they are expelled from their proper domain to have forced upon them a calling which is alien and altogether unnatural to them. They are meant to be rendered a great service when a moral end has been substituted for the frivolous object of giving delight, and their very evident influence upon morality is called upon to sustain such an assertion. It is seen as a contradiction that the same art, which promotes the highest object of humanity to such a great degree, should accomplish this end only by the way and should make its final aim so vulgar a thing as pleasure is supposed to be. But this seeming contradiction could easily be resolved by a substantial theory of pleasure and a complete philosophy of art, if we had them. [. . .] But for the appreciation of art it is a matter of complete indifference whether its purpose is a moral one or whether it can only attain its purpose by moral means, for in both cases it has to do with morality and must act in the closest accord with moral sentiment; but for the perfection of art it is very far from indifferent which of the two is the end and which is the means. If the end is itself a moral one, it loses that through which alone it is powerful, its freedom, and that through which it is so universally effective, the charm of pleasure. Playfulness is turned into a serious business; and yet it is precisely play which enables it best to execute its business. It is only by achieving its *highest* aesthetic effect that it will exercise a beneficent influence upon morality; but only by exercising its complete freedom can it achieve its highest aesthetic effect.

It is moreover certain that every pleasure in so far as it flows from a moral source improves man's morality, and that here the effect must again turn into a cause. [...] Just as a blithe spirit is the assured destiny of a morally excellent person, so moral excellence will tend to accompany a blithe spirit. Art therefore has a moral effect not merely because it gives delight by moral means but also because the pleasure itself which is given by art becomes a means towards morality. [...]

The general source of every pleasure, including the sensual, is adaptation to purpose. The pleasure is sensual if the purpose is not recognised by the powers of the mind, but merely has the physical consequence of the sensation of pleasure by the law of necessity [...]

Pleasure is free if we are conscious of the adaptation to purpose and the agreeable sensation [of this] accompanies this consciousness: all notions therefore by means of which we experience agreement with and adaptation to purpose are sources of a free pleasure, and to that extent capable of being used by art for such a purpose. [...]

The touching and the sublime agree in producing pleasure and displeasure, i.e. making us feel (pleasure springing from adaptation to purpose and pain from its reverse) an adaptation to purpose which presupposes a contrariety to purpose.

But in determining the proportion of pleasure to pain in our emotions, we have principally to ascertain whether the violated end surpasses the attained end in importance, or the attained end that which is violated. No adaptation to purpose moves us as much as a moral purpose, and nothing surpasses the pleasure we feel concerning this. Natural adaptation to purpose might still be problematical; in moral things it is proven. It alone is founded upon our rational nature and upon an inner necessity. For us it is the one that is closest, most important and at the same time most recognisable, because it is not determined by external things but by an inner principle of our reason. It is the palladium of our freedom.

This moral adaptation to purpose is recognised most vividly if it keeps the upper hand in conflict with other purposes; only then does the moral law manifest its entire power when it is shown contending with all the other forces of nature, and all of them lose their power over a human heart beside it. [...] The more terrible the antagonists, the more glorious the victory; resistance alone can render the power visible. [...]

So the species of poesy which affords us moral delight to an exceptional degree has for that very reason to employ mixed sensations and to delight us by means of pain. This is done to an exceptional degree by *tragedy*, and its domain comprehends all possible cases where some natural purpose is sacrificed to a moral one, or one moral adaptation to purpose to another of a higher order. [...]

But the suffering of a criminal delights us tragically no less than the suffering of the virtuous person; and yet we here receive the impression of a moral contrariety of purpose. The contradiction of his acts to the moral law should fill us with indignation, the moral imperfection underlying his conduct, with pain, even without our taking into account the misfortunes of the innocent who have become his victims. Here there is no satisfaction with the morality of the persons capable of compensating us for the pain which we feel concerning their actions and sufferings – and yet both constitute a very fruitful theme for art upon which we may dwell with great delight. It will not be difficult to bring this fact into accord with what we have stated so far.

It is not merely obedience to the moral law that gives us the idea of adaptation to moral purpose, but pain caused by its violation does so as well. The sadness which springs from the consciousness of moral imperfection is purposeful inasmuch as it stands as the reverse of the satisfaction which accompanies morally right conduct. Repentance, self-condemnation, even in their highest degree, in despair, are morally sublime since they never could be felt if, deep in the criminal's heart, there did not lie awake an incorruptible feeling for right and wrong, asserting its claims even against the most ardent interests of self-love. [...] A man who despairs on account of a violation of a moral law, returns by this very means to his obedience to it; and the more terribly his self-condemnation manifests itself, the more powerfully we see the moral law hold sway over him.

But there are cases where the moral pleasure is purchased only by a moral pain, and this happens if a moral duty has to be violated in order to act more in accord with a higher and more general duty. [...]

But no moral phenomenon will be judged by people in so many different ways as this very one, and the reason for this difference is not far to seek. The moral sense is indeed inherent in all men, but not in all of them with the degree of strength and freedom required in judging these cases. For most men it is enough to approve of an act because its correspondence with the moral law is easily grasped, or to reject another because its opposition to this law is self-evident. But a clear understanding and a reason independent of every natural force, even including moral impulses (to the extent that they are instinctive) are required in order correctly to determine the relation of moral duties to the highest principle of morality. Hence the same act in which some few men recognise the highest adaptation to purpose, may strike the multitude as a revolting contradiction, even though both are passing a moral judgement; hence it is that the emotion kindled by such acts cannot be shared universally as the unity of human nature and the necessity of the moral law might lead one to expect. [. . .] A small soul sinks under the load of such great concepts or feels painfully distended beyond its moral dimensions. [. . .]

So much for the sense of moral adaptation to purpose in so far as tragic emotions and our delight in suffering are based upon it. But there are nevertheless enough cases where a natural adaptation to purpose seems to give us pleasure even at the expense of the moral purpose. We are evidently delighted at a villain's superior logic in setting up his engines, although both contrivances and object offend our moral sense. Such a man is capable of exciting our liveliest sympathy and we tremble at the failure of the very same plans, the defeat of which, if it were really the case that we referred everything to moral purposes, we should most ardently desire [. . .].

Under all circumstances adaptation to purpose, either with no reference to morality at all or in direct contradiction to it, affords us pleasure. This pleasure remains unalloyed as long as we do not remember a moral end which is contradicted by it. [. . .] But if it occurs to us to refer this end and its means to some moral principle and we then discover a contradiction between it and the end; in short, if we remember that it is the act of a moral being, then a deep indignation takes the place of the former pleasure, and no intellectual adaptation to purpose whatsoever is capable of reconciling us to the idea of a want of moral contrariety of purpose. We should never be too vividly aware that this Richard III, this Iago [. . .] are human beings, otherwise our sympathy will inevitably turn into its opposite. But the fact that we possess and often enough exercise the faculty of turning our attention voluntarily from one aspect of things and directing it to another, the fact that pleasure itself, which is only possible for us by virtue of this selectivity, invites us to do this and keeps us there – these are confirmed by daily experience.

In *Die Braut von Messina* (1803), Schiller took his idealistic drama to its furthest extreme by borrowing the convention of the chorus from classical Greek tragedy. (For the contemporary reception of the play, see **225–6**.) *Die Braut von Messina* has not kept its place in today's German repertoire with the frequency of other Schiller plays; but what is significant from the theoretical point of view is that in the preface to the play Schiller lucidly argued the case for the chorus in the modern theatre – a device attempted in post-Renaissance drama from Racine to Yeats and T.S. Eliot – on explicitly anti-naturalistic grounds. This preface, in fact, calls for detachment or distanciation on the part of the spectator as a necessary part of a truly aesthetic experience, in contrast to the emotional involvement claimed by sentimental middle-class drama.

187   Schiller on the chorus in tragedy, 1803

J.C.F. Schiller, Preface to *Die Braut von Messina: Über den Gebrauch des Chors in der Tragödie* (The Bride of Messina: On the Use of the Chorus in Tragedy) (Tübingen: Cotta, 1803), pp. iii–xiv. A short excerpt reproduced in Nagler (1952), pp. 442–4. Translated in full in A. Lodge, *The Works of Frederick Schiller* (London: Bell and Daldy, 1871), vol. 3

[. . .] True, everyone expects from the imaginative arts a certain emancipation from the bounds of reality, he wishes to take delight in possibilities and give scope to his fancy. [. . .] But he knows well enough that he is only playing an idle game, that is only literally taking delight in dreams, and when he returns from the theatre to the real world, the latter enfolds him again with all its oppressive narrowness, he is its victim as he had been before, for it has remained what it was and nothing has changed in him. So nothing has been gained thereby but a pleasing delusion of the moment which vanishes on awakening.

And precisely because a mere passing illusion is aimed at here, only a semblance of truth or the much-favoured verisimilitude is required, which people are so ready to substitute for the truth.

But true art does not aim merely at a short-lived game; it has the serious purpose of not merely wafting man into a momentary dream of freedom but to *make* him free in actual fact, and to do this by arousing, exercising and forming a strength in him to move to an objective distance the entire sensory world which otherwise only burdens us as undigested matter, pressing down on us a blind power, and to transform it into a free working of our spirit and to dominate matter by our ideas. [. . .]

But how art can at the same time be wholly ideal and yet in the deepest sense real – how it ought, and is able to, depart from reality altogether and yet correspond to nature exactly, that is what few understand and what makes opinion concerning poetic and plastic works so squint-eyed, because in the common view the two demands seem absolutely contradictory. [. . .]

The two demands are so little in contradiction with one another that on the contrary – they are identical; art is true only by departing from reality altogether and becoming purely ideal. Nature itself is only an idea of the mind which is never present to the senses. It lies beneath the guise of appearances but it never appears itself. Only the art of the ideal is granted the power, or rather it is entrusted with the task, of seizing that spirit of the universe and binding it in a corporeal form. [. . .]

What is true of art and poetry in toto also holds good as to their various subdivisions, and we can easily apply what has just been stated to tragedy. Here, too, it has long been and still is necessary to combat the common notion of *naturalness*, which in truth cancels out and destroys all poetry and art. A certain ideality has at a pinch been conceded to painting [...]; but in poetry, and especially dramatic poetry, what is demanded is *illusion*, which even if it were feasible would never be any more than a miserable sleight-of-hand. All the externals of a theatrical representation are opposed to this notion; everything is merely a symbol of the real. The very daylight in a theatre is but artificial, the set is only symbolical, the metrical language is itself ideal; yet they would have the action real and the part destroy the whole. Thus the French, who were the first wholly to misread the spirit of the ancients, introduced on their stage the unities of time and place in the most banal empirical sense, as if there were here any place other than the merely ideal space, and any time other than the steady continuity of the action.

However, an important step towards poetic tragedy has already been taken by the introduction of metrical language. A few lyrical experiments have been successful on the stage, and poetry has by its own living energy won some victories here and there over the prevailing prejudice. But single actions avail little unless error is overturned altogether, and it is not enough merely to tolerate as a poetic licence that which is really the essence of all poetry. The introduction of the chorus would be the final, the decisive step – and even if it only served to declare a frank and open war on naturalism[1] in art, it should be a living wall for us which tragedy erected around itself, to shut itself off entirely from the real world and to maintain its ideal soil, its poetic freedom. [...]

Ancient tragedy, which originally only dealt with gods, heroes and kings, needed the chorus as a necessary accompaniment; it found it there in nature and used it because it found it. [...] In modern tragedy it becomes an organ of art, it helps to *produce* poetry. The modern poet no longer finds the chorus in nature, he must create and introduce it by poetic means, that is, he must so alter the story he is treating as to take it back to that naive period and to that simple form of life.

The chorus therefore renders an even more substantial service to the present-day tragic playwright than to the ancient poet, precisely because it transforms the commonplace modern world into the old poetical one, because it rules out for his use whatever is repugnant to poetry and thrusts him towards the most simple, original and genuine motives of action. The palace of kings is closed now, the courts of justice have withdrawn from the gates of cities to the interior of buildings, writing has replaced the living word, the people itself [...], when it does not operate as brute force, has turned into the state and hence an abstract concept, the gods have returned within the bosom of mankind. The poet must reopen the palaces, he must lead the courts of justice out under the canopy of heaven, he must put the gods back in their place, he must restore everything immediately tangible that has been abolished by the artificial arrangement of actual life [...].

But just as the painter spreads the ample drapery of garments around his figures in order richly and gracefully to fill up the spaces of his picture, in order to combine its several parts harmoniously into well balanced masses, in order to give due play to colour which charms and delights the eye, [...] just so the tragic poet interweaves and envelops his strictly designed plot and the firm outlines of the characters of his action with a tissue of lyrical magnificence in which, as in a flowing robe of purple, the persons of the action move freely and nobly, with measured dignity and high serenity. [...]

Now man is so constituted that he wishes always to go from the particular to the general, and reflection must therefore have its place in tragedy too. But if it is to merit this place, it must regain by diction what it lacks in sensory vividness; for if the two elements of poetry, the ideal and the sensory, do not act *together* in intimate alliance they must act *side by side*, or poetry ceases to exist. If the balance is not in perfect equipoise, equilibrium can only be restored by a rise and fall of the two scale pans.

And that is what the chorus effects in tragedy. The chorus is not itself an individual but a general conception; but this conception is represented by a mighty palpable body which impresses the senses by its imposing presence. The chorus leaves the narrow sphere of the action in order to dilate upon past and future, upon distant times and nations, upon human affairs at large, in order to sum up the grand results of life and to pronounce the lessons of wisdom. [...]

The chorus thus *purifies* the tragic poem by keeping reflection separate from the action, and by this very separation equipping it with poetic vigour [...].

But just as the painter sees himself obliged to strengthen the hue of the living in order to counterbalance the prepotent materials, so the lyrical language of the chorus obliges the poet to elevate all the language of the poem proportionately and thus strengthen the sensory power of expression generally. It is only the chorus that entitles the poet to [employ] this elevation of tone which fills the ear, exerts the spirit and enlarges the whole mind. This one giant figure on his canvas obliges him to mount all his figures on the buskin and thereby give a tragical grandeur to his picture. [...]

[...]

As the chorus gives *life* to the language, it imparts calmness to the action – but that fair and lofty calmness which must be the characteristic of a noble work of art. For the mind of the spectator should maintain its freedom even in the most violent passion; it should not fall prey to impressions but always calmly and serenely detach itself from the emotions it is undergoing. That which a common-place judgement will blame the chorus for – that it spoils the illusion, that it disrupts the power of the feelings – is what constitutes its highest recommenda-tion; for this blind power of the feelings is the very thing the true artist avoids, this illusion is what he disdains to excite. If the blows tragedy directs at our heart were to follow one another without interruption, suffering would win out over action. We should merge with the subject and no longer soar above it. By keeping the parts separate and interposing itself between the passions with its calming reflection, the chorus gives us back our freedom which would be lost in the tempest of the emotions. The characters of tragedy, too, themselves need this intermission, this repose, in order to collect themselves; for they are not real beings who merely obey the impulse of the moment and merely represent the individual, but ideal figures and representatives of their species who enunciate the profound things of humankind. The presence of the chorus, who listens to them as a judging witness and mitigates the first eruptions of their passion by its interposition, motivates the circumspection with which they act and the dignity with which they speak. [...]

[1] Note this early use of the term 'naturalism' – here seen in a wholly negative light.

C. INDIVIDUAL PLAYS

Miss Sara Sampson (Lessing)

Lessing's bourgeois tragedy, Miss Sara Sampson, which was largely instrumental in establishing this English-derived genre in the German theatre, was performed by Acker-mann's company in Frankfurt-on-Oder on 10 July 1755, shortly after it had been written. Indeed, before its appearance in the programme of the National Theatre in Hamburg at quite an early stage in the latter's brief history, that city had already seen it in a successful production by Schönemann on 6 October 1756. When it was performed at the National Theatre in 1767, this was not primarily a tribute to its resident 'theatre poet' Lessing, nor was it designed to implement the exemplary repertoire policy as laid down by Löwen (see 170); unfortunately there was to be little enough of that in actual practice (see Robertson (1939), p. 40): in fact, Miss Sara Sampson was intended to show off the acting skills of the formidable Mme Hensel who had played the title role previously with the Schuch company in Berlin. There were to be four repeats of the play at the National Theatre.

188   Mme Hensel's impressive death scene, 1767

Lessing, Hamburgische Dramaturgie, (12 June 1767). Reproduced in Werke (1925), pp. 75–6

'*Miss Sara Sampson*' was performed on the eleventh evening (Wednesday 6 May). Nothing more can be demanded of art than Mme Hensel performs in the role of Sara, and altogether the play was very well done. It is a little too long, and therefore it is cut in most theatres. I rather doubt if the author is entirely satisfied with all these cuts. But we know what authors are like; the moment you deprive them of as little as the head of a pin, they scream at once, 'You're killing me!' To be sure, the play's excessive length is but poorly remedied by mere omissions, and I do not see how you can shorten a scene without altering the whole run of the dialogue. But if the author doesn't care for somebody else's cuts, let him make them himself if he thinks it is worth doing and he isn't one of those fellows who put children into the world and then fail to care for them ever after.[1]

Mme Hensel died with immense propriety; in the most picturesque attitude; and there was one trait that I found extraordinarily striking. It has been noted in dying people that they begin to pick away with their fingers at their clothes or bedding. She used this observation in the most felicitous manner; at the moment when her soul was departing from her a mild spasm manifested itself, but only in the fingers of the arm which had grown rigid; she pinched her skirt, which was lifted a little and at once dropped again: the last flicker of a dying light; the final ray of a setting sun.[2]

---

[1] Clearly Lessing is being somewhat ironical here at the expense of a play he had written some twelve years earlier and the style of which he had by now outgrown. But the fact that he was not responsible for the revised, or rather the cut, version as staged by the National Theatre would seem to illustrate his limited influence in that organisation.

[2] Karoline Schulze, Mme Hensel's predecessor with Ackermann in Hamburg who had left the company before it was transformed into the National Theatre, claimed that her rival had copied much of the business for Sara Sampson from her. She had had ample opportunities in her calamitous early life to study death-bed scenes at close quarters. See E. Benezé (*SGTG* 1915), vol. 1, pp. 222, 224, or Buck (1988), p. 135, and Robertson (1939), p. 35.

Minna von Barnhelm (Lessing)

Just as *Miss Sara Sampson* had been performed before being staged at the National Theatre, the first performance there of Lessing's comedy of character, *Minna von Barnhelm*, on 30 September (or 1 October) 1767 was not an actual première either. It had been staged shortly before, on 21 March 1768, in Berlin by the Döbbelin company – so successfully that it ran for nineteen nights. Considered an important breakthrough in German playwriting, it persuaded educated Berlin citizens, who had previously preferred French drama, to go to see German plays. But the Hamburg production was a much more distinguished event than the Berlin one. With sixteen performances, *Minna von Barnhelm* proved to be quite the most popular play in the National Theatre's repertoire. From 1774 onwards the play was also performed abroad. In 1786 it was the first play of German origin to be staged in England in an adaptation by James Johnstone, *The Disbanded Officer; or, the Baroness of Bruchsal* (London: T. Cadell 1786); it ran at the Haymarket for nine nights.

189   Qualified praise of the performance, Hamburg, 16 May 1768

Unterhaltungen (Diversions) (Hamburg: December 1768), pp. 537–40. Reproduced in Julius W. Braun, *Lessing im Urtheile seiner Zeitgenossen* (Lessing in the Judgement of his Contemporaries), vol. 1 (Berlin: Friedrich Stahn 1884), pp. 228–31; reprinted Hildesheim: Olms, 1969

– Thursday 19 May: *Minna von Barnhelm*, or *The Soldier's Fortune*, a comedy by Herr *Lessing* in 5 acts. In view of the infancy of our German theatre, the manhood of which will not perhaps be seen even by our grandchildren, we may regard our *Lessing* as the German *Livius Andronicus*.[1] [...] Germany, this country so unappreciative of the fairest of the liberal arts, does not deserve a *Lessing*; a man who unites all the beauties of Plautus and Terence in his plays and who has often surpassed them both. [...] We do not, though we have heard many people say so, wish to blame Herr *Ekhof*, who plays Major Tellheim, for the situation being false in which he seeks to place himself on seeing Minna. – Actually it is not. It is wholly appropriate to his sensitive character. Overjoyed one moment on seeing his Minna; gloomy and serious the next moment on considering his present situation.[2] If we were to criticise anything in this, in every other respect excellent, actor we might well wish that he played Tellheim with more dignity [...]. *Minna* is played by Mme *Hensel*. One actually forgets in most parts of her performance that she is too mature and no longer quite young enough for this role: she does the serious scenes splendidly; but whenever she has to act the playful girl, you detect some strain and insincerity in her voice, her gestures and her acting. She has difficulty in overcoming the lassitude all too noticeable in her comic roles which she usually sheds only when strong and flashy passages carry her along forcibly. [...] Just one word about Franciska.[3] This darling of a part, which does as much honour to the playwright as to the actress, is currently played outstandingly well by Mme *Mecour*.[4]

[1] Lucius Livius Andronicus (second half of the third century BC), the first to translate Greek tragedies and comedies into Latin. The writer uses this comparison to place Lessing in the history of German drama as an important forerunner of greater authors to come.
[2] Major von Tellheim, the over-scrupulous hero of the play, refuses to marry Minna, whom he loves and who loves him, because he is destitute after the end of his army career.
[3] Minna's maid.
[4] Susanne Mecour (1738–84), an excellent soubrette, had insisted that Lessing should not mention her, either favourably or unfavourably, in his *Dramaturgie*.

190   Scene from *Minna von Barnhelm* (etching by Chodowiecki) Act 2, sc. 9: Minna and v. Tellheim

Theatre Collection, University of Bristol

190

Minna was, and continues to be, a very popular role for German actresses. Friederike Bethmann-Unzelmann (1760–1815), who was a star of the Berlin Royal National Theatre to which she belonged from 1788 to 1815, playing as many as 284 different roles, and who also did a good deal of touring (Munich, Hamburg, Vienna, Prague etc.), sought to break with acting clichés and infuse her parts with psychological verisimilitude as well as a high style. How she did this in the title role of *Minna von Barnhelm* can be gauged from the following account written by an anonymous admirer, whose detailed notes on her playing of various roles during her guest performance in Breslau (Wroclaw) in 1801 were only published posthumously (see also **195**). Frau Bethmann-Unzelmann was somewhat less successful in poetic drama: her performance of the title role in Schiller's *Maria Stuart* did not altogether meet with the author's approval. (See *Schillers Briefe*, vol. 6 (1892), letter 1715, pp. 300–1. Reproduced in Carlson (1978), p. 159.)

191   A subtle reading of the title role, Breslau, 1801

Anon., 'Die verstorbene Bethmann/Friederike Unzelmann' (The late Frau Bethmann/
Friederike Unzelmann), in *MBGDKL*, vol. 3, no. 3 (June 1828), pp. 245–9. Herzog-August-
Bibliothek, Wolfenbüttel, Wd 567 i

They [i.e. German actresses] make Minna into a romantic, perhaps even an adventurous girl. The cruder colouring pleases; vox populi is held to be in the right, and the true Minna has to keep silent. – The representation by our actress was true to Lessing's original portrait. She sits gracefully at the table, speaks in an easy and pleasing tone, plays with her curl, supports her head with, without quite putting it into, her right hand, and leaps up when Franciska accuses Tellheim of infidelity ... [...] The landlord enters; she sits down again and remains quite detached until Franciska's teasing coaxes from her a smile, but no more. [...]

Her scene with Riccaut de la Marliniere revealed such mastery and such deep study that a precise description would be a very difficult task.[1] She takes on a very dignified air, hardly looks him in the face, smiles at his miserable pettiness all but unnoticeably, at least as far as he is concerned; [...] so that I know of no better representation of the way to dismiss such tiresome characters and their imperti- nences, no better representation of Minna's noble soul whose feelings are so well hidden. How beseechingly and insinuatingly she passes the cup of coffee to Franciska! – After a brief serious reflection she resumes her humorous tone. Werner comes in with his parade-ground step.[2] Minna is standing downstage. There is a chair in the sergeant-major's direct line towards her. That would upset his forward march; she quickly goes upstage and puts the chair to one side. [...] When she pretends to be angry with Tellheim in the last act, she uses every silent moment to exchange smiles with Franciska about her teasing; and she continues her scenes in this attitude until she lies in Tellheim's arms.

Vivid as are the hues of her portraiture, she could not in any way be accused of exaggeration. She does it all so unostentatiously; she seizes on every nuance so undemonstratively that nothing, nothing whatever reminds us of the artist standing in front of an audience [...].

---

[1] Riccaut is a comic French adventurer and card-sharper.
[2] Major von Tellheim's former sergeant-major, now his batman. For his and Franciska's popularity with audiences, see 174.

Emilia Galotti (Lessing)

Written after Lessing's retirement from practical involvement in the theatre, this prose tragedy was premiered in Brunswick by Döbbelin. The original production of *Emilia Galotti* seems to have been unworthy of a play of outstanding merit which was henceforth to enter the German tragic repertoire.

192   The first performance, Brunswick, 13 March 1772

'Aus einem Briefe von Braunschweig, den 15. Merz' (From a Letter from Brunswick, 15 March), in *Hamburgische Neue Zeitung* (*New Hamburg Journal*, 21 March 1772), front page. Reproduced in Hans Henning, *Lessings 'Emilia Galotti' in der zeitgenössischen Rezeption* (Lessing's 'Emilia Galotti' in its Contemporary Reception) (Leipzig: Zentralantiquariat der Deutschen Demokratischen Republik, 1981), p. 157

On 13th, the birthday of Her Grace our Duchess, the Döbbelin company staying here[1] performed a new tragedy by Herr Lessing, *Emilia Galotti*. This excellent play received its well merited applause although it was performed in a very mediocre manner. [. . .] Mme Döbbelin played Emilia, but how coldly! [. . .] Herr Döbbelin played old Galotti; but how stiffly! No! I did not shed any tears, but they shall flow when a better company again mounts this excellent play by the German Sophocles.

[1] Döbbelin (see 174, note 1) did not stay permanently in Berlin after establishing himself there in 1767 but continued to go on tour; he was in Brunswick as a court actor in 1772. He had staged *Minna von Barnhelm* in Berlin in 1768, and he was to be the first actor to play the eponymous hero of *Nathan the Wise* in Berlin (see 196).

193   'Emilia Galotti' in a different context, Hamburg, 1772

Anon., 'Anmerkungen über die Vorstellung der Emilia Galotti auf der Hamburgischen Bühne' (Notes about the Performance of Emilia Galotti on the Hamburg Stage), in *Beytrag zum Reichs-Postreuter* (Altona, 21 May 1772). Reproduced in Braun, *Lessing* (1884), pp. 383–5

[. . .] My second preliminary remark concerns a change made in the performance of *Emilia Galotti*. This was performed with a prologue and an epilogue in the manner of the English stage: it was accompanied neither by a ballet nor by an afterpiece, and the prologue, like the epilogue, was serious, not replete with crude jests and inappropriate satire as is commonly the case in the English theatre. An innovation which merits my whole-hearted approval [. . .]. Just one further comment. Herr *Schröder*, as the chamberlain Marinelli, spoke the prologue. [. . .] Herr Schröder's deportment did not suit the chamberlain at all; he spoke pretty inaudibly too, but being the chamberlain he must needs give the address. Herr *Borchers*[1] spoke the epilogue in the character of old *Galotti* with much propriety but alas! he could not be heard properly because his voice was too deep in his chest. But perhaps the fault lies with the current layout of the playhouse, which has gained greatly in terms of splendour as a result of the alterations undertaken but has lost a good deal in terms of audibility in the pit.

[1] For Borchers, see 115, note 2.

The role of Odoardo Galotti, the heroine's father, was one of Ekhof's great roles. He left an unforgettable impression on spectators, as the following account shows, written long after the actor's death.

194   Ekhof's business in the role of Odoardo

C.F. Nicolai, 'Ueber Eckhof' (Concerning Ekhof), in *Almanach für Theater und Theaterfreunde auf das Jahr 1807*, ed. A.W. Iffland (1807), pp. 35–8. Reproduced in Kindermann, *Conrad Ekhofs Schauspieler-Akademie* (1965), pp. 60–2

In the [. . .] scene between Orsina and Odoardo (Act 4),[1] when the latter, having received the dagger from the Countess, only discovers gradually who she is, Ekhof began during this discovery to pick away at his plumed hat several times, from time to time directing meaningful sideways glances at the Countess. His mute action made it obvious that the thought he expresses in the following scene, 'What has offended virtue to do with the vengeance of vice?' had inwardly touched him, all the more so as Orsina pours out her [desire for] vengeance more and more furiously. [. . .] In the following [. . .] scene, between the Prince, Marinelli and Odoardo,[2] the latter attempts to remain outwardly calm as best he can. Then when the Prince bedazzles him with courtierlike courtesy, he forgets himself to the point of asking Marinelli with a kind of triumph, 'Now what about that, Sir?' Thereupon the latter unfolds his cunning scheme bit by bit. Odoardo now comes to understand the frightful secret, and since Marinelli at last has the effrontery to say that he suspected a rival of Count Appiani had tried to do away with him, Odoardo loses his control altogether though still endeavouring not to show this, so that he falls into a sullen silence. Ekhof then recommenced the unconscious plucking away at his plumed hat, and when Odoardo's inward rage, which he was forced to hide, rose to its highest pitch, [. . .] Ekhof convulsively pulled *one* feather out of the trimming of the hat. Everything in his acting was so well co-ordinated, his inner feelings manifested themselves through tiny external movements so unexpectedly and yet with such terrible clarity, that the spectator was seized by cold horror at the plucking out of this little feather.

[1] In Act 4, Sc. 7, Countess Orsina, the cast-off mistress of the Prince of Guastalla, is almost beside herself as she seeks to inflame Colonel Galotti against the Prince, his daughter Emilia's would-be seducer.
[2] In Act 5, Sc. 5, the Prince and his scheming advisor Marinelli try to persuade Odoardo that they are seeking to investigate the murder of his daughter's fiancé, Count Appiani, for which in fact they are responsible, and that Emilia will have to be kept in confinement pending the trial. Odoardo comes to realise that this is a device to yield her up into the Prince's hands.

Friederike Bethmann-Unzelmann gave as much psychological depth to the character of Countess Orsina – a stellar role although she only appears in Act 4 – as she had done to her portrayal of the title role of *Minna von Barnhelm* (see **191**).

195   Friederike Bethmann as Orsina, Breslau, *c.* 1801

'Die verstorbene Bethmann/Friederike Unzelmann', in *MBGDKL*, vol. 3, no. 3 (June 1828), pp. 222–7

She entered, and with her first steps there entered the character of her subsequent scenes. – A murmur running through the audience had announced her long awaited coming, and rapturous applause greeted her. [...]

The way she generally handled this role was infinitely removed from the usual method. She does not come rushing in; she enters in a perturbed but graceful way, without any undue haste; she does not bellow out her first words – because that is not the way the proud Orsina behaves; she speaks to Marinelli on a note of indifference [...] with her face half averted; she only looks at him with deliberate hauteur when she says, 'How he stands there etc.';[1] she only permits herself a slight touch of emotion when she says, 'I bet he is in the room where I heard the squeaking, the screeching'.[2] [...] She calms down again and lets her tongue run on until – the unread letter.[3] 'Not read?' she exclaims, picking up Marinelli's last syllable, the second time she says it more softly so that Marinelli would not hear her – and for the third exclamation, 'Not even read it?', Lessing calls for a tear. I think – I saw her do more. She bursts out again more violently when she answers Marinelli with, 'Contempt?' She utters this word as quickly as possible and as it were throws it at Marinelli's feet. Ordinary Orsinas tend to stretch out the word, thinking to make it more significant that way.[4] – She speaks those beautiful words about indifference quite unemotionally, but her soulful eye accompanies each word, always follows the gentle hand movements; you can tell that all this flows from her lips unprepared, new-born. – And are not these words generally trumpeted out?[5] – The Prince appears. Orsina only meets him halfway; while he speaks with her she directs her glance at him – and who would care to share this look with him? He leaves, and without changing her posture, without raising her drooping arms, she casts her eyes down.[6] – [...] On her words of sympathy with Emilia's fate, 'Poor dear girl etc.' she quickly turns away from Marinelli – as she does with every, even the slightest, expression of feeling. – She carries through the whole scene with Marinelli in such a thoroughly individualised way. – Now Odoardo appears; she comes back and throws herself into the chair; and how closely she listens to him; how her eyes already prefigure the sympathy which is going to tie her to Odoardo! Let me only point out the most significant traits. I must skip a good deal and pick her up again as she sings out to the father an unhappy oracle – his fate.[7] She says, 'Only wounded? Appiani is dead!', and she gently closes her eyes – even her sympathy must be tactful and therefore spoken not harshly but softly and in a melancholy manner – [...]. Soon after, she lets her sleeping rage burst out for the first time, and her imagination feasts on the idea of the group of abandoned women tearing him to pieces some day.[8] Every facial muscle is tensed, her eye contracts in wild mockery and her mouth grows distorted in the representation of disgust; but she does not cry out loudly. – [. . .]

There is always this same sure agility of her entire body, this unforced, uncluttered accompaniment of her hand gestures – the free use of whatever she is in touch with, such as her fan [. . .] the business with which would be a study in itself, [and is] a Garrick-like talent of Mme Unzelmann's.

¹ Marinelli tries to keep Countess Orsina away from the Prince (Act 4, Sc. 3).
² Emilia Galotti and her mother Claudia are in the room next door, shortly after the assassination of Emilia's fiancé.
³ The Prince has insulted his ex-mistress by not even reading a note she had sent him to arrange to see him.
⁴ She rejects the possibility of the Prince having acted contemptuously towards her as being below her dignity.
⁵ Orsina speaks ('mockingly' according to the stage direction) about indifference in a lover.
⁶ The Prince has snubbed her in the presence of Marinelli.
⁷ The scene referred to in 194.
⁸ Orsina is here speaking for all the women seduced, humiliated and abandoned by the Prince.

Nathan der Weise (Nathan the Wise – Lessing)

This drama in iambic pentameters, Lessing's plea for religious tolerance, has long been a respected repertoire item in the German theatre: it was one of the first plays to be performed widely after the end of World War Two. But its initial reception was nowhere near the enthusiasm with which *Minna von Barnhelm* had been greeted.

196   Poor audience support for the première of *Nathan der Weise*, Berlin, 1783

Anon., 'Vom hiesigen deutschen Theater' (News of the Local German Theatre), in *LTZ*, 3 May 1783. Reproduced in Braun, *Lessing*, vol. 2 (1893), p. 341

The most curious item on our stage so far this year has been *Nathan der Weise* by *Lessing*. This dramatic poem [. . .] was performed on 14, 15 and 16 April. Herr *Döbbelin* has spared no expense to stage this masterpiece in as dignified a manner as possible. New sets and costumes were made for it, and one might have thought he would have been repaid a thousandfold for this expenditure. The first day the play went well enough. There was a solemn silence, each touching situation was applauded [. . .], it was thought that the public would take the house by storm, but this public stayed away almost entirely at the third performance of Nathan. The Jewish community whom one might very much have counted on for this play, was, as they put it themselves, too modest to listen to an apology which, to be sure, was not written for the Jews of today, and so there were only very few who had a stomach for Nathan. [. . .] Herr *Döbbelin* himself was Nathan, playing him with much warmth; his acting still reminded us of his theatrical merits of banishing Harlequin and teaching us a taste for purer enjoyments.[1]

[1] Döbbelin, who began his theatrical career with the Neubers (see **174**, note 1), banished Hanswurst from the Berlin stage and favoured regular plays, especially tragedies.

Götz von Berlichingen (Goethe)

Götz von Berlichingen was a key play in German theatre history for several reasons. First, it established Goethe, who in 1773 had published this dramatised chronicle of an historical sixteenth-century knight and freedom fighter, as an exciting new playwriting talent, although he had not in fact intended the text for stage production. Second, when the play was premièred in Berlin in the year following publication, it was immediately felt to be a great breakthrough in German theatre. Structurally *Götz* broke radically with neo-classical drama in defying the three unities, even the unity of action, in a way held to be the Shakespearean manner; its authentically German tone of voice contrasted refreshingly with the Frenchified style hitherto cultivated in the better kind of German theatre; and its portrayal of a bold fighter in the troubled times of the Reformation and the Peasants' War struck what was felt to be a patriotic note. In putting on this colourful and rather rambling play, German directors saw the need for more characteristic settings and costumes than had served hitherto: in fact, *Götz* introduced archaeological staging to the German theatre. (See **79**.) Dresses for the Berlin première were designed by Johann Wilhelm Meil (1733–1805), considered an expert in costume history. The following newspaper report reflects the play's favourable reception.

197 Götz von Berlichingen described as a Shakespearean type of play, Berlin, 16 April 1774

Berlinische privilegirte Zeitung, 16 April 1774. Reproduced in Braun, *Goethe im Urtheile seiner Zeitgenossen*, (Goethe in the Judgement of his Contemporaries), vol. 1, 1773–1786 (Berlin: Friedrich Luckhardt, 1883), pp. 32–3. Reprinted Hildesheim: Georg Olms Verlagsbuchhandlung, 1969

The drama which has caused such a stir in Germany:
Götz von Berlichingen with the Iron Hand
has been performed three times running at the German theatre here with great acclaim. It is a German story of chivalry, entirely in the Shakespearean manner. It would of course be very strange if one were to judge it according to the rules of so-called regular drama; but even stranger if one were to call to mind the arbitrary rules adopted from the Greeks and the French and determine the value of this piece accordingly. [...] Neither unity of action nor preparation from one incident to the next: but to make up for it, more of the German manners and ways of

thinking of that period than the keenest wit would extrapolate out of a Germany history book in folio.

[...] So, if this play had no other merit (and it certainly has plenty more!) than the one of acquainting us with the times of German chivalry, that by itself would be reason enough for every German to listen to it not once but many times. [...]

If applause is an indication of a good performance by the actors, it can on this occasion be termed excellent; and even if they had not won this applause, the impartial observer would still confess that such a play, beset as it is with many difficulties, could on the whole not be performed better by any company, in the present state of the German theatre. Especially the principal roles were very well done, and the costumes [...] will have to be praised even by antiquarians. It will be repeated tonight by popular demand.

Koch's production was so successful that it was performed as many as seventeen times. But not everybody was taken with the quality of the performances.

198   A dissenting view of the première of 'Götz von Berlichingen', 1774

'Auszug eines Briefs, über die Vorstellung des Goez von Berlichingen auf dem kochischem Theater' (Excerpt from a Letter about the Performance of Götz von Berlichingen at Koch's Theatre), in *Magazin der deutschen Critik* (Magazine of German Criticism), vol. 3, pt. 2 ed. Schirach (Halle, 1774), pp. 207–10. Reproduced in Braun, *Goethe*, vol. 1 (1883), pp. 418–20

The curtain went up, and I was thoroughly annoyed that they proposed to play Götz on a stage that seemed built only for afterpieces. But gradually I began to form a more favourable judgement, at least of the bold decision to stage the play at all, although I was but rarely satisfied with the actors. Brückner sometimes carried me away but he had not fully mastered his part.[1] He only gave a middling sort of performance of *good honest Götz* and did not know how to blend the roughness and stiffness of the knight in armour with the good nature of the honest fellow. But whenever he played the *passionate, stubborn Götz*, he was masterly. [...] Klotsch played Georg, and Withöft Lerse quite tolerably well.[2] Neither Mme Starke as Elisabeth nor yet Mme Heinsch as Maria quite hit the character of their roles.[3] Heinsch gave rather a mediocre performance as Weislingen.[4] [...] The dinner conversation at the Bishop's table was insufferably boring, but that was probably not the actors' fault. You may laugh at my taste when I tell you that I liked the gypsy scene enormously, although others around me turned away and spat ... [...] Nothing was more miserable than the secret tribunal. Just imagine the 'Woe! woe! woe' and 'Accuse! accuse! accuse!' reeled off in the tone of a boys' school.[5] One could have wished Götz [. . .] would drive them off the stage. – But it was not, and it is not, my intention to give you a complete critique of the performance of Götz, all I meant to tell you was that before seeing the play I would not have believed it possible to stage it and that now I am convinced of the contrary. But of course, the conditions would be demanding. If the theatre were twice the size of the one in Leipzig; if the company were strong enough to cast all parts well, even allowing for doubling (as indeed was the case in B.); and if there were an assembly of spectators not spoilt by sweet French manners and dramatic theories who had read enough Shakespeare to get used to now being here and now there and to take leaps of years in between scenes: then we should see what an impression Götz would make.

[1] Johann Ferdinand Brückner (1730–86): a man of versatile talent though somewhat old-fashioned in his technique, formerly with Schuch and now a leading member of Koch's company.
[2] Georg – Götz's squire; Lerse – an honest mercenary who volunteers to join Götz's troop of soldiers. Karl Wilhelm Withöft (1728–98), who had been with Frau Neuber early in his career, worked for Koch chiefly in comic roles.
[3] Elisabeth – Götz's wife; Maria – his sister. Johanna Christiana Starke (1732–1809) had been a member of the Schönemann company with her husband Johann Ludwig Starke (1723–69) before becoming an important member of the Koch ensemble.
[4] Weislingen, Götz's treacherous courtier friend – a key role in the play: he becomes engaged to Maria but abandons her for the adventuress Adelheid von Walldorf, who marries and subsequently poisons him.
[5] The secret tribunal which condemns Adelheid to death in absentia was one of Goethe's most daringly novel scenes in the play.

Later that year, *Götz* was staged in Hamburg by Schröder's company. Contemporary comparisons suggest that this production by what was at the time the best ensemble in German-speaking countries was superior to the one in Berlin. Between 1774 and 1786, further productions of *Götz* took place in Breslau, Leipzig, Frankfurt-on-Main, Vienna (at the Kärntnertortheater) and Mannheim.

199   'Götz von Berlichingen' in Hamburg, 1774

Theatralisches Wochenblatt (Theatrical Weekly), ed. J.J.C. Bode (Hamburg, 1774), nos. 10, 11 & 12. Reproduced in Fritz Winter, *Erste Aufführung des Götz von Berlichingen in Hamburg* (First Performance of G.v.B. in Hamburg), TGF, 2 (Hamburg/Leipzig: Leopold Voss, 1891), pp. 46–55

Whenever a new or curious phenomenon appears in the heavens, everything on legs will gather in crowds, young and old, men and women [. . .]. You can well imagine that it is no mean amusement on such an occasion to mix with the multitude [. . .] and to listen how opinions are divided this way and that [. . .]; certainly, no mean amusement!

And I have enjoyed it! enjoyed it two nights running, when they first performed the play: *Götz von Berlichingen with the Iron Hand*, last Monday 24 October and repeated it the following day. [...]

I hope the poet *Göthe* [sic] may read and hear from all parts of Germany tidings such as I can here write with a clear conscience so that he may feel to some extent rewarded for his precious gift [...].

I defy any company of German actors to [show] more interest in this play, to perform it with greater care and exactness, with more diligence, than our company under the direction of Mme *Ackermann* and Herr *Schröder!*[1] [...]

It is beyond question [...] a great recommendation of Mme Ackermann *vis-à-vis* her public that out of respect for the same she will not leave anything undone, will spare no expense and will set a thousand hands in motion when it is a matter of increasing the pleasure of her friends and patrons [...]. – Herr *Göthe* is honour-bound to take a courteous bow to our management for having done everything to the point of extravagance to secure him a good reception [...]. In short, costumes, splendour, good order, exactness, the actors' performance – everything vied patriotically to introduce the new patriotic author to the public in the best way possible. [...]

It would be a sin not to mention a man whom there is really no need to mention in the light of his deserts. Herr *Zimmermann*, [...] who for many years studied the art of scene painting at the Brunswick court under the most approved masters, then himself [...] continued working there in their company [...], has as the current scene painter of the Hamburg theatre enriched the same with two main settings for the performance of this drama, which honour him and Hamburg.[2]

One is a room in *Götz's castle*, entirely in the taste of that period, Old German and simple. Instead of the bedside table, you see underneath the mirror a table draped with a simple tapestry [...]; on the right, an antique cupboard ornamented with graduated jars; on the left, a fireplace; instead of wallpaper, the bare thick walls are hung all around with the portraits of knights of the Berlichingen family [...]; the ceiling of the room consists of rafters put together with such art, arranged with such taste that one's eye is amazed [...]. – The *other* thing he has produced is *the underground passage to the secret tribunal*, which is transformed into a *prison* by the dropping in of a single column. I should grow prolix if I were to enlarge on the light of a suspended lamp placed so happily upstage, and other beauties which at a first glance reveal the masterly hand of the refined artist. [...]

In addition to the theatrical décor [...] there were all the costumes as they have been handed down [by tradition] from those days, which delighted the eye and fed the imagination. Knights and squires in their armour, monk's cowl and bishop's gown, court and town dresses, everything transported us to where we were meant to be, everything assisted the illusion, everything conspired to praise Mme *Ackermann's* attention [to detail], with no expense spared.

[...] Too bad that our friend *Göthe* can only learn what you have done for him by cold hearsay and reading! that he has not himself enjoyed the keenly rewarding pleasure of being moved by his own work through your efforts! [...]

There was a *Götz* (Herr *Reineke* [*sic*]), worthy and chivalrous as he should be;[3] hero and father of his family, a rugged warrior and a good amiable fellow. [...] He had made Götz's face, Götz's tone, Götz's whole manner his own. We never knew we were in a playhouse! [...] There was a *Weislingen* (Herr Brokman [*sic*]), tepid and changeable, born to be good-natured but subject to his passion; worthy among the worthy and false among the false.[4] This could be read syllable by syllable from the artist's face who had studied and digested his character perfectly and played him most felicitously. [...] One of our public sheets has reviewed the performance of this play favourably, which is fair enough; only adding the wish at the end that *Weislingen might fall asleep more gently*. Some time ago a similar reproach was levelled at the same actor in the part of the Gamester[5] at an amateur performance, saying he did not die *with decorum*. What sort of decorum – French decorum perchance? The French must have a different fashion in dying from ours in this country [...]; for in Germany a dying person has more to do than worry about decorum. [...] Not only does *Götz* pursue him in his dreams; *Marie*, too, the sister of the man innocently condemned,[6] *good gentle Marie*, abandoned by him for a loose woman, comes to arouse *every sleeping memory* in his soul. Not only has he been poisoned; he must also learn that he has been so, and by whom? By his wife! [...] My view of this matter is that with all these emotions it is not possible to fall asleep gently.[7]

There was an *Adelheid* (Demoiselle *Ackermann the Younger*), bewitching and proud;[8] as a lover and wife devious and imperious; drowned in her own lusts and intemperate in the satisfaction of the lusts of others; seductive cunning in her eyes and voluptuous deceit in her face. Delicate as it may be for young women to shine in roles of this sort, the actress succeeded without giving any facetious scoffers an occasion for their impertinence. [...] For she presented the lustful *Adelheid* as the court lady intoxicated with high ambition trying to scale the topmost heights, and thus gave her that veneer of pride for which, with all its consequences, we are much more accustomed to give the female sex credit than that pointless luxuriousness of culpable desires without any ambition.

There was a *Marie* (Demoiselle *Ackermann the Elder*), gentle and good; quiet loving comfort in her eyes and the serenity of her soul upon her cheeks.[9] [...] One merely had to see her to know what she was going to say. She spoke without speaking; for her heart lay as an open book upon her face.

[...] There was an *Elisabeth* (Mme *Reineke*), Götz's jewel and comfort; sensible yet obliging; the whole-hearted, good, busy housewife looking after her own.[10].
[...]

There was a Brother *Martin* (Herr *Schröder*), quite the honest cleric he – was forced to be;[11] poor and patient; full of the sentiment of his vocation and yet resigned and gentle. The entire wealth of humane sentiments the author so appropriately put into this character poured from the actor's lips into our hearts. [...]

There was a *Lerse* (Herr *Schröder*), honest and faithful, the genuine, unadulterated, rough, good old German manner in his face, sure of his courage and yet not overbearing or arrogant in his strength.[12] The actor showed in this role how much he could multiply himself. Brother Martin was gone and in his place stood *Franz Lerse*, as if he had been born not to be a monk but solely a cavalryman.

[1] After his stepfather Konrad Ackermann's death in 1771, Schröder had taken over the direction of the Hamburg company with the assistance of his mother, Sophie Charlotte Ackermann (1714–92). (For Mme Ackermann, see **85**; for Schröder's directorial work, see Paul F. Hoffmann, *Friedrich Ludwig Schröder als Dramaturg und Regisseur* (F.L.S. as a Dramaturg and Director) (Berlin: SGTG 52, 1939).

[2] Before joining Schröder, Zimmermann worked for Nicolini's children's theatre in Brunswick. Nicolini, who had been the Brunswick court's *directeur des spectacles* from 1752–63, was well known for his attention to effective décor (see **96**). Note that even a production so dependent on spectacle as *Götz* still employed a good deal of stock scenery.

[3] Johann Friedrich Reinecke (1745–87), a handsome and talented actor of the new *kraftgenialisch*, i.e. passionate, school of acting; a difficult colleague.

[4] For Brockmann, see **103, 200–2, 204, 220.**

[5] The role of Beverley, the hero of Edward Moore's *The Gamester* (1753). A translation of this English play had long been popular on the German stage: Ekhof, too, had played the lead.

[6] I.e. Götz. For Maria, see **198**, notes 3 & 4.

[7] The naturalism brought in by the new drama was felt by many to be offensive. The question of how to portray death was discussed more than once in theatre journals of the period. See 'Ueber das Sterben auf der Schaubühne' (How to Die on Stage), in *LTZ*, 24 July 1779, pp. 468–71, which argued in favour of restrained conventionalised realism.

[8] Charlotte Ackermann (1757–75), Schröder's versatile and popular half-sister, who had played such roles as Franziska (in *Minna von Barnhelm*) and Emilia Galotti with great acclaim. She died before the age of eighteen, possibly by committing suicide.

[9] Karoline Dorothea Ackermann (1752–1821), elder sister of the former. Though as talented as Charlotte (she was an accomplished Orsina in *Emilia Galotti*), she abandoned the stage in 1778.

[10] Sophie Reinecke (1745–88), wife of Johann (see note 3); noted for passionate roles.

[11] A monk, who is probably (though not explicitly) Martin Luther before he abandoned the monastic life, makes a brief appearance in the play.

[12] See **198**, note 2. Schröder not only doubled the roles of Brother Martin and Lerse – he also played the senior judge of the secret tribunal. *Götz* and subsequent 'Ritterstücke' (plays of chivalry) called for much larger casts than neo-classical dramas and thus made a good deal of doubling unavoidable.

Schröder's Hamlet

Schröder's readiness to stage such irregular dramas as *Götz von Berlichingen* and Klinger's *Die Zwillinge* (The Twins) in Hamburg prepared the way for his production of *Hamlet* – a landmark in German theatre history in that it meant a turning away from French models, both in dramatic structure and acting style. Various versions of *Hamlet* had in fact been familiar on the German stage since the seventeenth century (see **26, 34, 50**) but they were distortions of the original.

More recently, Wieland, Eschenburg and Heufeld had prepared new versions (the latter was published in 1772). During a stay in Prague in 1776, Schröder saw the Heufeld version staged and was inspired to attempt the play in Hamburg. His own version, based on the three other texts and without a tragic ending, was premièred on 20 September 1776. He played the Ghost, the Reineckes the King and Queen, and Dorothea Ackermann Ophelia (see **199**). Brockmann (see **103, 199, 201–2, 204, 220**) scored a huge success in the title role. In the following year he went to Berlin to give guest performances with Döbbelin's company, including the role of Hamlet. On that occasion he used Schröder's second version of the text, published in 1777 (there was to be yet another one in 1778). The impression Brockmann created in Berlin was no less shattering than in Hamburg, as is shown by the following newspaper account in the form of a letter.

200   The audience response to Brockmann's Hamlet in Berlin, 1777–8

'Brockman', in *TJD* (1778), no. 5, pp. 54–9

Berlin

20th January 1778

What can be more pleasant for a German than to speak of a man who does honour to the Germans? So it is with the greatest pleasure that I comply with your request to give you a detailed account of Herr Brockmann's presence here in Berlin.

For three weeks we have enjoyed the inestimable pleasure of seeing him – him, the pride of the German stage – and had the proof that Germany has its Garrick.[1] Be assured that word of mouth can never do full justice to this man. Mother Nature has granted him everything: a handsome figure; an expressive face; a sonorous voice and a truthful, sensitive soul. All this united with the greatest artistry makes Brockmann one of the most complete actors of our age. – This great actor arrived here on the 14th of December [1777]. All of Berlin had been looking foward to his arrival for many weeks. – A proof of how German, how patriotic is our public's disposition! [. . .] On the 17th, Brockmann appeared as Hamlet for the first time. I take it you will believe me, without my having to take an oath on it, that the house was full to bursting; that many hundreds of people had to be turned away for lack of space. Every spectator entered the playhouse with the highest expectations, and there was probably not one whose expectations were not exceeded. I should be glad to describe all the fine points of his playing of Hamlet; I should be glad to show how he followed the trail of Shakespeare's magnificent ideas, entered into the greatest subtleties and portrayed Hamlet's character truthfully and convincingly, but forsooth I cannot: only a Lessing could do so. Suffice it for me to say that he played him inimitably, in a masterly style, and let all our local scholars bear me out in this. [...] The applause Brockmann garnered this very first night was extraordinary. Never before have I left the playhouse with so much emotion: how proud I was as a German; how entranced as a human being! – Hamlet was repeated on the 18th, the 20th, the 21st, the 22nd, the 23rd, the 24th: the crowds grew bigger each day.

On the 18th, owing to carelessness on the part of the stage manager, the curtain was lowered too soon at the end of Act 4 when Hamlet is about to drag off Oldenholm,[2] and Brockmann could not deliver his last speech. The audience noticed this mistake and would not give over until the curtain had gone up again and Brockmann could speak the last 6 lines. [...]

On the 8th [of January], after the end of the play, Brockmann was called out – an honour never before bestowed here on any actor – and he once again reaped the most general and best deserved applause any German actor has ever received.[3] He could only utter a few words to express his gratitude to the audience: tears stopped his speech. This scene was indeed the most beautiful and touching imaginable: we all wept with him. – On the 9th he again departed for Hamburg, and now our jubilation and our delight have turned to justified sorrow that he cannot be ours for ever. – At the request of many persons the skilful local medallist Abramson has made a silver medal – the first ever to be struck in honour of a German actor. – As a supplement to the fourth issue of our Litteratur und Theaterzeitung an engraving has been made by the famous Chodowiecki,[4] which represents the scene in which Hamlet is with his mother and the Ghost appears.

[1] Garrick was frequently cited by German critics as the non plus ultra in acting, the model to which German actors should aspire.
[2] Oldenholm was the name of Polonius in the Schröder version of the play.
[3] This was an exceptional though not altogether unprecedented honour at the time. (See 220, note 8.) In later years, calling out an actor for a special curtain call became so common as to constitute a nuisance: some audience favourites were summoned up to thirty or forty times at the end of a scene or an act. (See Düringer & Bartels, *Theater-Lexikon* (1841), pp. 574–6.)
[4] Daniel Nicolas Chodowiecki (1726–1801), Berlin painter and engraver who illustrated a number of plays, including *Macbeth*, Lessing's *Minna von Barnhelm* (see 190), and Schiller's *Kabale und Liebe* (Intrigue and Love). He became the Director of the Berlin Academy of Art in 1797. For further details, see Bruno Voelcker, *Die Hamlet-Darstellungen Daniel Chodowieckis und ihr Quellenwert für die deutsche Theatergeschichte des 18. Jahrhunderts* (D.C.'s Hamlet Illustrations and their Significance as Sources for German Eighteenth-Century Theatre History) (Leipzig: TGF 29, 1916).

201 Brockmann as Hamlet in the Queen's closet scene, with Döbbelin as the Ghost and Mme Hencke as the Queen.

Chodowiecki's engraving, published in *LTZ*, 24 January 1778, p. 55. Theatre Collection, University of Bristol

Note Brockmann's expressive gesture. The attempt, characteristic of this decade, to begin to break away from the costume convention of French court dress in tragedy was clearly not supported by any detailed knowledge of costume history. (See also (132.)

201

The playwright and journalist Johann Friedrich Schink (1755–1835) wrote a short book about Brockmann's performance in Berlin; while not wholly uncritical, this gives a generally enthusiastic account of the actor's interpretation of the role. The central place of *Hamlet* in the thinking of the *Sturm und Drang* generation of theatrical innovators as well as playgoers – much of it due to Brockmann's performance – is reflected in Books 4 and 5 of Goethe's theatrical novel, *Wilhelm Meisters Lehrjahre*. For a full treatment of the subject, see Adolf Winds, *Hamlet auf der deutschen Bühne bis zur Gegenwart* (Hamlet on the German Stage up to the Present Time) (Berlin: *SGTG* 12, 1909).

202   Brockmann's Hamlet described, 1778

Johann Friedrich Schink, *Ueber Brockmanns Hamlet* (Notes on Brockmann's Hamlet) (Berlin: Arnold Wever, 1778), pp. 10, 16–17

[...] In the first scene in which he appears he walks about slowly and tremblingly, with the most eloquent expression of grief, with downcast looks, arms akimbo, an ideal model for a painter who would depict grief! While the King is speaking and he stands by silently, his silence is [...] more eloquent than a great many words [would be]. He fetches deep sighs from his breast, his eyes seem to be awash with tears and his knees to be trembling beneath him. However, in the midst of these signs of dejection you notice the battle of the stronger passions clearly enough. His displeasure becomes distinctly visible in the looks of contempt he casts from time to time at the King and his mother, and it suddenly erupts on being addressed by the King, 'My beloved son!' in the words, 'Better not such close friends and less beloved!'[1] Although he has only thrown away these words he is quite well aware that he has allowed himself to be carried away further than he had intended, so he collects himself and relapses into a state of melancholy. [...]

What distinguishes Brockmann particularly as a great actor is the extra-ordinary eloquence of his face. [...] His face is as it were a book in which the least feelings of his soul are inscribed. [...] The scene I now wish to anatomise is an example of this. His eye wet with tears is fixed rigidly on the ground – and a dark pall of black thoughts wreathes his forehead. His friends enter, he recognises them, dries his eyes, and his tears are as it were nipped in the bud. A pleasant smile invades his cheeks and his eyes – but it is only the smile of an overcast day. Amidst the rays of good humour there is a sombre melancholy which carves a couple of gloomy furrows on his forehead; like the sun when it breaks through black clouds in faint rays after a thunderstorm. He hastens towards his friends, welcome and trust on his lips, jests with them and asks what has brought them hither. On Gustav's reply,[2]

'My lord, I came to see your father's funeral', the smile in his eyes begins to die away, the melancholy cast of his forehead grows stronger; but as he collects himself he mixes a touch of merry humour with this gathering melancholy and seeks to cover his embarrassment by jesting [...].

There is only one thing Herr Brockmann seems to have forgotten [...] which is that he only acts the fool, only pretends to be but is not actually mad, and precisely because he only acts the fool must often forget himself, often drop this pretence of folly, [...] with the stronger passion, his deep inner melancholy, his dislike and horror of the King and the Queen often overcoming his disguise, and with the foolish, humorous note very often lapsing into bitterness and sadness [...]. There is after all a difference between being a madman and only pretending to be one. But Herr Brockmann seems to forget this.

¹ The rather prosaic as well as inaccurate rendering of: 'A little more than kin, and less than kind.'
² Horatio was called Gustav in the Schröder version of the play. Both quotations refer to Act 1, Sc. 2 of
Hamlet.

Opposition to the new trend in German theatre

The innovations brought about by the production of the works of Shakespeare and of new
German playwrights disrespectful of the neo-classical rules was not to everybody's taste.
King Frederick II, wholly French-orientated in his cultural sympathies, attacked these
trends in his short book (characteristically written in French), *De la Littérature allemande*
(1780). The King's argument that German literature was, for historical reasons, not to be
compared either to that of the ancients or that of Italy, France and England was broadly
tenable but his knowledge of recent developments seems to have been limited: Lessing was
not mentioned once. In particular, he was almost totally out of sympathy with recent
theatrical trends, though there is no reason to suppose that he had any first-hand
knowledge of them. The one play of which he approved was von Ayrenhoff's all but
forgotten comedy, *Der Postzug* (see 111, note 2). A German translation of the King's book
by C.W.v. Dohm, *Ueber die deutsche Litteratur*, came out in the same year as the original
French version.

203   Frederick II on Shakespeare and Goethe, 1780

*De la Littérature allemande; des defauts qu'on peut lui reprocher; quelles en sont les causes; et par
quels moyens on peut les corriger* (German Literature; the Faults for which it can be Blamed;
how these are Caused; and by what Means they might be Corrected) (Berlin: G.J. Decker,
1789), pp. 46–8. Reproduced in *DLD*, 16 (1883), p. 23; reprinted Kraus Reprint (Nendeln/
Liechtenstein, 1968)

In order to be convinced what poor taste prevails in Germany up the present, all
you have to do is visit our public spectacles. There you will find performed the
abominable plays of Shakespeare translated into our language, and the whole
audience utterly delighted with these ridiculous farces worthy of the savages of
Canada. I call them so because they offend against all the rules of the stage. These
rules are by no means arbitrary; you find them in Aristotle's Poetics where the
unities of time, place and action are prescribed as the only means of rendering
tragedies interesting; instead of which, in these English plays the action extends
over a number of years. Where does that leave verisimilitude? Now porters and
grave-diggers appear who talk no better than you would expect, and then are
followed by princes and queens. How can this bizarre mixture of the base and the
elevated, of clowning and tragedy please anyone? You can forgive Shakespeare
for his strange extravagances; for the arts at their birth are never what they are in
their maturity. But here is a Götz von Berlichingen appearing on the stage, a
detestable imitation of those bad English plays, and the pit applauds enthusiasti-

cally and calls for those nauseating platitudes to be repeated. I know there is no arguing about taste; nevertheless permit me to say that people who take an equal pleasure in tightrope walkers, in puppets, and in the tragedies of Racine desire nothing more than to kill time [...].

Clavigo (Goethe)

Goethe wrote *Clavigo* – a play based on Beaumarchais's Memoirs – after *Götz von Berlichingen*. It was published in 1774 and premièred by Schröder's company in Hamburg in the same year.

204   The première of *Clavigo*, Hamburg, 1774

'Theatralische Neuigkeiten' (Theatrical News), in *Der Teutsche Merkur* (The German Mercury) (Weimar, June 1775), pp. 271–3. Reproduced in Braun, *Goethe*, vol. 1 (1883), p. 113

(Hamburg). – [...] *Clavigo* was performed for the first time on 21 August [1774]. Herr *Brockmann* is now the leading actor in the company, and so he was cast as Beaumarchais.[1] Although he receives equal applause as Mellefont and Essex[2] and his training supports him in all roles, he nevertheless seems to possess dignity and noble pride rather than flexibility and liveliness, which is why his Prince in Der Edelknabe[3] is better than his Beaumarchais. Herr *Reinecke*,[4] who normally specialises in affectionate fathers, played Clavigo, and in many scenes he succeeded in this difficult role which calls for coldness and fire at the same time. Herr *Schröder* excels in low comedy roles, and so the humour of Carlos did not always seem the thing for him.[5] Mlle *Ackermann* the elder may play Sara and Orsina, but tender roles undoubtedly come more naturally to her, and so Marie was very much the part for her.[6]

[1] For Brockmann's Hamlet, see 200–2. The role of Beaumarchais (based on the contemporary French playwright) is an important one in the play: he seeks to protect his sister Marie's honour against the influential journalist Clavigo who has broken his promises to her and abandoned her.
[2] Mellefont – the seducer in *Miss Sara Sampson*. Essex – the hero of a conflation by C.H. Schmid of four English tragedies (by Banks, Brooks, Jones and Ralph) on this perennially popular theme.
[3] *Der Edelknabe* (The Squire), by J.J. Engel (1775), playwright as well as theorist of acting (see 131, 132–3, 136–7, 183).
[4] For Reinecke, see 199, note 3. Like Beaumarchais, the eponymous villain-hero was based on a real person – the Spanish writer Clavijo y Fajardo.
[5] Carlos is Clavigo's friend and evil genius.
[6] For Dorothea Ackermann, see 199, note 9. The other roles referred to are the heroine of *Miss Sara Sampson* and the Countess in *Emilia Galotti*.

Stella (Goethe)

Published in January 1776, this new play of Goethe's was premièred by Döbbelin in Berlin on 13 March of the same year. Like *Clavigo*, it also deals with a man's betrayal of love – in this instance, of two women.

205   The première of *Stella*, Berlin, 13 March 1776

'Vom hiesigen deutschen Theater' (Local Theatre News) in *Berlinisches Litterarisches Wochenblatt* (Berlin Literary Weekly) (Berlin & Leipzig, 13 April 1776). Reproduced in Braun, *Goethe*, vol. 1 (1883), pp. 271–2

The applause this drama receives in performance is due to the incomparable playing of Mlle *Döbbelin* and Herr *Brückner*.[1] We see the dear, sweet and romantic creature act with the sentiment with which she must be acted if she is to be Stella. Mlle *Döbbelin* draws tears from the spectators – tears no one need be ashamed of. The author himself, had he been present, could not have wished for any other Stella. – The soliloquy at the beginning of Act 5, how movingly, how heart-rendingly does Mlle. *Döbbelin* not speak it?[2] At this moment we must feel that Fernando is a villain. [...] And how excellent are Mlle Döbbelin's miming and attitude at the end of this soliloquy, when she makes as if to stab the portrait with her knife, drops it and collapses in a flood of tears in front of the chair on which the picture is standing! – Herr *Brückner* shows us as Fernando that he is *Brückner* and lets us feel that he is Fernando. You young actors who are always under the delusion that it is the part that makes the actor, and not the actor the part, come hither and learn the contrary from a master! Let Fernando be acted not badly – let him just be acted in a mediocre way, and he will be an intolerable figure on the stage. Herr *Brückner* turns everything into action, into life.

[1] Karoline Maximiliane Döbbelin (1758–1829), Karl Theophil Döbbelin's daughter, who played the title role, was celebrated in the role of sentimental young lovers. For Brückner, see **198**, note 1. The part of Fernando which he played is one that could easily lose the sympathy of the audience altogether.
[2] A moonlight scene in which Stella addresses her faithless lover's portrait.

Die Räuber (The Robbers – Schiller)

The first performance of Friedrich Schiller's *Die Räuber* at the Mannheim National Theatre on 13 January 1782 was undoubtedly one of the key events in German theatre history. It was this production, rather than the play's appearance in print the previous year, that established the author as an outstanding young playwright. (He was twenty-two years old at the time, an army physician by profession.) Like *Götz von Berlichingen*, *Die Räuber* struck an exciting new note in the theatre and brought a permanent addition to the German repertoire. Like *Götz*, it was not originally written with a view to being staged – and thus could afford to be utterly heedless of the so-called rules. But unlike *Götz*, the play was not an exercise in recreating the German past. The sixteenth-century guise in which it was premièred at Mannheim was due to the intervention of the head of the theatre, Baron v. Dalberg, and not to Schiller who had conceived the story as taking place in his own century. Dalberg wanted to set the action as far away in the past as possible so as to avoid any embarrassing political conclusions to be drawn from this tale of insurrection and defiance of the law.

The announcement of the play quoted below was written by Schiller at Dalberg's request; it was the wording of the playbills which were posted in public places. Its tone catches the play's excited and sensational character; but it also reflects Dalberg's concerns in that it defuses some of the moral ambiguities of the story by stressing the author's essentially orthodox intentions.

206   Announcement of the first performance of *Die Räuber*, Mannheim, 1782

Playbill in the Schiller-Nationalmuseum, Marbach. Reproduced in *Schillers Werke/NA*, vol. 22, ed. Hermann Meyer (Weimar: Hermann Böhlaus Nachfolger, 1958), p. 87

The portrait of a great soul gone astray – equipped with all superior gifts, and for all these gifts, lost. Unquenchable fire and bad companions corrupted his heart – flung him from vice to vice – until in the end he captained a gang of incendiaries, heaped horrors upon horrors, plunged from abyss to abyss, into all the depths of despair. – Great and majestic in misfortune and by misfortune redeemed, led back to excellence. Such a man you will weep for and detest, abhor and love in the [person of the] robber Moor.

You will see a hypocritical, treacherous intriguer unmasked and hoist with his own petard. An all too weak, pliant over-indulgent father. – The pangs of romantic love and the torments of a ruling passion. Here too you will, not without horror, glimpse the inner workings of vice and learn from the stage how all the gildings of fortune fail to kill the worm of conscience, and fright, anguish, remorse, despair follow hard on its heels. Let the spectator today weep – and recoil – before our scene and learn to bend his passions under the law of religion and of reason; let the youth regard the end of unbridled debauchery with horror, nor let the grown man leave the playhouse without [learning] the lesson that the invisible hand of Providence can employ the very malefactor as an instrument of its intentions and judgements and is able to undo even the most tangled knots of fate.

The following review of the Mannheim production of *Die Räuber* was written by Schiller himself, in the guise of a letter received from a friend. The somewhat critical note regarding the play may have been directed partly at himself, but also partly at Dalberg who had insisted on considerable alterations to the text. Whatever its shortcomings in terms of text and performance, the production made an enormous impression on the public of Mannheim and of neighbouring cities as well. Not the least reason for its success was the virtuoso characterisation of the villainous Franz Moor by Iffland – a performance which at a stroke placed him in the front rank of German actors. For details of the première and the prompt book of the original production, see Herbert Stubenrauch & Günter Schulz, *Schillers Räuber/Urtext des Mannheimer Soufflierbuches* (S.'s Robbers/the Original Text of the Mannheim Promptbook) (Mannheim: Bibliographisches Institut, 1959). *Die Räuber* was to stay in the Mannheim repertoire for some time: by 15 January 1786 it had been performed ten times. It was also staged in Leipzig, Hamburg and Altona in the same year, and in Berlin, Rostock, Stuttgart and Mainz in 1783. In 1798, an English version carefully pruned of all subversive matter was given an amateur performance at the home of Lady Craven at Hammersmith.

207   Review of *Die Räuber* première, Mannheim, 13 January 1782

'Über die Vorstellung der Räuber' (The Performance of The Robbers), in *Wirtembergisches Repertorium der Litteratur* (Württemberg Anthology of Literature), ed. Friedrich Schiller, Johann Jakob Abel, Johann Wilhelm Petersen & Jakob Atzel vol. 1 (1782), pp. 165–9. Reproduced in *Schillers Werke/NA*, vol. 22 (1958), pp. 309–10

The play has been performed several times at Mannheim. I hope to oblige my readers by communicating to them a letter written at my request by my correspondent who had gone there for the purpose of seeing the play.
Worms, 15 January – 82.

The day before yesterday the performance of *The Robbers* at last took place. I have just returned from the trip and, with the impression still warm, I sit down to write to you. First let me express my astonishment at the seemingly insuperable obstacles President von Dalberg[1] had to overcome in order to serve up the play to the public. The author has of course adapted it for the stage, but how?[2] Certainly only for those inspired by Dalberg's active spirit; for all others, at least the ones I know, it is still an irregular drama. It was impossible to confine it to five acts; the curtain was lowered twice in between scenes to give the stage crew and actors more time; there were interludes, and that made seven acts. But nobody noticed. All characters appeared in new costumes, two magnificent sets had been made specially for the play, Hr. Danzy [*sic*] had also provided new compositions for the interludes,[3] so that the expenses of the first performance came to a hundred ducats. The house was unusually crowded so that a great many people were turned away. The play ran for four hours, and I felt the actors were hurrying.

But – you will be impatient to hear about the success [of the play]. On the whole it made a splendid effect. Herr Boeck[4] as the bandit chieftain fulfilled his role as far as it was possible for the actor to be in a continual torment of emotion. I can still hear him in the midnight scene by the tower, kneeling by his father's side, conjuring the moon and the stars with high pathos.[5] – I want you to know that the moon slowly moved across the backdrop, something I have never seen in the theatre before, and spread a fearsome natural light over the scene during its course.[6] – Too bad though that Herr Boeck has not the right personality for his part. I had imagined the bandit lean and tall. I liked Herr Iffland who acted Franz [...] best of all. Let me confess to you, I had considered this part which is not at all suitable for the stage a total loss, and I have never been so agreeably surprised. Iffland showed himself a master in the latter scenes. I can still hear him, in his expressive posture, confronting all of Nature's loud affirmation with a damnable *No* and then again, as if touched by an invisible hand, faint away [...].[7] – You should have seen him kneeling and praying when the rooms of the castle were already burning all around him. If only Herr Iffland did not swallow his words and speak in quite such a rush! Germany will find a master actor in this young man.[8] [...] I at any rate like Mme Toskani immensely.[9] I was at first worried about this part; for the author has botched it in many places. Toskani played very gently and delicately, she was very expressive in the tragic situations, but with too many theatrical mannerisms and [spoke] in a tiresome, tearfully lamenting monotone. Old Moor could not possibly succeed, having been spoilt by the author from the start.[10]

If I am to give you my candid opinion – the play is none the less not a play for the stage. Take away the shooting, scorching, burning, stabbing and the like, and it is tedious and difficult for the stage. I should have liked the author to cut a good deal [...]. Also it seemed to me that he had crammed too many things into it which unbalance the main impression. You could have made three dramas out of it, and each one would have been more effective. [...]

---

[1] For Dalberg, see also **176–8**.

[2] Dalberg had suggested several alterations, in addition to placing the action in the past which made it seem less subversively topical. Some of these changes – the drastic pruning of the text, the elimination of some essentially practical. Dalberg also insisted that the villainous brother Franz, far from committing suicide at the end of the play, should be sentenced by the robbers to lifelong imprisonment; and that on the other hand Amalia, the bandit chieftain Karl's love, should commit suicide rather than be killed by him. These were substantial changes which Schiller resisted but had to concede.

[3] Franz Danzi (1763–1828), the music director at the National Theatre in Mannheim, who was later to work in Munich, Stuttgart and Karlsruhe. He also wrote some operettas.

[4] Johann Michael Boeck (1743–93), leading actor of the Mannheim ensemble. (See **107**.) Not to be confused with Heinrich Beck (see **210**, note 1).

[5] In Act 4, Sc. 5.

[6] This was a movable device with a tin mirror. Note the increasing interest in stage lighting effects in the last quarter of the eighteenth century – compare **81** and **199**.

[7] In Act 5, Sc. 1.

[8] Iffland was twenty-six years old when he created the role of Franz Moor. Schiller's prediction of a great future for the actor turned out to be accurate.

⁹ Anna Elisabeth Toskani (or Toscani), a pupil of Mme Hensel, specialised in 'tender' roles. She played the role of Amalia von Edelreich, the only female part in *Die Räuber*. See 107 for Mme Toscani's place in the Mannheim company.
¹⁰ Clearly, this is a piece of self-irony on Schiller's part.

A far more detailed description than Schiller's own account of Iffland's acting in the role of Franz Moor (see 207) was that given fourteen years later by Karl August Böttiger (1760–1835), archaeologist, headmaster of the local *Gymnasium* and between 1795 and 1803 editor of the Weimar magazine, *Journal des Luxus und der Moden*. From 28 March to 25 April 1796, Iffland gave a series of guest performances with the Weimar company at Goethe's invitation in order to raise the local company's rather modest acting standards by his immensely accomplished example. The strikingly different roles he played, chosen deliberately to show off his astonishing powers of self-transformation, were described by Böttiger in considerable detail. In the book from which the following quotation is taken, Böttiger shows clearly how Iffland constructed his characterisations by the meticulous piling up of well thought-out individual traits and how his technique oscillated from role to role between psychological realism and picturesque stylisation.

Note that the text of *Die Räuber* referred to below is the 'Trauerspiel' (tragedy) version (1782) as used in the Mannheim production, and not the 'Schauspiel' (drama) version of 1781.

208   Iffland's Franz Moor, Weimar, 16 April 1796

Carl August Böttiger, *Entwickelung des Ifflandischen Spiels/In vierzehn Darstellungen auf dem Weimarischen Hoftheater im Aprillmonath 1796* (Iffland's Acting Described/In 14 Performances at the Weimar Court Theatre in the Month of April 1796) (Leipzig: G.J. Göschen, 1796), pp. 299–318. BL 11795.b.40

Cowardly guile is the main trait in the monster's character. So his initial coldness goes very well with the rest of his pretence, and it would be blameworthy only if the artist had not on several occasions let the passion boiling and raging inside him shine through. But in this performance there was not the slightest lack of these preparatory hints, indeed of their most artful gradation, according to which they were bound to become more and more frequent and violent with the accelerating progress of the play.

Rather than trying to prove my point, let me only here quote the soliloquy at the beginning of Act 2, in which he calls up the inner furies with which he is planning to torture his father to death. [...] We saw horror, picturesque and convincing down to the last detail, in the convulsive tremor of his hands and in the backward-leaning posture. He seemed to be sensing the ice-cold embrace of this giant [force] inside him. But how subtly the artist's nice judgement knew how to differentiate between the [mere] *picturesqueness* of facial and gestural miming, which was all we were supposed to take *this* expression of horror for, and the expression of truly felt horror in one of the play's last acts! How frightful, and yet how revealing of the bottomless evil in this villain was the insinuating smile with which he calls upon those beneficent Graces, the Past and the Future, to be executioners and helpmates of his plan, and how accurately judged was the hellish jubilation, 'Triumph! triumph! the plan is made!' with which the monster exits![1] Another actor might have preferred to sound the loudest note in this paean of triumph, and he would have been all the more certain of applause in that for ordinary spectators the greater or lesser agitation of their ears is in exact proportion to their louder or lesser applause. But the scheming treacherous villain *never* rejoices so noisily and audibly. Even walls have ears. Iffland spoke this conclusion with firm self-confidence but without any screeching overemphasis.

I found Iffland's acting equally deeply pondered and true when, during the story which Hermann in disguise tells old Moor of the death of his beloved son, he, standing behind them, his arm on the back of the chair in which his father is sitting, with murderous gestures and a wild glow in his eye, takes keen pleasure in the grief his vile trick is causing his father and Amalia, and then he watches with neck extended well forward and eyes bulging in order to spy out every trait of the devouring pain on the face of Amalia, weak with grief.[2] The wretch pretends to be gentle as a lamb when he reads out the fictitious bloody inscription on the sword. But all the more horrifying is the swift yet most subtly shaded transition from the red heat of rage to the pallor of trembling impotence when all his arts in dealing with Amalia have come to naught and he now, when he sees himself alone, furiously throws down his sword and with an infernal grin, exclaims, 'My arts are lost on this stubborn creature!'

With the last two acts his force, hitherto muted and only half used, reached its climax of activity. [. . .] The coldest of spectators was seized by involuntary horror.

What gradation did his acting not run through, from the first startled moments to the most violent shocks, and hence to immobility, rooted to the stage floor, when Franz stands opposite his brother Karl's portrait in the gallery! What swelling and rising of passion from the first start on the exclamation, 'Cunning, malicious hell!' to the expression of horror when he shrinks back from the phantom of fratricide and, after the most violent but transitory shock, stammers out in a broken and yet cutting tone his ghastly, 'Hah! Hah! Horror quivers through my limbs!' with staring eyes and limbs paralysed as if cast in iron. [. . .]

The high point or crown of the entire performance, in the soliloquy in which he broods on fratricide, must be [. . .] his seeing the phantom created by his own disordered imagination. After the ominous pause when shock had congealed all his vital spirits, fear set in. Iffland was certainly not thinking of *Engel's* description of the frightened man[3] [. . .]; and yet it was precisely this stepping backward with eye staring fixedly and arms held out before him that gave his miming the greatest conviction and force. One particular subtlety in this was notable. His right hand is held out further than his left, which is bent backwards more at an acute angle and as it were is lying in wait as a succour to the right. Suddenly he touches his own side quite by chance with his left hand. This suddenly gives him, as if by an electric shock, the idea of being seized from behind by another frightful creature. He starts once again, turns in a flash because he wants to protect himself against the ghost behind him, and – vanishes.[4]

In the scene when he puts the honest old servant Daniel so terribly on the rack with his suspicions, the gesture with which he falls upon the poor wretch, holding in his hand the plate with the glass, was very well calculated to make a dramatic tableau.[5] But it also made an effective contrast. His affectionately and caressingly pressing up against this same Daniel immediately afterwards gave one a creepy feeling. The way in which he seized his hand to win his trust and the insinuating, sweetly disarming tone in which he put the question, 'But isn't it true he put money in your pocket?', were worthy of a Spanish Grand Inquisitor.

He played the discussion scene with *Hermann*, in which the latter throws off his own mask and also tears Franz's mask off his face, with equal mastery.[6] [...] He scorned the device suggested by the author of flinging himself into an armchair [...]. Even a mere mechanical motion of reaching out for something can disturb the unity of playing at certain moments when everything has to hang together. So Franz already has the pistol in his pocket without first taking it down from the wall as demanded by the stage directions. In fact I consider the lack of movement in this scene in which two villains, both the one who does the unmasking and the one who is being unmasked, are viciously fighting each other at close quarters, far more effective than the wild, furious rushing around the stage as is normally done in this scene [...]

I have little to say about the final scene when he suffers desperate fury-haunted pangs of conscience before he is fetched by the robbers. One has to see it and then try to assess whether this portrayal of the Last Judgement leaves anyone sufficiently detached to be able to analyse what one has seen. [...] With eyes horridly turned upwards, glowing and glittering at first and then turning into a petrified stare, with a sweeping, then immobile rooted-to-the-spot attitude in which the right hand reaching upward and forward seemed defiant, while the left hand convulsively lowered towards his chest seemed protective, he cried out, 'Is there an avenger there beyond the stars?' There follows a pause. – A quiet, frightened, fear-squeezed, 'No!' – Another pause. – The feared thunderbolt fails to come crashing down. – The atheist's blasphemous courage increases. – 'No!' he roars a second time, gratingly, raising his fist heavenwards and noisily stamping his foot. – Now he had slain the One beyond the stars as well. But suddenly all hell seizes hold of him. His hairs bristle, his knees brokenly stagger forward. – A pause of the most deeply felt annihilation! – A flash of lightning streaks across his benighted soul in which the universal judge appears to him, with the scales suspended in heaven. – 'But what if there were?' – he mumbles, and the words emerge rattling from deep within his bosom.

[1] Act 2, Sc. 1. Note the distinction Böttiger is making between merely picturesque (i.e. external) and psychologically truthful acting.
[2] Act 2, Sc. 5.
[3] J.J. Engel, in his *Ideen zu einer Mimik*, vol. 1 (1785), p. 166. (See 131).
[4] Act 4, Sc. 9. Note how Iffland contrives an immensely effective exit for himself.
[5] Act 4, Sc. 6.
[6] Act 4, Sc. 8. Hermann, Franz's fellow in villainy, has come to realise that he will never obtain his prize – Amalia – and therefore turns against his master.

Kabale und Liebe (Intrigue and Love – Schiller)

More than a year after the première of *Die Räuber*, Schiller was engaged as resident playwright at the Mannheim National Theatre (September 1783). His first contribution to the theatre's repertoire, *Die Verschwörung des Fiesco zu Genua* (The Conspiracy of Fiesco in Genoa) (1784) was not well received. However, his next play, the bourgeois tragedy *Kabale und Liebe* was, and has ever since continued to be, an enormous popular success. Schiller attended the rehearsals; his deep personal involvement in the play has been described in the following terms by his friend Andreas Streicher.

209   Schiller's reactions at the première of *Kabale und Liebe*, Mannheim, 15 April 1784

Andreas Streicher, *Schillers Flucht von Stuttgart und Aufenthalt in Mannheim von 1782 bis 1785* (S.'s Flight from Stuttgart and Stay at Mannheim 1782–1785) (Stuttgart & Augsburg: J.G. Cotta, 1836), pp. 174–6. Reproduced (in part) in Karl Berger, *Schiller/Sein Leben und seine Werke* (S./His Life and Works). vol. 1 (Munich: Oskar Beck, 1921), pp. 379–80, and (*in toto*) in Hans Henning (ed.), *Schillers 'Kabale und Liebe' in der zeitgenössischen Rezeption* (The Contemporary Reception of S.'s 'Intrigue and Love') (Leipzig: Zentralantiquariat der Deutschen Demokratischen Republik, 1976), pp. 202–4

[...] During this revision work Iffland staged his *Das Verbrechen aus Ehrsucht* [Crime from Ambition].[1]

He had the courtesy to hand it over to Schiller before the performance and to leave it up to him what the title of this family drama should be, which was given the significant name it retains to this day. The extraordinary success obtained by this play worried Schiller's friends not a little, fearing that *Louise Millerin* would be overshadowed by it[2] [...].

Not long after, it was the turn of our author's new tragedy to be performed, which Iffland, to whom it had been passed previously, entitled *Intrigue and Love*. In order to be able to be present at the performance quite undisturbed, Schiller had reserved a box and invited his friend S. [i.e. Streicher] to join him there.

Calmly, in good spirits but turned in upon himself and only exchanging a few words, he waited for the curtain to rise. But once the performance had started – who could describe his deep expectant look – the action of his lower against the upper lip – his frown whenever anything was not spoken quite as it should be – his flashing eyes whenever passages designed for an effect actually produced it! – During the whole of the first act he let slip not a single word, and only at the end of it he uttered, 'It's going well.'

The second act, and especially its conclusion, was performed in a very lively manner, with such fire and compelling veracity that after the curtain had been lowered, all spectators rose up in a way quite unusual at that time and burst into a storm of unqualified cries of approval and applause. The playwright was so surprised at this that he stood up and took a bow towards the audience. His expression, his noble and proud deportment reflected his consciousness of having done himself justice as well as his satisfaction at his merits being recognised and duly honoured.

---

[1] As in the case of *Die Räuber*, Schiller had to revise *Kabale und Liebe* extensively before it could be performed on the Mannheim stage. Even with these alterations, Dalberg chose not to extend Schiller's appointment after this production of what was inevitably read as a socially critical play. Iffland, the outstanding actor in the Mannheim ensemble, was already becoming well known as a playwright too.
[2] The original working title of *Kabale und Liebe*.

Schiller included theatrical reviews in his magazine, *Rheinische Thalia*, only one number of which actually appeared. His comments on *Kabale und Liebe* suggest that the performances were not all equally accomplished. Curiously enough, Iffland, who played the part of the intriguer Wurm, is not mentioned at all.

210   Schiller's review of a Mannheim performance of *Kabale und Liebe*, 1785

Rheinische Thalia, ed. Schiller (Mannheim: Schwan, 1785), pp. 186–7. Reproduced in Henning (1976), p. 212

18 January. *Intrigue and Love*. Herr *Bek* [*sic*] as the Major surprised even the author several times by the greatness of his tragic acting.[1] Mlle *Baumann* played Louise Miller quite splendidly, and notably in the final acts with much feeling.[2] Mme *Rennschüb* did some things excellently in the role of the Englishwoman, but she is not quite *equal* to it.[3] Nevertheless Mme Rennschüb would be one of the best actresses if she always paid attention to the difference between emotion and screaming, weeping and howling, sobbing and deep feeling. Herr *Beil* was adequate in the lively role of the musician, at least whenever he knew it by heart.[4]

Herr *Rennschüb* played the court-marshal quite excellently.[5] Herr *Pöschel*, too, was liked as the prince's valet.[6]

[1] Heinrich Beck (1760–1803), a leading member of the Mannheim company, linked with his fellow actors Iffland and Beil in an attempt to raise acting standards. (See 107.) He was also a playwright. The Major is Ferdinand von Walter, whose love for Louise Miller, a musician's daughter, contravenes the social code and leads to the suicide of both lovers.

[2] The handsome young actress Katharina Baumann (1766–1849) played juvenile leads.

[3] Karoline Wilhelmine Rennschüb (b. 1755). Her role was that of Lady Milford, the Prince's English-born mistress.

[4] Johann David Beil (1754–94), a highly gifted but undisciplined actor with a particular talent for comic roles; also a playwright. (See 107.) The somewhat cross-grained musician Miller is the heroine's father.

[5] Johann Ludwig Rennschüb (b. 1755), husband of Karoline R. (see note 3), a useful actor as well as director: director of the Frankfurt National Theatre from 1792 onwards. The role of Court-Marshal v. Kalb, a foppish courtier, is an essentially satirical portrait.

[6] The valet – a cameo role of considerable importance – complains to Lady Milford about the sale of pressed German soldiers to serve the British crown against the insurgent Americans.

Egmont (Goethe)

When Goethe took over the direction of the Weimar theatre, he asked Schiller to prepare a stage version of *Egmont* which had been published in 1788. This was the text Iffland used in one of his guest performances in Weimar in April 1796. (See 208.) Böttiger's description of Iffland's performance in the title role shows that, much as he admired the actor, he was not wholly unaware of his limitations. Iffland was a highly calculating virtuoso, entirely sure of his effects, rather than an instinctive or charismatic actor. (See 122 and 124.)

211   Iffland as Egmont, Weimar, 25 April 1796

Böttiger (1796), pp. 353–71

Iffland could not and would not impersonate the Egmont who [. . .] is *a benevolent, merry and open personality, friend to the whole world, full of naive trust in himself and others, amiable and gentle, sensual and in love, a light-hearted worldling*, since he really never plays the role of the fine gentleman or the first lover [. . .], no amount of art quite being able to supply the requisite qualities for this.[1] So he took away from him some of that light easy-going nonchalance and youthful impetuosity and instead gave him more manly fortitude, deeper feeling, profound seriousness. It must be confessed that the impression this made on the *greater* part of the audience seemed to be stronger and more appropriate to the idea of a tragedy [. . .] than if Egmont had been presented, according to the author's notion, more from the angle of his charming good nature and insouciant carelessness.

But for that very reason the love scenes with Klärchen, the author's greatest achievement in this play, could not be acted with the careless abandon and playfulness which sit so well on Goethe's Egmont. [. . .] The beautiful picturesque scene [...] in which Klärchen kneels on a stool in front of Egmont [...] did indeed make a handsome tableau in this production: but a certain something was missing which can only be breathed into this romantic scene by the sweet delusion that here two lovers are united by a bond of which one cannot say who is giving and who is taking more [...].[2]

Iffland as Egmont [in prison] lies on his right side,[3] his head resting on his folded arm, turned entirely towards the spectators. The lower part of his body up to the navel remains almost entirely immobile during the whole dream vision; an action based on subtle physiological observations which tell us that during the dream the lower parts of the body move but little [...], since the weight of the body presses more on the lower extremities, whereas nothing obstructs a freer movement in the upper ones.

The visionary's entire gestural pattern consisted of nothing more than three very simple movements following one another at certain intervals [...]. A slight twitching at the back of the neck announced the beginning of the imaginary spectacle. The heavenly figure appears. The slumbering, lowered head half rises up to inform us that an interesting image is hovering before him. *First moment.* After a short pause during which his head has remained in this half raised viewing position, it rises up wholly into ecstatic contemplation. It tilts back as if looking at heaven. The lofty heavenly figure shows him the bundle of arrows and the cap of liberty. *Second moment.* The figure floats down closer to him and appears to be about to crown him with the wreath. It is Klärchen herself in the fair embodiment of the goddess of liberty. The sleeper's chest rises visibly. He groans and at the same moment closes both arms as if trying to seize hold of the angel hovering above him. His head had sunk back loosely for a moment since continued rigidity would have been unnatural; but on stretching out his arms it resumed its ecstatic, backward tilted angle. *Third moment.* Martial music approaches. He awakes. But he does not now leap up abruptly while reaching for the dream vision's wreath on his head, and observes the greatest decorum in the gradual lowering of his feet.

[1] Iffland's increasingly rotund figure disqualified him from romantic parts.
[2] Act 3, Sc. 2.
[3] The last scene of Act 5.

Die Sonnenjungfrau (The Virgin of the Sun – Kotzebue)

August von Kotzebue (1761–1819) was the most exuberantly prolific playwright of the (partly overlapping) classical and romantic periods of German drama: he himself lost count of the number of plays, operettas, farces etc. he had written, but they are reckoned to come to approx. 230. Critics tended to look down on him while the public adored him. Even

Goethe had to admit his theatrical craftsmanship. Of the 4,156 performances of the Weimar theatre under Goethe's direction, over 600 were plays by Kotzebue.

Not only was he extremely popular with German audiences – he also appealed to the theatre-going public in France and Britain. His *Menschenhass und Reue* (Misanthropy and Repentance) (1794) was a great success in England in Benjamin Thompson's version as *The Stranger* (1797–8). Important as his plays were in the German, French and English theatres during the nineteenth century, only a few of them have kept their place in the German repertoire up to the present.

Die Sonnenjungfrau (1791) – first translated by A. Plumptre under the title, *The Virgin of the Sun* (1799) and followed by further English versions – was a spectacle play set in Peru at the time of the Spanish Conquest. Iffland included it in his series of exemplary performances in Weimar in 1796 (see **208**, **211** & **213**). The role of the High Priest gave him an opportunity of displaying the formal side of his talent, with much emphasis on controlled movement and picturesque poses.

212   Iffland as the High Priest in *Die Sonnenjungfrau*, Weimar, April 1796

Böttiger (1796), pp. 249–70

Over the long white priest's tunic tied with a plain black belt there flowed down a cloak or upper garment which formed a wide fold from the left shoulder over the chest and almost completely covered the undergarment from the belt down. The amplitude of this artfully draped cloak rounded off everything sharp, angular and, if I may put it that way, *restless* about the extremities everywhere [...]. Everything was oscillating and flowing in wavy lines. The material for this was [...] neither taffeta nor satin but a fine woollen fabric, a serge which makes the softest folds [...]. One end of this upper garment usually rested on the right lower arm so lightly and softly that at times it was held by the tip with the fingers bent gently inwards, but at other times thrown off completely in a passionate gesture, whereby the cloak was given a more close-fitting circumfluent appearance; this produced the highest effect of picturesque expressiveness particularly on the words, '*I wish to cast aside the priest!*', since now he really seemed to be standing only in his undergarment, stripped of all priestly pomp. Just as in this case the effect was produced by the swift flowing down of the garment from the hand, similarly, when the garment was very lightly draped over the lower arm and the latter was raised aloft in gesticulation, the soft vibrations and folds with which it rose from the ground contributed greatly to preventing any dry stiffness and uniformity in the frequently repeated arm movement.

The man's very walk was expressive and adapted to the various situations in which he appeared, either gliding along softly, or deliberate and measured, or firm and prophetic. How different was his walk when appearing in the priests' assembly for the tribunal or when leaving its circle, indignant about the oppression of mankind!

Whatever can be produced by way of beauty and picturesqueness through costume, facial expression and gestures in harmony with the character and the situation, Iffland brought together in the two scenes of the solemn interrogation, and when the Inca is to pronounce sentence. With pious dignity [...] the High Priest announces the fearful purpose of their present assembly, then returns centre stage in a slow solemn walk and sinks down [...] gently and almost imperceptibly onto his knees. He puts his arms across his chest with slow deliberateness and makes the vow to be a just judge in a simple solemn tone expressing the most absolute reverence [...]. Now for the interrogation itself. Here every word of the dangerous confession was mirrored in the reactions of the sympathetic High Priest. Every incriminating statement Cora makes augments the fears of the anxious old man.[1] Each word is as it were a dagger, and each thrust is depicted with stronger facial reactions. Now he can no longer raise his arms, they droop lifeless by his side, he leans half fainting against a priest onto whose shoulder his head declines. But when Alonzo begins his self-accusation, a new ray of light strikes the fearful High Priest's soul. He rallies; his head bends forward; he approaches the speaker by several steps as if trying to catch his words before the others. When Alonzo spoke the words, 'Was it not I whose lascivious glances drove the fire into your cheeks?', he extended his right arm against the criminal with the floating movement admired so often during the whole performance, [...] whereas his left arm, raised only slightly and half bent, seemed to bespeak sympathy and compassion. But when Cora again seeks to take all the guilt upon herself, he recoils once more, dismay and despair in his face; and when the woman in her frenzy goes so far as to fling herself into Alonzo's arms, he no longer shades his forehead with one hand as he had done previously when she made her all too candid confessions, no, he covers his whole face with both hands. [...]

The crown of every work of art based on successive events is the gradual rise [in tension] as it proceeds towards the end. (Indeed here, too, the High Priest's miming in the last act, trembling before Rolla[2] as the latter comes rushing in wild agitation, outdid all that had gone before in terms of truthfulness and variety, and disclosed [...] a new gallery of picturesque postures and theatrical tableaux. The forward inclination with arms longingly outstretched towards the raging madman, the humbly beseeching posture towards the Inca, and finally the total sinking down to impress a kiss on Ataliba's hand,[3] these were three attitudes each one of which deserved to be seized by the draughtsman's hand and exhibited for permanent inspection.)

[1] Cora, the Virgin of the Sun, had broken her sacred vow of chastity by her love affair with the Spaniard Alonzo.

[2] The noble hero whose death was featured in Kotzebue's sequel, *Die Spanier in Peru, oder Rollas Tod* (The Spaniards in Peru, or Rolla's Death) (1796); adapted for the English stage under the title, *Pizarro*, by Sheridan in 1799.

[3] Ataliba – the Inca, or King of Peru in the play.

Der Spieler (The Gambler – Iffland)

Iffland was not only an outstandingly successful actor and director; he was also a fertile author of effective, predominantly sentimental dramas – many of them of the 'family portrait' variety. Some few of these still have an occasional place in the German repertoire of today. In his time, Iffland's plays – like Kotzebue's – figured much more prominently in the repertoire of German theatres than Lessing's, Schiller's or Goethe's. Not surprisingly, when he gave his guest performances in Weimar in 1796 (see above), he included no fewer than six of his own works in the programme. Böttiger's description of Iffland playing the eponymous gambler Captain v. Posert gives an idea of his keen attention to physical detail in building up a character.

213   Iffland as Captain von Posert in *Der Spieler*, Weimar, 9 April 1796

Böttiger (1796), pp. 174–6

The make-up of this demon of gambling was chosen with great intelligence. The scanty hairpiece, sewn onto flesh-coloured taffeta in such a way that the temples rose high up on both sides and thus formed a high bleached forehead, whilst hardly any hair stood up at the back where a humiliating bald patch shone through, by itself gave the contour of the head, bloated by candle fumes and night vigils, a miserable squat look which the heavy application of powder made all the more masklike. A black plaster over the left eye was stuck in the place where the eye itself had been before. This monocularity [. . .] hardly calls for any explanatory comment [. . .] in a gambler. It uglified him without depriving his muscles of their mobility and gave all the more expressiveness to the avid glance of the eye left uncovered, whenever once in a while the harpy of greed shone out of its lacklustre bleariness. The rest of the thick-set body, the broad-shouldered back, the well stuffed belly, the fat thighs, the fleshy, well padded arms and calves were in the most exact proportion to this thick flat skull.

The Wallenstein Trilogy (Schiller)

Schiller turned his back on the theatre after *Don Carlos* (1787) and devoted himself to history and philosophy; in 1789 he obtained the chair of history at the University of Jena.

But from 1791 onwards he began to wrestle with the problem of trying to find an adequate dramatic form for the theme of the fall of Wallenstein, the Imperial general in the Thirty Years' War. Goethe took a close interest in the development of the idea and encouraged him to make it a verse drama. The work was not concluded until the end of the decade and resulted in three interlinked but structurally different plays. Schiller's tragic treatment of this historical subject was boldly innovative though to some extent indebted to the Greeks and Shakespeare; contemporaries immediately recognised the trilogy as a milestone in the history of German drama and theatre.

I. Wallensteins Lager (Wallenstein's Camp)

The first, scene-setting play in one act, Wallenstein's Lager, did not feature Wallenstein, the principal character, at all; instead, it filled in the background to his tragedy by means of a broad panorama of military life during the Thirty Years' War. The language here is not the iambic pentameter of the other two (full-length) plays but a traditional German doggerel verse. Wallensteins Lager, like the rest of the trilogy, was premièred in Weimar and directed by Goethe who paid particular attention to movement and grouping as well as diction. The crowd work was remarkable for the period and anticipated nineteenth-century developments in stage directing.

The première of Wallensteins Lager on 12 October 1798 was given particular lustre by the fact that the totally renovated theatre in Weimar opened with this performance (as well as a Kotzebue play). Schiller wrote a prologue which combined a celebration of the new playhouse with a statement of the subject of the trilogy and an affirmation of rhyme as a distancing device in a realistic subject.

214   Schiller's justification of the form of *Wallensteins Lager*, Weimar, 12 October 1798

Schiller, *Prolog/Gesprochen bei Wiedereröffnung der Schaubühne in Weimar im Oktober 1798* (Prologue/Spoken on the Occasion of the Reopening of the Weimar Theatre in October 1798), in *Allgemeine Zeitung (General Journal)* (Tübingen: Cotta), 24 October 1798. Reproduced in *Schillers Werke/NA*, vol. 8 (1949), pp. 5–6. English translation by F.J. Lamport in *Schiller/The Robbers and Wallenstein* (Harmondsworth: Penguin 1979), pp. 168–9.

[. . .]
It is not he himself[1] who will appear
Upon these boards today. But in the hosts
Of gallant men his mighty word commands,
His spirit moves, you may perceive his shadow,
Until the timid muse at last may dare
To bring his living shape before your eyes;
For it was his own power seduced his heart,
His camp must help us understand his crime.

And so forgive the poet, if he does
Not sweep you all at once with rapid stride
To the catastrophe, but only brings
A row of captive scenes before your eyes,
In which those great events unfold themselves.
So let our play today win back again
Your ears and hearts to unaccustomed tones;
Let it transport you to that time of old,
On to that unfamiliar stage of war
Which soon our hero with his mighty deeds
Will fill.[2]
   And if today the gentle muse,
The goddess of the dance and melody,
Should with due modesty insist upon
Her ancient German right, the play of rhyme,
Then do not scold her, but be thankful rather
That she should thus transform the sombre hues
Of truth into the realm of art serene,
Create illusion, then in honesty
Reveal the trick she plays, and not pretend
That what she brings you is the stuff of truth.
Life is in earnest, art serene and free.

[1] I.e., Wallenstein himself.
[2] Wallenstein appears in person in parts 2 and 3 of the trilogy.

In spite of some shortcomings in the cast, the première was considered a great success. If Goethe's view as given below might seem unduly partial, the fact is that *Wallensteins Lager* was very well received.

215   Goethe on the exemplary verse speaking and crowd work in *Wallensteins Lager*, Weimar, 12 October 1798

Goethe, 'Eröffnung des Weimarischen Theaters' (Inauguration of the Weimar Theatre), in a supplement to *Allgemeine Zeitung*, 7 November 1798. Reproduced in *Goethes Werke*, WA, series 1, vol. 40 (1901), pp. 10–11, 33, and partly (in English translation) in Carlson (1978), p. 113

I have already communicated the *prologue* to you. Herr Vohs recited it in the costume in which he will appear later as the younger Piccolomini[1] [...]. This excellent actor displayed his full talent here; he spoke in a thoughtful, dignified and elevated manner and yet with such perfect distinctness and precision that not a syllable was lost in the furthermost corners of the house. His way of handling iambics aroused in us a well grounded expectation for the following plays. And what satisfaction will it not give us when we shall shortly see our theatre cured of the all but general rhythmophobia, this resistance to rhyme and metre afflicting so many German actors! [...]

The prologue ended, a cheerful military music gave an indication of what to expect next, and even before the curtain went up a boisterous song was heard. Soon the stage was discovered and there appeared before the spectator's eyes the colourful confusion of a camp. Soldiers of all types and colours were gathered in and around a canteen tent. In one place tradesmen's and hucksters' stalls had been put up, in another empty tables that seemed to be waiting for more guests; over on one side Croats and sharpshooters lay around a fire with a cauldron hanging over it, and not far from there some lads were playing dice on a drum, the canteen-woman and her assistants were running to and fro in order to serve high and low with equal attention, while the rough soldier's song kept resounding from the tent as a perfect expression of the temper of this company. [...]

As far as the soldiers in the mass were concerned, they could of course only be presented symbolically by some few representatives on our stage; actually, everything went quickly and well, and only the awkwardness of some extras showed how little time had been spent on rehearsals.

The costumes had been designed according to the illustrations available to us from those times, and we expect to see the principal characters of both the following plays to be dressed in the same manner.[2] [...]

Weimar, 15 October 1798.

---

[1] Max Piccolomini only appears in the second part of the trilogy. For the prologue, see **214**; for Vohs, see **217**, note 3.

[2] The costume design was based on extensive research into seventeenth-century clothes by Goethe's lifelong friend, the Swiss-born painter and art historian Johann Heinrich Meyer (1759–1832), who was also responsible for the set design. Meyer had been appointed professor of draughtsmanship at the Weimar art school at Goethe's instigation.

216   Scene from *Wallensteins Lager*. Coloured engraving by Christian Müller, from the painting by Georg Melchior Kraus.

Nationale Forschungs- und Gedenkstätten der klassischen deutschen Literatur, Weimar, Fotothek

II. Die Piccolomini

The second part of the trilogy was premièred in Weimar on 30 January 1799 – a date chosen in celebration of the birthday of Duchess Luise, the wife of Duke Karl August of Saxe-Weimar. On that occasion the first four acts of the play were compressed into two, the fifth act became the third, and the fourth and fifth acts were the first two acts of the following play, *Wallensteins Tod*. The scene references in the review quoted below therefore do not entirely correspond to the printed version.

The Berlin première followed within less than a month. See 219; also Julius Petersen (ed.), *Schillers 'Piccolomini' auf dem Kgl. National-Theater in Berlin. Ifflands Regiebuch zur Erstaufführung am 18. Februar 1799* (S.'s 'Piccolomini' at the Royal National Theatre in Berlin. Iffland's production scheme for the première on 18/2/1799) (Berlin: SGTG 53, 1940)

217   Schiller on the original production of *Die Piccolomini*, Weimar, 30 January 1799

Schiller, in an article written jointly with Goethe, in *Allgemeine Zeitung*, nos. 84–90 (25–31 March 1799). Reproduced in *Goethes Werke*, WA, series 1, vol. 40 (1901), pp. 64–6

Our *Graff*'s sensitive performance felicitously revealed the hero's dark, profound, mystical nature; whatever he said was deeply felt and came from within.[1] His moving recitation of the soliloquy, his words full of foreboding (in the scene with Countess Terzky) when he makes the unfortunate decision, the narration of the [...] dream swept all spectators along with them.[2] Only occasionally, carried away by his feelings, he put too much gentleness into his expression which did not quite correspond to the hero's manly spirit.

Vohs, as Max Piccolomini, was the public's delight, and he deserved to be.[3] He always stayed in the spirit of his part, and he knew how most happily to express the most subtle and tender feelings.

The scene in which he attempts to dissuade Wallenstein from the unhappy deed was his highest achievement, and the spectators' tears confirmed the penetrating truthfulness of his delivery.[4]

Thekla von Friedland was played tenderly and gracefully by *Mlle Jagemann*.[5] Her performance and her diction were characterised by a noble simplicity, and she was likewise able when necessary to elevate both to tragic dignity. A song sung by Thekla gave this excellent singer an opportunity to delight the public with this talent also.

Mme Teller, who recently joined the Weimar theatre, executed the important role of the Countess Terzky with the most careful exactitude.[6] She contributed greatly to the success of the play by her precise and lively diction in the key scene with Wallenstein in which everything depends on Countess Terzky's eloquence.

Becker presented the Imperial emissary in the camp with decorum and dignity and managed skilfully to avoid the pitfall of being ridiculous, to which this figure of a courtier, jeered at by a proud and insolent soldiery, was easily exposed.[7]

Malkolmi as Buttler, *Leissring* as Count Terzky, *Kordemann* as Illo, *Mme Malkolmi* as the Duchess of Friedland, *Weyrauch* as the Cellarer, *Beck* as the Astrologer, *Genast* as Isolani[8] felicitously caught the spirit of their roles and proved by the ease with which they managed to solve the problems of rhythmic diction that a more general use of metrical language on the stage might well be established.[9]

Hunnius as the Swedish envoy extremely aptly and happily represented in his own person the simple, straightforward and honourable warrior, the thoughtful, cautious negotiator, the religious Protestant well versed in the Bible, the mistrustful but at the same time bold and self-confident Swede.[10] [...]

Schall is greatly to be commended for the theatrical arrangement of the entire, very complicated performance with which he had been entrusted, and the hard work he put into his own considerable part, that of Octavio Piccolomini, did not prevent his devoting his attention to the whole.[11]

The management spared no expense by way of sets[12] and costumes in order to realise the poetic drama's meaning and spirit worthily, and to solve the task of delighting the eye with such barbaric period costumes as had to be represented, and of achieving a decent mean, to the best of their ability, between the absurd and the elevated.[13] [. . .]

---

[1] The role of Wallenstein was created by Johann Jakob Graff (1768–1848). For Graff, see William Charles Hicks, 'A Weimar actor under Goethe and Schiller', in *Publications of the English Goethe Society*, NS 11 (1935), pp. 60–85.

[2] The scenes are now to be found in pt. 3 of the trilogy, *Wallensteins Tod* – Act 1, Sc. 4, Act 1, Sc. 7 and Act 2, Sc. 3 respectively.

[3] Heinrich Vohs (d. 1804), a leading member of the Weimar court theatre from 1792–1802, often in charge of rehearsals. He spoke the prologue to the trilogy (see 214–5).

[4] Now in *Wallensteins Tod*, Act 2, Sc. 2.

[5] Karoline Jagemann (1777–1848), talented singer and actress in the Weimar company (see 141, 221 & 228). Thekla's song in Act 3, Sc. 7 was specially written for her by Schiller.

[6] Marie Luise Teller appears to have been noted more for her diction than her other acting qualities.

[7] The Imperial emissary – i.e. War Commissioner v. Questenberg. Heinrich Becker (1764–1822), an occasionally refractory member of the Weimar company: see Eckermann (1930), pp. 45–6, conversation of 26 February 1824, for Becker's difficult behaviour; Amalie Malcolmi's first husband (see note 8).

[8] Karl Friedrich Malkolmi (or Malcolmi; d. 1819), a widower who tended to play crusty old gentlemen, old peasants, comic or noble fathers in the Weimar company. Together with his two daughters Anna Amalie Christiane and Franziska, he served as a model for the itinerant old actor in Book 2, Ch. 7 of *Wilhelm Meisters Lehrjahre*. August Leissring (1777–1852), a minor actor in the company. Mlle Malkolmi (1780–1851), i.e. Amalie, the elder of K.F. Malkolmi's daughters who was to marry Goethe's favourite pupil Pius Alexander Wolff and work together with him at the Royal National Theatre in Berlin during Count von Brühl's management. Vincent Weyrauch (b. 1765), singer and actor. Johann Beck, brother of the better known Heinrich Beck (see 210, note 1). Anton Genast (1765–1831), actor and director who was with the Weimar company for virtually the whole of the Goethe regime. His son Eduard Genast (1797–1866), whose acting career began in Weimar, provided a principal source book for the Weimar theatre under Goethe's direction in his *Aus dem Tagebuche eines alten Schauspielers* (From an Old Actor's Diary), 4 vols. (Leipzig: Voigt & Günther, 1862–6).

[9] Teaching actors how to speak verse properly was one of Goethe's major preoccupations as a director and teacher (see 135, esp. pars. 18–33, and 215).

[10] The Swedish envoy – i.e. Colonel Wrangel. Friedrich Wilhelm Hermann Hunnius (1762–1835), a useful though not outstanding actor and capable administrator, had been with the Weimar company since 1797. The scene with the Swedish envoy is Act 1, Sc. 5 of *Wallensteins Tod*.

[11] Karl Schall (1780–1833), minor actor who carried out some directorial tasks; his being cast in such an important role suggests the limitations of the Weimar company. He later also became a playwright.

[12] The scenery was painted by Johann Jacob Michael Friedrich Haideloff and Conrad Horny. For further details on the sets of *Die Piccolomini* (as well as the whole of the trilogy), see Gertrud Rudloff-Hille, *Schiller auf der deutschen Bühne seiner Zeit* (S. on the German Stage of his Time) (Berlin: Aufbau-Verlag, 1969), pp. 107–30, 410–15, and Carlson (1978), p. 99–132. Note that the system of alternating shallow and deep stages was used; compare 17 and 81.

[13] Goethe clearly wanted the period authenticity of costumes to be modified by aesthetic considerations.

III. Wallensteins Tod (Wallenstein's Death)

The last play of the trilogy – *Wallensteins Tod*, originally performed under the simple title, *Wallenstein* – was premièred at Weimar with substantially the same cast as *Die Piccolomini* on 20 April 1799. This had been preceded by a revival of *Wallensteins Lager* on 15 and of *Die Piccolomini* on 17 April, thus unfolding Schiller's grand design in a series of linked performances. The run on tickets was such that seat prices were raised, some by a third, some by a half. The reception was rapturous, as the journalist and playwright Johann Friedrich Rochlitz was to recall years after the event.

218   First-night audience reactions to *Wallensteins Tod,* Weimar, 20 April 1799

Quoted in Kindermann, *Theatergeschichte der Goethezeit* (1948), pp. 640–1

I was actually in Weimar when Schiller's Wallenstein was staged for the first time. Heavens above! I feel as if I could at this moment see the noble poet's pale and grave face with his penetrating, blazing eyes shining out from his very small, narrow box which was immediately to the left of that of his gracious prince [. . .]. I say nothing about the grave solemnity of the entire assembly, not merely during the long performance but already before its beginning; nothing about how [. . .] a few hundred young Jena students came marching in with well chosen songs of praise and adorned with green sprigs as for a national celebration, sat down in the stalls, there established and managed to everyone's satisfaction a sort of private police with the greatest order, calmness and truly dignified conduct towards each other and other people present; I say nothing about the running, pushing and sending for works on the history of the Thirty Years' War in the libraries of scholars and particularly the Grand Duke's, which is open daily for general use, on the part of so many people of all ranks and both sexes the days before [the performance]; I say even less about the performance itself, although it offered the most perfect Max [Piccolomini] that ever trod the boards in the person of Vohs who alas! died so young and who [. . .] by his characterisation, tone and conduct of the whole [part], showed a consistency, clarity, dignity and strength such as I have never since encountered anywhere else among the many brilliant and magnificent performances of the play, not even in Berlin.

Iffland, who had been offered the directorship of the Weimar court theatre by Goethe at the time of his guest appearances there in 1796 (see **208, 211–13**), preferred to accept, on 14 November 1796, the alternative offer of running the Royal National Theatre in Berlin which gave him far more scope, both in terms of the talent and the resources at his disposal. He was to mount a number of spectacular productions of Schiller plays in Berlin. On 18 February 1799 he staged *Die Piccolomini*, on 17 May *Wallensteins Tod*, i.e. only weeks after the Weimar premières, with a much greater deployment of theatrical means and an on the whole stronger cast. Note, however, the *Wallensteins Lager* was not performed at the time, for fear of giving offence with its partly satirical portrayal of military life. (It was in fact staged in Berlin in 1803.)

In the Berlin cast, Iffland as Octavio was greatly superior to Schall in Weimar, and Henriette Meyer as Countess Terzky) to Wilhelmine Teller. But it was the interpretation of the principal role by Johann Friedrich Ferdinand Fleck (1757–1801) that made the Berlin production so memorable. Years after the event, Ludwig Tieck recalled Fleck's utterly compelling, psychologically profound reading of Wallenstein.

219   Fleck's Wallenstein, Berlin, 1799

Ludwig Tieck, 'Esslair zu Dresden. Brief an einen Freund zu B.' (Esslair in Dresden. Letter to a Friend in B.), first published in the Dresden *Abendzeitung* (Evening News), reproduced in *Dramaturgische Blätter* (Dramatic Journal) (1826), and in *Kritische Schriften* (Critical Writings), ed. Eduard Devrient, vol. 3 (Leipzig: Brockhaus, 1852), pp. 73–4

It may well be no easy task to represent the role of Wallenstein adequately and as a whole, to reconcile all the seeming contradictions, to unite the marvellous with the commonplace, the astrologer with the general, the communicative man of feeling with the solitary brooding misanthrope. The hardest thing is always to give a truthful and convincing representation of the astrologer with his magical beliefs, with his doctrine which he passionately preaches on any and every occasion, sometimes out of season. It was precisely this peculiarity that Fleck seized upon in order to make it the hero's predominant characteristic. The moment he entered the spectator felt as if an invisible protective power went with him; with every word the proud and melancholy man referred to a supernatural glory in which only he had a share; hence he spoke seriously and truthfully only to himself; with everybody else he was condescending and even while talking to them was absorbed in his dreams. So one felt that the general, so multifariously, so strangely complicated, was caught up in a great horrendous madness, and whenever he raised his voice in order actually to speak about the stars and their influence, we were seized by a mysterious horror, for it was precisely this seeming wisdom which stood in too glaring a contrast with reality and its demands.

This gave conviction and tragic depth to everything, even some things where the reader might think that the author had yielded too much to his poetic bias.

Iphigenie auf Tauris (Iphigenia in Tauris – Goethe)

The first (prose) version of *Iphigenie* was performed in Weimar on 6 April 1779 by amateur actors, with the singer Corona Schröter playing the title role and Goethe himself the role of Orestes; Goethe's performance in particular won high praise. (For amateur theatricals at the Weimar court, see 111.) This very successful production in Greek costume was repeated locally several times. But the later verse *Iphigenie*, curiously enough, was premièred not in Weimar (where it was only presented on 15 May 1802) but at the Burgtheater in Vienna, on 7 January 1800. At the time the Burgtheater was famous more for the quality of its acting than for its choice of plays: much of the credit for making this event possible was due to Kotzebue who, shortly before, had been employed as 'theatre secretary' there.

220   Première of *Iphigenia* in verse, Vienna, 1800

Journal des Luxus und der Moden (Weimar), February 1800, pp. 80–8. Reproduced in Braun, *Goethe im Urtheile seiner Zeitgenossen*, vol. 2 (1883), pp. 330–5

Tuesday, 7 January 1800. [...] On the occasion of the safe arrival of the Archduke Palatine[1] and his spouse from St. Petersburg, Iphigenia in Tauris was performed at the Imperial and Royal Theatre of the Hofburg. It is said that this play was selected by the Emperor in person from amongst a number of outstanding German plays suggested; the cream of the nobility was invited by the Emperor for the evening to this performance. Also foreign ambassadors and ministers, top military men, persons of rank, high law officers and the leaders of commerce were given free entry in exchange for the tickets they had been sent, so that only the most polite and best educated part of the public was admitted to share in the admiration of this masterpiece. The theatre was handsomely illuminated with more than 500 wax candles and adorned with masses of garlands. The stage itself was relieved of one of its most annoying illusion-destroying drawbacks – the prompter's box,[2] and entirely covered with green baize. The curtain went up and you saw an open copse; on the left-hand side Diana's temple, on the right some cypresses through the trunks of which a view opened up onto the town of Tauris and the sea bathing the same. I do not know who was responsible on this occasion for the arrangement of the scenery; it is certainly the case that this décor by the usually skilful hand of the distinguished designer, the court painter *Plazzer* [*sic*],[3] did not seem quite as relevant as one might have wished. [...]

If only a little more thought had been given to the geography of Taurica, to wild mountainous Scythia, this featureless open landscape would undoubtedly have been avoided. It would be absurd to claim that in Taurica there is no friendly plain anywhere; but the notion of that country tends to be associated with the idea of a wilderness and steep mountains, and even the area around Diana's temple should show some traces of this. [...] Now for the performing artists.

Mme *Roose* had the distinction, in spite of her youth, [...] of demonstrating her outstanding dramatic talent in all its lustre in the very difficult role of Iphigenia.[4] It is not the purpose of this article to analyse all the various subtleties of her playing

[. . .]. – But it is impossible not to touch upon the profound penetration with which this artist grasped and presented the character, the precision of her declamation and the heartfelt notes with which she either filled the auditors with deep melancholy or shook them to the core, nor altogether to deny her due praise for a *perfect* performance. [. . .]

Herr *Lange* deserves equal praise as Orestes.[5] [. . .]

Herr *Brockmann* declaimed [the part of] Thoas with somewhat excessive dignity and calm.[6] His tone, deportment and expression were rather those of a well spoken and well bred Greek and hence not quite in harmony with the description of him given by Arcas at the very beginning.

Herr *Ziegler* was Pylades.[7] He seemed not to be entirely familiar with the art of declaiming iambics. He often fell into a singing tone. [. . .]

Also, it was noticeable that he seized Iphigenia's hand and put his arm around her neck in almost every speech. Was this due to his not knowing what to do with his hands in this strange dress without any trouser or waistcoat pockets, or total ignorance of Greek manners and religious customs?

Herr *Bergopzoom* [sic] was the only one whose performance gave one overall cause for dissatisfaction.[8] He stressed the iambics with extraordinary harshness and made such a Scythian mess of the words that no German soul could comprehend him. The management should have had so much consideration for such a deserving veteran as not to expose him to going astray [. . .] in that unaccustomed territory.

But if the artists deserved all praise and the full respect of the public, whom they had sought to entertain to the best of their ability, for the exemplary rendering of this excellent piece, one might have thought these select, polished and well bred spectators would have responded with undivided attention and sympathy to the performers' palpably eager efforts. But one would be mistaken. All the high nobility present were magnificently attired. At noon they had shown off their splendid carriages, costly gowns and a wealth of jewels at court. But the court, in its noble simplicity, pays little attention to glitter. Then the stones sparkle more in artificial light than in daylight. So what was more natural than [. . .] dazzling the stalls with the display of the family jewels and thus keeping them in awe? Even the august example of Their Majesties the Imperial couple and their family who gave their undivided attention to the spectacle was unable to restrain an outbreak of boorishness. The chief offenders were those who, having sufficiently exhibited their sumptuous clothes and their painted faces, went home again after the second act.

---

[1] Archduke Joseph, the Palatine, i.e. Viceroy, of Hungary (1776–1847) was the brother of the Holy Roman Emperor Francis II (subsequently Francis I, Emperor of Austria, 1768–1835).

[2] In line with Continental usage, the prompter's box was, and is, downstage centre.

[3] Joseph Platzer (1751–1806), scene painter who worked for both the Burgtheater and the

Kärntnertortheater from 1784 until 1806. He also provided sets for the (German-language) National Theatre in Prague. His work represented a transitional style from baroque to neo-classicism.

⁴ Betty Roose (1778–1808), leading tragédienne at the Burgtheater ensemble under the Brockmann regime, noted for her power to move audiences and her melodious voice.

⁵ Josef Lange (1751–1831), handsome Burgtheater actor whose consciously picturesque deportment and influential views in matters of costuming were due to his having been trained as a painter. He published his memoirs under the title: *Biographie des Josef Lange, k.k. Hofschauspielers* (Biography of J.L., Imperial & Royal Court Actor) (Vienna: Peter Rehms sel. Witwe, 1808).

⁶ For Brockmann, who had been director of the Burgtheater since 1789, see 103, 199–202, 204.

⁷ Friedrich Wilhelm Ziegler (1760–1827), actor as well as playwright. For his ideas on auditioning for a theatre school, see 251.

⁸ Johann Baptist Bergopzoomer (or Bergopzomer) (1742–1804), formerly director of the (German-language) Prague theatre, then with the Burgtheater ensemble; given to violent physical effects in tragic roles but more natural in low comedy; the first actor in the German-language theatre to be called out for an individual curtain call (Vienna, 4 June 1774), even before Brockmann in Berlin (see 200, note 3).

Maria Stuart (*Mary Stuart* – Schiller)

The rehearsals for this historical tragedy which was premièred in Weimar on 14 June 1800 were conducted by Schiller himself. Karoline Jagemann (see 141, 217, 228), who had initially resisted being cast as Queen Elizabeth, in fact had her first triumph as a tragic actress in this role. The play was extremely well received from the start; it has become an integral part of the German theatrical repertoire.

221   Karoline Jagemann as Queen Elizabeth in *Maria Stuart*, Weimar, 16 June 1800

Weimars Album zur vierten Säkularfeier der Buchdruckerkunst (Weimar Album on the Occasion of the Quater-Centenary of the Art of Printing) (Weimar, 1840), p. 154. Reproduced in English translation in Carlson (1978), p. 146. (Translation taken from Carlson.)

Dem. Jagemann triumphed as Elizabeth. Never an instant passed when she was not the Queen. The spectator could have no doubt of her hypocrisy and yet it never degenerated into pettiness or vulgarity; it seemed to arise from necessity, not mere sentiment. She presented herself with the haughtiness of a great queen, which the poet perhaps left too much with the actress and indicated too slightly in the text. Mme Wolff, who played Elizabeth later, never approached Jagemann in this respect.[1]

While the rounded charming features gave Mary an air of friendly benevo-lence,[2] the sharply chiselled features, the regular classical profile, the deep spiritual eyes of loveliest blue marked Elizabeth, on the other hand, as the superior being in majesty and cold strength. In a quite unique way, which surprised even Schiller, the much discussed scene of the dispute between the two queens miscarried in that Mary appeared to triumph over the humiliated Elizabeth.[3]

[1] For Mme Wolff, née Malcolmi, see **217**, note 8.
[2] Mary Stuart was played by Friederike Vohs, the wife of Heinrich Vohs – see **217**, note 3.
[3] In Act 3, Sc. 4 – the fictitious encounter between the two queens, the unhistorical character of which tends to shock some British spectators of the play.

From 1791 onwards, the Weimar company used to play a summer season (June to August) at the small nearby spa of Lauchstädt. Although there was usually a complement of students from the University of Halle present, the public was far from ideal: essentially what was looked for was light entertainment. The success of *Maria Stuart* in such a venue was all the more remarkable.

222   The success of *Maria Stuart* at the Lauchstädt theatre, 3 July 1800

Heinrich Becker, quoted in Karl Berger, *Schiller/Sein Leben und seine Werke (S./ His Life and Works)*, vol. 2 (Munich: C.H. Beck, 13th edn 1921), p. 485. Reproduced (in English translation) in Carlson (1978), p. 147

The play was so successful that I cannot remember any similar sensation. The unanimous opinion of all spectators was that it was the most beautiful play ever presented on the German stage [. . .]. There was no need for the box-office attendant to come to the box office at all. By half past three in the afternoon all the tickets had been collected from his apartment. People's fury about the smallness of the house was so great that we removed the musicians from the orchestra onto the stage and crammed their places full of spectators.[1] They offered each other eight-groschen tickets for three dollars. Even so, more than two hundred people had to be turned away. To pacify them we promised to repeat Maria Stuart.

[1] The theatre at Lauchstädt, the auditorium of which contained fourteen rows of benches, could accommodate only a limited number of patrons. When it was rebuilt by the Weimar architect Johann Götze in 1802, it was large enough to hold more than 600 spectators.

Die Jungfrau von Orleans (The Maid of Orleans – Schiller)

Schiller's poetic – and very free – dramatisation of the life of Joan of Arc was premièred in Leipzig on 11 September 1801; this was followed on 23 November of the same year by the Royal National Theatre, Berlin, where under Iffland's direction the spectacular aspect of the play was given pride of place. This was notably the case in the coronation procession in Act 4, Sc. 2 when Charles VII was crowned King of France: some 200 extras appeared on stage! Although Schiller disapproved of this excessive pomp, the production was a great success; there were another thirteen performances within five weeks. Performances in Hamburg, Magdeburg, Dresden, Vienna, Frankfurt, Kassel, Schwerin, Nuremberg, Stuttgart and Mannheim followed in quick succession; a number of these used seriously mutilated texts, especially in Vienna where even the author's name was suppressed.

223   The coronation procession of *Die Jungfrau von Orleans* in Iffland's production, Berlin, 1804

Engraving by Fr. Jügel, 1806. Nationale Forschungs- und Gedenkstätten der deutschen klassischen Literatur in Weimar, Fotothek

When *Die Jungfrau von Orleans* was put on in Weimar – as late as 23 April 1803, owing to Duke Karl August's initial resistance to the play – there was no possibility of rivalling the extravagance of the Berlin production.

224   A modest production of *Die Jungfrau von Orleans*, Weimar, 1803

Eduard Genast, *Aus dem Tagebuche eines alten Schauspielers*) (*From an Old Actor's Diary*), 4 vols. (Leipzig: Voigt and Günther, 1862), vol. I, pp. 140–1. Reproduced in English translation in Carlson (1978), pp. 196–7. (Translation taken from Carlson.)

The coronation procession presented a particularly difficult problem with our limited means; in order to present it in an even moderately suitable manner, the financial commission of which I was a member had to grit its teeth and make all sorts of purchases. Woollen serge that was available in handsome colours and small bits of gold and silver were the basis of our creations; pasteboard helmets and armour with taffeta capes of gold and silver were created. The royal gown, however, was the real stumbling block. The enormous expense of it staggered Kirms,[1] and since he was in charge of all the supplies of the court, he tried to pass off an old blue silk curtain for this purpose. Both Goethe and Schiller protested strongly. Finally the good Kirms gave in and gave his approval, though with glum looks, to the creation of a real coronation robe. It was, to be sure, of imitation velvet, and from now on had to be passed down from king to king like a grandmother's wedding gown in the old days. In such ways as this savings were effected whenever possible, and yet the public was delighted with it all. Indeed, they viewed the coronation procession that was created with wide-eyed astonishment.

[1] Franz Kirms (1750–1826), Weimar court official responsible for the financial management of the Weimar court theatre and its co-director during Goethe's regime.

Die Braut von Messina (The Bride of Messina – Schiller)

This, the most uncompromisingly classical play that Schiller ever wrote, was – in contrast to the other plays of his late period – not based on history. Goethe directed the first production (Weimar, 19 March 1803) which was very well received, although its rigorous formalism did not court popularity in any way. Working on *Die Braut von Messina* clearly helped to define Goethe's later staging ideas: a number of examples in his 'Rules for Actors' were drawn from it. (See **135**; see also **143** which illustrates the last act of the play in a Weimar revival dated 1808–9.) Schiller's justification of his, at the time altogether unusual, use of the chorus, was written as the preface to the published version of the play (see **187**).

The following quotation shows the attention which both Schiller and Goethe gave to stage lighting. (Compare **81**, *Wilhelm Tell*.)

225   Lighting in *Die Braut von Messina*, Weimar, 1803

Zeitung für die elegante Welt (Journal for the World of Elegance), 31 March 1803. Reproduced in Julius Braun, *Schiller und Goethe im Urtheile ihrer Zeitgenossen* (Leipzig, 1882), ser. 1, vol. 3, p. 286, and in English translation in Carlson (1978), p. 194. (Translation taken from Carlson.)

In the last act the major lighting [. . .] is from a twelve-branched candelabra above the action which has a lovely effect, giving a chiaroscuro of heavy shadows and painterly light, particularly in the striking scene where the brother's corpse is brought in on a bier and at the end where the illuminated chapel can be seen with the burial place of the Countess of Messina.

The romantic poet Clemens Maria Brentano (1778–1842), who during his stay in Vienna was an unpaid contributor to the theatre journal, *Dramaturgischer Beobachter* (Theatrical Observer) (edited by Carl Bernhard, Vienna, 1813–14), saw the production of *Die Braut von Messina* at the Burgtheater. Also having witnessed the Weimar production of the play he was in a position to compare the two – to the advantage of the latter. Note that the Burgtheater was far from being totally committed to Schiller: its productions of *Die Jungfrau von Orleans* (1802) and of *Kabale und Liebe* (1808) used texts politically bowdlerised to meet any censorship objections. *Die Braut von Messina* offered no such difficulties.

226 The Weimar and Vienna productions of *Die Braut von Messina* compared, 1814

Clemens Brentano in *Dramaturgischer Beobachter*, no. 11 (Vienna), 26 January 1814. Reproduced in Heinz Kindermann, 'Brentano und das Burgtheater', in *M & K*, 22 (1976), pp. 102–5

Schiller struggled to find the right form in none of his works more than in The Bride of Messina; the choruses stand like echoing pillared halls, the mother and the children like the group of Niobe between them, the whole is almost architectural and made of stone; but they are sounding stone monuments, Memnon's columns of ancient times which resonate because the wonderful aurora of modern romantic art bathes their forehead in its rays and magically brings them to life.[1] This writer first saw the tragedy performed in Weimar according to Schiller's plan and intention. The whole thing was immensely strange but you were soon reconciled [to it], as with all well balanced architecture, by the simplicity of the storyline, the beautiful symmetry of the characters and the very rich language. [...] The whole performance which reflected the author's ideas was immensely firm, clear and serene. [...]

A truly perfect performance of this work is beyond the capacity of the German theatre as currently constituted. All players in this, the most beautifully conceived, work of the noble, good, beloved poet, must be entirely pure of heart, with a soul moved only by the beautiful dignity of art, without the least hint of mannerism, [...] full of a decent feeling for propriety, full of rhythm, full of superior tact, nay full of a superior divine innocence [...]. The perfect performance of this most noble piece calls for the strictest direction by a thinker of deep and purely poetic feelings in whom the laws of all the arts are united [...].

I have seen many performances of The Bride of Messina, not one of them perfect, some of them approximations, many nearly ridiculous. [...] The current production was at some moments not too bad, at some *moments* quite good, the position and grouping in all the major encounters was mostly haphazard, often very faulty. The choruses spoke quite well, the leader of Don Manuel's chorus [did so] excellently most of the time, the third leader of the chorus, Don Cesar's, extremely well in the few words he had to say.[2] – The mother is surely an excellent actress in a good many other roles; here this worked against her.[3] This play does not permit any extraneous excellence, its excellence is unique and belongs to it alone. She never spoke a false note, but mostly with too much verisimilitude, with too much feeling. If the whole story had been in another play, in a modern noble house, her playing would have been excellent. [...]

There was too much movement, too much emotion, in a sense she acted the mother who had experienced this, too well; but she was no *Niobe*. [...] – I recall one single passage in The Bride of Messina in which she [...] spoke in a manner which according to all the laws of art is false but which has unfortunately been adopted by the wretched declaimers on the stage and which makes its effect; [...] this is the pictorial manner[4] [...]. When she told her sons of her dream, she painted all the monsters she had seen and all their movements with her voice; she painted extremely well, but you do not paint with sounds in a speech[5] [...]. I say once again, this actress played very well indeed but not in the correct style. Don Manuel came closest to perfection as regards style,[6] apart from his chorus leader; they were equally excellent. If they had all played in the same style and if the composition of the figures had been more architectural, this would have been one of the best performances after the Weimar one. [...]

Last of all let me turn to the dear, sweetly pleading, pure Beatrice who often sounds absolutely magical, for she is conceived differently in this poem from anyone else;[7] the rest are a pillared hall which collapses on top of all that is innocent, melodious and human, she alone is allowed to be fully human, a virgin, a lover, and a bride [...] In order to conclude with praise [...], let me voice my criticism first. In the *declamatory* passages [there was] an almost false rising of her tone at the end of single periods; in the passages denoting expectancy or surprise [...] [she was] a few times too quick, forceful, loud and bold, and hence untrue. This is the worst and indeed all I can reproach her with, and this only applies to those declamatory passages where her heart is not speaking. But whenever it does speak, what a heart, what language, what infinitely childlike, innocent, mild and humanly pure-sounding tone of voice; no song can move as much, and yet she is only speaking [...]. I have never seen an actress with such splendid gifts.

[1] Niobe, the daughter of Tantalus, King of Lydia, was turned to stone when her sons were killed by Apollo and her daughters by Diana. The statue of Memnon, King of Ethiopia, uttered a melodious sound every day at sunrise.

[2] *Die Braut von Messina* has, strictly speaking, not one chorus but two – the followers of the two enemy brothers, Don Manuel and Don Cesar, and the speeches were not in fact spoken in unison but subdivided. The third leader of Don Cesar's chorus was Nikolaus Heurteur (1781–1844), an important Burgtheater actor who played heroic roles.

[3] Isabella, the tragic mother of the piece, was played by Johanna Franul von Weissenthurn (1773–

1847), member of the Burgtheater ensemble since 1789, who frequently acted in sentimental roles; she also wrote a number of history plays.

4 Pictorial in the sense of descriptive or demonstrative.

5 In Act 2, Sc. 5.

6 Don Manuel was played by Maximilian Korn (1782–1854), who had joined the Burgtheater ensemble in 1802 and was to become an important member of the company, directing as well as acting.

7 The role of Beatrice, the only guiltless person in the tragedy, was played by Toni Adamberger (1790–1867), an important member of the Burgtheater. She had been the fiancée of the poet Theodor Körner, killed at the age of twenty-one in the Wars of Liberation against the French.

Period III: 1815–1848

XV Contractual and organisational documents

Directorial appointments

In the course of the nineteenth century it became more and more common, particularly in major theatres, for the director not to be an actor but, as often as not, a man with a literary background. An outstanding example was Joseph Schreyvogel (1768–1832), a Viennese journalist with some playwriting experiences who after having spent some three years in Jena and Weimar in the Goethe-Schiller circle was appointed the Burgtheater's 'theatre secretary' in 1802. Leaving the post after two years without having made much of an impact, he was offered it again in 1814 with a very wide brief by the then lessee of the two court theatres (see **68–9, 71**), Count Ferdinand Palffy (1774–1840). Count Palffy, who was also the owner of the Theater an der Wien, had assigned distinct functions to the Burgtheater and the Kärntnertortheater, the former being dedicated to the spoken, the latter to music drama. Schreyvogel's original appointment included administrative and financial responsibilities for these three theatres; within less than a year he had to shed the non-artistic side of his functions. However, what was left still constituted a daunting workload, as the following letter explains.

227 Schreyvogel's range of duties as theatre secretary defined, Vienna, 19 March 1815

Letter from Ferdinand Count Palffy to Josef Schreyvogel. Reproduced in Karl Glossy, 'Josef Schreyvogel und Graf Ferdinand Palffy', in *Jahrbuch der Grillparzer-Gesellschaft*) (*Yearbook of the Grillparzer Society*), 31 (Vienna, 1932), pp. 145–7

If the management of the two court theatres and the Theater an der Wien is to succeed in its unceasing efforts most effectively to combine the interests of the enterprise with the requirements of art and the public, special provision for the artistic side is urgently necessary [. . .].

In view of the fact that court theatre secretary and deputy director of the Theater an der Wien Schreyvogel has on the one hand demonstrated quite outstanding abilities, talents, experience and tact specifically in the field of art and literature and on the other hand a special preference and liking [for them], in addition to having expressed a definite wish to that effect, I have decided to reserve these areas exclusively for you [. . .]

283

Your new range of duties and the obligations arising out of them will therefore be defined [as follows]: First. You will see to it that a new full-length play comes out every fortnight both in town[1] and [at the Theater] an der Wien, indeed every week at the latter theatre [. . .], the opening night to be on a Saturday, to which end you will procure the latest theatrical products both domestic and foreign as soon as possible, [. . .] assess these jointly with all members of the directing staff and then cause to be undertaken without any delay all such improvements, cuts or alterations as may prove necessary, and [. . .] submit suggestions for the necessary encouragement and payment of authors in this country and abroad in order to obtain good new plays in time. Second. If good foreign-language works have to be resorted to, you will have to choose the best translators and meticulously check the works submitted, just as in the case of tried and tested old plays [. . .] you will actively concern yourself with the necessary adapting of the same and, if need be, improving the dialogue.

Third. You will also take a particular interest in seriously dealing with censorship matters and having the censor's requirements attended to in the shortest possible space of time [. . .]. Once sufficient stage material [. . .] has been obtained, you will, fourth, have to consult, as per regulation, with the directorial staff about the plays, operas and ballets to be staged, and about the casting and the mode of production, and to submit the result of your consultation to the central commission forthwith; therefore, fifth, you will chair all meetings of the directing staff for drama as well as opera and ballet and see to it that the minutes of the meetings and other deliberations of the directing staff are submitted instantly and without delay to the central commission, and that all reports and submissions in the artistic field are drawn up with the respect and courtesy due to the management, the stage directors' freedom of speech notwithstanding. Sixth, you will turn up at the read-throughs of a new play as indeed at all subsequent stage rehearsals and actively ensure that performances attain the required degree of precision and perfection, and seventh, [. . .] you will see to it that the dress rehearsal is invariably held at least one day before the actual performance so that the play's success is not left to chance but before the [public] announcement [of the play] the necessary alterations will have been made, and if the latter require more time the performance of the play may be postponed. Eighth, you will have to make yourself responsible for all the correspondence regarding the theatre with outside writers, composers, actors, singers etc. [. . .].

Ninth, in order to give you all the assistance, time and space needed in your new range of duties, you will have set aside for you an office for your exclusive use [. . .]. Vienna, 19 March 1815.

Palffy.

[1] Meaning the Burgtheater and the Kärntnertortheater.

In fact, Schreyvogel long outlasted Court Palffy who was deprived of his post by the Emperor in 1817. During his regime from 1814 until his abrupt dismissal in 1832, Schreyvogel was to make the Burgtheater the premier playhouse in the German-speaking world. Skilfully circumventing some of the rigours of censorship, he featured the Weimar authors as well as Shakespeare and the Spanish Golden Age playwrights in the Burgtheater repertoire; and in promoting the work of the Viennese playwright Franz Grillparzer (1791–1872), he helped to give Austria an important voice in German-language drama. He also assembled the strongest ensemble in the German-speaking world, including the tragédienne Sophie Schröder (1781–1868) – not to be confused with Sophie Charlotte Ackermann-Schröder (see 85) – Heinrich Anschütz (1785–1865), who was to play leading roles at the Burgtheater for half a century (see 265), the character actors Joseph Koberwein (1774–1857) and Karl Ludwig Costenoble (1769–1837) – see the latter's *Tagebücher aus dem Burgtheater 1818–1837* (*Burgtheater Diaries*) (Vienna: Konegen, 1889) – Friedrich Wilhelm Wilhelmi (1788–1852) who played coarse and comic roles, Karl Fichtner (1805–1873) who started off as a juvenile lead, Nikolaus Heurteur and Maximilian Korn (for the latter two, see 226, notes 2 & 6), and Sophie Müller (1803–30) (see 246).

Goethe's influence on such institutions as the Burgtheater was profound in respect of repertory-planning; it was less so as regards acting style. But his ideas were not uncontested even in Weimar. Tensions came to a head over an incident when a melodrama by Ignaz Castelli, *Der Hund des Aubry de Mont-Didier, oder Der Wald bei Bondy*, adapted from René Charles Guilbert de Pixérécourt's *Le Chien de Montargis, ou la forêt de Bondy*, which featured a dog in the lead, was presented at the Weimar theatre at Duke Karl August's insistence over Goethe's strenuous objections. No doubt this was not the only cause of disharmony: the actress Karoline Jagemann, the Duke's mistress, had long been undermining Goethe's authority (see 141); but this clash of wills led to his dismissal from his directorial post in a somewhat curt letter from the Duke.

228   Goethe's dismissal from the Weimar theatre, 13 April 1817

Reproduced in Hans Wahl & Dora Zenk (eds.), *Carl August von Weimar in seinen Briefen* (Karl August in his Letters) (Weimar: Gustav Kiepenheuer, 1915), pp. 148–9, in Hans Wahl (ed.), *Briefwechsel des Herzogs-Grossherzogs Carl August mit Goethe* (Correspondence of the Duke/Grand Duke C.A. with G.), vol. 2 (Berlin: E.S. Mittler & Sohn, 1916), p. 185, letter 592, and in an English translation in Carlson (1978), p. 291

Dear Friend!

Various remarks of yours which have come to my eyes and ears have persuaded me that you would be pleased to be relieved of the troublesome business of running the theatre, but that you would be glad to support the directors with your advice and help whenever they might request it of you, as is frequently likely to be the case. I am glad to meet your wishes in this matter, while thanking you for the many good things you have achieved in this very knotty and tiring business, begging you to maintain an interest in the artistic side of it, and hoping that the lessening of vexation will benefit your health and prolong your years.

I am enclosing an official letter concerning this change and I send you my best wishes.

Weimar, 13 April 1817.

Administrative practices

Throughout the previous century it had been the custom in the German theatre (as in the theatres of other countries) for an actor to step forward at the end of a performance in the costume in which he or she had just performed, in order to advertise the next play to be given. This custom known as 'Harangieren', i.e. haranguing, was often criticised but it persisted nevertheless until the early years of the nineteenth century. A playbill shows that a more up-to-date practice was introduced in Leipzig in 1815.

229   Announcement of next play abolished in Leipzig, 1815

C. 19th playbill, quoted in Heinrich Blümner, *Geschichte des Theaters in Leipzig. Von dessen ersten Spuren bis auf die neueste Zeit* (History of the Theatre in Leipzig. From its First Traces until the Most Recent Times) (Leipzig, 1818), p. 359. Reproduced in Maurer-Schmoock (1982), p. 134

Since every stage representation must be regarded as an artistic whole complete within itself, it cannot fail to disrupt this effect when, as has been happening until now, a member of the cast as it were steps out of character and takes it upon himself to announce the following play. In order to avoid this disruption, it has been arranged starting today that the next performances will always be mentioned on the announcement of the [current] performance (playbill) as well; in addition, the name of the forthcoming play will be written up on a specially designated board by the theatre exit. The customary announcements from the stage will therefore cease henceforth.

Towards the end of the eighteenth century and in the first half of the nineteenth, new theatres rose not only in major centres but in relatively small towns as well. Playing times differed according to the size of potential audience, as this quotation from a theatrical encyclopaedia shows.

230   Acting days in small towns

Düringer & Bartels (1841), p. 1070

Acting day [Theatertag]. In the larger towns theatres play every day, with the exception of certain days ([...] Holy Week, days of fasting and prayer etc.);

however, in smaller towns, depending on local living conditions or habit and custom, [they play] only on 3, 4 or 5 fixed days per week on which the public habitually goes to the theatre; these are the so-called acting days. If theatrical performances are once in a while to take place on other days, for instance because of benefits, guest performances or [special] celebrations, these must be advertised very conspicuously [...]. As a rule a great many more patrons can be expected to turn up on acting days, for which reason it is advisable to secure these days contractually for guest performances and benefits.

Authorities continued to keep a close eye on audience behaviour in the theatre so as to ensure the maintenance of public order.

231   Policing of theatres in the nineteenth century
Düringer & Bartels (1841), p. 1,123

Guard. For playhouses this consists of (1) military guards at court theatres; (2) police guards for municipal and provincial theatres. The men on duty have to fall in in the vestibule giving onto the boxes and thence move to their posts before the theatre is thrown open to the public. Normally all entrances used by the public as well as the stalls and the upper galleries are occupied by guards, whereas the stage door is only guarded by a janitor and, in the cases of court theatres, by a permanently employed so-called theatre sergeant-major. These guards are responsible for the maintenance of public order, and if there is any danger of this being disturbed, their numbers are to be doubled. [...] Above all, on the box-office [...] being opened, guards have to keep back pushy and obstreperous persons in a firm but calm and humane manner; on the other hand they have to arrest trouble-makers, quarrellers and drunks. In court theatres, guards will take instant action against any open expression on the part of spectators which contravenes the orders and directions given by the prince, whereas in municipal and provincial theatres police actions only take place if there is any reason to fear public disorder and lawlessness, and this means that the public is usually given greater licence in the latter theatres. Guards are permitted to fall out only after the house has been entirely vacated by the public.

A theatre owned by shareholders

Like Hamburg with its short-lived National Theatre half a century earlier (see **170**), Brunswick saw the creation of a theatre by a joint-stock company in 1817: five wealthy local citizens took over the existing Brunswick theatre with a share capital of 24,950 dollars, termed it a National Theatre and appointed the author August Klingemann as director. Klingemann was determined to run an ambitious programme: on 1 April 1818 he opened with Schiller's *Die Braut von Messina*. He remained in post until the company, which had needed constant subsidies, collapsed in 1826, and he continued as artistic director when the playhouse was turned into a court theatre. One of his great achievements in this latter phase of his career was to have staged the first professional production of Goethe's *Faust* (on 19 January 1829), with the author's blessing.

232   Share No. 25 of the Brunswick National Theatre
Niedersächsisches Staatsarchiv, Wolfenbüttel, 30 Slg 21/9

The text reads:

The undersigned administrative commission of the National Theatre in Brunswick hereby certifies the correct receipt from . . . . . of *fifty rixdollars of 'convention currency'*[1] being half the amount of a signed share of 100 rixdollars, which sum will be used for the necessary equipment of the said theatre, such as the acquisition of the wardrobe, new scenery, music and texts, and the setting up of the enterprise generally.

The administrative commission of the National Theatre in Brunswick promises to pay in cash four per cent interest annually on the above-named sum of *fifty rixdollars of 'convention currency'* for three years from today onwards (for which reason three interest coupons made out for the sum of the interest are appended to this share) and to submit an annual account of the business entrusted to it, which will give a clear statement of the state of the institute.

Given in Brunswick on 1 March 1818.

The Administrative Commission of the National Theatre here.

---

[1] By a convention arrived at in 1753, the currency of Brunswick-Wolfenbüttel and some other German states was linked with the Cologne mark at a fixed rate. See Walter Horace Bruford, *Germany in the Eighteenth Century: The Social Background of the Literary Revival* (CUP, 1935), p. 330.

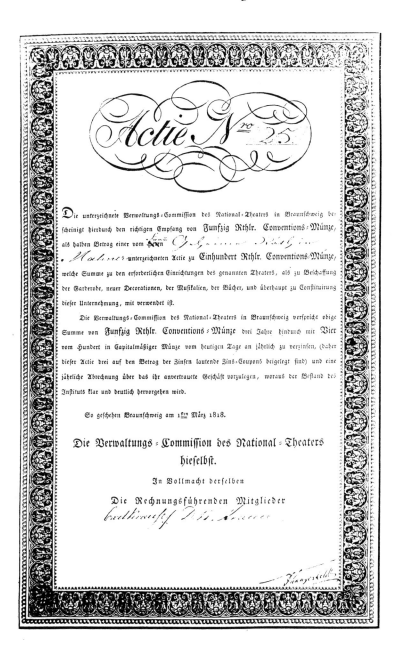

Basing a theatre on the joint-stock principle was not unique: there were comparable institutions in Breslau (1798), Hanover (1819), Bremen (1826) and Düsseldorf (1832 – see 258).

XVI Playhouses

In the nineteenth century, many newly built German theatres fell into line with the general neo-classical trend in architecture. An outstanding representative of this development in its earlier stages was the Prussian architect Karl Friedrich Schinkel (1781–1841) who designed the restored Royal Theatre as well as other important buildings in Berlin. The earlier Royal Theatre by Karl Gotthardt Langhans (1732–1808), which had opened on 1 January 1802 and which became popularly known as the 'Trunk' because of its somewhat squat shape, had burnt down in 1817. The new, severely classical edifice, which Schinkel designed in consultation with Iffland's successor, Count Karl Friedrich Moritz von Brühl (1772–1837), Director General of Berlin theatres, was inaugurated on 26 May 1821 – appropriately enough with a performance of Goethe's *Iphigenie auf Tauris*. Some time in the summer of 1818 Schinkel had submitted some plans for the new theatre to King Frederick William III (1770–1840) with the comments quoted below; significantly, in addition to aesthetic questions, considerations of safety loomed large (compare **235**).

Schinkel, who in his earlier years had been a painter of dioramas and panoramas, was also a distinguished scenic designer; he drew his inspiration largely but not exclusively from classical concepts of form and sought to simplify the stage picture.

233 Schinkel's plans for the new Berlin theatre, 1818

'Schinkel's Bericht an den König' (Schinkel's Report to the King), in Alfred Freiherr von Wolzogen, *Aus Schinkels Nachlass/Reisetagebücher, Briefe und Aphorismen* (From S.'s Papers/ Travel Diaries, Letters and Aphorisms), 4 vols. (Berlin: R. Decker, 1863), vol. 3 pp. 175–82

The idea which Your Royal Majesty deigned to put forward in your order in council[1] concerning the purpose of the new playhouse – that it should serve only for comedy, operetta and intimate drama in which no great scenic effort would be called for and in which too large a stage would be detrimental to performance, for which reason [...] it should be given the right dimensions both in respect of stage and auditorium while making use of the old walls[2] – is in every way a more advantageous disposition than the former one was [...]

The first point, the functional nature of the interior, I have ensured by dividing the building into three main parts according to its natural purpose: in the middle the theatre as the most essential part; on one side the concert hall with all its rooms; on the other the wardrobes, management offices, dressing-rooms for the actors and extras, meeting rooms, rehearsal rooms etc.

The functionally different entrances arise directly out of this arrangement; those for the playhouse are different for pedestrians and for coaches, and the latter can easily drive up [to the door] for alighting under full cover. A special entrance on the side of the concert hall leads directly into the tea-room of Your Royal Majesty's side-box, and from the same room a special flight of stairs leads into the royal box in the concert hall so that, the occasion arising, both play and concert can be enjoyed in the greatest comfort. [...]

Even though the stage area will be less by 1,300 square feet than in the previous state, it will nevertheless be quite sufficient for the most convenient presentation of the plays Your Majesty has in mind. The arrangement introduced into all new theatres, whereby scenery is flown straight up, has been applied here too because of its great advantages. Not only is this immensely helpful in preserving the painted scenery but it also avoids all tiresome errors in scene changes; there are great savings in the running of the theatre in that it is possible to hang four times as much scenery as under the old arrangement [...].

The auditorium is laid out in such a way that nearly all the boxes have the stage directly in front of them, and from the worst seat you can see the whole downstage area and more than half of the rear of the upstage area.

[...]

The parapets of the gallery and boxes run in a semicircle which is highly favourable from the point of view of sightlines and audibility and at the same time permits a beautiful dividing up of the ceiling decoration.

The boxes are supported by slim little iron columns such as have been used in several English theatres, which do not interfere with the sightlines. [...]

The paintshop for scenery is situated above the auditorium. The scene docks are all in the basement of the building [...].

The second point, internal and external beauty, I have also ensured by the arrangements mentioned under point one.

The fact that the theatre as the essential part occupied the middle of the building has resulted in less elevation being needed for the wings, and thereby the long uniform mass of the old building has been broken up and the whole thing brought into a pyramidal shape. Flat roofs with their frontispieces arranged towards the entrances could give the building a noble appearance in the manner of Greek architecture. The basement needed for the scene docks at the same time adds immensely to the noble style of the building in that the edifice is thereby elevated above the normal town buildings. [...]

The design of all the façades has been carried through with all due rigour in the Greek manner in order to match the [...] portico [...].

The regular distribution of the interior space allows for functional ornamentation everywhere, and the shape of the auditorium in particular with the beautiful lines of the semicircle is in itself more pleasing and can be made extremely appealing through the arrangement of the ornamentation [...]. The whole house, in white decorated with gold, would have a most attractive appearance when illuminated.

The third point, safety from fire hazards, I have likewise secured by the aforementioned dispositions. The building has been divided into three main sections which do not lie under one roof and hence are separated by very thick walls like different buildings. Added to this there are the flat roofs which in case of an accident will not permit any flames to rise high and will collapse more towards the interior and thus enable fire-fighting to take place from outside at close quarters. If an accident were to occur, only one-third [of the building] at most would be consumed, especially since on the [different] floors and corridors there are stairs with vaulted ceilings which will inhibit the fire and facilitate rescue measures. Even the stage is divided off from the auditorium by a massive proscenium which, vaulted on top, allows for a parting-wall in the roof which separates the most endangered part, the stage, from the rest of the space and in which a curtain made of iron, in the manner of an English theatre, could easily be mounted whereby the proscenium opening itself could be shut off.[3]

Similarly the placing of the scene dock in vaulted rooms in the basement of the building contributes greatly to fire safety. The main reason why the red heat in the roof of the old house rose to such an extraordinary extent during the fire was that there was such a sizable accumulation of scenery under the roof, the weight of which also constituted a daily peril for the audience.

The fourth point, maximum economy in design, has also been satisfied by the arrangements outlined above. [...]

As for the spatial dimensions of the theatre, I believe that in being designed for approximately one thousand six hundred people, it will strike a balance between the opera-house which seats approximately three thousand people and another third theatre yet to be built.

---

[1] The King had ordered the Royal Theatre to be rebuilt by an order in council dated 2 April 1818.
[2] The old building had not been destroyed totally, and Schinkel planned to incorporate some structural elements in the new playhouse.
[3] Note that the idea of an iron curtain was still something of a novelty at the time. The highly ornamented iron curtain which actually was installed was removed later on account of its weight.

234   The New Royal Theatre in Berlin, designed by Schinkel, 1821

Photograph by Stoedtner, Berlin. Franz Benedikt Biermann, *Die Pläne für Reform des Theaterbaues bei Karl Friedrich Schinkel und Gottfried Semper* (K.F.S.'s and G.S.'s Plans for Reforming Theatrical Architecture) (Berlin: *STGT* 38, 1928), pl. 29

Theatre fires

The burning down of the old Royal Theatre, Berlin, in 1817 was not a unique event: theatre fires unfortunately were frequent occurrences in Germany as elsewhere during the eighteenth and nineteenth centuries. Thus the theatre at Graz burnt down Christmas 1823, and the Weimar theatre was destroyed by fire less than two years later, on 22 March 1825. A vivid description of the latter disaster, which was a repetition of an earlier fire in the same town half a century earlier (see 72), is to be found in Eckermann (1930), pp. 90–100. (For similar calamities in other European countries, see 314 – the burning down of the Schouwburg in Amsterdam in 1772. A number of theatre fires have also been listed in Laurence Senelick (ed.), *TIE: National Theatre in Northern and Eastern Europe, 1746–1900* (CUP, 1991), pp. 66, 87–8, 111–12, 115, 133 and 273–4.) The complete incineration of the Karlsruhe theatre near the end of our period, on 28 February 1847, had been preceded a little earlier by what was perhaps the most spectacular disaster of its kind in Germany: the fire at the Royal Opera-house in Berlin in 1843. The following account of this latter event appeared in a Berlin newspaper.

235   The fire at the Berlin Opera, 18–19 August 1843

Berlinische Nachrichten von Staats- und gelehrten Sachen (Berlin Political and Scholarly News), 21 August 1843 (Haude & Spener, ed. S.H. Spiker). Reproduced in Weddigen, vol. 1 (1904), facing p. 247

Berlin, 20 August. [. . .] In the night of Friday to Saturday, 18 to 19 August, Berlin lost one of its finest architectural monuments, *the Royal Opera-house* which had stood for over a hundred years since its completion, as the result of a terrible fire.[1] There had been a performance there on the evening of 18th [. . .]. The show was over and the theatre closed when shortly after ten o'clock the fire was spotted, initially in and above the third window from the end on the eastern side facing the Catholic church, whence indeed it soon made its way through the ceiling and the roof [. . .]; it is very likely that the fire was caused by the gunfire in the final ballet, perhaps as a result of a tampion that went astray [. . .]. The fire had quickly taken hold of the wardrobe and the stage, and the mass of highly inflammable material, of canvas drenched in oil and varnish, of scenery and masses of dry woodwork was bound to be extraordinarily favourable to the rapid spread of the fire. Opera officials as well as citizens, officers, artists and strangers penetrated into the burning building with great resolution and boldness and saved whatever could be saved: some flats, some wooden frames and a considerable quantity of music; however, this was barely more than an insignificant fraction of the valuable objects stored in the opera [. . .]. After only an hour, around 11 o'clock, practically the entire building was in flames and afforded a terrible sight, its whole interior ablaze [. . .]; the flames rose in tremendous concentrated masses of fire and lit up all of Berlin and its environs for miles as if with daylight. The fire was even seen a great distance away in the countryside. [. . .] At times the mighty columns of smoke pouring heavenwards reminded one of an eruption of Vesuvius [. . .]. The fire glittered in all colours according to whether it seized on objects painted with various metallic paints or on other chemical materials: now the whole blaze looked pink, now white and blue, now all these colours blended into a multi-coloured sea of fire [. . .]. Not only did the zinc roof melt but the metal itself burnt in the most beautiful green Bengal light and sparkled down from on high like so many stars and fire-balls.

The army had hastened to the spot early on and occupied a large circle around the burning building in order to keep back the people who had come flocking there in vast numbers [. . .]. The crowd stood in silence, showing exemplary discipline on this occasion [. . .]; in the free space there moved about some officers, some carts collecting the few objects which had been dragged out, and some fire brigade units with vats of water; but soon any idea of saving even a part of the burning building had to be abandoned [. . .]. So the conflagration went on for *hours* without substantially changing its character [. . .]. From time to time the galleries collapsed into the interior of the building with a thunderous crash [...]. The most breath-taking moments were the *collapse of the roofspace*, of the rows of boxes and the corridors, and at 1 o'clock the *collapse of the concert hall* [...]. It was not [...] until 2 o'clock in the morning that the water was beginning to have some effect, and now the firemen turned their attention from all sides towards the burning building.

We all know what treasures have perished in this building. It was a beautiful edifice, world-famous for its suitability for its purpose as well as its attractiveness [...]. Now this magnificent building, which graced one of the most beautiful squares in the world, is but a huge pile of rubble [...]

---

[1] In fact, the opera-house was just a little over a century old: it had been opened on 7 December 1742 in the presence of Frederick II.

XVII Stage presentation

A. SCENERY AND COSTUMES

The trend in the early nineteenth century towards more and more lavish staging – exemplified by some of Iffland's sumptuous productions in Berlin (see 223) – was not of course peculiar to the German-language theatre which shared this characteristic with other Western theatres such as those of England and France. It reflected a growing demand for illusion in the theatre, whether in the 'realistic' (often archaeologically accurate) sets of serious drama or the fantastic scenery of opera and popular theatre such as the Viennese *Zauberposse* (or 'magical farce'). While the public applauded these scenic extravagances, they were often deplored by critics who feared that they would deflect attention from the literary aspect of drama.

236   The nineteenth-century trend towards spectacle, 1828

H. (probably Karl von Holtei), 'Ein Seufzer' (A Sigh), in *MBGDKL*, vol. 2, no. 2 (February 1828), pp. 142–3, Herzog-August-Bibliothek, Wolfenbüttel, Sign. Wd 567 e

The splendour of the larger and richer theatres has seduced even the smaller and poorer ones into at least attempting to suggest the same, and [artistic] demands have declined to the point that nothing is wanted but the satisfaction of the coarsest sensuality; that the most repulsive spectacle plays, which enrich (and at the same time deplete) the box-office in big cities are imitated in market and provincial towns. [. . .]

The greater part of the public, including, alas!, educated spectators, grasps at trivia. People want to *see*, actually to see with their own eyes and if possible to be amazed. A pretty story has been made up about the alleged union of all the arts in the theatre. Painting, too, is supposed to be part of it. Scenery is no longer the dark, merely sketched-in and suggestive background which lifts and supports the overall picture. No, it has been turned into an independent work of art subject to criticism on its own, which disturbs and takes away all the more from the actual point the more successful it may be in and by itself. Correctness of costume has been developed with scrupulous conscientiousness. A certain race of connoisseurs seems to feel the need to be able to refer to the sources on which directors and dressmakers have based their work. What piles of costume drawings! What a library for researching the dresses of all nations and tribes since the creation of the world! And what rejoicing in all this in boxes and stalls! What close attention and discussion, altogether distracting from playtext and actors, of the scenery both dead as well as alive. For what are many of the performances other than exhibitions of mobile, colourfully draped pieces of scenery?

One critic deploring the 'realistic' trend of early nineteenth-century theatre was E.T.A. Hoffmann (1776–1822), best known outside Germany as the author of fantastic tales. In fact, Hoffmann was an extraordinarily versatile artist – composer, conductor, muralist and caricaturist – as well as a perceptive music critic; much of this multifarious activity ran side by side with his work for the Prussian government service. He had close first-hand knowledge of the theatre, having been on the staff of the Bamberg theatre from 1808 till 1813 in various capacities – music director, director of several operas, scenic designer and scene-painter; in his later life in Berlin he was a friend and drinking companion of the leading romantic actor Ludwig Devrient (1784–1832) – see **243–5**. An essay in dialogue form, from which the following extracts are taken, reflected some of his practical experiences.

237   Stage illusionism criticised, 1818

Ernst Theodor Amadeus Hoffmann, *Seltsame Leiden eines Theaterdirektors* (Strange Sufferings of a Theatre Director) (Berlin: Maurersche Buchhandlung, 1819). Reproduced in *E.T.A. Hoffmanns Sämtliche Werke* (E.T.A.H.'s Complete Works), vol. 10, ed. Rudolf Frank (Munich & Leipzig: Rosl & Cie., 1924), pp. 17, 94

Playwrights and composers now count for little in the theatre, they are usually regarded as mere handimen since they only provide the pretext for the actual spectacle which consists of magnificent scenery and splendid costumes. [. . .] But nevertheless our stage should not resemble a peepshow. The real point of theatrical décor is usually missed. Nothing is more ridiculous than attempting to take the spectator, without exercising his own imagination, to the point where he actually believes in the painted palaces, trees and rocks for all their disproportionate size and height. It is all the more ridiculous when [. . .] something is constantly happening that at a stroke shatters the illusion which one is thus attempting to create. I could name a hundred examples, but just to mention one, let me remind you of the wretched practicable windows and doors which are placed between the flats, instantly destroying the most artful architectural perspective, which of course can appear correct only when viewed from one angle.

Let the faithful imitation of nature, in so far as it is possible, serve the scenic painter not for ostentation but only for the purpose of creating that higher illusion which is produced in the spectator's breast by means of the performance. That false tendency of making an impact with large crowds, the childish display with a great many extras who move awkwardly in sumptuous costumes and destroy all harmony [...] has also produced the demand for large, needlessly deep theatres which are totally opposed to dramatic effectiveness. On our over-large stages the actor [...] is lost like a miniature in a huge frame.

The characteristically Viennese tradition of popular theatre, which continued into the middle of the nineteenth century, also made use of spectacle; but here illusionism, far from seeking to imitate everyday reality, set out to make magic incontrovertibly convincing. This can be seen clearly in the following stage directions from one of the best beloved plays by the actor-playwright Ferdinand Raimund (1790–1836), *Der Alpenkönig und der Menschenfeind*, which has remained popular to this day.

238   Spectacular effects in Viennese popular drama, 1828

Ferdinand Raimund, *Der Alpenkönig und der Menschenfeind* (The King of the Alps and the Misanthrope) (1828), in *Sämtliche Werke*, ed. J.N. Vogl (*Complete Works*, Vienna: Rohrmann & Schweigerd, 1837), vol. 1, pp. 190–2. Reproduced in *Ferdinand Raimunds Werke*, ed. Franz Hadamowsky, 2 vols. (Salzburg/Stuttgart/Zürich: Verlag Das Bergland-Buch, 1971), pp. 481–2

(i) Act 2, Sc. 7

The cottage continues to burn. Heavy rain. Howling storm and thunder; the floodtide keeps rising higher and higher until it reaches the mouth of Rappelkopf[1] who has sought refuge on the top of the tree, so that only half his head is visible. [...] Astragalus[2] quickly sails close to his head in a golden boat [...]. Rapid transformation: the boat changes into two ibexes with golden horns, the tree on which Rappelkopf is standing [changes] into a beautiful cloud chariot with Rappelkopf and the King of the Alps in it. The water vanishes and is transformed into a picturesque scene of rocks representing the Devil's Bridge in Switzerland, on which children, dressed as grey Alpine marksmen, fire mortars while the cloud chariot crosses the stage.[3]

[1] Rappelkopf ('Churl') is the play's misanthropic anti-hero.
[2] Astragalus is the beneficent King of the Alps whose magic teaches the misanthrope to mend his ways.
[3] The employment of children in this Alpine scene is clearly intended to create a sense of perspective. Compare **81** – Schiller's suggestion for the staging of Act 1, Sc. 4 of *William Tell*.

(ii) Act 3, Sc. 1

Throne room in Astragalus' ice palace embellished with tall columns which give off a silvery light. Downstage a tall throne of picturesque aspect, as if irregularly made of ice; upon it [sits] Astragalus as the King of the Alps; a long light blue, white-embroidered tunic, wide Greek cloak, white beard; on his head an emerald crown. In a circle in front of him kneel fancifully dressed Alpine spirits; short white tunics decorated with large green leaves.

The pictorial emphasis of early nineteenth-century theatre with its larger stages directed greater attention to problems of lighting, as can be seen from an article by the Brunswick director August Klingemann (see 232). Lighting principles were a matter for debate well before the introduction of gas lighting, which arrived rather later in the German-language theatre than in England and France. (By the early 1840s, the only fully gas-lit theatre in Germany was the one in Cologne.)

239   The limitations of early nineteenth-century lighting

August Klingemann, 'Einige Bemerkungen über die deutsche Bühne im allgemeinen, und über die hier in Braunschweig neu begründete insbesondere' (Some Comments about the German Theatre in General, and about the Newly Founded Theatre here in Brunswick in Particular), in *Braunschweigisches Magazin* (Brunswick Magazine), vol. 28 (8 April 1815), pp. 225–6. Niedersächsisches Staatsarchiv, Wolfenbüttel

[. . .] Above all, the former [system of] lighting from the proscenium has been criticised, partly because it was too feeble and partly because of the smoke spread by the tallow; it seemed to impart an oscillating motion to everything in such a way that, more than anything, the actors' mimetic expression was deformed and totally distorted. In spite of all the obstacles, lighting by Argand lamps, which produce a *firm* and *clear* light, has now been introduced.[1] Tallow candles are still being used only in the side wings for lack of lamps, with the result that the upstage contrasts with the downstage area and remains steeped in semi-darkness.[2] – In fact, correct lighting arranged according to pictorial principles is impossible on the stage; because apart from the fact that, in contradistinction to *natural* light, the stage is illuminated equally from *all angles*, the main rays of light cannot fall down from *above* but come, in their main effect, up *from below*, as it were out of the ground, which will always be in contradiction to sunlight or daylight illumination.[3] What has now and again been urged concerning more effective stage lighting, i.e. that light should be projected from above, from the righthand side towards the left, cannot in my view be put into practice, because artificial light can never attain the strength and effectiveness of natural light, and *shadows* would on the contrary be *blacker* and *more nocturnal* in the case of the former.[4] By the way, very few actors know how to place themselves in the proper illumination and find the right light, which is a study in itself.

[1] The lamp invented by the Swiss physicist Aimé Argand (1755–1803) was an oil lamp with a chimney; using a reflector it had the brightness of a dozen wax candles and set higher standards of stage lighting.

² It is interesting to observe that, though Argand lamps were in use in German theatres at the time, they were employed – at least in some theatres – together with candles which had a very much lower light output. Note the continuing use of tallow, as against the more efficient wax, candles.

³ Complaints against the unnatural lighting angle of footlights were not unusual, even in the previous century, and they were to continue until quite recent times.

⁴ Note that this was written before the introduction of gas lighting. Although Klingemann seems here to be condemning something akin to modern lighting methods, he was of course right in suggesting that *undiffused* light would cast unnaturally heavy shadows.

B. TECHNICAL JOBS AND THEATRE REGULATIONS

The following two quotations from the Düringer and Bartels *Theater-Lexikon* describing current practice in mid-nineteenth-century theatres suggest that by and large things had improved organisationally, if not necessarily artistically, in the last fifty years or so. The wardrobe regulations recall those laid down by Schröder in Hamburg in 1792 (see 90) but they are somewhat more detailed. The signalling systems described were an obvious necessity in theatres with a large staff handling increasingly elaborate machinery.

240   Wardrobe regulations in the 1840s

Düringer & Bartels (1841), pp. 495–8

1) The authority directly responsible for the wardrobe staff will see to it that the theatre personnel are treated respectfully by them and that the ordinary rules of decency and politeness are not neglected by *anybody*. [. . .] Whatever any member of the wardrobe staff can do to satisfy the actors and actresses should be done speedily and without any argument [. . .]. However, no one is required to put up with any improper conduct, let alone with being abused. [. . .]

3) Shoes soiled in the street may not be cleaned in the dressing-rooms. Neither may any clouds of dust be raised by powdering in the dressing-rooms, nor tables and walls be dirtied with make-up or in any other manner.

4) [. . .] Anyone damaging an item handed out by the wardrobe is liable for its replacement. Anyone soiling a wardrobe item with make-up, gum etc. pays the appropriate fine and is obliged to pay for the damage.

5) Two hours before the beginning of the performance the dressing-rooms must be opened for the acting personnel and tidied up, and the wardrobe staff has to be on duty.

6) At the same time (2 hours before curtain-up) all costumes needed for a given show, together with all other wardrobe requirements down to the least detail, have to be in serviceable condition and correctly laid out in every person's place.

7) The members of the wardrobe staff so instructed (tailor, shoemaker, hairdresser, and obviously the property master) will have to be present at each dress rehearsal.

8) All new costumes and shoes must be tried on in the early hours the day before the performance.

9) After the first performance, the wardrobe items selected for this by the management are to be entered in the wardrobe ledgers.

10) No other items of clothing etc. than those indicated by the management may be issued [. . .].

11) No one may take home any items from the wardrobe, regardless of whose name they are registered under, or lock them away in his cupboard. If anyone is granted a dispensation from this, he has to return the borrowed clothes at an agreed hour the next day. [. . .] If anyone (by way of exception, of course) wishes to change at home, he has to give proper notice of this to the stage management. [. . .]

15) The wardrobe supervisor has to see to it that the dressing-rooms as well as the furniture etc. located there are kept clean. The wardrobe staff has to make itself responsible for the installation of proper lighting, for clean fresh air, for proper but not excessive heating in winter, for looking after fire and lights, and is liable for any damage caused by negligence. [. . .]

21) Any disturbance caused by the consumption of comestibles and beverages of an improper kind at an improper time in an improper place is subject to the statutory penalty. Spirits are absolutely prohibited.

241   Stage signalling
Düringer & Bartels (1841), pp. 1,137–8

[. . .] At the start as well as the conclusion of the music [. . .] the stage manager signals with a handbell, or preferably by means of a wire cord which causes a hammer to strike a steel plate near the conductor in the orchestra, which is certainly the best way in that ringing bells within the public's hearing is too reminiscent of the Punch-and-Judy or the marionette theatre. For bringing the curtain up, the safest thing is for the signal to be given via the bell-pull leading to the fly-floor machinery either by the stage manager himself [. . .] or, at his direct command, by a machinist or stage servant [. . .]. For lowering the curtain, the first sign is *not* a ringing of the bell which might be disturbing, but the prompter puts out from the prompt-box a little white stick tied to a small chain so far onto the stage that it can be seen by the fly-man, following which the latter has to make the necessary preparations; at the prompter's second signal, [given] by means of the bell-pull, the curtain is then to be lowered. Whenever the curtain is to be dropped noiselessly, slowly and gently, the prompter is to give the second signal by means of a wave with the stick. The signals for scene changes are all to be given by the prompter by means of the bell-pulls leading to the fly-floor and machinery in the cellar which all come together in one cord [. . .] The signal for traps and all actions involving the machinery in the cellar is given by the prompter using special bell-pulls, the ringing of which must be either so soft or so damped with wrappings that they cannot be heard up above. In cases where something special is to be done on the fly-floor there must be, apart from several speaking-tubes going up the stage walls for the exclusive use of the machinists, a similar bell-pull leading from the prompt-box to the upper levels, in addition to several spring-levers from various points in the wings.

XVIII Actors and acting

A. FRENCH ACTORS

Berlin had often hosted French acting companies from the early eighteenth century onwards (see 33 and 91). A French company under the actor Delcour was once again established there on a permanent basis in 1829, surprising as this may seem after the recent upsurge of German patriotism in the Wars of Liberation against Napoleonic rule. Delcour was to remain the head of this French enterprise, which presented current boulevard fare rather than a classical repertoire to upper-class Berlin audiences, until 1845; St Aubin, another actor in the company, then took over until 1848 when the French theatre disbanded for good.

Working conditions were so favourable that the manager of the French company had no difficulty in attracting serious talents from France, as is made clear in a list of comparisons drawn up by St Aubin in the late 1840s.

242 Working conditions for actors in France and Berlin compared, late 1840s

St Aubin, *Aperçu comparatif de la condition des artistes du Théâtre français à Berlin avec celles des artistes des théâtres de France* (A Brief Comparison of the Conditions of the Artists of the French Theatre in Berlin with those of Artists in the Theatres of France) (n.d.), printed in Siegfried Söhngen, *Französisches Theater in Berlin im 19. Jahrhundert* (French Theatre in Berlin in the Nineteenth Century) (Berlin: SGTG 49, 1937), pp. 89–90

IN FRANCE: You have to play every day from 6 o'clock till midnight.

IN BERLIN: You only play twice a week and only from 6 till 9 o'clock.

IN FRANCE: You have to learn one play a week.

IN BERLIN: You learn one play a month.

IN FRANCE: Daily rehearsals which last 3 or 4 hours.

IN BERLIN: Rehearsals of one or two hours.

IN FRANCE: The audience is sometimes noisy, often unfair.

IN BERLIN: The audience is always quiet and well disposed.

IN FRANCE: You play tragedies, dramas and melodramas which exhaust and use up the artist's vitality.

IN BERLIN: You only play one comedy or two vaudevilles which are not very tiring.

IN FRANCE: Except in Paris, engagements only run for 8 months.

IN BERLIN: The shortest engagements run for 9 months, and you have a chance of making profitable use of the three months in the off-season in neighbouring capitals.

IN FRANCE: The wages of actors who only play comedy and vaudeville are wretched, and they risk not being paid in full because of bankruptcies.

IN BERLIN: Wages are much higher than anywhere in France, and payments take place with scrupulous exactness and punctuality.

IN FRANCE: Artists are absolutely obliged to supply all costumes, hairpieces and footwear.

IN BERLIN: Except for street clothes, the royal stores provide artists with everything.

IN FRANCE: In big cities life is very expensive.

IN BERLIN: Life is very cheap.

IN FRANCE: Payments are deducted when an artist is off sick for a fortnight.

IN BERLIN: You are given whatever time it takes to get well again.

B. GERMAN ACTORS

Concurrently with the rise of romantic literature in Germany, a more emotional and intuitive acting style began to make itself felt on the German stage. A leading exponent of this type of acting was Ludwig Devrient (1784–1832) whose life coincided almost exactly with that of Edmund Kean in England with whom he shared many characteristics. He excelled in such Shakespearean roles as Falstaff, Shylock and Richard III; in the German repertoire, Franz Moor was a favourite role.

Through his nephews Karl (1797–1872), Eduard (1801–77) and Emil (1803–72) the Devrient dynasty was to be a force in German theatre which extended into the twentieth century through the sons of Karl and Emil. Eduard Devrient was not only an actor but also a scholar, whose 5-volume *Geschichte der deutschen Schauspielkunst* (History of German Acting) (Leipzig: J.J. Weber, 1848–74) has remained a standard work to this day; he was also a keen advocate of more systematic actor training than was available in the first half of the nineteenth century (see **252**). His description of his uncle's acting style was based on first-hand experience.

Ludwig Devrient

243   Ludwig Devrient's character as an artist

Eduard Devrient, *Geschichte der deutschen Schauspielkunst*, vol. 3 (1848), pp. 358–63. Reproduced in Devrient, ed. by Rolf Kabel & Christoph Trilse (1967), vol. 2, pp. 53–6

The enthusiastic acclaim which Ludwig Devrient found in Breslau[1] made a very wide range of different sorts of parts available to him, often thrust him into tasks unworthy of him and seduced him into some which were quite incompatible with his artistic personality. That included all those [parts] demanding a well-balanced, noble attitude in speech and gesture, decorum, dignity or worldly polish. He was opposed to the Weimar School, and he failed in all merely rhetorical roles. He possessed neither grace nor nobility and fluency of speech, his diction had a hollow, nasal and guttural tone and a hard emphasis, as a result of which verse in particular was as often as not mangled. To represent [an image of] man idealised and fairly proportioned was not in Ludwig Devrient's line; beauty of form was not at his beck and call; his spirit pursued, with a kind of demonic glee, human borderline situations in their most extreme manifestations.

The extraordinary, the horrific, the gruesome, the bizarre and the ridiculous, from the most slight and subtle traits to the uttermost degree of expressiveness: that was the territory he commanded with brilliant characterisation and truly poetic humour. Here his brittle voice rang the greatest vocal changes with the most astonishing flexibility; his slight figure of medium height managed virtually to transform itself into a hundred different shapes; his longish face with the rather flabby cheeks, the hooked pointed nose, which was oddly bent to one side from the top of the bridge, changed [...] not only for every role, nay, from one expression to another in the most wonderfully swift muscular action. His large fiery eyes, as black as his rich soft hair, could in the most striking correspondence with his indescribably expressive mouth shoot out truly terrifying flashes of the wildest passion, of the most savage scorn, but it could also charm with the most lovable roguishness.

The altogether demonic power in Ludwig Devrient's artistic personality made it possible to endow the representation of the character of Franz Moor with a hitherto unsuspected, highly poetic magnetism and individual truth.[2] This role must be regarded as his peak achievement in tragedy; he manifested in this creation all the boldness of his imagination, all the infallibility of his touch, down to the ghastliest depths of human nature. [...]

By the sincerity and purity of his acting Ludwig Devrient seemed destined to undo all that was dangerous in Iffland's example. There was no pretentiousness, no effort to draw attention to himself, no flirting [with the audience], no mosaic of single, carefully prepared moments;[3] Ludwig Devrient's performance issued solely from the nature and the inherent necessity of his characters as he had created them. He *lived* his parts, he did not *act* them. That is why he had no tricks up his sleeve to make something, at any rate, of parts which were not suited to him, which he could not master completely; or at least brilliantly to hide their defects as Iffland knew how to do in masterly fashion. Whatever Ludwig Devrient could not achieve perfectly he failed in totally; in certain declamatory and formal parts he was downright amateurish; artistic technique was in his power to the highest degree only when he had grasped the inmost vital nerve and secret life of a human character.

¹ L. Devrient was with the Breslau theatre from 1809 until his move to Berlin in 1815.
² See the following item.
³ This is clearly an unfriendly description of Iffland's method.

Devrient was greatly admired by E.T.A. Hoffmann in his favourite role of Franz Moor, the villain of Schiller's *Die Räuber* – a performance described in the following terms by Ludwig Rellstab (Act 4, Sc. 2). Compare the performances of Iffland (**207–8**) and Seydelmann (**248**) of this key role in German theatre.

244   Ludwig Devrient as Franz Moor

Ludwig Rellstab, *Ludwig Devrient*, in *Gesammelte Schriften*, (*Collected Writings*) vol. 9 (Leipzig: Brockhaus, 1860), p. 321. Reproduced in English translation in Simon Williams, *German Actors of the Eighteenth and Nineteenth Centuries* (Berlin/New York: De Gruyter, 1985), pp. 71–2. (Translation taken from Williams.)

Never have I seen a more splendid, physically sensitive performance than Devrient's. Each step, each twitch of his hand, each turn of his head had meaning. He hastily threw back his black coat, for he was still in mourning for his father, as if his involuntary contact with it had terrified him. He looked around timidly, as if wanting to see whether the spectre in his breast were actually following him. At last he dared to turn around completely and stood once again with his face to the audience. But he was no longer the same person whom a few moments before we had seen leaving, fall of resolute malice. His features were pallid, his muscles quivered as if trembling with fever, his teeth rattled together, his hollow eyes rolled uncertainly here and there, his hair was standing on end in terror.

245   Ludwig Devrient in the role of Franz Moor

Pen-and-ink drawing by the Henschel brothers. Nationale Forschungs- und Gedenkstätten der klassischen deutschen Literatur in Weimar, Fotothek. Reproduced in Eduard Devrient, *Geschichte der deutschen Schauspielkunst*, vol. 2 (1967), pl. 128

Sophie Müller

Sophie Müller (1803–30) began her brief career at the National Theatre in Mannheim and then, in 1823, moved to the Burgtheater in Vienna where she was regarded as one of the most enchanting actresses of the Schreyvogel era (see 227). The daughter of a well known actor, she began to appear on the stage as a child; one such performance – in Müllner's fate tragedy, *Die Schuld* (Guilt) – was described by the authoress Johanna Schopenhauer.

246   Sophie Müller's touching performance in *Die Schuld*

From Johanna Schopenhauer's autobiographical writings, reproduced in H. (Karl v. Holtei?), 'Von dem Berufe für's Theater' (Concerning a Vocation for the Stage), in *MBGDKL*, vol. 2, no. 3 (March 1828), pp. 198–9. Herzog-August-Bibliothek, Wolfenbüttel, Wd 567 f

I will only mention one other performance, Müllner's *Die Schuld*, because the superb performance by a very young girl, enchanting little Sofia [*sic*] Müller, really struck me as utterly delightful. She played the boy Otto[1] so unsurpassably well that I would have wished the author had had the pleasure of seeing it. This child's part [...] is often made insufferable by the usual way in which it is done. The author has given it a strong, at times somewhat sharp, characterisation which, if it is made too blatant, turns the child into a saucy unattractive creature [...]. This Otto as presented by the charming Sophie appeared entirely different. Everything that needed to be softened she softened with the utmost delicacy so as not to make the child's speeches revolting, yet for all that without depriving the boy's character of its individuality; she expressed his affection for his beautiful native land masterfully and yet avoided any exaggeration of Spanish *grandezza*. She recited the excellent description of the bullfight[2] like a child glad to tell his grandfather about a curious event of which he had been an eyewitness and carried away by the torrent of his own speech, whereas others playing this part declaim it with affected rhetorical pathos and face the stalls directly while doing so. All the movements of this very young actress bespoke the purest childlike character. When she spoke about having seen her father in his coffin, a painful emotion kept rising within her with every word, until she mentioned the horrendous circumstance of his breast having been opened in order to embalm him with precious spices, for there must be something frightful in this thought for any child; at this point her feelings overcame her, her voice broke and at the end of the speech she buried her face in her mother's gown, weeping.[3]

[1] Otto is the son by a first marriage of Elvire, the Spanish wife of the Nordic Count of Oerindur.
[2] This is a long virtuoso speech in Act 3, Sc. 1.
[3] Act 2, Sc. 5.

Karl Seydelmann

Karl Seydelmann (1793–1843) followed Ludwig Devrient, his senior by about ten years, in becoming the German-language theatre's outstanding character actor, shining in roles such as Carlos in Goethe's *Clavigo*, Alba in the same author's *Egmont*, President v. Walter in Schiller's *Kabale und Liebe* and King Philip in his *Don Carlos*, as well as Iago, Richard III and Shylock. In contrast to Devrient, however, he was not so much an intuitive actor as a careful plotter of strong effects: hence his heavily annotated playtexts in which he carefully set down his character analyses, business and prop lists (see **249–50**). The characterisation given below must be taken with a grain of salt: the actor-director-author August Lewald (1792–1871) wrote his booklet on Seydelmann as a puff when the latter gave his first guest performances in Berlin in 1835. In fact, Seydelmann had to compensate by sheer hard work for the physical and vocal advantages he lacked. The following piece may therefore be read in part as an example of the burgeoning theatrical publicity industry.

247   A eulogy of Seydelmann, 1835

August Lewald, *Seydelmann und das deutsche Schauspiel* (*S. and the German Theatre*) (Stuttgart: S.G. Liesching, 1835), pp. 1–2, 22–4. BL 11795.d.12

As many actors as I have seen until this moment – and there were famous ones among them – I have never yet met any one who has such a range of aptitudes for his art as *Seydelmann*.

His marvellous, easily stimulated imagination shows him instantly such an apt and characteristic image of the person to be represented that he could vie with the most superb painter in this respect; the gift of impersonation he possesses in the most perfect degree; his body, all his limbs, are soft wax, clay, material from which he forms his creatures, now this way, now that; his voice, his diction, features and gestures are his paints, tints and glazes by means of which he individualises and imparts life. [...]

Seydelmann is fortunate in having been favoured by nature even in his appearance. His height is to be classed as neither tall nor short; but by some skilfully applied aids on the stage it can easily be made to have whatever stature seems indispensable for certain historical characters. A fair-haired person stays young longer than a brown-haired one, so he, though forty years old, can still look a youth when dressed to advantage. There is nothing very marked in his face; his features are pleasant and extremely mobile; his eye is intelligent though light-coloured; it can become piercing or romantic only for moments; but when calm it does not roll and flash as is the case with Devrient. His cheeks are fleshy but not fat [...].

Seydelmann's body possesses great agility and mobility; it serves him slavishly, whatever demands he may make upon it. His voice [...] is capable [...] of infinite modulations, nay of total transformation. [...] Seydelmann's voice in its natural state is a pleasant-sounding soft baritone, with considerable volume in the tenor and bass ranges. He has his voice so much in his power that he will speak entire parts in the lower register with an enormous effort, while he will do others entirely in the tenor range.

The role of Franz Moor naturally fitted into Seydelmann's repertoire of remarkable villains. (Compare 207–8, 244–5.)

248   Seydelmann as Franz Moor, 1833

O. Müller, 'Seydelmann als Franz Moor', report from Darmstadt in *Frankfurter Konversationsblatt*, 12 February 1838. Reproduced in Heinrich Stümcke (ed.), *Rollenhefte Carl (Karl) Seydelmanns/Aus den Handschriften veröffentlicht* (K.S.'s Playtexts/Published from the Manuscripts) (Berlin: SGTG 25, 1915), p. 3

This Franz in his broodiness, with his dry burning kisses, his hissing diction which under the pressure of his diabolical personality sometimes declines into mere mumbling heavy as lead, this unfathomable destructiveness in his unmoving treacherous eyes, this avid convulsion of all human passions and rage which frequently causes ten fingers to contract inconspicuously and then to open out again: this Franz indeed is not Schiller's, he is solely Seydelmann's.

Many of Seydelmann's detailed annotations to the roles he was working on were preserved after his death. This is his thumbnail sketch of the villainous President in Schiller's *Kabale und Liebe*.

249   Seydelmann's notes for President v. Walter, 1839
Stümcke (1915), p. 25

Not at all in the customary theatrical stiffly elegant 'lordly' manner, head thrown back – no, a personality showing the most exquisite manners – scintillating in the subtlest, smoothest, most pleasant colours; covering the volcano inside him with flowers.

Already in deep conflict with his conscience, sensing defeat; brooding on thoughts of how to prevent his downfall. Reserved – distracted – with flashes of harsh humour and violent passion, but without any shouting or theatrical trickery.

Similarly Seydelmann noted down the characterising props he would need for the above role.

250   Seydelmann's prop list for President v. Walter, 1839
Stümcke (1915), p. 23

Simple eye-glass (in his waistcoat pocket)
Ribbon of an order around his neck
Star on his chest
Rings
Small box for his Spanish snuff
Steel watch-chain
Trousers and buckles on his shoes
White silk handkerchief

Act 5: An open letter

C. ACTOR TRAINING

Various earlier attempts at training novice actors systematically such as those of Ekhof and Goethe (see **129** and **135**) having been of short duration, the call for the founding of a theatre school was reiterated in the first half of the century. One of the advocates of such a step, for which the acting profession seemed to show no great enthusiasm, was the actor-playwright Friedrich Wilhelm Ziegler (1760–1827), who did not merely plead for such an institution in the abstract but offered a number of ideas on how to run it. His suggestions for auditioning are not likely to commend themselves to teachers of acting today. In fairness to Ziegler it should be stated that he advocated a style of psychological verisimilitude rather than pure formalism. For Ziegler, see **220** and **258**, note 28.

251   The need for a theatre school: suggested auditioning procedures, 1820

Friedrich Wilhelm Ziegler, *Systematische Schauspielkunst in ihrem ganzen Umfange/Für die Freunde der dramatischen Kunst und ihre Schüler* (A System of the Art of Acting in all its Aspects/For the Friends of the Art of Acting and Its Students) (Vienna: Anton Pichler, 1820), pp. 22–5. BL 11795. aaa. 4(1)

If there are still to be artists and the art of acting in days to come, a true school of art is now a desperately urgent necessity; *without such a, not very expensive, institution there will no true art nor any artists in future, but only comedians.*[1]

The *future* has every right to demand [the provision of] both *artists* and *art* from those who are responsible for them, and the latter are owed an obligation to maintain this profession by *strict laws* and a *professional school*. Not all actors desire the former, and the latter they have until now regarded as impossible, because they disguise their own inadequacy with this [alleged] *impossibility*. The world is meant to find infinitely difficult that which they do without any hard work and effort. [...]

But if those who are responsible for the next generation wish to set up a training school for actors at minimal expense [...], the *institution* must be entirely above suspicion; only parents and guardians are to have free access at all times, and absolutely no frivolous female pupils are to be admitted; for the stage can more easily do without talent than without people's respect.[2] [...]

Anyone whom the probing eye recognises at a glance [... to be] physically suited to the great and noble profession qualifies for an examination of [his or her] intellectual gifts.

It is not passages from plays but *Schiller's* Song of the Bell that must be selected for the auditioning of candidates, because it is so rich in varied poetic beauties and simple truths.[3]

After a detailed and complete explanation of the words and the mythical sense of the words of this great poet, let a thoughtful and outstandingly *sensitive* actor recite for the male or female student carefully selected passages of the poem several times with a keen and lively imagination [. . .].

If the examiner finds the student, who is to be constantly watched during the recitation, inwardly and outwardly moved, if his lips and cheeks grow flushed and pale in rapid alternation, if his gestures are significant, if his hands and fingers begin to stir and his breath grows shorter while he is being strongly affected, the performing master has discovered a talent worth more than the famous pearl *Cleopatra* destroyed with a corrosive liquid. – Then he moves the student from a passive into an active role. He has him speak himself what has been recited to him before, until he finds that the springs of feeling have been opened up and found their direction; then physical and intellectual training will begin simultaneously. [. . .] – Brief military training will give the male students a manly posture, were this to be lacking. If the female student has had some moral training and the male student a scientific education, both, given constant diligence, can make a brilliant appearance on the stage within a year, and within two years they will acquire the name of artist, although they will never achieve this without a feeling for psychology.

---

[1] See 97, note 1.
[2] Note that in spite of the much greater social acceptance of the profession in recent decades, actors were still anxious to be considered respectable.
[3] Schiller's poem, which traces the entire course of human life through the metaphor of the casting of a bell, had been adapted for stage use by Goethe; it was premièred in Weimar on 10 August 1805 as a tribute to the recently deceased Schiller and performed again repeatedly.

The scheme for a theatre school outlined by the actor and author Eduard Devrient (see p. 304) twenty years after the publication of Ziegler's book will strike the reader today as in many respects much sounder than the earlier work – but there was no direct follow-up to this either.

252   A suggested curriculum for a theatre school, 1840

Eduard Devrient, *Über Theaterschulen/Eine Mitteilung an das Theaterpublikum* (Concerning Theatre Schools/A Message to the Theatre-Going Public) (Berlin: Jonas Verlagsbuchhandlung, 1840), pp. 29–45. BL 11795. aaa. 4(2)

Organisation of the Curriculum

As far as this is compatible with teaching, the sexes are to be kept separate during lessons.

The students are to be divided into at least two classes so that the advanced students are not held back by the less mature ones. [...]

The subjects of instruction are the following:

1. Speech

This begins with regulating the pronunciation of individual sounds and syllables, in order to get rid of provincialisms, defects and sloppiness of diction. Then students will be made aware of the accentuation of syllables, correct inhalation when reading, proper punctuation, phrasing, modulation of the voice and precise conscious placing of the accent in speaking. So at first the student should only learn how to read distinctly, clearly, intelligibly and euphoniously according to meaning. [...]

After that, reading exercises progress to narratives into which speakers are now introduced. Then on to novels in passionate language, with speeches [...] – and only now the reading of dramatic writings is to be tackled. At first only prose pieces should be chosen [...], comedies, then more serious plays, and then high-flown, tragic ones, in which the subtlest shading of expression and modulation of the voice are to be insisted on.

As soon as the German language course has meanwhile advanced as far as the explanation of the [different] kinds of verse, the reading exercises move on to metrical poems. First in simple, then in complex metres and, once the first inhibition in verse-speaking has been overcome, verse dramas are read at last [...]. These exercises will be learnt by heart and recited as soon and as much as possible, since the speaker has only mastered his material after he has made it entirely his own. [...]

2. Music

Those students who want to train specially for opera will receive

Singing lessons

in special classes and to make up for it will spend less time on speech exercises [...].

Singing lessons for acting students

But singing lessons must not be limited to opera students only, they are also up to a point necessary for students of the spoken drama, and only those rare individuals to whom nature has denied a singing voice altogether may be excused from it. The feeling for rhythm, one of the most essential requirements for verse-speaking, is most surely cultivated by singing lessons, as is the consciousness of modulation in speaking [...]. What will be most useful for acting students is to practice polyphonic singing because this trains them to adapt themselves to other voices, and to adjust their own accordingly and bring them into harmony, and these are things also demanded for dramatic speech.

3. The language of gesture

In order to be enabled to express inner states by means of postures, movements and facial expressions, the student must first of all acquire a general command over his body, hence the exercises of *riding* and *military drill* are necessary,[1] which give the body a firm, assured posture and balance, of *fencing* and *gymnastics*,[2] which give it strength and agility, and of *dancing*, which give it ease and gracefulness. The female students will benefit, apart from dancing, from some suitable gymnastic exercises and especially from military drill, in order to correct the sloppy walk, the unattractive tottering movement of the leg often induced by long, enveloping dresses. [. . .]

The student must learn how to stand, walk, greet, enter, exit, wave, sit, kneel down etc., and to be able to do all this not only with assurance and grace but also expressively according to variety of rank, circumstance and feeling. [. . .]

After the students have thus gradually been initiated into the language of gesture, they pass from the dancing-master's instruction into the higher class and begin at once to carry out more complicated plastic tasks on the school's studio stage. [. . .]

The audience-chamber scene in Don Carlos would for instance be well suited for these exercises in order to learn ceremonial dignity.[3] The postures, uncovering of one's head, bowing, kissing of hands, kneeling, the presenting of the cushion with the order etc. are all things which have already cropped up in the dancing lessons but which in combination will call for an astonishing number of corrections.

Another exercise would be the [. . .] scene from The Maid in which Joan prevents the fight between Burgundy, La Hire and the Bastard.[4] The constant mutual attacks and various [acts of] preventing, interposing etc. call for attentive practice and careful calculation of the groupings.

Furthermore, the teacher will design exercises linking up the everyday occurrences of life [. . .]. A servant's way of announcing someone, of entering and leaving, of serving etc., how a stranger enters, how people greet each other and sit down (the stranger in a different way from the host), how you open and read a letter, how you introduce a lady, how the latter has to conduct herself, how a letter is to be written and sealed on stage etc. etc., all these are things which everybody thinks he can do easily and which nevertheless have to be arranged with extreme care if they are to be presented gracefully and naturally on stage.

7. The art of performance

The student obviously must not enter upon this final stage of instruction, which puts all the preliminary studies discussed so far into practice and leads to actual dramatic performances on the studio stage, until he has been adequately prepared [...]

The same method as in the speaking exercise is to be followed here; the beginning should be the representation of familiar features of everyday life in order to be able to demand a natural approach from the student. A budding talent can venture to tackle circumstances and characters of a stronger, idealised expression, of a more emotional tone [...] only after he has made himself at home in this area. In following this method, the budding talent will best be preserved from those unnatural and affected mannerisms in speech, movement and expression which are criticised as such a general vice in our theatres [...].

So the students will first be trained in comedies and middle-class plays. In addition to plays by Schröder, Engel, Goldoni, Iffland, which are the easier ones, more demanding comical tasks from Holberg and Shakespeare will not fail to be selected.[5] Lessing's and Goethe's prose plays will lead on those by Schiller, and individual scenes from verse masterpieces will only then be chosen as the last and highest task. [...].

In order to stimulate the students' own creativity, it would be useful to get them to *improvise* some scenes, then short *playlets*. This is perhaps the most effective way of bringing individual talents to full development.[6]

In order to oblige students to have definite, sharply defined ideas about their projects, *explications of the contents and the meaning of the plays and analyses of individual roles* will be demanded. But these should be given orally, not in writing, so that students are directed at all times towards living speech as the element most proper to them. [...]

What is to be avoided in this class is students being cast entirely according to their bent; on the contrary they should be obliged to attempt different types of roles. [...]

A teacher in this class will not be able to keep occupied and closely supervise more than eight students; but to prevent his artistic individuality impressing itself too palpably on his charges, an exchange of students among the teachers should be undertaken from time to time.

---

[1] Ziegler, too, had recommended some military drill for male acting students in his book on theatre schools (see **251**).

[2] There had been a great upsurge of interest in gymnastics in Germany as a result of the activities of Friedrich Ludwig Jahn (1778–1852), the so-called 'Turnvater' ('Father of Gymnastics'), who opened the first open-air gymnasium in 1811 and trained young people to become physically fit for the fight against French domination.

[3] Act 3, sc. 7 of Schiller's *Don Carlos*.

[4] Act 2, sc. 20 of Schiller's *Die Jungfrau von Orleans*.

[5] For Schröder, see **90, 102, 120–1, 124, 134, 193, 199, 200, 204**; his comedies, more in the English taste, avoided the sentimentalism of Iffland's domestic dramas. – For Engel, see **183**. The Danish

playwright Ludvig Holberg (1684–1754) had long been popular on the German stage: some of his plays figured both in the Weimar and the Burgtheater repertoires.

6 Compare Brandes' views on improvisation (128).

But the fact that even by the middle of the nineteenth century the theatrical profession was by no means convinced of the value of actor training can be gathered from an entry in the *Theater-Lexikon* referred to previously. (It should be borne in mind that both its authors were practical men of the theatre.)

253   The need for a theatre school questioned, 1841
Düringer & Bartels (1841), p. 1,069

Theatre school. We do not boast any special institution for training actors in Germany. Attempts have been made by, before and since Iffland but without being successful or long-lasting. The upkeep of a perfect theatre school would involve greater sacrifices than would be justified by its usefulness [...]. A theatre school will no more form an artist than a great master would be able to do if the student were lacking in *talent* [...]. Nowadays excellent academic institutions exist everywhere for acquiring the necessary scholarly background knowledge, and the greatest training school for the talented born artist is, as it always has been, *life.* – We do not hereby mean to condemn institutions intending to take on the education and training of actors, we only deny their absolute necessity.

XIX Audiences

The nineteenth century saw a striking improvement in the status of the theatre in German-speaking countries. Theatre-going had become respectable and very much part not only of upper-class but of middle-class life; in some places, notably in Vienna, it attracted the broad masses of the people.

254 Changing attitudes towards the theatre, 1841

Eduard Devrient, *Über Theaterschule* (1841), p. 8

Not only has the German theatre come to occupy an honourable place among all the arts in the course of the last fifty years, it has actually become a social necessity.

In all the princely capitals [*Residenzen*] you find richly equipped theatres, all important towns vie with each other in building magnificent temples to the art of drama and establishing it within their walls. The greatest minds have devoted their interest and their activity to the theatre, every sphere of society is open to actors, and the dubious insinuations formerly current about the theatre in respect of morality and religion are only heard in some few isolated circles.

In spite of a pettifogging censorship, Vienna in the 1820s and the 1830s was an exceptionally lively theatrical city both on the popular and the literary level. This was the period of intense dramatic productivity of Franz Grillparzer whose work was mainly staged by the Burgtheater during the Schreyvogel regime. Grillparzer was later to make the following positive assessment of Viennese audiences of that (or perhaps a slightly later) period.

255 The Viennese theatre-going public in the 1830s

Franz Grillparzer, unpublished note conjectured to have been written in the spring of 1849, in *Sämtliche Werke* (Complete Works), ed. August Sauer, vol. 14 – *Prosaschriften II – Aufsätze über Literatur, Musik und Theater* (Prose Writings II – Essays on Literature, Music and Theatre) (Vienna: Anton Schroll & Co., 1925), p. 122

Fifteen or twenty years ago we had an excellent public in Vienna. Not over-educated but endowed with common sense, correct feeling and an excitable imagination, it naively yielded itself up to its impressions. Mediocre things often went down well because people wanted above all to be entertained, but good things never failed, with the exception of some cases of highly inadequate performance.

A less flattering picture of audiences was given by Grillparzer's friend and fellow playwright Eduard von Bauernfeld, looking at the recent past and the present in 1849, in a booklet directed particularly at the Burgtheater.

256   Class distinctions in the Burgtheater, 1849

Eduard von Bauernfeld, *Flüchtige Gedanken über das deutsche Theater. Mit besonderer Rücksicht auf das Hofburgtheater in Wien* (Passing Thoughts about the German Theatre. With Special Reference to the Burgtheater in Vienna) (Vienna: Ignaz Klang, 1849). Reproduced in E.v.B., *Gesammelte Aufsätze* (Collected Essays), ed. Stefan Hock (Vienna: Verlag des Literarischen Vereins in Wien, 1905), pp. 217–18

[. . .] In the boxes sat the high aristocracy – I do not know how many ancestors had to be certified – and just occasionally a few super-rich bankers. Highly respected families spent years vying for the favour of getting a quarter or an eighth of a box, and then their 'right-mindedness' had to be beyond all doubt. Common mortals, even if they could offer loads of money, never found out what the interior of a box in that sad and gloomy temple of the Muses looked like. The orchestra stalls were taken over by privy councillors and diplomats, who usually occupied them free of charge, and by habitués. [. . .] Playwrights who worked exclusively for the Burgtheater received complimentary tickets for standing room in the stalls which of course for various reasons they hardly ever set foot in, preferring to pay cash for their seats in the orchestra stalls for the few interesting performances. The real audience sits and stands in the rear stalls and the two galleries, all the less able to satisfy its craving for spectacle at new productions because in the past some 1200 (and currently still some 900) complimentaries would pre-empt the best seats. Which courtiers enjoy free admission I cannot say; the most disagreeable impression in any case used to be created by the court ladies-in-waiting whom one saw in the front stalls standing among the jostling officers and cadets of all branches of the service.

With the spread and consolidation of theatres, the rather patriarchal ticket-selling arrangements of former times (see 157), which only survived in small touring companies, yielded to more business-like and streamlined methods, although echoes of old practices could be detected in the personal attention given to season-ticket patrons. In the nineteenth century, season tickets had become an integral part of selling a show, as the *Theater-Lexikon* clearly indicated.

257   Box-office arrangements and season tickets
Düringer & Bartels (1841), pp. 194–6

Box office. [...] The *ticket collector* or *box-keeper* can, in spite of all supervision [...], seriously damage the management's takings, partly by the free admission of friends of his, partly by a private season-ticket arrangement or other kinds of corruption. The only safeguard against this is a daily change of ticket collectors, as in Berlin and other places, where they have to draw lots every day for the places at which they are to stand. [...] The *season ticket* either runs for a whole year, six months, three months or one month, sometimes for some weeks or only for a particular series or species of performances, e.g. guest performances or operas. [...] Once the management has published an advertisement announcing this, persons assumed to be subscribers or persons one wishes to enrol as such have subscription lists brought to their homes by the box-office manager in person or by the relevant box-keepers, and at the same time such lists are deposited in the box office for signing. Season-ticket subscriptions, particularly in princely capitals, are often significant, since apart from cheapness (with a usual reduction down to two-thirds of the full price) they offer the advantage that one always occupies the same seat and only comes into contact with persons with whom one is on closer terms by reason of a similarity of circumstances. [...] For the management the season ticket has the advantage [...] of making it possible to forecast expenditure, especially the wages bill [...]. The drawbacks, consisting of the supposed claims and demands of the season-ticket holders and various vexations [...] brought on by them, e.g. orders concerning the repetition of plays, the hiring or firing of actors, etc., are outweighed by the advantage of having a secure and definite income in hand in advance and of being able to count on a public used to going to the theatre. However, the so-called *military season ticket* [*Militär-Abonnement*] always has the greatest disadvantages for the management, not only because the price of admission is mostly reduced to one-third or even one quarter, and the house is full while the box office does badly, but also because the numerous military personnel, chiefly concentrated in the stalls, exerts too great an influence on the mood and judgement of the rest of the audience [...] (the same thing is true of student season tickets). [...] The sale of *tickets sold by the dozen [Dutzend-billets]* is [...] advantageous for very small touring companies, as long as no abuses creep in, because the interest of the public can be deduced from their ready sale, enabling the management to adjust its regular expenditure accordingly [...]. – *Box-office management for small companies* is very simple: the tickets are normally sold during the day in the director's apartment and in the evening by the director, his wife or some other member of the family at the box office by the entrance to the theatre, joined in exceptional circumstances for benefits by the beneficiary or a proxy appointed by him. After the show the contents of the cash-box is counted up and compared with the tickets taken, and this as well as the further use of the money remains confidential information for the director.

XX Repertoire, dramatic theory and criticism

A. REPERTOIRE

In the period following Goethe's and Schiller's work in Weimar, many complaints were voiced about the general decline in the standard of the German-language stage. However, Schreyvogel in Vienna (see 227) was not the only person to attempt to create an exemplary German repertoire in the early decades of the century. For a short time in the 1830s, Düsseldorf, then a town of a mere 30,000 inhabitants, stood out for the ambitious nature of its theatre, both in terms of programming and production quality. This was entirely due to the work of one man, Karl Immermann (1796–1840), a provincial court judge posted there in 1827. At first involved only in amateur productions, Immermann then did a number of 'exemplary' productions with the local professional company in 1833 and 1834. As a result of this, he gave up his judicial post and became the director of the company under the auspices of a 'Theaterverein' (Theatre Club). This enterprise lasted a mere thirty months; nevertheless it showed what could be achieved in far from lavish conditions by principled repertory-planning. Immermann was at first seconded in this venture by Felix Mendelssohn-Bartholdy as music director; that association, however, was only to be short-lived. He also attached the playwright Christian Dietrich Grabbe (1801–1836) to the theatre. Grabbe had not contributed any plays to the repertoire before he, too, broke with Immermann, but he wrote some reviews as well as the booklet on the Düsseldorf theatre from which the following quotation is taken; it gives some facts about that unusual setup and the programme it offered.

For the history of this venture, see R. Fellner, *Geschichte einer deutschen Musterbühne. Karl Immermanns Leitung des Stadttheaters zu Düsseldorf* (History of a German Exemplary Theatre. K.I.'s Direction of the Municipal Theatre in Düsseldorf) (Stuttgart: Cotta, 1888).

258 Immermann's theatre in Düsseldorf, 1834–5

Christian Dietrich Grabbe, *Das Theater zu Düsseldorf mit Rückblicken auf die übrige deutsche Schaubühne* (The Düsseldorf Theatre with a Backward Glance at the Other German Theatres) (Düsseldorf: J.H.C. Schreiner, 1835), pp. 23–31. Reproduced in C.D.G., *Werke und Briefe/Historisch-kritische Ausgabe in sechs Bänden* (Works and Letters/Historical-critical edition in six volumes), ed. Alfred Bergmann (Emsdetten: Verlag Lechte, 1966), pp. 132–6

Founding of the Present Düsseldorf Theatre

The majority of the most educated and most noble citizens of this city [...] have for years felt the inadequacies of the former theatre administration. This administration was a private enterprise and had the faults from which any private enterprise suffers in such a risky business. [...].

As a result of the praiseworthy, self-sacrificing efforts of the local friends of art, the institution took the following shape around the middle of last year [i.e. 1834]: the private management was given up but soon a sum of 10,000 dollars was raised for the theatre by issuing shares at 250 dollars each.[1] Besides, every theatre-lover in the city who had not taken any shares was asked to make an annual contribution to the fund, and if the contribution comes to 5 dollars or more, the contributor becomes an honorary member of the association, with consultative status at its general meetings. The actual direction of the theatre was passed on to a management committee which consists of the Lord Mayor, four shareholders elected by the joint-stock company, two members of the city council elected by the councillors, the director and the music director. This management committee leads and supervises the whole organisation, and takes decisions by a majority vote. For the first two years the members are to have tenure, after that new elections will take place but the former members can stand again. The immediate supervisory, aesthetic and technical running of the entire theatrical organisation is in the hands of the director [*Intendant*], besides opera direction which is in the hands of the music director. Also, it is only those two who take the initiative in aesthetic and technical matters and in the composition of the company [...]. If there is any clash between them, the management committee will decide. The director and the music director will have to submit guest performances, engagements, buildings etc. to the management council for approval, and a full account will be rendered at the annual general meeting.

A better constitution [...] will be found neither in England nor in France. [...]

Immermann was elected director and *Felix Mendelssohn-Bartholdy* the music director – names that call for no further comment.[2]

Immermann [...] kept on the better members of the former company and filled the gaps with a fair number of outstanding talents. I suspect he discovered them on his last trip through Germany [...].[3] It must be an easy matter for an author and connoisseur to spot gifted though as yet undeveloped people on quite a few stages where not many people would have suspected them. [...] What was required in handling these individuals was above all good will as well as seriousness and discipline. Furthermore tireless effort, repeated study sessions, many general read-throughs, individual reading rehearsals, the greatest possible opening up of minds to poetry, and – keeping one's temper in all that nerve-wracking business. And Immermann's sole reward for all this self-sacrifice: to see the work of art he has directed being performed just as it had been written.

Repertoire

[...] Our repertoire would be admirable for its richness and splendour even if it were badly acted. But that was by no means the case. Before Immermann took over the reins, exemplary productions undertaken by him, Uechtritz and Mendelssohn had taken place earlier: *Emilia Galotti, Stille Wasser sind tief, Der standhafte Prinz, Prinz Friedrich von Homburg,* [...] *Egmont, Nathan der Weise, Die Braut von Messina,* [...].[4]

When he took over the direction, there were newly produced and performed between 28 October [1834] and 1 April [1835], *among other things,* [the following] tragedies, historical and romantic dramas: *Prinz Friedrich von Homburg, Käthchen von Heilbronn,*[5] *Macbeth, Hamlet, The Merchant of Venice, King John,*[6] *Das Leben ein Traum,*[7] *Stella, Maria Stuart, Wallensteins Tod,*[8] *Maria Tudor,*[9] *Struensee,*[10] *Emilia Galotti, Raffaele,*[11] *Herr und Sclave,*[12] *Boccaccio,*[13] *Die Räuber,* and further items in the programme will be Tieck's *Blaubart,*[14] *Der Arzt seiner Ehre,*[15] *Die Jungfrau von Orleans,*[16] Raupach's *Heinrich VI,*[17] *König Enzio,*[18] *Alexis.*[19] Should one not [...] feel a tremendous thrill at all these spirits from so many different theatres rubbing shoulders with one another within such a short period of time? Perhaps you may ask, is there any space left for something quite different? That [space] has been found, or rather, genius has shown the way and *created* that space. Among major conversation pieces, *Minna von Barnhelm, Die Schule der Alten,*[20] *Donna Diana,*[21] *Die beiden Klingsberg,*[22] *Die Stimme der Natur,*[23] *Das Epigramm,*[24] *Der beste Ton,*[25] *Die vier Sterne,*[26] *Die Aussteuer,*[27] *Die Mohrin,*[28] *Richards Wanderleben*[29] were performed during the same period.

---

[1] See also 232.

[2] Jakob Ludwig Felix Mendelssohn-Bartholdy (1809–47), celebrated as a musical child prodigy, had already been made the music director for Düsseldorf in 1832, with a responsibility for church music and concerts. He stayed in Düsseldorf until 1835, leaving when he was appointed director of the Gewandhaus in Leipzig.

[3] The existing company, led by Josef Derossi (1768–1841), was by no means distinguished and needed an infusion of new blood. It was not uncommon for directors to have to travel far afield throughout the German-speaking world in search of acting talent.

[4] The writer Friedrich von Uechtritz (1800–75) was one of Immermann's close associates in the Düsseldorf theatrical venture. Like Immermann he was an official at a provincial court of law. Lessing's *Emilia Galotti* was given as the first of the 'exemplary performances' on 1 February 1833, then repeated on 22 December 1834 and 22 May 1835. F.L. Schröder's *Still Waters Run Deep* was based on Beaumont and Fletcher's *Rule a Wife and Have a Wife* (staged 2 March 1833; repeated on 20 February 1835). A.W. Schlegel's translation from the Spanish of Pedro Calderón de la Barca's *El príncipe constante (The Constant Prince),* had been performed at Weimar in 1811; Immermann's 5-act redaction was staged in Düsseldorf on 9 April 1833. Kleist's *Prince of Homburg* in Immermann's version, performed on 25 April 1833; repeated as the opening play of the newly constituted

company on 28 October 1834. *Egmont*, with the Beethoven score rehearsed under Mendelssohn's direction (18 January 1834). The title role of Lessing's *Nathan the Wise* was played by Karl Seydelmann as guest artist (February 1834). For Seydelmann, see **247–50**. *The Bride of Messina* (19 April 1834). Note that some of these exemplary productions were repeated subsequently, but others were not.

5   These two plays by Kleist (the latter staged on 3 and 18 February 1835) had already been performed successfully at the Burgtheater.

6   Goethe, Calderón and Shakespeare were Immermann's favourite playwrights. The respective dates of the Shakespeare productions were 2 November 1834 (repeated 25 January 1835); 28 December 1834 (repeated 27 February 1835); 13 March 1835; and 1 April 1835 (repeated 6 May 1835).

7   Calderón's *La vida es sueño (Life is a Dream)*.

8   The respective performance dates were 25 February and 20 March 1835; 15 February and 11 March 1835; 8 March and 10 April 1835. Schiller's plays, with 30 performances, outnumbered those of any other author in Immermann's repertoire.

9   Note that this play by Victor Hugo had only been premièred in Paris as recently as November 1833.

10   By Michael Beer (1800–33), the brother of the composer Giacomo Meyerbeer, staged 7 December 1834.

11   A play by the then immensely popular playwright Ernst Benjamin Salomon Raupach (1784–1852), staged 9 November 1834. As fertile as Kotzebue, Raupach wrote 117 plays altogether. Although Immermann did not care for his work, he put on 26 Raupach plays at Düsseldorf, as a concession to audience tastes. (See notes 17 & 18.) Immermann's repertoire was by no means pitched at a consistently taxing intellectual level.

12   *Master and Slave*, tragedy by Joseph Christian Baron von Zedlitz-Nimmersatt (1790–1682), staged 26 November 1834.

13   By Johann Ludwig Ferdinand Deinhardstein (1794–1859), Schreyvogel's successor as chief of the Burgtheater; staged 17 November 1834.

14   *Bluebeard* (3 May 1835).

15   Another Calderón play, *El médico de su honra* (The Surgeon of his Honour); staged 29 June 1835.

16   *The Maid of Orleans*, staged 17 May 1835.

17   *Henry VI* by Raupach. Probably staged May 1835. This play about the German emperor is not to be confused with Grabbe's play of the same title (let alone Shakespeare's).

18   *King Enzio*, also by Raupach. Staged 6 December 1835.

19   Only the first two parts of this trilogy by Immermann were staged, on 20 and 21 April 1835.

20   Casimir Delavigne's relatively recent play, *L'École des vieillards* (The School for Old Men) (1823); staged 5 January 1835, repeated 13 February.

21   Schreyvogel's German version of Agustín Moreto y Cabaña's *El desdén con el desdén* (Disdain Conquered by Disdain), staged 8 December 1832 and 19 March 1835.

22   Kotzebue's *The Two Klingsbergs*, staged April 1834 and 23 March 1835.

23   F.L. Schröder's *The Voice of Nature* (19 December 1834 and 27 April 1835).

24   Kotzebue's *The Epigram* (19 November and 15 December 1834).

25   *The Best Breeding*, by Carl Töpfer (30 November 1834 and 4 March 1835).

26   *The Four Stars*, by Wilhelm Vogel (1 December 1834).

27   *The Dowry*, by A.W. Iffland (28 January 1835).

28   *The Negress*, by F.W. Ziegler (6 February 1835). For Ziegler, see **220** and **251**.

29   Johann Georg Kettel's *Richard's Life as a Stroller*, based on John O'Keeffe's *Wild Oats* (16 March 1835).

By March 1837 Immermann's direction of the Düsseldorf theatre had come to a close; for all its artistic success, the venture failed for lack of funding. On the whole, the 1830s and 1840s were not a particularly productive time for the German theatre in terms of the repertoire or indeed anything else, as Eduard von Bauernfeld stated in his polemical booklet (see **256**; compare also **236–7**).

259   The poor state of the German theatre after Goethe and Schiller

Eduard von Bauernfeld (1905), pp. 188–9, 194–6

What has been done for the German theatre, after Goethe and Schiller, by all those involved in it? – Nothing, or practically nothing. [...]

Since our two dramatic heroes have withdrawn their hands and their hearts from the stage, nothing has been done in Germany, apart from Immermann's laudable but short-lived efforts,[1] to maintain the theatre at least as an artistic institution, even if it were not to be a national institution.[2] Governments have always looked down on the theatre with elegant disdain and have had no influence on it other than by way of censorship, and that was not exactly a beneficial one.[3] The directors of private enterprises have been out for profit; the directors of court theatres no less so since their meagre subsidies were rarely adequate. Major playwrights [...] more or less scorned having to bow to the miserable demands of routine, the box office and censorship, abandoned the theatre to its own devices, only retained a kind of ideal dramatic form and finally came to write more for the eye and the mind than for the ear and physical representation. [...]

With the disappearance of the good old plays, including the middle-class dramas in which there were at least some characters to be represented, as in Iffland, and with the flood of modern translations, the old solid art of acting is almost dead and buried. These plays and playlets can easily be reeled off, like painting 'by stencil'; the actors do not have to exert themselves. In Paris where these sprightly pictures arise directly from life and are presented with vivid grace [...], these witty little creations have a double value: an aesthetic and a social one. In Germany things are different! The German actor, especially in the smaller capitals, knows nothing of good society or of good breeding. [...] However, in order to express and represent modern life to some extent anyway, the German theatre has invented something called a 'conversational tone' [*Konversationston*], by means of which it usually turns French gracefulness into its opposite in the poor and mostly ill-memorised German prose in which it is offered. [...] If you add that one actor speaks with a somewhat Prussian, another one with a somewhat Saxon, a third with a somewhat Swabian, and a fourth with a Viennese accent,[4] that they stress what is least significant and crudely highlight a fleeting witticism to make quite sure it is not missed, that they entirely follow the prompter, resulting in a pace fit to make you despair – if you cast an eye over the hideous décor, the few tables and chairs in the fashion of the day before yesterday which [...] are set in routinely straight lines like soldiers, over the dim, sad German lighting, finally over the audience which sits there serious and pensive like a jury, never moves a muscle, never laughs, hardly ever smiles and regards the whole bag of tricks like a business which just has to be got through – taking all these things into account you may believe in a future for Germany, but hardly in one for the German theatre.

It is hardly worth while wasting a word on artistic and general managers of theatres. These gentlemen are everywhere much of a muchness with few exceptions. One pays more attention to the box office, another to the pretty actresses; art is the last thing they think of, or rather they do not think of it at all. [...] Most court theatres have hitherto been headed by a nobleman, who naturally enough handled things in an amateurish way. Hardly any are backed by a dramaturg.

Criticism used to have a lot of time for the theatre; by and by it fell silent since no new creations turned up to be assessed [...].

[1] See 258.
[2] See 170–4 and 260.
[3] See 175 and 261.
[4] This was not a new complaint: see Goethe's Rules for Actors, 135, pars. 1 & 2.

The question of a National Theatre, desirable as it might have seemed in the circumstances, was not very much on the agenda around the middle of the nineteenth century – a point made in a theatrical encyclopaedia.

260   The concept of a National Theatre from a nineteenth-century perspective, 1841

R. Blum, K. Herloszsohn, H. Marggraf, vol. 5 (1841), p. 345

National Theatre. A theatre which exclusively presents plays belonging to its people (i.e., not translations) like the *Théâtre français* in Paris [...], which thus represents the character of the people both through these plays and by the manner of presenting them, and hence can be regarded as an exemplary stage. We have no institution of this kind in Germany, which is due not so much to a lack of German national plays [...] as to a lack of nationality itself, which has been destroyed by virtue of a calamitous condition of political dismemberment. What people were formerly, and still are, pleased to call NT, the theatres in Berlin, Mannheim, Brunswick, Frankfurt etc. were German theatres like any others, i.e. such as had absolutely no national character. We can have an NT only when there will once again be *one* Germany.

B. CENSORSHIP

Censorship – particularly in Austria – continued to inhibit free expression on the stage. The five-day imprisonment of the satirical Austrian actor-playwright Johann Nepomuk Nestroy (1801–62), Raimund's successor as the provider of Viennese popular drama, was a case in point, although his offence was not a directly political one: he had merely improvised some dialogue on stage ridiculing the unfriendly critic Franz Wiest (1814–47). Nestroy's letter from prison was addressed to his friend, the court actor Carl Wilhelm Lucas (1804–57).

261   Nestroy in prison, 1836

Johann Nestroy, letter to Carl Lucas, National Library, Vienna. MS. Collection 53/58. Reproduced in Johann Nestroy, *Briefe* (Letters), ed. Walter Obermaier, in *Sämtliche Werke* (Complete Works), (Vienna/Munich: Jugend und Volk, 1977), pp. 34–5

Zwing-Uri.[1] Prison, 17 January 1836

Dear Friend Lucas!

I'm stuck fast between 4 walls. No chance of my getting pinched. Now no one can deny that I'm a *settled* sort of a fellow. [. . .] There's no card-playing here, it's not done in prison. So your books and my bottles are my sole occupation, I'm draining the contents of both at leisure. I've been gaoled for two days for improvising in *Mädchen in Uniform* (Girls in Uniform) and then so as not to get out of practice, for another three because of that bastard Wiest. [. . .] My detention is entirely according to the principles of prison etiquette. The locks on my door are the size of those generally met with on the prison doors of men guilty of high treason. The precautions against any possible escape are so thorough I might have forged IOUs to the value of two million, raped seven 13-year-old virgins and murdered several kids and various adults. [. . .] I'm only writing you these wretched things so you can have an idea of how much they respect art and artists in Vienna, and with what marvellous humanity they treat them for minor breaches of the law. – So I'm sitting in the most delicious solitude; only once in a while the gentle skyblue of an attendant policeman makes a change in the monotonous white of my prison cell. [. . .]

Your friend
J. Nestroy
Singer, actor, comic, author
and prisoner, and heaven knows
what else.

[1] Zwing-Uri: a jocular reference to the oppressive fortress in *William Tell*. See 81, Act 1, Sc. 4.

C. DRAMATIC THEORY

Probably inspired by Schiller's *Die Braut von Messina* (see **143, 187, 225–6**), a number of German playwrights achieved a temporary popularity in the early decades of the nineteenth century with a genre of drama termed *Schicksalstragödie* (i.e. 'tragedy of fate'). Notable examples were *Der vierundzwanzigste Februar* (The 24th February) by Zacharias Werner (1768–1823) which was premièred in Weimar in 1810 and published in 1815, and G.A. Müllner's two plays, *Der neunundzwanzigste Februar* (The 29th February, 1812), clearly modelled on Werner's melodrama, and *Die Schuld* (Guilt, 1815 – see **246**). Revelling in strong *coups de théâtre*, these plays were far from Schiller's lofty tragic aims. Grillparzer's first play to be performed (on 31 January 1817, at the Theater an der Wien) was likewise a tragedy of fate – *Die Ahnfrau* (*The Ancestress*). His essay in reply to a violent press attack on the play was a defence of his own concept of fate as a dramatic device; probably written in September 1817, it was, however, not published at the time.

262 Grillparzer on the proper role of fate in tragedy, 1817

Franz Grillparzer, unpublished essay, *Über das Fatum* (Concerning Fate). Published in *Sämtliche Werke* (Complete Works) (1925), vol. 14, p. 18.

[. . .] In drama it is the agents who speak, and here it is in the playwright's power so to arrange the characters, so to direct the tempest of their passions that the idea of fate is bound to arise in them. The moment that word has been uttered or the idea stirred up, the spectator's soul is struck by lightning. All he has pondered, heard, suspected or dreamt about this in hours of agony comes alive, the dark powers awaken and he becomes a fellow actor in the tragedy. But never let the playwright step forward and declare his characters' belief to be his own. Let the same obscurity which envelops the nature of fate also envelop his mention of it; his characters may clearly pronounce their belief in it but let it remain a moot point for the spectator whether to ascribe the fearful catastrope to the random flux of life or to a hidden destiny; let him suspect the latter but it must not be made clear to him, for any explicit error repels.

It is thus that Müllner has used the idea of fate, it is thus that I flatter myself I have used it, and the effect it has also made on the educated section of the public confirms me in my opinion.

Perhaps the ones least satisfied with this statement will be precisely those keenest champions of fate who think they are rendering the latter a great service in seeking to link it with the principles of the Christian religion and assigning to tragedy goodness knows what high moral function. But let them beware. It is just the Germans' misfortune that they *will* be taking all their learning to market and do not think they have made a proper tragedy unless it can also pass, if need be, as a compendium of philosophy, religion, history, statistics and physics, so that you find everything in their dramatic works except drama.

Maria Magdalena (*Mary Magdalen*, 1844) by Christian Friedrich Hebbel (1813–63) was one of the first modern problem plays. Hebbel's attempt to root serious drama in the great underlying conflicts of the age marks a distinctive break with the earlier theory and practice of tragedy, as does his placing of the eighteenth-century genre of bourgeois tragedy not in the facile area of sentimentalism but on the borderline of clashing world views, the struggle of the old with the new. His preface to the play was an attempt to break through misunderstandings and prejudices.

263   Hebbel on modern social tragedy, 1844

Friedrich Hebbel, *Vorwort zur 'Maria Magdalena', betreffend das Verhältnis der dramatischen Kunst zur Zeit und verwandte Punkte* (Preface to 'Mary Magdalene', Concerning the Relation of Dramatic Art to the Age and Similar Points) (Hamburg: Hoffmann & Campe, 1844), pp. 1–47. Reproduced in F.H., *Sämtliche Werke/Historisch-kritische Ausgabe*, (Collected Works/Historical-Critical Edition) ed. Richard Maria Werner (Berlin: B. Behr, 1904), pt. 1, vol. 11, pp. 39–65

Drama, as the highest of all the arts, is intended to illustrate the *condition of the world and of humanity* at any given time in its *relation to the idea*, i.e. to the moral centre governing everything, which we must assume [to be] in the universal organism if only for its self-preservation. Drama [. . .] is *possible* only when a decisive *change* is taking place in this condition, hence it is entirely a product of its age, but to be sure only in the sense that such an age is itself the product of all preceding ages, the connecting central link between a concatenation of centuries which are ending and a new one which is about to begin.

So far history has only two crises to show in which the highest drama could manifest itself, and indeed it has manifested itself only twice: once among the *ancients*, when the world view of antiquity passed from its original naivety to being moved, at first in a disintegrating and then in a destructive way, by reflection; and once among the *moderns* as the Christian [world view] underwent a similar dichotomy. Greek drama unfolded when paganism had outlived itself and it devoured the latter, [. . .] it created fate. [. . .] Shakespearean drama developed with Protestantism and emancipated the individual. Hence the fearful dialectic of his characters. [. . .]

I say to you, you who call yourselves dramatic authors, if you are content [merely] to stage anecdotes, historical or other, it matters not which, or at the very most to dissect a character in his psychological mechanism, you are in no way superior, no matter whether you squeeze the tear-glands or tickle the ribs [. . .], to that well known cousin of Thespis who makes the puppets dance in his booth. Your art has no business except where there is a *problem*; but wherever such a one strikes you, wherever *life* in its *ruptured nature* comes forward to meet you at the same time as, in your minds, [...] the [...] idea in which it finds its *lost unity* again, seize hold of it and pay no attention if the aesthetic mob wishes to have *good health* demonstrated *in the very disease* [...].

[...] dramatic art is intended to help complete the world-historical process which is taking place in our times and which aims not to overthrow the existing institutions – political, religious and moral – of the human race but to give them a deeper basis, i.e. actually to secure them against revolution. In *that* sense, like all poetry that seeks to be more than redundant and ornamental, it should be *in tune with the times*, as is all genuine [poetry] in *that*, and in *no other*, sense [...].

So much for general comment. Now for a word in connection with the play I am herewith submitting to the public. [...] It is a *bourgeois tragedy*. Bourgeois tragedy has fallen out of favour in Germany, mainly by reason of two defects. More than anything because it was built up not out of its *inner* elements peculiar to itself, out of the harsh isolation in which some individuals totally incapable of any dialectics were facing each other within the narrowest of circles and out of the dreadful *limitation of life* in *one-sidedness* which springs from this, but was patched together out of all kinds of *externalities*, e.g. lack of money coupled with plentiful hunger, but above all out of the clash of the third estate with the second and first in matters of love. Now that undoubtedly produces much that is sad but nothing tragic, for the tragic must from the start present itself as something based on necessity, as something, like death, inherent in life itself and not to be avoided; as soon as one can console oneself with: *If only he had had* (thirty dollars [...] etc.), the impression which should have been moving becomes trivial [...]. And then, too, [bourgeois drama is out of favour] because our writers, once they condescended to the people, [...] always first ennobled the common folk [...] with fine speeches lent them out of their own treasuries, or else they thought it necessary to depress them below their actual status in the world by making them stubbornly bone-headed, so that their characters struck us either as enchanted princes and princesses, whom the magician out of malice had transformed not even into dragons and lions [...] but into lowly bakery servant-girls and journeyman tailors, or else as animated blocks who amazed us if they were able to say Yes or No. Now the latter was if anything even worse [...] since everybody knows that ordinary folk and peasants pick their figures of speech, which they use every bit as much as do the heroes of drawing-rooms and promenades, not from the starry heavens and the ocean, but that the craftsman gathers them from the workshop, the ploughman from behind his plough; and [...] that these simple people, even if they do not converse, know quite well how to speak vividly and how to put together and illustrate their ideas. These two defects make the prejudice against bourgeois drama understandable but they cannot justify it, because they are obviously the fault not of the genre but only of the hacks who have made a botch of it. It is by itself a matter of indifference [...] whether an action significant in itself, i.e. symbolical, takes place in a lower or higher social sphere.

D. INDIVIDUAL PLAYS

The production at the Burgtheater in 1848 of *Maria Magdalena*, with its questioning of a conventional code of morals, was felt to be a momentous occasion, a reflection of the revolutionary events shaking Vienna in that year. It was not actually the first staging of the play which had been premièred in Königsberg on 13 March 1846, then performed in Leipzig on 19 October of the same year and in Berlin, at the Königsstädtisches Theater, on 17 April 1848; but clearly it was a matter of far greater significance to have it performed in Vienna, the arch fortress of theatrical conservatism.

264   *Maria Magdalena* at the Burgtheater, 8 May 1848

Siegmund Engländer, 'Die Aufführung der Maria Magdalena von Hebbel auf dem Hofburg-theater zu Wien im Mai 1848' (The Performance of Mary Magdalene by Hebbel at the Vienna Burgtheater in May 1848), in *Jahrbuch für dramatische Kunst und Literatur* (Yearbook for Dramatic Art and Literature), ed. H.Th. Rötscher (Berlin, 1848), vol. 2, pp. 195–9. Reproduced in H. Wüttschke (ed.), *Hebbel in der zeitgenössischen Kritik* (Contemporary Criticisms of Hebbel), (Berlin: DLD, 1910), pp. 204–10. Reprinted Kraus Reprint (Nendeln/Liechtenstein, 1968)

The abstract notion that we Austrians, too, have won our freedom is turned into a vivid feeling of jubilation by every concrete fact which may be regarded as an expression of freedom. [...] Another such fact confirming our really becoming liberated was the *performance of Mary Magdalene at the Burgtheater*. All one has to do is to know what the Burgtheater used to be like in order to appreciate such a performance. The Burgtheater was the great big cooker in which poetry was stewed to a mush, it was the private place of entertainment for a pampered aristocracy who would observe the gamboling of the shadowy figures on the stage from the easy chairs in their boxes.[1] The high nobility, hair dressed according to the French fashion journal, would be joyously watching yet another French article of fashion in the translations which were being staged. The common people were represented by nothing other than Iffland's low-life plays, which made the spectators in the boxes feel like ancient Romans as they bought their slaves and first inspected them stark naked; the aristocracy observed the anatomy of a famished stomach and the heavy, depressing weight of an empty purse with the keenest delight, and they cast contemptuous glances through their eye-glasses at the spectators in the galleries who wept with the humiliation of having their domestic secrets given away. Now the people have in truth taken possession of the stage; [...] a genuinely popular drama which must scare a certain part of the audience has been performed to a tremendous concourse of spectators. The performance of *Mary Magdalene* at the Burgtheater without any cuts or alterations is a *political event*, a manifestation of the liberated people, and it is generally described here as a landmark in the history of the Burgtheater. Hebbel has celebrated a triumph in a way that was not at all to be expected in view of the terrifying elements in his writing [...].

[1] Compare 256.

It may be interesting to compare Hebbel's subjective reactions to the above event as recorded in his diary.

265   Hebbel at the Burgtheater performance of 'Maria Magdalena', 8 May 1848

Friedrich Hebbel, note in his third diary (begun 30 June 1846 in Vienna), pp. 175–6 (9 May 1848). Reproduced in Friedrich Hebbel, *Tagebücher*, ed. Richard Maria Werner (Diaries) (Berlin: B. Behr, n.d.), vol. 3, pp. 303–4

Last night the Imperial and Royal Hofburgtheater presented my Mary Magdalene uncut and unaltered. The play was an educational test for the *Viennese* public, but it received the most unqualified acclaim and did not stir up any prudish reactions even at its touchiest moments. [...] For no person is so stupid as to rebel against necessity; now the core of the play being precisely the physical demonstration of necessity, its success is assured as far as the main thrust [of it] is concerned, and the only question is whether the recognition which it cannot be denied manifests itself in the form of love or mere respect. In my case respect and love were mingled. Of course the acting was beyond compare; Anschütz as Master Anton presented an image of iron,[1] and Tine laid bare a bleeding heart so shatteringly that I quivered and trembled for her.[2] I had gone up to a gallery, firmly resolved not to appear in case I was called out, and I stayed put in spite of this event arising as early as the end of the first act and being repeated at the end of the second. But then Tine had me called down and in spite of my disgust at this exhibition of my supererogatory person, I had to go through with aping what a score of fools had acted out before me. I felt the actors were not mistaken in their assertion that everything was at stake for me and my future plays, and I bowed to necessity.

1 Heinrich Anschütz (1785–1865), one of the pillars of the Burgtheater ensemble, played the tragic role of the stubborn and dogmatic father of the heroine.
2 Christine ('Tine') Enghaus (1817–1910), Hebbel's wife since 1845, played the heroine Klara who commits suicide at the end of the play.

Dutch theatre, 1600–1848

EDITED BY WIEBE HOGENDOORN

Introduction

Any introduction, however brief, to the history of the theatre in the Netherlands between 1600 and 1848 should mention at least the main political facts that influenced its development.

The establishment of the Dutch state took a first step around 1565 with the revolt of a number of high noblemen headed by William of Orange (1533–1584), against Spanish-Austrian rule under the House of Habsburg. Traditionally the Union of Utrecht (1579), a treaty of seven Northern provinces, is seen as its formal beginning. The new state was a republic, governed by representatives of the provinces who gathered in the States General. The reigning princes of the House of Orange, called Stadtholders, had military leadership as their main function. This form of government lasted until 1795, when the country was occupied by France. After the liberation of 1813 it became a monarchy, modernised under constitutional law in 1848.

The Southern Netherlands continued as part of the Habsburg dominions until the French occupation. Afterwards they were united with the new kingdom of the North. The revolt of 1830 against Holland was the beginning of the Kingdom of Belgium as an autonomous state.

Some terminological indications follow from this historical summary. Whenever 'the Netherlands' are mentioned here, this means the whole area of the Southern and Northern Low Countries. Present-day Belgium is indicated by 'the Southern Netherlands'. The union of the Northern provinces is called 'the Northern Netherlands' or 'the Republic' or 'Holland', as the case may be. The adjective 'Dutch' is used in two senses: in connection with 'language' and 'theatre' it concerns the whole area, including the Flemish culture of the South, while in any other context (Dutch government, taste etc.) it only applies to the North.

The political and social developments resulting from the Dutch revolt had a profound impact. The conquest of Antwerp by the Spaniards in 1585 caused a large-scale immigration of merchants, intellectuals and artists into the North. The result was a spectacular growth of economic power and of culture in the new state and particularly in Amsterdam. One of the effects in the field of theatre was the development of professional acting. Side by side with the traditional locally based amateur performances of the Rederijker ('Rhetoricians') companies, there had always been small groups of professionals. These now became more important, partly following the example of and in connection with the strolling actors from England.[1] The new Dutch companies also travelled to neighbouring regions such as Germany and the Baltic countries; they were especially successful in Sweden. At the same time the professional actors gradually replaced the Rhetoricians in the Dutch cities. The repertoire was modernised as well and in 1638 the Amsterdam 'Schouwburg' opened, the first permanent municipal theatre of the Netherlands.[2]

By way of contrast, the uncertain political identity of the Southern Netherlands and the fact that they were 'the battlefield of Europe' for more than a century prevented any such development there. There were some important Southern playwrights, but theatre practice continued to be determined by the old school drama and Rederijker activities. The cultural emancipation of the Flemish had to wait until after the separation from Holland in the nineteenth century, and the first professional Dutch-speaking theatre company of the South came into being after the period covered by this volume.

As a result, the selection of documents for this survey of Dutch theatre is inevitably lop-sided: against the many testimonies from the North only a few items deal with the Southern Netherlands.

The documents on the theatre in Holland are also of necessity unevenly balanced. The vast majority of them refer to its capital Amsterdam, and particularly its municipal theatre, the Schouwburg. Most of the sources are from Amsterdam; no new developments took place anywhere else. Documents from such important provincial towns as Utrecht, Leiden, Groningen and Rotterdam are in the minority and generally reflect what had happened before in the capital. There is one exception though: The Hague. The remarkable division between the country's capital on the one hand and its court and seat of government on the other was also expressed by a diversity in theatrical culture which one could summarise as 'Dutch bourgeois' against 'French aristocratic'. As it is, however, the sources on theatre life at The Hague are fewer and less informative than those on Amsterdam. Moreover, the predilections of the Stadtholder's court were by no means representative of the country as a whole; it did not function as the cultural centre of the nation. Dutch theatre in general reflected the taste of the 'burghers', with a distinct preference for strong didacticism based on spectacular pictorial effects. The continuous popularity of *tableaux vivants* as a part of drama performances is clear evidence of this preference.

A common element with Germany was the fact that most cities were too small to maintain their own permanent theatre companies. Apart from Amsterdam,

The Hague and much later Rotterdam, they would have only one venue awaiting performances by travelling actors. Even in Amsterdam the audience was not large enough to allow continuous runs of the same play for a prolonged period. Therefore the repertoire had to change frequently. In the first half of the seventeenth century, the production of original Dutch drama could still meet the demands to a certain extent, although there were also many adaptations of Spanish and early French plays. After the theatre had become fully professional, however, the choice had to widen. Translations and adaptations, often of foreign successes, now came to constitute approximately 65 per cent of the repertoire (except for farces which were more often home-brewed). Especially later in the period many English and German plays were put on, but in general French neo-classicism was dominant, both in the choice of foreign plays in translation and in the production of original Dutch dramas. The latter were written in enormous quantities but rarely proved to be first-class. French influence was felt in stage practice as well: great actors who were also essayists, such as Corver in the eighteenth century and Jelgerhuis in the nineteenth, derived most of their ideas from France.

While outstanding Dutch dramas in the later periods were few and far between, excellence can be found in other aspects of stage art. The pictorial arts ranked very high in Holland, and theatre accounts show that many painters of good quality were involved in the production of sets. Moreover, there was a market for scenic illustrations: especially in the eighteenth century a large number of theatrical drawings and engravings was produced, unparalleled for their accuracy and therefore an invaluable source for Dutch stage history.

The quality of acting is of course more difficult to gauge. From a variety of eye-witness accounts, both Dutch and foreign, it has to be assumed that, among many others who are not mentioned here, actors such as van Germez in the seventeenth century, Punt and Corver in the eighteenth, and especially Wattier, Snoek and Jelgerhuis in the nineteenth would have been considered excellent on any European stage. However, compared with other countries the social and financial situation of Dutch actors left much to be desired. There was continuous opposition from the Protestant Church and until 1795 a large part of any company's revenues had to go towards municipal poor relief, as had been the case in England up to 1642. The emancipation of stage artists – meaning better education, regular pensions and a hesitant acceptance by the bourgeoisie – was only realised by the end of the nineteenth century.

As a result of its specific development in the Northern Netherlands, Dutch theatre history has been periodised differently from the German part of this book. Period 1 covers the years between 1600 and 1664, roughly spanning what is known as the Dutch 'Golden Age', the era of the young republic's economic growth, international power, and the flourishing of the arts and sciences. A new drama repertoire of a high standard was created by such playwrights as Bredero, Hooft and Vondel, the latter two guided by the new classical ideals as formulated by such scholars as Heinsius. Professional acting centred in the unique Schouwburg built by Jacob van Campen. When this theatre was pulled down in 1664, it marked the end of an era, giving way to the Italian-type neo-classical stage with a proscenium arch and fully changeable scenery.

Period II, running from 1665 to 1794, covers the age of neo-classicism and the Enlightenment. Such unity as it has is to be found in the preponderant French influence on drama and theatre – at least as far as the taste of the *literati* is concerned. In 1665 the second Amsterdam Schouwburg opened, built after the Italian-French model. Four years later the literary society 'Nil Volentibus Arduum' was established, strongly advocating the rules of neo-classicism that were to influence Dutch drama and theatre for the entire period. Strong original drama now gave way to many translations. Acting flourished under company leaders like Corver. The later part of the period saw a flood of theatre magazines, pamphlets and essays, as was also the case in England, France and Germany. The season of 1794 was the end of the long period in which the theatres were employed by the municipal alms-houses. This rule was abolished in 1795 when the French occupied the Netherlands.

Period III covers the years 1795 to 1850. The first two decades were a high period for the art of acting. Gradually theatre organisation was modernised, with private ownership or subsidies by state and municipalities, attempts also being made to establish a school and a pension fund for actors. After 1820 the Schouwburg declined, mainly providing the lower and middle classes with French vaudevilles or melodramas by Kotzebue. Dutch drama production lagged. The best foreign repertoire, dramas and operas, was to be found in the French and German theatres of Amsterdam. *Cafés chantants* and vaudeville theatres became popular.

Just as with the German part of this book, the documentation covering the theatre in the Netherlands if of necessity highly selective, aiming at characteristic examples rather than completeness.

The spelling of Dutch names has been made uniform except in titles. The translations are as literal as possible but often involved minor changes in syntax and punctuation. The English version of all quotations is by W. Hogendoorn unless otherwise indicated – but invaluable help with translation has been given by Catriona O'Daly, by Helen Anne Ross and above all by George Brandt.

I also wish to express my gratitude for information and suggestions received from Dr Ben Albach, Amsterdam; Henny Ruitenbeek, Almere; and Dr Mieke B. Smits-Veldt, The Hague.

[1] For the Continental tours of English actors at the end of the sixteenth and during much of the seventeenth century, see Glynne Wickham (ed.), *TIE: England 1530–1660* (CUP, forthcoming).
[2] See 272–4.

Period I: 1600–1664

XXI Contractual and organisational documents

Apart from school drama and the repertoire of the odd professional company, before 1600 all drama performances in the Netherlands had been in the hands of the Chambers of Rhetoric (*Rederijkerskamers*). These were local literary societies on an amateur basis, whose members not only wrote and performed serious, mainly allegorical drama[1] and farces, but also practised non-dramatic poetry and took part in the organisation of various civic or religious festivities. Their important social function was reflected by a strict organisation along guild lines, with among others a president ('prince' or 'emperor'), deans, a book-keeper, a 'factor' who was their main author and supervised their productions, and a fool. Each Chamber had its heraldic blazon, most often on an allegorical-religious theme, and a maxim matching it.

When the revolt of the country against Spanish rule had failed in the South – the fall of Antwerp in 1585 serving as a landmark – a ban was pronounced on all Chambers there, since many of their plays had been of a revolutionary political nature. With other artists and intellectuals, many of their members fled to the North, where their presence not only led to the establishment of new Chambers but had a vital innovating effect on the cultural life of the young Republic in general. It is in their circles that Renaissance drama came to flourish in Holland.

The absolute peak in the life of any Chamber of Rhetoric would be the organisation of a 'Landjuweel', a regional prize-giving competition. An official invitation would be conveyed to its fellow Chambers, asking them to take part with a play on an assigned theme, as well as a ballad on a set refrain and other activities. On the appointed day they would solemnly enter the city where for several days the festivity was going to take place. The 'Landjuwe-len' at Ghent (1539) and especially Antwerp (1561) were famous for their lavish productions, commemorated in illustrated official reports and play editions.

The 'Landjuweel' at Haarlem (1606) was a late one, even for the North.[2] Twelve Dutch Chambers took part, each competing with a different play some 800 verses long, as an answer to the following question:

> He who gives loving care to the poor, what reward may he expect?
> Also, what punishment for him who heartlessly despises them?

The set theme for the refrain of the ballad was of the same import: 'If you love Christ as the Head, you should comfort His members.' It was probably felt that the answers would not only reflect upon a general Christian truth but also upon the position of the Chambers within the civic system for the relief of the poor (see **267** and **268**). So if, on the one hand, the festivity was traditional in its set-up, on the other its importance in the new context of any Northern city's theatre organisation is clear.

The prize list of this competition gives an impression of its many activities and of its social status. The rewards of the winning Chambers consisted traditionally of silver (later also pewter) tableware, with the highest prizes for the winning Chambers' Entry into the city, their emblematic play and their gift to the poor. That a competition like this one was an expensive affair for the organising city may be guessed from the amount of silver involved in the prizes (which of course was only part of their expenses). At Haarlem this came to more than six and a half kilogrammes. From the list it appears that the Chamber 'The White Columbine' from Leiden was the festival winner, taking home the most as well as the best prizes, followed by Amsterdam's 'White Lavender'; but the jury took care that all participants had their share, with the traditional exception of the organising Chamber.

[1] *Elckerlyc* (the origin of *Everyman*) is the best-known example. Their most renowned non-allegorical play is *Mariken van Nimweghen* (Mary of N.).
[2] The last of such competitions in the North was held at Vlaardingen in 1616; in the Southern provinces only Malines was later (1620).

266   Prizes at a Rhetoricians' Competition, Haarlem 1606

Const-thoonende Iuweel, By de loflijcke stadt Haarlem, ten versoecke van 'Trou moet blijcken', in 't licht gebracht: Waer inne duydelick verclaert ende verthoont wordt alles wat den mensche mach wecken om den armen te troosten, ende zijnen naasten by te staan, In twaalf spelen van sinne [. . .] (Art-showing Jewel, [organised] by the worshipful City of Haarlem, at the bidding of 'Fidelity must show itself': In which everything that may move man to comfort the poor and support his neighbour is clearly explained and shown, In twelve Emblematic Plays) (Zwolle: Zacharias Heyns, 1607)

Prizes, awarded with honour by the Jury (appointed by the City).[1]

For the Entry

The first prize to 'The Marigold' from Gouda	A Cup of 20 'lood'
The second to 'The Red Rose' from Schiedam	A Cup of 16 'lood'
The third to 'The White Columbine' from Leiden	A Cup of 12 'lood'

For the most beautiful Blazon

The first prize to 'The White Lavender' from Amsterdam	A Cup of 12 'lood'
The second to 'The Cornflower' from The Hague	A Cup of 10 'lood'
The third to 'The Marigold' from Gouda	A Cup of 8 'lood'

For the Emblematic Play

The first prize to 'The White Columbine'
from Leiden   A Cup of 24 'lood'
The second to 'The Hazel' from
Hazerswoude   A Cup of 18 'lood'
The third to 'The White Lavender' from
Amsterdam   A Cup of 14 'lood'

For the best Performance

The only prize to 'The White Columbine'
from Leiden   A Goblet of 6 'lood'

For the best written Ballad

The first prize to 'The Orange Lily' from
Leiden   A Cup of 10 'lood'
The second to 'The White Lavender' from
Amsterdam   A Cup of 8 'lood'
The third to 'The Red Rose' from Schiedam   A Goblet of 6 'lood'

For the most successful Orators

The only prize to 'The White Lavender'
from Amsterdam   A *tazza* of 8 'lood'

The best Song

The first prize to 'The Red Rose' from
Schiedam   A Cup of 8 'lood'
The second to 'The Ear of Corn' from
Katwijk   A Cup of 6 'lood'
The third to 'The Orange Lily' from Leiden   A Cup of 4 'lood'

For the best Singing

The only prize to 'The Oak Tree' from
Vlaardingen   A *tazza* of 6 'lood'

For the most beautiful and significant Fireworks

The first prize to 'The White Columbine'
from Leiden   A Cup of 10 'lood'
The second to 'The White Lavender' from
Amsterdam   A Cup of 8 'lood'
The third to 'The Oak Tree' from
Vlaardingen   A Cup of 6 'lood'

For having travelled the greatest Distance

The only prize to 'The Oak Tree' from
Vlaardingen[2]   A Cup of 8 'lood'

For the highest Deposit[3]

The first prize to 'The White Columbine'

from Leiden   A Cup of 20 'lood'

The second to 'The Red Rose' from

Schiedam   A Cup of 16 'lood'

The third to 'The White Lavender' from

Amsterdam   A Cup of 12 'lood'

[...][4])

---

[1] Weights are given in *lood*. One *lood* was half an *ons* ('ounce'). One *ons* was presumably $\frac{1}{12}$ of an old Amsterdam *pond* ('pound'), which was the equivalent of 494 grammes. If this is correct, one 'lood' was 20.6 grammes.

[2] Vlaardingen is about forty-seven miles from Haarlem.

[3] Each visiting Chamber donated a sum of money for the poor in the Haarlem almshouses.

[4] A list of 'additional' and 'honorary' prizes follows.

After 1598 Amsterdam had two Chambers of Rhetoric: the Old Chamber, 'The Eglantine' (which in the first two decades of the new century became instrumental in the establishment of Dutch Renaissance drama), and the rather more old-fashioned Brabant Chamber, 'The White Lavender'. Their performances took place in temporary venues, but when from *c.* 1610 they started to admit a paying audience to their performances and literary exercises, the need arose for a permanent and well-equipped building. In 1617, one of the leaders of 'The Eglantine', the highly energetic physician and playwright Samuel Coster, had a wooden hall erected on the Keizersgracht. It was not only meant to be a theatre but also a general cultural and academic centre – unlike Leiden, Amsterdam had as yet no university – hence its name 'The First Dutch Academy'. Unfortunately, as early as 1622 Church pressure put a premature end to the idealistic enterprise, because of Coster's own tragedy *Iphigeneia*, in which he lampooned the clergy. The building was sold to the city (see also **282**), which now put it at the disposal of the rival Chamber.[1]

As a general rule, civic permission to perform was given to visiting companies of foreign actors only on the condition that part of their takings would go to the benefit of the almshouses, more specifically the orphanages. Gradually this regulation was extended to performances by Rhetoricians' Chambers and, later, by Dutch professional resident or visiting companies. Theatre as part of poor relief became important for the city finances and grew into a typical Dutch tradition, lasting until the end of the eighteenth century. For their part the theatre companies also benefited by the regulation, because they could, and often did, use it as a successful argument in their struggle against the clergy. The agreement marks the formal beginning of this regulation for Amsterdam, where the Orphanage was now going to profit by theatre performances. After 1632, the Old Men's Home became another beneficiary, receiving one third of the profits against two thirds for the Orphanage.[2]

---

[1] Both Chambers were to merge in 1632.

[2] The regulation concerned the resident company only; visiting troupes had to pay part of their revenues to another of the city's social establishments, the Spinning House (a workhouse and penal institution for women).

267   Agreement between Dr Samuel Coster and the Governors of the Orphanage at Amsterdam, 1617

City Archives Amsterdam (Former Archives City Orphanage), P.A. 367, nr 72. Reproduced in C.N. Wybrands, *Het Amsterdamsche Tooneel van 1617–1772* (The Theatre at A. from 1617–1772) (Utrecht: J.L. Beijers, 1873), p. 36

In the following manner an agreement has been made between Jan Willemsz. Bogaert, representing Doctor Samuel Coster, on the one hand, and Rychart Gerritsz. Kieft, representing the Governors of the Orphanage of the City of Amsterdam, on the other. Given the fact that the above-mentioned Samuel Coster has erected a certain suitable building and venue, which is, and will be, his property, including the costumes and all the other things belonging to the place, situated in the new town[1] on the Keizersgracht, in order to establish there a Dutch Academy and also to perform and to present there some comedies, tragedies, and other exercises, made by himself or others, meant for the edification and amusement of everyone; and the afore-mentioned Coster being inclined to put the receipts of his plays and exercises to the benefit of the aforesaid Orphanage; to that end the above-mentioned Jan Willemsz. Bogaert, representing [the former] as above, promises hereby to leave to the aforesaid Orphanage for the first six years (as from date) a rightful third part from the profits of the plays and other exercises, and after the expiration of these six years a rightful half. And that the afore-mentioned Dr Samuel Coster will for the first six years benefit by the remaining two thirds of the profits of his plays and exercises to alleviate his past and future costs, such as building, costumes and other, and after the expiration of these six years the other half. [. . .].

Amsterdam, 23 September 1617
(*signed*) Samuel Coster
Jan Willemsz. Bogaert
Rychart Gerritsz. Kieft
[and three others]

[1] The construction of the great canals, one of which was the Keizersgracht, was a recent enterprise, starting in 1615. The city had been steadily expanding, since the political and religious upheavals caused many people from the South to settle there. In 1600, Amsterdam counted 60,000 inhabitants; forty years later there were 135,000, three quarters of them born elsewhere, with many foreigners among them.

After the opening in 1637 of the Amsterdam *Schouwburg* (see 269 and 272–4), which was the first professional Dutch city theatre, the city's Chambers of Rhetoric ceased to exist. However, the financial regulation with the two almshouses remained unchanged, and this was reflected by the manner in which the theatre was governed. Six Heads or Governors were yearly nominated by the Burgomasters on the recommendation of the trustees of the Almshouses who now financed the enterprise.[1] Any conflict arising between the two parties was to be solved by the Burgomasters. Over the years this proved to be no easy task, given the inherent tension between artistic ideals and the aim of maximum profits. Nevertheless, apart from a short-lived experiment with an autonomous theatre government in the eighteenth century, this form of theatre government survived until 1795.

[1] Cooption of these Heads (who for the most part were from the middle or upper-middle class) became the normal practice.

268   The task of the Theatre Governors and the manner of payment

T. van Domselaer, *Beschrijvinge van Amsterdam* (Description of A.) (Amsterdam: 1665), p. 201. Reproduced in B. Hunningher (1959), pp. 34–5

[The Governors of the Theatre][1] command, read and supervise all tragedies and comedies, *tableaux vivants* and farces, before they are performed on the stage, and take care that nothing is shown, either in word or deed, slandering or mocking the established government of the state or the city, the church or any religion, or any particular person. They ban from the stage [all] lecherous, wanton dissoluteness, too lewd and flippant for the young and other tender ears.

Every night the box-office takings are brought to the said governors and directors in their office on the first floor; they pay all the costs from them, keeping account of all receipts and expenditures, and presenting the remainder, two or three times per annum, to the almshouses. So that the earnings, which had been in arrears these past seventy years, now come to more than eleven thousand guilders every year, over and above all costs, two thirds being for the benefit of the Orphanage and one third for the Old Men's Home. Also, they allot each player his part, and decree in what clothes and with what props he will appear on stage, and order the sets and set changes, according to the requirements of the plays.

[1] The merchant and historian Tobias van Domselaer (1612–1685) was one of them, being in office, with intervals, for no less than 23 years (1638–41; 1655–72; 1678–81).

After some skirmishes with the clergy, the Schouwburg opened on 3 January 1638 with *Gysbreght van Aemstel* by Joost van den Vondel (1587–1679). Over the years this topical tragedy on the early history of Amsterdam, comparing the city with ancient Rome and its title-role with Aeneas, would prove to be one of the most popular plays of Dutch theatre history, performed annually around the turn of the year, a tradition that lasted until 1968.

That January, *Gysbreght* had eight performances (no other play was staged) and its last (thirteenth) performance of 1638 took place on 16 February. The revenues amounted to *f*[i.e. florins] 2457–8–0.[1] The source (417 written pages) is extremely important: with only a few gaps, it accounts for the daily Schouwburg receipts and expenses from the opening night till 2 February 1678. Other accounts in the Amsterdam City Archives complete the survey until 1754.

Most of the names mentioned below are those of the first generation of actors playing in the Schouwburg, even if they were paid for odd jobs like making costumes, selling candles, copying parts, etc. It appears that even a first-class performer like Adam van Germez could not live on his earnings as an actor alone.

¹ Guilders-stivers-cents: a guilder is 100 cents, a stiver 5.

269   Payments for the performance of the first play at the Schouwburg 1638

Ontfant en Uijtgift Van d'Amsterdamsche Schouburg Van de Jaere 1637 (Receipts and Expenses of the A.S. from the Year 1637), City Archives Amsterdam (Former Archives City Orphanage), P.A. 367, nr 425. Reproduced in Albach (1937), pp. 135–8

Payments by Mr Jacob Block for the play of Lord Gysbreght van Aemstel, the first drama played in the New Schouwburg, 3 Jan. 1638.¹

January

1	paid a bill to Pieter de Bray for the making and repairing of hoods²	13–6–0
[...]		
6	paid a bill to Harmen van Ilt for making costumes in *Aemstel*	41–10–0
[...]		
18	paid a bill to Maritje Huyberts for monks' serge and the like	113–13–0
[...]		
8 ditto	paid to Pelgrim for 3 weeks' rent of a carpet	3–12–0
[...]		
1	paid to Thomas de Keyser³ a bill for candles	49–10–0
[...]		
	paid to Pieter de Bray a bill for washing and starching and cleaning some linen	2–5–0
[...]		

February

[...]		
8 ditto	paid to Victorius for beer	17–10–0
12 ditto	paid a bill to Adriaan Bon in the Warmoesstraat for velvet	54–12–0
[...]		
14 ditto	paid to Adam van Germez⁴ for copying the parts of the play by Jan Vos and his farce *Oene*⁵	9–0–0

17 ditto	paid to Jan in de Harp for playing	22–0–0
	paid to Adam van Germez[6]	22–0–0
[...]		
18 ditto	paid to Pieter de Later for walking on three	
	times	1–16–0
	also paid to the drummer	0–12–0
[...]		
27 ditto	paid to all the playing characters [sic], from	
	the leading to the minor ones, the amount of	200–10–0
[...]		

Sum total the payments for *Gysbreght van Aemstel* come to

1363–15–12

---

[1] What follows is a short selection. Some entries do not really concern *Gysbreght*, e.g. the copying of other plays. Also, other payments for Vondel's tragedy are mentioned later in the accounts, such as a pair of swan's wings for the angel Raphael who is the *deus ex machina* (23 March 1638, for *f* 4). The document should therefore be read as a survey of the general costs made at the time when *Gysbreght* had its first performances.

[2] De Bray was the main performer of female roles, see **297**.

[3] See **297**.

[4] See **296**.

[5] The play is *Aran en Titus* (see **283** and **316**), like his *Oene* for some unknown reason printed and performed only later, in 1641 and 1642, respectively. Van Germez was to play Titus; at least, he did so in 1658/59.

[6] For playing.

Although the financial regulation with the almshouses now more or less safeguarded the work of resident companies, for visiting troupes it remained of course necessary to flatter the authorities in order to gain permission to perform or to secure later visits.

In 1648 and 1649 Archduke Leopold William of Austria, who was the Governor of the Southern Netherlands from 1648 to 1656, had given permission to a company of Dutch actors to play at his Court at Brussels (see **292**). These 'Brussels Comedians of the Archduke',[1] led by Triael Parkar and Jan Baptista van Fornenbergh (see **32, 280, 292, 293, 309, 333**), now gained easy access to the Amsterdam stage which had been refused them a few years earlier. In September 1654 the civic authorities even made the rare gesture of attending one of their performances, perhaps as part of some festivities to celebrate the fact that the Peace of Westminster had just concluded a naval war with England.

The playwright Vondel, who was quite friendly with these actors from the time he had instructed some of them for his play *Gebroeders* (The Brothers) (see **284**) twelve years earlier, wrote a poem for them to welcome the civic authorities at the beginning of the performance. It is of course a eulogy of the City Fathers, but also implicitly draws their attention to the fact that favouring the arts is an international sign of wealth and power, and that art is a means of making economic growth prestigious and widely known.[2]

[1] Companies which had performed at some foreign court, used the name of their royal patron to facilitate permission elsewhere (see **1, 5, 6, 59, 60**).
[2] The date of this performance and thus of the poem is mostly given as 1653, but Gunilla Dahlberg (1984) has argued that this is probably incorrect as the company was in Sweden at the time and that 1654 seems more likely.

270   Vondel flatters the authorities, 1654

Hollantsche Parnas (...) (Dutch Parnassus) (Amsterdam: Jacob Lescaille, 1660), p. 360. Reproduced in *De werken van Vondel* (The Works of V.), vol. 9 (Amsterdam: De Maatschappij voor Goede en Goedkope Lectuur, 1936), pp. 290–1

The 'Theatre brothers' under the patronage of the Archduke
    LEOPOLDUS
To the Magistrate[1] and Aldermen of Amsterdam;
When they honoured the stage with their presence.

Be praised, o noble Lords of the Amstel,
    Who did not turn down our request,
    And with your presence here
Have honoured the tragic stage.
    Even so our roles were played
In the light of the Danish crowns,[2]
And thus we were permitted to show our art
    To the Imperial Leopold
And in Holstein, both Holland's allies,
    Devotees of the buskin,
    Who feed the humanities and the sciences
At courts and in proud palaces.
    Now Athens flourishes in Amsterdam,
Spreading her favours liberally
And crowning the capital of navigation
    With arts and laurels from Parnassus.
May thus the new city-hall rise,[3]
    And the East and West for long centuries
    Enrich your stock exchange and bank.[4]
May we thus praise your courtesies.
    Worshipful Fathers, may your welfare
    Extend farther than any sail.

[1] The word probably indicates the presence of both Bailiff (see **352**) and Burgomasters.
[2] From 1649 the company had also played at the courts of Holstein (see **293**), Denmark and Sweden. In the Scandinavian controversy over the control of the Sound the Amsterdam merchants took the side of Denmark, which is probably the reason why Vondel does not mention Sweden here.

³ The old city-hall had burnt down in 1652; the new one (the present Royal Palace on the Dam), built by the Schouwburg architect Jacob van Campen, opened in 1655, Vondel publishing an extensive inaugural poem for the occasion.

⁴ Referring to the colonies in the East Indies and in America. These had already been systematically exploited by Dutch commercial companies for a few decades and vastly contributed to the country's wealth.

XXII   Playhouses and performance venues

271   Sketch of the stage for the Rhetoricians' festival at Haarlem, 1606

Const-thoonende Iuweel, frontispiece

The competition ('Landjuweel') of 1606 at Haarlem (see **266**) used a simple Rhetoricians' stage of the traditional type. Its front had three compartments, shown here with their curtains closed. Only the middle part had an upper floor.[1] The curtains have been opened to reveal the Lady Rhetorica (being the Patroness of any Rederijker activity), surrounded by the nine Muses and four town musicians. This upper compartment could be used for *tableaux vivants,* scenes with a royal throne or, in fact, any other dramatic action. The temple structure encompassing this main compartment and the Corinthian pillars at both ends of the stage, supporting an architrave, show classical influence, but there is no further suggestion of a unified stage: each compartment had its own function, derived from the drama to be played there, and permitting a variety of simultaneous and successive practices.[2] The city arms on top of the building indicate the provenance of some of the participating Chambers, and the fronton shows a pelican feeding its young from its own blood, as an emblem of the organising Chamber, 'The Pelican'. On the architrave of the compartments we see the beginning of the maxims on which the competing Chambers had to write and present a play and a refrain; and part of another accompanying verse at the bottom of the illustration.

---

[1] More elaborate stages would have a first floor covering the full width of the stage.
[2] Kernodle's idea that the façade of the Rhetoricians' stage could form a symbolic unity, presenting different successive meanings, has been refuted by Hummelen (1970) as being based on insufficient knowledge of the plays: such a stage is no more than an architectonic frame where compartments and entries may have divergent meanings, whether fixed or changing.

271

Around 1635 it was felt that the Academy, now the only theatre venue in the swiftly expanding city, had become derelict and too small. The Governors of both Almshouses decided therefore to build a new theatre, and the commission was given to the famous architect Jacob van Campen. The Academy was pulled down and in its place on the Keizersgracht the new theatre arose between April and December of 1637. The sum total of the building costs amounted to slightly more than thirty thousand guilders. From the beginning this theatre was called 'Schouwburg'; the word, a composite of 'to watch' and '[elevated] stronghold or city' was coined by the playwright Vondel as a translation of Greek *theatron* and has since been the regular Dutch word for any official city theatre. It appears from the accounts that well-known painters and sculptors took care of its decoration, but also that this work and many other parts of the interior were finished much later than the official opening on 3 January 1638.

The outcome of Van Campen's work is a theatre that, while on the one hand presenting a monumental unity, is on the other hand, in its mixture of styles unique in theatre history. In the extensive and detailed (mainly Dutch) literature on the building attempts have been made to trace the influence of Palladio (Teatro Olimpico), Scamozzi (Sabbioneta), Mahelot (Hôtel de Bourgogne) or Inigo Jones (the Cockpit), but to no avail. Van Campen has both realised some of his neo-classical ideals and taken pains to satisfy the wishes of the Rhetoricians (soon to become professionals). The building is clearly a hybrid, built to house both the traditional fare and the modern Renaissance repertoire. Recent studies have shown that it presented very practical solutions for the presentation of both. In the rather short period of its existence (until 1664) it was the main place where the change to professionalism took place and a new style of acting was presented, and where Dutch Renaissance drama, first created in the Academy, established itself.

Having passed a small gate and a courtyard the audience entered into a foyer and then into the actual theatre. Apart from this entry-room, there was a 'room for the players' and a tiny storage space for sets, props, etc. A spiral staircase on the immediate right of the entrance led to the boxes on the first floor and the amphitheatre on the second. Straight on was the pit. The theatre had excellent sightlines, the stage being extremely wide (14.15 m along the stage front) and shallow (a mere 4.5 m from the stage front to the back of the central 'Throne'). These measurements may seem clumsy from a modern point of view, but were in fact very suitable for the polytopic style of the Rhetoricians' stagings.

A room marked 'Back-stage' behind the 'Throne' was also very wide and shallow. Back-stage on the extreme right were two 'Dressing rooms for the women', meaning for the actors playing female parts (those for the male parts were on the first floor); and on the left of the stage, invisible to the audience, the 'Place for the Musicians'; in 1638 there were six.[1]

[1] The instruments were violin, bass, flute, two trumpets, drum. There were also singers and dancers.

272 The stage of the first Schouwburg, Amsterdam

Engraving by Salomon Savry (1658). Nederlands Theater Instituut, Amsterdam, TL 66–14

In 1658, Salomon Savry produced an engraving of the stage and one of the auditorium (273) in Jacob van Campen's Schouwburg. This was long after it had opened, but these illustrations may go back to earlier drawings. Although much of what we see in them was not yet present in 1638, they give a good general impression of the theatre from its early days.

Very striking in the combination of the two illustrations is the enormous barrel vault running straight from the central half-round window above and at the back of the audience to the throne as the central set piece of the stage. This was a practical, although old-fashioned, solution by Van Campen of the lighting problem. The performances started at four and ended around seven, and the vault permitted daylight to come in, adding to the effects of the chandelier, candles, oil-lamps and torches. Of itself, the theatre was not dark anyway: it consisted of wood, painted to give the impression of light-coloured marble.

The central set piece is built in two stages: the 'throne', forming a canopy covered by a triangular pediment, and above it a balcony, with a painting at its back, showing the Judgement of Paris. This balcony was, among other effects, used for appearances from Heaven, having at its back a stage lift with a cloud machine. Some of the stage machinery (and settings) had been taken over from the stock of the Academy (see 282).

Below the side galleries, we see flats between pilasters, the front ones with ornamental medallions, and those at the back painted in an Italian-style perspective. The large side flats downstage show a prison setting. The conflation of different symbolic elements, some decorative, others having a function in a play, points to multiple staging, and the same was true when the flats were removed, so that the spaces between the pillars and pilasters could be used as different mansions for interior scenes or *tableaux vivants*. But this stage could also be played in a monotopic style. The flats would then be homogeneous; also the central throne and the galleries could be taken away altogether, giving way to greater unity of place, for instance with a city or palace gate at the back (see **283**).

Instant scene changes as in the later wing system were not possible, but the use of the curtain was of great help here – not a front curtain in the proper sense,[1] but rather a large traverse. In the illustration, where it features the city colours black and red, it is open, hanging above the side galleries. When closed, it would cover the central scene and the four 'mansions', leaving the forestage available for continued acting.

All the sculptures in niches on the stage were illusionistic paintings; they represent mythological figures and philosophers from antiquity, each having an emblematic or didactic value. The coats of arms (of the reigning theatre Governors) and the inscriptions against the stage front were added by the engraver in 1658 and have no documentary value for the building.

One more remarkable aspect of this venue is its profuse decoration with didactic verses, not only on the stage and in the auditorium, but also at the entrance, in the foyer and green-room, and in the Governors' office. Many of them were written for the occasion by Vondel, others were quotations in Latin from Virgil and other poets. Almost all of them are moralistic comments on the purpose of the theatre, showing a fundamentally didactic attitude, even though allowance has been made, in the Horatian tradition, for a mixture of entertainment and instruction. Like many other parts of the interior, these maxims were installed some years after the official opening.

---

[1] A front curtain immediately behind the proscenium arch (also lacking here) was introduced with the rebuilding of 1665.

272

273   The auditorium of the first Schouwburg, Amsterdam, 1658

Engraving by Salomon Savry (1658). Nederlands Theater Instituut, Amsterdam, TL 66–15

The illustration of the auditorium shows an audience in the boxes and the 'amphitheatre' or gallery, with class distinctions marked by their dresses. Van Campen's neo-classical style is demonstrated in the giant Corinthian order supporting the boxes; this also stresses the new taste and wealth of the upper classes seated there. The pit however, a brick-paved standing room for the populace, is empty here.

Initially, performances took place on Mondays and Thursdays, also on Saturdays at the week of the annual September fair, which was the beginning of the season, but if a play proved to be very popular, the other days (including Sundays) could be chosen as well, and in the end there were performances each afternoon.

It is thought that the Schouwburg could contain about 900 spectators at most. How much they paid is not exactly known for the early years; in the Old Chamber the entrance fee had been three stivers, and this may have remained the same for the Schouwburg pit for some years (in 1678 it was six); the spectators in the gallery paid a few extra stivers, those in the boxes much more, up to a few guilders.

273

274   Interior of the first Schouwburg, Amsterdam, with a comedy scene

Oil painting by Hans Jeurriaensz. van Baden (attr.) (c. 1650). Nederlands Theater Instituut, Amsterdam, Inv. No. 187, on loan from Ringling Museum of Art, Sarasota

Van Baden's painting of a performance in the first Schouwburg gives the idea of a living experience, with most of the stage and part of the auditorium in sight and with both actors and spectators being present. The play may be I. de Groot, *De bedrooge Speckdieven* (The Deceived Bacon Thieves) (1653). The main points of interest lie in the differences with Savry's engraving (272), showing the changeability of this theatre; further, in the figures on the stage gallery, who are probably spectators; and finally, in the Commedia style of acting, which at first glance one would not expect in this type of theatre. The figures and the balustrade in the foreground have no documentary value but serve only as a pictorial *repoussoir*.

274

XXIII   Stage presentation

A. STAGING METHODS

275   Preparations for an open-air performance by Rhetoricians at a village fair, c. 1608

Engraving by Willem Isaaksz. Swanenburch after David Vinckboons (c. 1608) (fragment).
Atlas Van Stolk, Rotterdam, Suppl. 1600–50

One of many variations on the same theme shows a farmers' fair with a procession of rhetoricians on their way to a booth stage where they will give a performance. In the illustration the Chamber's blazon-bearers have reached the stage (only part of which is seen) and are hoisting their burden onto the stage façade, where it is to be fastened.[1] Behind the blazon the prompter is looking on through a chink between the curtains. The Chamber's drummer is half-way up the ladder leading to the stage floor. Behind him two of the traditional emblematic characters[2] are approaching, one dressed as a soldier and the other, wearing a mask, probably as an animal (a wolf?).[3] They are followed by a royal couple (the Queen representing the Lady World, also a traditional character), and further by a monk, soldiers, farmers and a standard-bearer who may be the Chamber's ensign. All in all some thirteen actors are involved. Beside the procession, the Chamber's fool, with cap and bells and pointed shoes, is teasing and chasing the audience with his bauble, thereby clearing a path for the actors.[4] The Chamber has not been identified, and neither has the play, which was in all certainty a serious one, not a farce, and may have been of a political nature.

---

[1] Probably on the crossing of the pilaster and the cove in front of the curtains, so as not to obstruct the opening and closing of the latter during the performance. Above the stage we see some billboards, to be used for coats of arms or maxims.
[2] Dutch: 'sinnekens', cf. 'vices'.
[3] In general, the Rhetoricians rejected the use of masks, being a characteristic of the despised professional players.
[4] He will take no part in the performance, because in Rhetoricians' plays vices and fools are mutually exclusive.

275

276   Royal Entry in Antwerp, 1599

Reproduced in Irmengard von Roeder-Baumbach, *Versieringen bij Blijde Inkomsten [...]* (Decorations at Royal Entries), (Antwerpen: De Sikkel, 1943), plate 60

Tableaux vivants and royal entries had always been inseparable, with the Gate as the main architectonic structure for showing the emblematic truths the cities wanted to confront the high visitor with. At Antwerp visiting royalty, after entering through the ordinary city gate, were traditionally welcomed with a poem by the City Virgin, Antverpia. She sat on an elevated throne under an ornamental gate, with her retinue of emblematic maidens and guards on the stairs and the platform in front of the throne. In 1582 this stage had been put on a large pageant car, which was put immediately behind the city gate as the first station on the route; it remained in use for several subsequent entries. In 1599, at the entry of the new sovereigns Albert of Austria and Isabella of Spain, Antverpia came down to street level to offer a golden lily to the royal couple.

276

277   *Tableaux vivants* on the Dam at Amsterdam on the occasion of the Twelve Years' Truce with Spain, 1609

Engraving by Cornelis Visscher (1609). Atlas Van Stolk, Rotterdam, Cat. No. 1239

The presentation of *tableaux vivants* now grew into one of the most typical traditions in the theatre history of the Netherlands, both South and North. They persisted well into the nineteenth century, not only for royal entries or other open-air solemnities, but also inside the theatre, to highlight important issues or theatrical climaxes in the dramatic action, like weddings, enthronements or executions. From quite early on, the *tableaux* were a speciality of the Rhetoricians' Chambers, and the practice continued in the time of professionalism. Most of them were of an allegorical or emblematic nature, or had in any case the intention of providing a succinct moral lesson to the spectators, even if at the same time they simply gave the audience an occasion to gape at magnificent or blood-curdling scenes. Apart from royal entries, these lessons had mostly been of a religious nature (and as such played a role in the religious struggles concerning the establishment of Calvinism in the Netherlands), but at the beginning of the seventeenth century the *tableaux* were more and more expressly used by the civic authorities of the North to present political messages, often connected with the revolt of the country against Spanish rule. To that end, they would command a Chamber or one of its members, who might be the Chamber's 'factor' or in Amsterdam such prominent authors as Samuel Coster or Pieter Cornelisz. Hooft, to choose a suitable theme and devise the show. In the seventeenth century, these themes were preferably chosen from supposed parallels in antiquity, like the uprising of the Batavian Claudius Civilis against the Romans.

Actors presented the main characters of the *tableaux*, but the more elaborate ones made ample use of the pictorial arts, so that live human beings intermingled with painted effects, for instance in the case of beheaded bodies or large crowds of people on stage, or when a royal carriage had to be drawn by lions. The succinctness of the message made some explanation necessary; this came in the form of short verses, on placards fixed to the stage or spoken by an actor.

On 5 May 1609, the proclamation of the Twelve Years' Truce between Holland and Spain presented the occasion for such an elaborate *tableau*, after a day's procession held at night by torchlight in the centre of Amsterdam. A temporary theatre with a façade in the classical style, probably 60 feet wide, was built by the well-known architect, Hendrik de Keyser. P.C. Hooft devised the show for the Rhetoricians' Chamber 'The Eglantine' and wrote the accompanying explanatory verse for its ten scenes, taken from the (legendary) early Roman history of Tarquin, Lucretia and Brutus. The message was clear: it vindicated the right to rebel against tyranny.

277

278   A floating *tableau vivant* in the river Amstel at the triumphal entry of Maria de Médicis, Amsterdam, 1638

Engraving by S. Savry after S. de Vlieger. Casparus Barlaeus, *Medicea Hospes, sive Descriptio publicae gratulationis (...)* (The Medicean Guest, or Description of a Public Welcome ...), (Amsterdam: Johannes and Cornelis Blaeu, 1638), Plate 6

In the 1630s the Queen-Mother Maria de Médicis roamed around in Western Europe, trying to get back to France and to bring about a reconciliation with her son Louis XIII and her arch-enemy Richelieu. Everywhere she negotiated with the authorities, trying to use them as go-betweens. In 1638, after she had stayed in Brussels and Antwerp, it was Holland's turn.

Her stay in Amsterdam, lasting for four days at the beginning of September, formed one of the climaxes of her visit, and among the many spectacles presented to her – designed by such prominent authors as S. Coster, P.C. Hooft and C. van Baerle – the floating *tableaux vivants* at the head of the river Amstel were the most magnificent. Two theatres had been erected there, the one with its back to the other (a second illustration, not given here, shows the other one), so that the spectators had to go around, by boat or on foot, to see the whole show. These theatres were in fact the upper compartments of triumphal gates used elsewhere for Maria's entry into the city. They remind one of the setting in Van Campen's Schouwburg (see **272**), but in fact their façades were flats, made of battens and cloth and painted in perspective. The connection with the Schouwburg is not coincidental, however, for a few days later some of these *tableaux* were repeated there for other authorities and the general populace.

The illustration shows Maria, the Princess of Orange and the city authorities being rowed to the island in a state sloop, decorated with tapestries. In her suite we see a classical conch with Neptune, and a boat with the City Virgin and the god Mercury, both vessels drawn and accompanied by sea-creatures; quite a feat, technically speaking. In the theatre a performance is going on[1] showing Maria's ancestor, Maximilian I, offering the city of Amsterdam an emperor's crown[2] (1488): a very aptly chosen subject, because it stressed the historical relationship between the Queen and the City. The whole reason for the City Fathers entertaining Her Majesty so lavishly was, in fact, the opportunity to show, on an international level, the expansion and supremacy of Amsterdam as a commercial and sea-faring power.[3] This is also quite apparent from *Medicea Hospes*, the official report of the royal entry (the first one of its kind in the Northern Netherlands) which appeared that same year,[4] profusely illustrated and written by the eminent scholar of the city's Athenaeum Illustre, Caspar van Baerle.

[1] Seen at a difficult angle, but the official report mentioned below has a description and another engraving showing it frontally.
[2] Also seen on top of the city's coat-of-arms at the summit of the theatre façade.
[3] Hence Mercury and Neptune. Mercury also had a (painted) sculpture on the stage of the Schouwburg (see 272).
[4] In Latin. A French and Dutch translation, the latter by Vondel, appeared a year later.

278

On 2 February 1654, the première was given of *Lucifer*, the impressive tragedy by Joost van den Vondel (1587–1679) on the fall of the archangels. Because of the subject matter, the Governors of the Schouwburg had high expectations for its success and had a new and costly celestial setting painted. Especially the Governor Jan Vos (1620–67), himself a playwright (see **283** and **316**), but unlike Vondel preferring exciting spectacles to drama following Aristotelian or Horatian poetics,[1] did his best to make it a theatrical success. He wrote Vondel a letter suggesting the addition of several dances. Vondel, who considered the power of language and adherence to classical prescriptions to be of central importance and who was not keen on spectacular effects, nevertheless allowed himself to be persuaded. All the conditions for a box-office hit had now been created. But after two well-attended performances, the clergy threw a spanner in the works. They sent a delegation to the Burgomasters with a fierce protest against the exhibition of religious matters on the stage. The authorities gave in and the performances were prohibited; the Burgomasters even banned the publication of the tragedy – with the predictable outcome that the first edition of a thousand copies was sold out in eight days and that six subsequent editions appeared that same year. However, the prohibition meant a great loss in income for the theatre. Vondel managed to confine the damage marginally by writing a new tragedy, *Salmoneus*, in which the celestial setting could be re-used.

---

[1] Vos' ideas on drama are to be found in the Preface to his tragedy *Medea* (1667), the main argument being that plausibility based on one's experience of human nature is more important than formal doctrines adopted from antiquity.

279   Jan Vos adds dances to Vondel's *Lucifer*, 1653

Letter from Jan Vos to Vondel, reproduced in Vondel, *Werken*, vol. 5 (1931), p. 938

Dear Sir,

The dance of the angels, of which you have spoken to me, will in my opinion not be advisable, because you make the angels appear on stage with sad faces, owing to Lucifer's fall (a valid reason). I have invented a new one,[1] which, I believe, will be more admired by the spectators, for in this one the sequel to the play will be presented: the Golden and Silver Ages. [...]

While Adam and Eve, who are naked, are busy building a cabin, an angel appears, with terrible wrath flaming from his eyes. He chases the seduced pair from the garden of Eden with the burning sword that he carries in his clenched hand. Hunger, Poverty, Labour, Old Age and Death join the first exiles. The Golden Age is driven off by the Iron Age. Time jumps nimbly onto the stage, accompanied by Ambition, Envy, War, Plunder and Murder. After these horrors have danced for a while, they disperse over the world. Love, Innocence, Fidelity and Honour are carried to the heavens in a cloud full of stars.

Now cease Love, Fidelity and Honour; the Plagues are mounting.
  Hunger, Labour and Death enter upon the earth.
Food can only be obtained by care and sweat.
  Ambition, Cruelty, Plunder and every disaster
Assume full power, to rule the world.
  These horrors can only be averted by the shield of Virtue.[2]

[...]
Sir,
I have added the melodies for the dances, now sad, now merry, after the
qualities of the said characters.

Your Hon.'s
most affectionate servant
JAN VOS.

---

[1] In fact, the stage directions for three dances follow; those for the second one are given here.
[2] The explanatory rhyme to the *tableau*.

An ordinary playbill may suggest which elements of stage presentation were attractive to a
Dutch audience around the middle of the seventeenth century (and presumably in earlier
and later times as well):

> An exciting topical theme, preferably based on historical reality and strengthen-
> ing national consciousness. The tragedy announced here, by Reinier Bontius
> (1645), is one of the approximately twenty plays which in the course of Dutch
> theatre history were devoted to the Siege (by the Spaniards) and the Relief (by the
> troops of William the Silent) of the city of Leiden (1584). Bontius' play was the
> most popular one, performed almost yearly until well into the nineteenth century
> all over the country, especially at fairs. It ran through some 75 editions and
> reprints, often illustrated.
>
> *Tableaux vivants.* Those mentioned here had only just been designed by the
> playwright Jan Vos. They were in use until about a century afterwards, always
> attracting new (and old) audiences. Descriptions of these *tableaux*, especially the
> one by Vos himself, were also published and saw several editions.
>
> Clowning, singing and dancing in the after-piece. Pickleherring (Dutch:
> *Pekelharing*) had been known as a carnival clown or quack's assistant since the
> Middle Ages. On the seventeenth-century stage he became extremely popular in
> consequence of the performances of the strolling players from England: some of
> their clowns, performing in jigs and farces, came soon to be identified with
> Pickleherring, who now grew to be the main character in a number of Dutch
> farces. Later he was in his turn identified with Harlequin or Pierrot (hence he may
> be 'white-powdered' on the playbill). One of the best-known performers of the
> part in the first half of the century was the English actor Robert Reynolds, who

founded his own Dutch-English company. Reynolds performed first in English, then in Dutch and also travelled to Germany and Denmark. (See **2**.) An English visitor to Danzig noted: 'It is said of him that he could so frame his face and countenance that to one half of the people on the one side he would seem heartily to laugh and to those on the other side bitterly to weep and shed tears.'[1] The farce mentioned here may have been an adaptation of an English jig by Isaac Vos or the anonymous *Singende klucht van Domine Johannes, ofte den jaloersen Pekelharing* (Singing Farce of Parson John, or Pickleherring's Jealousy) (1658). 'The Dutch Comedians' were the excellent company of Fornenbergh (see **32**, p. 352, **292**, **293**, **309**, **333**) and his associates.

[1] P. Mundy, *The Travels*, quoted in Schrickx, *Foreign Envoys*, p. 238–9.

280   A playbill, 1660

City Archives, Leiden, Bibl. nr. 2461

THE DUTCH COMEDIANS

by the favour and permission of the Bailiff of Heemstede, will on Wednesday 28 January 1660 and some following days open their Curtains, with the memorable and true history of the

Siege and Relief

OF THE CITY OF

LEIDEN,

TRAGEDY WITH A HAPPY END.

The same will be presented more magnificently yet, that is with more and rarer *Tableaux Vivants* than were shown at Valkenburg or Weesp or ever before.

And after that, our white-powdered Pickleherring will do his utmost, every day, to double the delight of our supporters, to let them depart in full joy and merriment.

The venue of the Show is a very suitable and warm Shed, in the House called the Thorn Tree, on the Herenweg, opposite the Hout [Wood], outside the Groote-Hout Gate.

On Stage at two o'clock sharp, sharp.

B. SETS AND PROPS

For the popularity of the Siege and Relief of Leiden, see **280**. The first known play on the subject was written by Jacob Duym (1547–before 1624), a military man from the South, who established himself at Leiden, where he became the head of the Flemish Chamber, 'The

Orange Lily'. Duym is the author of six historical and six more or less allegorical plays, both showing a mixture of traditional and Renaissance elements. His very practical stage directions indicate the simultaneous use of different locations on a wide stage which is typical for the Rhetoricians.

281   A simultaneous set for an historical play, 1606

Jacob Duym, *Benoude Belegheringe der stad Leyden [...]* (Precarious Siege of the City of Leiden) (Leiden: Henrick Lodowixsoon van Haestens, 1606), p. A 3 v°–4 r° (the Preface).

If anyone wanted to present this theatrically to the people, a large stage, platform or pageant car will have to be made, and on one side, in the farthest corner, the image of a city, which will be Leiden, with a gate for entrances and exits, and on top at the inner side a passageway to look and speak over the battlements. On the opposite side at the very front will be the church and the village of Zoeterwou,[1] to be panelled with canvas, showing compartments, where the Spaniards and their followers will enter and exit. Also, very near to Zoeterwou, the redoubt at Lammen, and a bit further to the back almost near the town, the redoubt at Boshuizen. These redoubts will be made of light wood, slats or else light sticks, square, fixed at the bottom with hooks and eyes, and at the top also connected by hooks, and they must be covered with cloth from the top to the bottom, and painted as earthen walls; this will remain on the floor till the time arrives [in the play] for the redoubts to be made; but at the back they will have to be open for exits and entrances. The wall of the city of Leiden will have to be equipped with ropes on one side, to let it fall down at the end before the relief has been completed. The rest, including entrances and exits, will become sufficiently clear from the marginal notes and drawings in the following comedy.[2] But the captains of the city must all have red and white sashes, those on the side of the Prince [William the Silent] orange, white and blue, and on the part of the King [Philip II] bright red ones; apart from that, the costumes will take care of themselves.[3]

---

[1] One of the fortifications of the besieging Spaniards stood there. The other two are mentioned further on: Lammen and Boshuizen.
[2] Comedy: only because of its happy ending.
[3] Note the combination of historical colours and emblematic succinctness in this costume direction.

When Samuel Coster sold his Academy to the Amsterdam Orphanage (see **267**), some scenery and properties belonging to him were included in the agreement. The list is interesting both for the (rather conjectural) stage technique of the Academy, and for the question which of these elements continued to be used in the Schouwburg of 1637. Play texts and especially costumes are strikingly absent from the list; perhaps these were the property of the individual members.

282   Sets and props of the Old Chamber sold to the Orphanage, 1622

[...] in this sale will be included and remain for the benefit of the buyers:
all the painted revolving cloths being on the stage[1]
22 coats of arms of the main princes[2] painted on ovals
9 square coats of arms of the Union[3] and six princes' coats of arms on cloth, –
2 big screens from which the lamps hang, painted on the other side, with their pulleys and ropes,[4]
the descending heavens with capstan and ropes and pulleys[5]
3 tables surrounding the place[6] with their trestles and benches
another smaller table with two trestles
3 pieces by means of which the stage is enlarged[7]
a prison door made with bars[8]
2 big wooden bars made for the play of *Harcilia*[9]
the screens made for the heavens
2 big black linen curtains with which the stage is closed[10]
all the spare parts in the highest attic
the tomb of Achilles[11]
the triumphal chariot
the square small altar
different kinds of fireworks[12] lying in the attic

[1] It is not known how these 'cloths' (meaning *flats*) revolved: whether horizontally, or as a kind of (two-sided) *periaktoi*; but it may also simply mean that they were changed by hand, without any turning device. One side showed a landscape, the other (part of) a building.

[2] The leaders of the combined Chambers of Rhetoric, fused in the Academy.

[3] The Union of seven Northern provinces and some cities (1579), later considered as the beginning of the Dutch Republic.

[4] It is not clear how or where these screens were used.

[5] See 272.

[6] 'Place' (for Dutch *plein*) as a technical term for the pit of the theatre (compare the older Latin *platea*). Perhaps (upper-class) spectators were sitting at these tables during performances, in which case they must have been on a raised level, maybe in boxes. They may also have been used at lectures, given the double purpose of the Academy (see 267). During rehearsals non-playing members (factor – see p. 345 – prompter, waiting actors) would also sit at them, cf. a painting by Job Berckheyde in the Jagdschloss at Grunewald, Germany, showing such a rehearsal.

[7] Meaning unknown.

[8] See 272.

[9] A tragedy by A. van Mildert, printed 1632. The play, more or less after Boccaccio, gained some reputation in its time because of its main character dying in the middle of the word 'victo-ry' ('*dies without speaking the last two letters*').

[10] Not the front curtain, but a traverse (see 272).

[11] In Samuel Coster's tragedy *Iphigenia* (1617).

[12] Probably torches, braziers, etc.

283   The last scene of 'Aran en Titus' by Jan Vos

Amsterdam: Jacob Lescaille, 5th ed., 1656, frontispiece

We see some stage machinery in action in a frontispiece of a famous Senecan horror-drama, *Aran en Titus* (Aaron and Titus) by Jan Vos. The play, written in 1638 and first performed in 1641, was admired by intellectuals and the populace alike and put on for more than a century, not only in city theatres, but also on the stages of the annual fairs all over the country. Apart from its many editions, it gave rise to some German adaptations and to a translation into Latin for a school performance; satirical poems on the play and parodies of it were also highly successful (see 316). The subject is the same as in Shakespeare's *Titus Andronicus*.[1]

The illustration shows the Schouwburg stage at the end of the play where, as with Shakespeare, most of the main characters have been horribly maimed and executed or are now awaiting their deaths. On the left the Moor, who had been taken prisoner, is falling through a trap in the ceiling (that is, in the side-gallery) into a trap in the floor, surrounded by spikes, in which a fire is blazing. From this trap he will in vain cry for mercy, with his head rising amidst the flames, while being burned alive. The trap in the ceiling has been opened by a chain, fixed to a pillar, and another, heavier chain has been fastened to Aran's left foot, probably meaning that the actor did not jump (that would have been a height of approx. five metres, and the trick was dangerous enough as it was), but was slowly eased down from above, greatly adding to the thrills of pleasure in the audience.

The central throne (see 272) has been replaced by a gate. On its architrave, the figure of a fox (Dutch *vos*) is an allusion to the name of the author.

[1] Travelling English actors had played one of Shakespeare's source dramas in the Netherlands. This was given a Dutch version (now lost), *Andronicus* by Adriaen van den Bergh, of which Vos' play is in its turn an adaptation (see also p. 378).

283

A manuscript, probably written by the author himself, prescribes the casting, the costumes, sets and props for Vondel's Biblical tragedy *The Brothers* (1640), presenting King David's revenge on the descendants of Saul. It is a unique document: not only does it show how Holland's main tragedian in the early stages of his playwriting career took a close interest in stage presentation – we know that he also rehearsed the actors – but it is equally important as a survey of what was needed in this period for the performance of a tragedy. Only part of the list, mainly concerning set pieces and properties, is quoted.

284   The author Vondel prescribes sets and props, 1640

Reproduced in Vondel, *Werken*, vol. 3 (1929), pp. 900–901

THE ARK must be like a square chest, two and a half cubits long and wide, and one and a half cubits high (a cubit being twenty-four inches or six hand-breadths), gilded all over, and with ornamental borders all around at the top and the bottom. On either side it should have two gilded rings, with two gilded poles passing through them. On top of the lid should be two gilded children, a boy and a girl, having instead of arms two wings each, flapping against each other just like [the seat of] a [folding] chair.

THE CANDELABRA should be gilded, with seven arms, at its foot like a man's thigh, then a knob like a goblet, with a lily springing from it, and above it an apple from which the seven arms come forth, one straight up and the other six, three on either side, strongly bent. All seven have three knobs like goblets, and above, an apple with flowers, with on top a lamp in the shape of a human eye. It [the Biblical one] weighed a quintal or 125 pounds of gold.[1]

[There follows a description of the costumes for the priests and the high-priest.]

> Two tin trumpets.
> 2 other trumpets.
> 8 white linen coats for the priests.
> 8 white linen caps with curls.
> An open crown for David.
> A helmet.
> A collar.
> The Ark with the cherubim.
> The candelabra.
> The niche [for the throne].
> The canopy of the throne.[2]
> A carpet on same.
> The rock, or mountain, at the side of the st[age].
> Seven gallows with seven ropes.
> A small mirror [for the plastron of the High Priest].
> A big chain with seven ladders [needed for the execution scene].
> Two leather whips [for the executioners].
> A small stool.
> White and black crepe for Rispe [the female protagonist].
> A parasol.
> Trumpet players.
> Thurible.

¹ Two very clumsy drawings of the Ark and the Menorah are added in the margin of their descriptions.
² The word for 'canopy' means literally *small loft* or *garret*, and may indicate that this canopy also served as the floor of the central balcony in this theatre, under which the throne stood (see **272**).

C. COSTUMES

Costumes were the main properties of a travelling company. A stage could be built from boards, trestles and an old curtain, all perhaps provided by some inn-keeper, but costumes had to be brought along. Although this was different with permanent companies, they also took great care of costumes. In Amsterdam, where these always gave rise to high entries in the book of accounts, there was an extra reason for this care, female dress being the most important means for the performance of women's roles by male players.

285   Costume storage and dressers at the Amsterdam Schouwburg, 1663

Dr O.D.[apper], *Historische beschrijvingh der Stadt Amsterdam* (Historical Description of the City of A.) (Amsterdam: Jacob van Meurs, 1663) p. 433

Because the entire theatre, regarding both supervision and actors, has been organised very effectively and in all respects in an orderly fashion, there is no lack whatever of costumes and adornments for dressing the characters, either in men's or in women's apparel. To that end there are two particular rooms; in one of them the clothes are kept in which the men appear on stage and in the other those for the women, or men appearing as women. For each room a different person has been appointed: one of them has as his only task dressing the men as men, and the other dressing the women, or men in women's clothes.[1]

[1] The first professional actress had made her debut in 1655 (see **297**), but apparently cross-dressing remained the custom for some time.

286   Exotic Costumes

Catharina Questiers, *Casimier of gedempte hoogmoed* (C. or Thwarted Pride) (Amsterdam: Ger. Smit, 1656), frontispiece.[1]

[1] Left margin cut. The play is an adaptation of Lope de Vega's *Engañar para reinar* (Deceiving in Order to Rule).

Initially, costumes will have been chosen and distinguished according to the sex, age, profession, social status, country of origin, etc. of the *dramatis personae*. Historical accuracy did not matter much; it became only gradually important from the second half of the eighteenth century. The main costume categories in the serious seventeenth-century repertoire were roughly geographical: Roman, Eastern (or Turkish), Spanish, and Old-Dutch. In actual stage practice, mixtures of these were quite common. In farces and most comedies, and later also in many tragedies, costumes were contemporary and more or less the same as in real life; of course they might be old-fashioned or modish (see **25**, **85**).

The illustration shows a mixture of costume categories; the three men in the foreground wear 'Polish' dress (for which the braids are characteristic), the man on the right adding an 'Eastern' turban.

XXIV Actors and acting

A. COMPANIES

The companies dealt with here concern strolling players from England; French visiting companies; and a Dutch company abroad. Information on Dutch companies at home is included in other chapters.

Strolling Players from England

The English companies that in the late sixteenth and the first half of the seventeenth century wandered all over Europe, invariably entered the Continent via the Low Countries. Most of them played there only on their way to Germany, nevertheless often calling themselves 'niederländische Comödianten' afterwards, because of the success of their performances en route. Others stayed for a longer time, and the Netherlands were the first country to undergo the impact of Elizabethan drama and acting.

The first troupe of English players to visit Holland came over with the Earl of Leicester in 1585. Other companies were soon to follow, playing at Leiden, Arnhem, Utrecht, Flushing, Groningen and many other cities, also in the Southern Netherlands, at Brussels, Louvain and especially at Ghent. Unfortunately there are no detailed reports on their performances; but from the many short entries in city accounts etc., the names are known of such actors as Robert Browne, John Green, Robert Reynolds (see pp. 369–70), John Payne, William Roe, and others (see 2, 5–7, 28–30). Their lively style of acting made a tremendous impression, because it differed greatly from the rather more static and pictorial declamation of the Rhetoricians. Also, they took care to include a great deal of pantomime, dance and acrobatics in their performances, well aware that hardly anyone in the audience understood any English. Nevertheless, some plays from their repertoire were adapted by Dutch authors, for instance Kyd's *Spanish Tragedy*, which became the very popular *Don Jeronimo* (1621), written by the Utrecht author Adriaen van den Bergh, who adapted a version of *Titus Andronicus* as well (see 283, p. 418). The English stage clown Pickleherring also entered the Dutch stage (see 280).

The English troupes set the example for the formation of Dutch professional travelling companies, the first one being established in 1619 as the 'Batavian Comedians' – the name is programmatically competitive with the English. Later, Dutch actors entered into partnership with the English strolling players, sometimes acting as 'English Comedians', sometimes as 'Dutch Comedians'. The best-known example is that of Jan Baptist van Fornenbergh (see 32, p. 352, 292, 309 and 333), who in 1645 formed a company with John Payne. Gradually, as some of the English became settled and learned to speak the language, their performances were given in Dutch. After 1650 the separate English troupes disappeared, having merged into Dutch companies.

287   An English company permitted to play in Leiden, 1604

Magistrate's Diary F, City Archives Leiden, Secr. Arch. 1575–1851, no. 9254, fol. 5v.
Reproduced in *De Navorscher* (Amsterdam: Frederik Muller, 1853), vol. 3, Bijblad III, p. xli.

On the recommendation of His Excellency[1] and the request of John Woods, Englishman, the Magistracy of Leiden permits and consents that during the present fair[2] he and his troupe will be allowed to perform a certain honest play for the amusement of the populace, provided that from each person (coming to see the play) he will receive and enjoy no more than twelve pennies,[3] and specifically, that he will pay an earnest of four guilders to Jacob van Noorde, [the Magistracy's] usher bearing the rod, for the benefit of the poor.

[1] Prince Maurice, the Stadtholder.
[2] The fair at the beginning of October to celebrate the relief of the city from the Spaniards.
[3] Dutch *penningen*; the nominal value of 12 *penningen* in modern currency is 3.75 cents.

Very little has come to light about the appearance of English actors in Amsterdam in the early days of their travels. They were probably kept out by the authorities because of their competition with the flourishing Chambers of Rhetoric. A few performances there have been recorded, however, and that these made a very strong impression becomes clear from two texts by the eminent poet and playwright Gerbrand Adriaensz, Bredero (1585–1618). First a written address, perhaps dating from 1613, to the audience of 'The Eglantine'.

288   The playwright Bredero criticises the English Comedians, c. 1613

G.A. Brederoods Nederduytsche Poëmata *(Dutch Poems)* (Amsterdam: Cornelis Lodewijcksz. van der Plasse, 1632). Reproduced in *Memoriaal van Bredero. Documentaire van een dichterleven*, samengesteld door Garmt Stuiveling (B.'s Diary. Documentary of a poet's life, compiled by G.S.) (Culemborg: Tjeenk Willink/Noorduijn, 1975), p. 123

[...]
Young ladies, rich in virtues! We are amazed that some lasses have not come and seen our play, but have avoided it as if it were an indecent thing, whereas, without any shame and with a passionate zeal, they run daily after the light-footed foreigners, to whom all villainies seem to be permitted. And is it not highly

amazing that such a laudable citizenry and this honourable community have been deluded for such a long time by the clever tricks of these light-fingered and thievish people? Tell me, you supporters of the foreign vagabonds, what instructive arguments have you ever heard from them? what edifying admonitions, from which others might benefit, have you ever seen in them? what virtuous morality have you ever discovered in them? what royal dignity have they ever shown? O you bewitched people! I had hoped that your enchanted eyes would have been opened by this happy age of poetry. But what happens? Many of you people stay wilfully blind. You madmen! And must you not admit that you have heard and seen nothing but ridiculous follies, and a farrago of vulgar and indecent gibberish, and many useless wanton frivolities? I will not deny that two or three of them play rather well. But, my dear listeners, what about the rest? For the most part [they present] nothing but ranting and raving, blood and guts, stuff and nonsense.[1] [. . .]

---

[1] An exact translation of the last sentence is impossible, the extremely colourful Dutch original being full of colloquialisms and rhyming effects.

Four years later, in 1617, Bredero published his play *Moortje* [Little Blackamoor]. Its action is adapted from Terence's *Eunuchus*, but so freely that the characters and the dramatic situation became typical of contemporary Amsterdam. In a passage of this play Bredero again takes up the topic of the English comedians in the Netherlands and now admits that their style of acting is a lot more attractive than that of the Chamber of Rhetoricians who, moreover, had to contend with internal squabbles, which caused a decline in public attendance. In Act III, scene iv, a young man tells how, the day before, he and his friends stood around discussing where to go to find some entertainment.

289   Characters in a play prefer the English players to the Dutch, 1617.

G.A. Brederoos Moortje waar in hy Terentii Eunuchum heeft Naeghevolght. En is gespeelt op de Oude Amstelredamsche Kamer Anno MDCXV (G.A.B.'s Little Blackamoor. In which he imitated Terence's *Eunuchus*. And in 1615 it was performed in the Old Amsterdam Chamber) (Amsterdam: Cornelis Lodewycksz. van der Plasse, 1617). Reproduced in the ed. by P. Minderaa and C.A. Zaalberg (The Hague: Martinus Nijhoff, 1984), pp. 234–5, vss. 1448–1471

Well, said Lichthart,[1] we've been standing here long enough,
Good fellows, advise me, where shall we go?
Come, let's go to the Hall[2] and see the members perform,
But Packe-bier[3] said: I cannot stand their scoffing,
I'd rather be in the pub with an excellent wench;
I cannot endure the Rhetoricians for such a long time:

For these fellows mock all men continuously,
And, like the monkey, they cannot cover their behinds;
They recite their lessons so gravely and so stiffly,
As if their bodies were lined and filled with staves![4]
Would they were the English, or some other foreigners,
Whom one hears singing and sees dancing so merrily
That they reel and spin like a top ...
These speak from their hearts, ours do it by rote.
Quite right, I said. Just so, said Eelhart[5] snappishly,
The difference is too great when one compares them!
[But] The foreigners are frivolous, our people advise good behaviour,
Indirectly and sweetly chastising what is bad.
It were nice, said roguish Jan, if they avoided bickering,
But they're at it all the time, arguing and answering back.
They teach the audience to refrain from envy and quarrelling,
But they themselves are misbehaving all the time.
What harm in that, I said, if they quarrel sometimes?
More refined people do the same, even if they aren't members of the
    Chamber.

[1] Lightheart, a 'telling name' in many comedies.
[2] At the time, the Chamber was housed on the upper floor of a 'meat hall'.
[3] Literally Take-a-beer.
[4] Meaning the curved pieces of wood forming a barrel.
[5] Nobleheart, see note 1.

French visiting companies

If the English strolling players appealed chiefly to Dutch spectators from the lower and middle classes, the many French companies visiting the Netherlands in the first half of the seventeenth century addressed themselves to an aristocratic or at least upper-class audience. The main goal was to perform at the courts of Brussels and The Hague, with excursions to neighbouring cities. In Brussels, performances in French were a matter of course, but it is to be noted that the Stadtholder's court at The Hague continuously employed French companies (see also p. 408, 353). In 1613 Valleran le Conte of the Hôtel de Bourgogne, considered the best actor of his time, played at the court of Maurice of Orange and at Leiden. In 1638, another French troupe played Corneille's *Cid* on the occasion of a royal wedding at the court of Frederick Henry, only a few months after its first performance in Paris.

The Stadtholders Maurice (in office from 1585 to 1625), Frederick Henry (1625–1647) and William II (1647–1650) each patronised a French company, performing as 'Les comédiens du Prince (d'Orange)' and also using this title in the Southern Netherlands and in France. After the death of William II (who had spent enormous sums on jewellery for French actresses) the Republic did without a Stadtholder until 1672, in which year all theatres were closed for more than five years because of the war with France; as a result of both events, no French company is documented between 1650 and 1680.

290   Letter of safe conduct by Prince Maurice, 1618

Reproduced in J. Fransen, *Les Comédiens français en Hollande au XVIIe et au XVIIIe siècles (The French Actors in Holland in the 17th and 18th Centuries)* (Paris: Librairie Ancienne Honoré Champion, 1925), pp. 52–3

His Excellency permits the bearers of this, French actors who are in his service, to proceed from here to France or elsewhere, wherever it will please them, in order to perform their comedies and tragedies there during this summer-time until 1 October, for a period of the next six months. Commands therefore all who are under his authority, both on land and water, and requests all the others to whom this may concern, to show the said comedians their favour and attention, both when they pass by and when they perform their comedies and tragedies.

> Given at The Hague, 17 April 1619
> Maurice of Nassau

That Corneille was well-known appears from the affectionate letters exchanged between himself and the famous poet and secretary to the House of Orange, Constantijn Huygens. In 1648 Corneille asked the actor Floridor, who at the head of his troupe was to visit the Netherlands, to present Huygens with a copy of his newly published *Oeuvres*, modestly adding in a letter: 'You won't find anything supportable in it, except *Médée*.' Nothing else is known about Floridor in Holland.

291   Huygens employs a French actor to tell Corneille that he is popular in Holland, 31 March 1649

J.A. Worp (ed.), *Lettres du Seigneur de Zuylichem à Pierre Corneille* (Paris-Groningen: 'Revue d'Art Dramatique', J.B. Wolters, 1890), pp. 4–8. Reproduced in Fransen (1925), p. 78–9

Sir, I have asked M. Floridor to make good the deficiencies of my pen and to testify to you *viva voce* how I esteem that precious proof of friendship you have favoured me with by sending me, by his hand, *mirabile visu coelatumque novem musis opus.*[1] [Huygens goes on to praise *Médée*.] This is my feeling about it and you will find reasons to disparage it; but the voice of a great people supports me and I relate to you the topic of conversation everywhere in Holland [. . .]. Permit me to rely for that subject on my first witness. If he will do justice to us, and to you, Sir, and to himself, he will never tire of reporting to you how great the applause was in our theatres at the time when he declaimed you, or, if you will permit me the phrase, when he spoke Corneille [. . .]. I could quote persons of consequence to support this, Sir, and you would find some cause for satisfaction in it; but again, please learn everything from M. Floridor, and if he would condescend to naming me *in hac nube testium*,[2] please love him for his kindness in so far as it is related to your own [. . .].

---

[1] 'This work, wonderful to see, and wrought by the nine Muses' (Horace, *Epist.*, II, ii, 91–2).
[2] 'In this cloud of witnesses' (Hebr. 12:1).

Dutch companies abroad

The actors' growing professionalism made it possible (and often necessary) to perform abroad. The Southern Netherlands were of course first to be considered: they were nearby, the people spoke or at least understood the Dutch language, there were many cities and an art-loving court at Brussels, which often employed foreign companies. In 1648 Archduke Leopold William permitted the troupe led by Jan Baptist van Fornenbergh to perform at the Brussels court (see p. 352). It consisted of young actors in their twenties, who had associated four years earlier and were established at The Hague. This was the first of their many foreign travels; the year after they revisited the South, both times also playing in Flemish cities.

292   A Dutch professional company in Brussels, 1648

Dépenses de la Cour d'Archiduc Léopold-Guillaume, Archives Générales du Royaume, Brussels, Cartulaires et Manuscrits, No 1374. Reproduced in J. Lefèvre, 'La cour de l'archiduc Léopold-Guillaume 1647–1652' (The Court of Archduke Leopold William), *Archives, Bibliothèques et Musées de Belgique, Bulletin mensuel de l'Association de conservateurs*, vol. v, No. 5, 15 May 1928, p. 73

On 26 February 1648 a sum of 750 florins was payed to Jean Baptiste Foremberg [*sic*] and Trial Parker, Dutch actors, who had performed five plays[1] before the Court. Trial Parker had, moreover, danced a ballet.[2]

---

[1] The French text has 'comédies', which may mean any kind of play.
[2] The name of the actor and dancer (Pieter) Tria(e)l Parker or Parkar (dates unknown), who like Fornenbergh was also a painter, may indicate an English origin. From 1640–1646 he acted at the Schouwburg, after which he stayed in Fornenbergh's company for twenty years.

Northern Germany and Scandinavia were also favoured by Dutch travelling companies, because these were countries where the Netherlands had a great commercial and political influence. Dutch and Flemish merchants, bankers etc. had been working in Northern Germany and Scandinavia for generations. The rapidly growing economic influence of Amsterdam made the Dutch language understood and spoken everywhere in the old

Hanseatic countries (the city of Göteborg, built by the Dutch, was even officially bilingual), so the travelling actors could stick to their own repertoire, without adding any extra visual effects. Their influence on the budding German drama is clearest in the fields of 'Spanish' dramas and of farces.

In 1649, when the political situation in Holland was troubled and when the opposition of the church made the situation of Fornenbergh and his partners rather awkward, it seemed attractive to them to make a further trip abroad, this time to Germany. At their first arrival in Hamburg, a very important city for gaining an audience, their request to perform was turned down, but they met with more luck at the Gottorp Palace (just outside the harbour of Schleswig), where a royal wedding was in progress. Afterwards their host, the Duke of Holstein, sent an effective letter of recommendation to the authorities of Hamburg, to which city they now returned with good results. – For their later performances in Sweden, see p. 437.

293   The Duke of Holstein-Gottorp recommends Dutch actors to the Hamburg authorities, 1649

Hamburger Staatsarchiv, Cl VII Lit. F 1, Nr 1, Vol. 1. Reproduced in Herbert Junkers, *Niederländische Schauspieler und niederländisches Schauspiel im 17. und 18. Jahrhundert in Deutschland* (Dutch Actors and Dutch Theatre in the seventeenth and eighteenth Centuries in Germany) (The Hague: Martinus Nijhoff, 1936), p. 71

By the Grace of God Frederick, Heir to Norway, Duke of Schleswig, Holstein, Stormarn and Ditmarsh, Count of Oldenburg and Dellmenhorst.

First Our most gracious salute, Honourable, Highly Learned and Wise, Dear and Loyal Sirs.

By this We let you know with all grace, that the actors of the Lord Archduke of Austria,[1] Our dearly beloved uncle, have recently arrived here and have presented themselves most humbly and besought Us most obediently to grant Our gracious permission to them to perform their plays, to which We have graciously consented. Whereupon they have [. . .] given their performances, in such a manner that the Kings, Princes, Noblemen and other persons present were fully satisfied.[2]

Because the said actors are now leaving for Hamburg, where they also want to perform for some time, they have at their departure most humbly requested Us to give them a letter of recommendation, which, things being as they are, We were happy to provide.

And therefore We put most graciously to your consideration, not only to permit and grant the above-mentioned actors their performances, also with regard to a venue, but especially and for Our sake to take good care of them in other respects as well.

With all good grace and specifically good intentions to be favourably disposed
towards you,
Given at Our castle,
Gottorp, 25 September, Anno 1649.
Frederick.

¹ See 270 and 292.
² Apart from the Duke and his family, the Danish royal couple and two Archdukes of Saxony were
present at the wedding.

B. INDIVIDUAL ACTORS

It is very seldom that we hear about ham acting and actors' jokes during rehearsals or
performances in the seventeenth century. Willem Ruyter (1584–?), who had been one of
the first actors to associate with English colleagues (see **287**), played the venerable old
Bishop Gozewijn in Vondel's tragedy *Gysbreght van Aemstel* (1638).
   The source is an anonymous poem, written after the death of the satirical minor poet
M.G. Tengnagel (1613–1652), describing how he meets the ghosts of his dead colleagues
in the hereafter. Among them are quite a few actors. See also **297**.

294   An actor's joke at a rehearsal

Anon., *De Geest van Mattheus Gansneb Tengnagel, In d'andere werelt by de verstorvene Poëten*
(The Ghost of M.G.T. in the Other World with the Dead Poets) (Rotterdam: Iohan Neranus,
1652, unpaged). Reproduced in Mattheus Gansneb Tengnagel, *Alle Werken* (Collected
Works), ed. J.J. Oversteegen, (Amsterdam: Athenaeum/Polak & Van Gennep, 1969),
p. 547, vss. 505–12

Willem Ruyter, that Bishop,
   Rehearsing for *Amstel*, at the height of his age,
Said, instead of 'mitre':
   'Now put the shit-pot on me,
For it will not be unsuitable,'
   He continued, 'on my anointed head.'
It was not thought that this would amuse
   Vondel, who heard about it.

295   An actor in his dressing-room, by Rembrandt

Probably Willem Ruyter as the Bishop Gozewijn in Vondel's *Gysbreght van Aemstel* (1638).
Drawing, Chatsworth House Trust Ltd

In the 1630s Rembrandt became interested in the theatre and, among other theatrical themes, his drawings of the period show scenes and characters from Vondel's *Gysbreght*. Some of them, formerly connected to the subject of St Augustine, are now recognized as pictures of an actor playing a bishop. In all probability they represent Willem Ruyter in the part of Gozewijn. One of them portrays him before the performance, sitting in his dressing-room, his episcopal costume hanging casually on a peg.

C. ACTING TECHNIQUE

Petrus Francius (1645–1704) was a Professor of History, Philosophy and Greek at Amsterdam, and a Governor of the Schouwburg from 1678 to 1681. About 1696, he commemorated the greatest actor of the Dutch seventeenth century, Adam Carelsz. van Germez (1612–67) (see also 269), of whom, alas, no portrait survives. Van Germez died before the main contemporary treatises on classical rhetoric, like the one by Le Faucheur, had been translated into Dutch, but from what Francius writes, it becomes clear that the influence of Cicero and Quintilian on the vocal delivery and gestures of the first generation of professional players was none the less very strong; most of them would not have read the classical prescriptions, but picked up the technique in a practical way from authors, scholars, paintings and in school performances. The document is important as a rare testimony of the reverse influence: actors teaching orators. Francius in his turn instructed the actor Enoch Krook who became the teacher of the generation of actors preceding Jan Punt (see 335).

296 A professor remembers being taught rhetoric by an actor

Petrus Francius, *Posthuma*, Amsterdam 1701, translated in A. van Halmael, *Bijdragen tot de geschiedenis van het tooneel* (Contributions to Theatre History) (Leeuwarden: G.T.N. Suringar, 1840), pp. 16–7, 20. Reproduced in Albach, *Langs kermissen*, app. B, pp. 147–8

I speak [. . .] of a man of the people, unschooled, ignorant of, and inexperienced in all matters, other than poetry and eloquence. Cicero and Quintilian he had not read, perhaps he had not even heard of the latter's name. However, he expressed with his voice and his gestures and all the movements of his body all that Tully prescribes, or Fabius, to perfection and true to life. [. . .]

As a young man he used to rise very early, go to the top of his house and occupy himself with declamation for some hours, until he was all in a sweat. By doing so he made his body soft and supple and capable of all kinds of movement; thus he formed and fashioned himself to such an extent that subsequently he could express anything he wanted and transform himself into all sorts of guises. [. . .]

What they have in common, the performances of the actors and those of the orators, is shown by M. Tully, who demands the voice of the tragedian, meaning a similar one, in the orator, and for both nearly the same tone. Because I was of the same opinion, I have applied myself to imitate the voice, the gestures, the stance and the whole bodily attitude of that man, in whom, whenever I heard and saw him, I thought I was hearing and seeing the Ancients themselves. I would never have known what the eloquence of those Ancients, what a Cicero, what a Roscius had been, if I had not heard him, the man who has taught me all those things. [. . .]

Before women entered upon the Dutch stage, female parts were played by men, some of whom were specialists in this line. It appears from the quotation that, in contrast to England, this specialism was not restricted to boys and that some actors continued as drag artists into ripe old age.

The first woman to get an official appointment as an actress in the Amsterdam municipal theatre was Adriana van den Bergh. This was in March 1655. The year is rather late, an indication of a conservative official policy regarding women on stage. Long before, although infrequently, women had played in a few Chambers of Rhetoric;[1] and with travelling companies it had always been normal to involve the wives (and children) of the actors. It is interesting to note that female singers (needed for the choruses in 'classical' drama) were also from the start quite common among the Schouwburg personnel, at a time when actresses were still anathema.

Adriana (c. 1620–61), who was the daughter of the actor and playwright Adriaen van den Bergh (see 283, note 1) and also married to an actor, had years of experience behind her when she made her contract with the Theatre Governors. She was given a salary of f 4.50 per performance, from which she had to pay for her costumes (and a year later f 3. – 'except clothes'): the earnings of a first-rate actor and the same income as her husband. From the start of her career she had to play many female protagonists, taken over from the men who had impersonated them. In the season 1658–59 she appeared in no less than fifty different parts. Happily, her example soon brought other actresses to the stage; for some time, however, men continued to play women as well. Unfortunately, there are no documents of much interest concerning this first Schouwburg actress.

---

[1] In 1600 for instance, Jakob Duym (see 281) prescribes two fake breasts for a female character, 'unless she were [played by] a woman'.

297   Female impersonators

Anon., *De Geest van Tengnagel* (1652); ed. Oversteegen, (see 294) pp. 546–547, vss. 465–468, 497–503

There's de Bray[1] who presented them all,
  Damsel, Whore or Queen,
Proudly, when Keyzer[2] played the Emperor,
  He would play the Empress.

[...]

There's the great drag artist,[3]
  Who had his beard shaved
Till he was old. Of course, he became
  Hardly prettier, indeed quite ugly,
Both with age and because of the make-up.

But he would not retire
Before death ordered him to.

<hr />

¹ Pieter de Bray, d. 1639 (see also **269**).
² Thomas Gerritsz. de Keyzer (1597–1651, see also **269**.) The line contains a pun, because the name of the actor means 'the emperor'.
³ This concerns an otherwise unknown actor, Jan Bos.

XXV   Audiences

In contrast to later times, separate documents and important observations on audiences and audience behaviour are virtually non-existent in this period. Some information has been given in **288–9**, and for different kinds of audiences in illustrations, see **273–8**.

The opening scene of *Griane*, a tragicomedy by Bredero (see **288–9**) for the first time performed on 23 September 1612 by 'The Eglantine' of Amsterdam, presents a satirical portrait of audience behaviour, mainly among the lower classes, with many topical remarks. The characters lampooning the spectators are themselves lower class, a farmer and his wife, who serve to supply the comic relief in an otherwise tragically coloured melodramatic main action set in aristocratic circles. Scenes like this are not uncommon in the non-classical repertoire of the period, and one of their characteristics is that the actors play *to* the audience and involve them in the action on stage. Primary emphasis is laid on the rowdiness of youths.[1]

---

[1] The scene is written in rhyming couplets with lines of differing length, a type of verse used to characterise the lower classes and hence typical for comedies and farces in the first half of the seventeenth century. The Dutch farmer's dialect spoken here and the references to names and events make the passage hard to translate; the English version is but an approximation.

298   The playwright Bredero lampooning the audience, Amsterdam, 1612

G.A. Bredero, *Griane [...]*, Amsterdam: Cornelis Lodewycksz. van der Plasse, 1616. Ed. F. Veenstra (Culemborg: Tjeenk Willink/Noorduijn, 1973), pp. 119–22, vss. 3–44

Enter Bouwen-lang-lijf with his wife, Sinnelijcke Nel van Goosweghen[1]

BOUWEN [...] I cannot but believe that half the entire town is present.
  Well, why is this soft-head gaping![2] Have you never seen any people in your life before?
  Look at him, standing there,[3] grinning with all his teeth.
  Well, you dear little ninny! you darling, keep your hands to yourself.
NEL Shame on you slobbering and smoking tobacco here!
  Remember that other people almost get sick and retch from this fug,
  Your belching does not suit us, nor your stench,

Go to the tobacco-pubs, if you want to smoke.

BOUWEN Thirsty Dick is crying and raving and ranting and shouting,
>   And if he hears something beautiful, he's quite at a loss.

NEL Look! Meck and Lauwter are throwing peelings at each other,
>   If kids were doing it, they would have their bottoms smacked.

BOUWEN Dear me, how glad Machtelt is to be with her handsome boy friend,
>   She laughs so much, her mouth is nearly a fathom wide.

NEL O these braggarts! they don't know their arse from their elbow,
>   And this shrew over here, what a racket she makes on arriving.
>   [. . .]

BOUWEN This rabble from the rough parts of town,[4]
>   They're forever moving about and throwing shells at each other.
>   Lord, how badly these people behave! don't they? don't they?
>   [. . .]
>   Come, let us be off, o come, my Sinnelijcke Nel.

Enter Florendus, the Greek prince. [. . . and the aristocratic melodrama is about to begin.]

---

[1] The names could be translated as Baldwin Longbody and Tidy Nell.
[2] Someone in the audience.
[3] Most of the people mentioned here would be standing in the pit.
[4] Literally: from the ramparts or from the alleys.

XXVI Repertoire, dramatic theory, opposition to the theatre

A. REPERTOIRE

It is instructive to compare the repertoire of the first year in the Schouwburg at Amsterdam with that of one of its last seasons. The accounts are quoted for a few months of 1638 (**299**) and of 1662 (**300**). Expenses have not been given, only the takings. Authors' names are not mentioned in the accounts, but have been added here. With translations or adaptations (for the seventeenth century the difference is not relevant) the author and the name of the original play are added.

In the first year of the Schouwburg sixty-four performances were given of twelve plays, including one *tableau vivant*.[1] There were no performances from May up to and including August. The combination of a main play and an after-piece occurred only once; for the rest a performance consisted of one play. The vast majority were original Dutch plays.[2] About half of them had been performed before in the Dutch Academy (see **267**), for the others it was their première. Most of them were tragedies, either after the classical or after the 'Spanish' model; the latter provided also tragicomedies. Two entries concern comedies.

Of the plays mentioned for this year *Gysbreght van Aemstel* was the most popular (see **269**); during the lifetime of the first Schouwburg (1638–64) it had 110 performances. Runners-up were A. van den Berg's *Don Jeronimo* (see p. 378) (62 performances) and P.C. Hooft's historical tragedy *Geeraerdt van Velsen* (54 performances).

The brief conclusion is that for the first year of the new theatre an accent was put on original, mainly serious plays, partly written for the occasion.

---

[1] Meaning as a separate performance, not the *tableaux* within the plays.
[2] Of course their subjects and structure could have been derived from earlier sources, e.g. Hooft's comedy *Warenar* (see below).

299 Repertoire of the Amsterdam Schouwburg, 1638

Ontfang en Uijtgift (see **269**). Reproduced in E.Oey-de Vita and M. Geesink, *Academie en Schouwburg. Amsterdams toneelrepertoire 1617–1665* (Academy and Schouwburg. The Amsterdam Theatre Repertoire 1617–1665) (Amsterdam: Huis aan de Drie Grachten, 1983), pp. 86–7.

January

   3   J. van den Vondel, *Gysbreght van Aemstel*   228   4   –[1]

5	*Gysbreght van Aemstel*	211	15	–
6	*Gysbreght van Aemstel*	215	17	–
10	*Gysbreght van Aemstel*	263	9	–
11	*Gysbreght van Aemstel*	239	15	–
14	*Gysbreght van Aemstel*	187	12	–
17	*Gysbreght van Aemstel*	84	13	–
28	*Gysbreght van Aemstel*	168	17	–
31	*Gysbreght van Aemstel*	180	–	–

[...]

September

7	The Queen-Mother[2]	127	17	–
8	The Queen-Mother	120	17	–
16	Th.Rodenburgh, *Batavierse Vryagie*[3]	82	–	–
19	Anon., *Clorimond en Gloriana*[4]	184	9	–
20	*Clorimond en Gloriana*	273	19	–
21	*Batavierse Vryagie*	197	5	8
22	*Batavierse Vryagie*	135	11	–
23	*Clorimond en Gloriana*	126	6	8
24	*Clorimond en Gloriana*	114	18	–
26	*Batavierse Vryagie*	98	4	8
27	*Clorimond en Gloriana*	120	17	–

[...]

December

12	P.C. Hooft, *Warenar*[5]	78	5	–
13	*Warenar*	73	4	–
19	*Warenar*	69	9	8
20	*Warenar*	69	2	–
26	*Warenar*	100	8	–
27	*Warenar*	92	18	–
28	*Warenar*	38	15	–

---

[1] Guilders – stivers – cents; see **269**.
[2] The *tableaux vivants*, first shown on the river Amstel, at the entry of Maria de Médicis (see **278**).
[3] (Batavian Courtship), a pastoral play (1616).
[4] An unknown play.
[5] From 1616; like Molière's *Avare*, adapted from Plautus' *Aulularia*.

Twenty-five years later, the year's repertoire was both different from and similar to that of 1638.

The number of performances – ninety-two over the whole year – had grown into what was required for a full-fledged theatre in a large city. More plays were needed (approx. fifty main plays and about as many after-pieces) and it was therefore no longer possible to present so many premières as in 1638: most of the fare dated from a few decades ago, with an occasional new play coming in. The result was that instead of fairly continuous runs a constant change of plays took place (except for guest performances or the period of the fair and other occasional shows). The combination of a main play (nearly always a tragedy or tragicomedy) and a farce had now become standard, while a ballet might be added in between or replace the farce altogether. Ballets were no longer exceptional, and the Schouwburg could also be used for concerts: French 'Court Musicians' played there for the whole month of July. In 1662 the Schouwburg was closed only for August.

Most of the plays were still original Dutch ones.[1] When adapted, Spanish drama continued to be preferred; classicism had not yet set in. Of the serious plays, *Gysbreght* was now followed in popularity by *Le Cid* (79 performances for 1638–1664), Lope de Vega's *El amigo por fuerza* (Enforced Friendship) and *La fuerza lastimosa* (The Grievous Violence), and *Het Beleg en Ontzet van Leiden* (The Siege and Relief of Leiden) by Bontius/Vos (see **280**).

---

[1] It should be noted, however, that many farces, given as original works here, were in fact adapted from (foreign) novellas, collections of anecdotes and the like.

300   Repertoire of the Amsterdam Schouwberg, 1662

Ontfang en Uijtgift (see **269**). Reproduced in E. Oey-de Vita and M. Geesink (see **299**), pp. 142–4

January

2	*Gysbreght van Aemstel* / Is. Vos, *Klucht van de Moffin*[1]	169	14	–
5	*Gysbreght van Aemstel* / J. van Daalen, *Aardige Colikoquelle*[2]	100	5	–
9	Corneille, *Le Cid* / Is. Vos, *Robbert Leverworst*[3]	185	6	–
12	R. Anslo or L. van den Bosch, *Parysche Bruiloft / Paris Oordeel* / J. van Daalen, *Kale Edelman*[4]	192	–	–
16	*Le Cid* / W.D. Hooft, *Stijve Piet*[5]	180	1	–
19	G. Brandt, *Veynzende Torquatus* / Ballet[6]	169	3	–
23	Calderón, *La Vida es Sueño* / B. Fontein, *Sulleman*[7]	231	14	8
26	Lope de Vega, *El amigo por fuerza* / J.S. Colm, *Malle Jan Tot*[8]	179	13	–
30	Lope de Vega, *La fuerza lastimosa* / *Spanjaards Ballet*[9]	226	–	–

[…]

September

25	R. Bontius / Jan Vos, *Belegh ende Ontset van Leiden*[10]	488	6	–

26	Belegh ende Ontset van Leiden	401	16	–
27	Belegh ende Ontset van Leiden	319	12	8
28	Belegh ende Ontset van Leiden	333	3	8
29	Belegh ende Ontset van Leiden	246	4	8
30	Belegh ende Ontset van Leiden	159	5	8

[...]

December

4	Boisrobert, Le Couronnement de Darie / A.B. de Leeuw, Huwlijk van Niet[11]	199	6	8
7	Bredero, Moortje / Paris Oordeel[12]	87	2	8
11	Regnault, Blanche de Bourbon[13]	105	10	–
14	Blanche de Bourbon / Kale Edelman	113	9	–
18	Blanche de Bourbon / Robbert Leverworst	99	15	–
21	Blanche de Bourbon / Bolbackers Jan[14]	154	1	–
27	Gysbreght van Aemstel / Ballet	222	12	8
28	Gysbreght van Aemstel / Huwlijk van Niet	220	1	–

[1] (Farce of the Kraut Woman, 1642).
[2] (Fickle C.), a farce, (1655).
[3] (R. Liverwurst), a farce, (1650).
[4] (The Parisian Blood-Wedding), either the tragedy of that name by Reyer Anslo (1649) or that of Lambert van den Bosch (1645); (The Judgement of Paris), a ballet; (The Penniless Nobleman), a farce (1657).
[5] (Stiff P.), a farce (1628).
[6] (Feigning T.), a 'Senecan' tragedy (1645).
[7] Calderón's play 'Life is a Dream' (approx. 1636) was often performed (from 1645); Mr. Sullemans Soete Vriagie (Master Softy's Sweet Courtship), a farce with songs (1633), freely adapted from the English, The Black Man.
[8] Malle Jan Tots Boertige Vrijerij (Foolish J.T. Farcical Courtship) (1633).
[9] (Spaniards' Ballet).
[10] See 280. The play is by Bontius. Jan Vos, mentioned as co-author here, is the designer of its tableaux vivants. The exceptionally high revenues are partly due to these tableaux, partly to the fact that September was the time of the annual fair and all visitors would traditionally also attend a performance at the Schouwburg.
[11] The tragedy by François le Metel de Boisrobert, 'The Coronation of Darius', dates from 1641; De Leeuw's farce (1662) is after A.J. de Montfleury, Le Mariage de rien (The No-Marriage, 1660).
[12] For Moortje, see 289.
[13] Blanche de Bourbon, Reine d'Espagne (Blanche de Bourbon, Queen of Spain, 1641).
[14] (Roll-Baker's J.), a farce (1659).

B. DRAMATIC THEORY

Early Renaissance drama did not yet follow Aristotelian rules. As regards plot, it is characterised by a loosely connected series of situations, rather than by logical development; not even a thematic unity is guaranteed in every case. The situations often focus on stock elements from Seneca, formulated in fixed rhetorical forms and demonstrating moral truths, while the action in between serves only to connect these static elements into a story.

Some of all this is discernible from the Preface of one of the many plays on the murder of William the Silent in 1584.

301   Play structure before classicism

G. van Hogendorp, *Truer-spel van de Moordt begaen aen Wilhelm, by der Gratie Gods Prince van Oraengien, etc.* (Tragedy of the Murder committed on William, by the Grace of God Prince of Orange, etc.) (Amsterdam: Cornelis vander Plasse, 1617). Reproduced in Dr. F.K.H. Kossmann (ed.), *De spelen van Gijsbrecht van Hogendorp* (The Plays of G.v.H.) (The Hague: Martinus Nijhoff, 1932), pp. 51–2

The play is divided into five parts. In the first part one is shown the King [of Spain]'s grandiloquent bragging, the consultation with the Inquisition, the qualities of False Religion and Superstition, their connection with the Inquisition, who at their desire summons Megaera, Tisiphone and Alecto up from hell. It finishes with a chorus.

The second act shows the nature of the hellish Furies that motivate most Papists, and above all those accursed murderers. There is also the dispute between False Religion, Superstition and the Murderer. Then follows the farewell of the Murderer from the Court of Parma. The Chorus relates the main cause of Spain's anger against these countries.

The third part shows a conversation between the Prince of Orange and his Steward; during which the Princess Louise enters and relates the depressing dream she had. Following which, a song in praise of the Prince and his lineage – then there is the arrival of the Murderer at the Prince's court, and the sly way he glosses over the [real] reasons for his coming there. It finishes with a song in praise of the defence of the Fatherland.

In the fourth part there is a conversation between the Princess Louise and her Nurse. The Murderer is supported by False Religion and hotly encouraged in his schemes – she also warns the hellish Furies not to leave until the murder has been committed. There follows a narration of many events in the Prince's life. After that, this most pious-hearted Prince's unworthy end. It finishes with a lament.

The fifth part: the laments of the extremely sorrowful Princess Louise; her Nurse's comforting words; laments from the States General, vowing nevermore to forget this wicked murder. Time concludes the play, explaining what revenge for the death of the Prince has been taken by the bravery of his children and the heroes of his blood.

The neo-classical principles of Renaissance drama found their most renowned expression with Daniel Heinsius, whose *De tragoediae constitutione* influenced scholars and authors all over Europe, and especially in France. Heinsius (1580–1655) was not only active as a Professor of Poetry, Greek, Politics and History at Leiden, but also as a poet in Latin and

Dutch and as a playwright in Latin. He first published his treatise on drama in 1611 as an addendum to his edition of Aristotle's *Poetics*, rewriting and enlarging it for its second edition of 1643 into a very clear exposition of Aristotelian dramatic theory, with his own comments and examples. The fragment on dramatic unity quoted here should be read in contrast to the model of drama structure implied in 301. The first edition of Heinsius' text precedes Van Hogendorp's drama by a few years: obviously it took some time before the new ideas on drama structure were put into practice.

302   The neo-classical model

Dan. Heinsii de tragoediae constitutione (...), 2nd enl. edn. (Leiden: Elzevier, 1643 (1611), pp. 33–8). Quoted from: Daniel Heinsius, *On Plot in Tragedy*, trans. by Paul R. Sellin and John J. McManmon, ed. Paul R. Sellin (Northridge, California: San Fernando Valley State College, 1971), pp. 25–7.

One must also observe whether the action has unity. For the most part, things are considered to have unity in two ways. Either they are separate and simple [...], or, being composed of many parts, they acquire unity after the several parts have blended together. No learned person has said that the fable must have unity in the former sense. Indeed, we have already suggested that in tragic action there are two requirements: right magnitude, and equal proportioning of its parts among themselves. Neither seems possible if the action is one and simple [...]. Even since antiquity, this has misled many, and still continues to do so. Thus not a few in the past believed the action of one person to be one (think of Hercules, Theseus, Achilles, Ulysses and others), which is stupid and false insofar as generally it is possible for many things to happen through one and the same agent that cannot readily be conjoined and related to the same end. [...]

Besides, just as a house does not consist *of* a single thing, but *is* one, so the action of a tragedy does not consist *of* one thing but *is* one. For unity to emerge from multiplicity, however, above all requires such parts as agree and can be fitly joined together. This likewise holds for an action too. An action does not become one from all kinds of disconnected actions, since an action becomes one only from actions so inter-related that if one of them is posited, another follows out of either necessity or verisimilitude. This is evident in any properly constructed tragedy. Consider, for example, Sophocles' *Ajax*. Deprived of his weapons Ajax grows indignant, and because he is angry at being checked, he storms and rages. In such a condition, he therefore acts with hardly a jot of sense, and at last he insanely slaughters the sheep instead of Ulysses. When he comes to himself, however, he is overwhelmed with disgrace, takes his own life, and is denied burial. It is these events, rather than all the things that ever happened to Ajax throughout his entire life, which fittingly hang together. But not just any one of them suffices *per se*. All those which truly belong together form that single action of which they are the parts. [...] A part of a whole is a true one when, if it is omitted, either the whole is disturbed or no longer remains a whole. For if a part is such that either its absence or presence leaves the whole unaffected, it cannot be called part of the whole. Such is the nature of episodes, which we shall discuss later,[1] or of very disparate actions by one and the same man. Such, for example, is Ajax's duel with Hector, as described by Homer in detail, which has no relevance to the *Ajax* of Sophocles.

---

[1] Heinsius does leave room for digressions, once the unity of the plot has been established. 'Indeed, what household articles and furnishings are to a home, digressions and episodes are to a tragedy' (p. 25).

C. OPPOSITION TO AND DEFENCE OF THE THEATRE

From the beginning, the Reformation and condemnation of the theatre went hand in hand, partly continuing what the Church Fathers had taught in the matter. Nowhere was the opposition as strong and enduring as in Holland and Scotland, with England, parts of Germany, France and Switzerland following at some distance. The first Dutch vituperations date from the last quarter of the sixteenth century, and from the 1630s a plethora of treatises were published, including excerpts and translations from famous foreign authors, like Prynne and, later, Witherspoon. Performance, not drama, was the main target, especially the performance of sacred subjects.

Gysbertus Voetius (1589–1676), clergyman and Professor of Theology at Utrecht, was one of the main representatives of orthodox Calvinism in Holland. His *Disputatio* of 1643 is written in the time-honoured scholastic form, with numbered questions and answers, theses, arguments, refutation of counter-arguments, conclusions, etc.

303   A theologian's objections to the theatre, 1643

Gysberti Voetii Disputatio de Comoediis, Dat is, Twist-redening van de Schouspeelen. Gehouden en voorgestelt in de Hooge-School van Uitrecht. Uit de Latijnsche in de Neerduitsche taal vertaalt door B.S. (Gysbertus Voetius, D. d. C., Being a Critical Argument on Theatrical Performances. Given and proposed in the Illustrious School of Utrecht. Translated from Latin into the Dutch Language by B.S.) (Amsterdam: Jasper Adamsz Star, 1650)

After an introduction Voetius raises the question what kind of performances could be allowed under Christian rule. Guided by his own religious convictions and by numerous spiritual authorities, mainly Church Fathers and contemporaneous fellow theologians, he is out to condemn nearly all plays. The only kind of performances for which Voetius makes a grudging allowance, because he does not think them intrinsically evil, are those which represent the actions of strong and virtuous heroes, demonstrating not their faith (Christian subjects are forbidden) but general qualities like justice, generosity, etc. There is, however, one strict proviso:

[These might be permitted] if the [existing] performance practice were to be changed, that is, if the following would be banned: disguisings, women mixing with men, men posing as women, abuse of God's name, mockeries or old plays,[1] follies, improper jests, dancing and all that goes with it, and the implements of jugglers, fools and such like. Thus purified, performances seem to be allowed by some, as an exercise in eloquence. And therefore if they are nothing else but discourse or enunciation of dialogue, I see no reason why one should try to attract competent actors, rather than masters and students of eloquence. [...] And if the intention were to add something resembling a performance, this could perhaps not be judged as in itself strictly forbidden; but one should seriously consider: 1. whether it is of any use; 2. whether it is rather harmless; 3. whether it does not seem to look like the art of playing; 4. and whether no pretext is found for defending the theatre and for making it easier to lapse into it. [pp. 37–8]

Voetius' explicit arguments for this condemnation, known from a long tradition, result in a set of propositions and more detailed conclusions:

1. That stage actions may not be presented when their subject is, or has the semblance of, holy matter; which is allowed to the present day by Popedom [...], being a public imitation of paganism.
2. That stage players, and especially hired ones,[2] or those who make acting their profession, even when they play purposely for nothing, are not to be admitted to the community of the church, or to remain there. [...]
3. That Christians may not watch them. This goes especially for girls and women. The propriety of that sex must not be seduced by such actions, to avoid their falling in the end into too much looseness of speech, immorality, shamelessness, not to mention worse things; – because they dress up and adorn themselves as if vying with one another, and are taken there by men or youths, coming to watch, but also to be watched themselves. [...]
4. That the faithful should be kept away from those performances by ecclesiastical punishments. This has always been the practise of the old church, which permitted nobody to be baptised, unless they had renounced the Devil with all his decorated theatre performances; which is also the custom in the present-day Reformed Church [...].
5. That Ministers may never be permitted to attend performances, not even private ones. [...]
6. That actors, who have said farewell to their living, may not be encouraged to attend church services, at least not as a rule. [According to St Augustine] they who had married an actress were excluded from the holy congregation. What should be done in exceptional cases, as occasioned by necessity or other important reasons, is to be investigated prudently.

7. That those people are not without sin who furnish the costs for these performances, or act as theatre governors, or show them to the people, or produce them to be shown, or secretly train the actors, demonstrating what they will have to ape. [...]

8. That those people are not innocent either who write plays for these actors and supply the same to them. [...]

9. That it is particularly horrendous and damnable to make or perform plays which mock the word of God, orthodox religion, holy worship, and church services. [...] [pp. 75–9]

---

[1] Probably meaning classical comedies (Plautus, etc.).
[2] In 1643, the year of Voetius' *Disputatio*, professional acting in Holland had not yet fully developed, 'hired players' meaning semi-professional ones.

From the end of the 1630s, Vondel was a main target for the Protestant clergy. The author had not only been converted to Roman Catholicism but also started to write a series of Biblical plays which (initially) were highly successful in the Schouwburg. Moreover, he was naturally polemical, challenging and lampooning the clergy in his poetry whenever an occasion presented itself. The Prefaces to some of his plays present an introduction to dramatic theory or a defence of the theatre. He also published a separate essay to the same end.

304   Vondel defends the theatre, 1654

Joost van den Vondel, *Berecht aan alle kunstgenooten, en begunstigers van de tooneelspelen* (Message to all Fellow Artists and Patrons of Drama), Preface to his tragedy *Lucifer* (Amsterdam: Abraham de Wees, 1654). Reproduced in Vondel's *Werken* (see 270), vol. 5, 1931, pp. 607–14.

It is true that the Fathers of the old Church banned actors, even when converted, from the community of the Church, and vehemently opposed the theatre of their days; but it is to be noted that both the times and the arguments were completely different from ours. In many places the world lay still deeply sunk in pagan idolatry. [...] Therefore the aim of these performances was indeed to serve as a powerful support of the blind idolatry of paganism, to the glory of its gods. This was a deep-rooted horror, and its destruction cost the first heroes of the cross and the ever struggling Church much sweat and blood – but it has long since died out and leaves no vestiges in Europe today. That the Holy Fathers rebuked the theatre, not only for the reason mentioned, but also because it was an immoral abuse, publicly and shamelessly showing young men, women and virgins naked, together with other obscenities, was therefore necessary and honourable, and still would be so under the same circumstances. But when this has been considered, let us not all too readily dismiss the usefulness of edifying and amusing plays.[1] Holy and virtuous examples serve as a mirror to teach the espousal of morality and religiousness; and the avoidance of lapses and the miseries ensuing. The aim and intention of true tragedy is to purge people by fear and pity. The theatre is an exercise for schoolchildren and adolescents, to learn languages, eloquence, wisdom, discipline, morality, and good manners; and it impresses those tender hearts and senses with virtues and apt behaviour that will stay with them into old age [...].

As regards biblical material, it is held against us that one ought not to play with holy matters; and this would seem to be justified, because our language happens to make use of the word *play*. But even for those who can only stammer a word or two in Greek, it is common knowledge that the word is not used in this sense in Greek and Latin: for *tragoidia* is a compound, originally meaning Goat Song (...). So if we are to be chided mercilessly for the word *play*, what are we to do with organ playing, with David playing songs on the harp, with playing the ten strings of the psaltery[2] and other flute- and string-playing, introduced by several non-Catholics in their religious services? They who understand this distinction may still rebuke the abuse of the stage, but will no longer criticise its rightful use and will not begrudge our youth and art-loving citizens this marvellous and indeed divine invention, this virtuous pastime, this honey-sweet relief from the worries of life [...].

[1] Meaning tragedies and comedies.
[2] The instrument is mentioned in Psalm 32:2.

The position of the civic authorities regarding the theatre had always been a sensible middle distance between the opposing parties, trying on the one hand to keep the clergy at bay and the populace quiet, and on the other to maintain their right as the sole judges to decide whether to permit or ban theatre performances. They always had to be careful, though, because a political issue was involved, the clergy and populace being the strongest adherents of the Stadtholder. P.C. Hooft (1581–1647), the pre-eminent poet, playwright, historian and high magistrate, presents the authorities' point of view. The quotation concerns the year 1562, but is equally applicable to Hooft's own time.

305   The position of the authorities *vis-à-vis* the theatre, 1642

P.C. Hooft, *Nederlandsche Historiën* (*History of the Netherlands*) (Amsterdam: Henrik Wetstein and Pieter Scéperus/Leiden: Dan. van Dalen/Utrecht: Willem van der Water, 1703), I, p. 36. (1st edn Amsterdam: Louis Elzevier, 1642)

[The Rhetoricians] were accustomed not only to publish and hand out diverse poems but even to perform, in public, complete plays with speaking characters. In these they confronted everyone, now jokingly now seriously, with their duties. An edifying amusement and a kind of song which is of no small service to curb the emotions of the masses – provided that the authorities beat the time. Orators having disappeared now, there are only two ways left to lead the people by the ears: the pulpit and the stage. Therefore the government has no means more powerful than this to drill the mob into quiet submission and to maintain their proper behaviour. This runs counter to the authority of the clergy, because it seems they are bound to thwart the governing powers of those who do not manage to come up to their standards. And nobody should imagine that the distribution of pamphlets or printed books could prevail over the sharpness of a glib tongue, able to persuade a great number of different people in no more than an hour, and failing this, to convey the emotions of the speaker by other means.[1]

[1] It is not quite clear whether the last sentence concerns the preachers or the actors. Perhaps both, and in any case Hooft is stressing the power of vocal delivery and gesture versus written matter as regards their effect on the general public.

Period II: 1665–1794

XXVII Contractual and organisational documents

In Amsterdam, as elsewhere in the Netherlands, the establishment of the civic theatre as a professional enterprise entailed an ever growing number of laws and regulations for the actors and audience. These were issued by the Bailiff and/or by Burgomasters and Aldermen, so that the Theatre Governors could appeal to the highest city authorities. Over the years these rules tended to become more detailed and bureaucratic.

306 Preservation of order, 1687

City Archives Amsterdam, Handvesten, p. 278. Reproduced in Wybrands (1873), pp. 246–8.

The Gentlemen of the Court of the City of Amsterdam, having ascertained that a large number of misdemeanours are committed daily by wanton and wilful people, tending to the ruin of the Theatre; and also that an additional ruling concerning actors is required; have agreed to order, decree and rule as follows:

I.

That no one is permitted to make any clamour or din or be a party to any other wantonness in the Theatre, either in word or deed, on pain of a fine of three guilders for the first time, and the same for the second time plus, in addition, a correction to be effected by the judiciary.

II.

That no one is to tear down the playbills announcing what will be performed, on pain of a 25-guilder fine for the first time, and for the second time the same fine plus a correction by the law, according to the circumstances.

III.

Neither shall anyone be permitted to put up playbills in the city or to publish any on behalf of those who might come to perform outside the jurisdiction of this City;

the fine will be fifty guilders for the first time, and for the second time the same penalty of fifty guilders, plus judicial correction.

IV.

That no authors or others, shall be allowed to connive, form cliques or associations so as to insult the Theatre or its Governors and to ruin the income of the said Theatre on pain of a thousand-guilder fine for the first time and the same penalty for the second time plus judicial correction over and above that, according to the circumstances.

V.

And in order to avert any wilfulness, rowdiness or any other misconduct in the Theatre, the aforementioned Gentlemen of the Court have hereby authorised the Lord Bailiff to place two of his servants in said Theatre to escort those who have been charged by the Governors to be guilty of misdemeanour, and also to report them to Their Lordships, if necessary.

VI.

And finally, that the actors and actresses, having made their contracts with the Governors of the Theatre, and having signed them, shall abide by and live up to them faithfully; and that if they should happen to break them, leave their job, or enter the employ of others in order to play elsewhere, action shall be taken against the same, just as it is usual to start proceedings against servant-girls who leave their position or carry on in any irregular way.[1]

All the above-mentioned fines to be distributed as follows: one third in aid of the Orphanage and Old Men's Home, one third in aid of the Governors of the Theatre and the remaining third for the benefit of whoever will be administering the fine. – Thus decreed on the 13th of June, 1687. [...]

---

[1] Seventy years later (1757) this penalty was specified (and made more severe because of the incessant violations) in one of the many sequels to these rules: offenders were to be put on bread and water for a period of six weeks.

307   Theatre laws, 1748

Wetten voor de Speelders en Speelsters op den Schouwburg (Laws for the Actors and Actresses at the S.), City Archives, Amsterdam. Reproduced in N.C. Vogel, 'De arbeidsovereenkomst van tooneelisten' (The Employment Contract of Theatre Artists), diss. Univ. of Amsterdam (Amsterdam: C.A. Spin & Zoon, 1899), p. 176

LAWS FOR THE ACTORS AND ACTRESSES IN THE SCHOUWBURG

1. On the usual acting days actors and actresses are obliged to be present in the

Schouwburg at 3 o'clock, whether they are to play or not, under penalty of 6 stivers.[1]

2. All will have to content themselves with such costumes as will be assigned to them by the costumier, under penalty of 12 stivers.

3. Anyone who does not make his entrance at the proper time and without having to be warned by others, will be fined 1 guilder.

4. Anyone who does not know his part, so that he will be hissed or jeered at, will be fined 1 guilder.

5. Anyone who is absent from a rehearsal or arrives after the fixed time, will be fined 10 stivers.

6. In winter no one may leave his dressing-room before showing the house manager that fire and light have been put out, under penalty of 10 stivers.

7. Anyone found drunk will be fined 1 guilder.

8. Anyone abusing someone, or if they abuse one another, will be fined 1 guilder each.

9. Anyone hitting someone, or if they hit one another, will be fined 6 guilders each.

10. Dressers[2] will have to be present in the Schouwburg at half past two and may not leave at night before they have assisted the costumier in putting the costumes away, under penalty of 10 stivers.

11. Anyone smoking tobacco[3] behind, under or above the stage, will be fined 12 stivers.

12. On performance days no actors or actresses will be allowed to take a seat in the pit.

---

[1] A stiver is five cents, the twentieth part of a guilder; see 269.
[2] The Dutch has the female form.
[3] Meaning pipe tobacco; cigars appeared only later.

B. OTHER RELATIONS WITH THE AUTHORITIES

Dutch culture in the seventeenth and eighteenth centuries was an affair of the 'burghers' themselves, unencumbered by the governing standards of a central royal court. The House of Orange and their Stadtholder's Court at The Hague were nevertheless not without importance as patrons of the arts.

The *Tooneel-aantekeningen* [*Theatre Notes*] of Marten Corver (see 332), were written in the form of a long polemical letter to the author Simon Styl, who in his *Leven van Jan Punt* (Life of J.P.) (1781) – the first biography of a Dutch actor – had defended the old theatrical style and attacked Corver's reforms (see 339). Corver's long stage experience and the wealth of concrete information he provides make his book one of the most impressive and authoritative sources for the Dutch theatre of the eighteenth century.

308   Patronage of the Stadtholder's court, 1767–1774

M. Corver, *Tooneel-Aantekeningen, vervat in een omstandige Brief aan den Schrijver van het Leven van Jan Punt (...)* (Theatre Notes, Comprised in an Elaborate Letter to the Author of the Life of J.P.) (Leiden: Cornelis Heyligert, 1786),. p. 154

With regard to the patronage of the court [...], His Highness[1] took a subscription in 1767 for six months of the year; and so I was obliged to play here[2] during six months for 3000 guilders, a sum on which I often lost, especially in the years 1770, 1771 and 1772,* when because of the prejudices of our country I lost 5000 guilders – a hefty blow to a growing concern. For seven years I received the aforementioned sum of 3000 guilders from His Highness.

* [Corver's footnote] In the three years mentioned, there was no permit in Rotterdam and in the first two, there was no permit in Utrecht; both due to the death of cattle.

[1] The Prince Stadtholder William V.
[2] At The Hague.

In 1660 The Hague got its first public theatre, built by the actor and theatrical *entrepreneur* Johan Baptist van Fornenberg (see 32, p. 352, 280, 292, 293, 333).

There was a difference between theatrical life at The Hague and that of the other cities, including Amsterdam. Being the residence of the Stadtholder and his court, The Hague had always had performances intended for the aristocracy only. The courtiers generally spoke French and therefore rarely visited Dutch performances, but went to see French standing or visiting companies, who had their own theatre in the Stadtholder's riding-school or the adjacent fives court. The French actors had to obey court rules, whereas performances by Dutch companies at The Hague came under the same municipal rules as elsewhere. Apparently, the Stadtholder prevented any general regulation which could disadvantage the French companies.

Meanwhile, the regulation quoted here was extremely profitable to Fornenbergh. Not only did he obtain the monopoly of the public theatre at The Hague, but also he was obliged to pay a mere 10 cents (2 stivers, Dutch: *stuivers*) for the poor out of an extremely expensive fee of four shillings for the pit (a Dutch *schelling* was 30 cents, so this meant 120 cents or 1.20 guilders). Shortly before, he had buttered up the authorities by promising to give a lump sum of *f* 200 to the poor, promising to double the amount if the French actors did not cause him too much disadvantage. See also 310, note 3.

309   The Hague: the Stadtholder prevents the authorities fixing new entrance fees; Fornenbergh gains the monopoly, 1679

Reproduced in E.F. Kossmann (ed.), *Das Niederländische Faustspiel des siebzehnten Jahrhunderts (De Hellevaart van Dr. Joan Faustus)* (The Dutch Faust Play of the seventeenth C. (The Descent into Hell of Dr J.F.), The Hague: Martinus Nijhoff, 1910), p. 115

On 17 November 1679 the Burgomasters earnestly urged and instructed Johan Baptist van Fornenbergh, leader of the Dutch comedians, and his companions, that each person visiting the theatre would have to pay two stivers for the poor. Being the same stivers contained and included in the four shillings which are paid for sitting in the pit, and for the taking of which a qualified person would be appointed by the authorities. Which the aforesaid John Baptist undertook to obey, and requested on his part that if from time to time another troupe of Dutch comedians were to ask permission to perform here in The Hague, they should not be given leave to do so, unless their performances were to take place in the theatre built some years ago by himself, Baptist, on the Denneweg, which they would have to rent from him for a reasonable sum; which the aforesaid Burgomasters also granted to said Baptist. A short time afterwards the Burgomasters heard that the aforesaid two stivers would not be taken, because they were given to understand that His Highness [the Stadtholder] did not wish the French comedians to be thus burdened, even though the same levy had been imposed on them by the Lords of the Court.

C. CONTRACTS

Jacob van Rijndorp (1663–1720), playwright, actor and company leader, was Fornenbergh's successor at The Hague and in 1705 built the first municipal theatre of Leiden. His troupe also travelled frequently to foreign countries, performing in Copenhagen, Hamburg and Brussels. Italian companies had been visitors to the Netherlands, albeit irregular ones, since the late sixteenth century.

310   An Italian company rents the theatre in Leiden, 1717

Reproduced in E.F. Kossmann (1910), p. 148

Today 27 August 1717 there appeared before me, Johan van Castel, [...] Mr Jacob van Rijndorp, director of the respective theatres of the cities of Leiden and The Hague, known to me, notary, on the one hand, and Sr Augustus Babron on the other. Said parties declare that they have come to an agreement with one another, to the effect that the latter party will perform [items] from the Italian repertoire, with the latter party's own Italian troupe, from 8 November to 18 December next in the theatre of the first party in Leiden, which the latter party shall have at his reasonable disposal, on condition that the latter party shall ensure that all damage done to same theatre will be charged to the latter party and shall be fully made good.

The first party shall supply the latter party with four sets for reasonable use during the aforementioned period, to wit a Wood, a Court, a Street, and a Chamber, together with four suits of Roman clothes, being three men's and one woman's apparel; [furthermore,] a doctor's coat, two Fury costumes, two Turkish and two modern coats, ditto two farmer's clothes for men. At the expiration of this contract, all these shall be returned undamaged by the latter party to the first party without any further ado.

This being agreed, the latter party is obliged to provide a good troupe of actors and actresses, together with musicians, attendants and a person who furnishes light and heating (the latter to be appointed by the first party, though all costs are to be charged to the latter party). And in case at night, after the performance, a fire were to break out in the theatre (which God forbid), the latter party will not be obliged to pay for any damage to the aforementioned theatre. Furthermore, the latter party will be required to bear the costs of candles and oil, the printing and posting of playbills, and whatever else may be required for the performances.

For all the aforementioned items the latter party has promised, which he hereby confirms, to pay the first party a net third part of the complete proceeds [...].

The latter party is obliged to have the playbills printed in Dutch, though the titles of the plays and the comedies[1] may be in French. [...]

Similarly, the first party shall receive a rightful third part of the profits on [the hiring out of] foot-stoves[2] and cushions, to be drawn and received in the manner mentioned above; that is, after the costs thereof have been deducted.

The alms for the poor, which will have to be paid in the aforementioned place at the aforementioned time, will be deducted from the third part of the first party.[3] [...]

Furthermore, the respective parties are also in agreement that if, within the space of six weeks, the latter party can obtain official permission to perform in The Hague from 10 or 11 January for a period of four to five weeks, the first party will make its theatre in the Buitenhof[4] at The Hague available to the latter party, on all the foregoing terms [...].

---

[1] I.e., the main pieces and the farces (after-pieces).
[2] Foot-stoves served to support the feet, but mainly to warm them, a small brazier with smouldering coals or peat having been put inside.
[3] How much the poor received could vary according to period and city. For Van Rijndorp's predecessor Fornenbergh see **309**. In 1702, Van Rijndorp had to hand over a lump sum of ƒ 300, – per year. If this amount is stated correctly, he also came off cheap: in 1711 at Utrecht for instance, the theatre had to pay ƒ 1000, – for twenty performances; in 1712 ƒ 20, – and later ƒ 10, – per performance; in 1719

ƒ 500, – for the period from 10 July to 26 September; in 1728 ƒ 620, – for the same period.
⁴ Lit. The Outer Court, a street in The Hague where two of the temporary theatre venues were.

Until the end of the eighteenth century Rotterdam, as yet no more than a provincial trading town with only 55,000 inhabitants, had to be content with temporary theatres for travelling companies. It was only in 1765 that a liveryman opened a more permanent accommodation in the form of a wooden theatre in a storehouse. After the Amsterdam theatre fire in 1772 (see 314), a number of Amsterdam actors settled there under the leadership of Jan Punt. This was the first (permanent) company of professional players in Rotterdam. However, the venture did not succeed, for the actors were too old, did not possess any good costumes and could not offer what people most wanted to see, namely opera. Finally a few merchants took the decision to provide Rotterdam with a well-equipped stone-built theatre. This opened a year later, in 1774. Punt was initially in charge, but the Governors were soon on the look-out for a new director to take his place. They invited his rival Marten Corver and expressed the wish to engage him, first as an actor. Since a full engagement was not what he wanted (he had his own company at The Hague and Leiden), Corver suggested playing 'some roles' in Rotterdam.

That he was allowed to choose, cast and direct the plays in which he was going to perform, shows his rank in the theatre hierarchy, and also that from the start he was in fact to function as a director. Two years later, in 1776, he was appointed as such. Punt hung on for another year, acting and house-managing, then took his leave. Corver's directorship did not last long either.

311 Proposal for a director's contract, Rotterdam, 1774
Corver (1786), pp. 166

Whereupon we began to discuss the fee and came to an agreement to perform twice a month. This meant eighteen plays every nine months (because they closed down for three months during the summer). I was to decide on the choice of the plays myself. I was to be in charge of arranging them, the afterpieces included. I was to set up three rehearsals for each play and direct them and the performances by myself; and all this for the sum of 1400 guilders,[1] on condition that I supply my own costumes and pay for my own transport there and back and my own board and lodging. This agreement was made without any written contract or signature, on our word of honour; and for two years, we faithfully observed it.

[1] At the time, ƒ 2000 would be the top salary for a first-class full-time actor. The average income amounted to approx. ƒ 700 and a novice actor or an extra would get not more than ƒ 300 (technical personnel and musicians would receive even less). Most actors had to have some job on the side. On the other hand, acting was often a family business, so that the joint income of husband, wife and children could represent a less gloomy state of affairs; and during the summer vacation, their work as members of travelling companies provided some extra money. In 1774/75, when he was the leader of the Rotterdam company, Punt and his wife earned a combined income of ƒ 4000 plus ƒ 300 for the management of the theatre.

XXVIII   Playhouses and Performance venues

In the 1660s the form and technique of the Amsterdam Schouwburg (see 272–4) were no longer considered to be in accordance with modern taste. The baroque repertoire required quicker scene changes and more machinery for spectacular effects. Also, French classicism, which was soon to become the dominant style, needed a central perspective and a deeper stage. Foreign theatres could provide the example of what such a fashionable stage looked like and how it worked.

At the end of 1663 the Schouwburg governors gave the architect Philip Vingboons the commission to design a new theatre on the site of the old one. This second Amsterdam Schouwburg opened on 26 May 1665.[1] Its building had cost ƒ 36,663.

The reference to Venice in the quotation is interesting, but no specific Venetian theatre or other connection with Venice has been found to explain it.

[1] After only nine performances it was closed for half a year because of the war with England.

312   Why the first Amsterdam Schouwburg needs rebuilding, 1664

T. van Domselaer, *Beschrijvinge van Amsterdam*, 1665 (see 268), p. 201

But this stage [of Van Campen's theatre, built in 1637], being too wide and too shallow, and also because its weight and unwieldiness do not allow easy changes every time the plays require it, will presently be knocked down, together with most of the interior of the entire theatre, in order to replace it by a new stage after the Italian fashion, now in use in Venice, with all imaginable and swift changes of perspectives [...] and many sorts of flying works, called machines; so that the spectators will be able to observe all details of the location of the plays, such as palaces, cities, villages, halls, landscapes, courts, woods, rocks, mountains, dunes, beaches, seas, heaven, hell, with their appropriate swarms of all kinds of spirits, animals, birds, fish, &c., as natural as they are lively, together with the actions and movements of the players, while they hear them speak their parts. About which not only this city, but all of Holland, nay all the Netherlands, never having seen such novelties before, will be full of admiration and high rapture.

313   General View of the Stage, Seen from the Auditorium

Engraving by N. van Frankendaal after W. Writs, 1772–74. *Atlas van de Waereldberoemde Koopstad Amsterdam [...] (Atlas of the World – Famous City of A., J.B. Elwe, 1804), pp. 11–12. (1st ed. Amsterdam: R. Ottens a.o., 1767–75)*

The foreground in Writs' illustration of the stage and part of the auditorium shows the parapet, separating the pit from the standing-room. We note that the ground floor was lit by lanterns. The set in the illustration is The New Sun Court, representing the heavenly palace of Apollo in an adaptation of Vondel's tragedy *Phaethon* (1663); see also **320, 325**. The orchestra pit seated sixteen musicians. Conspicuously absent in this citizens' theatre was a royal box; when in June 1768 the Stadtholder William V and his family visited this theatre for the first time, a magnificent and large box was made for the occasion, but after the summer, when all and sundry had admired it, the royal seat was taken away again.

It is not known for certain how many people this theatre could seat in all its different periods. In 1678, a year for which the accounts do for once mention the number of spectators for the different classes of seats and their fees, a successful performance would have some 700 people in the audience. The spectators first paid a general entrance fee and afterwards a surcharge according to the kind of ticket they had bought. Prices varied from 20 cents for the gallery to 70 cents for the dress circle. The price of a box, regardless of whether one came alone or with five others, was ƒ 3.15.

The boxes were built as late as 1768, i.e. shortly before the print was made. In the same years a separate exit at the back of the theatre was made for the populace. Both reflect the wish of the higher *bourgeoisie* to keep a greater distance from the masses and to adopt clearer class distinctions (see also **383**).

At the front of the stage one saw on both sides two round columns and behind these two flat pilasters, both of the Corinthian order. Their shafts were red, and the bases and capitals represented white marble.[1] The columns were covered by a cornice, with an arch on top of it, likewise representing red marble. Between these columns one saw two well-made statues on their pedestals, which statues also showed white marble, and the pedestals red. One of these statues, representing the Muse Melpomene, stood on the right side of the stage;[2] she was provided with a sceptre, a crown, and a poniard, as emblems expressing Tragedy. The other one, representing the Muse Thalia, stood on the left side of the stage; she was identified by a mask and a shawm, being signs of Comedy. Both statues, but mainly the first one, had been sculpted most skilfully. Under the said arch hung five chandeliers, each counting twelve candles, as can be seen in the illustration. Behind the arch and the columns hung the curtain.

[1] In fact, they were made of wood, like everything else in the building and also the building itself.
[2] Meaning stage-right.

313

314   The Fire of the second Amsterdam Schouwburg, 1772

Engraving by S. Fokke, 1772. Nederlands Theater-Instituut, Amsterdam, GD 101–19. The caption reads: 'Portrayal of the first blazing flame in the Amsterdam Schouwburg on Monday 11 May 1772 in the evening just after half past eight.'

Theatre fires have been rare in the Netherlands. On 13 August 1754 a newly built 'French Comedy' for opera and drama burnt down in Amsterdam, a few hours after a performance of Molière's *Misanthrope* and La Ribardière's 'opéra-comique' *Les Soeurs rivales* (The Rival Sisters). When the fire was discovered there was no help from the fire-brigade because in order to avoid the city jurisdiction the venue had been erected outside the city walls, and an old law forbade the gates to be opened after 9.30 in the evening. This did not cause any stir because foreigners were involved.

The fire of the second Amsterdam Schouwburg on 11 May 1772 on the other hand was followed by tremendous commotion. The disaster took place during a performance of P.A. Monsigny's opera *Le Déserteur* (The Deserter),[1] played by a Flemish opera company under the direction of Jacob Toussaint Neyts, who had rented the theatre for the summer season. Too much tallow had been put into the wing-ladders, and because their bolts had been closed to create darkness in a prison scene, one of the wings grew too hot and caught fire. Only minutes later the wooden building was ablaze. The audience, some five hundred people, panicked, some exit doors did not work, attempts to extinguish the fire were to no avail and in less than two hours the theatre had burnt down, with luckily no more than eighteen casualties.

The after-effects of the disaster were to be expected. It greatly activated the Protestant church in its opposition to the stage, and although the authorities admonished them to keep quiet, many ministers rose in their pulpits to present the accident as an intervention and a warning by the Almighty. Violent polemics followed, with no fewer than nearly two hundred pamphlets and many poems from both sides, some well-known authors taking part. The disaster was portrayed in at least a dozen different engravings.

The illustration has again a high degree of exactness in so far as the startled characters on stage exactly fit the action taking place according to the play. Up stage at the far right, two stage hands appear to see what is happening. Note the practicability of the door at the left, known from many plays and illustrations, and again showing some similarity to the English stage.

¹ After Mercier's play of the same name.

314

XXXIX   Stage presentation

A. STAGING METHODS

The innovations in the staging methods of this period generally followed what was happening in France. National characteristics appear from their mixture with time-honoured traditional elements which persisted throughout, even if they did not show up in fashionable performances of the more up-to-date repertoire such as the new bourgeois drama or the opera.

315   An open-air theatre with a performance of *Pyramus and Thisbe*, 1708

Painting by Matthijs Naiveu, Stedelijk Museum 'De Lakenhal', Leiden. Photo A. Dingjan

First, the continuing tradition of open-air performances at village fairs and other festivities. Over the years their staging remained much the same and there is no fundamental difference between playing on a booth stage in the late sixteenth century and doing so in the eighteenth. In the painting by Matthijs Naiveu (1647–1721) the stage façade has become a neo-classical structure: a gate or perhaps an inner stage, with a door on either side flanked by columns and an architrave and cornice on top. The stage itself, though, is bare as ever – and full of actors. These are performing a Pyramus and Thisbe scene. The characters are clearly recognisable: from left to right the Lion (being fed or teased by a member of the audience); a director-prompter in a Harlequin costume, using a pointer and with an enormous playscript unrolled in front of him; Wall, with the wall curled up under his left arm; Moon, played by a woman presenting Diana with a crescent on a stick; Thisbe, an actress again, lifting her skirts in order to stab herself with the sword she brandishes; the dead Pyramus; and a man carrying a small (mulberry?) tree who represents the Well at Ninus' tomb.[1]

The scene had been performed before, with great success, in the Schouwburg of 1637. This was the version by Matthijs Gramsbergen. In his *Kluchtige tragedie van de Hertog van Pierlepon* (Farcical Tragedy of the Duke of P.) (1650) some travelling actors play it before a farmer whom they have introduced as a duke to an inn-keeper at Leiden. The similarity to Shakespeare's text is such that Gramsbergen must have known some version of *A Midsummer Night's Dream*, probably from a performance by English travelling actors. The version played here, however, is a rather bad translation, *Klucht van Pyramus en Thisbe*

(Farce of P. and T.) (1669) by the actor A.B. Leeuw of *Absurda comica oder Herr Peter Squentz* (1657), the German adaptation by Andreas Gryphius.[2]

In other respects the painting leaves much room for guesswork. The audience are an odd assortment, clumsily painted, who do not give the impression of reality. The tower in the background may belong to a Leiden city gate,[3] but the surrounding landscape does not match this. It is not clear why the figure of Mercury is looming above the back of the stage. Most interesting is the British coat of arms, flanked by the lion and the unicorn, on top of the façade. If this indicates a group of 'English Comedians', their presence is later than theatre history assumes.

[1] Mentioned by Ovid, but not a Shakespeare character.
[2] In 1659 De Leeuw had translated Gryphius' *Leo Arminius*. See also 51.
[3] The Hogewoerdspoort – information kindly supplied by the architectural historian Wouter Kuyper.

Fun-fairs were traditionally held at the end of the summer, mostly in the middle of September. There was no fair without theatrical performances. The new theatre season would not have started yet, and the professional companies travelled from fair to fair in cities and villages. But performances were also given there by local amateurs, still organised in Chambers of Rhetoric. Of course the theatre would have to compete with the other fairground entertainments. Therefore plays were chosen which had proved to be box-office successes in the regular theatres because of their historic interest enhanced by picturesque *tableaux vivants*, like Bontius' *Beleg en Ontzet van Leiden* (Siege and Relief of L.) (see **280**, **300**), or their blood-curdling melodrama, like Vos' *Aran en Titus* (see **283**).

In 1708 the author Lucas Rotgans published his farcical epic poem *Boerekermis* (The Farmers' Fun-fair), presenting a parody of the different kinds of fairground entertainment. Prominent in this poem is the mocking description of a Rhetoricians' company performing *Aran en Titus*, followed by the traditional neo-classical condemnation of such wild and immoral shows.

316   Theatre at a village fair, 1708

Lucas Rotgans, *Boerekermis* (Amsterdam: Samuel Halma, 1708). Reproduced in the edition by L. Strengholt (Gorinchem: J. Noorduijn, 1968), pp. 57–62, vss. 929–1062

[...] According to their Chamber's laws,
The stage was discovered to the sound of flourishing trumpets,
And there was King Saturninus, wearing a paper crown
And displaying a wooden sceptre, sitting on a rickety chair.
I was told that his great-great-grandmother
Used this chair when diarrhoea plagued her
Discharging her excreta with great groans through a hole,
For her convenience cut into the matting.
This was the seat of the Roman Catholic sceptre-bearer.
[...]
But Aaron, whom you see here, is a skinner's servant,
[...]
He has plastered his mug with thick soot,
Wears a sash, representing his General's insignia;
The chain which confines him as a slave, after his capture,
Is used by his old lady for the cauldron on the hearth.
Even yesterday, she was busy for six hours
Scouring it till it was smooth and bright.
A lassie from the village gave him an apron
Made of red silk, but for a long time left lying in a corner:
His turban was made from it [...].
[...]
Proud Tamora, played by Neighbour Lubber,
Came with a spear for killing swine in his rough fist
And quarrelled with Roslyn and squire Bazian.
Tempers rose high [...],
The young brawler lost his life, she her virginity.
Then came the crafty Moor [...].

Presently a piercing scream sounded so gruesomely,
That, stiffened by shock and trembling from the noise,
I thought: if these people are that cruel, and if this raving continues,
Even the spectators will be murdered in the end.
So then I left [. . .].

In amateur performances, the traditional Rhetoricians' style persisted well into the age of
neoclassicism and Enlightenment. This is especially true of the Southern Netherlands,
where this tradition was unchallenged and formed an unbroken line until the nineteenth
century.

317   Pageant-wagon with a religious scene, Malines, 1770

Anon., *Prael-treyn, Verrykt door Ry-benden, Prael-Wagens, Zinnebeelden en andere Oppronkingen, Toegeschikt aan het duyzent-jaerig Jubilé van den [. . .] Heyligen Rumoldus [. . .]*
(Magnificent Pageant, Ornated by Troops of Horse, Floats, Emblems and other Pomp. On
the Occasion of the Thousand-Year Jubilee of [. . .] Saint Rombaut [. . .] (Malines: Joannes-
Franciscus vander Elst, n.d.)

In 1770 the city of Malines celebrated the 'Millenary Jubilee' of its Patron Saint, Rombaut.
On this solumn occasion ten allegorical floats formed the main body of an historical pageant
in chronological order, commencing in pagan times and culminating in the establishment
of Christianity in the city. The last waggon presented the succeeding monarchs in the
reigning House of Austria, ending with Maria Theresa and her son Joseph II. The setting is
of course highly baroque, but the presentation and its context are in accordance with old
customs. The illustration shows the second float, paid by the Guilds of the Gardeners and
the Hatters. The description explains:

On the top of this waggon a sacrifice is made to the idols Delia, Pan, and Neptune.
Down below Malines is sitting, totally blinded by the darkness of paganism. This
is bemoaned by the Holy Church, sitting at the front of the waggon, but she is
comforted by Divine Providence and Omnipotence.

The waggon is conducted by Blind Stupidity, having as his motto 'Ignoto Deo
(*Acts* 17): To an unknown God'.

317

318   **Five medallions with scenes from Vondel's *Gysbreght van Aemstel***

Central, and larger than the other scenes, the *tableau vivant* showing the murder of the bishop and nuns. Engraving by S. Fokke, 1775. Nederlands Theater Instituut, Amsterdam, GD 104–1

Tableaux vivants also formed a continuing tradition in Dutch theatre. Frozen scenes of high drama (mainly murder, marriage and enthronements) always attracted the audience. It is thought that the reason for their popularity, lasting well into the nineteenth century, was their mixture of theatricality, painting and didactic verses. To the Dutch mind painting ranked (and probably still ranks) highest among all art forms, and its combination with living actors and a morally instructive explanation must have been irresistible. The best-known examples are provided in Vondel's *Gysbreght* (1637), with its unique tradition of regular performances every year (see p. 350).

318

The *tableaux* always caused astonishment to foreign travellers. Louis (Luigi) Riccoboni mentions those in *Gysbreght* in the context of examples of coarse realism and melodramatic effects.

319   Riccoboni on realism, *tableaux,* and scenes of blood and horror, 1738

Louis Riccoboni, *Réflexions historiques et critiques sur les différens théâtres de l'Europe. Avec les Pensées sur la Déclamation* (Amsterdam: Aux Dépens de la Compagnie, 1740) (Paris: Guérin, 1738), pp. 144–6

In the old [Dutch] tragedies they represented the action on stage as it had happened: for instance in *Egmont en Hoorne* they cut the heads of these two earls on stage. In another piece the Hero stabs himself & falls dead after having inundated the scene with all the blood contained in a bladder which he hides in his armpit. In *Aman* they hang Haman, & Mordecai tours the stage mounted on a jade. In *Tamerlan* that prince appears on a horse with Bajazet.[1] [...]

Another peculiarity of the old theatre is what they call *Vertoning (tableau vivant)*: they lower the curtain in the middle of an act, and arrange the actors on the stage in order to represent, in the manner of the pantomime, some main action of the play's contents. Thus, in *Gysbrecht van Aemstel* they raise the curtain, & the theatre shows the soldiers of Egmont, Gysbrecht's enemy, who plunder a nunnery; each soldier takes hold of a nun and treats her as it pleases him. The Abbess lies down in the middle of the stage, holding on her knees the venerable Goswin, the banned bishop of Utrecht, who is then slaughtered in his pontifical clothes, the mitre on his head and the cross in his hand. At the end of *The Siege of Leiden*[2] there are eight or ten living emblems to represent the weight of the Spanish tyranny, the valour of the Dutch, Religion Triumphant, the arts re-established, etc. There are more than three hundred characters on the stage,[3] and an Actress with a baton in her hand explains them to the audience, who marvel at them: one can say in truth that this makes a beautiful show.

[1] These were all very popular plays. *Egmont en Hoorne* is by Thomas Asselijn, 1685. *Aman* is *Hester, oft verlossing der Jooden* (E., or Liberation of the Jews) (1659), an adaptation from Lope de Vega's *La hermosa Ester* (Fair Esther) by Joannes Serwouters, which held the stage for more than a century. The same author wrote *Tamerlan*, 1657 (see also 333).
[2] By R. Bontius, 1645 (see 280 & 300).
[3] A gross exaggeration.

B. SETS, PROPS AND MACHINERY

In the 1670s the Amsterdam Schouwburg began for various reasons to suffer losses. The Burgomasters now allowed an experiment and let out the enterprise to private management. This lasted until 1688, with changing directorship, but it was not financially successful and the city took over again, a conveyance which involved an inventory of the Schouwberg contents, not only of the sets and costumes (for the latter see 331), but also of props, machinery and all sorts of odds and ends dispersed through the building. The sum total of the estimation was *f* 7388:16, the costumes excluded.

320   A theatre inventory, 1688

MS, State Archives, Utrecht, Huydecoper Family Archives, No 164. Reproduced in Albach, 'Een inventaris [. . .]', (An Inventory), *Scenarium* 8 (1984), pp. 63–72.

Sets, wings, etc. which were in the Schouwberg A.D. 1687 around the time of the fair, and were recorded there again on 27 November 1688, and have been assessed in the following way.[1]

On the Stage.

[. . .]

A Street Scene, being a street consisting of 8 wings, with two doorsteps, a well, with the balcony, three hundred and twenty five guilders[2]   *f* 325:–

A Forest of 8 wings, among which four with frames, and ten

boughs, added to which 10 new wings, newly made for this   ƒ 363:–
A Garden of eight wings, added to which ten new wings and a
new backcloth, and two of the old ones repainted[3]   ƒ 413:10
A Rock, consisting of eight wings, now improved with another six
new small winglets; and on the other side of the aforesaid eight
wings the Clouds of *Phaethon*,[4] together   ƒ 320:–
A Farce Scene of five wings, the first cloth patched in three places,
otherwise undamaged   ƒ   90:–
[...]
A Tent Scene consisting of eight wings, with its perspective,
undamaged, painted by Mr Lairesse   ƒ 100:–
A backcloth with a bedstead painted by Lairesse, representing an
Alcove with multicoloured hangings, with fringes and tassels   ƒ   80:–
[...]
A dropping Heavens, the Cloud, slightly damaged, but since
repaired   ƒ   40:–
[...]
A scene, representing a Royal Hall and an enclosed room,[5]
painted by Lairesse, now valued at   ƒ 1050:
[...]
Six iron sheets used in *The Fire of Troy*[6]   ƒ   18:
The flying machine, consisting of four flying chariots and horses,
and the ship for *Amadis*[7]   ƒ   80:–
All the ropes newly made, also some renewed with some new
pulleys, 15 to 16 strings, with two heavy ropes, and as it was
found, together   ƒ 120:–
[...]
Lamps and trays to put lights on, about eighty pieces   ƒ   50:–
[...]
Handcuffs, fountain, a tree, some poles, a table, a pedestal, some
wood, a cupboard, two footstools, a case, and four ladders   ƒ   96:–
[...]
The dragon in *Armida*,[8] and two horses, a peacock, an owl,
together   ƒ   24:–
[...]
Whatever might be in the lofts, which hasn't been mentioned here   ƒ   12:–
[...]
The following wings, scenes, etc. have been made by [order of] the
Governors of the Schouwburg since the fair, A.D. 1687 and have
been assessed as follows: –

On the Stage

A scene, consisting of six wings with a backdrop, representing the
Madhouse Hospital⁹   ƒ 175:

A scene, consisting of eight wings with a backdrop, representing
the Elysian Fields¹⁰   ƒ 400:

On the back of the first four wings of the Elysian Fields the Quaker
Church has been painted, with a separate backdrop to the
church¹¹   ƒ 36:–

A scene, consisting of eight wings with a backdrop, representing a
Hell, with four big and eight small borders¹²   ƒ 400:

[...]

In the Lofts

A chariot of Pluto without wheels, a chariot of Juno with two
peacocks in front, a big eagle, a chariot of Pallas with two owls in
front, a chariot of Night with bats, two pairs of swans, a dragon, a
white shell made of osiers, an eagle of Jupiter, a lightning, three
sword guards,¹³ some small shepherd's crooks, two statues
belonging to a garden scene, being Hercules and Venus, three
wooden frames for bowers, together   ƒ 70:

Two wooden shafts where the ropes run through   ƒ 10:

A Sea painted on cloth, consisting of eleven pieces, used in the
opera of *Perseus*¹⁴, plus six hanging waves and their ropes, with
the Sea in *The Relief of Leiden*,¹⁵ mended   ƒ 60:

The printers' workshop, installed in the second gallery, and a
printing press standing there with cut dies, a big pair of scissors, a
wooden pipe, three knives¹⁶   ƒ 36:–

[...]

Four vertically and four horizontally moving machines under the
stage newly made, with a one-hundred-pound iron weight¹⁷   ƒ 75:

[...]

---

[1] The names of sets which are known from illustrations or descriptions have been capitalised.

[2] The Street, better known as 'The Italian Street' was painted by Jacob Vennekool (1632–1673).
Further on, the inventory mentions a backcloth (not given here) painted for this set by the famous
Gerard de Lairesse (1640–1711) who among the items of this inventory also did the Forest (1680?),
the Old Royal Hall (1681, see 321), a Scene with Tents (1682?), the Farce Scene, also known as the
Furnished Room (1687), and a backcloth representing an Alcove. Prices are given in guilders and
stivers.

[3] This set and its painter are unknown.

[4] A play by Joost van den Vondel (1663), see 313, 325. It appears that wings could be painted on
both sides to represent different scenes, no doubt as a matter of economising on canvas. Given the
fact that the first four wings were profiled, being set at an angle on a raked floor, they would
presumably have to be installed on the opposite side of the stage for each separate use.

⁵ See 321. The Old Court Gallery, as it is commonly known, is the most expensive item on the list. The 'enclosed room' is the shortened Royal Hall with a different backcloth and a throne under a canopy put in front of it.

⁶ A play by Govaard Bidloo (1649–1713), date unknown. Bidloo, a Professor at Leiden and the personal physician of William III, was the author of several plays and opera libretti; he defended Vondel against the attacks of 'Nil Volentibus Arduum' (see 356). The iron sheets were thunder-sheets, shaken to imitate the sound of thunderbolts.

⁷ An opera libretto translated by Thomas Arendsz (1687) after *Amadis de Gaule* by Quinault (1684). The music was by Lully.

⁸ *De Tooveryen van Armida, of het belegerde Jeruzalem* (The Magic Tricks of A. or Jerusalem Besieged), adapted by A. Peys (approx. 1683), perhaps from a Dutch version of Tasso's *Gerusalemme liberata*. It precedes Quinault's *Armide* (1686), with which it has only the subject in common. The play was quite successful. In later times Czar Peter the Great attended a performance at Amsterdam (1697); it was in the repertoire of a travelling company under Anthonie Spatzier, playing it in Hamburg in 1740.

⁹ For W.G. van Focquenbroch's popular play *De Min in het Lazarushuis* (Love in the Lepers' Hospital) (1694) – the Amsterdam lepers' hospital was used as a lunatic asylum. See 355.

¹⁰ Probably painted by Chr. Lubienietzki (1688) for the opera *Proserpine* by Quinault/Lully, see 323.

¹¹ See note 3. Quakers were mocked in several comedies; it is not known which one is referred to here.

¹² See 323.

¹³ The words could also mean 'brackets or braces for guns'.

¹⁴ *Persée* (1682) by Quinault/Lully. It had just been performed, in the summer of 1688, by a visiting French company.

¹⁵ By Bontius (1645), see 280.

¹⁶ Presumably, this press was used for printing playbills. The publication of the plays themselves was in the hands of established publishers, who would have their own printers working for them.

¹⁷ Unfortunately, nothing is known about these machines, which must have controlled the change of the wings (the horizontally moving ones) and that of the borders and the backcloth (the vertically moving ones); see also 326.

The sets of the second Amsterdam Schouwburg have been portrayed in a large number of engravings that are of great importance for stage history. Among other Dutch theatre illustrations, they have been praised for their 'unparallelled completeness and accuracy',[1] and this refers not only to the sets as such, but also to what they reveal about stage technique, acting and costumes. All in all they comprised approx. 50 illustrations and the main ones were presented in two series of fifteen engravings, published in instalments between 1749 and 1770 by J. Smit at Amsterdam. Smit no doubt intended them for the moneyed classes; excellent care was taken of their production and after their publication many of them were exquisitely coloured.

The engravings of each series show a fixed frame or passe-partout representing the front of the Schouwberg interior with an audience; and of a middle part or medallion portraying scenes from different plays.[2] The passe-partout varies for the two series. The first one, engraved before 1742[3] by N. van der Laan after Hendrik de Leth, shows elaborate chandeliers and festoons hanging in the proscenium arch. The other has simple cande-labra, a larger orchestra pit and a different audience; it dates from approx. 1770 and was sketched and engraved by Simon Fokke.

All in all these engravings show fourteen stock settings, dating from different periods between 1665 and 1766. They are, in chronological order:[4] The Italian Street, The Forest, The Old Court Gallery, The Furnished Room, The New Forest, Mt Parnassus, Hell, The Common Neighbourhood, The New Court Porch, The Wallpapered Room, The Court of the

Sun, The Convent Church, The New Garden and The New Court Hall.[5] In the course of time many of them were repaired or renewed. All of them were lost in the fire of 1772.

321   De Aloude Hofgallery [The Old Court Gallery] (1681)

Drawing and engraving by Jan Punt, approx. 1740; published by J. Smit, 1749. Nederlands Theater Instituut, Amsterdam, TL 44–4

The Old Court Gallery or Hall,[6] painted in 1681 by Gerard de Lairesse (see 320, notes 2&5) was praised as the most magnificent set of the Schouwburg. Corver declared that he had not seen its like in the Southern Netherlands or in Paris; foreign visitors also admired it. Two of its attractions were its strict symmetry in a Louis XIV style and its deep perspective, the four wings on each side being repeated on the backcloth. The statues on the sides were all painted. Some characteristics of the acting technique shown in the illustration are the clear distinction between first-rank and second-rank roles and the frontal position of the actors.

The scene is taken from the tragedy *Het huwelyk van Orondates en Statira* (The Marriage of O. and S.) (1670), adapted by David Lingelbach for the society 'Nil Volentibus Arduum' from a French play of the same name by Jean de Magnon (1648) and meant to be an exemplary demonstration of neoclassical rules. The rhyming inscription, admonishing the main characters to remain firm in their adversity, was added by the engraver or the publisher.[7]

---

[1] Gascoigne, *World Theatre* (1968), p. 179; see also Gascoigne, 'Shuffling the Schouwburg scenes' (1968).
[2] There are also copies without the passe-partout. Many of the medallions were engraved by the actor Jan Punt (see 335).
[3] Probably on the occasion of the Schouwburg's centenary in 1738.
[4] Of the sets, not of the engravings.
[5] The older ones are mentioned in the Inventory of 1688 (see 320).
[6] 'Old' to distinguish it from the later Palace Courts.
[7] The same is true for the inscriptions to the other engravings.

321

322   Stage set: *De Gemeene Buurt* (The Common Neighbourhood) (date unknown)

Jan Punt after P. van Liender, approx. 1760. Nederlands Theater Instituut, Amsterdam, TL 3–11

'The Common Neighbourhood' is a simple set for farces playing in front of the houses of a typical Dutch street. It is exceptional in the series, because it does not represent the scene as if it were a closed space, but shows the separations between its three wings, backcloth and borders; and also, in that some air and leaves were painted on the wings above the houses. That the shadows of some characters on stage run in opposite directions indicates an equally realistic treatment of the implied light sources. When not practicable, doors and windows in the set were painted.

The painter of this set is unknown. The scene is from a farce *Het verliefde Brechje* (B. in Love) by P.W. van Haps (1708).

322

323   Stage set: *De Hel* (Hell), 1688? or 1738

Engraving by N. van der Laan(?), 1738. Nederlands Theater Instituut, Amsterdam, TL 1–2

In 1738 the centenary of Amsterdam's City Theatre (see also 354) was celebrated with a gala performance of an allegorical play *Het Eeuwgetyde van den Amsterdamschen Schouwburg* [*The Centenary of the A.S.*] by Jan de Marre. It had four sets, published immediately afterwards in a lavish jubilee volume, and also separately and as part of the two series of engravings. The most spectacular of the four represented Hell, a set which may have existed before, in which case it was probably painted by Christoffel Lubienietzki (1660/61–1729), a Polish artist who had settled in Amsterdam.[1]

Because the engraving can be compared with De Marre's stage directions in the play and also with some extant notes of a stage manager, it is known exactly which mythological figures have been depicted and also which actors played the allegorical characters on stage. The latter are Envy, Slander, Discord, Ignorance and Deceit, laying a plot against the Schouwburg. Their costumes, described in the minutest detail, are partly based on Cesare Ripa's *Iconologia*.

[1] At the opening of this theatre in 1665 a Hell set had been promised for the near future and the Inventory of 1688 (see 320) mentions one, valued at ƒ 400, – the most expensive set after Lairesse's Royal Hall. The latter may have been used in 1688 for the opera *Proserpine* by Quinault/Lully, which needed a 'Palais de Pluton' (Pluto's Palace).

323

It would be a mistake to think that stock scenery like this exhausted all the scenic possibilities of the theatres of the time, being used in a static way, repeated from one performance to the next and obeying the rules of unity of place. In actual stage practice these sets were most of the time varied in four different ways: a. by the succession of different sets in one and the same performance, even in the strictest neoclassical plays prescribing one single place of action; b. by the combination of widely different wings and backcloths in a composite set, for instance a garden corner and part of a hall for the wings, and the sea in the background; b. by reducing a set, using only a few wings, thereby for instance converting a hall into a room or a landscape into a forest clearing; c. varying the meaning of a set by different pieces of scenery, e.g. changing a room in a monastery into a prison cell by the application of barred windows. The illustrations by Writs show the second variation. In 324 the first pair of wings of the Royal Hall form a huge royal tent, with the statues (see 321) covered by panels of military trophies and the border provided with a curtain and tassels. This is combined with two forest wings, with set pieces in the form of tents placed in front of them, and a sea, painted on the backcloth. The fall of Phaethon in Vondel's play of the same name is shown in 325.

324   Stage set: *The Army Tents and the Calm Sea*

Drawing and engraving by W. Writs, 1772. *Atlas van [...] Amsterdam* (1804)

325   Stage set: *The Rocks and the Stormy Sea*

Engraving by S. Fokke (1774) after W. Writs (1760). *Atlas van [...] Amsterdam* (1804)

326   Machinery for changing the scenes in the Schouwburg

Anon., *Historie van den nieuwen Amsterdamschen Schouwburg. Met fraaijen afbeeldingen* (History of the new A.S., with beautiful illustrations) (Amsterdam: G. Warnars/P. den Hengst, 1775), p. 29–30

All these flats [of the theatre since 1665] slide in levelled grooves, in which iron bars and metal pulleys have been fastened,[1] so that they can be moved and changed in a very easy way. – The manipulation of the borders and back drops takes place by changing the same, also by means of machinery. They slide on pulleys, all provided with the necessary counterweights, which are separated from each other by wooden shafts; and, heavy as they are, one by one and with little effort, they are manipulated by one person. [. . .] All this is mainly achieved by a great number of copper and pockwood pulleys, which have been fastened to several blocks in the attic above the stage and are estimated to come to more than eight hundred. Subsequently, all the components have, by means of cords, been conducted to the south side of the stage, where more than eighty thousand pounds of weight are hung, in order to set all those instruments in motion.

[1] Read: with bars and pulleys fastened to the flats.

On 10 August 1773, the architect de Witte was asked by the Burgomasters to build a maquette of the proposed new theatre in order to test scene changes and to clear up other space problems. On 27 August he showed them his model. Following the example of the Schouwburg of 1665, the model showed the first four grooves at oblique angles. Apparently, the repeated choice of oblique wing positions needed some defence. In a memo de Witte explains their advantages.

327   An architect's arguments for oblique wings, 1774

Minuut-memoriën en Memoriën, Keuren en Contracten van J.E. de Witte (1772–1777) (Minutes and Memoranda, Statutes and Contracts of J.E. de W.), City Archives Amsterdam, Archief van het Fabrijksambt of Stadswerken en Gebouwen, Nos 4/5, p. 43. Reproduced in Sluijter-Seijffert (1976), p. 32

–fewer oblique wings will be needed than straight ones
–oblique wings take up less room in the width of the theatre than straight ones
–oblique wings mask better
–wings when oblique have a larger width than straight ones, therefore they present more painting surface
–the obliqueness aids the perspective automatically, provided the painter knows its rules
–the space between one [wing] and the next one is wider, and so it is easier for an actor to go through and to exit quickly

–with straight wings one sees too little to represent architecture, except on the big stages where one has plenty of space

–all the noise from behind the wings comes directly onto the stage and annoys the player and the spectator

–the only advantage of straight wings consists in that they can be better lit and are easier to paint for a painter who understands perspective only passably well. The first point can be taken care of by painting the oblique ones brighter and the second by an increased skill in perspective.

Since all the stock scenery of the old Amsterdam theatres had been destroyed by the fire of 1772, new sets had to be painted for its successor. Twenty of these, dating from its opening in 1774 until 1794, are known from engravings, again published by J.W. Smit. Some old localities appear among them: a Forest, a Roman Court Gallery, an Italian Street, etc.; others show new preferences: The Gothic Palace, The Poor Man's House, The Winter Forest, etc. – and indeed, all of them were painted in a grander classical style.

328   Stage set: *De Straat van Londen* (The London Street) (1774), with a scene from *Beverley* (after Moore, *The Gamester*)

Engraving by C. Brouwer after J. Bulthuis, 1788. Nederlands Theater Instituut, Amsterdam, TL 4–11

The illustration of 'The London Street', painted in 1774 by J. Andriessen and H. Numan, shows a scene from *Beverley*, one of three Dutch adaptations from the French version by B.J. Saurin of Edward Moore's popular *The Gamester*, which was also directly translated. Stage realism is not to be expected: the set got its name from the backcloth, showing a distant view of St Paul's Cathedral, but the wings have no connection with London at all, and the first flat on the left even portrays a recently built house on an Amsterdam canal.

329   *De armoedige woning* (The Poor Man's House) (1776)

Engraving by R. and H. Vinkeles after R. Vinkeles, 1777. Nederlands Theater Instituut, Amsterdam, TL 3–30

'The Poor Man's House', a set made in 1776 by A. van der Groen, shows a scene from one of three Dutch adaptations of L.S. Mercier's *L'Indigent* (1772) (see 357). The set is modern as regards its subject, but not in its construction, for although ostensibly a box set it consisted of wings and borders. Apart from the furniture on stage and a practicable door, everything else in this set was painted.

C. COSTUME

The first of eight letters requesting new costumes brings the stinginess of the Schouwburg financiers into relief. The demand was repeated with mounting exacerbation and a variety of arguments, not the least one being the fact that several actors were leaving the theatre because their contracts had not been observed properly. By the end of May, the Governors of the City Almshouses had still failed to comply. As early as 1668 a request for costumes had reached the Burgomasters, who admitted that the Governors *did* have the funds for the production of expensive costumes, but clearly preferred to use the existing ones as long as possible so as not to diminish the profits of the Almshouses.

330   Request for new costumes, 1681

City Archives Amsterdam, Archives City Orphanage, P.A. 367. Reproduced in Wybrands (1873), pp. 239–240

To the Honourable Lords Governors of the Orphanage and the Old Men's Home at Amsterdam

Your Honours.

In accordance with the instructions given to us, both in writing and orally, by the Noble Lords the Burgomasters, we have often ordered from Yr Hons the things we need for the theatre, which Yr Hons have not delivered according to Yr Hons' duty. And because we cannot think otherwise but that our placing of an order should be acted upon: therefore, we let Yr Hons know that the clothes and props are dilapidated for lack of repair and of the making of new ones, to such an extent that the plays cannot be presented properly; so that the theatre attracts small houses and the authors are robbed of their pleasure of delivering something to the theatre. And we let Yr Hons know this in order never henceforward to be blamed for being in any way the cause of these inconveniences; and at the same time to admonish Yr Hons to deliver what is needed as a general provision:

2 Roman men's, and

2 Roman women's dresses, together with

2 modern men's coats, and

1 embroidered field cloak after the new fashion.

Also, that proper repair be done to plumes, hats, bows, jewellery, swords, shoes, &c. with the fabrication of as many new items as are needed. And it will be advisable that the above will not be ordered with Yr Hons' usual slowness, but diligently and without delay, to prevent a further total dilapidation which will otherwise be unavoidable, and to preserve the Theatre as best we can. We remain, Hon. Lords,

Yr Hons' affectionate
friends and confrères,
The Governors of the Theatre.
L. MEIJER, Acting Secretary.

Given at Amsterdam,
20 January 1681. [...]

Theatre costumes are a very important subject in the Inventory of 1688 (see **320**). Their enumeration takes up 37 pages, whereas the sets have 14. The total estimate for the costumes is ƒ 6484:5, against ƒ 7388:16 for the sets. The average value per item will be no more than ten guilders or less, but some costumes fetched a high price, the most expensive one being 'A large red woman's dress, embroidered with satin, with a [separable] skirt and sleeves and bodice', which was valued at ƒ 125. Unfortunately, only a minority of the items are described in detail or linked up to particular plays, roles or performance.

331   A costume inventory, 1688

MS, State Archives, Utrecht, Huydecoper Family Archives. No 164 (see **320**)

[...]

A Moor's dress with feathers[1]	ƒ 13: –
Four Sosias' dresses, with four caps[2]	ƒ 44: –
A dress for Scapin	ƒ 4: –
A red satin jerkin, with *passementerie*	ƒ 7: –
A ditto	ƒ 9: –
A dress for *Nieuwsgierig Aagje*[3]	ƒ 6: –
Three timbrels	ƒ 4: 10
A red Turkish pendent cloth, lined with red satin, and on it a dolphin	ƒ 38: –

[...]

---

[1] Perhaps for Aran in Jan Vos' *Aran en Titus* (see **283**, p. 418).
[2] For Molière's *Amphitryon*, which had been performed at the end of the seventies.
[3] [*Nosey A.*]. There are two farces of this title, by A. Bormeester (1662) and by A. Bogaert (1679).

332   Jan Punt stands corrected: his dress not suited to the character

Corver (1786), pp. 21–2

Dressed in his Roman suit, Punt (who certainly had never read Homer's *Iliad*), came walking across the stage for the beginning of the play:[1] he was wearing a big black wig with two queues, one of which hung over his chest and the other over his back, and he had made himself two handsome moustaches with Indian ink. Jacobus Jordaan, an excellent actor,[2] who also happened to be walking across the stage, seeing Punt rigged out like that, began to laugh. Punt asked him: *Why are you laughing, Koos?* Jordaan answered him: *At my own stupidity. Wherein does it lie?* rejoined Punt. *In that up to now,* answered Jordaan, *I have always imagined Ulysses to have been a sensible and crafty man, but that now I must confess to seeing the opposite; he was a complete madman. Because,* continued Jordaan, *he went to so much trouble [...] to disguise himself as a merchant, adding a helmet, a sword and a shield to his wares. It was by going for these that Achilles was discovered, whereas without any further ado he could have been easily distinguished from so many virgins by his black leonine head of hair and by his moustaches.* Punt fell silent, went directly to his small dressing-room, washed off the moustaches and instead of the large black one, he put on a small, what is known as a powdered 'fox' wig, and came sauntering back on stage, saying to Jordaan: *Is this more to your liking?* who replied: *Yes, now you look more like Achilles; but what gave you that idea just now?* Punt said: *To make him more awe-inspiring, as I look very young. The younger Achilles' face looks, the better,* continued Jordaan. *Yes, even if there is something feminine in it; it can't do Achilles any harm; and make him especially light of foot, if you want to portray him well.*

---

[1] On Punt, see 335–7. The play was Balthasar Huydecoper's *Achilles*, 1719. (See 335 & 345).
[2] (1716–?).

XXX Actors and acting

For the latter half of the seventeenth and the first quarter of the eighteenth century travelling to foreign countries continued, and Sweden remained an important goal. In 1666 Fornenbergh's company (see **270, 293**) visited the country for the second time. At the Swedish Court they were received warmly; they even acquired, a rare distinction for travelling actors, a state appointment as the official resident company for the period of one year. The climax of their stay was no doubt the opening of their own permanent venue. This was the first permanent public theatre of Sweden, established near the royal palace in the Lion's Den ('Lejonkulan'), where in former days Queen Christina had kept a lion. The stay of the Dutch actors in Sweden is hardly documented, but most of their repertoire is known: on the opening night of the 'Lejonkulan', 22 February 1667, they performed *The Marriage of Orondates and Statira* (see **321**).

On their way back to Holland in 1667, they gave two performances in Hamburg, which were attended by the Swedish traveller Urban Hjärne. Unfortunately the short notices in his (Latin) diary do not mention the actors' names or the titles of the plays. The first one must have been the ever popular *Tamerlan* (Tamburlaine) by Joannes Serwouters (1657). (See also **32.**)

333   A Dutch performance in Hamburg, 1667

Reproduced in Kossmann, *Nieuwe Bijdragen* (1915), p. 4. Kossmann refers to O. Wieselgren in *Sveriges Teaterhistoriska Samfund, Årsskrift*, 1912, p. 47

25 June. After lunch I went out to visit Queen Christina,[1] but coming to the Market I discovered the house where they were giving a performance. After paying 8 stivers I entered [...] on a higher floor, where I watched the complete tragedy, which had begun late. It was the history of Tamburlaine and his subjection of Bajazet. It was quite remarkable because [...] of the way in which they represented Turks and Tartars. Especially Tamburlaine himself with a red spot on his face.[2] Further esp[ecially] the mistress thought to be a jester,[3] Tamburlaine's horse on the stage, Bajazet's submission.[4] Poison is given to Tamburlaine, etc.

[1] The former Queen of Sweden stayed there at the time.
[2] The meaning of this is unclear.
[3] For 'mistress' Hjärne's Latin has *mulier moecha*, 'adulterous wife', which does not make sense here. In the play Bajazet's Turkish mistress, far from being adulterous, disguises as a jester in order to free her lover from Tamburlaine's camp.
[4] He is put in a cage.

At the end of the eighteenth century a resident theatre company in a big city was a large enterprise, not so much because of the number of actors, but because dancers, singers and musicians were involved as well. Another difference with a modern theatre was the specialisation of the actors according to standard lines of business, a feature Holland shared with the theatres of England, France and Germany. At the end of the eighteenth century this division into more or less fixed types, ages, etc. developed into a very detailed system (see 107).

The best sources for lines of business are the *tableaux de la troupe*, given in theatre almanacs, which in Holland began to appear in 1770. The tableau for 1793, rather a simple one for its time, is quoted only for the actors; the specification of their types is followed by those of the male and female dancers, the male and female singers, and by the orchestra members with their instruments.

334   A *tableau de la troupe* and lines of business at the end of the eighteenth century, 1793

Algemeene Amsterdamsche Schouwburgs Almanach, voor 't Jaar 1793, met fraaje Tooneel-plaatjes (General Amsterdam Theatre Almanac, For the Year 1793, With Beautiful Stage-Illustrations) (Amsterdam: J. van Gulik), pp. 115–16

At present the following Gentlemen are now acting in the Dutch theatre of Amsterdam:

W. BINGLEY,	
D. SARDET,	for the first roles.
J. CROESE,	
S. KRUIS,	
A.W. HILVERDING,	for the princes.
A. VAN MAERLEN,	tender fathers.[1]
H. ANGEMEER,	roles *à manteaux*.[2]
J. HELDERS,	Stage Manager; dry roles.[3]
D. OBELT,	peasants and comical characters.
J. DE LA PLAS,	first servants.
K. VAN DER STEL	dry roles.
N. KNOLLEMAN,[4]	
H. 'S-GRAVESANDE.	
J. VAN WELL,	

D. KAMPHUIZEN,
J. HILVERDING,   for the children.

ACTRESSES.

J. SARDET, *née* WOUTERS,
J. WATTIER,   for the first roles.
RYNVELDS, *née* VAN NES,   for the second roles.
H. MOLSTER, *née* VAN THIL,   for the old princesses.
M.E. VAN MAERLEN, *née* GHYBEN,   ridiculous roles and Dutch maids.
J. 'S-GRAVESANDE, *née* RAMP,   the mothers in the farces.
A.M. HILVERDING *née* GISSER,
HELENA HILVERDING,
FREUBEL, *née* SMALWOUD,   servant-girls.
H. HILVERDING,   lovers.
A. HILVERDING,   for the children.

¹ This line of business shows the influence of the modern bourgeois *drame*. 'Noble fathers' would have
  been traditional.
² At the time, 'roles *à manteaux*', originally characterized by the wearing of a cloak, was a collective
  term for different men's parts in tragedy or comedy, which had in common the fact that the
  character was of a certain age and moved with some dignity, for instance *financiers* (men of private
  means) or *grimes* (elderly comical parts). In later times the specific indications are more common.
³ Characters with a dry wit (?).
⁴ When no line of business is mentioned, the actor in question may have been a general utility,
  meaning that he was used for several (smaller) parts; or else that the author did not always know
  who was what. H. 's-Gravesande for instance, who was 51 when this Almanach appeared, gets no
  qualification, but was in fact well known as a player of first roles in comedies and of lovers and 'third
  characters' in serious plays; and also as a translator of drama and a company director.

B. INDIVIDUAL ACTORS

335 Self-portrait of Jan Punt as Achilles, 1770

Engraving. Nederlands Theater Instituut, Amsterdam, TL 52–1A

Jan Punt (1711–1779) is generally considered the greatest Dutch actor of the eighteenth
century. He was the main representative of the neo-classical style of acting and excelled in
tragic heroes like those of Corneille, playing them in a grand rhetorical manner, full of
pictorial effects and showing strong emotions at the same time. He was the first Dutch actor
to be the subject of a biography (see p. 407). For financial reasons Punt also worked as an
artist and he is especially known for his excellent engravings (see 321–2). To this activity
we owe his self-portrait, made at the end of his career, in one of his most admired parts, the
title role in *Achilles* by Balthazar Huydecoper (1719). (See 332.) It is one of the extremely
rare portraits of a Dutch actor in the eighteenth century. Huydecoper's play
was vastly popular, not the least because of Punt's performance. The portrait of course

depicts the climax of the play, when Achilles has heard about Patroclus' death and at last takes the decision to go into battle once more, in a stirring tirade which the whole of theatre-going Amsterdam knew off by heart.[1] The actor wears the customary *'habit à la romaine'* and his body is positioned in accordance with the doctrine of contrasts.

Punt made a deep impression when he played the title role in *Don Luis de Vargas*, adapted by D. Heynk from Alarcón's *El tejedor de Segovia* (The Weaver of Segovia), which was played and reprinted for more than a century. He always remained partial to Spanish drama, as he did to Vondel and Corneille. The climax of the play is the scene where Don Luis, thought

---

[1]   Its opening lines form part of the portrait's inscription (omitted here).

dead, takes off a mask, a wig and some plaster and makes himself known to his opponent, a villainous count. The quotation is not only remarkable for the extent to which the youthful Punt identified with his part, but also for the fact that apparently none of the actors had at the time had any fencing lessons or experience.

336   Jan Punt impresses a fellow actor and the audience, *c.* 1740
Corver (1786), pp. 13–14

The face, the posture and the tone with which Punt thrust the line
I am the same and I shall give you proof
at Schmidt, who was playing the count, caused the latter's face to freeze, so that people standing in the pit said to each other in a low voice: 'Look! Look at the count! Look at how Schmidt is changing!' and the amateurs[1] whose place at the time was usually behind the orchestra, said delightedly to the others: 'So much for the count!' [...] Many a time after that, when I [Corver] was a player in the Schouwburg and Punt was no longer there, I heard Schmidt say that when Punt said to him: '*I am the same*', it was as if a bucket of cold water was being poured over his body. Also, it almost cost Schmidt his life, because the duel which immediately follows the above-mentioned exchange was so fiery on Punt's part and was accompanied by so much perplexity and confusion on the part of Schmidt, that (though neither of them understood the art of sword-fighting) Punt gave Schmidt such an almighty blow that if it hadn't hit a button on the belt of his trousers, which split in two, and if it hadn't been for a sudden fall, (which he accompanied with the words *Oh, Jesus!*), Schmidt would have received a dangerous wound in the abdomen; as it was, he turned as white as a sheet, and Punt was greatly shocked and kept his eyes trained on the floor to see if there was any blood flowing. In the pit the people shot to their feet to see what was happening, as everybody was sure the thrust had gone home. As chance would have it, this was a beautiful, though dangerous display.

[1] These were amateur players who had been accepted as student actors. They also took part in performances and could, if coming up to expectation, be selected for a contract as company members. Punt himself came from among their ranks; so did Corver and many others.

337   Punt as a social climber
Corver (1786), p. 79

It pleased Punt to be elevated above the middle classes. At the time that he was the [theatre's] house-manager,[1] he must in my opinion certainly have earned about seven or eight thousand guilders as an artist and as an actor, if account is also taken of his painting and engraving. Yes sir, I don't think it would have been much less than that. He was always very fond of horses and could now devote himself to that hobby by buying them and acquiring a 'faragon', a cart and a 'fools' sled'.[2] This really put some of the patricians' noses out of joint, even some of the burghers'; and at that time I once heard an affluent gentleman air his views on the matter vociferously. *Who does Mr Punt think he is?* he said to me, *is he such a great gentleman that he can keep a carriage? It befits him well, the son of a weighing-house porter!*

[1] Jan Punt and his wife, herself a first-class actress, acquired this lucrative additional job both in Amsterdam and in Rotterdam (see 311). A homely detail is given in a review from the magazine *De Hollandsche Tooneel-beschouwer* [*The Dutch Theatre-Observer*] of 28 Sept. 1762: 'Mrs Punt is kindly requested not to leave her ironing board in the hall of the theatre next time there is a performance; for it has obstructed the exit of many people.' (p. 44).

[2] Different kinds of carriages. The sledge (but why a fool's sledge?) was the most common kind of vehicle: it consisted of the body of a coach, without wheels, mounted on a sledge and drawn by one horse; it seated four persons.

Initially ranking second after Jan Punt, whose pupil and colleague he was, Marten Corver (1727–1794) became important as an actor, a company leader, a teacher and the main stage reformer of his time, propagating the modern repertoire of Voltaire, the *drame bourgeois* etc., and a more 'natural' style of acting, congenial to the ideas and practice of Lekain in France and Garrick in England. After playing for many years at the Amsterdam Schouwburg, he headed his own company, set up in the theatres of The Hague, Leiden and Rotterdam. Punt and he had now become competitors and even enemies, and the history of Dutch theatre in the eighteenth century is to a large extent the history of their different opinions. Corver won in the end, because he was the new man, the stronger company leader and the better teacher. In his *Theatre Notes*, however (see 308), he has a keen eye for Punt's greatness and tries to dispel the impression that he ever slighted his predecessor.

As an actor, Corver evoked highly divergent sentiments. Most intellectuals adored him for his 'natural' style, comparing him to Garrick and Talma and opposing him to Punt, whom they thought bombastic. They called Punt an 'orator', Corver an 'actor'. Indeed, the old style of acting had declined from the middle of the century and Punt, it was felt, exaggerated.

338   Corver honoured as an actor, 1773

Anon., *Brief over het Vertoonen van den Vader des Huisgezins, door de Haagsche Tooneelisten* [. . .] (Letter on the Performance of the [Diderot's] Father of the Family by the Actors at The Hague) (Gedrukt voor den Autheur [Private Print], n.p., n.d. [Amsterdam, 1773]), pp. 6–7

Let me admit that I have never seen our Amsterdam actors and actresses play with such a relaxed liveliness, nor with such fire, for I have always detested the Amsterdam stiffness and that horrible shouting [. . .]. The people in Mr Corver's company[1] do not shout at any time, they speak naturally [...]. They are used to their easy and natural style, and [will never relapse because they] have learned too much from their Master, whom we acknowledge as the greatest actor known in the country, now and perhaps ever.

[1] Established at The Hague and Leiden at the time.

Simon Styl, a physician, historian and playwright from Harlingen in Friesland, wrote Punt's biography (see p. 407). Styl is much fairer than Corver's grim answer, the *Theatre Notes* of 1786, would lead one to suspect, but he preferred the classical manner, both in acting and writing, and therefore gave short shrift to Corver, especially criticising his voice. Other opponents disapproved of his meagre appearance and the way he stood on stage, in one instance comparing his attitude to that of someone who had been with a *fille de joie* and had brought home more from her than he needed.

339   Corver slighted as an actor, 1781

Anon. [= Simon Styl], *Levensbeschryving van eenige voorname meest Nederlandsche mannen en vrouwen, Deel 9. Het leven van Jan Punt* (Biography of Some Outstanding Men and Women, mostly Dutch. Vol. 9. The Life of J.P.) (Amsterdam: [publisher unknown], 1781), pp. 87–8

This man, well-favoured in the Schouwburg at Amsterdam, but not thought to be of the highest rank, [had gone to The Hague]. There he thought to enjoy the proud heroic roles which they had not dared to entrust him with in Amsterdam. But because the good fellow had both a *hincorrect prownownciashun* and a false squeaking voice, he had to look for some remedy to compensate for these faults. In The Hague there is no readier expedient than to ape the French: that is, to gabble as quickly as breath will fly through the nose and the mouth. The result is unintelligible and therefore faultless. He has also borrowed a new way of acting from some common French players, especially a few postures which have chanced to raise some applause. In addition he made a trip to Paris, and lo and behold, my Lord Corver is frenchified and capable of being compared to Lekain or Grandval).[1] But we cannot refrain from conjecturing that the first Frenchmen he imitated must have had a kind of Neapolitan rattle in their throats, and that by a similar coincidence their limbs were also stiffened. Otherwise it is impossible to explain the hoarse sounds and distorted spasms which are the greater part of his 'new' manner.

[1] Charles François Racot de Grandval (1711–84), distinguished French tragedian.

C. ACTING TECHNIQUE

340   In praise of touring, 1786

Corver (1786), p. 43

A travelling actor always has more experience than one who has never played anywhere but in his native city. He continually has to appear before a different audience, one not used to him, and usually he doesn't stay in any one place long enough to be able to form a clique; whereas an actor who always plays in his native city has more opportunity to do so. The audience is used to him, and he to the audience; this means that they will both always be satisfied with each other. Is there any actor in France or England or in Germany, who has not travelled and who has not played on different stages?

Rehearsing

341   Learning many roles

Corver (1786), p. 51

[. . .] during the period of six years that I spent with Punt,[1] I learned approximately as many as a hundred roles by heart, without using any feeling. All of them were in the most important line of business: heroes from Melpomene's train, all the Roman and Greek fellows. These came in very handy a few years later, when I took on the aforementioned stereotype, because I had that number already in my memory and so didn't have to learn them.

[1] As a young man, when he was already a supernumerary, Corver took acting lessons from Punt.

342   Rehearsing in private, 1753

Corver (1786), pp. 58–9

Meanwhile, the time approached for Punt to make his debut:[1] three days beforehand, he asked me to come to his house every morning for an hour or two, to rehearse the passages with him that we had to do together (because I had to play Patroclus). This I did; we were soon in agreement and our interaction was swiftly arranged. He had brought something new to it, namely that he armed me on the stage, he put a helmet on my head and handed me the sword and shield: what he devised was a dumb-show and later on he always retained it. His reappearance on stage was on 22nd December, which was the Saturday before Christmas 1753. He played Achilles excellently. The theatre was completely full, but his voice was found to be duller than it had been a few years earlier; and in the second act I noticed it for the first time, when he came to stand beside me and I had to adjust my tone a little to suit his. I told him just after our exit, saying that: *It would have been better to rehearse our passage in the theatre instead of at his house.*

[1] Punt had left the Amsterdam Schouwburg from 1745–1753. The 'debut' concerns his re-appearance there. He had of course chosen Huydecoper's *Achilles* (see 335).

The earliest Dutch theatre magazines date from 1762. The first one, published at The Hague and written in French, *L'Observateur des spectacles*, covered mainly the French theatre in Holland. Like so many to follow it was short-lived, lasting only for six months. *De Hollandsche Tooneel-beschouwer*, a bi-weekly, appeared in 20 numbers, reviewing the performances in Amsterdam from 30 Aug. 1762 to 24 May 1763; and afterwards in book form. Its anonymous author was a member of one of the many literary societies in Amsterdam.

343   Rehearsals too short, 1762

De Hollandsche Tooneel-beschouwer (The Dutch Theatre-Observer), no. 7, 23 November 1762; pp. 118–19 of the book edition, n.p., 1763

[. . .] sometimes one has the added grief of seeing one's play being pitifully torn apart by the actors. Just imagine how it could be otherwise: two weeks before the play is to be performed, each actor receives a printed text, from which to learn his part. Time enough, though, to commence the job, but instead of starting to study the play, they go and lend it to their good friends to read it [. . .] and in this manner the play is known and has been criticised before it has ever even been performed. Then, finally, the time for performance draws near and about two or three days beforehand they start a hasty reading of their parts without even knowing the play. Then, on the Friday before, it is rehearsed in the presence of the Lord Governors (a single run-through is deemed sufficient), and when it is performed on the following Monday, none of the actors know their parts properly and they excuse themselves by saying: Yes, it's a new play and it's not so easily done! What a wonderful excuse!

The actor's technique

344   The use of the voice, 1762

De Hollandsche Tooneel-beschouwer (The Dutch Theatre-Observer), No. 8, 7 December 1762, pp. 127–8 of the book edition, n.p., 1763

[. . .] Mr Punt, who was to personify Pyrrhus,[1] stepped out of the wings. He began thus:

Leave me. a moment. alone. with my father.

I consulted my edition at once[2] and found that it said:

Leave me a moment alone, with my father.

Glaucias answered this in the following manner:

Step up. my Helenus! come. you, ultimate support
Of a King. whom fate. oppresses. with severe abuse.
Now breaks the fatal dawn. that. in immeasurable grief.
Shall cause me to die. of shame. or break my heart. forever.

If the verses of a tragedy should be pronounced in such a way as I have here reproduced them, then all those people who have laid down the laws of the stage for us and have spoken of the declamation of verses on the stage must either be great ignoramuses or our actors must have no knowledge whatsoever of recitation. If one reads the treatment of pronunciation and gesture by Mr Le Faucheur,[3] one finds that their whole manner of declaiming and gesturing is in opposition to the lessons of this man and quite in conflict with reason. [...] I cannot understand why every verse must be specifically divided in four – unless it is that our actors have faulty memories so that they may be better helped out by the prompter when speaking in that manner; or it must be that their breath is beginning to fail with age and that they can continue with greater ease that way without caring whether the spectator is satisfied or not. I am certain that this manner of acting is no art [...]. Shakespeare gives splendid instruction to the Players in his tragedy *Hamlet* and nicely demonstrates the gross failings daily committed by them. I cannot resist letting it follow here in the hope that our actors will make use of it one day:

Speak the speech, I pray you, as I pronounced it to you ... [the rest of Hamlet's address follows].[4]

[1] Crébillon, *Pyrrhus* (1726).
[2] Playtexts were sold in the theatres before the performance. They were often consulted during the play (the house lights stayed on).
[3] Michel Le Faucheur, *Traité de l'action de l'orateur et de la prononciation et du geste* (Paris, 1657). This influential treatise was translated into Dutch in 1701 (there were also English, German, Spanish and Latin translations).
[4] The quotation from *Hamlet* is derived from a passage in the Dutch translation of Steele's *Tatler* (no. 8, 7 December 1762, pp. 128–30). Most Dutch translations and performances of Shakespeare followed the French version by Ducis, translated into Dutch in 1777. The first Dutch Shakespeare translation (in prose) which to a certain extent followed the original, consists of a selection of his plays, published 1778–82, in a series of five volumes.

345   Actors do not feel the emotions of their role

Corver (1786), p. 53

Farewell! I am going to Death! farewell in eternity![1]
[. . .] If it is true that Punt really felt all those [. . .] passions and emotions while he chanted this line, it is absolutely impossible that he could have communicated them to the onlooker by his facial expression and posture.[2] [. . .] How could it be possible, at a distance of thirty feet, where this passage usually took place in the former theatre[3] and where the middle drop curtain [. . .] obstructed the light to such an extent that that spot was always in the shade, how could it be possible, I say, for a spectator to perceive all the aforementioned emotions in an actor who had his back turned at that moment,[4] or who, if he wished to be histrionic, could at most be seen in profile?

[1] A line from Punt's famous tirade in Huydecoper's *Achilles* (see 335).
[2] Corver adds that he often stood close by in many supporting roles, but never discovered any real emotion in Punt or any other actor taking the part of Achilles.
[3] The second Amsterdam Schouwburg (1665–1772).
[4] Note that it is often said that acting rules in this period would not allow actors to turn their backs to the audience.

In other instances complete identification is seen as the ultimate aim of art. Cornelia Bouhon-Ghijben (1733–90), playing Zaïre in Voltaire's play, was given to understand between the second and the third act that her old father had just died. The source is an anonymous adaptation from Servandoni d'Hannetaire's *Observations sur l'art du comédien* (1775), interspersed with examples from Dutch theatre.

346   The true greatness of acting is to overcome artificiality

Anon., *De Tooneelspeler en zijn Aanschouwer kunstmaatig beschouwd, of Grondregelen voor beiden. Gevolgd van een Handleiding om zich in de Tooneelspeelkunde te onderwijzen.* (The Actor and his Spectator, Considered in the Light of Art, or Basic Rules for both. Followed by a Manual to Teach Oneself the Art of Acting.) *Delectat et erudit.* (Amsterdam: W. Holtrop, 1791), p. 83

A flood of tears did credit to this sensitive woman. She entered again, and coming to the lines

Grey-haired Lusignan, succumbing under his strains,
Ended his life and horrible misfortunes,

her emotions became so heartfelt, that the spectators, unaware of this curious incident, could not withhold their tears or refuse her a general applause. [. . .] They took so much delight from the imitation that they forgot the imitation, and only thought of the thing itself: and this is the true greatness of acting.

347   The actor should copy body positions from the pictorial arts, 1786

Corver (1786), pp. 69–70

You quote Karel van Mander[1] and refer the actors to it [drawing], in order that they adjust their posture and contrasts[2] properly. This is all good and true; but very few actors, both here and elsewhere, know the proper use of it and it is all Greek to some of them. But a good ballet-master, who knows the art of serious, beautiful dancing, will achieve this even better than the art of drawing. In the grand Opera in Paris, people make drawings of the *Attitudes* of dancers during their performance; and I have seen two dancers there, forming the pose of Hercules and Anthaeus – which is produced in plaster – perfectly beautifully. However, experience has shown me that drawing is indeed of use to an actor [...].

[1] The Dutch Vasari; his *Schilderboek* (The Art of Painting) appeared in 1604.
[2] The doctrine of putting one's limbs in opposition to each other in order to obtain elegance and harmony.

348   Lines of business: Queen Mothers difficult to play

Corver (1786), pp. 98–99

You say that Miss Van Thill[1] exaggerated. If that is true, I would not be amazed. In her youth, she played the 'Jeunes premières', as the French call them, and also some leading roles as the Sentimental Heroine. She had not been on stage for twelve years and was making her [second] debut in April of the year 1762 with the part of Clytaemnestra in *Iphigenia in Aulis*[2] (no mean difference indeed) and then had to take the whole line of business of the Queen Mother upon herself. Do you think that this difference in roles would demand no exercise or that the nature of an actress would be prepared for this without any further ado? Often six or seven years can go by before such a part is done properly, and especially in Amsterdam, since *Rodogune*,[3] *Iphigenia in Aulis* or other plays where Queen Mothers appear, are not put on there for six, seven or more times a year. When the same play is put on many times consecutively, one has the opportunity to adjust one's manner and posture. The point is that this line of business does not consist of a great number of roles, but requires a great deal of study; therefore, it would not be any wonder if someone were to exaggerate a little in the beginning.

[1] Hendrina Margaretha van Thill (1722–95).
[2] Racine.
[3] P. Corneille.

349   Hierarchy of stage positions, but all actors equal, 1786

Corver (1786), p. 152

I pray you, sir, what is this highest rank you speak of? Do you think that backstage in Amsterdam, we observed the same rank amongst each other as on stage, where the King or Hero and his confidant are distinguished*? Oh no, we were equal in rank and position, unless one had to take charge as stage manager; but since this applies mostly to menial work and rarely to actors, I see this hierarchy you speak of as sheer madness.

* [Corver's footnote:] In my time this stage rank was in Amsterdam as follows. The King always had to stand in the middle, like a tea-pot on the hob, with the cups and saucers on either side. The Princess always had to stand upstage, with her confidante on her left, and no matter what the situation was, even in extreme confusion, one always attempted to keep to these positions. I banned this mad and unnatural stiffness from the stage; but what difficulties I encountered here in Amsterdam! For most of my fanatical brothers I was a heretic in the art, and they would gladly have roused the mob to stone us.

350   Good acting is the same in all ages, 1786

Corver (1786), pp. 157–9

I always have to laugh when I hear people say that I have invented a new method of acting. It is an unfounded opinion and reveals, plainly and clearly, the ignorance and inexperience of our nation with regard to acting. This so-called new method has existed for a hundred years and more before our time; and in his early days, before he left the stage, Punt himself acted in this manner. Later on, his acting could be described as singing rather than speaking, and if anything it is this that could bear the name of a new manner, unacceptable to intelligent people, but welcomed by poetry fanatics – and by young idiots. [. . .] Everything that good French actors do agrees perfectly with the lessons to be found in our good old authors. Shakespeare illustrates this manner clearly in his *Hamlet*;[1] therefore, it is quite old, and there is but one good way throughout the whole world. I have seen Dutch, French, German, English and Spanish actors, and those who were good had the same way of acting, simply based on reason and nature, without any force; firm and not roaring in that false so-called Dutch heroic tone:

> Phoe, pha, tra la la la, oh Lord, govern my strength
> Fa, foo, twiddle twaddle, lee la, tra la la la la length,

which bellowing I, and anyone who shares my knowledge, regard as the work of fools.

¹ Probably, Corver had become acquainted with Hamlet's advice from *De Hollandsche Tooneel-beschouwer* of 1762 (see 344). Fifteen years later, in The Hague and Rotterdam, he directed the first Dutch *Hamlet* in the adaptation by Ducis, playing the title role (at the age of 49).

The status of actors and acting

351   The difficulties in providing for one's old age as an actor, and especially as an actress, 1791

Anon., *De Tooneelspeler en zijn Aanschouwer kunstmaatig beschouwd* (1791, see 346), pp. 111–12

After reaching a certain age, it is best for actors and especially actresses to leave certain types of roles alone. It is disgusting to see heroes and lovers performed by elderly players. 'Ah!' the answer will be, 'but if that would mean leaving the stage altogether, what are we going to live on?' In Holland, actors' wages are too low to put something aside for old age. We live in a country in which commerce, not art, is the main thing. Our actors may never hope to earn the same high wages, remuneration and gifts as in countries where so-called entertainment is the people's main concern. [...] The set-up of the theatres in France and England is such that actors' wages may be substantial. In those countries audience attention is greater and more continuous; moreover, their famous actors work under conditions which are more profitable than ours: there a single so-called benefit night offers much more to an outstanding player than an excellent colleague would earn over a whole year in this country. Apart from that, a French actress who is competent and pleasing, is never without hope of providing herself with an infinitely larger income outside the stage than on it, owing to the generosity of upper-class members of the male sex, and to the compliance on the part of the stage heroine or chamber maid; a compliance which is not without its examples in this country, but of a rarer occurrence and far from being so richly recompensed, because this nation has vastly different views on moral behaviour than the lively French. On the whole, our actresses are more virtuous and reticent than those of France, where, on discovering a pleasing woman on stage, it is not considered disgraceful to ask openly and at once: *Est-elle à avoir?* ['*Is she to be had?*'] – Small wonder then, things being what they are, that it is easier there to provide for one's old age than in this country!

XXXI Audiences

In 1667–69 Cosimo de' Medici (1642–1723), son and in due time successor of Ferdinand II, Grand Duke of Tuscany, made two educational journeys through Europe, on both occasions including the Dutch Republic. One of the many honours bestowed upon Cosimo was a gala performance of Jan Vos' tragedy *Medea* in the theatre of Amsterdam.

352 Gala performance for Cosimo de' Medici, 1667

The official travel report, reproduced in G.J. Hoogewerff (ed.), *De twee reizen van Cosimo de' Medici Prins van Toscane door de Nederlanden (1667–1669), Journalen en Documenten* (The Two Journeys of C.d.M., Prince of Tuscany, through the Netherlands (1667–1669), Diaries and Documents) (Amsterdam: Johannes Müller, 1919), pp. 69–71

At about two o'clock [on Friday 30 Dec. 1667] Blaeu[1] came to collect H[is]. H[ighness]. The latter had sent his retinue on along to the theatre, not wishing to go with the whole group, for fear of attracting crowds. This was arranged in order to accommodate the desires of H.H., who had made it known that he wished few people to be about. At the gate of the theatre there was a guard of halberdiers; and the Bailiff, the Burgomasters and a few Magistrates greeted him in the street. He was led into the auditorium in between the Bailiff, that is the Praetor, who is the head of the criminal justice department, and the governing Burgomaster, Reynst, and was offered a box in a seat just above the ground floor, where they also took their seats, surrounding him on both sides. At his entrance to the theatre, he was greeted with a loud flourish of trumpets. Indeed, there was no one else there, presumably to show that the ceremony was organized for H.H. alone. Thus the best ornament was missing: the crowd and the ladies, of whom there were [only] fifteen seated in the boxes that surrounded the said auditorium in a double row, an auditorium which because of its emptiness, appeared cold. The work was performed by the official actors of the city and the subject was provided by Jason and Medea on their journey to the Golden Fleece. It was a skilful touch that they compensated for the absence of a common language by introducing a large number of actions, flying activities, and various machines for heaven and earth, evoked by the incantations of Medea, and it all went went extremely well.[2] And at the end they finished with some eulogies for H.H., who had been entertained by the Bailiff with all sorts of conversations. [...] During the performance, the Commander of the garrison came to ask H.H. for the password [for that night]. When at eight o'clock the party was over, the Burgomasters firmly insisted on being permitted to escort H.H. home, or at least on having the halberdiers accompany him, but they were not permitted to do anything of the kind, so that they took their leave of him at the gate to the flourish of trumpets, and each went his way. H.H. then dined at home and withdrew shortly afterwards.

¹ Cosimo's guide during his stay in the city.
² Cosimo's treasurer Cosimo Prie notes in his own journal: '(The play) was elaborately got up, had five acts, after each of which there was a scene change, but with curtains closed every time and not in view of the audience.' And again, complacently: 'For those of us who had seen things in Italy, there was no lack of great weaknesses. But as actors and novices in the manipulation of scene changes and machines, they conducted things tolerably well.'

Nowhere in Holland was the French theatre so much in fashion as in the aristocratic city of The Hague. In the late eighteenth century, French opera and drama companies played no longer in court theatres only, but also in various other venues visited by courtiers and upper bourgeoisie alike.

About 1730 the French company of The Hague split up. There followed a fierce competition between the two offshoots, the French opera performing in the theatre in Casuariestraat, and the French 'comédie' playing spoken drama in the Voorhout, both of them tiny venues. After two years the victory went to the latter, but to small avail, since in 1733 all theatres were closed down because ship worm (teredo) had affected the (wooden) sea-walls of the western part of the country and a national disaster was feared.

The theatre in Casuariestraat remained active till 1804, the year in which the Royal Theatre opened (see **366**). It catered for plays and operas in French. In 1781 its leading actor was Collot d'Herbois, better known later as a member of the National Convention and the butcher of Lyons.

Justus van Effen (1684–1735), the anonymous author of the following report, is one of the main Dutch Enlightenment authors. He was the initiator of *De Hollandsche Spectator* (1731–1735), a weekly in which he wrote no less than 400 essays, showing himself to be influenced by Addison's *Tatler*. Van Effen, who was equally fluent in French and English and had edited several French magazines before he started the *Spectator*, was a Fellow of the Royal Society, a friend of Swift, conversant with Newton and Pope, and had translated Shaftesbury and Mandeville.

353   Two French companies divide the theatre buffs of The Hague, 1731

De Hollandsche Spectator (Amsterdam: Hermanus Uytwerf), vol. I, no. 12 (5 November 1731), pp. 93–4

[...] The two theatres were opened one after another and both companies declared war on each other. Hereupon all of The Hague was divided into two public parties and the whole affair was taken to heart with extreme zeal. Just as in the civil war between Caesar and Pompey, no one was permitted to remain neutral, one was forced to side openly with either the 'Voorhoutians' or the 'Casuarists'. Even families were divided: Sir was seen riding to one theatre and Madam to the other, just as in some families the wife goes to Mass and the husband to Service. The fierce faction-fighting was the topic of all conversations. Both sides formed cliques, and plotting and scheming was resorted to with the most inexpressible animosity. The first thing that was asked in company was: 'Were you in the Voorhout or in the Casuariestraat? Were there lots of people there?' And the answer would cause happiness in the one and sadness in the other. The *beaux esprits* concerned themselves in no small way either; an investigation was carried out on the comparative merits of both companies: each actor, each actress was balanced against the other [...]. The most industrious of all were the ladies, they mustered all the attractions Nature had given and Art had lent them, in order both to back up the party they had taken under the wing of their charm and to inflict the greatest possible losses on the opposition. [...]

354   Invitation to attend the Schouwburg centenary, 1738

See 323. Reproduced in Wybrands (1873), p. 251

.... is invited, with his Wife, or a Lady, and a Child of his own that can take care of itself, to attend the CENTENARY of the AMSTERDAM SCHOUWBURG on Tuesday, the 7th of January, 1738, in the Afternoon at 4 o'clock sharp. N.B. A Servant may be brought, whose place will be in the upper Gallery.

Coaches please arrive from the Old City; and in the evening please arrange their assembly on the Westermarkt before half past eight, where everybody will be shown his place by a Deputy Bailiff, so as to prevent congestion.

This ticket will serve only for the invited persons mentioned above, and therefore it is requested to hand it in on arrival.

355   Corver deplores 'monkey business' being necessary to attract audiences

Corver (1786), p. 178–80

Has it ever been possible to keep the theatre in Amsterdam going or even in existence without buffoonery? Not in the last forty or fifty years at any rate. Would your people want to see *De Min in het Lazarushuis*[1] if this comedy (which is rather good, as long as it is performed properly) was not marred by monkey tricks? A board laid across two supports like a tightrope cord; making people stand still as if bewitched and then smearing their faces with syrup and sticking feathers in it; and creating a hundred other tomfooleries even baser than what is shown on the platforms in front of fairground entertainments: this is what makes your fellow townspeople come to the theatre in droves. And this buffoonery is so well known in our country that wherever I have performed this play, I have always been forced to fall in with this madness, if I wanted to earn any money doing that play. Yes, I kept making it more and more ridiculous, in the hope that the public would start getting disgusted with it. In a certain city I even brought a live ox onto the stage in the play mentioned, and had Marten and Klaasje[2] raffle it off: the people really did come to see the ox. In the end I got tired of it and here in The Hague I left out all the monkey business and simply performed the play, but it dragged. [...]

I remember that I once helped to destroy *De Tooverijen van Armida*[3] seven times in a row: I have seen box-seats being rented solely in order to see the monkey, very attractively played by Schmidt's child. The whole city was full of the little monkey in *Armida*; yes, at the end of the play people arrived backstage in entire parties to visit the monkey. The ladies cried out: *What a sweet monkey! Look, look, what a lovely monkey! Come here, little monkey, come to me!* The poor boy was still walking around in his monkey suit at ten in the evening,[4] receiving compliments for his monkey tricks and was dripping wet when he took it off.

---

[1] See 320, note 9.
[2] Two characters in the play.
[3] See 320, note 8.
[4] Theatre performances started at four o'clock in the afternoon and generally ended around eight, or sometimes later when the afterpiece was long.

XXXII   *Dramatic theory, repertoire, criticism*

A. DRAMATIC THEORY, REPERTOIRE

In the second half of the seventeenth century neo-classicism came to dominate drama
theory and practice. Its main propagator was the Amsterdam literary society 'Nil
Volentibus Arduum', established in 1669. 'Nil' strongly opposed the ever popular
tragicomedies and melodramas with spectacular stage-effects. Their ideal was to instal the
'civilised taste and high morals' of the French repertoire. To that end and in accordance
with the name of their society they encouraged authors to polish their language ceaselessly
and to translate French plays or to revise the existing Dutch repertoire rather than to write
their own. Many 'improvements' of existing dramas were now published, and when the
Amsterdam Schouwburg re-opened in 1677 after a five years' closure owing to the war
with France, members of 'Nil' took over its government and controlled stage practice. Their
polemical attitude gave rise to much opposition from authors with different views, and of
course popular taste remained unchanged. After a decade 'Nil' lost its power, but its ideas
continued to influence drama and official theatre policy for more than a century.

One of the main spokesmen of 'Nil' was the lawyer and playwright Andries Pels (1631–
81), who wrote a long didactic poem to propagate his views. Jan Vos' *Aran en Titus* (see **283**,
p. 418) was his black sheep, Corneille's *Cid* his most admired example. But although a
staunch advocate of French neo-classicism, Pels was not dogmatic and he admitted the
qualities of the English and Spanish type of drama.

356   Andries Pels defends neo-classicism, 1681

A. Pels, *Gebruik én Misbruik des Tooneels* (Use and Misuse of the Theatre) (Amsterdam: Albert
Magnus, 1681. Reproduced in the edition by Maria A. Schenkeveld-van der Dussen,
Culemborg: Tjeenk Willink/Noorduijn, 1978), vss. 1049–84

Those plays bring in money and are received favourably,
In which one perceives language and good manners
According to the rules of art. Let the French ones be our example.
How decent is their language! how rich in morals! how fine
Their art of arrangement, their passions and ideas.
[...]
There is nothing wrong with many beautiful Spanish plays

And English ones, if only one would carefully divide them
Into acts and scenes: then one would watch them
With as much pleasure as the French plays, or probably more so,
Because of their many actions and their abundant
Invention. [...][1]
Their arrangement of time and place is wild; but all the world,
Both the Learned and the Illiterate, praises their subject matter.
[...]
If, once in a while, we want to derive a play from the English,
Imitate their vigour *and* at the same time take care of the proper rules,
Then it would easily reach the top
And surpass all French fiction.
For if the rules of art are well-observed,
Would any less money therefore flow to the Almshouse?
Oh no, but more; for truly, entertainment sustained by art
And morals, deserves all the world's favour.

---

[1] Pels mentions some popular adaptations from Spanish plays here: *Het verwarde hof* (The Confused Court), thought to be adapted from Lope de Vega's *El palacio confuso*, but in reality an original play by L. de Fuyter (1647); *El cuerdo loco* by Lope, adapted as *Voorzichtige Dolheid* (Prudent Madness) (1650); *El tejedor de Segovia* (The Weaver of S.) by Alarcón, adapted as *Don Luis de Vargas* (1668, see also p. 440); and one other. It is a random and minimal choice from a plethora of Spanish plays in adaptation that proved to be box-office successes in the Netherlands. For seventeenth-century adaptations from English drama, see p. 378; for the eighteenth century, Shakespeare's collected plays are to be added (see **344**, note 4), as well as, among others, plays by Addison, Garrick, Lillo, Moore, Otway, and Sheridan.

More than a century later, Corver deplored what he saw as a general decay of European drama, and especially the activities of the members of the literary societies who, in his view, had nothing to say and who wasted their time touching up other people's translations of plays and churning out rhymed versions of prose plays according to barren neo-classical norms. It is remarkable that in Holland the bourgeois drama was popular with the audience, but not with most authors. Consequently, for the sake of the theatre there were many contemporary translations of the foreign box office successes in this *genre*, while original Dutch bourgeois plays were scarce. Corver often included the new kind of drama in his repertoire, while also pleading for the revival of the older tragedies.

357   Corver on the decay of drama, 1786

Corver (1786), pp. 186, 191, 196

[...] whether what one puts on stage is a tragedy, a comedy or what is called a *drame* doesn't matter, as long as the play is good. It is certain that, however much one may concentrate on beautiful words and elegant expressions, in two hundred years' time people will express themselves differently. And then, just as they do now, people will say that the language has been greatly improved, and what we speak now will be old-fashioned. Good ideas can be extracted from a language which has fallen into decay, but there is nothing to be drawn from words that are beautiful, but contain no thought. [. . .]

The *Tragedy of George Barnwell* is too good, or at least there is too much good in it, to be put into verse. It would rob it of just as much of its real value as [has been done to] the *Déserteur* by Mercier, the *Graf Olsbach* by Brandes, the *Indigent* and the *Jenneval* by Mercier and to be brief, everything that has been transposed from prose into verse that appears on our stage.[1] Besides, it provides no mean source of ruination for the actors, as it thoroughly destroys their natural gifts and talents.

[. . .] but as long as poets fritter away their time remodelling prose *drames* into verse and verse into prose, both of which I find equally insane, or retranslating plays that have long been translated, in order to display their virtuosity in spelling and coining words, nothing valuable will appear on our Helicon [. . .] Mercier and Falbaire[2] are unjustly dismissed, because they threaten to rip away the plasters from the festering wounds; and for that reason, it seems, people want to resume the Spanish taste, of which *Le Barbier de Séville* and *Le Mariage de Figaro* may serve as proof. But neither the bourgeois tragedies, neither the acting of comedies or *drames* in prose, yes, not even the operetta, that poison for the soul of true acting, will ever be able to suppress the tragedy – if only one can produce a Vondel, a Hooft,[3] a Corneille, a Shakespeare, a Voltaire or a Lessing. We have to have good authors, and good actresses and actors to perform them well, and if then victory is not gained, I forfeit my head; but without them trying to please by force will always be the same as catching the moon.

[1] Lillo's *London Merchant* (1731): there is a late Dutch translation (1779), but the play had become popular as *Jenneval ou le Barnevelt français*, Mercier's adaptation (1768), translated into prose in 1770, which translation was put into rhyme in 1776. In 1775 the same translator had also made a rhyming version after a prose translation of Mercier's *L'Indigent* (The Pauper) (1772), under the title of *Doriman en Melanide*. This play proved very popular: in the same period, three other translations were published, each under a different title. Mercier's *Le Déserteur* (1770) was translated six times in verse or in prose. Brandes' *Graf Olsbach* (Count Olsbach) (1768) saw three translations.
[2] Fenouillot de Falbaire's most popular play was *L'Honnête criminel* (The Honest Criminal) (1767), three times translated.
[3] P.C. Hooft, see 277, 299, 305.

Some essays in dramatic theory from the literary societies of the time have a more modern ring. An anonymous author published an excellent piece on stage directions, doing justice to their value for theatre practice. Comparable essays on stage dialogue and on the aside are by the same hand.

358   The nature of stage directions in plays, 1786

Nederlandsche Dicht- en Tooneelkundige Werken, van het Genootschap Onder de Spreuk: Door Natuur en Kunst (Dutch Works on Poetry and Drama, by the Society under the Motto: By Nature and Art) (Amsterdam: Willem Holtrop, 1786), pp. 121–39

[It is certain that] denoting silent passages and actions everywhere in the plays [by stage directions] must offend and irritate the great actor. It follows that the dramatist should take the greatest care here, for otherwise he leaves too little to the actor and moreover spoils the pleasure of emotional sensation for the spectator by taking him by the hand and demonstrating from gesture to gesture what he can expect. [...]

The question is therefore: whether one can determine any limits here, to the extent that common sense will be really convinced of their necessity. [...] We must consequently look into: I. Where the dramatist places the directions needlessly; II. where they may be useful; III. where one cannot do without them without hurting the play itself as well as the main actors.

I. Where the text itself is clear enough, it is useless to clarify it by additional prose; and the poet who takes this most into consideration, is in this the most praiseworthy. [...]. II. The first kind of *useful directions* are, in our opinion, those which indicate entrances and exits when two actors may not catch sight of each other. [...] Likewise, it is also not inexpedient to point out where a character has exited when another has to follow or look for him. [...] We consider to be the third useful kind those where the dramatist cannot clearly express his particular objective. [...]

> Mélanie: Where am....
> (*She becomes aware of her father and throws herself in fright into the arms of her mother.*)
>   What do I see ... .?[1]

Would one not also be able to *act* the exclamation, 'Where am ... What do I see ...?', fixedly staring at the father with a posture begging for mercy? – We believe this to be so. But the dramatist, steeped in his characterisation, felt otherwise and wished terror and amazement to maintain the upper hand over begging for mercy. [...]

III. We regard as indispensable those directions where the leading actor or actress depends to a great extent on the minor characters, the walk-ons in particular. [...] On nearly every stage people are hired as body-guards, retinue, mute citizens, who (especially if their number has to be rather large) know nothing of the play, who are just as if they had been picked up off the street; and through this, infinite errors are made in the richest and the most beautiful of scenes. Now if in such cases stage directions are written down, it will be infinitely easier for the stage manager, when directing the walk-on characters, to make them understand the passage by letting them read it themselves than if he lets them repeat his own prepared plan ten times or more. [...] Then the dramatist has done his duty in coming to the aid of the stage manager, who, however competent he may be, will get less done orally than the dramatist with his well-written prose that everyone can read, mull over and envisage.

¹ From Jean-François de la Harpe's *Mélanie* (1770), Act II, Scene 6.

B. CRITICISM

In the new eighteenth-century genre of the theatre review, the comparison with the drama text was often applied as a standard for judgement. Deviations from the printed dialogue sometimes met with boos from those literati in the audience who had bought a playtext in the theatre and consulted it during the performance. On one occasion, a Dutch actor being thus stopped had to prove that his error was due to a misprint in his own copy before he was allowed to go on. But deviations from the stage directions also met with an unfavourable reception.

359   Unfavourable criticism, because playtext is not followed, 1773

Anon., *Compleete Verzameling van Vyftig Brieven, Van een Rotterdamsch Heer*, etc. (Complete Collection of Fifty Letters, by a Gentleman from Rotterdam) (printed by the author, n.p., n.d. [1774]), p. 34

But Gerald's house¹ was used poorly, because first it had to serve as a farmer's dwelling and then again as the house of a philosopher. Likewise, the stage did not represent a street as prescribed [in the playtext] under [the list of] players or characters, to wit in the third and fifth acts. Also the Chamber was not a proper room for such a small house, being much too stately and distinguished. [...] [Also, when a character in the play remarks:] 'The doorstep is too high', while such a step is absent, certainly Gerald would have to answer: 'There is no doorstep in front of my house.'

¹ In the anonymous farce *De malle wedding of Gierige Geeraard* (The Foolish Bet or Stingy Gerald) (1750)

The same reviewer shows that historic accuracy in stage dress also started to matter. In 1773 in a Rotterdam performance of Bontius' evergreen *The Siege and Relief of Leiden*, set in 1584 (see **280**), the actors wore modern costumes, but the Burgomasters had in addition donned seventeenth-century full-bottomed wigs. Corver (1786, p. 60) mentions that these wigs were an idiosyncrasy of Jan Punt, who played the main Burgomaster. However, the wigs had some advantages.

360   Costumes unhistorical – but to good effect, 1773

Vijftig Brieven (Fifty Letters), p. 130. (See also **359**)

Their appearance was proper, according to each character. The costumes, however, were not historical but modern, following the tradition of the Amsterdam theatre for this play. The same for the Burgomasters, who appeared with big wigs, known as full-bottomed. While this was not in accordance with former times and even differed from what the Honourable Governors of Leiden are accustomed to today, yet it made a dignified impression and necessarily caused feelings of respect in the audience. This succeeded all the better, because there was another advantage: three of them, who had to play double roles, could not be recognised. This caused incompetent spectators, present in large quantities, to be favourably impressed, thinking that each character was played by a different actor.

Period III: 1795–1848

XXXIII   *Contractual and organisational documents*

Over the years theatre regulations had become much more detailed and draconian (see 306–7). Directors had absolute power, actors none, and offences against the rules carried high fines (compare 90). It is only after approximately 1840 that we hear of actors appealing to justice against some rule or penalty imposed by theatre directors.

Among the many new regulations of public life during the French occupation of the Netherlands, i.e. from 1793 in the South and from 1795 in the Dutch Republic, those for the theatre put an end to the connections between it and the civic almshouses, which had lasted for two centuries. The cities now governed the theatres directly; also, a short experiment took place with a central state government (1798–1800) and theatres were let to private persons, mostly associated actors. In 1805 the Amsterdam Schouwburg was governed by civic Commissioners.

361   Rules of the Amsterdam theatre, 1805

Contracten van acteurs enz. (Contracts of actors, etc.), Univ. Libr. Amsterdam, Port.ton. fo. X. 1–62. With theatre laws 1803–10. Reproduced in Vogel (1899), pp. 182–7

The Commissioners of the Municipal Theatre having nothing closer to their hearts than that this institution, entrusted to their care, should attain its true purpose, namely to be a useful breeding ground of national taste and a school of virtue and morality, and being convinced that discipline, determined by appropriate rules, is to this end definitely required, have judged it necessary to stipulate the following articles in order to have them observed and followed precisely, without exception.

I. All actors and actresses, male and female dancers who belong to the Schouwburg must clearly declare their place of abode to the stage manager under penalty of three guilders for every week that they are in default.

II. None of them may absent themselves from the city during the theatre season without having asked and obtained permission to do so from the Commissioners, under forfeit of one month's salary, the second time two months' [salary] and the third time under penalty of dismissal.

III. Neither may any of them play, dance or perform any service at any other theatre, in or outside the city, under any sort of pretext or colour whatsoever, be it of Societies, Colleges, amateur companies or otherwise during the Schouwburg season, under penalty of dismissal.

IV. All actors and actresses, male and female dancers who are not required on stage, are obliged to remain at their domiciles until six o'clock so that the Commissioners may always, before or after, call on them upon a sudden change of one of the plays; and on absenting themselves from home after this time, must leave information about where they are to be found if necessary. Anyone who acts against this will forfeit twenty-five guilders for each occurrence.
[...]

VII. Every actor and actress must take care to be ready with their allotted role or vocal part at the time stipulated and none may excuse themselves on whatever pretext; illness, of whatever nature, shall henceforth no longer be an exception. Anyone who acts against this shall forfeit half of a hundred and twenty-fifth part of his contract for every occurrence, about half of what he earns per performance.
[...]

VIII. Those who do not know their roles properly or who do not deliver their cues quickly enough shall forfeit a fine of six guilders in either case.
[...]

X. Those who are appointed as walk-ons on the cast list must perform the roles with fitting discipline according to the demands of the play. But as the Commissioners have experienced what disadvantage the plays suffer as a result of the frivolous pretexts with which some actors and actresses attempt to excuse themselves from the walk-ons, they deem it right to lay down the following statute:
That the walk-ons will be divided into three classes from now on:
1. in which people come on stage as soldiers or only as body-guards without performing any special action;
2. in such as occur in diverse plays, whether as citizens, soldiers, servants, farmers, etc. and to whom some form of silent action is assigned, albeit very little;
3. in which more action is required or action on which the success of a play or the good or adverse outcome of a role may depend, the judgement of which remains reserved for the Commissioners.
Women as well as men belong to the last two classes.
All actors and actresses whose contract is for more than ƒ 800 are excused from the second class.
No one shall be excused from the third class, whilst all actors or actresses, from the

first to the last, must willingly lend themselves to such walk-on parts as indicated above and as the Commissioners impose upon them.

And the fines with respect to all these classes shall be the same as those stipulated with respect to the speaking parts, and no more than with those will illness be an excuse; and the least refusal shall be held to be disobedience to the law.

XI. Everyone must provide himself with the necessary effects the plays require, the effects belonging to the head and feet of the actors and actresses to be out of their own pocket along with the flesh-coloured tights and pantaloons, the white and yellow pantaloons, and the modern trousers which do not explicitly belong to any particular costume – and they are obliged to procure them to the requirements of the play to be performed. By effects, as is customary, should also be understood the purchasing of decent swords, plumes, hats and caps, dagger sheaths, epaulets, shoulder belts, and sashes, everything in the style of the play to be performed, and those persons who do not appear on the stage decently dressed or whose effects do not fit the requirements of the play in which they are performing, and are therefore not neat and in good order, will forfeit a fine of six guilders for each occurrence.

[...]

XVI. [...] in the evening of every acting day, after the show, the stage manager shall deliver a written list to the Commissioners of those who have violated these articles and shall be held to observe these laws strictly without respect of persons under penalty of paying double the statutory fines himself, if he should be guilty of any connivance in this.

The fines shall be deducted from the salaries on the usual payday.

By order of the Commissioners of the Municipal Theatre, Amsterdam, 1 May 1805.   (*signed*) W. Haverkorn, Willemsz., Secretary.

Contracts were also formulated along strict lines, even for a first-rate actor like Andries Snoek, who had at the time made his name as one of the greatest Dutch actors of tragedy and would shortly be appointed as a company director at Amsterdam.

The income offered to Snoek (f 1900) was well above the average. Top salaries were an exception, like those of Mrs Wattier or the dancer Polly Cunninghame in the season 1809–10, who each received f 4000. A beginner would earn no more than f 300 per season of nine months, with costume accessories such as hats, swords or shoes being at his own expense. Figures like these make it clear what the fines for misdemeanours amounted to: an actor earning f 600 per season and running into a f 25 fine would lose half a month's salary.

Snoek's contract does not mention any lines of business. He was appointed as *premier rôle et premier amoureux*, but the contracts obliged every actor to be ready for all possible roles, including walk-ons.

When Snoek himself had become one of the company directors (1810),.he simplified the contracts, no longer mentioning specific conditions in them.

362   Andries Snoek's contract, 1807

Contracten (see 361). Reproduced in De Leeuwe (1978), p. 105

CONTRACT

by which the undersigned pledges himself to the service of the Royal Dutch Schouwburg[1] and is appointed by the Commissioners for the next season, beginning 7 August 1807 and ending in the following month of May, for as many performances as will please the Commissioners.

I, the undersigned, pledge myself by this contract to the service of the Royal Dutch Schouwburg, to perform there during the next season as many times as the Commissioners of that Schouwburg will deem necessary such characters and plays, mute characters not excepted, as will be assigned to me, and to play the parts in which I shall be cast according to the lists which will be handed over to me or will be lying in the office of the Stage Manager.

I also pledge myself to take part in the necessary rehearsals in the required costume at the discretion of the Commissioners.

Further I pledge myself for the period of my engagement to subject myself to the commandments and laws issued by the said Commissioners, or which they will issue, and especially to the theatre laws and fines decreed by them on 1 May 1805, of which a printed copy has been added hereafter, which laws I undertake to obey as if they were included in this contract verbatim.

I promise to conduct myself in all respects according to my duty and to fulfil strictly all the conditions stated above, and this for such wages as I have stipulated and which have been mentioned below.

Amsterdam, ... May 1807.
  [Signed:] Andries Snoek

According to the above contract, the Commissioners of the Royal Dutch Schouwburg have appointed in the service of the same Schouwburg, for the season beginning on 7 August 1807 and ending the following month of May, for as many performances as it will please the Commissioners, for the sum of [handwritten] nineteen hundred guilders, as an [handwritten] Actor [: Andries Snoek.]

Amsterdam, ... May 1807.
  By order of the said Commissioners,

                                                    [Signature missing.]

1 'Royal' because from 1806 to 1810 Holland was a kingdom under Napoleon's brother Louis
Napoleon who had accepted the patronage of the Schouwburg.

From the second half of the eighteenth century, complaints are heard about the lack of
provision for the actors' old age (see 351); fixed pensions were of course non-existent. Also,
their education had to be bettered: instead of the traditional learning routine through
amateur companies and individual lessons from established actors, institutional theatre
education was now called for in order to raise the level of performances. In 1808 the actor
Johannes Jelgerhuis (see 371–2, 381–1, 385, 388) was the first to urge the necessity of
establishing a theatre academy. It was not until 1821 that the Commissioners of the
Schouwburg set up a Fund in order to tackle both problems in a uniquely combined way,
providing pensions for those actors who would be willing to teach drama students in
accordance with the Fund regulations. The enterprise turned out to be a success. It is not
known how long the Fund lasted, presumably until the middle of the century. Several other
pension funds gradually came into being. With the Fund, the school ceased to exist. From
1820, a Society for Public Eloquence provided training for young actors, but the first Dutch
theatre school in its own right was established in Amsterdam as late as 1870.

363   Theatre education and actors' pensions, 1821

*Reglement voor het Fonds, ter Opleiding en verdere Onderrigting van Tooneelkunstenaars, voor den
Stads Schouwburg, te Amsterdam* (Regulations for the Fund for the Education and Further
Instruction of Stage Artists on behalf of the Municipal Theatre of Amsterdam), n.p., 1821,
University Library, Amsterdam, Port.ton. fo. X 1–62

Art. 1.

A Fund shall be set up to find the requisite expenses to allow actors or those suited
to the dramatic arts to enjoy a sound training in that art.
[...]

Art. 3.

The necessary monies for the establishment and maintenance of the Fund will be
found from:
1. The gross profit, with no deduction of any costs, of three special performances
per year;
2. the forfeited fines received in accordance with the theatre regulations;
3. such monies as can be specially collected by subscription or from other
approved resources or contributions.

Art. 4.

For their efforts remuneration will be granted from the Fund to those whom the
Commissioners elect to give the aforesaid instruction in the dramatic arts, and

who by the acceptance of this become members of the Fund according to the amendments stipulated hereafter.

Art. 5.
The members of the Fund must give instruction to all those assigned to them by the Commissioners in all aspects of the dramatic arts necessary to train them as competent stage performers.
[...]

Art. 7.
The number of members may be less but not more than eight persons.[1]

Art. 8.
No one other than the dramatic artists of the Amsterdam Municipal Theatre or those who through age or disability have had to leave it may be nominated a member of the Fund.

Art. 9.
The members of the Fund shall be divided into benefiting members and anticipatory members.

Art. 10.
The benefiting members shall be those who have had to leave the service of the Theatre through age or disability, yet remain committed to the ongoing teaching of the persons assigned them by the Commissioners. These have immediate enjoyment of the remuneration mentioned in art. 4. In so far as they may through advanced age or disability become completely incapable of any further teaching, this will not curtail the right once granted and they shall continue to enjoy their annual pension. The decision in respect of this remains entirely with the Commissioners.

Art. 11.
The anticipatory members are those who are still under contract to the Theatre; they may not receive any direct benefit from the Fund, but on being forced to leave the Theatre through old age or disability they become benefiting members automatically and immediately.

Art. 12.
The annual pensions from the Fund to its benefiting members will be made as follows. If there is only *one* benefiting member, he shall enjoy one third of the

revenues mentioned in art. 3. over the previous year. In case of there being two, each a third. In case of there being three, collectively two thirds. In case of there being four, jointly three quarters. In case of five, jointly six sevenths. In case of six to eight, collectively the whole, each with an equal part.

Art. 13.

The balance not paid out from the annual revenue as specified in art. 3 shall be invested to obtain a fixed capital, the fruits of which will likewise be invested as capital.
[...]

Art. 15.

If an anticipatory member leaving the service of the Theatre through old age or disability and thus moving to the rank of benefiting member is recognised by the Commissioners, due to his circumstances, as no longer being fit to give the instructions mentioned in art. 5, he shall nevertheless enjoy to the full all the privileges related to benefiting membership.

Art. 16.

If an anticipatory member should pass away before moving to the rank of benefiting member, a block gratuity shall be granted from the fund capital of a twentieth part of the last ten years of the revenue referred to in art. 5 (or less according to the time he had been active as an anticipatory member) to his widow or, failing her, to his legal children and, failing them also, to any person appointed in writing by the member himself to the Commissioners.
[...][2]
Thus ratified at Amsterdam, 24 April 1821.
Commissioners of the Municipal Theatre

(Signed) D. Hooft Jbz.
By order of the same: A. Tauney
Secretary

(Underneath)   Seen and approved by the Honourable Lords Burgo-masters of the City of Amsterdam, 9 May 1821.
By order of their Honours:
(Signed) W.J. Backer.

---

[1] In 1836 the rules for a limited membership were abolished, so that from then on all retired Schouwburg actors who were willing to teach would be sure of a pension.
[2] There are five more articles.

In the first half of the nineteenth century, dramatic censorship conformed to a variety of regulations. Since 1803, during the French occupation, the Chief Commissioners of Police had acted as licensers. Quite a number of patriotic plays, most of them in the guise of historical dramas, stood no chance of being passed by them, with the result that in 1813 the Minister of Justice drew up a whole list of banned plays. After the liberation of that same year the Burgomasters reclaimed of course their right to make the final decisions regarding all forms of public entertainment – this time with maintenance of religion, morality and public order as criteria. However, the practical execution of this right remained in a state of uncertainty for some time – for who was going to read all those plays? For the official Municipal Theatres the boards of commissioners were expected to supervise their repertoire, but the many smaller venues and companies which had now come into existence raised a problem. Finally in 1835, a separate censor was appointed. This measure did not work very well, as the banned plays were performed after all; that is, on Sundays at private performances. In 1866 the post of censor was abolished, but the Burgomasters have maintained – and often exercised – their right to forbid performances to this day.

364   Censorship, 1836

A letter from the Censor to the Burgomasters of Amsterdam. City Archives, Amsterdam, Arch. 5181, Portef. 212, Doc. 3514

Amsterdam, 9 April 1836

We have the privilege of advising Your Honours, in reply to your missive of 31 March, that we have examined the changes made by the director of the French Theatre in the play *Don Juan d'Autriche*.[1] We have concluded however, that for the most part they consist only in that whenever mention is made of Jews or ceremonies of the Israelitic religion, this has been replaced by Moors and quotations from the Koran, without any improvement of the continuous offence against the Roman Catholic religion, which offence is so interwoven with the whole play that it cannot possibly be removed. The play is a *tableau* of the suppression of the Jews in Spain under Charles the Fifth and Philip the Second, painted in the French manner, vigorous and incisive, but harshly delineated. To change this in such a way that not the Jews but the Moors suffer from this suppression may spoil the historical aspect of the play, but it does not diminish the continuous defamation of the Roman Catholic Church.

And so we remain of the opinion that the performance of such a play cannot be but highly displeasing to all the members of that Church.

[...]

The Commissioner,

P. van Marselis Hartsinck.

---

[1] Casimir Delavigne, *Don Juan d'Autriche ou la Vocation* (Don John of Austria, or The Vocation) (1836).

XXXIV   Theatre venues

In the last quarter of the eighteenth and the first half of the nineteenth centuries, a wealth of new theatres were established in Amsterdam, all much smaller than the Schouwburg, some of them short-lived, others more permanent. A rough sociological division would be as follows:

1. Upper- and upper-middle-class theatres, presenting the best and latest taste in drama and opera. These were the French Theatre on the Erwtenmarkt (1785–1855)[1] and the High-German Theatre in Amstelstraat (1791–1852). Both venues seated approx. 500 spectators.

2. The Schouwburg, still catering for all ranks, but gradually suffering from the competition of the French and Germans and for economic reasons[2] giving in to the lower-class preference for melodrama, vaudeville and the like, much to the distress of the intellectually minded members of the audience (see 387).

3. Popular theatres, presenting all kinds of entertainment, from high opera to magic tricks. A few of these were of good quality, like the Grand Salon of the Duport family in the Nes (1839–1867) or the Salon des Variétés in Amstelstraat (1844–1914): some of the greatest actors began their career in these venues. Others were of a lower status, being all at once a pub, a dance-hall, a café chantant and a drama theatre. One of the latter was 'De Ooievaar' ['The Stork'] in Sint Anthoniesbreestraat (1776–1876).

365   De Ooievaar [*The Stork*], an Amsterdam Café Chantant, 1808

Engraving by Daniel Veelwaard after Jacob Smies. A. Fokke Simonsz., *Amsterdamsche Winteravond-uitspanningen* (Amsterdam Winter Night's Entertainments) (Amsterdam: J.C. van Kesteren, 1808. Reproduced from Fokke's *Werken* [Works], vol. 6, *ibid.*, 1833), p. 171

Whoever entered the premises was obliged to order a drink immediately, preferably a glass of the best red wine or punch. The waiters would ask: 'What will it be?' (thus the caption on the print, omitted here). People would then walk around the hall with their drinks, trying to find a seat, beside a 'lady of entertainment' if so desired.

The hall was 50 ft long up to the stage and 30 feet wide; the stage itself had a depth of 20 ft. It was low, its floor was not raked and no one took off their hats: that is why the stage could only be seen by part of those present, some eighty or ninety people in the front. At the back of the hall people sang and talked loudly. – The café kitchen served as the actors' dressing-room and foyer.

The actors did not perform complete plays, but scenes from operas or from comedies, and in between, after a short break, they sometimes sang burlesque arias and duets. After the performance, when the respectable citizens had gone home, the auditorium turned into a dance-hall; it stayed open till three in the morning. – Note the statues of Melpomene and Thalia (see 313).

---

[1] The building, now called 'De Kleine Komedie' (The Little Comedy) is today's oldest theatre of Amsterdam.

[2] The municipal subsidy, on which the Schouwburg depended after the connections with the Almshouses had been discontinued, was always too low; in the twenties it amounted to no more than 25,000 guilders *per annum*.

366   Façade of the Koninklijke Schouwburg, The Hague

Lithograph by Desguerrois & Co. after P. Lauters, 1850, Municipal Archives, The Hague

The Koninklijke Schouwburg [Royal Theatre] at The Hague was certainly an upper-class theatre. Its beautiful façade showed (and still shows) its origin: the theatre was housed in the former palace, built in 1766–73, of Prince Charles Christian of Nassau-Weilburg, a brother-in-law of the last Stadtholder William V. After a reconstruction of its interior by the architect J. van Duyfhuis, who built an intimate auditorium for no more than 712 spectators, the Schouwburg opened on 30 April 1804 with a Dutch performance of Voltaire's *Sémiramis*, given by the company of Ward Bingley (see 373), with the renowned *tragédienne* Johanna Wattier (see 374–6) in the title role. Until his death in 1818 Bingley was to be the theatre's first director. The French taste of the audience at The Hague is shown by the fact that alternating performances in Dutch and French were given for most of the nineteenth century. The French repertoire was mainly opera; from 1830 to 1853 the French opera company at The Hague ranked third among the opera houses of Europe, after Paris and St. Petersburg. At first the Royal Theatre was privately owned, afterwards either the King (William I and II) or the city took possession, the city being supported by a large Royal subsidy.

XXXV   Stage presentation

A. STAGING METHODS

Tableaux vivants remained popular as ever (see **277–8, 318–9**). In this age of melodrama, however, they aimed less at moral instruction by means of allegory than trying to bring a tear to the eyes of the sensitive spectator. An example is provided by the end of Maarten Westerman's play *The Relief of Leiden*, where the starved citizens welcome their liberators.

367   A moving *tableau*, 1809

M. Westerman, *Het Ontzet der Stad Leiden, Geschiedkundig Tafreel in drie bedrijven* (The Relief of the City of L., An Historical *Tableau* in Three Acts) (Amsterdam: H. Moolenijzer, 1809). Quoted from the 4th edn (1836), pp. 80–1

The ships enter amidst loud music. The crowd has flocked in from all sides and cheers merrily. The bridge on the Vliet is chock-full of people of every rank, sex and age. The sailors hand out food to the crowd. [. . .] Happiness, gratitude and rapture show on every face. The members of the city council exhort the crowd through gestures to thank heaven, and form a dignified group. The sailors wave their caps. The citizens clash their weapons. In the foreground one sees several moving groups. Van der Laan and his wife have given their child a piece of bread; they lift him up together and while he bends forward he raises his hands and turns his eyes heavenwards. Here one sees a mother kneeling in a grateful attitude with a child at her breast and surrounded by three others, with the food she has received in her hand; there a married couple hug each other tightly, surrounded by their children. Others bedew their bread with their tears and are unable to enjoy it because of their ecstasy. [. . .] The whole scene is a moving *tableau*, supported by the music. After it has stood still for a moment, [the Admiral] Boisot disembarks, followed by [. . .] the ship's officers, and they are saluted by the councillors and welcomed with happy cheers.

At the end of 1813, after the defeat of the French at Leipzig and the establishment of the Kingdom of the Netherlands, the cultural ties with England were strengthened again. Within a few months a large contingent of English theatre artists crossed the North Sea.

474

First, a travelling company arrived, calling themselves grandiosely 'Their Majesties' Servants from the Theatre-Royal of London and Windsor'. During their stay in Amsterdam, from May to the beginning of July 1814, they were to perform no less than twenty different productions, each consisting of a main piece and an after-piece. These took place in the German Theatre.[1] Most of the visitors' plays were light and visually explicit fare,[2] for just like the strolling players of two centuries earlier the English visitors were apparently aware that the majority of the audience did not understand their language. One of the spectators thus handicapped was the actor Johannes Jelgerhuis (see p. 467, 371–2, 380–1, 385, 388) who, moreover, had never seen an English performance before. His notes and sketches – jotted down under the modest motto 'What shall we say about that which we do not understand' – stress what he felt to be characteristic of the English performance style, as an indirect comment on what was typical for Continental stage presentation.

---

[1] See p. 471.
[2] Mainly now forgotten English comedies, with G. Colman Jr. as the most frequently played author. But they also performed plays by Shakespeare (*Hamlet*), Goldsmith (*She Stoops to Conquer*), Lillo (*The London Merchant*), Beaumarchais (*Figaro*), and of course Kotzebue.

368   English guest productions, 1814

Iets over het Engelsche Tooneel, waar genoomen in de maanden Maij en Junij 1814 Door J.Jelgerhuis Rz [,] Hollandsch Acteur te Amsterdam (Some Observations on the English Performances in the Months of May and June 1814 by J.J., Dutch Actor at A.), MS, Univ. Library, Amsterdam, 23 pp., unnumbered.[1]

[...] The dialogues were spoken very swiftly, and the women spoke in a high-pitched and thin tone which I cannot say I have found very pleasing. [The play] had five acts, each with numerous scenes which changed with the curtain open. Now they were here, now there, and back again in the same room with the same characters.

[...] The performance took place without a prompter; the cover of his box was closed and lamps were put on it.[2] I was told for sure that they did not even have a prompter. [...]

Their blocking was most remarkable, often spread out over the entire stage. They passed one another and intermingled, thereby indicating natural confusion, which nevertheless showed a visible order, because they never masked each other. However, they were free from that visible order which reigns on the French and Dutch stages, meaning that most characters gather round the prompter and pass behind each other with some formalities. Their spreading out [also] makes the speaking of asides possible and convincing. [...]

The play was in prose [...] and their national taste showed up specifically in that most of the time the characters entered while speaking before they were to be seen; also in their positioning just mentioned.

[1] Part of the translation is taken from E. de Wijs-Maher, who translated Albach (1977).

[2] This shows that the prompter's place was as yet only a hole in the stage floor, without a hood. The centrally placed prompter's box probably appeared on the Dutch stage after the French occupation of 1795. Earlier, Holland followed the same tradition as England in placing the prompter behind the first wing (although at the Amsterdam Schouwburg stage right, i.e. the reverse of the traditional English position).

B. SETS

369   A miniature model theatre for demonstrations at home

Nederlands Theater Instituut, Amsterdam

In the eighteenth century miniature theatres were an attraction of the fun-fairs or were exhibited in special venues,[1] presenting all kinds of townscapes and landscapes or the places where recent famous events had taken place. Such miniature theatres were also used by gentlemen of leisure in their homes, not to present plays in them, but to demonstrate different Schouwburg sets and the technique of scene-changing to their friends in *soirées* organised to that end. Some of these theatres and their settings have been preserved and the most accomplished one was built in 1781 for (the later Baron) Hieronymus van Slingelandt. It comprised eight sets, a sea and a cloud, all copied from the Schouwburg scenery by one of its best set painters, Pieter Barbiers. Slingelandt's son Hieronymus Nicolaas, who was a Schouwburg Commissioner (with special responsibility for its scenery) continued this hobby until his death in 1844 and had another six sets, a new front curtain and some furniture and figurines[2] made by the most prominent Dutch scene painter of the nineteenth century, François Joseph Pfeiffer (1778–1835). The set shown here is 'The Winter Wood' (1824). The theatre's façade has been much changed in the nineteenth and twentieth centuries. The stage opening measures 75 by 86 cm.

[1] Such a venue is shown in Edward Burney's illustration of De Loutherbourg's Eidophysikon in the British Museum.

[2] These have also been preserved, together with a host of designs, programmes, accounts and notes concerning this theatre, covering the whole period from 1781 to 1844.

370   F.J. Pfeiffer, Design for *La Muette de Portici*

Undated (approx. 1828). Pencil, pen and washed ink, 27 by 50.3 cm. Nederlands Theater
Instituut, Amsterdam, TL 38–37

Pfeiffer, who was employed by the Schouwburg for nearly forty years, designed and made
dozens of sets for drama, opera and ballet, not only for the actual theatre, but also for a
'théâtre optique' which he owned and used for public performances. Scenery and its usage
had gradually changed since the eighteenth century. Stage effects like the moving sea and
the descending cloud were no longer fashionable, scene-changes took place with the front
curtain closed and, most important, at least some sets were made which formed no part of
the stock scenery, as they were meant to be used in one production only. Such a set was
made by Pfeiffer for Auber's opera *La Muette de Portici* (1828), showing the bay of Naples
with the smoking Mt Vesuvius in the background, suffusing all the surroundings with a red
glow. As elsewhere, the back-cloth was a transparent screen which, with lamps lit behind
them at the right moments, would suggest moonlight or the eruption of the volcano. The
asymmetrical disposition, the suggestive use of colour and the large view of a fantastic
landscape are all typical of Pfeiffer as a romantic artist, and the same is true for his many
sets depicting castles, churchyards, prisons, ruins and the like. The design shown here, one
of many for the same set, was intended for his 'théâtre optique', as a copy of the real thing in
the Schouwburg. Auber's opera happened to play a political role as the incentive for the
Belgian uprising against the Northern Netherlands: after its performance at Brussels in
1830, the excited audience took to the street, crying for independence.

C. COSTUME

Johannes Jelgerhuis (1770–1836) was one of the most important stage artists of the early nineteenth century: an excellent actor in serious parts, an accomplished draughtsman and painter, both of theatrical and non-theatrical subjects, a costume designer, and above all a tireless chronicler of the performances he had watched or taken part in, with a keen eye for the technical aspects. Jelgerhuis' greatest merit, however, lay in his work as a teacher and a theoretician (see 380–1). He had chosen to play King Lear (in Ducis' adaptation) for his *début* in the Schouwburg in 1804.

371   Jelgerhuis, Self-portrait as King Lear, 1805

Water colour. Caption: 'King Lear 1805 Middle Ages'. Nederlands Theater Instituut, Amsterdam, GD 3–36

372 How to dress as King Lear? Jelgerhuis considers his own practice, 1811

Toneel Studien. Bevattende Ontwikkelingen en Gedachten van Onderscheiden Toneel Studien. Welke slegts tot op de helft van het voorgenomen plan zijn afgeschreven. Door den Hollandschen toneelspeler J. Jelgerhuis Rzn. Dezelven zijn meestal geschreven bij ziekte mijner huijsgenoten, en zittende tot derzelver oppassing en gezelschap (Theatre Studies. Containing Developments and Thoughts from Various Theatre Studies. No more than half of what was originally planned having been written down. By the Dutch actor J. Jelgerhuis Rzn. They were mostly written during illnesses of members of my family, while sitting at their side to nurse them and keep them company), MS, 1811, Nederlands Theater Instituut, Amsterdam, pp. 4–13

[. . .] My predecessor always changed his dress.[1] His last one was much better than his first one, but yet, in my opinion, he had not sufficiently attuned it to the age and the national character [. . .]. I have always found the best solution in what follows. I kept in mind that in the age of Lear the English and Scots will have closely resembled each other. The best engravings confirmed this: I studied and followed them as far as the costume stock in the theatre permitted. In doing so the result became very similar to Engel's illustration, which provided me with the concept.[2] I took great care to dress Lear in an undergarment, serving as a short skirt to cover the nakedness of the entire lower part of his body. It was of a quiet and sombre colour, and a red sash wound its way around it in a disorderly manner, falling down from the shoulder; it looked quite poor and therefore fitted the text. The remaining traces of royalty were provided by a black velvet gown, with the ermine fur which is the prerogative of kings. [. . .]*

Further, I made my own footwear, in the form of a boot. I would have liked to use puttees instead, in the manner of the old Scots; but as the other characters in the play went around in boots, I would have been too conspicuous. [. . .] Boots, however, are all right, as long as they do not look like the top boots of the sixteenth and seventeenth centuries; so that the footwear I made stood midway between them, as the illustration shows.[3] It consisted of leather gaiters, shoes, and loose tops. [. . .]

Properly using my paint-brush according to the art of physiognomy, I provided this monarch with a handsome face, adding a grey beard and a pate that had soon grown white and bald from grief and sorrow. The pate was covered with flesh-coloured taffeta and had some hair at the back. The eyebrows were pasted on, consisting of evenly coloured grey wool. [. . .]

*[Note by Jelgerhuis.] It causes no end of difficulties to find satisfactory costumes in theatre stock. As a result one is often compelled to dress quite contrary to the way it ought to be, because for one reason or another nothing else can be found. [. . .]

---

[1] That is, from one performance of this role to the next. The predecessor in question was Ward Bingley (see 373).

² J.J. Engel's *Ideen zu einer Mimik* (1785–86) had been translated into Dutch as *De kunst van nabootzing door gebaarden* (The Art of Imitation through Gestures) (Haarlem: Jan van Walré, 1790). (For Engel, see 131–3, 136–7).

³ The illustration in this text shows the same actor and costume as 371, but with a different attitude.

XXXVI   Actors and acting, direction

A. INDIVIDUAL ACTORS

The prominent actor and director Ward Bingley (1757–1818) (see also p. 472) was praised by most for the powerful or even fierce way he played tragic heroes, villains and proud fathers. An appendix to the important theatre magazine *De Tooneelkijker* (1816–1819), which was very critical of the acting style and repertoire of its days, judges him differently from his confrères. Implicitly it sketches the desiderata for the new style of acting which would only very gradually come into being: psychological insight instead of fixed passions; sensitiveness instead of rhetoric; muted instead of vehement climaxes; and harmonious unity of all the actor's physical means instead of salient vocal effects.

373   Bingley, or the new style of acting

Anon., *Verslag der tooneelvertooningen van W. Bingley te Amsterdam; door de schrijvers van Den Tooneelkijker* (Report on the Theatre Performances of W. Bingley at Amsterdam, by the authors of The Theatre-Observer), Appendix to vol. IV of the magazine (Amsterdam: St. Delachaux, 1819), p. 14

A more difficult task now needs to be done: to evaluate Bingley's acting in the role of Talland, the Father.[1] How can we fully praise him, when the whole country watches him rapturously perform a part in which he cannot possibly be equalled, let alone surpassed [. . .]. We would have to indicate to you from scene to scene what he uttered powerfully, what with insight into human nature, what sensitivity. We would have to tell you that his sadness did not amount to shouting, nor his fear to weeping or screaming; nor his madness to the violence of a drunken sailor; that his death was not horrible, but natural and gentle; that all the emotions of his part were not only apparent from his voice, but also from his face, his gestures and his attitude. Words fail us to express all this with dignity, and to judge Bingley in the part of Talland, the Father, another Bingley would be needed.

---

[1] In A.W. Iffland, *Das Gewissen* (Conscience) (1799). Bingley played the part in 1802.

374   Wattier as Lady Macbeth in the sleepwalking scene

D.P.G. Humbert de Superville, pen drawing in brown, washed in grey, 1802. Print Room of the University, Leiden, PK 1467

Johanna Cornelia Wattier (1762–1827)[1] is the most renowned actress in Dutch theatre history. Like Bingley (see **373**) she was a pupil of Corver. She began her career at Rotterdam, but changed to Amsterdam where she was a first actress for 35 years, venerated alike by the *literati*, her colleagues, royalty and the general audience. Tragic heroines from the classical French repertoire such as Chimène, Phèdre, Iphigénie or Sémiramis were her forte, but she was excellent in comedies as well. It was felt that her combination of 'poetic nobleness' and 'truthfulness' was unequalled and her silent acting was especially praised. She was extolled in many poems, paintings, essays and spoken eulogies; the highest possible salary (see p. 465) and a regular gift of laurel wreaths and jewellery confirmed her fame. Napoleon called her the greatest actress of Europe and granted her an annuity. She was admired by Talma, with whom she played in a guest performance of Ducis' *Macbeth* in Paris (1806) and subsequently made a 'pensionnaire' of the Théâtre Français. All agreed that the sleepwalking scene of Lady Macbeth – called Frédégonde by Ducis – was one of the high points of her acting career. See also **384**

[1] Or Ziezenis-Wattier, after her marriage to the architect B.W. Ziezenis (1801).

374

375   Wattier's entrance in the sleepwalking scene

C.G. Withuys, *Lofrede op Johanna Cornelia Wattier* [Eulogy on J.C.W.], Amsterdam, 1827. Reproduced in Albach (1956), p. 126

[...] but how high the emotion rose in the last act, when the imperious Lady Macbeth entered sleeping, destined by the revenging gods to thrust the dagger with which she wanted to stab the Crown prince of Scotland, into the breast of her own son! – Her entrance in the sleepwalking scene was both studied and natural, so that, even before she appeared on stage, the least observant spectators were aware of the sleeping woman's approach from her heavy breathing. Indeed, her actions in the speaking dream, in which she presented that female monster with alternating feelings of hatred and tenderness, bloodthirstiness and fear, triumph and remorse, formed a masterpiece of genius and technique, so sublime, perfect and unique as will perhaps never be imagined.

376   Wattier's silent acting

Matthijs Siegenbeek, *J.C. Wattier Ziezenis, eerste toneelkunstenaresse van Nederland, in eene redevoering geschetst* (J.C.W.Z., the First Actress of Holland, Sketched in an Oration) (Haarlem: De Erven François Bohn, 1827), pp. 30–2

[...] I want to draw your attention to a particular quality which in my opinion makes Wattier's artistic fame complete [...]. No doubt you will already have some idea which most noble and, alas! most neglected aspect of the art of the theatre I am referring to. When it is practised well, it causes the audience never to perceive the genuine artist as an actor, but only as the character he has to play, even when he is but a silent participant in the stage action. Now Wattier used to take care of this aspect of her art to such a degree of perfection that I for one do not remember having seen any artist who was not far inferior to her in this respect. [...]

In the last conversations I had with her about her way of acting, more than two years before her death, I remember that she enlarged upon the importance of the part of Badeloch in *Gijsbrecht van Amstel* by the famous Vondel, and did so with much vividness and fire. She complained that this role was seldom performed decently. Now what do you think she saw as its most important aspect? Perhaps the highly poetic report of her dream, in which her niece Machteld van Velzen appeared to her, or any other magnificent part of her role? Far from it [...]: most important to her were the different sensations and emotions which Badeloch had to express while listening to the elaborate reports of Arend and Gijsbrecht van Amstel and especially of the messenger – emotions which were noticed by perhaps a bare twenty out of a thousand spectators, while the eye and the mind of the majority were fixed on the speaking actor only [...].

377   Andries Snoek in the title role of Voltaire's *Oreste*

Engraving by W. van Senus after J. Kamphuysen, n.d. [*c.*1800]. Nederlands Theater Instituut, Amsterdam, GTL 3–14

Andries Snoek (1766–1829) was the male equivalent of Mrs Wattier, for twenty-five years playing next to her in the Amsterdam Schouwburg, where for some time he was also a director (see **362**). With his athletic body and powerful voice, Snoek became the first tragic actor of his time, like Wattier admired by all and sundry. When in 1811 Napoleon visited the Netherlands and the Théâtre Français performed in the Schouwburg, alternating with the Amsterdam company, Talma, who had Hamlet in his repertoire, saw Snoek play the same role and was so impressed by it that he refrained from performing it himself for the rest of his stay. (See also **388**.)

Anton Peters (1812–72), a pupil of Jelgerhuis, was one of the most important actors of the 1850s and also a theatre director in several cities. He started as a tragic actor, but gained renown in melodrama. The playwright and novelist H.J. Schimmel explains why, on the strength of a performance of von Holtei's *Lorbeerbaum und Bettelstab* (Bay-tree and Beggar's Staff).

378   An actor's limitations may serve him well for melodrama

H.J. Schimmel, 'De dichter in de maatschappij [...]' ('The Poet in Society'), *Kunstkronijk uitgegeven ter aanmoediging en verspreiding der Schone Kunsten* (Art Chronicle for the Furtherance and Propagation of the Fine Arts) (The Hague: K. Fuhri, 1850), vol. 11, p. 70–1

Rightly judging the qualities of the dramatic genre he had to choose, Peters applied himself to gesture, and that made him a truly great artist. He felt that he could never be a tragedian because he lacked the physical stature to present a giant or a demigod; and also felt that his voice was inferior to that of his lower-ranking colleagues, who would always surpass him in rattling off and bawling out the traditional alexandrine, which was designed for this effect. Peters could not be a tragedian, but he became a player of dramas; he is no reciter, but rather a true actor in the highest sense. [...]

When I attended a performance [of Holtei's play], someone whispered excitedly into my ear: 'It is great to express the feelings of the heart by means of the voice, but it is infinitely greater to do so by means of gesture, silently.' This is what Peters did [...]. How excellently he plays the 11th scene of the 3rd act, where the 'Geheimrat' chases him away. He stoops to pick up his stick, but falls down in the act. When he rises, the greatest of changes has taken place. He has gone mad. All those who were agape at how the artist presented this, at how he conveyed that great change by the trembling of his facial muscles and by every movement of his body, and at how he even made it clear by groping around as if he were blind when a moment earlier he knew his whereabouts, – surely they will all have shed tears of compassion and not withheld their due admiration from him.

B. ACTING TECHNIQUE

In his treatise on the desired future of Dutch dramatic art, the classical scholar Van Limburg Brouwer also made a suggestion to heighten the standards of acting. (Compare 133.)

379   Actors need an intellectual education

P. van Limburg Brouwer, *Verhandeling over de vraag: Bezitten de Nederlanders een nationaal toneel met betrekking tot het treurspel? [...]* (Essay on the Question whether the Dutch have a National Theatre as far as Tragedy is concerned?), n.p., n.d. [Leiden, 1823]

The actor should not only know the way in which he has to pronounce the words of the poet, he should not only *feel*, but he should also know the things he is going to talk about. In brief, the actor should have if not a scholarly, at least a so-called 'lettered' education. How else will he be able, not only in his dress but also in his attitude, his gestures, yes, even in his smallest nuances, to strike the notes of the age and the nation to which the play belongs in which he performs, if he does not know the history, the customs and traditions, and what's more the mentality of that age and nation to which he at that moment must belong? When the author presents us with Greeks and Romans on the stage, what's the use if the whole play breathes the spirit of antiquity, while the actor's performance gives constant proof that he has not got the slightest notion of it?

Would it be impossible to establish a School for young theatre artists?

Jelgerhuis' *Theoretical Lessons* are a rich source for all aspects of acting technique in the early nineteenth century; 'the text is detailed, extensive, concrete and authoritative' (Barnett (1987), p. 487). The book contains the *verbatim* notes and the illustrations for the course given by Jelgerhuis during four winters for the Educational Fund of the Schouwburg (see 363). The book was published in two volumes, the first containing the text of thirty-eight lessons, treating, respectively, the stage and how to enter and leave it; how to stand, walk and sit down; the positions and gestures of the body, the legs, the arms, the hands and the fingers; facial expressions and make-up; and costume. The second volume contains hundreds of expert drawings illustrating the lessons.

Jelgerhuis epitomized the neo-classical ideas of the preceding century, always stressing grace, nobleness and beautiful 'attitudes' as the essence of acting and basing himself on such earlier authorities as Van Mander, Le Brun, Lairesse, Le Faucheur, Sainte-Albine or Engel, whom he referred to in his lessons. In this respect he is a late representative of a closing tradition. In others, however, he is very much a child of his age, for instance in his plea for historical studies as a means to obtain accuracy as a condition for total illusion.

Jelgerhuis' *Lessons* have been published in English, with an important introduction, by Alfred S. Golding, *Classicistic Acting* (New York/London: Lanhem, 1984), whose translation is only partly followed here.

380   How to enter and exit, and how to move on stage

J. Jelgerhuis, Rz., *Theoretische lessen over de gesticulatie en mimiek. Gegeven aan de kweekelingen van het Fonds ter Opleiding en Onderrigting van Tooneel-Kunstenaars aan den Stadsschouwburg te Amsterdam* (Theoretical Lessons on Gesticulation and Mimic Expression. Given to Pupils of the Fund for Training and Instruction of Dramatic Artists, Playing in the Municipal Theatre at Amsterdam), 2 vols. (Amsterdam: P. Meyer Warners, 1827), pp. 34–8

The aim is to tread the boards in the right attitude for each character and especially to appear on it with the appropriate gait and movement.

Let us speak for the moment about the way of walking [...]. A certain conventional stage gait is not always suitable: it should be modified according to the character represented. This goes without saying, for it would be ridiculous to make a peasant walk like a nobleman. If the former walks in a natural way, the latter treads proudly; but this provides us with a warning against going to extremes. We must not copy the military march here and very carefully avoid its imitation, even when playing the hero of a tragedy, and yet we must walk nobly and even tread in a stately and brave manner. So, if we have thrust out one leg, A, in a dignified fashion, the rear one must not follow with the knee stiffened; – the consequence is a rolling motion of the entire body, which is indecorous.

I shall draw this action so that you may better understand my meaning.[1] We must equally avoid pacing with the knees bent, but follow the joints which Nature has given and move hips and knees freely.

We must also avoid dragging the feet when walking, a practice observed in some French actors, who move one leg ahead in a dignified way only to bring up the rear one with the toes gracefully scraping the floor. It transcends the bounds of nature and becomes an affectation, which can only be effective if one wants to provoke laughter in comedy when portraying a conceited fool, and it is therefore allowed in the high style only for representing a haughty man, because, serious as he may be, he is meant to invite mockery through disgust.

These examples automatically demonstrate the golden mean: our walk on stage should be firm and bold, but without any evidence of haste. In tragedy, especially, we should not take too short a step or one too large for the performer to negotiate. So that is the way to appear on stage, to enter it.

[. . .]

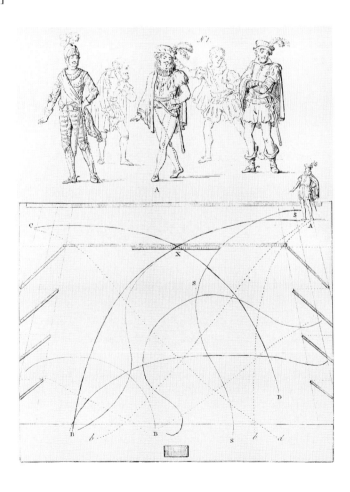

Plate 3 shows a floor or ground-plan for a well-arranged stage. The actor A is on the point of entering and has decided at rehearsal or in his previous private study that at first he will move to position B on the forestage. Now, if his movement is to acquire decorum (let alone grace and nobleness), he should not follow the dotted line from A to b, but the curved line from A to B, whether the stage is empty or whether a door or gate between the two points is opened to him, as at X. In doing so he should carefully avoid entering or exiting through a half-open door, which is unbecoming and therefore quite forbidden; this practice has to be left to the comical actor, who will apply it profitably according to circumstances. He should not go from A to b in a miserable way around the corner of the wing, but rather from C to D or from A to B. He should not go from C to d, but rather from C to D, as indicated just now. [...]

When exiting, he has only to be careful to prepare himself a little shortly before he leaves the stage, in order to avoid a ridiculous impression, like a soldier who makes a short turn left or right. Going off along a gracious ample curve, he should regard it as a law to be observed as much as possible (I repeat, as much as possible) always to cross and exit on the opposite side from where he entered. If the blocking of his exit does not allow this, he should go to the centre from where he stands and also follow a curved line (indicated at SSS), whether or not exiting through the door or gate.

Following this lesson, the stage will remain large in the eye of the spectators, whereas by following the dotted lines it will seem small and cramped, even if it were large. – I must also add that one should carefully avoid entering through the wings if no gate has been painted on them: or else the actor will seem to be breaking through a wall. [...]

All these important notions are especially valid for tragedy [...] and for comedy [...]; in bourgeois drama, they need less attention, but will still need application to the characters represented and in any case should never be neglected *completely*. [...]

---

[1] See illus.

381   How to collapse in despair

Jelgerhuis, 1827 (see 380), p. 64

We now come to the attitude which is encountered so frequently on the stage, that of collapsing in despair across a table. More often than not, in this situation all the rules of stage decorum are violated.

First let me give you an absolutely incorrect posture as seen in no. 7. We shall see that it is hardly possible to mend it, so we must think of a better disposition for expressing despondency and desperation than this one. The legs are badly positioned; indeed, the whole attitude remains wrong, even when the right leg is set more appropriately. The same is true for both arms, and while changing them may improve the representation slightly, it does not make the deportment completely graceful. The entire attitude, despite its common usage, I regard as ill-considered and reprehensible.

But now for no. 8. What grace, what contrast! How much better, how decorous; and the hand hanging limply down by the right knee makes the entire posture the true image of despondency and desperation. So let me show you that merely to collapse onto a table in a highly emotional manner is insufficient. Decorum must continually assist the stage artist in his work, without being harmful to his emotions or diminishing them, if it is ever to deserve being called beautiful.

C. DIRECTION

If an important actor headed a company, he would traditionally also direct. Direction as a separate function was unheard of. Although the call for a supervisor as yet does not indicate directorship in the modern sense, the requirement that he should mould the actors into an *ensemble* is part of a new performance concept. The anonymous author will have adopted his ideas from France, where they had been expressed earlier.

382   A call for directors, 1817

De Tooneelkijker (The Theatre Observer), 4 vols. (Amsterdam: S. Delachaux, 1816–19), vol. II, pp. 405–6

The manner of staging and the casting of the plays should be entrusted to an accomplished *supervisor*,[1] to a man or to men who have attained fame as artists and who would theoretically know how the less experienced should approach matters in practice [. . .]. This experienced and acknowledged artist should enjoy full confidence, and should be able to act freely [. . .]. It is by this means that a unity can be created, an *ensemble* which will form the basis of the performance. He will work in harmony with the board of directors in monitoring the morality, customs and costumes of the characters in his plays, and in this way each step will be a step forward, both for the actors themselves and for the audience. [. . .] These sub-directors are to have absolutely nothing to do with the receipts or expenditures. They are to be able to act freely as artists, not as speculators.

[1]   The text has '*régisseur*', only later the common Dutch word for 'director', but at this time still having the French meaning of stage manager.

XXXVII   *Audiences*

At the Amsterdam Schouwburg the lower classes had always resented any attempt to remove them from their familiar standing room at the back of the pit. When at last around the turn of the century they were definitely put into the upper gallery, their noisiness caused the same trouble as ever.

383   Mob behaviour in the gods, 1808

A.L. Barbaz, *Amstels Schouwtooneel*, 2 vols (Amsterdam: Willem van Vliet, 1808–9), vol. 1, 1808, p. 36

It is there [i.e. in the gods] that the mob, in the upper part of the house divided into two sections, by shouting, cursing, swearing and other outrages, expose the respectable members of the audience, who are seated below them, to multifarious kinds of unpleasantness, specifically by spitting and by throwing all sorts of filth into the pit, just as carelessly as if there were not any people down below. It is therefore that I am accustomed (and in my opinion not without reason) to call the pit the spittoon of the gods: indeed! spittle, chewed-up tobacco, apple and pear skins, nutshells, hats, bottles, pieces of glass, etc. cascade into it like a shower of rain or hail; once it even happened that something as brittle as glass, to wit a human body, flopped into it, but less at the expense of the one who fell down than of the one who received this weighty load on his shoulders. Those who usually stand on either side in the pit are the most generously sprinkled of all, and the kettledrummer and bass player, at the extreme ends of the orchestra pit, also receive their liberal share, and one could apply to them what Gysbreght van Aemstel says to Father Willebrord:

You have not been disfavoured in war's mild blessings.[1]

[1] Vondel, *Gysbreght van Aemstel* (1637), vs. 206.

There are many complaints about audience behaviour in the early nineteenth century. That things could be quite different when both play and performance were compelling, was proved by the performance of *Macbeth* in the Amsterdam Schouwburg, with Snoek and Wattier in the main parts (see 374–7).

384   The audience enthralled

C.G. Withuys, 1827 (see 375). Reproduced in Albach (1956), pp. 125–6

Whenever it was given, there was a solemn atmosphere in the audience, even before the performance started. The spectators were already under the impression of the fearsome beauty at hand, and of the high art to be seen and heard in all its awe-inspiring majesty. I cannot imagine a more excellent whole than this tragedy. The terror of its plot, the dark beauty of the verse, and the compelling performance of the two main characters got both actors and spectators in one and the same sombre mood and expectation. This caused everyone, even in the cheapest seats, to hold their breath, so that the house, although invariably packed, was silent, which was nearly as impressive as the play and the performance themselves.

Flanders had seen renewed cultural activities since the end of the War of the Austrian Succession in 1748, but professional theatre life had to wait until well after the end of the French occupation and the separation from the Northern Netherlands. The first professional Flemish company was established in 1853. Guest performances from the North took place from time to time and in 1816 the indefatigable Jelgerhuis took notes.

385   The Amsterdam Company badly received in Flanders, 1816

Johannes Jelgerhuis, Rzn., *Aanteekeningen gehouden op eene Ryze naar Brabandt in den jaare 1816 verrijkt met de noodige schetzen. Te Antwerpen, voorts naar Gent en terug naar Holland* (Notes on a Journey to Brabant in the year 1816, embellished with the necessary Sketches. At Antwerp, then on to Ghent, and back to Holland), *MS*, City Archives Amsterdam. Reproduced in A.E. d'Ailly (1938), pp. 80–94

[Antwerp] Our performances met with much applause and audience attention; small wonder, it must have impressed them as lightning in a pitch-dark night; those lads had never seen such a thing, for in long years they had only had little French operas, two or three per night. [...]

The second night's work in the theatre amazed me: this was the second performance and the auditorium was empty. We discovered that everywhere the announcements in Dutch had been torn off from under the French words on the playbills. [...] How will it be possible to make Dutchmen of these people?

[Ghent] The theatre is an old building made over into a playhouse. It is rather big, much bigger than at Antwerp. They have boxes in the proscenium arch so that the heads of the spectators at the bottom are on a level with the feet of the actors. There are even small glass windows in the columns of the proscenium arch, and they are watching [the play] through them while drinking a bottle of wine.

[Brussels] The theatre was reasonably full, but the hatred against the Dutch nation is greater here than anywhere else. The play bores them, for they cannot understand it, they all speak French. [...]

They did not applaud Snoek's entrance. Being used to it, I was horrified by this omission [...]. Today it was rumoured that the performance would be hissed so that the Dutch would not perform here again. Indeed, this happened at the end of each act, but at the end [of the performance] it was also uncommonly strong, and yet, there were people among my colleagues who thought nothing of this and called it the doings of a clique which one had to rise above, whereas I called it an insult, never to be forgotten.

XXXVIII   Repertoire, dramatic theory, criticism

Around the turn of the century and until a few decades later, there were lively discussions on traditional and modern literature, repeatedly concentrating on the question of what were the requirements for a good new theatre repertoire. Romanticism had little influence in the Netherlands, and in their quest for new standards most intellectuals upheld the ideal of (neo-) classical tragedy. One of them was Van Limburg Brouwer, who did not advocate slavish imitation of Greek tragedy, but maintained its aesthetics as an ideal for all time. About Shakespeare he had the usual mixed feelings, but German romanticism was his *bête noire*.

386   Shakespeare unique but Schlegel to be condemned, 1823

P. van Limburg Brouwer, *Verhandeling*, 1823 (see 379), pp. 140–3

I admire him [Shakespeare] as a genius, as a man of the finest feeling, as a true poet, and among these as one of the greatest judges of human nature. [...] But if you ask me whether I would recommend him as an example for a national theatre, I must confess that I would by no means venture to do this. Shakespeare is unique and, it seems to me, the least suitable to be imitated in every respect. Let authors study his character-painting, his true expression of the passions, and, if that were given to anyone, imitate those and make them their own. If they have the same fine understanding of what is tragic, let them follow his art in order to express it in their own works in the same moving way. But why should the strange form of his works, his puns, his mixture of jokes and seriousness, yes even his ridiculous anachronisms and inaccuracies be forced upon us? If we are to believe Schlegel,[1] Shakespeare is perfect. [...] I want to declare war upon Schlegel and his Germans, for not only do they want to recommend Shakespeare's merits and flaws alike, but also to present both as a model [...]

Schlegel begins by corrupting the prerequisite of any literary work: its unity.[2] Causes and effects belong to a plot, therefore [according to S.] you may begin and end where you want. So you may start with Leda's egg if you wish to sing Hector's death, and possibly add the flight of Aeneas [...]. Schlegel certainly does not regard this as unity, he wants a deeper, more intimate and secret unity than that which pleases most judges of art. [. . .] But why make a secret of what should be clear? [. . .] Just as I believe that the example I have given will not be considered to possess any unity, nobody will deny that *King Oedipus* does. [. . .]

---

[1] In what follows, his criticism is mainly directed against (A.W.) Schlegel's *Ueber dramatische Kunst und Literatur. Vorlesungen* (1809–11).
[2] Cf. the twelfth 'Vorlesung'.

After 1815 the Amsterdam Schouwburg went through a difficult period (see p. 471) which was to last for half a century. While the foreign and popular theatres were thriving, the Schouwburg was generally felt by the connoisseurs to be in a state of decay. The municipal theatres elsewhere fared no better. Complaints, analyses and proposals for improving the situation appeared in abundance. Actual reform had to wait until the seventies. When he was a student at Leiden, the author Kneppelhout devoted one of his sketches of student life to the theatre of his days, criticising it fiercely.

387   The vulgar repertoire of the municipal theatres, 1840

Klikspaan (= Johannes Kneppelhout), *Studentenleven* (Student Life) (Leiden: H.W. Hazenberg, 1844); quoted from the 6th edn (Leiden: A.W. Sijthoff, n.d.), pp. 243–4

But if in the enjoyment of the traditional theatre fare, leaving aside the manner in which it is performed, a civilised man should hope to relax from his social affairs, how greatly deceived he will be! French and German melodramas, of the coarsest literary merit, rough-hewn, ungainly, clumsily conceived, best for those who stand at the back of the house or sit up in the gods, this is what is being performed nowadays in the big theatres of this country: a *Naufrage de la Méduse*, a *Steffen Langer*, a *Kaspar Hauser*, a *Jeanne de Naples*, a *Forêt de Bondy*,[1] trash of the worst kind, pearls of the murkiest water, which a properly educated man would be ashamed to find entertaining, pieces at home on the boulevard stages of Paris; and all this for the benefit of sailors and housemaids, while the higher ranks watch like blind owls, lacking the independence of thought and the understanding of art needed to abhor all this and to avenge the insult by loud and open signs of unanimous disapproval. The spectator is condemned to untranslatable vaudevilles, which paint customs and use expressions foreign to a Dutch audience and the Dutch way of speaking, incomprehensible to two thirds of the public. But a product of our own soil, an original play – even if performed a hundred times – remains forgotten and despised. [. . .][2] Indeed, would our ham actors be conversant with the names of the first of our authors, would they ever have thought about Dutch theatre works, would they know what poetry is? Seriously speaking, I doubt it.

¹ L. Desnoyer and A.Ph. d'Ennery, *Le Naufrage de la Méduse* (The Wreck of the Medusa) (1838); Charlotte Birch-Pfeiffer, *Steffen Langer*; probably Wilhelm Thiel, *Kaspar Hauser, der arme Findling* (K.H., the Poor Foundling) (1828); J.F. de la Harpe, *Jeanne de Naples* (1781); R.C. Guilbert de Pixérécourt, *Le Chien de Montargis ou la forêt de Bondy* (The Dog of Montargis, or The Forest of Bondy, 1814) (see **228**).
² Klikspaan mentions Vondel's *Gysbreght* and some nineteenth-century Dutch playwrights here. The fact that the latter have long since passed into a justified oblivion provides an ironic comment on his endeavours to see more contemporary Dutch dramas performed.

B. CRITICISM

388   Ducis' 'Hamlet' at the Amsterdam Schouwburg, 1816

De Tooneelkijker (see **382**), vol. I, 1816, pp. 145–53

[...] the verse play entitled *Hamlet* is generally considered one of the most elevated and with the most vivid of characters. We uphold this judgement from the bottom of our heart, if one will allow us to consider as indelible stains on this masterpiece by the English Bard the Gravediggers' scene in the fifth act and the means Hamlet uses to prove to himself that his mother and Claudius are the murderers of his father (a stage play, which must have been unknown in the Dark Ages, especially in Denmark, and is therefore improbable). [...]

The play is perfectly well acted by Snoek, Miss Grevelink, Jelgerhuis, Westerman and Van Hulst. Snoek was unsurpassable: he does not yield to the Frenchman Talma in his interpretation of this role, one of the most sublime of his profession; and Miss Grevelink has often reminded us of Wattier: this is to extend the greatest praise to her. The costumes, with the exception of that of Struik, were very good, especially that of Jelgerhuis: nevertheless we would have wished to inject more dignity into this worthy actor in the fifth act (the most weakly played of all), and in particular the unseemly laugh during the monologue of the fifth scene might have been dropped. His daughter, Miss Jelgerhuis, deserves all encouragement, although she did nothing more than recite her part rather coolly and in the most monotonous fashion. When she came on during the seventh scene of the last act, she committed an unforgivable error by 1. entering through the wall, and 2. stepping over the corpse of Claudius, for she asks for him immediately afterwards. Thus she destroyed the entire illusion and made the scene ridiculous.

The theatre was reasonably full; the play was listened to with attention and applauded with discretion, and we hope that the theatre management will bid farewell at last to the mistaken theory that tragedies do not attract audiences. Any reasonably good tragedy will be attended again if what is required is executed – in décor and costume as well as in acting.

389   Acrobats at the Schouwburg, 1826

Anonymous cartoon. *Pandora, in bezit van het tooneelklokje* [*P., in Possession of the Stage-Bell*][1] (nos 1–6, 1825–6) (Amsterdam: Gebroeders Diederichs, n.d. [1826]), p. 144

[1]The strange title means that the theatre magazine *The Stage-Bell* had been taken over by *Pandora*.

In 1815 connoisseurs had been scandalized by melodramas in the Amsterdam Schouwburg in which animals played the leading role: R.C. Guilbert de Pixérécourt's *Le Chien de Montargis ou la Forêt de Bondy* (1814) (see **228**, **387**) and L.C. Caigniez and d'Aubigny's *La Pie voleuse* (The Thieving Magpie, 1814). These performances had been duly criticised by *De Tooneelkijker* (The Theatre-Observer). In 1826 things had grown worse, acrobats now filling the stage. A cartoon in one of the many short-lived theatre magazines depicts the Schouwburg façade decorated with an enormous flag on which some of their tricks are shown under the motto '*Non plus ultra* of good taste'. Lucifer is inviting spectators to enter the theatre. A magpie on the roof and a dog in the street (from the plays just mentioned) are protesting that this is going too far. An elderly gentleman with field glasses, representing the late *Theatre-Observer*, is looking on in amazement. At the left this new repertoire and the melodramas of 1815 are weighed on a pair of scales. The inscription (not reproduced here) reads: 'O miracle of miracles!! Enter, please, enter!'.

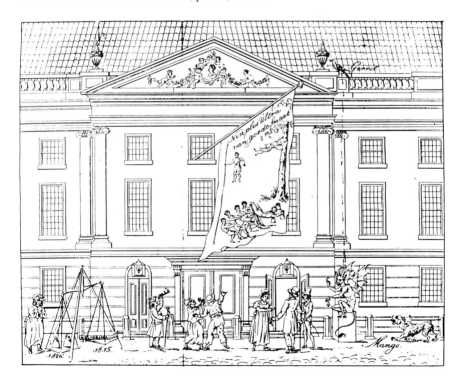

Select bibliography, 1600–1848

GERMAN-SPEAKING COUNTRIES

(1) General studies and works of reference

Anon. (allegedly Abraham Peiba). *Gallerie von Teutschen Schauspielern und Schauspielerinnen der ältern und neuern Zeit* (Vienna: I.N. Edler v. Epheu 1783; ed. R.M. Werner, Berlin: SGTG 13, 1910) [120]

Blum, Robert/Herloszsohn, Karl/Marggraff, Hermann (eds.). *Allgemeines Theater-Lexicon oder Encyklopädie alles Wissenswerten für Bühnenkünstler, Dilettanten und Theaterfreunde*, 7 vols. (Altenburg-Leipzig: Pierer/Heymann, 1839–46) [126, 260]

Devrient, Philipp Eduard. *Geschichte der deutschen Schauspielkunst*, 5 vols. (Leipzig: Weber, 1848–74; rev. and enlarged by Willi Stuhlfeld, Berlin-Zurich: Eigenbrödler, 1929; new edn. by Rolf Kabel & Christoph Trilse, 2 vols., Berlin: Henschelverlag, 1967) [35, 98, 110, 243, 245]

Düringer, Philipp Jakob & Barthels, H. *Theater-Lexicon* (Leipzig: Wigand, 1841) [127, 230, 231, 240, 241, 253, 257]

Eisenberg, Ludwig. *Grosses biographisches Lexikon der deutschen Bühne im 19. Jahrhundert* (Leipzig: List, 1903)

Fehr, Max. *Die wandernden Theatertruppen in der Schweiz/Verzeichnis der Truppen, Aufführungen und Spieldaten für das 17. und 18. Jahrhundert* (Einsiedeln: Waldstatt, 1949)

Glossy, Karl Ludwig. *Fachkatalog der Abteilung für Deutsches Drama und Theater der Internationalen Ausstellung für Musik und Theaterwesen in Wien* (Vienna: Ausstellungs-Commission, 1892)

Gregor, Joseph. *Geschichte des österreichischen Theaters von seinen Ursprüngen bis zum Ende der ersten Republik* (Vienna: Donau-Verlag, 1948)

Hadamowsky, Franz. 'Leitung, Verwaltung und ausübende Künstler des deutschen und französischen Schauspiels, der italienischen ernsten und heiteren Oper, des Ballets und der musikalischen Akademien am Burgtheater (Französisches Theater) und am Kärntnertortheater (Deutsches Theater) in Wien 1754–1764', *Jahrbuch der Gesellschaft für Wiener Theaterforschung*, 12 (Vienna, 1960), 113 ff.

Die Wiener Hoftheater (Staatstheater) 1766–1966: Verzeichnis der aufgeführten Stücke mit Bestandnachweis und täglichem Spielplan (Vienna: Prechner, 1966)

Kertz, Peter & Strössenreuther, Ingeborg. *Bibliographie zur Theatergeschichte Nürnbergs* (Nuremberg: Stadtbibliothek, 1964)

Kindermann, Heinz. *Theatergeschichte Europas*, 10 vols. (Salzburg: Otto Müller 1957–74), esp. vols. 3 (1959) [9, 28, 58], 4 (1961) [114], 5 (1962) [178], 6 (1964)

Knudsen, Hans. *Deutsche Theatergeschichte* (Stuttgart: Kroner, 1959)

Kosch, Wilhelm. *Deutsches Theaterlexikon/Biographisches und Bibliographisches Handbuch* (Klagenfurt-Vienna: Kleinmayr 1951–60; Berne-Munich: Francke, 1965–71)

Lebede, Hans. *Vom Werden der deutschen Bühne* (Berlin: Hartmann, 1923)

Nagler, Alois Maria. *Sources of Theatrical History* (New York: Theatre Annual Inc. 1952; repr. as *A Source Book in Theatrical History*, N.Y.: Dover, 1959) [82, 135, 138, 140, 187]

Nippold, Erich. *Das deutsche Theater von seinen Anfängen bis zur Gegenwart* (Gotha: Perthes, 1924)

v. Reden-Esbeck, Friedrich Johannes. *Deutsches Bühnen-Lexikon/Das Leben und Wirken aller hervorra-genden Bühnen-Leiter und -Künstler*, 1 vol. only (Eichstädt-Stuttgart: Krühl, 1879)

Richel, Veronica. *The German Stage, 1767–1890/A Directory of Playwrights & Plays* (Westport, Conn.: Greenwood Press, 1988)

Rub, Otto. *Das Burgtheater/Statistischer Rückblick auf die Tätigkeit und Personalverhältnisse 1776–1913* (Vienna: Knepler, 1913)

Schäffer, C. & Hartmann, C. *Die königlichen Theater in Berlin/Statistischer Rückblick auf die künstlerische Tätigkeit und die Personal-Verhältnisse während des Zeitraums vom 5. Dezember 1786 bis zum 31. Dezember 1885* (Berlin: Berliner Verlagscomtoir, 1886)

Schmidt, Leopold. *Das deutsche Volksschauspiel/Ein Handbuch* (Berlin: Erich Schmidt, 1962)

Schöne, Günther. *Tausend Jahre deutsches Theater, 914–1914* (Munich: Prestel, 1962)

Stammler, Wolfgang. *Deutsche Theatergeschichte* (Leipzig: Quelle & Meyer, 1925)

Trilse, Klaus/Hammer, Klaus/Kabel, Rolf. *Theater-Lexikon* (Berlin: Henschelverlag, 1978)

Voll, Matthaeus. *Chronologisches Verzeichnis aller Schauspiele, deutschen und italienischen Opern, Pantomimen und Ballette, welche seit April 1794 bis 1807 ... in den k. und k. Hoftheatern als auch in den k. und k. privaten Schauspielhäusern ... aufgeführt worden sind etc.* (Vienna: Wallishauser, 1807)

Walter, Friederich. *Archiv und Bibliothek des Grossherzoglichen Hof- und Nationaltheaters in Mannheim, 1779–1893*, 2 vols. (Leipzig: Hirzel, 1899)

Wollrabe, Ludwig. *Chronologie sämmtlicher Hamburger Bühnen nebst Angabe der meisten Schauspieler, Sänger, Tänzer und Musiker, welche seit 1230 bis 1846 an denselben engagiert gewesen und gastiert haben* (Hamburg: Behrendsohn, 1847)

Zedler, Johann Heinrich (publ.). *Grosses vollständiges Universal-Lexicon Aller Wissenschaften und Künste*, 64 vols. (Halle-Leipzig, 1732–50)

(2) Published sources

Anon. *Abschilderung der Ackermannischen Schauspieler, in einem Schreiben an einen Freund in Berlin* (Halle: Schwetschke 1755)

Ballet von Zusammenkunft und Wirckung derer VII. Planeten (Dresden: Melchior Bergens, 1678) [20]

Briefe über das versifizierte Drama/Ein Beitrag zur pragmatischen Geschichte der dramatischen Poesie (Leipzig: Wolf 1801)

Vergleichung der Ackermann- und Kochischen Schauspielergesellschaften (Hamburg-Leipzig, 1769) [65]

Anschütz, Heinrich. *Erinnerungen aus dessen Leben und Wirken* (Vienna: Sommer, 1866)

v. Ayrenhoff, Cornelius Hermann. *Ein und anders über Deutschlands Theaterwesen und Kunstrichterey* (n.p., 1782)

Bauer, Karoline. *Aus meinem Bühnenleben* (ed. A. Wellmer, Berlin: Decker, 1871)

v. Bauernfeld, Eduard. *Aus Alt- und Neu-Wien*, in: *Ausgewählte Werke*, vol. 4 (ed. Emil Horner, Leipzig: Hesse & Becker, n.d., repr. in edn by Rudolf Latzke, Vienna: Österreichischer Schulbücherverlag, 1923)

Denkschrift über die gegenwärtigen Zustände der Zensur in Österreich (1845), and *Flüchtige Gedanken über das deutsche Theater* (1849) [256, 259], in: *Gesammelte Aufsätze* (selected & edited by Stefan Hock, Vienna: Verlag des Literarischen Vereins in Wien, 1905)

Bäuerle, Adolf. *Memoiren* (Vienna: Lechner, 1858)

Becker, Gottfried Wilhelm. *Briefe über Ifflands Spiel in Leipzig zu Ende des Junius 1804* (Leipzig: Comptor für Litteratur, 1804)

Bergopzoom (sic), Johann Baptist. *Letztes Wort an das Wiener Publikum* (Vienna: Wiener Bibliophilen-Gesellschaft, 1954)

v. Bertram, Christian August. *Über die Kochische Schauspieler-gesellschaft/Aus Berlin an einen Freund* (Berlin-Leipzig, 1771)

Beuther, Friedrich. *Dekorationen für die Schaubühne, nebst einem Vorwort über Theatermalerei* (Brunswick, 1824)

v. Bielfeld, Jacob Friedrich. *Progrès des Allemands dans les Sciences, les Belles-Lettres et les Arts, particulièrement dans la Poésie, l'Éloquence et le Théâtre*, 2 vols. (3rd edn, Leiden: S. & J. Luchtmans, 1767)

Bittner, Norbert. *Theater-Decorationen, nach den Originalskizzen des k. k. Hoftheatermahlers Anton de Pian* (Vienna, 1818)

Bodmer, Johann Jakob. *Critische Betrachtungen und freye Untersuchungen zum Aufnehmen und zur Verbesserung der deutschen Schau-Bühne/Mit einer Zuschrift an die Frau Neuberin* (Berne: n.p., 1743)

Böttiger, Carl August. *Friedrich Ludwig Schröder in Hamburg im Sommer 1795* (Leipzig, 1818)
   Entwickelung des Ifflandischen Spiels in vierzehn Darstellungen auf dem Weimarer Hoftheater im Aprillmonath 1796 (Leipzig: Göschen, 1796) [**208, 211–13**]

Böwe, Kurt (ed.). *Über Schauspieler und Schauspielkunst: Ausgewählte Abhandlungen von A.W. Iffland und Johann Gottfried Seume* (Berlin: Ministerium für Kultur, 1954)

Brandes, Johann Christian. *Meine Lebensgeschichte*, 3 vols. (Berlin: Maurer, 1799–1800) [**72, 75, 95, 115, 128, 149, 152**]
   Die Komödianten in Quirlequitsch, in *Sämtliche Werke*, vol. 8 (Hamburg: Dyck, 1791) [**145**]

Braun, Julius (ed.). *Schiller im Urtheile seiner Zeitgenossen*, 3 vols. (Berlin: Luckhardt, 1882, 2nd ed. Leipzig: Schlicke, 1888)
   Goethe im Urtheile seiner Zeitgenossen 3 vols. (Berlin: Luckhardt, 1883–5; repr. Hildesheim: Olms, 1969) [**79, 111, 158, 197–8, 204–5, 220**]
   Lessing im Urtheile seiner Zeitgenossen 3 vols. (Berlin: Stahn, 1884–97; repr. Hildesheim: Olms, 1969) [**189, 193, 196**]

Bressand, Friderich Christian. *Cleopatra, Sing-Spiel* (Wolfenbüttel, Bissmarck, 1691) [**24**]

Breysig, Johann Adam. *Szenographie oder Bühnengemählde des neuen Königsberger Schauspielhauses* (Königsberg/Kalingrad, 1808)

v. Brühl, Alois Friedrich. *Neue Costüme auf den beiden Königlichen Theatern in Berlin*, 3 vols. (Berlin, 1819–30)

Burney, Charles. *The Present State of Music in Germany, the Netherlands and United Provinces*, 2 vols. (London: Becket, Robson & Robinson, 1773) [**69, 71, 106**]

Butenop, C.H. *Biographie des K.K. Hofschauspielers Herrn Philipp Klingmann* (Glogau n.p., 1825)

Castelli, Ignaz Franz. *Memoiren meines Lebens/Gefundenes und Erfundenes, Erlebtes und Erstrebtes* (Vienna-Prague: Kober & Markgraf, 1861)

Catel, Louis. *Vorschläge zur Verbesserung der Schauspielhäuser* (Berlin: Lange, 1802)

Christ, Joseph Anton. *Schauspielerleben im 18. Jahrhundert* (ed. Rudolf Schirmer, Munich-Leipzig: Langewiesche-Brandt, 1912)

Cludius, Hermann Heimark. *Grundriss der körperlichen Beredsamkeit* (Hamburg: Bohn, 1792)

Costenoble, Carl Ludwig. *Tagebücher von seiner Jugend bis zur Übersiedlung nach Wien (1818)*, 2 vols. (ed. Alexander v. Weilen (Berlin: SGTG 18/19, 1912)
   Tagebücher aus dem Burgtheater 1818–1837 (ed. Karl Glossy, Vienna: Konegen, 1889)

De Pian, Antonio. *Theater-Dekorationen, gestochen von Bittner* (Vienna, 1818)

Devrient, Otto (ed.). *Briefe von A.W. Iffland und F.L. Schröder an den Schauspieler Werdy* (Frankfurt: Rommel, 1881)

Devrient, Philipp Eduard. *Über Theaterschule/Eine Mitteilung an das Theaterpublikum* (Berlin: Jonas Verlagsbuchhandlung, 1840) [**252, 254**]
   Das Nationaltheater des neuen Deutschlands (Leipzig: Weber, 1849)
   Das Passionsspiel in Oberammergau und seine Bedeutung für die neue Zeit (Leipzig: Weber, 1851)
   Aus seinen Tagebüchern, vol. 1: 1836–1852; vol. 2: 1852–1870 (ed. Rolf Kabel, Weimar: Böhlau, 1964)

v. Dittersdorf, Karl Ditters. *Lebensbeschreibung, seinem Sohne in die Feder diktiert* (Leipzig: Breitkopf & Härtel, 1801; new ed. by Eugen Schmitz, Leipzig: Staackmann, 1940); Eng. trans. by A.D. Coleridge, *The Autobiography of K. von Dittersdorf*, London: Bentley, 1896) [**74**]

Dräseke, Johann Heinrich Bernhard. *Über die Darstellung des Heiligen auf der Bühne* (Bremen: Heyes, 1815)

Dressler, Ernst Christoph. *Theater-Schule für die Deutschen, das Ernsthafte Singe-Schauspiel betreffend*

(Hanover-Kassel: Schmidt, 1777)

Eckermann, Johann Peter. *Gespräche mit Goethe in den letzten Jahren seines Lebens*, 3 vols. (vols. 1 & 2, Leipzig: Brockhaus, 1836, vol. 3, Magdeburg: Heinrichshofen, 1848). English trans. by John Oxenford, *Conversations of Goethe with Eckermann and Soret*. (London: Smith, Elder & Co., 1850) [**82, 138, 140**]

Eder, Ruth (ed.). *Theaterzettel* (Dortmund: Harenberg Kommunikation, 1980) [**38**]

v. Einsiedel, Friedrich Hildebrand. *Grundlinien zu einer Theorie der Schauspielkunst/Nach der Analyse einer komischen und tragischen Rolle: Falstaf* [sic] *und Hamlet von Shakespeare* (Leipzig: Göschen, 1797)

Elmenhorst, Heinrich. *Dramatologia Antiquo-Hodierna, das ist: Bericht von denen Opern-Spielen, darinn gewiesen wird, was sie bey den Heyden gewesen . . . Ferner was die heutigen Opern- Spiele seyn . . . und von Christen ohn Verletzung des Gewissens geschauet und angehöret werden etc.* (Hamburg: George Rebenl. Wittwe, 1688) [*See* Rauch and Reiser]

Engel, Johann Jakob. *Die Apotheke* (Leipzig: Dyck 1772) [**183**]

   Ideen zu einer Mimik, 2 vols. (Berlin: Mylius, 1785–6) [**131–3, 137**]

Engelschall, Carl Gottfried. *Gedancken über die Frage: Ob ein Christ ohne Schaden und Gefahr seiner Seelen die Comödien und Schau-Spiele besuchen könne? Etc.* (Brieg, 1724)

Engelschall, Joseph H. *Zufällige Gedanken über die teutsche Schaubühne zu Wien von einem Verehrer des guten Geschmacks und der guten Sitten* (Vienna, 1760)

Flittner, Christian Gottlieb (ed.). *A.W. Ifflands Theorie der Schauspielkunst für ausübende Künstler und Kunstfreunde*, 2 vols. (Berlin: Neue Societäts-Verlags-Buchhandlung, 1815)

Flögel, Carl Friederich. *Geschichte des Groteskekomischen/Ein Beitrag zur Geschichte der Menschheit* (Liegnitz-Leipzig: Siegert, 1788)

Frederick II of Prussia. *De la Littérature allemande, etc.* (Berlin: Decker, 1789) [**203**]

Fuhrmann, M.H. *Die an der Kirchen Gottes gebauete Satans-Capelle* (Hamburg, 1682) [**36**]

Funck, Z. (Karl Friendrich Kunz). *Aus dem Leben zweier Schauspieler: August Wilhelm Iffland's und Ludwig Devrient's* (Leipzig: Brockhaus, 1838)

Furtenbach (or Furttenbach), Joseph. *Architectura civilis* (Ulm: Saur, 1628)

   Architectura recreationis (Augsburg: Schultes, 1640)

   Mannhafter Kunst-Spiegel (Augsburg: Schultes, 1663). Partly reproduced in Bernard Hewitt, *The Renaissance Stage* (University of Miami Press, 1958) [**11, 12, 16, 39**]

Gaedertz, Karl Theodor (ed.). *Archivalische Nachrichten über die Theaterzustände von Hildesheim, Lübeck, Lüneburg im 16. und 17. Jahrhundert* (Bremen: C.E. Müller, 1888)

Galli-Bibiena, Giuseppe. *Architetture prospettive dedicate alla maestà di Carlo Sesto imperador de' Romani* (Vienna: Pfeffel, 1740)

Gämmerler, Franz. *Theaterdirektor Carl/Sein Leben und Wirken* (Vienna: Wallishauser, 1854)

Genast, Eduard Franz. *Aus dem Tagebuche eines alten Schauspielers*, 4 vols. (Leipzig: Voigt & Günther 1862–6) [**86, 224**]

v. Goethe, Johann Wolfgang. *Theatrical prologues & addresses* in WA, sect. 1, vol. 13, pts. 1 & 2 (1901): 'Vorspiel zur Eröffnung des Weimarischen Theaters am 19. September 1807'; 'Was wir bringen/ Lauchstädt' (1802); 'Prolog bei Wiederholung des Vorspiels in Weimar' (1802); 'Was wir bringen/Halle' (1814); 'Prolog zur Eröffnung des Berliner Theaters im Mai 1821'; 'Theaterreden' (1791–4);

   Theatrical essays in WA, sect. 1, vol. 40 (1901): 'Weimarischer neudecorirter Theatersaal' (1798); 'Eröffnung des Weimarischen Theaters' (1798) [**215**]; 'Die Piccolomini' (1799), 'Einige Scenen aus Mahomet nach Voltaire' (1800); 'Dramatische Preisaufgabe' (1800); 'Weimarisches Hoftheater' (1802) [**179**]; 'Über das deutsche Theater' (1815); 'Prosperine' (1815); 'Zu Schillers und Ifflands Andenken' (1815); 'Französisches Schauspiel in Berlin' (1828); 'Regeln für Schauspieler' (1803–16) [**135**]

   Zum Schäkspears Tag (1771), (WA, sect. 1, vol. 37, 1896)

   Shakespeare und kein Ende (1813), (WA, sect. 1, vol. 41, 1902)

   Auf Miedings Tod (1782), (WA, sect. 1, vol. 16, 1894)

   Euphrosyne (1799) (WA, sect. 1, vol. 1, 1887)

Wilhelm Meisters theatralische Sendung (ed. Harry Maync, *WA*, vols. 51–2, 1911)

Wilhelm Meisters Lehrjahre (1795–6), (*WA*, sect. 1, vol. 21, 1898) [**99, 139**]

Die Weilburger Goethe-Funde/Blätter aus dem Nachlass Pius Alexander Wolffs (ed. Hans Georg Böhme, Emsdetten: DSB 36, 1950)

Goethe über seine Dichtungen, 4 vols., esp. vol. 2, *Die dramatischen Dichtungen* (ed. Hans Gerhard Gräf, Frankfurt, 1908, repr. Munich: Rütten & Loening, 1968)

Goethe und Schiller in Briefen (ed. Hans Gerhard Gräf, Leipzig: Reclam, 1896)

Goethes Gespräche, 5 vols. (ed. Flodard v. Biedermann, Leipzig: Biedermann, 1909–11)

Goethes Gespräche, 4 vols. (ed. Wolfgang Herwig, Zürich: Artemis, 1965–72)

Goeze (Goetze), J. Melchior. *Theologische Untersuchung der Sittlichkeit der heutigen Schaubühne, etc.* (Hamburg: Brandt, 1770) [**147**]

Gotthardi, Wilhelm (Moritz Wilhelm Gotthard Müller). *Weimarische Theaterbilder aus Goethes Zeit/ Überliefertes und Selbsterlebtes*, 2 vols. (Jena-Leipzig: Costenoble, 1865)

Gottsched, Johann Christoph. *Versuch einer critischen Dichtkunst für die Deutschen* (Leipzig: Breitkopf, 1730; further editions 1737, 1742, 1751; 1751 ed. repr. Darmstadt: Wissenschaftliche Buchgesellschaft, 1962) [**83, 180**]

Der sterbende Cato (Leipzig: Teubner, 1732) [**159**]

Nöthiger Vorrath zur Geschichte der deutschen dramatischen Dichtkunst, etc., 2 vols. (Leipzig: Teubner, 1757–65)

Grabbe, Christian Dietrich. *Das Theater zu Düsseldorf, etc.* (Düsseldorf: Schreiner, 1835) [**258**]

Gregor, Josef (ed.).*Wiener szenische Kunst*, 2 vols. (Vienna: Wiener Drucke, 1924–5)

Grillparzer, Franz. *Aufsätze über Literatur, Musik und Theater*, vol. 14 of *Sämtliche Werke*, 20 vols., (ed. August Sauer, Vienna: Schroll, 1925) [**255, 262**]

Gropius, Carl Wilhelm. *Dekorationen auf den beiden königlichen Theatern* (Berlin, 1827)

Grüner (Akatz), Carl Franz. *Die Kunst der Szenik in ästhetischer und ökonomischer Hinsicht; theoretisch, praktisch und mit Plänen etc.* (Vienna: Mausberger, 1841)

Gryphius, Andreas. *Freuden und Trauer-Spiele etc.* (Breslau/Wroclaw: Lischke & Trescher, 1658) [**51**]

Hadatsch, F.I. *Launen des Schicksals oder Szenen aus dem Leben und der theatralischen Laufbahn des Schauspielers Anton Hasenhuth* (Vienna: Ludwig, 1834; repr. Vienna: Wiener Bibliophilengesellschaft, 1941)

Haerle, Heinrich (ed.). *Ifflands Schauspielkunst/Ein Rekonstruktionsversuch auf Grund der etwa 500 Zeichnungen und Kupferstiche W. Henschels und seiner Brüder* (Berlin: SGTG 34, 1925) [**123**]

Hafner, Philipp. *Brief eines neuen Komödienschreibers an einen Schauspieler*, incl. two scenarios for improvised comedies, in vol. 1 of *Philipp Hafners gesammelte Schriften*, 3 vols. (Vienna: Wallishauser, 1812)

Harsdörfer, Georg Philip. *Frauenzimmer Gesprächspiele*, 8 vols., (Nuremberg: Endkern, 1641–9; repr. Tübingen: Niemeyer, 1969), esp. vol. 6 (1646) [**53**]

Hasenhuth, Anton. *Selbstbiographie* (ed. M.M. Rabenlechner, Vienna: Wiener Bibliophilengesellschaft, 1941)

Hebbel, Friedrich. *Vorwort zur 'Maria Magdalena'* (Hamburg: Hoffmann & Campe, 1844) [**263**]

Tagebücher 1835–1863, 4 vols. (ed. R.M. Werner, Berlin: Behr, n.d.) [**265**]

Henning, Hans (ed.). *Lessings 'Emilia Galotti' in der zeitgenössischen Rezeption* (Leipzig: Zentralantiquariat der DDR, 1981 [**192**]

Schillers 'Kabale und Liebe' in der zeitgenössischen Rezeption (Leipzig: Zentralantiquariat der DDR, 1976) [**209–10**]

Hoffmann, Ernst Theodor Amadeus. *Seltsame Leiden eines Theaterdirektors* (Berlin: Maurer, 1819) [**237**]

v. Holtei, Karl. *Vierzig Jahre*, 8 vols. (Berlin: Adolf, 1843–50)

Hosemann, Theodor. *Berliner Theater um 1840* (ed. Winfried Klara and Rolf Badenhausen, Berlin: SGTG 48, 1938)

Iffland, August Wilhelm. *Fragmente über Menschendarstellung auf den deutschen Bühnen* (Gotha: Ettinger, 1785)

Briefe an seine Schwester Louise und andere Verwandte, 1772–1812, 2 vols. (ed. Ludwig Geiger, Berlin: SGTG 5 & 6, 1904–5)
Über meine theatralische Laufbahn, in *Dramatische Werke*, vol. 1 (Leipzig: Göschen, 1798) [**176**]
Schillers Piccolomini auf dem Kgl. National-Theater in Berlin/Ifflands Regiebuch zur Erstaufführung am 18. Februar 1799 (ed. Julius Peterson, Berlin: SGTG 53, 1941)
Almanach für Theater und Theaterfreunde auf das Jahr 1807 (Berlin: Oehmigke, 1807) [**98, 194**]
Kostüme auf dem Königl. National-Theater in Berlin/Unter der Direction des Herrn Aug. Wilh. Iffland (Berlin: Wittich, 1812) [**87**]
Immermann, Karl Lebrecht. *Memorabilien*, 2 vols. (Hamburg: Hoffmann & Campe, 1840–3)
Theater-Briefe (ed. Gustav Heinrich Gans zu Putlitz, Berlin: Duncker, 1851)
Karl Immermann, sein Leben und seine Werke/Aus Tagebüchern und Briefen an seine Familie zusammengestellt, 2 vols. (ed. G.H.G. zu Putlitz, Berlin: Hertz, 1870)
Jagemann, Karoline. *Die Erinnerungen der Karoline Jagemann* (ed. E. Bamberg, Leipzig: Sibyllenverlag, 1926) [**141**]
Khevenhüller-Metsch, Count Rudolf & Schlitter, Hanns (eds.). *Aus der Zeit Maria Theresias/Tagebuch des Fürsten Johann Josef Khevenhüller-Metsch, Kaiserlichen Obersthofmeisters, 1742–1776*, 8 vols. (Vienna: Holzhausen, 1907–25) [**150**]
Kindermann, Heinz (ed.). *Conrad Ekhofs Schauspieler-Akademie* (Vienna: Sitzungsberichte der österreichischen Akademie der Wissenschaften 230, 1956) [**88, 129, 194**]
Klemm, Christian Gottlob. *Der auf den Parnass versetzte grüne Hut* (Vienna: Konegen, 1767; repr. Vienna: Konegen, 1883)
Klingemann, August. *Kunst und Natur/Blätter aus meinem Reisetagebuche*, 3 vols. (Brunswick: Mayer, 1819–28)
Einige Bemerkungen über die deutsche Bühne, etc., in *Braunschweigisches Magazin*, 8 April 1815 [**239**]
Knispel, Georg. *Erinnerungen aus Berlin an Karl Seydelmann, vom Spätherbst 1842* (Darmstadt: Leske, 1845)
Koller, Benedikt Josef Maria. *Aphorismen für Schauspieler und Freunde der dramatischen Kunst* (Ratisbon: Montag & Weifs, 1804; repr. Munich: Hanfstaengl, 1920)
v. Kotzebue, August. *An das Publicum* (Leipzig: n.p., 1793)
Fragmente über Recensenten-Unfug/Eine Beilage zur Jenaer Litteraturzeitung (Leipzig: Kummer, 1797)
Über meinen Aufenthalt in Wien und über meine erbetene Dienstentlassung (Vienna: Kummer, 1799)
Aus August v. Kotzebues hinterlassenen Papieren (ed. P.G. Kummer, Leipzig: Kummer, 1821)
Krapf, Ludwig & Wagenknecht, Christian (eds.). *Stuttgarter Hoffeste/Texte und Materialien zur höfischen Repräsentation im frühen 17. Jahrhundert* (Tübingen: Niemeyer, 1979) [**14–15**]
v. Küstner, Karl Theodor. *Rückblick auf das Leipziger Stadttheater* (Leipzig: Brockhaus, 1830)
Vierunddreissig Jahre meiner Theaterleitung (Leipzig: Brockhaus, 1853)
Album des königl. Schauspiels und der königl. Oper zu Berlin unter der Leitung von August Wilhelm Iffland, Karl Grafen v. Brühl, Wilhelm Grafen v. Redern und Karl Theodor v. Küstner für die Zeit 1796 bis 1851 (Berlin: Schauer, 1858)
Lang, Franciscus. *Dissertatio de actione scenica, cum figuris eandem explicantibus, et observationibus quibusdam de arte comica* (Munich: Riedlin, 1727); trans. & ed. by Alexander Rudin, *Abhandlung über die Schauspielkunst*, Berne-Munich: Francke, 1975) [**41–7**]
Lange, Joseph. *Die Biographie des Joseph Lange, k.k. Hofschauspielers* (Vienna: Rehms sel. Witwe, 1808)
Langhans, Carl Gotthard. *Vergleichung des neuen Schauspielhauses zu Berlin mit verschiedenen älteren und neueren Schauspielhäusern in Rücksicht auf akustische und optische Verhältnisse* (Berlin, 1800)
Grund und Aufriss des neuen Schauspielhauses in Berlin (Berlin: n.p., 1802)
Über Theater; oder Bemerkungen über Katakustik in Beziehung auf Theater (Berlin: Hayn, 1810)
Lediard, Thomas. *Eine Collection verschiedener Vorstellungen in Illuminationen und Feuer-Wercken, so in denen Jahren 1724 biss 1727 . . . zur Ehre des . . . königl. Gross-Britannischen Hauses . . . auf dem Hamburgischen Schau-Platze, unter der Direction und von der Invention T. Lediard's . . . sind vorgestellet worden, etc.*, 4 pts. (Hamburg, 1729)
Lenz, Jakob Michael Reinhold. *Anmerckungen übers Theater etc.* (Leipzig: Weygand, 1774)

Lessing, Gotthold Ephraim. *Briefe, die neueste Litteratur betreffend* (Berlin-Stettin: Nicolai, 1766) [100, 168]

Hamburgische Dramaturgie (Hamburg, 1767–9) [117, 119, 184, 188]

Lessings Briefwechsel mit Mendelssohn und Nicolai über das Trauerspiel (ed. Robert Petsch, Leipzig: Dürr, 1910)

Lewald, August. *Seydelmann und das deutsche Schauspiel* (Stuttgart: Liesching, 1835) [247]

Seydelmann/Ein Erinnerungsbuch für seine Freunde (Stuttgart: Gopel, 1841)

Entwurf zu einer praktischen Schauspielerschule (Vienna: Wallishauser, 1846)

Lindner, Heinrich. Introduction to *Karl der Zwölfte vor Friedrichshall* (Dessau: Aue, 1845) [52, 110]

Litzmann, Berthold (ed.). *Schröder und Gotter/Eine Episode aus der deutschen Theatergeschichte/Briefe Friedrich Ludwig Schröders an Friedrich Wilhelm Gotter, 1777 & 1778* (Hamburg-Leipzig, 1887)

Löbel, Renatus Gotthelf. *Anleitung zur Bildung des mündlichen Vortrags* (Leipzig, 1793)

Löwen, Johann Friedrich. *Kurzgefasste Grundsätze von der Beredsamkeit des Leibes* (Hamburg, 1755)

Erinnerungen an die Kochsche Schauspieler-Gesellschaft, bei Gelegenheit des 'Hausvaters' des Herrn Diderot (Frankfurt-Leipzig, 1776)

Geschichte des deutschen Theaters; Auszug aus einem Briefe eines Freundes; Vorläufige Nachricht von der auf Ostern 1767 vorzunehmenden Veränderung des Hamburgischen Theaters – in vol. 4 (1766) of *Schriften*, 4 vols. (Hamburg: Bock 1765–6, repr. and ed. by Heinrich Stümcke, *Johann Friedrich Löwens Geschichte des deutschen Theaters und Flugschriften über das Hamburger Nationaltheater*, Berlin: Frenssdorf, 1905) [118, 161, 165, 170]

v. Lyncker, Karl. *Am Weimarischen Hofe unter Anna Amalia und Karl August* (Berlin: Mittler, 1912)

v. Mailáth, János Nepomuk. *Leben der Sophie Müller, weiland k.k. Hofschauspielerin etc.* (Vienna: Ullrich, 1832)

Martersteig, Max (ed.). *Die Protokolle des Mannheimer Nationaltheaters unter Dalberg aus den Jahren 1781 bis 1789* (Mannheim: Bensheimer, 1890)

Menantes (Hunold, Christ. Friedrich). *Allerneueste Art zur Reinen und Galanten Poesie zu gelangen* (Hamburg: Liebernickel, 1707)

Meyer, Friedrich Ludwig Wilhelm. *Friedrich Ludwig Schröder*, 2 vols. (Hamburg: Hoffmann & Campe, 1819) [73, 108, 121, 134, 142]

Montagu, Lady Mary Wortley. *The Complete Letters* (ed. Robert Halsband, Oxford: The Clarendon Press, 1965) [21]

Moritz, Karl Philipp. *Anton Reiser*, 5 vols. (Berlin: Maurer, 1785–94)

Müller, Johann Heinrich Friedrich. *Genaue Nachrichten von beyden Kaiserlich-Königlichen Schaubühnen und andern öffentlichen Ergötzlichkeiten in Wien* (Pressburg/Bratislava-Frankfurt-Leipzig: Löwen, 1772) [68]

Theatral-Neuigkeiten/Nebst einem Lustpiele und der dazu gehörigen Musik etc. (Vienna: Ghelen, 1773)

Geschichte und Tagebuch der Wiener Schaubühne (Vienna: Trattner, 1776)

Müllers Abschied von der k.k. Hof- und Nationalschaubühne etc. (Vienna: Wallishauser, 1802)

Müller, Johannes (ed.). *Das Jesuitendrama in den Ländern deutscher Zunge vom Anfang (1555) bis zum Hochbarock (1665).* 2 vols., esp. vol. 2, *Materialien* (Augsburg: Filser, 1930)

Müllner, Amandus Gottfried Adolph. *Ueber das Spiel auf der Privatbühne/Dramaturgische Abhandlung* (Leipzig: Göschen, 1816)

Almanach für Privatbühnen auf das Jahr 1817 [–1819] (Leipzig: Göschen, 1817, 1818, 1819)

Vers und Reim auf der Bühne/Ein Taschenbüchlein für Schauspielerinnen (Stuttgart-Tübingen: Cotta, 1822)

Theater-Lexikon in vol. 1 of *Vermischte Schriften*, 2 vols. (Stuttgart-Tübingen: Cotta, 1824–6)

Nestroy, Johann Nepomuk. *Nestroys Briefe* (ed. Walter Obermaier, Vienna-Munich: Jugend und Volk, 1977) [261]

Nicolai, Christoph Friedrich. *Beschreibung einer Reise durch Deutschland und die Schweiz im Jahre 1781*, 12 vols. (Berlin-Stettin: Nicolai, 1783–95)

Niessen, Carl (ed.). *Frau Magister Velten verteidigt die Schaubühne* (Emsdetten: Lechte, 1940) [36–7]

Nölting, Johann Hinrich Vincent. *Herr Nölting an Herrn Senior Göze* (Hamburg: Harmsen, 1769)

Vertheidigung des Hrn. Past. Schlossers wider einen Angriff etc. (Hamburg: Harmsen, 1769) [**148**]
Zwote Vertheidigung des Past. Schlosser in welcher des Senior Göze Untersuchung etc. mit Anmerkungen begleitet wird (Hamburg: Harmsen, 1769)
Zugabe zu der Vertheidigung des Hrn. Past. Schlossers etc. (Hamburg: Harmsen, 1769)
Payer von Thurn, Rudolf (ed.). *Josef II. als Theaterdirektor/Ungedruckte Briefe und Aktenstücke aus den Kinderjahren des Burgtheaters* (Vienna: Heidrich, 1920)
Penther, Johann Friedrich. *Ausführliche Anleitung zur bürgerlichen Bau-Kunst etc.*, 4 vols. (Augsburg: Pfeffel, 1744–8), esp. vol. 4
Perinet, Joachim. *Mozart und Schikaneder/Ein theatralisches Gespräch über die Aufführung der Zauberflöte im Stadt-Theater, in Knittelversen* (Vienna, 1801)
Theatralisches Gespräch zwischen Mozart und Schikaneder über den Verkauf des Theaters (Vienna, 1802)
Hundegespräche über die theatralische Vorstellung: Der Hund des Aubri de Mont Didier, oder: Der Wald bey Bondy etc. (Vienna: Am Hundsturme, 1816)
Platzer, Josef Ignaz. *Theater-Decorationen, nach den Original-Skitzen des k.k. Hof Theater Mahlers Joseph Plater; radirt und verlegt von Norbert Bittner* (Vienna, 1816)
Plümicke, Carl Martin. *Entwurf einer Theatergeschichte von Berlin* (Berlin-Stettin: Nicolai, 1781)
Proelss, Robert. *Beiträge zur Geschichte des Hoftheaters zu Dresden in actenmässiger Darstellung* (Erfurt: Bartholomäus, 1879)
v. Quaglio, Johann Maria. *Praktische Anleitung zur Perspektive mit Anwendungen auf die Bühnenkunst* (Munich: Lithographische Kunst-Anstalt, 1811)
Rauch, Christoph. *Theatrophania/Entgegen gesetzet der so genanten Schrifft Theatromania* (Hanover: Schwerdimann, 1682). [See Elmenhorst and Reiser]
Reichard, Heinrich August Ottokar. *H.A.O. Reichard/Seine Selbstbiographie, 1751–1829* (ed. Hermann Uhde, Stuttgart: Cotta, 1877)
Reiser, L. Anton. THEATROMANIA *oder die Wercke der Finsterniss, in denen öffentlichen Schau-Spielen von den alten Kirchen-Vätern verdammt etc.* (Hamburg, 1681)
Der gewissenlose Advokat mit seiner THEATROPHANIA *kürzlich abgefertigt* (Hamburg, 1682). [See Rauch and Elmenhorst]
Risbeck, Johann Caspar. *Briefe eines reisenden Franzosen über Deutschland an seinen Bruder zu Paris*, 2 vols., (Zürich: Gessner, 1783), [**104**]
Rist, Johann. *Das Friedewünschende Deutschland* (Cologne: Bingh, 1649) [**25**]
Die AllerEdelste Belustigung Kunst- und Tugendliebender Gemüther (Hamburg: Naumann, 1666) [**32, 48, 54**]
Rost, Johann Christian. *Das Vorspiel/Ein Episches Gedicht* (n.p., 1742; repr. in *DLD* 142, ed. F. Ulbrich, Berlin, 1910) [**164**]
Rötscher, Heinrich Theodor. *Seydelmanns Leben und Wirken* (Berlin: Duncker, 1845)
Schauer, G. *Album des Königlichen Schauspiels und der Königlichen Oper zu Berlin für die Zeit von 1796 bis 1851* (Berlin, 1858)
Schiller, Johann Christoph Friedrich. *Theatrical essays* in *NA*, vol. 22 (1958): 'Die Räuber' (playbill 1782) [**206**]; 'Die Räuber-Besprechung' (1782); 'Über die Vorstellung der Räuber' (1782) [**207**]; 'Mannheimer Dramaturgie' (1785); 'Über die Mannheimer Preismedaille' (not publ. till 1901); 'Über Iffland als Lear' (1784); 'Repertoire des Mannheimer Nationaltheaters' (1785); 'Wallensteinischer Theaterkrieg' (1785); 'Dramaturgische Preisfragen' (1785); 'Über die erste Aufführung der Piccolomini' (1799) [**217**]; 'Dramaturgische Preisaufgabe' (1800)
Die Räuber/Urtext des Mannheimer Soufflierbuches (ed. Herbert Stubenrauch & Günter Schulz, Mannheim: Bibliographisches Institut, 1959)
Kabale und Liebe/Das Mannheimer Soufflierbuch (ed. Herbert Kraft, Mannheim: Bibliographisches Institut, 1963)
Die Räuber: Vorrede zur ersten Auflage (1781), Vorrede zur zwoten Auflage (1782) (Mannheim-Schwan, 1783)
Die Schaubühne als eine moralische Anstalt betrachtet (in *Rheinische Thalia*, Mannheim: Schwan, 1785)) [**185**]
Über den Grund des Vergnügens an tragischen Gegenständen (Leipzig: Crusius, 1802) [**186**]

Über den Gebrauch des Chors in der Tragödie (preface to *Die Braut von Messina*, Tübingen: Cotta, 1803) [187]

Schillers Briefe (ed. F. Jonas, Stuttgart etc.: Deutsche Verlags-Anstalt, 1892), 7 vols.

Schinck, Johann Friedrich. *Ueber Brockmanns Hamlet* (Berlin: Weber, 1778) [202]

Allgemeiner Theater-Allmanach [sic] *vom Jahr 1782* (Vienna: Gerold, 1782)

Bescheid auf die Beurtheilung des Theater-Allmanachs [sic] *in der Realzeitung* (Vienna, 1782)

Dramatische und andere Skizzen nebst Briefen über das Theaterwesen zu Wien (Vienna: Hörling, 1783)

Friedrich Ludwig Schröders Charakteristik als Bühnenführer, mimischer Künstler, dramatischer Dichter und Mensch (Leipzig, 1818)

Dramatisches Scherflein/Ein Taschenbuch für die Bühne (Lüneburg: Herold, 1810)

Schinkel, Carl Friedrich. *Decorationen auf den beiden Königlichen Theatern in Berlin unter der General-Intendantur des Herrn Grafen von Brühl*, 5 vols. (Berlin: Wittich, 1819–24)

Sammlung von Theater-Decorationen, erfunden von Schinkel/Vollständig auf 32 Tafeln dargestellt (2nd ed. Potsdam: Riegel, 1849)

Aus Schinkels Nachlass/Reisetagebücher, Briefe und Aphorismen, 4 vols (ed. Alfred v. Wolzogen, Berlin: Decker, 1863) [233]

Schlegel, Johann Elias. *Theatrical essays* in vol. 3 (1764) of *Werke*, 5 vols. (Copenhagen-Leipzig: Prost & Roth, 1764–73; repr. Frankfurt: Athenäum, 1971):

Schreiben über die Komödie in Versen (1740)

Vergleichung Shakespeares und Andreas Gryphs (1742)

Gedanken zur Aufnahme des dänischen Theaters (1749) [167]

Schmid, Christian Heinrich. *Über die Leipziger Bühne/An Herrn J.F. Löwen zu Rostock*, 2 vols. (Dresden, 1770)

Ueber einige Schönheiten der Emilia Galotti/An Herrn Friedrich Wilhelm Gotter (Leipzig: Müller, 1773)

Ueber Götz von Berlichingen (Leipzig: Weygand, 1774)

Chronologie des deutschen Theaters (Leipzig: Dyck, 1775; new edn by Paul Legband, Berlin: SGTG 1, 1902) [163, 169]

Schmidt, Friedrich Ludwig. *Dramaturgische Aphorismen*, 2 vols. (Hamburg: Hoffmann & Campe, 1820–8)

Dramaturgische Berichte (Hamburg: Nestler & Melle, 1834)

Denkwürdigkeiten des Schauspielers, Schauspieldichters und Schauspieldirektors, 2 vols. (ed. Hermann Uhde, Hamburg: Mauke, 1875)

Schmidt, Heinrich. *Erinnerungen eines Weimarischen Veteranen aus dem geselligen, literarischen und Theater-Leben* (Leipzig: Brockhaus, 1856)

Schmidt, Philipp. *Sophie Schröder, wie sie lebt im Gedächtnis ihrer Zeitgenossen und Kinder* (Vienna: Wallishauser, 1869)

Schneider, Louis. *Gallerie der Costüme auf historischen, nationellen und characteristischen Grundlagen für das Theater*, 12 vols. (Berlin: Winckelmann, 1844–8)

Aus meinem Leben, 3 vols. (Berlin: Mittler, 1879–80)

Schoch, Johann Georg. *Comoedia vom Studenten-Leben* (Leipzig: Wittigauer, 1658) [17]

Schönemann, Johann Friedrich. *Schönemannische Schaubühnne*, 5 vols. (Brunswick-Leipzig, 1748–51) [144, 151]

Schopenhauer, Johanna Henriette. *Ausflucht an den Rhein und dessen nächste Umgebungen im Sommer des ersten friedlichen Jahres* (Leipzig: Brockhaus, 1818)

Schreyvogel, Josef. *Der Roman meines Lebens* (Vienna: Jahrbuch der Grillparzer-Gesellschaft 9, 1899)

Josef Schreyvogels Tagebücher, 1810–23, 2 vols. (ed. Karl Glossy, Berlin: SGTG 2 & 3, 1903)

Schröder, F.L. *Friedrich Ludwig Schröder in seinen Briefen an K.A. Böttiger, 1794–1816* (ed. Hermann Uhde, Leipzig: Historisches Taschenbuch 45, 1875)

Schröder, Sophie. *Briefe von Sophie Schröder, 1813–1868*, 2 vols. (ed. Heinrich Stümcke, Berlin: SGTG 16 & 26, 1910, 1916)

Briefe/Gespräche (ed. Heinrich Stümcke, Berlin: KSGTG, 1913)

Schulze, Johann. *Über Ifflands Spiel auf dem Weimarischen Hoftheater im September 1810* (Weimar:

Landes-Industrie-Hof-Comptoir, 1810)

Schulze-Kummerfeld, Karoline. *Lebenserinnerungen der Karoline Schulze-Kummerfeld*, 2 vols. (ed. Emil Benezé, Berlin: SGTG 23 & 24, 1915) [**64, 85, 105, 154**]

Schütte, D. *Über den Vortheil stehender Theater vor reisenden; und Vorschläge zur Errichtung eines solchen in Bremen* (Bremen: Heysen, 1806)

Schütze, Johann Friedrich. *Hamburgische Theater-Geschichte* (Hamburg: Treder, 1794)

    Satyrisch-ästhetisches Hand- und Taschen-Wörterbuch für Schauspieler und Theaterfreunde beides Geschlechts (Hamburg: Verlagsgesellschaft, 1800)

    Dramaturgisches Tagebuch über Ifflands Gastspiele in Hamburg (Hamburg: Nestler, 1805)

Seydelmann, Carl. *Rollenhefte Carl Seydelmanns/Aus den Handschriften veröffentlicht* (ed. Heinrich Stümcke, Berlin: SGTG 25, 1915) [**248–50**]

Seyfried, Heinrich Wilhelm (Tlantlaquatlapatli). *Frankfurter Dramaturgie* (Frankfurt: Kämpfe, 1781)

    Schauspieler/Schauspielerinnen – Almanach auf das Jahr 1782 (Frankfurt, 1782)

    Ein dramatisches Wort zu seiner Zeit (Berlin, 1788)

Sievers, Georg Ludwig Peter. *Schauspieler-Studien/Ein unentbehrliches Handbuch für öffentliche Privat-schauspieler* (Brunswick, 1813)

Smekal, Richard (ed.). *Das alte Burgtheater, 1776–1888/Eine Charakteristik durch zeitgenössische Darstellungen* (Vienna: Schroll, 1916)

v. Sonnenfels, Josef. *Gedanken eines Philosophen von dem Lustspiel* (Vienna: v. Trettner, 1767)

    Briefe über die Wienerische Schaubühne, aus dem Französischen übersetzt (Vienna: Konegen, 1768; repr. & ed. August Sauer, Vienna: Konegen, 1883)

    Briefe von Sonnenfels (ed. H. Rollett, Vienna: Braumüller, 1874)

de Staël, Germaine. *De L'Allemagne* in vol. 11, *Oeuvres complètes* (Paris: Nicolle, 1813)

Staudlin, Carl Friedrich. *Geschichte der Vorstellungen von der Sittlichkeit des Theaters* (Göttingen: Rosenbusch, 1823)

Stranitzky, Joseph Anton. *Ollapotrida des durchgetriebenen Fuchsmundi, worinnen lustige Gespräche, angenehme Begebenheiten, artliche Ränck und Schwänck . . . sich in der Menge befinden* (n.p., 1711; re-issued by R.M. Werner, Vienna: Konegen, 1886)

Streicher, Andreas. *Schillers Flucht von Stuttgart und Aufenthalt in Mannheim von 1782 bis 1785* (Stuttgart-Augsburg: Cotta, 1836) [**209**]

Sturz, Helfrich Peter. *Brief über das deutsche Theater an die Freunde und Beschützer desselben in Hamburg*, preface to *Julie und Belmont* (Vienna: zu finden beym Logenmeister, 1779)

Sulzer, Johann Georg. *Allgemeine Theorie der Schönen Künste*, 2 vols. (Leipzig: Weidmanns Erben & Reich, 1771–4) [**181–2**]

Suphan, Bernhard Ludwig (ed.). *Urkunden aus den Zeiten der Theaterdirektion Goethes* (Weimar: Hof-Buchdruckerei, 1891)

Thürnagel, Emil. *Theorie der Schauspielkunst* (Heidelberg: Oswald, 1836)

Tieck, Ludwig. *Kritische Schriften*, 4 vols. (Leipzig: Brockhaus, 1848) [**124, 219**]

Tzschimmer, Gabriel. *Die Durchlauchtigste Zusammenkunft/Oder: Historische Erzehlung was Der Durch-lauchtigste Fürst und Herr/Herr Johann George* [sic] *der Ander/ Herzog zu Sachsen . . ./Bey Anwesenheit Seiner Churfürstlichen Durchlauchtigkeit Hochgeehrtesten Herren Gebrüder/dero Gemah-linnen/Prinzen/und Princessinen . . . in Dero Residenz und Haubt-Vestung Dresden im Monat Februario, des M.DC.LXXVIIIsten Jahres an allerhand Aufzügen . . . Schau-Spielen . . . Operen, Comoedien, Balleten, Masqueraden . . . aufführen und vorstellen lassen etc.* (Nuremberg: Hoffmann, 1680) [**20**]

v. Uechtritz, Friedrich. *Das Düsseldorfer Theater unter Immermanns Leitung/Blicke in das Düsseldorfer Kunst- und Künstlerleben*, 2 vols. (Düsseldorf, 1835)

Vogt, Nicolaus (ed.). *Pantomimische Stellungen von Henriette Hendel/Nach der Natur gezeichnet und in 26 Blättern herausgegeben* (Frankfurt: J.N. Peroux, 1810)

Wagenseil, Christian Jakob. *Unparteiische Geschichte des Gothaischen Theaters* (Mannheim, 1780)

Wagner, Heinrich Leopold. *Briefe, die Seylerische Schauspielergesellschaft und ihre Vorstellungen zu Frankfurt am Mayn betreffend* (Frankfurt, 1777)

Wahl, Hans (ed.). *Briefwechsel des Herzogs-Grossherzogs Carl August mit Goethe* (Berlin: Mittler, 1915) [228]

Weidmann, Franz Karl. *Maximilian Korn/Sein künstlerisches Wirken* (Vienna: K.K. Hof- und Staatsdruckerei, 1857)
  Die fünf Theater Wiens/Von ihrer Entstehung bis zum Jahre 1847 (n.p., 1847?)

Weise, Christian. *Lust and Nutzen der Spielenden Jugend* (Dresden-Leipzig, 1690) [40]
  Christian Weisens Freymüthiger und höfflicher Redner, das ist, Ausführliche Gedancken von der Pronunciation und Action . . . bey Gelegenheit gewisser Schau-Spiele allen Liebhabern zur Nachricht gründlich und deutlich entworffen (Leipzig: Gleditsch, 1693)

Weiss, Carl (ed.). *Die Wiener Haupt- und Staatsaktionen/Ein Beitrag zur Geschichte des deutschen Theaters* (Vienna: Gerold, 1854)

Weisse, Christian Felix. *Selbstbiographie* (ed. Christian Ernst Weisse & Samuel Gottlob Frisch, Leipzig: Voss, 1806)

Wittenberg, Albrecht. *Briefe über die Ackermannsche und die Hamonsche Schauspielergesellschaft in Hamburg* (Berlin, 1776)

Woetzel, Johann Carl. *Versuch einer völlig zweckmässigen Theaterschule oder der einzig richtigen Kunst und Methode, vollkommener Kunstschauspieler, Opernsänger, Pantomime und Ballettänzer im höheren Grade und in kürzerer Zeit zu werden, als auf dem bisherigen Wege* (Vienna: v. Mösle, 1818)

Wütschke, H. (ed.). *Hebbel in der zeitgenössischen Kritik* (Berlin: DLD 143, 1910; repr. Nendeln: Kraus Reprint, 1968) [264]

Ziegler, Friedrich Wilhelm. *Systematische Schauspiel-Kunst in ihrem ganzen Umfange* (Vienna: Pichler, 1820) [251]

(3) Studies

Adel, Kurt. *Das Jesuitendrama in Österreich* (Vienna: Bergland Verlag, 1957)
  Das Wiener Jesuitentheater und die europäische Barockdramatik (Vienna: Österreichischer Bundesverlag für Unterricht, Wissenschaft und Kunst, 1960)

Adrian, Karl. *Salzburgs Volksspiele, Aufzüge und Tänze* (Salzburg: A.H. Huber, 1908)
  Geistliches Volksschauspiel im Lande Salzburg (Salzburg/Leipzig: Pustet, 1936)

Alewyn, Richard & Sälzle, Karl. *Das grosse Welttheater/Die Epoche der höfischen Feste in Dokument und Deutung* (Hamburg: Rowohlt, 1959)

Alt, Heinrich. *Theater und Kirche/in ihrem gegenseitigen Verhältniss historisch dargestellt* (Berlin: Verlag der Plahnschen Buchhandlung, 1846; repr. Leipzig: Zentralantiquariat der Deutschen Demokratischen Republik, 1970)

v. Alvensleben, Udo & Reuther, Hans. *Herernhausen/Die Sommerresidenz der Welfen* (Hanover: Feesche, 1966)

Auch, Hans Günter. *Komödianten, Kalvinisten und Kattun/Geschichte des Wuppertaler und Schwelmer Theaters im 18., und 19. Jahrhundert, 1700–1850* (DSB 55, 1960)

Bab, Julius. *Die Devrients/Geschichte einer deutschen Theaterfamilie* (Berlin: Stilke, 1932)

Bachman, Claus-Henning & Frank, Gertrud (eds.). *275 Jahre Theater in Braunschweig* (Brunswick: Generalintendanz des Staatstheaters Braunschweig, 1965)

Bärensprung, Hans Wilhelm. *Versuch einer Geschichte des Theaters in Mecklenburg-Schwerin/Von den ersten Spuren theatralischer Vorstellungen bis zum Jahre 1835* (Schwerin: Hofbuchdruckerei, 1837)

Baesecke, Anna. *Das Schauspiel der englischen Komödianten in Deutschland* (Halle: Niemeyer, 1935)

Bauer, Anton. *150 Jahre Theater an der Wien* (Zürich: Amalthea-Verlag, 1952)
  Das Theater in der Josefstadt zu Wien (Vienna: Manutiuspresse, 1957)

Baur-Heinhold, Margarete. *Theater des Barock* (Munich: Callwey, 1966). English version: *Baroque Theatre* (London: Thames & Hudson, 1967) [10, 18, 70]

Beaumont, Cyril. *Fanny Elsler* (London: C.W. Beaumont, 1931)

Berger, Karl. *Schiller/Sein Leben und seine Werke*, 2 vols. (Munich: Beck, 1904–8) [222]

Biach-Sciffmann, Flora. *Giovanni und Ludovico Burnacini/Theater und Feste am Wiener Hof* (Vienna: Krystall, 1930)

Biberhofer, Raoul. *125 Jahre Theater an der Wien, 1801–1926* (Vienna: W. Karczag, 1926)

Biermann, Franz Benedikt. *Die Pläne für Reform des Theaterbaues bei Karl Friedrich Schinkel und Gottfried Semper* (SGTG 38, 1928) [234]

Binal, Wolfgang. *Deutschsprachiges Theater in Budapest/Von den Anfängen bis zum Brand des Theaters in der Wollgasse, 1899* (Vienna: Böhlau, 1972)

Bischoff, H. *Ludwig Tieck als Dramaturg* (Brussels: Université de Liège, 1897)

Bitterling, Richard. *J. Fr. Schink/Ein Schüler Diderots und Lessings* (TGF 23, 1911)

Bobbert, Gerda. *Charlotte von Hagn/Eine Schauspielerin der Biedermeierzeit, 1809–1891* (TGF 45, 1936)

Born, G. *Die Gründung des Berliner Nationaltheaters und die Geschichte seines Personals, seines Spielplans und seiner Verwaltung bis zu Doebbelins Abgang, 1786–89* (Borna-Leipzig: Noske, 1934)

Blümml, Emil Karl & Gugitz, Gustav. *Alt-Wiener Thespiskarren* (Vienna: A. Schroll, 1925)

Blümner, Heinrich. *Geschichte des Theaters in Leipzig* (Leipzig: F.A. Brockhaus, 1818)

Bolte, Johannes. *Drei Königsberger Zwischenspiele aus dem Jahr 1644* (Berlin: n.p., 1890)

Das Singspiel der englischen Komödianten und ihrer Nachfolger (TGF 7, 1893)

Das Danziger Theater im 16. und 17. Jahrhundert (TGF 12, 1895) [1, 2, 8, 55–6]

Brachvogel, Albert Emil. *Das alte Berliner Theater-Wesen bis zur ersten Blüthe des deutschen Dramas* (Berlin: Otto Janke, 1877)

Geschichte des Königlichen Theaters zu Berlin, 2 vols. (Berlin: Otto Janke, 1877–8)

Bruford, Walter Horace. *Germany in the Eighteenth Century/The Social Background to the Literary Revival* (CUP, 1935)

Theatre, Drama and Audience in Goethe's Germany (London: Routledge and Kegan Paul, 1950)

Burath, Hugo. *August Klingemann und die deutsche Romatik* (Brunswick: Vieweg, 1948)

Burkhardt, Carl August Hugo. *Das Repertoire des Weimarischen Theaters unter Goethes Leitung, 1791–1817* (TGF 1, 1891)

Carlson, Marvin. *Goethe and the Weimar Theatre* (Ithaca and London: Cornell University Press, 1978) [81, 122, 135, 179, 221–2, 224–5]

The German Stage in the Nineteenth Century (Metuchen, N.J.: Scarecrow Press 1972)

Cohn, Albert. *Shakespeare in Germany in the Sixteenth and Seventeenth Centuries* (Oxford University Press 1865; repr. Wiesbaden: Sandig, 1967) [5–7, 26, 28, 30, 34, 50]

Creizenach, Wilhelm Michael Anton. *Die Tragödie 'Der bestrafte Brudermord oder Prinz Hamlet aus Dänemark' und ihre Bedeutung für die Kritik des Shakespeare'schen Hamlet* (Leipzig: Hirzel, 1887)

Die Schauspiele der englischen Komödianten (Kürschners Deutsche Nationalliteratur 23, Berlin/Stuttgart: W. Spemann 1889, repr. Darmstadt: Wissenschaftliche Buchgesellschaft, 1967) [26, 31]

Crüger, Johannes. *Englische Komödianten in Strassburg im Elsass* (Leipzig, 1887)

Daffis, Hans. *Hamlet auf der deutschen Bühne bis zur Gegenwart* (Berlin: Felber, 1912)

Danzel, Theodor Wilhelm. *Gottsched und seine Zeit* (Leipzig: Verlag der Deutschen Buchhandlung, 1848)

Daunicht, Richard. *Die Neuberin/Materialien zur Theatergeschichte des 18. Jahrhunderts* (Berlin: Ministerium für Kultur, 1956) [84]

Deneke, Otto. *Göttinger Theater im 18. Jahrhundert* (Göttingen: Silvester, 1930)

Deutsch, Otto Erich. *Das Freihaustheater auf der Wieden, 1787–1801* (Vienna/Leipzig: Deutscher Verlag für Jugend & Volk, 2nd ed., 1937)

Deutschmann, Wilhelm. *Wiener Theater/Bilddokumente* (Vienna: Historisches Museum, 1972)

Devrient, Hans. *Johann Friedrich Schönemann und seine Schauspielergesellschaft* (TGF 11, 1895) [61–2, 144, 151]

Diebold, Bernhard. *Das Rollenfach im deutschen Theaterbetrieb des 18. Jahrhunderts* (TGF 25, 1913) [107]

Diem, Ulrich. *Aus der St. Gallischen Theatergeschichte* (St. Gall: Tschudy, 1955)

Dietrich, Margret (ed.). *Das Burgtheater und sein Publikum* (Vienna: Österreichische Akademie der Wissenschaften, 1976)

Doebber, Adolph. *Lauchstädt und Weimar/Eine theaterbaugeschichtliche Studie* (Berlin: Mittler, 1908)

Doerry, Hans. *Das Rollenfach im deutschen Theaterbetrieb des 19. Jahrhunderts* (SGTG 35, 1926)

Droescher, Georg. *Der Schinkelbau/100 Jahre Schauspielhaus* (Dresden: Waldheim, 1921)

Eberle, Oskar. *Theatergeschichte der inneren Schweiz, 1200–1800* (Königsberg/Kaliningrad: Gräfe und Unzer, 1929)

Ebert, Hermann. *Versuch einer Geschichte des Theaters in Rostock* (Rostock: Hinstorff'sche Buchdruckerei, 1872)

Eggert, Walther. *Christian Weise und seine Bühne* (Berlin/Leipzig: de Gruyter, 1935)

Ehrhard, Auguste. *Les Comédies de Molière en Allemagne* (Paris: Lacène & Audin, 1888)

Eichhorn, Herbert. *Das Schlosstheater zu Gotha* (KSGTG 13, 1955)
   Konrad Ernst Ackermann/Ein deutscher Theaterprinzipal (DSB 64, 1965)

Eloesser, Arthur (ed.). *Aus der grossen Zeit des deutschen Theaters/Schauspieler-Memoiren* (Munich: Rentsch, 1911)

Engelbrecht, Christiane, Brennecke, W. & Schaefer, Hans Joachim. *Theater in Kassel* (Kassel: Bärenreiter-Verlag, 1959)

Enzinger, Moriz. *Die Entwicklung des Wiener Theaters vom 16. zum 19. Jahrhundert*, 2 vols. (SGTG 28/29, 1918–19)

Falck, Robert. *Zur Geschichte des Liebhabertheaters* (Berlin, 1887)

Fellmann, Hans Georg. *Die Böhmische Theatertruppe und ihre Zeit* (TGF 38, 1928)

Fellner, Richard. *Geschichte einer deutschen Musterbühne/Karl Immermanns Leitung des Stadttheaters zu Düsseldorf* (Stuttgart: Cotta, 1888)

Fetting, Hugo. *Conrad Ekhof/Ein Schauspieler des 18. Jarhunderts* (Berlin: Henschelverlag, 1954)

Fischer, Ernst H. *Lübecker Theater und Theaterleben in frühester Zeit bis zur Mitte des 18. Jahrhunderts. Ein Beitrag zur Entwicklungsgeschichte einer norddeutschen Bühne bis zum Jahre 1765* (Lübeck: Gesellschaft Lübecker Theaterfreunde, 1932)

Flemming, Willi. *Andreas Gryphius und die Bühne* (Halle: Niemeyer, 1921)
   Geschichte des Jesuitentheaters in den Landen deutscher Zunge (Berlin: SGTG 32, 1923)
   Goethe und das Theater seiner Zeit (Stuttgart: Kohlhammer, 1968)

Freisauff v. Neudeck, Rudolf. *Geschichte des Salzburger Theaters* (Salzburg, 1875)

Frenzel, Herbert A.. *Brandenburg-Preussische Schlosstheater/Spielorte und Spielformen vom 17. bis zum 19. Jahrhundert* (SGTG 59, 1959)
   Thüringische Schlosstheater/Beiträge zur Typologie des Spielortes vom 16. bis zum 19. Jahrhundert (SGTG 63, 1965)

Frey, Dagobert. *Das Schönbrunner Schlosstheater* (Zürich: Amalthea-Verlag, 1924)

Fürst, Norbert. *Grillparzer auf der Bühne* (Vienna: Manutiuspresse, 1958)

Fürstenau, Moritz. *Zur Geschichte der Musik und des Theaters am Hofe zu Dresden*, 2 vols. (Dresden: Kuntze, 1861–2)

Gaedertz, Karl Theodor. *Das niederdeutsche Schauspiel/Zum Kulturleben Hamburgs* (Berlin: Hoffmann, 1884)

Genée, Rudolf. *Lehr- und Wanderjahre des deutschen Schauspiels vom Beginn der Reformation bis zur Mitte des 18. Jahrhunderts* (Berlin: Hofmann, 1882)
   Hundert Jahre des Königlichen Schauspiels in Berlin (Berlin: Hofmann, 1886)
   Iffland's Berliner Theaterleitung, 1796–1814 (Berlin: Buckdruckerei der National-Zeitung, 1896)

Glaser, Adolf. *Geschichte des Theaters zu Braunschweig* (Brunswick: Neuhoff, 1861)

Glossy, Karl Ludwig. *Zur Geschichte der Wiener Theaterzensur* (Vienna: Konegen, 1896)
   Zur Geschichte der Theater Wiens, 2 vols. (Vienna: Konegen & Amalthea-Verlag, 1915–1920)
   Das Burgtheater unter seinem Gründer Kaiser Joseph II. (Vienna: A. Hartleben, 1926)

Grandaur, Franz. *Chronik des königl. Hof- und Nationaltheaters in München* (Munich: Ackermann, 1878)

Gregor, Joseph. *Das Theater in der Wiener Josefstadt* (Vienna: Wiener Drucke, 1924)
   Geschichte des österreichischen Theaters/Von seinen Ursprüngen bis zum Ende der ersten Republik (Vienna: Donau-Verlag, 1948)

Gross, Edgar. *Die ältere Romantik und das Theater* (TGF 22, 1910)
   Johann Friedrich Fleck (SGTG 22, 1914)

Gugitz, Gustav. *Der weiland Kasperl (Johann La Roche)/Ein Beitrag zur Theater- und Sittengeschichte Alt-Wiens* (Vienna: Stracks, 1920)

Günther, Johannes. *Der Theaterkritiker Heinrich Theodor Rötscher* (TGF 31, 1921)

Hadamczik, Dieter. *Friedrich Ludwig Schröder in der Geschichte des Burgtheaters* (SGTG 60, 1961)

Hadamowsky, Franz. *Ferdinand Raimund als Schauspieler. Chronologie seiner Rollen nebst Theaterreden und lebensgeschichtlichen Nachrichten* (Vienna: Schroll, 1925)

Das Theater an der Wien (Vienna: Kataloge der Theatersammlung der Nationalbibliothek, vol. 1, 1930)

Die Figurinen der Wiener Hoftheater (Vienna: Kataloge der Theatersammlung der Nationalbibliothek, vol. 2, 1930)

Das Theater in der Wiener Leopoldstadt (Vienna: Kataloge der Theatersammlung der Nationalbibliothek, vol. 3, 1934)

Wien: Theatergeschichte von den Anfängen bis zum Ende des Ersten Weltkrieges (Vienna: Jugend und Volk, 1988)

Hänsel, Johann-Richard. *Der Autor auf dem Theaterzettel* (KSGTG 16, 1958)

Hagen, Ernst August. *Geschichte des Theaters in Preussen; vornähmlich der Bühnen in Königsberg und Danzig* (Königsberg/Kaliningrad: Dalkowski, 1854)

Hager, Luisa. *Markgräfliches Opernhaus Bayreuth* (Munich: Bayerische Verwaltung der staatlichen Schlösser, Gärten und Seen, 1952)

Haider-Pregler, Hilde. *The Theatre in Austria* (Vienna: Federal Press Service, n.d.)

Hampe, Theodor. *Die Entwicklung des Theaterwesens in Nürnberg von der zweiten Hälfte des 15. Jahrhunderts bis 1806* (Nuremberg: *Mitteilungen des Vereins für Geschichte der Stadt Nürnberg*, nos. 12/13, 1900)

Hartleb, Hans. *Deutschlands erster Theaterbau/Eine Geschichte des Theaterlebens und der englischen Komödianten unter Graf Moritz dem Gelehrten von Hessen-Kassel* (Berlin/Leipzig: de Gruyter, 1936)

Hartmann, August. *Das Oberammergauer Passionsspiel in seiner ältesten Gestalt* (Leipzig: Breitkopf & Härtel, 1880)

Hartmann, G. *Küstner und das Münchner Hofschauspiel* (Dresden, 1914)

Hefter, Rudolf. *Die moralische Beurteilung des deutschen Schauspielers* (DSB 14, 1936)

Heine, Carl. *Johannes Velten/Ein Beitrag zur Geschichte des deutschen Theaters im 17. Jahrhundert* (Halle: Karras, 1887)

Das Schauspiel der deutschen Wanderbühnen vor Gottsched (Halle: Niemeyer, 1889)

Heitmüller, Franz Ferdinand. *Holländische Komödianten in Hamburg, 1740 und 1741* (TGF 8, 1894)

Henning, Hans. *Schillers 'Kabale und Liebe' in der zeitgenössischen Rezeption* (Leipzig: Zentralantiquariat der DDR, 1976) [**209–10**]

Lessings 'Emilia Galotti' in der zeitgenössischen Rezeption (Leipzig: Zentralantiquariat der DDR, 1981) [**192**]

Hermann, Max. *Das Jahrmarktsfest zu Plundersweilen/Entstehungs- und Bühnengeschichte* (Berlin: Weidmann, 1900)

Herz, Emil. *Englische Schauspieler und englisches Schauspiel zur Zeit Shakespeares in Deutschland* (TGF 18, 1903)

Hess, Josef Hermann. *P. Marianus Rot (1597–1663)/Ein Kapitel Schweizer Theatergeschichte* (Basle: Hess, 1927)

Heym, Heinrich. *Frankfurt und sein Theater* (Frankfurt on Main: Kramer, 1963)

Hill, Wilhelm. *Die deutschen Theaterzeitschriften des 18. Jahrhunderts* (Weimar: Duncker, 1915; repr. Hildesheim: Gerstenberg, 1979)

Hinck, Walter. *Das deutsche Lustspiel des 17. und 18. Jahrhunderts und die italienische Komödie* (Stuttgart: Metzler, 1965)

Hodermann, Richard. *Geschichte des Gothaischen Hoftheaters, 1775–9* (TGF 9, 1894)

Hoffman, Paul F. *F.L. Schröder als Dramaturg und Regisseur* (SGTG 52, 1939)

Hoffman, Paul Theodor. *Die Entwicklung des Altonaer Stadttheaters* (Altona: Köbner, 1926)

Houben, Heinrich Hubert. *Hier Zensur – wer dort/ Antworten von gestern auf Fragen von heute* (Leipzig: Brockhaus, 1918)

Huesmann, Heinrich. *Shakespeare-Inszenierungen unter Goethe in Weimar* (Vienna: Böhlau, 1968)

Hummel, Georg. *Erfurter Theaterleben im 18. Jahrhundert* (Erfurt: Gutenberg-Druckerei, 1956)

Hysel, Franz Eduard. *Das Theater in Nürnberg von 1612–1863* (Nuremberg: publ. by author, 1863)

Jacob, Martin. *Kölner Theater im 18. Jahrhundert bis zum Ende der Reichsstädtischen Zeit, 1700–1794* (DSB 21, 1938)

Kaiser, Hermann. *Barocktheater in Darmstadt* (Darmstadt: Roether, 1951)

Kasten, Otto. *Das Theater in Köln während der Franzosenzeit, 1784–1814* (DSB 2, 1928)

Kaulfuss-Diesch, Carl Hermann. *Die Inszenierung des deutschen Dramas an der Wende des 16. und 17. Jahrhunderts* (Leipzig: Voitglander, 1905)

Kayser, Fritz. *Immermann und das Elberfelder Theater/Ein Beitrag zur Geschichte einer Musterbühne* (Wuppertal-Elberfeld: Stadtbücherei, 1935)

Kerry, Stanley Spencer. *Schiller's Writings on Aesthetics* (Manchester University Press, 1961)

Kersting, Kurt. *Wirkende Kräfte in der Theaterkritik des ausgehenden 18. Jahrhunderts* (Berlin: Theater und Drama 6, Elsner, 1936)

Kertz, Peter. *Das Nürnberger Nationaltheater, 1798–1833* (Nuremberg: Mitteilungen des Vereins für Geschichte der Stadt Nürnberg 50, 1960)

Kilian, Eugen (ed.). *Beiträge zur Geschichte des Karlsruher Hoftheaters unter Eduard Devrient* (Karlsruhe: Braun, 1893)

Der einteilige Theater-Wallenstein/Ein Beitrag zur Bühnengeschichte von Schillers Wallenstein (Berlin: Duncker, 1901)

Kindermann, Heinz. *Theatergeschichte der Goethezeit* (Vienna: Bauer, 1948) [63, 141, 218]

Shakespeare und das Burgtheater (Vienna: Böhlau, 1964)

Kindermann, Heinz & Dietrich, Margret. *Die Commedia dell'Arte und das Altwiener Volkstheater* (Rome: Österreichisches Kulturinstitut, 1965)

Klara, Winfried. *Schauspielkostüm und Schauspieldarstellung/Entwicklungsfragen des deutschen Theaters im 18. Jahrhundert* (SGTG 43, 1931)

Klein, Wilhelm. *Der Preussische Staat und das Theater im Jahre 1848/Ein Beitrag zur Geschichte der Nationaltheateridee* (SGTG 33, 1924)

Kneschke, Emil. *Zur Geschichte des Theaters und der Musik in Leipzig* (Leipzig: Fleischer, 1864)

Knudsen, Hans. *Heinrich Beck/Ein Schauspieler aus der Blütezeit des Mannheimer Theaters im 18. Jahrhundert* (TGF 24, 1912)

Goethes Welt des Theaters (Berlin: Tempelhof, 1949)

Koch, Gustav. *Adolf Müllner als Theaterkritiker und literarischer Organisator* (DSB 28, 1939)

Koffka, Wilhelm. *Iffland und Dalberg/Geschichte der classischen Theaterzeit Mannheims* (Leipzig: Weber, 1865)

Koeppen, A. *Die Geschichte des Schwedter Hoftheaters* (Schwedt: Schultz, 1936)

Kopp, Heinrich. *Die Bühnenleitung Aug. Klingemanns in Braunschweig* (TGF 17, 1901)

Kosch, Wilhelm. *Das deutsche Theater und Drama seit Schillers Tod* (2nd ed. Leipzig: Vier Quellen Verlag, 1922)

v. Kotzebue, Wilhelm. *August von Kotzebue/Urtheile der Zeitgenossen und der Gegenwart* (Dresden: Baensch, 1881)

Krause, Markus. *Das Trivialdrama der Goethezeit 1780–1805/Produktion und Rezeption* (Bonn: Bouvier Verlag Hermann Grundmann, 1982)

Krauss, Rudolf. *Das Stuttgarter Hoftheater von den ältesten Zeiten bis zur Gegenwart* (Stuttgart: Metzler, 1908)

Kroll, Christina. *Gesang und Rede, sinniges Bewegen/Goethe als Theaterleiter* (Düsseldorf: Goethe-Museum, 1973)

v. Krosigk, Hans Dedo Ludwig. *Karl Graf von Brühl, General-Intendant der königlichen Schauspiele* (Berlin: Mittler, 1910)

Kühling, Karl. *Theater in Osnabrück im Wandel der Jahrhunderte* (Osnabrück, 1959)

Kuhn, Waldemar & Delle, Eberhard. *Theater im alten Berlin* (Berlin: KSGTG 12, 1954)

Kürschner, Joseph. *Ekhofs Leben und Wirken* (Vienna: Hartleben, 1872)

Kutscher, Artur. *Das Salzburger Barocktheater* (Vienna: Rikola, 1924)

Vom Salzburger Barocktheater zu den Salzburger Festspielen (Düsseldorf: Pflugschar-Verlag, 1939) [9]

Lamport, F.J. *German Classical Drama/Theater, Humanity and Nation 1750–1870* (CUP, 1990)

Laskus, Irmgard. *Friederike Bethmann-Unzelmann/Versuch einer Rekonstruktion ihrer Schauspielkunst auf Grund ihrer Hauptrollen* (TGF 37, 1927)

Lebe, Reinhard. *Ein deutsches Hoftheater in Romantik und Biedermeyer/Die Kasseler Bühne zur Zeit Feiges und Spohrs* (Kassel: Roth, 1964)

Legband, Paul. *Münchener Bühne und Litteratur des 18. Jahrhunderts* (Munich: Verlag des historischen Vereins von Oberbayern, 1904)

Lentner, Franz. *Deutsche Volkskomödie und salzburgisches Hanswurstspiel* (Innsbruck: Wagner, 1893)

Lichterfeld, L. *Entwickelungsgeschichte der deutschen Schauspielkunst* (Erfurt: Bartholomäus 1882)

Litzmann, Berthold (ed.) *Schröder und Gotter/Eine Episode aus der deutschen Theatergeschichte/Briefe Friedrich Ludwig Schröders und Friedrich Wilhelm Gotters 1777–1778* (Leipzig: Voss, 1887)

Hamlet in Hamburg, 1625 (Berlin: Paetel, 1892)

Aus den Lehr- und Wanderjahren des deutschen Theaters (Berlin: Paetel, 1912)

Lothar, Rudolph. *Das Wiener Burgtheater* (Leipzig: Seemann, 1899; rev. & enlarged ed. Vienna: Szabo, 1934)

Lürgen, Bernd (ed.) *Chronik des Theaters in Altenburg* (Leipzig: Beck, 1937)

Lynker, Wilhelm. *Geschichte des Theaters und der Musik in Kassel* (Kassel: Kay, 1865)

v. Magnus, Peter. *Die Geschichte des Theaters in Lübeck bis zum Ende des 18. Jahrhunderts* (Lüneburg: Museumsverein für das Fürstentum Lüneburg, 1961)

Mahlberg, Paul. *Schinkels Theaterdekorationen* (Düsseldorf, 1916)

Martersteig, Max. *Pius Alexander Wolff* (Leipzig: Fernau, 1879)

Die Protokolle des Mannheimer Nationaltheaters unter Dalberg aus den Jahren 1781 bis 1789 (Mannheim: Bensheimer, 1890)

Das deutsche Theater im 19. Jahrhundert (Leipzig: Breitkopf & Härtel, 1904)

Martino, Alberto. *Storia delle teorie drammatiche nella Germania del Settecento, vol. 1: 1730–1780* (Università di Pisa, 1967)

Maurer-Schmook, Sybille. *Deutsches Theater im 18. Jahrhundert* (Tübingen: Niemeyer, 1982) [78, 84, 229]

Mausolf, Werner. *E.T.A. Hoffmanns Stellung zu Drama und Theater* (Berlin: Germanische Studien 7, 1920)

Mayerhofer, Josef. *Ausstellung 200 Jahre Burgtheater* (Vienna: Österreichisches Theatermuseum, 1976)

Wiener Theater des Biedermeyer und Vormärz/Ausstellungskatalog (Vienna: Österreichisches Theatermuseum, 1978)

Maync, Harry Wilhelm. *Immermann/Der Mann und sein Werk* (Munich: Beck, 1920)

Mayor, Alpheus Hyatt. *The Bibiena Family* (New York: Bittner, 1945)

Meissner, Johannes. *Die englischen Comödianten zur Zeit Shakespeares in Österreich* (Vienna: Konegen 1884) [29]

Mentzel, Elisabeth. *Geschichte der Schauspielkunst in Frankfurt a.M. von ihren Anfängen bis zur Eröffnung des städtischen Komödienhauses* (Frankfurt: Volcker, 1882)

Das alte Frankfurter Schauspielhaus und seine Vorgeschichte (Frankfurt: Rütten & Loening, 1902)

Merschberger, Prof. Dr. *Die Anfänge Shakespeares auf der Hamburgischen Bühne* (Hamburg: Realgymnasium des Johanneums, 1890)

Meyer, Curt. *Alt-Berliner politisches Volkstheater, 1848–1850* (DSB 40, 1951)

Meyer, Günter. *Hallisches Theater im 18. Jahrhundert* (DSB 37, 1950)

Meyer, Rudolf. *Hecken- und Gartentheater in Deutschland im 17. und 18. Jahrhundert* (DSB 6, 1934)

Meyer, Walther. *Die Entwicklung des Theaterabonnements in Deutschland* (DSB 32, 1939)

Michael, Friedrich. *Die Anfänge der Theaterkritik in Deutschland* (Leipzig: Haessel, 1918)

Mirow, Franz. *Zwischenaktmusik und Bühnenmusik des deutschen Theaters in der klassischen Zeit* (SGTG 37, 1927)

Morschel-Wetzke, E. *Der Sprechstil der idealistischen Schauspielkunst* (DSB 48, 1950)

Moser, Ernst. *Königsberger Theatergechichte* (Königsberg/Kaliningrad: Karg & Manneck, 1902)

Moser, Fritz. *Die Anfänge des Hof- und Gesellschaftstheaters in Deutschland* (Berlin: Theater und Drama 16, 1940)

Müller, Eugen. *Eine Glanzzeit des Zürcher Stadttheaters/Charlotte Birch-Pfeiffer 1837–1843* (Zürich: Orell Füssli, 1911)

Schweizer Theatergeschichte (Zürich: Oprecht, 1944)

Müller, Hermann. *Chronik des Königl. Hoftheaters zu Hannover* (Hanover: Helwing, 1884)

Müller, W. *Joseph von Sonnenfels/Biographische Studie aus dem Zeitalter der Aufklärung in Österreich* (Vienna; Braumüller, 1882)

Noch, Curt. *Grillparzers 'Ahnfrau' und die Wiener Volksdramatik* (Leipzig: Wiegandt, 1911)

Oberländer, Hans. *Die geistige Entwicklung der deutschen Schauspielkunst im 18. Jahrhundert* (TGF 15, 1898)

Olivier, Jean-Jacques. *Les Comédiens français dans les cours d'Allemagne au 18e siècle*, 4 vols. (Paris: Société Française d'Imprimerie et de Librairie, 1901–5) [33]

Pascal, Roy. *Shakespeare in Germany* (CUP, 1937)

Pasqué, Ernst Heinrich Anton. *Goethes Theaterleitung in Weimar* (Leipzig: Weber, 1863)

Patterson, Michael. *The First German Theatre: Schiller, Goethe, Kleist and Büchner in performance* (London: Routledge, 1990)

Petersen, Julius. *Schiller und die Bühne* (Berlin: Mayer & Müller, 1904; repr. New York: Johnson, 1967)

Das deutsche Nationaltheater (Leipzig/Berlin: Teubner, 1919)

Goethes Faust auf der deutschen Bühne (Leipzig: Quelle & Meyer, 1929)

Peth, Jakob. *Geschichte des Theaters und der Musik in Mainz* (Mainz: Prickarts, 1879)

Pfeiffer, Heinz Ernst. *Theater in Bonn von seinen Anfängen bis zum Ende der französischen Zeit* (DSB 7, 1934)

Piana, Theo. *Lodernde Flamme/Aufstieg und Untergang des Schaupielers Ludwig Devrient* (Berlin: Verlag Das Neue Berlin, 1957)

Pichler, Anton. *Chronik des Grossherzoglichen Hof- und Nationaltheaters in Mannheim* (Mannheim: Bensheimer, 1879)

Pies, Eike. *Das Theater in Schleswig 1618–1839* (Kiel: Hirt, 1970)

Prinzipale/Zur Genealogie des deutschsprachigen Berufstheaters vom 17. bis zum 19. Jahrhundert (Ratingen-Kastellaun-Düsseldorf: Henn, 1973) [35]

Pietsch-Ebert, Lilly. *Die Gestalt des Schauspielers auf der deutschen Bühne des 17. und 18. Jahrhunderts* (TGF 46, 1942)

Pirchan, Emil. *Therese Krones, die Theaterkönigin Altwiens* (Vienna: Wallishauser, 1942)

Potkoff, Ossip D. *Johann Friedrich Löwen/Der erste Direktor eines deutschen Nationaltheaters* (Heidelberg: Winter, 1904)

Proelss, Robert. *Geschichte des Dresdner Hoftheaters von den Anfängen bis zum Jahre 1862* (Dresden: Baensch, 1878)

Kurzgefasste Geschichte der deutschen Schauspielkunst von den Anfängen bis 1850 (Leipzig: Berger, 1900)

Protkhe, Josef Ernst. *Das Leopoldstädter Theater/Von seiner Entstehung an skizziert* (Vienna: Stockholzer von Hirschfeld, 1847)

Prutz, Robert Eduard. *Vorlesungen über die Geschichte des deutschen Theaters* (Berlin: Duncker & Humblot, 1847) [17, 40]

Pukánszky (Kádár), Jolan. *Geschichte des deutschen Theaters in Ungarn* (Munich: Reinhardt, 1933)

Raab, Ferdinand. *Johann Joseph Felix von Kurz, gennant Bernardon* (Frankfurt: Rütten & Loening, 1899)

v. Radics, Peter. *Die Entwickelung des deutschen Bühnenwesens in Laibach* (Laibach/Ljubljana: Kleinmayr & Bamberg, 1912)

v. Reden-Esbeck, Friedrich Johannes. *Caroline Neuber und ihre Zeitgenossen* (Leipzig: Barth, 1881) [59, 63, 114, 153, 161]

Reed, T.J. *The Classical Centre/Goethe and Weimar 1775–1832* (London: Croom Helm, 1980)

Reimann, Viktor. *Der Iffland-Ring/Legende und Geschichte eines Künstleridols* (Vienna: Deutsch, n.d.)

Richter, Horst. *Johann Oswald Harms/Ein deutscher Theaterdekorateur des Barock* (DSB 58, 1963)

Robertson, John G. *Lessing's Dramatic Theory* (CUP, 1939) [170]

Rommel, Otto. *Die grossen Figuren der Alt-Wiener Volkskomödie/Hanswurst, Kasperl, Thadäddl und Staberl, Raimund und Nestroy* (Vienna: Bindenschild-Verlag, 1946)
Ferdinand Raimund und die Vollendung des Alt-Weiner Zauberstückes (Vienna: Bindenschild-Verlag, 1947)
Johann Nestroy, der Satiriker auf der Altwiener Komödienbühne (Vienna: Schroll, 1948)
Die Alt-Wiener Volkskomödie/Ihre Geschichte vom barocken Welt-Theater bis zum Tode Nestroys (Vienna: Schroll, 1952)
Rosen, Elisabeth. *Rückblicke auf die Pflege der Schauspielkunst in Reval* (Melle-Hanover: Haag, 1910)
Rosendahl, Eric. *Geschichte der Hoftheater in Hannover und Braunschweig* (Hanover: Helwing, 1927)
Rub, Otto. *Die dramatische Kunst in Danzig von 1615–1893* (Danzig/Gdansk: Bertling, 1894)
Rudan, Helmar & Othmar. *Das Stadttheater in Klagenfurt* (Klagenfurt: Verlag des Landesmuseums für Kärnten, 1960)
Rudin, Alexander. *Franciscus Lang und die Bühne/Studien zur Theatergeschichte des 17. und 18. Jahrhunderts* (DSB 72, 1972)
Rudloff-Hille, Gertrud. *Das Theater auf der Ranstädter Bastei, Leipzig 1766/Geschichte des ersten Leipziger Theaterbaues* (Leipzig: Museum für Geschichte der Stadt Leipzig, 1969) [78]
Schiller auf der deutschen Bühne seiner Zeit (Berlin: Aufbau-Verlag, 1969)
Satori-Neumann, Bruno Thomas. *300 Jahre berufsständisches Theater in Elbing* (Danzig/Gdansk: Quellen und Darstellungen zur Geschichte Westpreussens 20, 1936)
Die Frühzeit des Weimarischen Hoftheaters unter Goethes Leitung, 1791 bis 1798 (SGTG 31, 1922)
Schiedermair, Ludwig. *Bayreuther Festspiele im Zeitalter des Absolutismus* (Leipzig: Kahnt, 1908)
Schiffman, Konrad. *Drama und Theater in Österreich ob der Enns bis zum Jahre 1803* (Linz: Verlag des Vereines Francisco-Carolinum, 1905)
Schlesinger, Maximilian. *Geschichte des Breslauer Theaters, 1552–1841* (Berlin: Fischer, 1898)
Schloenbach, Carl Arnold. *Beiträge zur Geschichte der Schiller-Periode des Mannheimer Theaters* (Dresden, 1860)
Schlösser, Rudolf. *Vom Hamburger Nationaltheater zur Gothaer Hofbühne/Dreizehn Jahre aus der Entwicklung eines deutschen Theaterspielplans* (TGF 13, 1895)
Schneider, Louis. *Johann Carl von Eckenberg, der starke Mann/Eine Studie zur Theater-Geschichte Berlins* (Berlin, 1848)
Schöne, Albrecht. *Emblematik und Drama im Zeitalter des Barock* (Munich: Beck, 1964)
Schreyvogel, Friedrich. *Das Burgtheater/Wirklichkeit und Illusion* (Vienna: Speidel, 1965)
Schulze, Friedrich. *Hundert Jahre Leipziger Stadttheater* (Leipzig: Breitkopf & Härtel, 1917)
Schumacher, Erich. *Shakespeares 'Macbeth' auf der deutschen Bühne* (DSB 22, 1938)
Schwanbeck, Gisela. *Sozialprobleme der Schauspielerin im Ablauf dreier Jahrhunderte* (Berlin: Colloquium-Verlag, 1957)
Schwarzbeck, Friedrich Wilhelm. *Ansbacher Theatergeschichte bis zum Tode des Markgrafen Johann Friedrich* (DSB 29, 1939)
Senn, Walter. *Musik und Theater am Hof zu Innsbruck/Vom 15. Jahrhundert bis 1748* (Innsbruck: Österreichische Verlagsanstalt, 1954)
Sharpe, Lesley. *Friedrich Schiller/Drama, Thought and Politics* (CUP, 1991)
Sichardt, Gisela. *Das Weimarer Liebhabertheater unter Goethes Leitung* (Weimar: Arion, 1957)
Siebert-Didczuhn, Rolf. *Der Theaterdichter/Die Geschichte eines Bühnenamtes im 18. Jahrhundert* (Berlin: Theater und Drama 11, 1938)
Sievers, Hartwig. *Hebbels 'Maria Magadalena' auf der Bühne/Ein Beitrag zur Bühnengeschichte Hebbels* (Berlin-Leipzig: Behr/Feddersen, 1933)
Sievers, Heinrich & others. *250 Jahre Braunschweigisches Staatstheater, 1690–1940* (Brunswick: Appelhans, 1940)
Sittard, Josef. *Zur Geschichte der Musik und des Theaters am Württembergischen Hofe*, 2 vols. (Stuttgart: Kohlhammer, 1890–91)
Sitwell, Sacheverell. *Theatrical Figures in Porcelain/German 18th Century* (London: Curtain Press, 1949)
Söhngen, Siegfried. *Französisches Theater in Berlin im 19. Jahrhundert* (SGTG 49, 1937) [242]

Sommerfeld, Kurt. *Die Bühneneinrichtungen des Mannheimer Nationaltheaters unter Dalbergs Leitung, 1778–1803* (SGTG 36, 1927) [76–7, 89]

Stabenow, Herbert. *Geschichte des Breslauer Theaters während seiner Blütezeit 1798–1823* (Breslau/Wroclaw: Hochschulverlag, 1921)

Stadler, Edmund & Nef, Albert. *Zweihundert Jahre Berner Theater 1700–1953* (Berne, 1954)

Stahl, Ernst Leopold. *Das Mannheimer Nationaltheater* (Mannheim: Bensheimer, 1929)

 Shakespeare und das deutsche Theater (Stuttgart: Kohlhammer, 1947)

Stahl, Ernest Ludwig. *Friedrich Schiller's Drama/Theory and Practice* (Oxford: Clarendon Press, 1954)

Steiner, Jacob. *Die Bühnenanweisung* (Göttingen: Vandenhoeck & Ruprecht, 1969)

Steinschneider, Moritz. *Purim und Parodie* (Frankfurt: Kauffmann, 1903)

Stiehl, Carl Johann Christian. *Geschichte des Theaters in Lübeck* (Lübeck: Borchers, 1902)

Streit, Armand. *Geschichte des Bernischen Bühnenwesens vom 15. Jahrhundert bis auf unsere Zeit* (Berne: publ. by the author, 1873)

Struck, Ferdinand. *Die ältesten Zeiten des Theaters zu Stralsund, 1697–1834* (Stralsund: Verlag der Königl. Buchdruckerei, 1895)

Stubenrauch, Herbert. *Wolfgang Heribert von Dalberg* (Mannheim: Nationaltheater Mannheim, 1957)

Stümcke, Heinrich. *Corona Schröter* (Bielefeld: Velhagen & Klasing, 1904)

 Die ältesten deutschen Theaterzettel (Berlin, 1911)

Suphan, Bernhard Ludwig. *Friedrichs des Grossen Schrift über die deutsche Literatur* (Berlin: Hertz, 1888)

Tardel, Hermann. *Studien zur bremischen Theatergeschichte* (Oldenburg: Stalling, 1945)

Teuber, Carl Oscar. *Geschichte des Prager Theaters*, 3 vols. (Prague: Hasse, 1883–88)

Thiele, Richard. *Die Theaterzettel der sogenannten Hamburgischen Entreprise, 1767–1769* (Erfurt: Güther, 1895)

Tintelnot, Hans. *Die Entwicklungsgeschichte der barocken Bühnendekoration in ihren Wechselbeziehungen zur bildenden Kunst* (Berlin: Gebr. Mann, 1938)

 Barocktheater und barocke Kunst (Berlin: Gebr. Mann, 1939)

Thompson, L.F. *Kotzebue/A Survey of his Progress in France and England/Preceded by a consideration of the critical attitude to him in Germany* (Paris: Librairie Ancienne Honoré Champion, 1920)

Trautmann, Karl. *Englische Komödianten in Nürnberg bis zum Schluss des Dreissigjährigen Krieges, 1593–1648* (Leipzig, 1886)

 Oberammergau und sein Passionsspiel (Bamberg: Buchner, 1890)

Uhde, Hermann. *Das Stadttheater in Hamburg, 1827–1877* (Stuttgart: Cotta, 1879)

Ullmann, Walter. *Adolph Müllner und das Weissenfelser Liebhabertheater* (SGTG 46, 1934) [112]

Vasterling, Heinz. *Das Theater in der Freien Reichsstadt Kaufbeuren* (Brunswick: Gutenberg, 1934)

Voelcker, Bruno. *Die Hamlet-Darstellung Daniel Chodowieckis und ihr Quellenwert für die deutsche Theatergeschichte des 18. Jahrhunderts* (Berlin: TGF 29, 1916)

Vogl, Frank. *Düsseldorfer Theater vor Immermann* (Düsseldorf: Lintz, 1930)

 Das Bergische Nationaltheater (Düsseldorf: Lintz, 1930)

Wagner, Hermann F. *Das Volksschauspiel in Salzburg* (Salzburg: Mayrische Buchhandlung, 1882)

Wallbrecht, Rosemarie Elisabeth. *Das Theater des Barockzeitalters an den welfischen Höfen Hannover und Celle* (Hildesheim: Lax, 1974)

Walter, Friedrich. *Geschichte des Theaters und der Musik am Kurpfälzischen Hofe* (Leipzig: Breitkopf & Hartel, 1898)

Weddigen, Friedrich Otto. *Geschichte des Königlichen Theaters in Wiesbaden* (Wiesbaden: Schnegelberger, 1894)

 Geschichte der Berliner Theater (Berlin: Seehagen, 1899)

Weddigen, Friedrich Otto (ed.). *Geschichte der Theater Deutschlands*, 2 vols. (Berlin: Frensdorff, 1904–6) [49, 235]

Weichberger, Alexander. *Goethe und das Komödienhaus in Weimar, 1779–1825* (TGF 39, 1928)

Weil, Rudolf. *Das Berliner Theaterpublikum unter A.W. Ifflands Direktion, 1796 bis 1814* (SGTG 44, 1932)

v. Weilen, Alexander (ed.). *Die Theater Wiens*, 2 vols. (Vienna: Gesellschaft für vervielfältigende Kunst, 1899–1906)

Die erste Aufführung der 'Jungfrau von Orleans' im Burgtheater (Prague: Bellmann, 1908)
Der erste deutsche Bühnen-Hamlet (Vienna: Wiener Bibliophilen-Gessellschaft, 1914)
Werner, Richard Maria. *Das Theater der Laufner Schiffleute* (TGF 3, 1891) [97]
Wild, P. *Über Schauspiele und Schaustellungen in Regensburg* (Ratisbon: Mayer 1901)
Williams, Simon. *German Actors of the 18th and 19th Centuries/Idealism, Romanticism and Realism* (Westport, Conn.: Greenwood Press, 1985) [244]
 Shakespeare on the German Stage, vol. 1: 1586–1914 (CUP, 1990)
Wimmer, Heinrich. *Das Linzer Landestheater 1803–1958* (Linz: Oberösterreichischer Landesverlag, 1958)
Winds, Adolf. *Hamlet auf der deutschen Bühne bis zur Gegenwart* (SGTG 12, 1909)
Winter, Fritz & Kilian, Eugen. *Erste Aufführung des Götz von Berlichingen in Hamburg* (Hamburg-Leipzig: TGF 2, 1891) [199]
Wlassak, Eduard. *Chronik des k.k. Burgtheaters* (Vienna: Rosner, 1976)
Wolff, Gustav. *Das Goethe-Theater in Lauchstädt/Seine Geschichte und seine Wiederherstellung im Jahre 1908* (Halle: Gebauer-Schwetschke, 1908)
Wolff, Christian. *Die Barockoper in Hamburg* (Wolfenbüttel: Moseler, 1957)
Zechmeister, Gustav. *Die Wiener Theater nächst der Burg und nächst dem Karntnerthor von 1747 bis 1776* (Vienna: Böhlau, 1972)
Zeidler, Jakob. *Studien und Beiträge zur Geschichte der Jesuitenkomödie und des Klosterdramas* (TGF 4, 1891)

(4) Periodicals
(In chronological order)

Critischer Musicus (J.A. Scheibe, Hamburg: v. Wierings Erben, 1738–40), 2 vols.
Beyträge zur Historie und Aufnahme des Theaters (ed. G.E. Lessing & C. Mylius, Stuttgart: Metzler, 1750), 4 nos. [91]
Theatralische Bibliothek (ed. G.E. Lessing, Berlin: Voss, 1754–8), 4 nos.
Theatralische Belustigungen (ed. G.K. Pfeffel, Frankfurt-Leipzig: 1765–74), 5 vols.
Briefe über die Wienerische Schaubühne aus dem Französischen übersetzt (ed. J.v. Sonnenfels, Vienna: Kurtzböck, 1767–9), 52 vols.
Hamburgische Dramaturgie (ed. G.E. Lessing, Bremen: Cramer, 1767–9), 104 nos.
Freie Beurtheilungen der Starkischen Schauspielergesellschaft (ed. J.M. Klefeker, Jena, 1768), 7 nos.
Wienerische Dramaturgie (ed. C.G. Klemm, Vienna: M.T. Schulzin, 1768), 26 sheets
Dramaturgie, Litteratur und Sitten (ed. C.G. Klemm, Vienna: Kurzböck, 1769), 39 nos.
Theaterchronik (ed. C.H. Schmid, Giessen: Krieger, 1772), 1 no.
Theatralkalender (later *Theatralalmanach*) *von Wien für das Jahr 1772 [–1774]* (ed. C.G. Klemm & F. Heufeld, Vienna: Kurzböck, 1772–4)
Theatralisches Wochenblatt (ed. K.K. Streit, Breslau/Wroclaw: Korn, 1772–3), 25 nos.
Theatralisches Wochenblatt (ed. C.P. Loeper, Prague: Mangold, 1772–3), 23 nos.
Magazin zur Geschichte des deutschen Theaters (ed. J.J.A. vom Hagen, Halle: Curt, 1773), 1 no.
Theatral-Neuigkeiten (ed. J.H.F. Müller, Vienna: v. Ghelen, 1773), 1 no.
Unsere Gedanken über das Prager Theater (Prague 1774), 11 nos.
Historisch-kritische Theaterchronik von Wien (ed. C.H.v. Moll, Vienna: Bader, 1774–5), 36 nos.
Der Theaterfreund (ed. G.F. Lorenz, C.S.v. Hebenstreit, Prague: Hochenberger, 1774–5), 25 nos.
Theatralisches Wochenblatt (ed. J.J. Christ, Hamburg: Bode, 1774–5), 24 nos.
Der dramatische Antikritikus von Wien (L.J. Boogers, Vienna: v. Ghelen, 1775), 12 nos.
Beiträge zur Geschichte des deutschen Theaters (ed. C.A.v. Bertram, Berlin-Leipzig: Birnstiel, 1775–6), 4 nos.
Wiener Dramaturgie (ed. K.v. Schelheim, Vienna: Trattner, 1775–6), 25 nos.
Theaterkalender auf das Jahr 1775 [–1800] (ed. H.A.O. Reichard, Gotha: Ettinger, 1775–1800), 25 vols.
Theaterwochenblatt für Salzburg (ed. C.L. Seipp, Salzburg: Waisenhausbuchdruckerei, 1775–6), 29 nos.

Theaterzeitung (ed. J.G. Bärstecher, Cleves: Bärstecher, 1775), 42 nos.

Bagatellen, Litteratur und Theater (ed. J.G. Bärstecher, Düsseldorf: Verlag der Expedition, 1777), 66 nos.

État actuel de la musique et des spectacles de S.A.S. Monseigneur le Landgrave Regnant de Hesse (ed. J.P.L. Luchet de Laroche du Maine, Kassel: Étienne, 1777), 1 no.

Theater-Journal für Deutschland (ed. H.A.O. Reichard, Gotha: Ettinger, 1777–84), 22 nos. [92, 113, 146, 172, 200]

Journal von auswärtigen und deutschen Theatern (ed. J.F. Schmidt, Vienna: v. Trattner, 1778–9), 3 vols.

Litteratur- und Theater-Zeitung (ed. C.A.v. Bertram, Berlin: Wever, 1778–84), 7 vols. [109, 155, 196, 201]; continued as *Ephemeriden der Litteratur und des Theaters* (ed. C.A.v. Bertram, Berlin: Maurer, 1785–7), 6 vols. [80, 157, 162, 174, 177–8]; continued as *Annalen des Theaters* (ed. C.A.v. Bertram, Berlin: Maurer, 1788–97), 20 nos. [101–2, 127, 130]

Theater-Wochenschrift (ed. F. Hasenest, Stuttgart, 1778)

Dramaturgische Nachrichten (ed. J.J.A. vom Hagen & G.F.W. Grossmann, Bonn: Abshoven-Rommerskirchen, 1779–80), 2 nos.

Theatralischer Zeitvertreib; eine Wochenschrift (ed. T.F. Lorenz, Ratisbon: Montag, 1779–80), 45 nos.

Mannheimer Dramaturgie für das Jahr 1779 (ed. O.H.v. Gemmingen, Mannheim: Schwan, 1780), 12 nos.

Meine Empfindungen im Theater (ed. F.v. Otterwolf, Vienna: Schmidt/Trattner, 1781), 26 nos.

Dramaturgische Fragmente (ed. J.F. Schink, Graz: Widmanstätten, 1781–4), 12 nos.

Wiener Theaterjournal vom Jahre 1781 (ed. J. Schwaldopler & F.C. Widermann, Vienna, 1781), 12 nos.

Der dramatische Censor (ed. J.M. Babo, L. Hubner, J.B. Strobel, Munich: Strobel, 1782–3), 6 nos.

Theatralisches Quodlibet für Schauspieler und Schauspielliebhaber (ed. G.F. Lorenz, Warsaw: Dufour, 1782–3), 12 vols.

Über die Berliner Schaubühne (ed. C.F.v. Bonin, Berlin: Hesse, 1783), 6 nos.

Allgemeiner Theaeralmanach vom Jahr 1782 (ed. J.F. Schink, Vienna: Gerold, 1782), 1 no.

Königsbergisches Theaterjournal fürs Jahr 1782 (ed. F.S. Mohr, Königsberg/Kaliningrad: Kanter, 1782) 21 nos.

Gratzer Theaterchronik (ed. J.F. Schink, Graz: Widmannstätten, 1783), 11 nos.

Der dramatische Faustin für Hamburg (ed. H.W. Seyfried, Hamburg: Matthiessen, 1784–5), 9 nos.

Raisonnirendes Theaterjurnal (sic) *von der Leipziger Michaelmesse 1783* (ed. J.F.E.v. Brawe, Leipzig: Jacobäer, 1784) [78]

Russische Theatralien (ed. Sauerwald, St. Petersburg, 1784), 2 nos.

Der Bote aus Eimsbüttel bringt mit viel Neuigkeiten, freimüthige Nachrichten über das Schrödersche Theater in Altona etc. (ed. G.T.M. Kühl, Hamburg, 1785–7), 91 nos.

Thalia (no. 1 identical with *Rheinische Thalia*) (ed. C.J.F. Schiller, Leipzig: Göschen, 1785–91), 12 nos.; continued as *Neue Thalia* (ed. C.J.F. Schiller, Leipzig: Göschen, 1792–3), 12 nos.

Journal de Moden, continued as *Journal des Luxus und der Moden*, then *Journal für Luxus, Mode und Gegenstände der Kunst*, then *Journal für Literatur, Kunst, Luxus und Mode*, then *Journal für Literatur, Luxus und geselliges Leben* (ed. F.J. Bertuch & G.M. Krause, later E. Ost & S. Schutze, Weimar: Industrie Comptoir, 1786–1827)

Journal über die Hamburgische Schaubühne unter der Direktion des Herrn Schröders (ed. A.G. Cranz, Hamburg: A.F. Schröder, 1786), 11 nos.

Almanach der k.k. National-Schaubühne in Wien (ed. F.K. Kunz, Vienna, 1788–9), 2 nos.

Dramaturgische Blätter (ed. A.v. Knigge, Hanover: Schmidt, 1788–9), 36 nos.

Dramaturgische Blätter (ed. A.W. Schreiber, Frankfurt: Esslinger, 1788–9), 39 nos.; continued as *Tagebuch der Mainzer Schaubühne* (ed. A.W. Schreiber, Frankfurt: Eichenberg, 1788), 13 nos.

Deutsche Schaubühne (Augsburg, 1788–95), 74 vols.; continued as *Neue deutsche Schaubühne* (Augsburg, 1800)

Kritisches Theaterjournal von Wien. (ed. K.v. Schelheim, R.v. Spalart, Vienna: Ludwig, 1788–9), 20 nos.

Neues Theaterjournal für Deutschland (ed. W.v. Bube, Leipzig: Schneider, 1788–9), 2 nos.

Theaterspiegel des Brünner Theaters (ed. J.B. Bergopzoom, Brünn/Brno: Trassler, 1788), 1 no.

Kleine Beiträge zur Hannoverschen Dramaturgie (ed. A.C. Wedekind & Beneke, Hanover: Helwing, 1789), 4 nos.

Theaterzeitung für Deutschland (ed. C.A.v. Bertram, Berlin: Unger, 1798), 26 nos.

Dramaturgische Monate (ed. J.F. Schink, Schwerin: Bodner, 1790), 12 nos.

Neue Hamburgische Dramaturgie (ed. H.C. Albrecht, Hamburg: Freder, 1791), 18 nos.

Dramaturgisches Wochenblatt (Hamburg: Freder, 1791), 3 nos.

Allgemeines Theaterjournal (ed. H.G. Schmieder, Mainz: Fischer, 1792), 5 nos.

Hamburgische Theaterzeitung (ed. J.F. Schink, Hamburg: Bachmann, 1792), 52 nos.

Dramaturgisches Wochenblatt für Berlin und Deutschland (ed. J.G.L. Hagemeister, Berlin: Petit & Schöne), 11 nos.

Annalen des Theaters und der dramatischen Litteratur (ed. J.F. Schink, Hamburg: Freder, 1793), 12 nos.

Dramaturgische Zeitschrift (ed. G.F.W. Grossmann, Hanover: Hahn, 1793), 24 nos.

Zeitung für Theater und andere schöne Künste (ed. H.G. Schmieder, Stuttgart, 1793–4), 12 nos.

Rheinische Musen (ed. H.G. Schmieder, Mannheim: Kaufmann, 1794–8), 7 vols.; continued as *Taschenbuch fürs Theater auf 1798 und 1799* (ed. H.G. Schmieder, Mainz-Hamburg: Vollmer, 1798); continued as *Neues Journal für Theater und andere schöne Künste* (ed. H.G. Schmieder, Hamburg: Mutzenbecher, 1799–1800), 3 vols.

Wiener Theater-Almanach (ed. J.F. Sonnleithner, Vienna: Kurzböck, then Camesina, 1794–6), 3 vols.

Theater-Kalender (ed. H.G. Schmieder, Mannheim, 1795–6), 2 vols.

Dramatischer Briefwechsel das Münchener Theater betreffend (ed. F.L. Reischel, Munich: Hübschmann, 1797–8), 6 nos.

Der theatralische Eulenspiegel (ed. F. Hegrad, Prague: Neureutter, 1797), 13 nos.

Thalia und Melpomene (ed. F.G.H. v. Soden, Chemnitz: Hoffmann, 1797), 2 nos.

Theatralischer und literarischer Anzeiger (Königsberg/Kaliningrad: Nicolovius, 1798), 83 nos.

Neue deutsche Dramaturgie (ed. J.G. Rhode, Altona: Schmid, 1798–9), 2 vols.

Allgemeine deutsche Theater-Zeitung (Pressburg/Bratislava: Landerer, 1798–9)

Hamburgisch- und Altonaische Theaterzeitung (ed. F.W.v. Schütz, Altona: Bechtold, 1798–1800), 40 nos.

Berlinische Dramaturgie (ed. J.M.F. Schulz, Berlin: Nicolai, 1799), 2 vols.

Schauspielkunde (ed. G.G. Schmidt, Frankfurt, 1799), 36 nos.

Nürnbergs Thalia (ed. H.v. Harrer, Nuremberg, April–June 1799), 12 nos; continued as *Nürnberger Theaterjournal* (Nuremberg, 1799), 3 nos.

Wiener Theater-Kritik (Vienna: Hohenleitner, 1799–1800), 2 vols.

Raisonnierendes Journal vom deutschen Theater zu Hamburg (ed. J.F. Ernst, Hamburg: Nestler, 1800–01), 50 nos.

Münchener Theater-Journal (ed. A.J.v. Guttenberg, Munich: Hübschmann, 1800), 7 nos.

Nürnberger Theater-Taschen-Almanach (ed. I. Schwarz, Nuremberg, 1800–02), 3 nos.

Allgemeine Theaterzeitung (ed. J.G. Rhode, Berlin: Frölich, 1800), 50 nos.

Sonntagsblatt. Eine Zeitschrift enthaltend das Tagebuch des Frankfurter National-Theaters (Frankfurt, 1801–2), 26 nos.

Annalen des neuen Kgl. Nationaltheaters zu Berlin und der gesammten deutschen dramatischen Literatur und Kunst (ed. F.R. Rambach, Berlin: Quien, 1802), 26 nos.

Annalen des Theaters und der dramatischen Literatur (ed. J.F. Schintz, Hamburg: Mey, 1802–3), 22 nos.

Dramaturgisches Journal für Deutschland (Fürth: Bureau für Literatur, 1802), 52 nos.

Wiener Hof-Theater-Taschenbuch (ed. H.J.v. Collin & I.F. Castelli, Vienna, 1804–16), 13 vols.

Der Freimüthige oder Berlinische Zeitung für gebildete, unbefangene Leser (ed. A.v. Kotzebue, then G. Merkel & others, Berlin: Sander, then others, 1803–40)

Monatsschrift für Theaterfreunde (ed. F. Linde, Vienna: Wallishauser, 1805), 12 nos.

Theaterblatt (ed. K.M. Plümicke, Danzig/Gdansk, 1805), 65 nos.

Wöchentliche Theater-Nachrichten aus Breslau (ed. G.H. Kapf, later W. Grattenauer, Breslau/Wroclaw: Gehe, later Max, 1805–10), 6 vols.

Allgemeines kritisches Theater-Journal (ed. J.E. Wiedemann, Vienna: Wallishauser, 1806–7), 27 nos.

Wiener Theaterzeitung (ed. A. Bäuerle & others, Vienna-Trieste: publ. by eds., 1806–59), appearing at various times as *Zeitung für Theater, Musik & Poesie; Allgemeine Theaterzeitung und Unterhaltungsblatt für Freunde der Kunst, Literatur und des geselligen Lebens; Illustrierte Theaterzeitung; Österrei-*

chischer Courier; Wiener Allgemeine Theaterzeitung; Wiener Theaterzeitung, 50 vols.

Almanach für Theater und Theaterfreunde auf das Jahr 1807 [–1812] (ed. A.W. Iffland, Berlin: Oehmigke, 1807–12), 6 vols.

Allgemeine deutsche Theaterzeitung (ed. K.W. Reinhold, Hamburg, 1807–8); continued under same editor as *Archiv für Theater und Literatur* (Hamburg 1809); as *Archiv für Literatur und Kunst* (Hamburg, 1810); as *Hamburgisches Unterhaltungsblatt* (Hamburg, 1811–15)

Prager Theater-Almanach (Prague: Calve 1808–9), 2 vols.

Almanach für's Theater (ed. F.L. Schmidt, Hamburg, 1809–12), 4 vols.

Thalia, ein Abendblatt den Freunden der dramtischen Muse geweiht (ed. I.F. Castelli & J. Erichsohn, Vienna: Geistinger, 1810–14)

Theatralische Mitteilungen (ed. T. Hell, Dresden: Arnold, 1811–15) 23 nos.

Taschenbuch vom k.k. priv. Theater in der Leopoldstadt (ed. G. Ziegelhauser, later C. Meisl & others, Vienna: 1811–40?), 30 (?) vols.

Theater-Almanach für das Jahr 1811 (ed. C.F.W. Borch, St. Petersburg 1811)

Allgemeiner deutscher Theateranzeiger (ed. D.G. Quandt, Prague: Enders, 1811–14), 4 vols.

Taschenbuch für Freunde des hiesigen Hoftheaters (ed. J.A. Moll, Darmstadt, 1812–15)

Dramaturgischer Beobachter (ed. J.C. Bernard, Vienna: Kupfer & Wimmer, 1813–14), 84 nos. [226]

Münchener Theater-Journal (ed. Carl Carl, Munich, 1814–16), 36 nos.

Breslauische Theaterblätter (Breslau: Holäufer, 1815–16), 26 nos.

Rigisches Theater-Blatt (ed. F. La Coste, Riga: Hartmann, 1815), 36 nos.

Theater-Journal der kgl. baierischen privilegierten Schaubühne zu Würzburg (Würzburg, 1815–31), continued as *Theater-Journal des Kgl. Baierischen Würzburger Nationaltheaters* (ed. K. Jaeger, Würzburg, 1832–3)

Dramaturgisches Wochenblatt in nächster Beziehung auf die Kgl. Schauspiele in Berlin (ed. K. Levezow, Berlin, 1815–17), 2 vols.

Kgl. Württembergisches Hoftheater-Taschenbuch auf das Jahr 1816 [–1817] (ed. B. Korzinsky, Stuttgart, 1816–17), 2 vols.

Tagebuch der deutschen Bühnen (ed. K.T. Winkler, Dresden: Winkler, 1816–35), 20 vols.

Taschenbuch für Schauspieler und Schauspielfreunde für das Jahr 1816 [–1823] (ed. J.W. Lembert & Carl, Stuttgart-Munich-Vienna, 1816–23), 8 vols.

Almanach für Privatbühnen (ed. A. Müllner, Leipzig: Göschen, 1817–19), 3 vols.

Ansichten von der Danziger Schaubühne (Danzig/Gdansk: Albert, 1820–21), 52 nos.

Dramaturgische Blätter für Hamburg (ed. F.G. Zimmermann, Hamburg: Hoffmann & Campe, 1821–2), 4 vols.

Zeitung für Theater, Musik und bildende Künste (ed. A. Kuhn, Berlin: Schlesinger, 1821–7), 7 vols.

Allgemeiner deutscher Theater-Almanach für das Jahr 1822 (ed. A. Klingemann, Brunswick, 1822), 1 vol.

Theaterblatt (Königsberg/Kaliningrad, 1822), 4 nos.; continued as *Königsberger Theaterblatt* (Königsberg/Kaliningrad, 1826), 15 nos.

Münchener Theater-Almanach den Freunden der Kunst und des geselligen Lebens gewidmet (ed. F. Holzapfel, Munich: Hübschmann, 1823–5), 3 vols.

Pistolen, gerichtet auf das Breslauer Theater in wöchentlicher Kritik (ed. Kapf, Breslau/Wroclaw: Fritsch, 1824), 23 nos.

Tagebuch des Kgl. Sächsischen Hoftheaters auf das Jahr 1824 [–1918] (Dresden, 1824–1918)

Berliner Schnellpost für Literatur, Theater und Geselligkeit (ed. M.G. Saphir, Berlin: Krause, 1826–9), 4 vols.

Monatliche Beiträge zur Geschichte dramatischer Kunst und Literatur (ed. K.v. Holtei, Berlin: Haude & Spener, 1827–8), 9 nos. [64, 85, 105, 116, 154, 191, 195, 236, 246]

Dramaturgische Blätter (ed. L. Tieck, Dresden: Wagner, 1827), 23 nos.; continued as *Dresdner Theaterzeitung* (Dresden: Wagner, 1828), 10 nos. [219]

Neue dramaturgische Blätter (ed. F.G. Zimmermann, Hamburg: Hoffman & Campe, 1827–8), 3 vols.

Der Berliner Courier/Ein Morgenblatt für Theater, Mode, Eleganz, Stadtleben und Localität (ed. M.G. Saphir, Berlin: Laue, later Krause, 1827–30), 910 nos.

Almanach für Freunde der Schauspielkunst auf das Jahr 1828 [1830] (ed. F. Viedest, Riga, 1828 & 1830),

2 vols.

Berliner Theateralmanach auf das Jahr 1828 (ed. M.G. Saphir, Berlin, 1828)

Theaterzeitung (ed. F.v. Caspar, Munich: Jaquet, 1828), 13 nos., continued as *Münchner Theaterzeitung* (ed. F. Stoepel, Munich: Finsterlin, 1828–9), 26 nos.

Almanach für's Aachener Stadt-Theater auf das Jahr 1829 (ed. Arndt, Aachen: La Ruelle & Dester, 1829)

Danziger Theater-Blatt (ed. C.A. Krause, Danzig/Gdansk, 1829), 27 nos.

Repertorium der Kgl. Schauspiele zu Berlin vom 1. Dez. 1828 bis Nov. 1830 (Berlin: Brettschneider 1830), 7 vols

Breslauer Theaterzeitung (ed. H. Michaelson, Breslau/Wroclaw: Gruson, later Hentze, 1830–6), 7 vols.; continued as *Nordische Theaterzeitung* (Breslau: Freund, later Friedländer, 1837–8), 2 vols., then as *Theater-Figaro/Für Literatur, Kunst und Künstlerleben* (Breslau: Bauschke, 1839–45), 7 vols.

Rheinische Theaterzeitung (ed. K. Köchy, Mainz: Kupferberg, 1830), 4 nos.

Breslauer Theater-Almanach für das Jahr 1831 [–1835] (ed. E. Philipp, later G. Roland, Breslau/ Wroclaw: Richter, 1831–5), 5 vols.

Allgemeine Theaterchronik/Wöchentliche Mittheilungen von sämmtlichen deutschen Theatern (ed. L.v. Alversleben, Leipzig: Sturm & Koppe, later Kölbel & others, 1832–75), 44 vols.

Jahresbericht des Herzogl. Hoftheaters von Coburg-Gotha (ed. C. Spielberg, Coburg, 1834–46)

Almanach der deutschen Bühnen (ed. E. Beurmann, Frankfurt, 1835)

Allgemeine Theater-Revue (ed. A. Lewald, Stuttgart-Tübingen: Cotta, 1835–7), 3 vols.

Thalia/Norddeutsche Theater-Zeitung und schönwissenschaftliches Unterhaltungsblatt (ed. C. Töpfer, Hamburg: Töpfer, 1836–9), 416 nos.

Jahrbücher für Drama, Dramaturgie und Theater (ed. E. Willkomm & A. Fischer, Leipzig: Wunder, 1837– 9), 2 vols.

Der Theaterfreund/Blätter für Mitglieder und Freunde des Theaters (ed. L.v. Alversleben, Halle, later Grimma, 1837–9)

Jahrbuch und Repertorium der Stadt Leipzig (Leipzig, 1842–4)

Bühnenwelt/Blätter für dramaturgische und belletristische Unterhaltung (ed. W.A. Lieboldt, Nuremberg: Winter, 1843–7), 5 vols.

Regensburger Theater-Revue (ed. K. Blankenstein, Ratisbon, 1843–4), 1 vol. & 38 nos.

Dramatik, Theater, Musik (ed. A. Gubitz, Berlin, 1844–5), 1 vol. continued as *Monatsschrift für Dramatike, Theater, Musik* (ed. A. Gubitz, Berlin: Vereinsbuchhandlung, 1846–8), 3 vols.

Deutsche Theaterzeitung/Archiv für das Gesamtinteresse der deutschen Bühne und ihrer Mitglieder (ed. J. Koffka, Leipzig: Reclam, 1844–5), 104 nos.

Theater-Lokomotive/Oeffentlichkeit für Bühnenwelt und Schauspielwesen (ed. J. Koffka, Leipzig, 1845–6), 2 vols.; continued as *Neue Theater-Locomotive/Blätter für Schauspieler und dramatische Kunst* (ed. W. Bernhardi, Berlin: Hirschfeld, 1847–8), 2 vols.

Der Theater-Horizont (ed. H. Michaelson, Berlin: Bote & Bock, later Schlesinger, 1846–62), 17 vols.

Illustrierte Theaterzeitung/Dramatische Werke und dramatische Abhandlung, Biographien und Charakteristiken, Bühnengeschichte und Theaterchronik (Leipzig: Weber, 1846), 39 nos.

Album für Liebhaber-Theater (ed. J. Koffka, Leipzig: Bruns, 1847–8), 8 nos.

Jahrbücher für dramatische Kunst und Literatur (ed. H. T. Rötscher, Berlin: Hirschfeld, later Trewitzsch, 1847–9), 3 vols.

Allgemeine Theaterzeitung/Originalblatt für Kunst, Literatur, Musik, Mode und geselliges Leben (ed. A. Bäuerle, Vienna: Gerold, 1848), 312 nos.

For further information, see Hill, *Die deutschen Theaterzeitschriften des 18. Jahrhunderts* (1915) and Joachim Kirchner, *Bibliographie der Zeitschriften des deutschen Sprachgebietes*, 4 vols. (Stuttgart: Anton Hiersemann, 1969–77), esp. vols. 1 & 2.

(5) Articles

Anon. 'Geschichte des deutschen Theaters in Wien vornehmlich seit den Zeiten Hilverdings'. *Theaterkalender von Wien für das Jahr 1772*, repr. in *M&K*, 2 (1956), 359–63

Alker, Ernst. 'Das österreichische Theater im Zeitalter der Barockliteratur'. *Neophilologus*, 13 (Groningen, 1928), 187–96

Alexander, Robert. 'George Jolly (Joris Joliphus), der wandernde Player und Manager/Neues zu seiner Tätigkeit in Deutschland (1648–1660). *KSGTG*, 29/30 (1978), 31–48

Asper, Helmut Gernot. 'Kilian Brustfleck alias Johann Valentin. Petzold und die Eggenbergischen Komödianten'. *M&K*, 16 (1970), 20–59

Baravalle, Robert. 'Franz Brockmanns Jugend'. *M&K*, 1 (1955), 47–53

Bergman, Gösta M. 'Der Eintritt des Berufsregisseurs in die deutschsprachige Bühne'. *M&K*, 12 (1966), 63–91

Boeck, Urs. 'Der barocke Komödiensaal des Celler Schlosses'. *Niederdeutsche Beiträge zur Kunstgeschichte*, 11 (Cologne, 1972), 101–18

Bolte, Johannes. 'Schauspiele am Heidelberger Hofe (1650–1687)'. *Euphorion*, 31 (1930), 578–91
'Von Wanderkomödianten und Handwerkerspielen des 17. und 18. Jahrhunderts'. *Sitzungs-Berichte der Preussischen Akademie der Wissenschaften, phil.-hist. Klasse*, 19 (1934), 448–87

Brachvogel, K. 'Liebhabertheater und Maskeraden an deutschen Fürstenhöfen'. *Bühne und Welt*, 1, pt. 2 (1898–9), 1084–9

Brockmann, Johann Hieronymus. 'Der erste Burgtheaterdirektor als Erzieher der Schauspieler'. *M&K*, 1 (1955), 54–62 [**103**]

Bruford, Walter Horace. 'Actor and Public in Gottsched's Time'. *German Studies presented to H.G. Fiedler* (OUP, 1938), 62–78

Brüggemann, Fritz. Introduction to *Gottsched Lebens- und Kunstform in den zwanziger und dreissiger Jahren* (Leipzig: Reclam, 1935), 5–16
Introduction to *Die Anfänge des bürgerlichen Trauerspiels in den fünfziger Jahren* (Leipzig: Reclam, 1934), 5–17
Introduction to *Das Drama des Gegeneinander in den sechziger Jahren/Trauerspiele von Christian Felix Weisse* (Leipzig: Reclam, 1938), 5–47

Chalaupka, Christl. 'Die "Erinnerungen" von Heinrich Anschütz/Ein Beitrag zur Quellenkritik'. *M&K*, 4 (1958), 220–9

Dessoff, Albert. 'Über englische, italienische und spanische Dramen in den Spielverzeichnissen deutscher Wandertruppen'. *Studien zur vergleichenden Literaturgeschichte* 1 (Berlin, 1901), 420–4

Diedrichsen, Diedrich. ' "Die Comödie in dem Tempel der Tugend" oder: Reform und Gegenreformation im Hamburg der Lessing-Zeit'. *M&K*, 30 (1984), 103–14

Dietrich, Margret. 'Einige Daten zu Josef Platzer'. *M&K*, 4 (1958), 134–41

Duncker, Albert. 'Landgraf Moritz von Hessen und die englischen Komödianten'. *Deutsche Rundschau*, 48 (Berlin, July-Sept. 1886), 260–75

Fischer, Friedrich Johann. 'Wandertruppen des 17. Jahrhunderts in Salzburg'. *Festschrift: Hundert Jahre Gesellschaft für Salzburger Landeskunde, 1860–1960* (Salzburg, 1960), 431–69 [3]

Flemming, Willi. Introduction to *Das Ordensdrama* (Leipzig: Reclam, 1930), 5–36
Introduction to *Das Schauspiel der Wanderbühne* (Leipzig: Reclam, 1931), 5–69 [**29, 58**]
Introduction to *Das schlesische Kunstdrama* (Leipzig: Reclam, 1930), 5–54
Introduction to *Die Oper* (Leipzig: Reclam 1933, 2nd impr. ed. Darmstadt: Wissenschaftliche Buchgesellschaft, 1965), 5–83
'Die Erfassung des Epochalstils barocker Schauspielkunst in Deutschland'. *M&K*, 1 (1955), 109–39
'Das Oberammergauer Festspiel als theatergeschichtliche Quelle'. *M&K*, 6 (1960), 147–57

Fratzke, Dieter. 'Die masstabgerechte Nachbildung des Theaters am Gänsemarkt von 1765, des späteren Hamburger Nationaltheaters'. *Lessing Yearbook*, xx (Detroit: Wayne State University, 1988), 1–14

Gerhäuser, Max Ferdinand. 'Die Planung der Theater und ihre Entwicklung in Hannover.' *Hannoversche Geschichtsblätter*, new series, vol. 23 (1969), 85–144

Glossy, Karl Ludwig. 'Josef Schreyvogel und Graf Ferdinand Palffy'. *Jahrbuch der Grillparzer-Gesellschaft*, 31 (Vienna, 1932), 138–48 [**227**]

Göhring, Ludwig. 'Theatervorstellungen im Altstädter Rathaussaal um die Mitte des 18. Jahrhunderts'. *Erlanger Heimatblätter* (Erlangen 5, 12, 17, 26 May & 2, 9 June 1928)

Greisenegger, Wolfgang. 'Schauspiel- und Ausstattungskunst im Zeitalter der Romantik in Deutschland'. *M&K* 19 (1973), 281–303

Gross, Gerda. 'Das Danziger Theater im 17. Jahrhundert. In: H. Kindermann, *Danziger Barockdichtung* (Leipzig: Reclam, 1939), 266–333

Grüner, Johann Sigismund. 'Über körperliche Beredsamkeit/Eine Rhapsodie'. *Gothaer Theater-Kalender auf das Jahr 1798*, repr. in *M&K*, 2 (1956), 182–6

Hadamowsky, Franz. 'Die Commedia dell'arte in Österreich und ihre Wirkung auf das Wiener Volkstheater.' *M&K*, 3 (1957), 312–16

'Das dramatische Werk Schillers in Wien'. *M&K*, 5 (1959), 208–12

'Die Schauspielfreiheit, die "Erhebung des Burgtheaters zum Hoftheater" und seine "Begründung als Nationaltheater" im Jahr 1776'. *M&K*, 22 (1976), 5–19

Haider-Pregler, Hilde. 'Das Rossballett im Inneren Burghof zu Wien'. *M&K*, 15 (1969), 291–324 [27]

'Wien probiert seine National- Schaubühne/Das Theater am Kärntnertor in der Spielzeit 1769–70'. *M&K*, 20 (1974), 286–349

Hicks, William Charles. 'A Weimar Actor under Goethe and Schiller [Johann Jakob Graff]'. *Publications of the English Goethe Society*, n.s. 11 (Cambridge, 1935), 60–85

Hüttner, Johann. 'Sensationsstücke und Alt-Wiener Volkstheater/Zum Melodrama in der ersten Hälfte des 19. Jahrhunderts'. *M&K*, 21 (1975), 263–81

Immerwahr, Raymond Max. 'Iffland in the role of Tieck's Kater'. *Modern Language Notes*, 70 (Baltimore, 1955), 195–6

Jordan, Gilbert B. 'Theatre plans in Harsdörffer's Frauenzimmer-Gesprechspiele'. *Journal of English and German Philology*, 42 (1943), 475–91

Kindermann, Heinz. 'Brentano und das Burgtheater/Mit Abdruck seiner kritischen Beiträge im "Dramaturgischen Beobachter" '. *M&K*, 22 (1976), 54–133 [226]

Król, Barbara. 'Joseph Kurz-Bernardon in Warschau'. *M&K*, 4 (1958), 142–54

McKenzie, John R.P. 'Cotta's Comedy Competition (1836).' *M&K*, 26 (1980), 59–73

v. Maltzahn, W. 'Julius Cäsar für die Bühne eingerichtet von A.W. Schlegel'. *SJB* 7 (Weimar, 1872), 48ff.

Mertz, Peter. 'Die Uraufführung des "Fiesko" war in Bonn'. *M&K*, 10 (1964), 282–303

Nagler, Alois Maria. 'The Furttenbach Theatre in Ulm'. *Theatre Annual*, 10 (New York, 1953), 45–69

'Gluck in Wien und Paris'. *M&K*, 1 (1955), 222–67

'Metastasio – der Hofdichter als Regisseur', *M&K*, 7 (1961), 274–84

Paludan, J. 'Deutsche Wandertruppen in Dänemark'. *Zeitschrift für deutsche Philologie*, 25 (Halle, 1893), 313–43

Pascal, Roy. 'The stage of the Englische Komödianten – three problems'. *Modern Language Review*, 35 (Cambridge, 1940), 367–76

Passow, Wilfred. 'Das gedruckte Szenarium in Deutschland'. *KSGTG*, 25 (Berlin, 1972), 45–59

'Johann Gottfried Dyks "Bermerkungen über theatralische Vorstellung"/Eine frühe deutsche Anregung zur professionellen Theaterarbeit unter der künstlerischen Leitung eines Dichter-Regisseurs'. *M&K*, 31 (1985), 7–15

Pietschmann, Kurt R. 'Calderon auf der deutschen Bühne von Goethe bis Immermann'. *M&K*, 3 (1957), 317–39

Rommel, Otto. 'Rokoko in den Wiener Kaiserspielen'. *M&K*, 1 (1955), 30–46

Rudin, Bärbel. 'Hanseatische Komödianten in Deutschland'. *KSGTG*, 23 (1969), 64–7

'Fahrende Schauspieler in Regensburg'. *Verhandlungen des Historischen Vereins für Oberpfalz und Regensburg*, 113 (1973), 191–205

'Der Prinzipal Heinrich Wilhelm Benecke und seine "Wienerische" und "Hochfürstliche Bayreuthische" Schauspielergesellschaft'. *Mitteilungen des Vereins für Geschichte der Stadt Nürnberg* (Nuremberg, 1975), 179–232 [4]

'Ein Würzburger Theaterprogramm des "Gebenedeyten Glücks" von 1684/Zur Geschichte des italienischen Dramas auf der Wanderbühne'. *Mainfränkisches Jahrbuch für Geschichte und Kunst,* 27 (1975), 98–105

'Eine Leipziger Studentenbühne des 17. Jahrhunderts/Universität und Berufstheater – Das Ende einer Legende'. *KSGTG,* 28 (1976), 3–17

'Hans Mühlgraf & Co., Sitz Nürnberg/Ein deutsches Bühnenunternehmen im 30jährigen Krieg'. *KSGTG,* 29/30 (1978), 15–30

'Frl. Dorothea und Der Blaue Montag/Die Diokletianische Christenverfolgung in zwei Repertoirestücken der deutschen Wanderbühne'. *Elemente der Literatur,* 1 (Stuttgart: Kröner, 1980), 95–113 [57]

'Wanderbühne'. *Reallexikon der deutschen Literaturgeschichte,* 4 (2nd edn, Berlin-NY: de Gruyter, 1984), 808–15

Rudloff-Hille, Gertrud. 'Das Leipziger Theater von 1766.' *M&K,* 14 (1968), 217–38 [66, 156]

'Die Bayreuther Hofbühne im 17. und 18. Jahrhundert'. *Archiv für Geschichte und Altertumskunde von Oberfranken,* 33, no. 1 (Bayreuth: Ellwanger, 1936)

Schindler, Otto G. 'Der Zuschauerraum des Burgtheaters im 18. Jahrhundert'. *M&K,* 22 (1976), 20–53

Schöne, Günter. 'Barockes Feuerwerstheater'. *M&K,* 6 (1960), 351–62

Schrögendorfer, Konrad. 'Die Bibliothek und das Archiv des Burgtheaters'. *M&K,* 3 (1957), 84–9

Schrott, Margarethe. 'Shakespeare im Alt-Wiener Volkstheater'. *M&K,* 10 (1964), 282–300

Singer, Herta. 'Die Akustik des alten Burgtheaters'. *M&K,* 4 (1958), 220–9

Skalicki, Wolfram. 'Das Bühnenbild der "Zauberflöte"'. *M&K,* 2 (1956), 2–34, 42–165

Speyer, Carl. 'Magister Johannes Velthen und die sächsischen Hofkomödianten am kurfürstlichen Hof in Heidelberg und Mannheim'. *Neue Heidelberger Jahrbücher,* new series 3 (1926), 54–77

Stanzel, Eva. 'Das Ballett in der Wiener Barockoper'. *M&K,* 7 (1961), 313–28

Terfloth, John H. 'The Pre-Meiningen Rise of the Director in Germany and Austria'. *Theatre Quarterly,* 21 (London: Spring 1976), 65–86

Trautmann, Karl. 'Italienische Schauspieler am bayrischen Hofe'. *Jahrbücher für Münchener Geschichte,* 1 (Munich: Lindauer, 1887), 193–312

'Französische Schauspieler am bayrischen Hofe'. *Jahrbücher für Münchener Geschichte,* 2 (Munich: Lindauer, 188), 185–334

Volkmann, Ernst. 'Chodowieckis Beiträge zur Theatergeschichte'. *M&K,* 1 (1955), 297–317

v.Weilen, Alexander. 'Aus dem Nachleben des Peter Squentz und des Faustspiels'. *Euphorion,* 2 (1895), 623–32

Witkowski, Georg. 'Englische Komödianten in Leipzig'. *Euphorion,* 15 (1908), 441–4

Wolff, Hellmuth Christian. 'Laterna magica-Projektionen auf dem Barocktheater'. *M&K,* 15 (1969), 97–104

Zielske, Harald. 'Andreas Gryphius' Catharina von Georgien auf der Bühne/Zur Aufführungspraxis des schlesischen Kunstdramas'. *M&K,* 17 (1971), 1–17

'Die deutschen Höfe und die Wandertruppen im 17. und frühen 18. Jahrhundert/Fragen ihres Verhältnisses'. *Europäische Hofkultur im 16. und 17. Jahrhundert,* vol. 1 (Wolfenbütteler Arbeiten zur Barockforschung 8, 1981), 521–32

Zobel, Konrad & Warner, Frederick E. 'The Old Burgtheater: a structural history, 1741–1888'. *Theatre Studies,* 19 (Columbus, Ohio, 1972–3), 19–53

Zucker, Adolf Eduard. 'Goethe and Schiller stage Wallenstein'. *Monatshefte,* 30 (1938), 1–12

Select bibliography, 1600–1848

THE NETHERLANDS

(1) General studies and works of reference

Aken, L.J.N.K. [Boeken-]van. *Catalogus Nederlands toneel Bibliotheek der Universiteit van Amsterdam, samengesteld door-*, 3 vols. (Amsterdam: Stadsdrukkerij, 1954–56)

Albach, Ben. *Drie eeuwen 'Gysbreght van Aemstel'. Kroniek van de jaarlijksche opvoeringen* (Amsterdam: Noordhollandsche Uitgeversmaatschappij, 1937), [**269, 317**]

Het huis op het plein. Heden en verleden van de Amsterdamse Stadsschouwburg (Amsterdam: Stadsdrukkerij, 1957)

'Bibliographie raisonnée du théâtre néerlandais', *Theatre Research/Recherches du Théâtre*, vol. 1, 1960, 88–98.

Duizend jaar toneel in Nederland (Bussum: C.A.J. van Dishoeck, 1965)

'De Amsterdamse geschreven bronnen van de Nederlandse toneelgeschiedenis', *Scenarium* (Zutphen: De Walburg Pers), vol. 1, (1977), pp. 92–113 [with a summary in English]

Langs kermissen en hoven. Ontstaan en kroniek van een Nederlands toneelgezelschap in de 17de eeuw (Zutphen: De Walburg Pers, 1977) [**270, 296**]

'De geschreven bronnen buiten Amsterdam van de Nederlandse toneelgeschiedenis', *Scenarium* (Zutphen: De Walburg Pers), 3, (1979) 89–101 [with a summary in English].

Barnett, Dene. *The Art of Gesture: the Practices and Principles of 18th Century Acting* (with the assistance of Jeanette Massy-Westropp, Heidelberg: Carl Winter Universitätsverlag, 1987)

Bientjes, Julia. *Holland und der Holländer im Urteil deutscher Reisenden 1400–1800* (Groningen: J.B. Wolters, 1967), 151–9 ('Das Theater')

Bottenheim, S.A.M. *De opera in Nederland* (Amsterdam: P.N. van Kampen & Zoon, 1946)

Coffeng, Joh.M. *Lexicon van Nederlandse Tonelisten* (Amsterdam: Polak & Van Gennep, 1965)

Fransen, J. *Les Comédiens français en Hollande au XVIIe et au XVIIIe siècles* (Paris: Librairie Ancienne Honoré Champion, 1925) [**290–1**]

Golding, Alfred Simon. *Classicistic Acting. Two Centuries of a Performance Tradition at the Amsterdam Schouwburg. To which is Appended An Annotated Translation of the 'Lessons on the Principles of Gesticulation and Mimic Expression' of Johannes Jelgerhuis, Rz* (New York–London: Lanham, 1984)

Groot, Hans de. 'Bibliografie van in Nederland verschenen 18de- en 19de- eeuwse toneeltijdschriften (1762–1850) en toneelalmanakken (1770–1843), *Scenarium* (Zutphen: De Walburg Pers), 4, (1980), 118–46 [with a summary in English]

Halmael Jr., A. van. *Bijdragen tot de geschiedenis van het tooneel, de tooneelspeelkunst, en de tooneelspelers, in Nederland,* (Leeuwarden: G.T.N. Suringar, 1840) [**296**]

Hellwald, Ferd. von. *Geschichte des holländischen Theaters* (Rotterdam: Van Hengel & Eeltjes, 1874)

Hilman, Johs. *Alphabetisch overzicht der tooneelstukken in de bibliotheek van –,* (Amsterdam: Gebroeders Binger, 1878)

Ons tooneel. Aanteekeningen en geschiedkundige overzichten. Naamrol van plaatwerken en geschriften, 2 vols. (Amsterdam: C.L. van Langenhuysen, 1879; (Register) Leiden: E.J. Brill, 1881)

Hogendoorn, W. 'Leiden in last op de planken', *Jaarboekje voor geschiedenis en oudheidkunde van Leiden en omstreken* (Leiden: A.W. Sijthoff) 60 (1968), 65–85 [**280–1**]

Junkers, Herbert. *Niederländische Schauspieler und niederländisches Schauspiel im 17. und 18. Jahrhundert in Deutschland* (The Hague: Martinus Nijhoff, 1936) [**293, 333**]

Kindermann, Heinz. *Theatergeschichte Europas*, 10 vols. (Salzburg: Otto Müller, 1957–74) vol. III (1959), 244–267; V (1962), 443–469; VI (1964), 194–208

Knuvelder, G.P.M. *Handboek tot de geschiedenis der Nederlandse letterkunde*, 4 vols. ('s-Hertogenbosch: L.C.G. Malmberg, 5th edn, 1970–1976), vol. II (1971), III (1973)

Kossmann, E.F. *Das niederländische Faustspiel des siebzehnten Jahrhunderts (De Hellevaart van Dr. Joan Faustus)*. *Herausgegeben von –. Mit einer Beilage über die Haager Bühne 1660–1720* (The Hague: Martinus Nijhoff, 1910) [**309–10**]

Nieuwe Bijdragen tot de Geschiedenis van het Nederlandsche Tooneel in de 17e en 18e eeuw (The Hague: Martinus Nijhoff, 1915) [**333**]

Koster, Simon. *Van Schavot tot Schouwburg. Vijfhonderd jaar toneel in Haarlem* (Haarlem: De Erven F. Bohn, 1970)

Komedie in Gelderland. Grote en kleine momenten uit driehonderd jaar theaterleven (Zutphen: De Walburg Pers, 1979)

Leek, Robert H. *Shakespeare in Nederland. Kroniek van vier eeuwen Shakespeare in Nederlandse vertalingen en op het Nederlandse toneel* (Zutphen: De Walburg Pers, 1988)

Leeuwe, Hans de. 'Das Theater in den Niederlanden', in Martin Hürlimann (ed.), *Atlantisbuch des Theaters* (Zürich/Freiburg i. Br.: Atlantis Verlag, 1966), 719–30

'Sechs Jahrhunderte komödiantisches Theater in Holland', *M&K* 15 (1969), 11–21.

In collaboration with Hans Mulder Westerbeek and Hans van Maanen, 'International Bibliography of the Dutch and Flemish Theatre. Publications in English, French and German', *Theatre Research/ Recherches Théâtrales*, 12 (1972), 175–90

Leeuwe, H.H.J. de and Uitman, J.E. *Toneel en dans* (Utrecht: Oosthoek Lexicons, A. Oosthoek, 1966)

Looijen, T.K. *Een geschiedenis van Amsterdamse theaters. Wie kwam er niet in de Nes?* (Nieuwkoop: Heuff, 1981)

Ornée, W.A. (ed.). *Van Bredero tot Langendijk. Een bloemlezing uit de Nederlandse kluchten van het begin van de zeventiende eeuw tot 1730* (Zutphen: De Walburg Pers, 1985)

Pennink, R. *Nederland en Shakespeare. Achttiende eeuw en vroege romantiek* (The Hague: Martinus Nijhoff, 1936)

Praag, J.A. van. *La Comedia espagnole au Pays-Bas au XVIIᵉ et au XVIIᵉ siècle* (Amsterdam: H.J. Paris, 1922)

Ronde, Theo de. *Het tooneelleven in Vlaanderen door de eeuwen heen* (Bruges: Keurboeken Davidsfonds no. 3, 1930)

Smeyers, J. 'De Nederlandse letterkunde in het Zuiden', in Hermine J. Vieu-Kuik and J. Smeyers, *De letterkunde in de achttiende eeuw in Noord en Zuid*, Geschiedenis van de letterkunde der Nederlanden, vol. 6 (Antwerp-Amsterdam: Standaard Uitgeverij, 1975) 333–49, 562–5.

Smits-Veldt, Mieke B. 'Tragedy, Tragicomedy, Comedy and their Variants', (forthcoming) in P. Béhar and H. Watanabe-O'Kelly (eds.), *Spectaculum Europaeum* (Wolfenbüttel)

Snoep, D.P. *Praal en Propaganda. Triumfalia in de Noordelijke Nederlanden in de 16de en 17de eeuw* (Alphen aan den Rijn, Canaletto, n.d. [1975]) [with a summary in English]

Sorgen, W.G.F.A. van. *De Tooneelspeelkunst te Utrecht en de Utrechtse Schouwburg* (The Hague: A. Rössing, 1885)

Thienen, Frithjof van. '"Gijsbrecht van Aemstel" de Joost van den Vondel, tradition presque "nationale" au théâtre d'Amsterdam', *Revue d'histoire du théâtre*, vol. 2 (1964), 152–60

Het doek gaat op. Vijfentwintig eeuwen in en om het Europese theater, 2 vols. (Bussum: De Haan, 1969)

Vogel, N.C. *De arbeidsovereenkomst van tooneelisten* (Amsterdam: C.A. Spin & Zoon, 1899) [**307, 361**]

Willekens, Emiel. 'Le Théâtre aux Pays-Bas', in Guy Dumur (ed.), *Histoire des spectacles*, Encyclopédie de la Pléiade, vol. 19 (Paris: Gallimard, 1965) 779–95.

Winkel, J. te. *De Ontwikkelingsgang der Nederlandsche Letterkunde*, 6 vols. (Haarlem: De Erven F. Bohn, 1922–1927)

Worp, J.A. *Geschiedenis van het drama en het tooneel in Nederland*, 2 vols. (Groningen: J.B. Wolters, 1904–1908)
Geschiedenis van den Amsterdamschen Schouwburg, 1496–1772. Uitgegeven met aanvulling tot 1872 door dr. J.F.M. Sterck (Amsterdam: S.L. van Looy, 1920)
Wybrands, C.N. *Het Amsterdamsche tooneel van 1617–1772* (Utrecht: J.L. Beijers, 1873) [267, 306, 330, 354]

Period 1, 1600–1664

(2) Sources

Anon. *Const-thoonende Iuweel, By de loflijcke stadt Haarlem, ten versoecke van 'Trou moet blijcken', in 't licht gebracht: Waer inne duydelick verclaert ende verthoont wordt alles wat den mensche mach wecken om den armen te troosten, ende zijnen naasten by te staan, In twaalf spelen van sinne [. . .]* (Zwolle: Zacharias Heyns, 1607) [266, 271]
De Geest van Mattheus Gansneb Tengnagel, In d'andere werelt by de verstorvene Poëten (Rotterdam: Iohan Neranus, 1652). Reproduced in Mattheus Gansneb Tengnagel, *Alle Werken* (ed. J.J. Oversteegen, Amsterdam: Athenaeum/Polak & Van Gennep, 1969, 523–568) [294, 297]
Barlaeus, Casparus. *Medicea Hospes, sive Descriptio publicae gratulationis [. . .]* (Amsterdam: Johannes and Cornelis Blaeu, 1638) [278]
Bredero, G.A. *Griane [. . .]* (Amsterdam: Cornelis Lodewycksz. van der Plasse, 1616; ed. F. Veenstra, Culemborg: Tjeenk Willink/Noorduijn, 1973) [298]
G.A. Brederoos Moortje waar in hy Terentii Eunuchum heeft Naeghevolght. En is gespeelt op de Oude Amstelredamsche Kamer Anno MDCXV (Amsterdam: Cornelis Lodewycksz. van der Plasse, 1617; ed. P. Minderaa and C.A. Zaalberg, The Hague: Martinus Nijhoff, 1984) [289]
G.A. Brederoods Nederduytsche Poëmata (Amsterdam: Cornelis Lodewijcksz. van der Plasse, 1632) [288]
D.[apper], O. *Historische beschrijvingh der Stadt Amsterdam [. . .]* (Amsterdam: Jacob van Meurs, 1663) [285]
Domselaer, T. van. *Beschrijvinge van Amsterdam [. . .]* (Amsterdam: Marcus Willemsz. Doornick, 1665) [268, 312]
Duym, Jacob. *Benoude Belegheringe der stad Leyden [. . .]* (Leiden: Henrick Lodowixsoon van Haestens, 1606) [281]
Heinsius, D. *Dan. Heinsii de tragoediae constitutione [. . .]* (2nd enlarged ed., Leiden: Elzevier, 1643 (1611)). Translated by Paul R. Sellin and John J. McManmon in Daniel Heinsius, *On Plot in Tragedy* (ed. Paul R. Sellin, Northridge, California: San Fernando Valley State College, 1971) [302]
Hogendorp, G. van. *Truer-spel van de Moordt begaen aen Wilhelm, by der Gratie Gods Prince van Oraengien, etc.* (Amsterdam: Cornelis vander Plasse, 1617). Reproduced in F.K.H. Kossmann (ed.), *De spelen van Gijsbrecht van Hogendorp* ('s-Gravenhage: Martinus Nijhoff, 1932, pp. 43–175) [301]
Hooft, P.C. *Nederlandsche Historiën* (Amsterdam: Louis Elzevier, 1642; Amsterdam: Henrik Wetstein and Pieter Scéperus/Leiden: Dan. van Dalen/Utrecht: Willem van der Water, 1703) [305]
Huygens, Constantijn *Lettres du Seigneur de Zuylichem à Pierre Corneille* (ed. J.A. Worp, Paris-Groningen, 'Revue d'Art Dramatique', J.B. Wolters, 1890)
De briefwisseling van Constantijn Huygens (1608–1687), vol. v (1649–1663) (ed. J.A. Worp, The Hague: Martinus Nijhoff, 1916) [291]
De Navorscher. (Amsterdam: Frederik Muller), vol. 3 (1853). Bijblad III, p. xli [287]
Voetius, G. *Gysberti Voetii Disputatio de Comoediis, Dat is, Twistredening van de Schouspeelen. Gehouden en voorgestelt in de Hooge-School van Uitrecht. Uit de Latijnsche in de Neerduitsche taal vertaalt door B.S.* (Amsterdam: Jasper Adamsz Star, 1650) [The Latin text had been published in 1643] [303]

Vondel, J. van den. *De werken van Vondel*, 10 vols. + index (Amsterdam: De Maatschappij voor Goede en Goedkope Lectuur, 1927–1940) [270, 279, 284, 304]

Vos, Jan. *Aran en Titus* (Amsterdam: Jacob Lescaille, 5th edn, 1656). Reproduced in Jan Vos, *Toneelwerken* (ed. W.J.C. Buitendijk, Assen/Amsterdam: Van Gorcum, 1975, 99–210) [283]

(3) Specialised studies and works of reference

Albach, Ben, 'De schouwburg van Jacob van Campen'. *Oud-Holland* (1970), 85–109 [with a summary in English] [272–4]

'Rembrandt en het toneel'. *De Kroniek van het Rembrandthuis* 31 (1979/2), 2–32 [295]

'Pekelharing, personage en potsenmaker'. *Literatuur* (Utrecht: Hes) 7 (1990), 74–80

Bachrach, A.G.H. 'Leiden en de "strolling players"'. *Jaarboekje voor geschiedenis en oudheidkunde van Leiden en omstreken* (Leiden: A.W. Sijthoff) 60 (1968), 29–37 [287]

Boheemen, F.C. van and Heijden, Th.C.J. van der. *De Delftse rederijkers 'Wy rapen gheneucht'* (Amsterdam: Huis aan de Drie Grachten, 1982)

De Westlandse Rederijkerskamers in de 16e en 17e eeuw (Amsterdam: Rodopi, 1985)

Briels, J.G.C.A. 'Reyn Genuecht. Zuidnederlandse Kamers van Rhetorica in Noordnederland 1585–1630'. *Bijdragen tot de Geschiedenis* 57 (1974), 3–89

Gudlaugsson, S.J. *Ikonographische Studien über die holländische Malerei und das Theater des 17. Jahrhunderts* (Würzburg: Karl J. Triltsch, 1938)

De komedianten bij Jan Steen en zijn tijdgenooten (The Hague: A.A.M. Stols, 1945)

'Jacob van Campens Amsterdamsche Schouwburg door Hans Jurriaensz, van Baden uitgebeeld'. *Oud-Holland* 66 (1951), 179–84 [274]

Hummelen, W.M.H. *De sinnekens in het rederijkersdrama* (Groningen: J.B. Wolters, 1958) [with a summary in German]

Inrichting en gebruik van het toneel in de Amsterdamse Schouwburg van 1637 (Amsterdam: Noord-Hollandsche Uitgevers Maatschappij, 1967) [272–4, 283, 286]

Repertorium van het rederijkerdrama 1500–ca. 1620 (Assen: Van Gorcum, 1968)

'Typen van toneelinrichting bij de rederijkers (. . .)', *Studia Neerlandica* (1970), 51–109 [271]

'Rembrandt und Gijsbrecht: Bemerkungen zu den Thesen von Hellinga, Volskaja und Van de Waal'. In O. von Simson/J. Kelch (eds.), *Neue Beiträge zur Rembrandt-Forschung* (Berlin: Mann, 1973, 151–61) [295]

'Types and Methods of the Dutch Rhetoricians' Theatre'. In C. Walter Hodges/S. Schoenbaum/Leonard Leone (eds.), *The Third Globe: Symposium for the Reconstruction of the Globe Playhouse. Wayne State University, 1979* (Detroit, 1981), 133–48

Amsterdams toneel in het begin van de Gouden Eeuw. Studies over Het Wit Lavendel en de Nederduytsche Academie (The Hague: Martinus Nijhoff, 1982) [267, 282]

'Toneel op de kermis, van Bruegel tot Bredero'. *Oud Holland* 103 (1989), 1–45 [with a summary in English] [275]

Hunningher, B. 'De Amsterdamse Schouwburg van 1637. Type en karakter', *Nederlands Kunsthistorisch Jaarboek*, 9 (1958), 109–71

Het toneel in de Amsterdamse Schouwburg van 1637 (Amsterdam: Noord-Hollandsche Uitgevers Maatschappij, 1959) [268, 272–4]

A Baroque Architect Among Painters and Poets'. *Theatre Research/Recherches Théâtrales*, 3 (1961), 23–31 [272–4]

Kernodle, George. *From Art to Theatre. Form and Convention in the Renaissance* (Chicago/London: The University of Chicago Press, 1944)

Kuyper, W. 'Two Mannerist Theatres'. *New Theatre Magazine*, 9, no. 3 (summer 1969), 22–9

'Een maniëristisch theater van een Barok architect'. *Bulletin van de Koninklijke Nederlandse Oudheidkundige Bond*, 69 (1970), 99–117 [with a summary in English]

Leeuwe, Hans de. 'La Médée de Jan Vos, contribution néerlandaise à l'histoire du théâtre européen'. In Jean Jacquot (ed.), *Le Lieu théâtral à la Renaissance* (Paris: Centre National de la Recherche Scientifique, 1964), 445–57

Lefèvre, J. 'La cour de l'archiduc Léopold-Guillaume 1647–1652', Archives, Bibliothèques et Musées de Belgique, Bulletin mensuel de l'Association de conservateurs, V, no. 5 (15 May 1928)

Limon, Jerzy. Gentlemen of a Company. English Players in Central and Eastern Europe, 1590–1660 (CUP, 1985)

Mak, J.J. De Rederijkers (Amsterdam: P.N. van Kampen & Zoon, 1944)

Meeus, H. Repertorium van het ernstige drama in de Nederlanden, 1600–1650 (Leuven: Acco, 1983)

Oey-de Vita, E. and Geesink, M. Academie en Schouwburg, Amsterdams toneelrepertoire 1617–1665, naar de bronnen bewerkt en ingeleid door – (Amsterdam: Huis aan de Drie Grachten, 1983) [299, 300]

Riewald, J.G. 'New Light on the English Actors in the Netherlands, c. 1590–c. 1660'. English Studies (Amsterdam: Swets & Zeitlinger) 41 (1960), 65–92

    'The English Actors in the Low Countries, 1585–c. 1650: An Annotated Bibliography'. In G.A.M. Janssens and F.G.A.M. Aarts (eds.), Studies in Seventeenth-Century English Literature, History and Bibliography [Festschrift T.A. Birrell], (Amsterdam: Rodopi, 1984)

Roeder-Baumbach, Irmengard von. Versieringen bij Blijde Inkomsten gebruikt in de Zuidelijke Nederlanden in de 16e en 17e eeuw (Antwerp: De Sikkel, 1943) [276]

Schrickx, W. 'Nederlandse en andere acteurs te Gent en elders in de XVIIde eeuw', Studia Germanica Gandensia 7 (1965), 25–53

    Foreign Envoys and Travelling Players in the Age of Shakespeare and Jonson (Wetteren: Universa, 1986)

Smits-Veldt, Mieke B. 'Vondel en de Schouwburg van Jacob van Campen'. In E.K. Grootes (ed.), Visies op Vondel na 300 jaar (The Hague: Martinus Nijhoff/Tjeenk Willink/Noorduijn, 1979), 247–69.

    'De opening van de 'Neerlandtsche Academia De Byekorf'. Melpomene presenteert: Gijsbrecht van Hogendorps Orangientragedie', Spektator (Groningen: Wolters-Noordhoff) 12 (1983), 199–214 [301]

    Het Nederlandse Renaissancetoneel (Utrecht: Hes, 1991)

Stuiveling, Garmt Memoriaal van Bredero. Documentaire van een dichterleven, samengesteld door – (Culemborg: Tjeenk Willink/Noorduijn, 1975) [288]

Uitman, J.E. 'Les Fêtes baroques d'Amsterdam de 1638 à 1660. L'intelligibilité de leurs motifs allégoriques et historiques pour un public contemporain'. In Jean Jacquot (ed.), Dramaturgie et société. Rapports entre l'oeuvre théâtrale, son interprétation et son public au XVIe et XVIIe siècles, vol. I (Paris, Centre Nationale de la Recherche Scientifique, 1968), 220–6

Waal, H. van de. 'Rembrandt at Vondel's Tragedy Gijsbreght van Aemstel', Miscellanea I.Q. van Regteren Altena (Amsterdam: Scheltema/Holkema, 1969), 145–9, 337–40. Reprinted in Henri van de Waal, Steps towards Rembrandt. Collected Articles 1937–1972, (Amsterdam: North-Holland Publishing Company), 73–89 [295]

Wille, J. 'De Gereformeerden en het toneel tot omstreeks 1620', in Christendom en Historie. Lustrumbundel van het Gezelschap van Christelijke Historici in Nederland (Kampen: J.H. Kok, 1931), 96–169; reprinted in J. Wille, Literair-historische opstellen (Zwolle: W.E.J. Tjeenk Willink, 1963), 59–142

Period 2, 1665–1794

(4) Sources

Anon. Prael-treyn, Verrykt door Ry-benden, Prael-Wagens, Zinnebeelden en andere Oppronkingen, Toegeschikt aan het duyzentjaerig Jubilé van den [. . .] Heyligen Rumoldus [. . .] (Malines: Joannes-Franciscus vander Elst, n.d.) [316]

[= S. Fokke] Historie van den Amsterdamschen Schouwburg. Met fraaije afbeeldingen (Amsterdam: G. Warnars en P. den Hengst, 1772)

Brief over het Vertoonen van den Vader des Huisgezins, door de Haagsche Tooneelisten [. . .] (Printed by the Author, n.p., n.d. [Amsterdam: 1773]) [338]

Compleete Verzameling van Vyftig Brieven, Van een Rotterdamsch Heer, Over het spelen van de aldaar zynde acteurs en actrices, aanvang genoomen hebbende op den 26ste May des Jaars 1773, en geëindigt zynde den 14de May 1774 (. . .). (Printed by the Author, n.p., n.d., [1774]) [359–60]

Historie van den nieuwen Amsterdamschen Schouwburg. Met fraaije afbeeldingen (Amsterdam: G. Warnars en P. den Hengst, 1775) [326]

Etat de la Comédie française à La Haye, à Pâques 1780 [. . .] (The Hague: H. Constapel, 1780) [353] [= Simon Styl] *Levensbeschryving van eenige voorname meest Nederlandsche mannen en vrouwen. Deel 9.*

Het leven van Jan Punt (Amsterdam: [publisher unknown], 1781) [339]

Nederlandsche Dicht- en Tooneelkundige Werken, van het Genootschap Onder de Spreuk: Door Natuur en Kunst (Amsterdam: Willem Holtrop, 1786) [358]

De Tooneelspeler en zijn Aanschouwer kunstmaatig beschouwd, of Grondregelen voor beiden. Gevolgd van een Handleiding om zich in de Tooneelspeelkunde te onderwijzen. Delectat et erudit. (Amsterdam: W. Holtrop, 1791) [346, 351]

Algemeene Amsterdamsche Schouwburgs Almanach, voor 't Jaar 1793, met fraaje Tooneel-plaatjes. (Amsterdam: J. van Gulik) [334]

Atlas van de Stad Amsterdam. (Amsterdam: R. Ottens, P. Yver, J. Smit, F.W. Greebe, A. van der Kroe, and J.C. Sepp, 1767–1775); reprinted as *Atlas van de Waereldberoemde Koopstad Amsterdam [. . .]* (Amsterdam: J.B. Elwe, 1804) [324–5]

Corver, M. *Tooneel-Aantekeningen, vervat in een omstandige Brief aan den Schrijver van het Leven van Jan Punt [. . .]* (Leiden: Cornelis Heyligert, 1786) [308, 311, 332, 336–7, 340–2, 345, 347–50, 355, 357]

Dongelmans, B.P.M. (ed.). *Nil Volentibus Arduum: Documenten en Bronnen. Een uitgave van Balthazar Huydecopers aantekeningen uit de originele notulen van het genootschap* (Utrecht: Hes, 1982)

De Hollandsche Spectator. (Amsterdam: Hermanus Uytwerf, 1731–1735) [353]

De Hollandsche Tooneel-beschouwer [1762–63] (no place, 1763) [337, 343–4]

Hoogewerff, G.J. (ed.). *De twee reizen van Cosimo de' Medici Prins van Toscane door de Nederlanden (1667–1669). Journalen en documenten* (Amsterdam: Johannes Müller, 1919) [352]

Pels. A. *Gebruik én Misbruik des Tooneels* (Amsterdam: Albert Magnus, 1681; ed. Maria A. Schenkeveld-van der Dussen, Culemborg: Tjeenk Willink/Noorduijn, 1978) [356]

Rotgans, Lucas. *Boerekermis* (Amsterdam: Samuel Halma, 1708; ed. L. Strengholt, Gorinchem: J. Noorduijn, 1968 [316]

(5) Studies and works of reference

Albach, Ben. *Jan Punt en Marten Corver. Nederlandsch tooneelleven in de 18e eeuw* (Amsterdam: P.N. van Kampen & Zoon N.V., 1946)

'Een inventaris van toneeldecors uit 1688'. *Scenarium* (Zutphen: De Walburg Pers) 8 (1984), 34–72 [with a summary in English]. [320, 331]

Boheemen, F.C. van and Th.C.J. van der Heijden. 'Kermis en toneel in Delft en Delfshaven gedurende de achttiende eeuw', *Scenarium* 8 (1984), 108–18 [with a summary in English].

Gascoigne, Bamber. *World Theatre. An Illustrated History* (London: Ebury Press, 1968)

'On Stage: Dutch Theatrical Prints'. *Delta. A Review of Arts, Life and Thought in the Netherlands* (Amsterdam: Delta International Publication Foundation) (1969), 5–20 [321–5]

'Shuffling the Schouwburg Scenes'. *Theatre Research/Recherches Théâtrales*, 9 no. 2, (1968), 88–103 [324–5]

Geelen, A. van. *Deutsches Bühnenleben zu Amsterdam in der zweiten Hälfte des 18. Jahrhunderts* (Nijmegen: 1947) (*Deutsche Quellen und Studien*, ed. W. Kosch, vol. 18).

Harmsen, A.J.E. *'Onderwys in de tooneel-poëzy'. De opvattingen over toneel van het Kunstgenootschap Nil Volentibus Arduum* (Rotterdam: Ordeman, 1989) [with a summary in French]

Haverkorn van Rijsewijk, P. *De oude Rotterdamsche Schouwburg* (Rotterdam: van Hengel & Eeltjes, 1882)

Hogendoorn, W. 'Sieraaden van het tooneel. Iets over vertoningen in de Amsterdamse schouwburgen van 1637 en 1665'. *Scenarium*, 2 (1978), 70–82 [with summary in English]

a.o. 'Een Rotterdamse koopman en zijn repertoirelijst (1774–1779)', *Scenarium*, 8 (1984), 119–44 [with a summary in English]

Jong-Schreuder, S. de. 'Een serie achttiende-eeuwse decorprenten van de Amsterdamse schouwburg aan de Keizergracht, MA thesis, Univ. of Leiden, 1969 [321–3]

Kuyper, W. 'Grooves on the Leyden Stages of 1809 and 1865, and Some Observations on the Amsterdam Stages of 1665 and Later', *Theatre Research/Recherches théâtrales*, 14 (1980), 54–61

Leeuwe, H.H.J. 'Der Erzengel Rafael in Vondels "Gijsbreght van Aemstel". Wandlungen in der Darstellung des Ueberirdischen auf dem holländischen Theater', *M&K*, 10, (1964) [Festgabe für Heinz Kindermann], 385–95

'11. Mai 1772: die Schauburg brennt!'. In Rolf Badenhausen/Harald Zielske (eds.), *Bühnenformen, Bühnenräume, Bühnendekorationen* (Festschrift Herbert A. Frenzel) (Berlin: Erich Schmidt, 1974, 108–27) [314]

'Holländisches Theaterleben um die Mitte des 18. Jahrhunderts'. In Roger Bauer/Jürgen Wertheimer (eds.), *Das Ende des Stegreifspiels – Die Geburt des Nationaltheaters: Ein Wendepunkt in der Geschichte des europäischen Dramas* (Munich: Fink, 1983, 51–9)

Mattheij, Th.M.M. *Waardering en kritiek. Johannes Nomsz en de Amsterdamse Schouwburg 1764–1810* (Amsterdam: Huis aan de Drie Grachten, 1980)

Meijer Drees, Marijke. 'De treurspelen van Thomas Asselijn (c. 1620–1701)', diss. Utrecht, n.p., 1989 [with a summary in English]

Niemeyer, J.W. *Cornelis Troost 1696–1750* (Assen: Van Gorcum, 1973)

Riccoboni, Louis. *Réflexions historiques et critiques sur les différens théâtres de l'Europe. Avec les Pensées sur la Déclamation* (Amsterdam: Aux Dépens de la Compagnie, 1740) (Paris: Guérin, 1738) [319]

Rössing, J.H. *Geschiedenis der stichting en feestelijke opening van den Schouwberg op het Leidsche Plein te Amsterdam* (Utrecht: J.L. Beijers, 1874)

Sluijter-Seijffert, Nicolette. 'De Amsterdamse Schouwburg van 1774'. *Oud Holland*, 90 (1976), 21–64 [with a summary in English] [327–9]

Thienen, F. van. 'Der Maler Gérard de Lairesse und die klassizistische Bühne'. *M&K*, 1 (1955), 140–7

Veltkamp, R.J.H. 'Het Eeuwgetyde van den Amsteldamschen Schouwburg. Een schouwburgfeest in 1738, naar zijn bronnen beschreven en geanalyseerd,' MA thesis, Univ. of Amsterdam, 1984. [323, 354]

Werkgroep 'De Schouwburg in Beeld'. 'De Italiaansche Straat: afbeeldingen van een decor uit de Amsterdamse schouwburg (1665–1772)'. *Leids Kunsthistorisch Jaarboek 1985* (Delft, 1987), 85–110 [with a summary in English]

Wren, Robert M. 'Grooves and Doors on the Seventeenth and Eighteenth-Century Dutch Stage'. *Theatre Research/Recherches Théâtrales* 7, no. 1 (1965), 56–7

Period 3, 1795–1848

(6) Sources

Ailly, A.E.d'. 'Rijze door Braband Aº. 1816 Antwerpen, Gent Brussel'. *Historia. Maandschrift voor Geschiedenis en Kunstgeschiedenis*, 4 (1938), 80–94 [385]

Anon. *Verslag der tooneelvertooningen van W. Bingley te Amsterdam; door de schrijvers van Den Tooneelkijker*, Appendix to vol. IV of the magazine *De Tooneelkijker* (Amsterdam: St. Delachaux, 1819), 14. [373]

Barbaz, A.L. *Amstels schouwtooneel*, 2 vols. (Amsterdam: Willem van Vliet, 1808–1809) [383]

Fokke Simonsz., A. *Amsterdamsche Winteravond-uitspanningen* (Amsterdam: J.C. van Kesteren, 1808) [365]

Jelgerhuis Rzn, J. *Toneel Studien. Bevattende Ontwikkelingen en Gedachten van Onderscheiden Toneel Studien. Welke slegts tot op de helft van het voorgenomen plan zijn afgeschreven. Door den Hollandschen toneelspeler – . Dezelven zijn meestal geschreven bij ziekte mijner huijsgenoten, en zittende tot derzelver oppassing en gezelschap*, MS., 1811, Nederlands Theater Instituut, Amsterdam. Introduced and partly edited in Ben Albach, 'Johannes Jelgerhuis over zijn rollen in *Gijsbrecht van Aemstel*. Twee van zijn *Toneel-studiën* (1811) ingeleid en uitgegeven', *Spektator* (Dordrecht: Foris Publications) 17 (1987–8), 415–30 [372]

Jelgerhuis, Rz., J. *Theoretische lessen over de gesticulatie en mimiek. Gegeven aan de kweekelingen van het Fonds ter Opleiding en Onderrigting van Tooneel-Kunstenaars aan den Stadsschouwburg te Amsterdam* (Amsterdam: P. Meyer Warners, 1827; reprint Amsterdam: Adolf M. Hakkert, 1970. English translation in Golding (1984) [**380–1**]
'Iets over het Engelsche Tooneel, waar genoomen in de maanden Maij en Junij 1814 door – , Hollandsch Acteur te Amsterdam, MS, Univ. Library Amsterdam, 23 pp., unnumbered [**368**].
'Schettzende Herrinneringen van de Representatien: gegeven in October 1811 door de Fransche Acteurs Talma, Damas, Duchinois, en Bourgoin op het Hollandsche Toneel te Amsterdam. Door – [,] Hollandsch Acteur. Ter Gelegenheijd dat de fransche Keijzer Napoleon zig in de Stad Amsterdam bevond.', MS., coll. Nederlands Theater Instituut, Amsterdam. Ed. Ben Albach, *Scenarium*, 10 (Amsterdam: NThI, 1985)
Klikspaan [= J. Kneppelhout] *Studentenleven* (Leiden: H.W. Hazenberg, 1844) [**387**]
Pandora, in bezit van het tooneelklokje. (Amsterdam: Gebroeders Diederichs, n.d. [1826]) [**389**]
Reglement voor het Fonds tot Pensionering van Tooneelkunstenaars, aan den Stads Schouwburg te Amsterdam. (n.p., 1821, University Library, Amsterdam, Port. ton.), fo. X 1–62. [**363**]
De Tooneelkijker. (Amsterdam: S. Delachaux, 4 vols, 1816–1819) [**382, 388**]
Westerman, M. *Het Ontzet der Stad Leiden, Geschiedkundig Tafreel in drie bedrijven* (Amsterdam: H. Moolenijzer, 1809) [**367**]
Withuys, C.G., *Lofrede op Johanna Cornelia Wattier* (Amsterdam, 1827) [**375, 384**]

(7) Specialised studies and works of reference

Albach, Ben. *Helden, draken en comedianten. Het Nederlandse toneelleven voor, in en na de Franse tijd* (Amsterdam: Uitgeversmaatschappij Holland, 1956) [**375, 384**]
'A Dutch Actor's Experiences with English Theatre in Amsterdam, May-July 1814', in David Mayer and Kenneth Richards (eds.), *Western Popular Theatre* (London/New York: Methuen 1977), 75–90 [**368**]
Albach, Ben and Blom, Paul. 'Uit in Amsterdam. Van schouwburgen en kermissen tussen 1780 en 1813', in Paul Blom a.o. (eds.), *La France au Pays-Bas. Invloeden in het verleden* (Vianen: Kwadraat, 1985), 89–151
Anon. *Tooneelkundige Brieven, geschreven in het najaar 1808. Ten vervolge op de brieven uit Amsteldam, over het Nationaal Tooneel en de Nederlandsche letterkunde, van C.F. Haug. Niet vertaald.* (Amsterdam: L.A.C. Hesse, 1808)
Berg, Tuja van den. 'Het miniatuurtoneel van Baron van Slingelandt'. *Ons Amsterdam*, 34 (Feb. 1982), 33–7 [**369**]
Boulangé, F. *Koninklijke Nederduitsche Schouwburg. Chronologische lijst van programma's, uitgevoerd door de 'Zuid-Hollandsche Tooneelisten' in de Koninklijke Schouwburg Den Haag (1815–1834)* (n.p., n.d. [Amstelveen, 1989])
Delaunois, Greta. 'Het Nederlandstalig toneel in Vlaanderen tijdens het Verenigd Koninkrijk', diss. Ghent, 1978
Gelder, H.E. van. *Het Haagse toneel-leven en de Koninklijke Schouwburg, 1804–1954* (n.p. [The Hague], book-ed. of the monthly 's-Gravenhage, 1954, no. 2)
Gilhoff, Gerd Aage. *The Royal Dutch Theatre at The Hague 1804–1876* (The Hague: Martinus Nijhoff, 1938)
Haar, Carel ter. 'Neoklassizismus und nationales Drama in den Niederlanden um 1800'. In Roger Bauer (ed.), *Der theatralische Neoklassizismus um 1800. Ein europäisches Phänomen?* (Bern etc.: Peter Lang, 1986), 257–77
Haug, C.F. *Brieven uit Amsteldam over het Nationaal Tooneel en de Nederlandsche Letterkunde. Uit het Hoogduitsch vertaald.* (Amsterdam: L.A.C. Hesse, 1805)
Jelgerhuis, *Johannes Rzn, Acteur-Schilder, 1770–1836.* (Catalogue of the Jelgerhuis exhibition at Nijmegen, Leiden and Amsterdam, 1969–1970, Nijmegen: Stichting Nijmeegs Museum voor Schone Kunsten, 1969)
Keyser, Marja. *Komt dat zien! De Amsterdamse kermis in de negentiende eeuw* (Amsterdam: B.M. Israel/ Rotterdam: Ad. Donker, 1976)

Leeuwe, H.H.J. de. 'De geschiedenis van het Amsterdamsch tooneel in de negentiende eeuw (1795–1925)', in A.E. d'Ailly (ed.), *Zeven eeuwen Amsterdam*, 6 vols. (Amsterdam, 1948), vol. v., 113–55
'Stilepochen des holländischen Theaters im 19. Jhahrhundert'. *M&K*, 3 (1957), 340–62
'De toneelspelersopleiding in Nederland in de 19e eeuw', *Scenarium*, (1977), 9–32 [with a summary in English]
' "Ik ondergetekende verbinde my . . .". Holländische Engagementsverträge und Theatergesetze im 19. Jahrhundert'. *KSGTG*, 29/30 (1978), 101–12 [362]
'Revolution durch Oper? Auber's 'Stumme von Portici' 1830 in Brüssel'. *M&K*, 30 (1984), 267–84
Limburg Brouwer, P. van. *Verhandeling over de vraag: Bezitten de Nederlanders een nationaal toneel met betrekking tot het treurspel? [. . .]*, (n.p., n.d. [Leiden, 1823]) [379, 386]
Panne, M.C. van de. *Recherches sur les rapports entre le Romantisme français et le théâtre hollandais* (Amsterdam: H.J. Paris, 1927)
Schimmel, H.J. 'De dichter in de maatschappij. Laurierboom en Bedelstaf enz. [,] tooneelspel van Carl von Holtei'. *Kunstkronijk uitgegeven ter aanmoediging en verspreiding der Schoone Kunsten* (The Hague: K. Fuhri) 11 (1850), 67–71 [378]
Siegenbeek, Matthijs. *J.C. Wattier Ziezenis, eerste tooneelkunstenaresse van Nederland, in eene redevoering geschetst* (Haarlem: De Erven François Bohn, 1827) [376]
Slechte, C.H., Verstraete, G. and Zalm, L. van der. *175 jaar Koninklijke Schouwburg 1804–1979* (The Hague: Kruseman, 1979)
Thienen, Frithjof van. 'Jelgerhuis und die richtige Körperhaltung'. *M&K*, 10 (1964), 455–67

Index